Maxim Jakubowski is a London-based novelist and editor. He was born in the UK and educated in France. Following a career in book publishing, he opened the world-famous Murder One bookshop in London. He now writes fu███████████████████████lling erotic anthologies ▓nd b▓oks on ero▓ic ▓▓▓▓▓ ▓▓ ▓▓▓▓ ▓▓ ▓▓▓▓▓ many acclair▓▓ ▓▓e collections. His novels inclu▓▓▓ ▓▓▓▓ ▓▓▓▓▓▓ ▓nt to *Kiss, Because She Thought She Loved Me* and *On Tenderness Express*, all three collected and reprinted in the USA as *Skin in Darkness*. Other books include *Life in the World of Women*, *The State of Montana*, *Kiss Me Sadly*, *Confessions of a Romantic Pornographer*, *I Was Waiting For You* and *Ekaterina and the Night*. In 2006 he published *American Casanova*, a major erotic novel, which he edited and on which fifteen of the top erotic writers in the world collaborated, and his collected erotic short stories as *Fools For Lust*. He compiles two annual acclaimed series for the Mammoth list: *Best New Erotica* and *Best British Crime*. He is a winner of the Anthony and the Karel Awards, a frequent TV and radio broadcaster, a past crime columnist for the *Guardian* newspaper and Literary Director of London's Crime Scene Festival. Over the past years, he has authored under a pen name a series of *Sunday Times* bestselling erotic romance novels which have sold over two million copies and been sold to twenty-two countries, and translated the acclaimed French erotic novel *Monsieur* by Emma Becker. His monthly review column appears at www.lovereading.co.uk.

Recent Mammoth titles

MBO New Sherlock Holmes Adventures
MBO the Lost Chronicles of Sherlock Holmes
The Mammoth Book of Historical Crime Fiction
The Mammoth Book of Best New SF 24
The Mammoth Book of Really Silly Jokes
The Mammoth Book of Best New Horror 22
The Mammoth Book of Undercover Cops
The Mammoth Book of Weird News
The Mammoth Book of Muhammad Ali
The Mammoth Book of Best British Crime 9
The Mammoth Book of Conspiracies
The Mammoth Book of Lost Symbols
The Mammoth Book of Body Horror
The Mammoth Book of Steampunk
The Mammoth Book of New CSI
The Mammoth Book of Gangs
The Mammoth Book of SF Wars
The Mammoth Book of One-Liners
The Mammoth Book of Ghost Romance
The Mammoth Book of Best New SF 25
The Mammoth Book of Jokes 2
The Mammoth Book of Horror 23
The Mammoth Book of Street Art
The Mammoth Book of Ghost Stories by Women
The Mammoth Book of Best British Crime 11

The Mammoth Book of Jack the Ripper Stories

Maxim Jakubowski

ROBINSON

ROBINSON

First published in Great Britain in 2015 by Robinson

Copyright © Maxim Jakubowski for the selection and individual stories by respective contributors, 2015
1 3 5 7 9 8 6 4 2

The moral right of the author has been asserted.

A CIP catalogue record for this book
is available from the British Library.

ISBN: 978-1-47213-584-1 (paperback)
ISBN: 978-1-47213-585-8 (ebook)

Typeset in Whitman by Hewer Text UK Ltd, Edinburgh
Printed and bound in Great Britain by CPI Group (UK) Ltd, Croydon CR0 4YY

Papers used by Robinson are from well-managed forests and other responsible sources.

MIX
Paper from
responsible sources
FSC   FSC® C104740

Robinson
is an imprint of
Little, Brown Book Group
Carmelite House
50 Victoria Embankment
London EC4Y 0DZ

An Hachette UK Company
www.hachette.co.uk

www.littlebrown.co.uk

First published in the United States in 2015 by Running Press Book Publishers,
A Member of the Perseus Books Group

Books published by Running Press are available at special discounts for bulk purchases in the United States by corporations, institutions, and other organizations.
For more information, please contact the Special Markets
Department at the Perseus Books Group, 2300 Chestnut Street,
Suite 200, Philadelphia, PA 19103, or call (800) 810-4145, ext. 5000, or e-mail
special.markets@perseusbooks.com.

US ISBN: 978-0-7624-5814-1
US Library of Congress Control Number: 2015944811

9 8 7 6 5 4 3 2 1
Digit on the right indicates the number of this printing

Running Press Book Publishers
2300 Chestnut Street
Philadelphia, PA 19103-4371

Visit us on the web!
www.runningpress.com

Printed and bound in the UK

Contents

Introduction

The looming spectre of the famous Whitechapel serial killer haunts us still. Evil and elusive, he emerged from the foggy East End of London at the end of the nineteenth century, one of the first heavily documented serial killer of note, and his shadow has weaved its compulsive spell over us ever since. Made more emblematic by the fact that he was never caught, of course, leaving the mystery wide open for generations to speculate wildly about his identity, his intentions, modus operandi and the reason he vanished into thin air, both at the scene of the horrible crimes he was responsible for as well as from existence altogether when the murders suddenly came to a halt.

Over a decade back, I compiled, with my colleague and author Nathan Braund, a non-fiction Mammoth volume about the facts behind Jack the Ripper, collecting some of the countless theories about his identity and motives from the prolific pens of many specialists, some of whom proudly call themselves "Ripperologists", together with a lengthy analysis of all the known facts behind his historical criminal spree. The volume did not intend to solve the mystery, just to offer various hand-fuls of theories as to what actually happened in the dark, narrow streets of Whitechapel on those fateful nights and to analyse the many efforts to catch the dreaded culprit. At the time it was, so to speak, a state of the art of Ripper knowledge. Needless to say that since, further theories have been advanced by new experts and researchers. And so it will go on and I personally doubt whether the case will ever be solved to anyone's satisfaction.

Despite the horrible nature of the killings attributed to Jack the Ripper, he has cast a seductive spell ever since in the imagination of readers, historians and the general public and has become a somewhat dubious icon who has been at the origin of what is a veritable industry, both on the page and the screen.

Rather than align yet new speculations and variations on the iden-tity parade of suspects, I thought it would be fascinating to gather a group of both noted and upcoming writers and novelists from the thriller and horror genres to resurrect Jack the Ripper, his aura and his shadow and influence in a series of brand-new short stories, not so much putting the terrible events he was involved in under a microscope, but looking at the way he has captured the imagination of the world and still survives today in the collective unconscious.

Some of the tales are fantastical, others wonderfully speculative, and seductiveness and horror share the page on an equal footing. Many adhere to the known facts and try to offer a new point of view, a look at the man behind the legend and the reasons behind his awful killing spree and his sudden disappearance, while others involve the sleuths and policemen hunting him down, but overall imagination set free was the order of the day and I believe our team of fictioneers have done a wonderful job in bringing the character –and he is indeed now a major character in the annals of writing – alive, albeit even more mysterious and elusive than he ever was.

Enjoy and walk carefully at night through those dark streets!

Maxim Jakubowski

———

Bertie
Barbara Nadel

---

8 November 1888

There were lots of myths about the Irish. They were all Fenians, they were dirty, they lived with pigs. Maybe. What did Shmuel Kominsky know of the Irish? He knew the Burke girls. Four little seamstresses to break your heart – Mary, Concepta, Dolores and Assumpta. All under twenty-five, red-headed with tiny fingers that flew along a hem like birds.

Unlike the Jewesses, they smiled and they didn't swear like the Cockneys. The Burkes were perfect ladies and, in another, better life, they would probably have all become nuns. But not in Spitalfields. Not even with that brother of theirs forever guarding their chastity.

Albert 'Bertie' Burke was a man to be reckoned with. Spare and small, he was a dour type, dark like a Romany and handsome enough to break a woman's heart. Not that he had. Too busy. People who did his sort of work always were.

'Come now, girls, it grows dark and if I'm to get back to my business it has to be now.'

Four red heads looked up and smiled. The rest of the women just carried on with their work. They all knew Bertie Burke. Even the most recently arrived immigrant knew what a moneylender looked like.

The Burke girls all curtsied before they left. Little fake ladies in a room full of bombazine and rat droppings. Who did they think they were? Whatever Bertie told them.

The older *menschen* could tell some tales. Cohen the milliner could remember when the skeleton woman and her boy had come from Ireland. Colleen was her name, probably not even twenty when she'd fetched up on Fashion Street, stinking and almost naked. The first of the Irish from the dead potato fields. Many had followed but none with a child in tow the like of Bertie Burke.

Right from the start the child had worked like a man. Eight? Ten? God alone knew how old he'd been, but he'd done anything, everything. Mainly he'd put flesh on the bones of his mother.

Had Bertie Burke ever had a father? No one, not even the old knew that. But Colleen had married. O'Rourke, the Paddies' own pawnbroker and father of the four shining girls who took his red hair but not his name. Bertie Burke wouldn't have it. What he did do was add O'Rourke's business to his own when the old man died. Now he was king of the pawnshop, of moneylending and was the best fence in the East End of London. He was also emperor of the women in his house and everyone knew it and that included Shmuel Kominsky.

'Dolores, will you come along now.'

Dolores was the dreamiest of the Burke sisters. And even though Bertie knew that Shmuel Kominsky wouldn't dare give his sister the sack – not with his brother Hymen in Bertie's debt – he felt he had to call her out on it whenever she slipped into another world.

'Ah, Bertie, there's such a pretty girl up there looking right at you.'

He knew.

He saw Assumpta glance at her sister with something he interpreted as wonder. She was the youngest and yet she knew more than any of her sisters. She knew where they were and what it meant. Flower and Dean Street was the most insanitary thoroughfare in London. Full of low boarding houses, thieves, whores and buyers of Bertie's considerable expertise. Up from this pit of filth and stink they'd drag themselves to seek him out with whatever they could pinch, whatever he deigned to give them a few coppers for.

'Assumpta, stop looking.'

If any of his sisters became a low woman it would be that one. Bertie saw how she looked at the young men with the hungry eyes who followed the Burke sisters' every move. Wouldn't they like the chance of a fine young virgin on their arm?

He shook her by the shoulder. 'Behave yourself! You want the Ripper to see you looking at men? You know what he does to bad women.'

'But I'm not a bad—'

'Be quiet now!'

He put a finger up to her soft lips. Full and pink. He pulled his hand away.

'This Ripper sees what he wants to see,' he said. 'It's why I come to collect you all from work every day. Unescorted ladies or ladies who look at men are what he likes.'

'And ladies who drink.'

'Yes and that too, Assumpta.'

'Well, we don't drink.'

'No. No, you don't.'

They walked on to Brick Lane. An old Jewess dressed in rags, her feet bare, shoved a basket of that bread the Jews like into his face. 'Bagel?'

He pushed it away. The dirt was so ingrained in her flesh he knew it would never come out however much she washed. His hadn't.

The milkman crossed the road with one of his cows. A Welshman, he spoke little and owed no one and was one of the few people Bertie respected. They nodded to each other, one businessman to another. If the milkman were not a Protestant, he could marry one of the sisters. But he was.

Fournier Street came into view through the gloom. They passed a butcher's shop and Bertie kicked a nameless lump of something out of his way. On this corner, opposite the Jews' synagogue, the road became a quagmire of human excrement, mud and animal hide. Shoeless children clutched the bits of cloth they called clothes to their skinny chests and looked at the Burkes with hungry eyes. Bertie knew what they were thinking. *Bog-trotting Irish scum!*

But he and his sisters were the ones with shoes. Bertie smiled.

'Mammy?'

The woman in the bed opened her eyes.

'Are my girls in?' she asked.

'They are.'

Bertie sat down. Neither he nor his mother made much of a dent on the soft mattress Mr O'Rourke had bought the sad, beautiful Colleen Burke when he married her. For the second time in her life, Colleen was wasting away. But this time there was no work Bertie could do to make it right. She coughed. He resisted putting a hand on her shoulder. He was her son. She had daughters for the sympathy.

'I will need to go out tonight,' he said. 'Can I get you anything?'

The coughing subsided. She shook her head. She wasn't an old woman. At most only fourteen years older than her son. But that made her sixty-one, which was ancient for a woman who had lost her soul in the rotting potato fields of County Clare.

'No.'

What she'd wanted was long gone. Her traveller boy lover to help her rear their baby and then, later, some food would have done. But it hadn't come. Not for a long time. And then her child had stolen it for her and she'd been so happy. But it had tasted like ashes. Always and forever like dust. Now it was nothing, she couldn't even think about it.

'Be careful of the Ripper,' Colleen said.

'Mammy he only rips bad women,' Bertie said. 'Not businessmen about their legitimate work.'

She looked into his eyes. 'You know what I mean, Bertie.'

He looked away.

To have a drink in his hands with the Irishman due wouldn't be a good idea. Arthur owed the bastard money and if he saw him spending what he was supposed not to have on gin, he'd have his liver. A Scotsman once told him that when the Irish were dying in the hungry forties they ate human flesh.

The door behind him opened and Arthur Manning shivered. Even over the sound of the whores laughing and the costers shouting, he knew the gentle tapping fall of those tiny Irish feet.

'Mr Manning.'

He looked up.

'Not drinking?'

'How can I?' Arthur said. He took his hat off and stuffed it in his pocket. 'I am financially embarrassed, sir.'

'Are you indeed?'

'I am.'

Bertie Burke sat down. Arthur knew that he was sweating but he couldn't help it. Why had he borrowed money from Burke? He was a moneylender yes, but also a fence. He worked with criminals. He was a criminal. But then who else but a criminal would lend money to someone like Arthur Manning?

'So if you're financially embarrassed what are we to do about your sovereign?' the Irishman asked.

Burke was not a fighting man. He rarely used his fists, which were, in all truth, puny. But he was quicksilver with a blade. And everyone knew it. Some more immediately than others.

'I will get it to you, Mr Burke.'

'And how might you do that?' He leaned forwards across the table. 'Will you be selling the wife?'

'No, I . . .'

'Or maybe you'll be after not sniffing around the whores on Millers Court any more.'

Arthur felt his face flush.

'Ah, you know I have eyes and ears everywhere. Don't try to hide yourself or your vices from me.'

'I . . .'

'Mr Manning I have a reputation to uphold here. If I let my guard down, or make exceptions for people, I will have my advantage taken from me and I don't want that.'

'No.'

'Not with my elderly mother and my four maiden sisters to consider.'

'No.' He was shaking as well as sweating now. In a minute, if he wasn't careful, he'd piss himself.

'So reparation will have to be made. And it'll have to be seen to have been made.'

'I'll get it for you tomorrow. I swear, I will!'

The blade Burke took out of his pocket was thin, shiny and pointed at one end.

'Put your right hand on the table, Mr Manning.'

It was said so calmly. It was also said in what had now become silence. It wasn't often possible to hear a pin drop in an East End pub. But when Bertie Burke had a blade out, everyone looked and listened or they got the hell away.

'Put your hand on the table, Mr Manning.'

He knew what was coming, he'd seen Burke do it before. He knew it wouldn't kill him. But Arthur shook. And when he finally managed to put his hand down in front of the Irishman, he was ashamed that his flesh trembled.

Men and women leaned across each other so they could see. How many of them owed Burke money? Most. And if they didn't they were inconvenienced by him in some other way. Shmuel Kominsky employed his sisters, who were good at their jobs but who Burke took out of the Jew's sweatshop whenever he felt like it. Burke knew everyone's fears and weaknesses. That, above fencing, pawnbroking and moneylending, was his real skill.

Arthur wanted to be defiant. Oddly he didn't want to look away from what Burke was about to do. Was that enough? When the silence became too much he said, 'God Almighty, Mr Burke, I can feel you see my very soul! I'd be willing to bet you even know who the Ripper is, don't you?'

The stab was so quick, in the skin between the thumb and forefinger, for a second, Arthur felt nothing. But as soon as Burke pulled the blade out it bled hard and fast. And it hurt. Arthur jumped up as if scalded and tucked his hand underneath his left armpit. As he ran towards the street door, he heard Burke say, 'Tomorrow, Mr Manning, or you'll not be so lucky next time.'

*   *   *

The Ten Bells was not Burke's local. He didn't have one. He knew that as an Irishman people expected him to drink. His stepfather, O'Rourke, had drunk himself to death. But Burke favoured control. He always had.

Once Arthur Manning had left, Burke made his exit. Behind him, he heard conversations, songs and swearing as the Ten Bells went back to normal in his absence.

Burke had imagined that his victim would have scuttled away after his spiking. But he was lying against the pub wall, a woman in his arms tying a rag around his hand. Manning panted.

'Good night to you, Mr Manning,' Burke said. His blade, now back in his poacher's pocket had given way to the cane he always kept up the sleeve of his coat.

'Mr Burke.'

The woman looked up. Hatless and plump, she was brazen even by local standards. And she smiled at him. She had to know the name, if not the face. And he knew her. One of the Millers Court tarts that Arthur Manning so favoured, her name was Mary Jane Kelly.

Would Manning be stupid enough to have the whore when he was out of cash and in hock? Probably. Burke walked away knowing that Mary Jane's smile was boring into his back. It was said she was an ambitious girl. Maybe too much so.

9 November 1888

'Oh, Holy Mary, he's struck again!'

A boy in the street had shouted it. Barefoot, running through the shit and the mist, he'd looked into Dolores Burke's face when she'd opened her bedroom window to see what all the fuss was about.

'Ripper's done another one!' he'd said.

She'd put a hand to her mouth before she'd burst out to her sisters.

Dolores cried. 'Maybe we shouldn't work any more,' she said. 'If the streets are so dangerous now!'

Assumpta shook her head. 'For whores. Not for us.'

'And sure Bertie comes to fetch us every day from work,' Mary said. 'And if I can't come one time?'

He stood in the doorway to their chamber, immaculate as he always was in his coal-black suit and silk top hat. But he was pale. So pale he could've been ill.

Assumpta took his arm. Even though he was her brother, she was a little in love with her handsome Bertie. 'Ah, but you always come,' she said. 'You're the best brother a girl could ever have.'

He smiled. Then he patted her hand once before he pulled away. 'That's grand of you to say so,' he said, 'but If I were ever held up and anything happened to you I'd never forgive myself.'

'Oh.' Mary began to cry.

'And I earn enough for all of us,' Bertie said. 'Business is good, you don't have to work, none of yous.'

Bertie was aware that someone was behind him but he didn't turn around to look. He knew who it was.

'But I like to work,' Assumpta said. 'I've made friends at Mr Kominsky's workshop.'

'Mr Kominsky is a crook and a bounder, who pays poorly.'

'Then why did you let us work for him in the first place?' Assumpta said.

Dolores, more timid than her sister said, 'It's best not to question . . .'

'No, I want to know!' Assumpta said. 'Bertie?'

Dolores and, to a lesser extent, Mary and Concepta too, held their breath. Bertie was the kindest, gentlest brother any girl could have but he didn't like to be interrogated. Not by anyone.

'Because I wanted to make you happy,' he said. 'Because good girls should be able to do what they want in life.'

It had been Mary who had started it. She'd been to school with a girl called Ruth Katz, who had been given a job by her uncle, Shmuel Kominsky. She'd begged Mary to come with her and Mary in turn had begged her brother. Bertie had, to his way of thinking, caved in. Then the other girls had followed. Then the Ripper had come . . .

'Bertie, I need a word.'

He turned to see his mother leaning on the arm of Rosie, the kitchen maid. 'Mammy, you should be in bed!'

'With women torn to pieces almost on my doorstep?' Colleen shook her once-red curls. 'I think not.'

And Bertie looked into her eyes and what he saw there frightened him. He avoided her gaze as he moved in her direction.

'Yes, Mammy.'

She sat in the chair beside her bed. Lying down was too uncomfortable. It made her feel as if she had a weight on her chest.

Rosie gave her a cup of cocoa and left.

'Bertie . . .'

He shut the door behind him and took a chair for himself opposite his mother.

'You didn't get home until dawn,' she said. 'And don't deny it. I sleep rarely these days. I know. What were you doing?'

'You really want to know?'

'I do.'

He sighed. Did she know? Was it worth lying? Ah, but it was his way . . . 'I was chasing a debt,' he said. 'A man who'd rather spend money on whores than pay his dues.'

'Oh, yes?'

'Yes.'

'So what did you do to this man when you caught up with him?'

'I watched him.'

'With a whore?'

Bertie said nothing.

'Or did you spike him before he could get his long johns down?' Colleen shook her head. 'I know what you do to get money out of people. And in the old days when we first came here, what could I say about what you did? Bertie, don't misunderstand me, I've always seen the violence in you and of course I've known why it's there. I put it there, may God forgive me. But then this is not about a debt, is it?'

He took one of her hands. 'You did what you did to save our lives, Mammy.'

'Did I?'

'You know you did!' He leaned in close so that he could whisper. 'What would your mother have done if you hadn't . . .'

She put a hand up to stop him.

Bertie sat back again. 'We would have been dead, Mammy, and you know it.'

There was a pause, then she said, 'But maybe that would have been better.'

'What?'

'This is all unnatural, Bertie, and you know it!'

'What's all unnatural, Mammy? What?'

She looked at him and then she said, 'You.'

He couldn't speak. His face went white.

'Because I may be dying but I am no fool,' his mother said. 'I know you've been out of this house every night upon which these women have been torn to pieces. And I know you, Albert Burke. I know what you really are. You've not forgotten, have you? Of course you haven't. That's why this is happening, isn't it?'

Bertie took his jacket off and laid it on his mother's bed.

She said, 'Your granny made me have you in the cow's barn. She told me if you were a girl I was to drown you in the ocean. Girls had no value except as sex for the English. She made us live in that cow barn until all the people she feared would laugh at a gypsy's bastard had become corpses. Then she died. We dug her grave. Do you remember?'

Bertie removed his boots. He didn't dare think.

'You do, I know,' Colleen said. 'I also know that what you're doing now is in place of words you cannot say. I'm aware I deserve it. But what was I to do?'

He unbuttoned his waistcoat.

'There are people like you all over Ireland. It's how many survived. If the potatoes hadn't rotted in the earth you would've gone to work for an English landlord and you would've had a job and a life.'

'Like the one I have here?' He threw his waistcoat on the floor.

'Ah, Bertie . . .'

'I'll pick it up later.'

'What's that?'

There was a patch, a stain of dark red on the front of his shirt.

He began to unfasten the buttons.

'Women have always made passes at me.'

'You look like your father,' Colleen said. 'Like a prince of Arabia.'

'An ageing prince of Arabia,' he said. 'You know these women, Mammy? The ones who try to pull me into doorways, lift their skirts and puff their ancient alcoholic breath in my face? These days they are old whores.'

'Rosie told me the woman who died last night was a girl . . .'

'Young but gin soaked, riddled with the pox. Makes you realise that life has passed and you've never been touched as you should.'

He threw the shirt to the floor and then the vest beneath it and stood before his mother, bare-chested.

The once-fine breasts, the two of them, squashed and flattened with rags for so many years, hung flat against prominent ribs, their nipples almost touching the waistband of Bertie's trousers.

Colleen's eyes filled with tears. She hadn't seen Bertie unclothed for over twenty years.

'Who would touch this, Mammy? And I mean a man because it is men that are my preference.'

'You are a girl. Still.' Looking made her wince. Then she saw the oozing blood.

Bertie, following her eyes, said, 'She stabbed me.'

'The girl . . .'

'Mary Kelly. Young, as you say. She fought. Turned my own blade against me, the bitch.'

'You must get a doctor to your wound.'

'No.' Bertie sat on Colleen's bed. 'It'll heal. And, if it doesn't, it's the end anyway. Isn't that why you called me to you? So it could end?'

Bertie's head drooped. 'And when you hear the details of her death, you'll not want me for your child, Mammy. She beckoned me in after servicing a man who owes me money. She told me she'd always wanted me. I knew that. I'd seen the way she looked at me. You think part of me doesn't want to be a real man? I'm nothing as I am! But I'm not a man and I want to be loved as a woman. Days come when I want to cut every cunt out of every woman in this world. The dirty whores! But I want what they have too and the fact I'll never have it makes me a madman.'

Colleen leaned forward and stroked Bertie's face. 'I did you such a wrong,' she said. 'But there was always an excuse for it. First your granny, then, as you grew, so you'd get work, so the English landlords wouldn't get you in the family way. Then we came here and I should've stopped it . . .'

Bertie kissed her. 'Mammy, we were all but dead when we came here. What would I have done as a girl? I would've gone on the streets like Kelly and Eddowes and Stride. I would've ended up an old whore. I'd be dead of the pox by now. As it was, I worked as a man and got respect as a man and it's not your fault that the price was so high for me.'

'And you saved me from the streets, my lovely child.'

Bertie looked away.

'And now it's made you this,' Colleen said. 'You have to stop, Bertie. Now.'

'I know. But, Mammy, there's only one way to do that,' Bertie said. 'And I fear for you and the girls. I make good money.'

'And you think that your sisters can't run a pawnshop? You think that just the name of Bertie Burke won't protect them? You underestimate what you've done. Those girls are bright and sharp and without you they will have to be their own protection. And the Ripper will be gone then, won't he?'

Bertie began to dress. 'When the girls have gone to work, I'll go.'

Colleen nodded. 'You may have anything in my wardrobe that will fit you. And you must take some money.'

'No.'

'Yes.' She grabbed his arm. 'You'll need money as a woman alone. I know. God Almighty, Bertie, if you hadn't done these terrible things, do you think I'd ever let you go? I love you. You are my beloved child! This consumption that will kill me soon will be a blessing when you have gone. I don't want to live without you in my life!'

She cried.

Bertie circled her with the arms of a man for the last time and said, 'Then we will both welcome death, Mammy, because then I will see you again.'

Bertie Burke left Colleen's room, never to return.

2 February 2015

The above represents a fictional account of the story that was told to my grandmother, Eunice, by her mother Dolores Burke. Too upset to go to work on the 9 November 1888, Dolores was in the house when Bertie Burke left and she witnessed her mother's consequent distress. Colleen Burke only ever told Dolores the truth about Bertie and, as far as I know, she never, ever passed that knowledge on to any living soul except my grandmother. Whether it's true or not is another matter. What is known is that after Bertie Burke left Spitalfields, the Ripper murders stopped.

Forcing girls into men's clothes so they could work for better wages was common in Ireland in the nineteenth century and so there were lots of 'Berties' at one time. Where my Great-great-uncle Bertie went and whether he ever wore his mother's clothes and found love with a man isn't known. I like to think that he did. There is a story about a skinny little Irish woman, handy with a blade by all accounts, who ran a moneylending operation in Southwark in the 1890s. Known only by the name Clare she never had a man and, by all accounts, spent any time away from her business in church. Bertie had been born in County Clare. And, although the family was never religious, did he finally atone for his crimes in the arms of the Church? Or was he praying for death so he could be reunited with his mother?

It will never be known now. But then will the identity of the real Ripper ever come to light? Could all of the above just be a family fairy tale told to further demonise the oppressors of 'fallen' women and the evils of the British Empire? I can only leave you with questions, reader. Because they are all that I have.

Bernadette Mary Elizabeth Chisholm
(known by her mates as 'Bertie').

The Guided Tour
Rhys Hughes

———

Yes, he felt uncomfortable about the ethics of what he did. After all, it was the misery and terror of real people he was exploiting. They truly *had* lived once upon a grimy time, had endured the appalling violence and died in loneliness and agony. And now he was here to benefit from the gory tragedies, to make a vocation from being a ghoul. But no one thought him vile. It was a respectable thing to do, helping to keep history alive.

He told himself this again and again but it didn't make him feel better. He was naturally too pensive, he decided, and really he ought to learn to grin wider with his mouth and smile with his eyes at the same time. So he attempted these minor contortions with his reflection but something was always wrong with the mirrors in his house, for they all just showed the same dour figure as before and none of the cheerfulness came back at him.

The crucial factor, he knew, was the separation in time between the crime and its utility as heritage. The more years in this respect, the less parasitical the process, the more morally acceptable it was.

But the results would inevitably be less accurate.

True, he was getting better and better at his job and really ought to take at least some comfort and pride from this fact. He remembered how he had started out, not exactly nervous but awkward and perhaps a little feverish, his mind full of interesting facts but a constriction in his throat that made his voice hoarse. It was always going to be difficult to jump into the deep end of this profession, to be instantly suave and capable and efficient.

His very first day he had been with mentors, two of them, who were there to support him, but he felt the pressure of their scrutiny as a negative force. On the corner of Brick Lane and Wentworth Street, he had taken a deep breath and regaled his audience with the details of the murder that had taken place here and how the victim was subjected to an assault involving a blunt instrument tearing her perineum. "Like *this* and *that*, my friends."

Gestures came only a little more easily to him than the words did, but the mentors seemed satisfied. They nodded approvingly and, when the description was done, they continued strolling along together. Later, back in his too-narrow dwelling, he went through his act again and dismay filled him that it all flowed more smoothly and amusingly now he was alone. "But few authorities believe that *she* was actually a victim of the Ripper . . ."

His mentors he would never see again. He had no clear idea of who they were anyway, or what qualified them to judge.

A re-enactment of the re-enactment and then a nightcap before bed, the brandy fumes stinging his eyes as he fluttered his eyelids on the pillow in sleep, jolting him awake periodically. But his dreams were untroubled, surely because he did feel confident that he was able to refine and keep refining to perfection. The next time he would be alone, without fraternal encouragement, and so in a sense that would be his actual loss of virginity.

But he was no longer scared by the prospect, because the ordeal would be a secret initiation ceremony, his shyness known only to himself. His audiences were more experienced than he was at this game, but not more in control. They might appear blasé, jaded, having done all this before an uncountable number of times in some cases. Yet he was always ultimately in charge, a facilitator of fate with the rigours of a fixed itinerary on his side.

It was almost as if his timetable was a sordid and human equivalent of a meteorological forecast, not quite inevitable or flawlessly accurate, subject to a number of delays and misinterpretations of force and duration, but good enough for practical purposes. "More generally accepted as his first victim, *she* ended up sprawled on the first-floor landing. This makes her important. The puddle of her blood spread slowly into a regular ellipse."

He experimented with different accents, with style.

Even if he failed to impress sufficiently next time, the blame would partly be with them, not his responsibility alone. They had to react properly, contribute to the drama, throw their gasps at him and roll their eyes. Audiences are part of the act too, they can be more shy than those on stage, especially when the stage is on the same level as they are, when the footlights are the reflections of street lamps and moonbeams on glistening pavements.

The build-up was crucial to the success of every tour. The incidentals and tangents assisted not only in setting the scene, coagulating the right atmosphere, but proved to be fascinating in their own right. Little things, everyday details, an accumulation of trivialities, as if building the monster from human parts. And, of course, there had to be leeway, speculations presented as likelihoods, the myths communicated as true history. That was his duty.

"*This* is a public house he might have drunk beer in. *Here* he was spotted by a witness who later described him to the police. Perhaps he bought the paper for the first letter he sent to Scotland Yard at *that* stationery shop. Can you now understand the panic, the morbid curiosity, the perverse arousal felt by so many inhabitants of this great city at the exploits of this diabolic creature who moved mysteriously among them, can you almost *feel* it?"

Clichés when boomed out can still be effective.

It is all about projection, both of resonance and shadows. Sending out a palpable series of waves of swirling darkness.

His voice lost its hoarseness and ripened deeply until it had a true retired actor's timbre, an assurance that would put anyone at their ease, that even made him feel safe as he caught its echoes from stone walls in alleys, courtyards and doorways. "The first to be abdominally mutilated, here in Buck's Row, and in the minds of the press and public the first genuine victim, the first *kosher* victim if you will excuse me for putting it that way, and so . . ."

He was torn between putting greater emphasis on the gory technicalities and highlighting the social aspects, the context that surrounded every slaying, the poverty and desperation, the general brutality of a world that comfortably framed such acts of explosive specific savagery. Also he wanted to make them laugh, an occasional chuckle and snort here and there, not so much to lighten a mood that was thickly black but to mock mirth itself.

And like so many performances in other art forms, such as music and drama and dance, there had to be a crescendo at the end. Something bigger and better than what had come so far, a logical conclusion, an instant of supreme triumph, a culmination that was an ending but also an analysis, a singular act that while unique was also a repository for all that had previously occurred, a destination but one in flesh, so that the hard voyage might be over.

For there was no doubt in his mind that the murders were a journey into the gathering dusk of the landscape of the human soul, in the same way that his tours were movements along those veins and pipes called city streets, and that these inner and outer pilgrimages were not open-ended but heading deliberately for a place of rest, a refuge. It was a temporary role for him, this progress along the network of death, and there would be peace at last.

Pinpricks on a map. Stab wounds in bodies. The correlation had a touch of voodoo about it, contrived black magic. Hanbury Street and a folded leather apron. Dutfield's Yard and black grape stains on a hand-kerchief. Mitre Square and the boot buttons. He paced himself well, gathering strength and momentum for what everyone knew was the focal point of the entire business, the climax of the raucous symphony, the last page of the banned book.

Namely, the comprehensive and thorough disembowelling of a woman in a place where there was little risk of disturbance, the back room of a sordid little house in Dorset Street. His preparations were impeccable. He dressed with more than usual care, trimmed the moustache he had cultivated especially for the job, wrote out and revised his speech and learned it by heart, not trusting this time to his skills at improvisation. There was too much at stake.

He was so prepared that he felt he had springs embedded in his heels, that he could jump clear over roofs, cushion any shock.

"And the viciousness of this particular attack is why it deserves attention more than those that preceded it. There is something absolutely *definitive* about it. We might even say that it contains the others as if they are subsets. Or to take an alternative approach we could compare it to a perfect flower arrangement in which previous flowers have been sacrificed in order to understand positioning in space and time. This, my friends, is the pure one . . ."

And yes, the checklist was long. The throat cut from left to right but the subsequent mutilation making it impossible for the police surgeon to be positive about this afterwards. The messy delving into the abdomen that betrays no skill at anatomy at all, despite the impression to the contrary that the public will have later, partly influenced by erroneous newspaper reports. The bloodstains all up the walls. The partly digested fish and potatoes.

"And here, lean forward, take a good look at this . . ."

Yes, at the scattered viscera, cast about the room randomly or positioned with esoteric meaning, who knows which? One breast under the head, one next to the right foot as if about to be kicked into the fireplace among the half-burned clothing, bonnet and melted kettle. "Can you imagine the screams in this room that night, can you? Indeed, they would have sounded like *that*, exactly right, well done. I ought to hand my job over to you."

Hands slick but deep in pockets and heart thumping greasily, his farewell is perfunctory and he makes his gradual way home, no need to rush, certain that tomorrow he will start seeking alternative employment. It is time. The guided tour is no longer his thing. There must be other opportunities out there. He has no regrets now. It is not that he thought there was any mistake in doing what he did. But his audiences were always modest.

Modest in size if not demeanour, which is hardly a surprise, for the tourist industry is still in its infancy. Just one person on each tour. Just one. The crucial factor. The separation in time between the crime and its utility as heritage. For the sake of accuracy, the overriding sake of accuracy, what happens when that separation in time is reduced to zero? When the reconstruction is simultaneous with the original act? When the overlap is total?

His shape is gone in the fog. More than a century later, a writer who feels uneasy about using the murders as material for a story designed to entertain, but who lacks the ability to create a work that not only expresses with full force the despair and horror but also sanctifies the memories of the victims, will seek an alternative method of handling the subject matter, a metafictional approach, even working himself into the final paragraph.

MARTHA
Columbkill Noonan

It was 2.45 a.m. on Friday, 31 August 1888, and Martha Adams sat miserably on the corner of the bed that occupied the better part of the room which she let along with her man, John, at the lodging house on Flowers and Dean Street. But it was her friend, Emily Holland, not John, who sat on the chair opposite her. It was Emily who sat with her, as it so often was nowadays, because John was out late, as he was wont to do, leaving Martha alone, worried and wondering, until dawn's light brought him stumbling home, drunk.

But, tonight, Emily was not there to merely sit with her friend as they waited for John to come home. Tonight, Emily had news for Martha, and it was this news that caused Martha to gaze dejectedly, first at her friend, and then at the near-empty bottle of gin that she held tightly in her hand.

The lodging house was a pitiful affair, drafty and dirty and dank, replete with vermin and fleas and dissolute drunks. In other words, it was exactly like all of the other lodging houses on Flowers and Dean, neither nicer nor more run-down. The name of the street was sadly ironic, for there were no flowers, nothing bright or cheery or pretty to ameliorate the dismal air of desperation that permeated the ramshackle buildings which leaned precariously over the uneven old cobblestones. Really, to even call Flowers and Dean a street was somewhat ambitious, as it was in actuality little more than an alley, as were so many of the streets in the corner of London's East End known as Whitechapel. Narrow and twisted, most of Flowers and Dean Street was hidden from the sun even on the brightest of days, and the profound darkness of its shadowy corners at night gave shelter to all manner of nefarious deeds as well as to the ne'er-do-wells and scoundrels who committed them.

Scoundrels, as Martha had suspected and was now finding out for certain, like her own man, John. For Emily had just told Martha that she had just come from Osborne Street, where she had run into her friend Polly Nichols. And, as Emily had concluded her conversation with Polly, made her goodbyes and begun walking up the street towards her own room, she had turned back to utter a word of caution, for Polly had been out prostituting as usual, and as usual had drunk away all of the money she had earned. Polly, eyes bleary with drink, had told Emily that she need only one more man in order to pay for a room for the night, and Emily, good friend that she was, thought it best to warn Polly that she had heard of attacks on women occurring lately in the area. So far, no one had been killed, but two women had been stabbed, quite gruesomely, and Emily thought Polly in no condition to protect herself, as drunk as she was.

As she turned to warn Polly, however, she had seen John, drunken and staggering and wearing a lecherous leer on his face, coming up to Polly. The two had spoken for a moment, and then, leaning heavily on each other and giggling, zigzagged their way along the dark street towards Buck's Row, a place that Polly, like many of the local prostitutes, often chose to service her customers.

Emily, seeing this, had known that Polly had thus secured her lodging money for the night. Further, she had known that Polly would be safe with John (or, as safe as anyone could be out in the streets in the wee hours of the morning in Whitechapel). So, she wasted no more time worrying for Polly's safety, and instead rushed to tell her friend Martha what she had seen.

The news, while not entirely surprising to Martha, nonetheless came as a heavy blow. John had been her man for nigh on three years. During their time together, he had always been a drinker, but so, for that matter, was Martha. No, Martha did not so much mind his drinking, so long as he did it at home, with her. But, in the past few weeks, something had changed.

For John had begun going out in the evenings. Oft-times, now, he stayed out until dawn, when he would crawl, stinking with drink, into the bed where Martha had lain awake with worry and suspicion throughout the long night. He turned to Martha less and less often to fulfill the needs of a man for his woman. But, perhaps most distressingly, was the sudden dearth of money for their household needs.

Never had the two of them had much. He a day laborer, she a seamstress; both took work where they could, and rarely had they been able to do much more than just get by. But always there had been money for lodging, and food, and, of course, drink. Until John began staying out all night, that is.

Now, the money needed for their basic necessities had run short, and Martha found herself scrambling to make ends meet. What Emily was saying now, that the missing money was being spent on prostitutes such as Polly, certainly made sense to Martha. And though she had suspected that such might be true, to have her fears enunciated, made real in the words from the mouth of her friend, filled her with pain, and shame, and, at last, a burning rage.

Martha felt herself flush with humiliation, and she lowered her eyes to stare fixedly into the bottle of gin that she held tightly in her fist as Emily tittered on and on, animated with the excitement of delivering such a terrible (yet delicious) bit of gossip. At last, seeing that Martha did not even appear to be listening to her remarks about the depredations of men in general and the shocking disrespect shown Martha by John in particular, Emily's prattle tapered off. Discomfited by the strange demeanor of her friend, as Martha sat staring into her bottle, as immobile as a statue, Emily fidgeted uncertainly for a moment. She was no longer enjoying her role as the deliverer of bad news, and wondered if she ought to leave Martha sitting there with no further ado. Her decision was made for her when Martha looked up suddenly. Her eyes seemed to look through Emily, instead of at her.

"Go now!" rasped Martha, her voice not entirely her own. But it was the look in Martha's eyes more than her words that rattled Emily and caused her to rise suddenly and make for the door. For the ice that had frozen Martha's heart at the telling of Emily's story shone in her eyes. Black in the dim light of the dingy room and utterly devoid of any emotion save for cold fury, Martha's eyes appeared to Emily as soulless as those of a dead fish. Looking into those eyes, thought Emily, was like staring into the cold pits of hell, and she hurried out in all haste.

It wasn't until she was halfway down the street, and certain that Martha, with those dreadful eyes, wasn't behind her, that Emily's unreasoning terror abated. "Crazy old hag," she muttered, resentful now that her erstwhile friend had shown so little gratitude for the news that she had gone out of her way to tell her, and had instead scared her half witless to boot. "No wonder John needs some softer comfort with the likes of Polly. I bet Polly don't look at nobody with crazy dead eyes like that."

As for Martha, there was no further thought spared for Emily once she had left the room. She took a deep swig from her bottle, finishing it, and let the warmth of the gin diffuse through her body. Rather than calming her, though, it seemed instead to further ignite the animus that she felt towards Polly. How dare that trollop, that dissolute tramp, use her sagging, wrinkled old body to steal that which belonged to Martha; namely, her man and the money that should have been spent on food and Martha's own drink, rather than on the disgusting favors of a pox-ridden whore. No, Martha could not abide the insult of this for another moment, and she made up her mind to seek out Polly and have it out with her.

So thinking, Martha rose and strode purposefully out of her room, down the stairs, and out of the lodging house on to Flowers and Dean Street. She walked quickly down the narrow street, outrage and anger making her surefooted despite the gin-fogged state of her body and mind. She made several turns on to ever-narrower alleys and passageways, until she came at last to Buck's Row.

Not seeing Polly, she hesitated a moment, confused as to what to do next. "Where could that whore have got to?" she muttered aloud to herself. But then, she heard a low, guttural grunt, as though from a man achieving satisfaction. Quickly, she made off towards the sound, hoping, yet dreading, to catch John and Polly in the act. She rounded a bend in the street, and was disappointed, yet relieved, to spy Polly a few feet away, leaned up against a brick wall, with a man who was not John in the process of disengaging himself from her. The man was short, where John was tall; he wore a mustache, where John was bearded; and he wore a fancy sailor's hat, whilst John disdained such frippery.

The man smirked as Martha approached, tipped his hat to Polly, and slipped away into the shadows behind the wall. Polly, straightening her skirts, began to utter a greeting to Martha, but in her husky voice Martha imagined that she could hear the tone of smug condescension of a woman who had just seduced another woman's man, and thus felt herself superior.

Anger overcame her, and she lunged for Polly. The last thing she remembered was stumbling, beginning to fall to the ground, as she called out, "Don't you never touch my man again, you filthy whore!" before the gin that soaked her brain overcame her and a cloud of blackness obscured all thought.

When Martha awoke, she found that she was lying atop the small bed that she shared with John. Someone, presumably John, had removed last night's dress and she wore only her shift. Mid-morning light oozed into the room through the dirty wax-paper window, but even its weak cheeriness seemed to stab at her throbbing, aching brain.

John was busy dressing himself, but turned to her when he heard the low groan that escaped her lips as she tried to rise. The expression on his face as he looked at her was full of disapprobation, sadness, and a touch of disgust.

"What happened?" she croaked, her throat scratchy with dehydration. "How did I get home?"

"Shhh," he replied tersely. "Never you mind about that."

"But, Polly—" she began.

He raised a hand, silencing her. He then made his way to the door and opened it as though to leave, but stopped and turned to her before going.

"You got to stop drinking so much, Martha," he said, shaking his head. "You don't act right when you're in the bottle."

So saying, he stepped out into the corridor and closed the door behind him, none too quietly, causing Martha's groggy head to ache and throb even more.

Some time later, when Martha had recovered somewhat and had even managed a few bites to eat, Emily stopped by.

"Did you hear?" Emily said, her eyes sparkling with the excitement of the sordid news that she was about to impart. "About Polly?"

Martha's interest was immediately piqued. Knowing Emily as she did, she quickly deduced from her manner that something quite horrid must have happened. "What about Polly?" she asked impatiently, a sick feeling forming in her gut. She vaguely recollected the events of last night, and Emily's words seemed to stir some sort of memory in the depths of her brain, but the exact nature of it remained elusive. "What, Emily?" she demanded. "Out with it, now!"

Emily savored the deliciousness of her secret a moment longer, then leaned forward excitedly. "She done been . . ." she began, then paused for dramatic effect, looking from side to side as though to see who else might be listening, even though they were alone in the room. "She done been murdered!" she finished at last.

Martha gasped, and stared at Emily, mouth agape. Emily, thoroughly enjoying herself, nodded emphatically. "They found her body this morning, all chopped up like. Slashes here—" Emily made a slicing motion across her neck "—and here," now making the same motion across her belly.

As Martha's initial shock subsided, she began to feel a touch of self-righteous satisfaction set in.

"Well," she humphed. "Seems to me like she got just what she deserved. You sell your body like that, you break up families and steal people's men, well, one day it's bound to catch you up."

Emily stared at her, confused and somewhat disappointed by her reaction. She had expected shock and horror, or at least some degree of fear and outrage, not this callous indifference. So, she made her goodbyes to Martha and headed out in search of a more satisfactory audience.

* * *

Next Friday night, Martha found herself once more sitting alone in her room, as John did not come home yet again. Midnight came and went, as Martha speculated and worried and raged by turns. Clutching her bottle of gin to her breast, she drank more and more deeply from it as the minutes marched inexorably towards dawn and John still had not returned.

Finally, as 5 a.m. came and went, impatience and drunken outrage got the better of sense, and Martha headed out to search for her wayward man. However, she was not relieved when at last she found him. Quite to the contrary, actually. For, as she turned a corner on to Hanbury Street and made her way along the darkened twists and turns, she heard the unmistakable sound of John's voice, whispering in the dark shadows. A woman giggled, and Martha crept closer.

Her stomach lurched with a queasy, jealous feeling as she came closer and the two people became clear to her vision in the dim light. There stood John, leaning closely in to none other than Dark Annie, a prostitute known throughout the East End to have syphilis, and to be quite mad from it.

Martha's thoughts began to spiral out of control as she beheld her man in what was clearly the initial stages of a sexual transaction. Why, she thought, does he need these filthy women? Why did he prefer their diseased bodies to her own? Dark Annie was yet another drunkard, fleshy and bloated from the drink, utterly worthless as far as Martha was concerned. So why then was her man preparing to fornicate with this disgusting creature against a garden fence in this sleazy alley? And paying for the privilege, no less!

"Filthy, filthy whore!" Martha screamed, as rage took over her mind. "Faithless, sinful man!" She moved forward, thinking to thrust them apart, to stop this travestying that was occurring right before her very eyes. But the world spun, and grew gray around the edges, and then Martha knew no more.

She woke up the next morning in her own bed, with John sleeping soundly beside her. She stirred, hungover and nauseated, and unable to remember anything that had happened after she had seen John and Annie together. Panic set in, and she shook John awake.

"Did I stop you in time?" she asked feverishly. "Did you have relations with that whore?"

His eyes fluttered open, and he looked tiredly at Martha before sighing deeply. He began to rise, but she forestalled him by grabbing on to his arm, her grip like iron in her desperation.

"Did you do the deed with Dark Annie?" she demanded. "I deserve to know if you got the syphilis or not!"

"No, Martha," he answered resignedly. "I ain't got the syphilis." He paused, and looked upon her with the same expression that he had the week before. "I can't keep picking up after you like this, you know. You're not yourself when you've had a bottle."

"Well," Martha responded peremptorily, "mayhaps I wouldn't drink if my man weren't cavorting with prostitutes all night. And you're lucky I saved you from that pox-ridden whore."

So saying, she turned her back and listened to the sounds of him getting dressed and leaving, and at last fell back to sleep. It wasn't until later that day that she heard the news: Dark Annie Chapman had been found in the early morning, dead, her body mutilated and cut in much the same way that Polly's had been. Martha heard the news, wondered if the gap in her memory obscured some knowledge of what had happened, and then shrugged. It was nothing to her what happened to another whore of the East End. The world was better without women such as that, anyway.

After that, John played the dutiful man for several weeks. He came home early, and curtailed his drinking, and Martha dared to hope that this unpleasant interlude in their lives had passed. Then, one Friday night, John was once again late coming home. Martha, half a bottle of gin warming her belly, at last went out looking for him until the early hours of the next morning, to no avail. But, as she at last gave up and went home, and made her way down the hall of the lodging house to her room, hoping that John might be inside, she noticed that the neighbors were casting strange glances at her, then covering their mouths to whisper and titter as she passed.

At last, she grabbed one by the arm, a woman by the name of Ellen, and demanded to know the cause of this. Ellen prevaricated, blushing and looking wildly towards the others in the hall for help, but everyone had suddenly bethought themselves of other places to which they must immediately go, and had thusly taken themselves hence in all haste.

Impatient, Martha gave Ellen a nasty pinch. "Answer me, girl!" she hissed.

"It's just . . . it's that . . ." Ellen stammered nervously.

"Out with it then!" Martha demanded, pinching Ellen again.

"John were with Elizabeth Stride last night," Ellen blurted at last. "You know, what stays in the room upstairs?"

Martha released the girl, and strode away, embarrassed and angry. She promptly took herself to the nearest tavern, where she spent her food money on a fresh bottle of gin. Nursing it, she walked the streets of Whitechapel for hours, becoming ever more drunk and despondent. She tried to fight her growing anger, but the gin gave fuel to it and at last she gave in. Oh, how she hated these women, with their decaying teeth in wrinkled faces, their sagging breasts, their gaping woman parts that they used to seduce her man. She wondered if he were with one even now. Perhaps he was with Elizabeth, or maybe that dreadful Kate Kelly who was always batting her eyelashes at men and trying to wheedle money from them.

At last she came to her last gulp of gin and, as she downed it, she decided that she must confront Elizabeth, teach the chit a lesson, tell the slut to keep her hands off her man. Swiftly, she made her way back to the lodging house. However, she had downed two bottles of gin, with no sleep in between, and before she even reached Flowers and Dean Street she felt the comfort of the alcohol's oblivion taking over, and remembered no more.

She awoke some time before dawn on the stairs inside the lodging house, arranged in such a way so that she was unsure if she had passed out on her way up to Elizabeth's room or on her way down from it. Groggily, she lurched downstairs to her own room, and climbed wearily into bed. She was still too drunk, however, to either see, or to care if she had seen the glint of suspicion in John's eyes as he watched her. Nor did she much care when she awoke, and John told her that Elizabeth had been found dead in her room, her throat slashed. Further, Kate Kelly, who lived just up the street, had been found as well, her body horribly mutilated. Her ear had been chopped off, and her intestines pulled out and draped over her shoulder like a gruesome sash.

People now feared a habitual killer, and the cases had taken over the collective imagination of the populace. Everyone talked of the brutality of the murders. What animus, what twisted hate drove a person to such deeds? The people of Whitechapel, indeed of the entire East End, were horrified by it, and delighted with their horror at the same time. The people could not get enough of the story, and the newspapers were happy to feed their appetites each and every day.

But, as John spoke of this to Martha, she simply shrugged, uncaring. What of it, she thought. I don't even know if I made it up there, or if I saw Kate, either.

So that was that, in Martha's mind, and she felt better knowing that yet two more sinful tramps were gone from Whitechapel. The place was lousy with women such as them, after all, and now there were two fewer to tempt her man, she thought with satisfaction. Too long had these women traded their disease-infested bodies for drink, and too long had stupid, weak men fallen prey to their sordid charms. It was about time someone did something about it.

"Where was you last night, Martha?" John asked quietly.

"Oh, here and there," she replied tartly.

"I'm serious, Martha," he said. "Answer me."

"Maybe I was where you was the other night," she spat. "Maybe I was socializing with the likes of them tramps you're so fond of nowadays!"

"Don't joke, Martha," John growled warningly. "You do things when you drink. Things that ain't funny. Ain't funny at all."

"You think I done . . ." She hesitated, gesturing vaguely at the places on her own body that were analogous to the knife cuts on the bodies of Elizabeth and Kate. "You think I done that!" she shrieked.

"Well, you don't remember nothing, now, do you? And there were that time last year, when you done got so jealous and threatened that one lady with her own scissors. You was right scary, then, Martha, and I ain't stretching the truth none when I say so."

"Well," said Martha in an aggrieved tone, "that was different. I didn't do in that lady with the scissors, now, did I? Just made my point, is all. So don't you never accuse me of such doings again, do you hear me?"

So saying, she turned her back and busied herself with tidying up the room, thereby ending the conversation and also hiding her face from John's view. She didn't want him to read in her eyes the thoughts that whirled wildly through her mind. What if, in her gin-addled state, she had given in to her jealousy and rage? What if she were the murderer everyone in Whitechapel so feared? She didn't think herself capable of such atrocities, but John was right on two points: she didn't remember things when she was drunk, and she had been known to indulge her anger, sometimes quite violently, when the drink was in her.

Uncomfortable with the way such thoughts made her feel, she shook her head, dismissing them. It was no use speculating on what might have happened, or on what she may or may not have done. If John would stop with the trollops, there would be no problem. Yes, she decided, the whole situation was entirely John's fault.

John sighed, and left the room without another word. With him gone, she stopped pretending to clean, and instead picked up the daily newspaper that John had tossed carelessly to the floor. She couldn't read very well, but she liked to look at the pictures, and she could make out enough of the words to get the gist of the headlines, at least.

There, on the first page, was a picture of Mr Lusk, whom Martha, along with everyone in the neighborhood, knew as the President of the Mile End Vigilance Committee. The prostitutes of the East End resented

Mr Lusk for his efforts to bring Christian morals to bear on the brothels, because as the brothels closed under the pressure exerted by Lusk and his friends, the women within them were displaced on to the streets and alleys where they were easy prey for rough and lawless men, including the killer whom the papers had dubbed "The Ripper". Of course, it was for this very reason that Martha approved of Mr Lusk very much.

In the print above Mr Lusk's picture, Martha, squinting as she slowly sounded out the words, could just make out that Mr Lusk had received some sort of letter from the killer. This letter was the latest of several that had been addressed to Mr Lusk. Along with Mr Lusk, the newspapers and even the police had received dozens of letters in the past few weeks, purporting to be from the killer. Most of the letters were probably hoaxes, but nonetheless each one printed by the papers caused a great deal of excitement as residents of the East End picked over them line by line, trying to glean some clue from them as to the identity of the murderer.

The text of this most recent letter to Mr Lusk was printed there on the page, and Martha, struggling to read it, picked out a few words. As best she could tell, the letter said something about a kidney being mailed to Mr Lusk, and it was signed, "From Hell."

Well, thought, Martha. There you had it. She knew that she herself hadn't written that letter; indeed, she could scarcely read it. Therefore, any doubts that she may have harbored as to the extent of her actions on the nights of the murders, when her memory failed her (and she remembered only feelings of anger and righteous outrage), must, of course, be unfounded. That most people said that the letters sent to Lusk, the newspapers, and the police, were most likely fakes, practical jokes perpetrated by sick-minded people who enjoyed stirring up panic, or by journalists looking to build a sensational story, was a thought that Martha found it convenient to disregard.

No, any suspicions that she had about herself were now firmly put to rest. Satisfied, she put down the paper and went about her day, and guilty thoughts troubled her conscience no more.

Meanwhile, whilst Martha was thus occupied, John, out and about in Whitechapel, crossed paths with Martha's friend Emily. The two greeted each other, and made the usual polite small talk about the weather, and mutual acquaintances, and such. Soon, however, Emily turned the conversation to the subject of Martha, and her strange reactions to the news of the murders, which so occupied the thoughts of the residents of the East End, particularly the prostitutes who suddenly found themselves fearing the very men from whom they needed to solicit business.

Most people were horrified and frightened by the murders (and if they also happened to be just the slightest bit excited and titillated, well, that could be excused as a natural morbidity that was simply part of human nature). But Martha's reaction had seemed very unnatural to Emily. Smug and self-righteous, Martha had shown no evidence of compassion or sadness at the news of the deaths of women whom she had known for her entire life. To Emily's mind, such unfeeling nonchalance was incomprehensible. It most certainly was not the way one responded to such things, even if one disapproved of the women to whom those things had occurred. In fact, when Emily considered how little Martha had cared when she heard of the murders, and reflected on Martha's soulless eyes that had so scared her, she could almost fancy that Martha herself was the murderer. After all, John had been with all of the victims, and Martha had most certainly known of each tryst of his, as secrets were hard to keep in the East End. No, it wouldn't surprise her at all if it turned out that Martha had killed those women, and she determined to ascertain John's thoughts on the matter. With that thought in mind, Emily told John of her conversations with Martha, and of Martha's strange attitudes.

John, hearing of Martha's cold, dismissive behavior towards Emily, grew quiet, and stroked his beard pensively. Emily, sharp-eyed and ready as always to glean gossip from whatever source she could, considered his reaction. She was surprised that he did not immediately speak out in Martha's defense, but rather simply stood there in the street before her, looking troubled. This, of course, stoked Emily's suspicions of Martha to even greater heights, and she strove all the harder to pry whatever information she could from him that she might have all the more delicious tidbits to disseminate among all of her friends.

"Where was Martha those nights the girls was killed?" she urged, leaning forward to press her bosom against John's arm as though by accident, that he might be more inclined to share Martha's secrets with her.

But John just sighed and shook his head. "I dunno," he said sadly. "I just dunno."

"I know she was mad at them," she prompted.

John nodded, non-committally.

"John," gasped Emily, purposefully breathless and batting her eyes up at him as she leaned in even more closely. "You don't think it were Martha what done them in, do you?" she whispered, her face the picture of concerned innocence.

Gently, John extricated himself from her grasp, and moved away a step. "No, no," he replied, not meeting Emily's eyes with his own. "Of course not. Now, if you'll excuse me . . ."

With that, he turned and walked off briskly, leaving Emily to wonder. True, he had denied that Martha was the killer, but he certainly hadn't looked as if he was at all certain of it. In fact, he had seemed rather more like a man who was trying to convince himself of his woman's innocence, instead of a man who knew that she was guiltless without a doubt.

To Emily, the idea that John so much as doubted Martha was enough to convince her of Martha's guilt. But rather than rush off to speak of this with everyone she knew, Emily found that she was too nervous to even think of mentioning it. If Martha was the killer, Emily reasoned, it would not do to provoke her. So, for once, circumspection held Emily's tongue, and she remained quiet on the matter, and spoke of it no more.

So, too, did John. If he watched Martha closely while she painstakingly read the paper each morning, looking for news on the Ripper, if he wondered at the avid interest she took in the speculations of the reporters, as though she were searching for some clue to solve a mystery known only to her, if he flinched every time she spoke of another woman with a tongue sharpened by jealousy, he said naught, but kept his own counsel instead.

As for Martha, her interest in the case became nearly obsessive. She devoured each badly written letter that purported to be from the Ripper, hating when the syntax sounded like her own cockneyed speech, sighing with relief when the writing seemed beyond her own limited capabilities. And, as the weeks went by, and the Ripper remained quiescent, so too did Martha's vigilance over the papers quiet, and did John's own vigilance over Martha.

At last, John felt that perhaps the ordeal was over. As he relaxed, the call of drink and novel feminine companionship became too strong to resist and John slowly returned to his carousing ways. In response, Martha also turned once more to her bottle of gin, and once again began to find herself waking up with no recollection of the night before.

Such was the case one morning in early November. John had not come home the night before; Martha, three sheets to the wind, had gone out in search of him. She vaguely recollected finding John near Miller's Court. Things grew hazy after that, the flow of time became disjointed and it seemed that her memories were not in their proper order. She recalled confronting him, remembered slapping his face in anger, remembered him saying to her, "This has to stop, Martha!' and her own reply, "I ain't done nothing!" But she had no idea to what, exactly, the conversation had been referring (had he been with another prostitute? had he resisted her attempts to bring him home?), nor did she know in what order these events had occurred, or what, if anything, had happened in between.

Nevertheless, despite the argument, and the gaping holes in her memory, and her throbbing head, she felt somewhat cheery when she awoke the next morning, alone in their room in the lodging house, and she sang a little tune to herself as she made ready for the day.

"Father and mother they have passed away/Sister and brother now lay beneath the clay/But while life does remain to cheer me I'll retain/This small violet I plucked from Mother's grave."

It was a melancholy song, to be sure, but Martha skipped about the room as she sang, a small smile lifting the corners of her mouth. She was still happily singing and flitting about the room when John burst in, brandishing the morning's newspaper like an accusation.

"Do you see?" he growled, shaking the paper in her face. "Is this what you done?"

Her cheery mood faltered in the face of his anger. "Done what?" she asked, confused.

"Done in Mary Kelly, that's what!" he yelled.

"Of course not!" she protested. "I was with you, weren't I?"

John sat heavily on the bed and slumped dejectedly. "Well, I think so," he said, calmer now that she had denied his accusation and enabled him to doubt his worst suspicions. "I know you was mad, and yelling, and cussing up a fit. But I don't know where you was before."

"Well!" she huffed, putting on an air of aggrieved dignity. "I most definitely weren't out 'doing in' another of your tramps, that's for sure."

"I just don't know, Martha," he said sadly. "And I don't know if you even know, neither. I don't like to think you coulda done them things. But you got a nasty streak in you what comes out when you're in your cups, and I don't rightly think I can take it no more."

With that, he stood and made to leave, but Martha blocked his way. "You rotten whoreson!" she screamed. "After all I done for you, all I put up with! And how do you 'spect me to pay the lodging fee if you leave me? You'd make me destitute, scrounging up bed money by using my body like them whores you like so much."

John reached into his pocket, took out a fistful of coins, and pressed them into Martha's hand. A few dropped to the ground and, as she bent to pick them up, he darted around her and made his escape.

"You'll be back!" she cried after him. "Best hope I ain't got myself a better man than you by then!"

She then hurled herself on to the bed, weeping hysterically. She didn't grieve so much for the loss of John, that whore-chasing bastard, as she did for the loss of financial help as well as for the blow to her pride. That he should leave her, when by rights it should have been the other way around! And the accusations he had made were simply outrageous.

But a small worm of doubt crept into her mind again. Were his accusations so outrageous, after all? It was true that John had been with each murdered girl, shortly before the Ripper had got to them. And it was also true that on each of the nights that the Ripper had struck, she, Martha, had gone out in search of him, dead drunk and in a blind rage. Further, on each of the nights in question, there were disturbing gaps in her memory. Might she be the Ripper, after all?

She shuddered with horror at the thought, for though she felt that the Ripper had done the world a service by removing those low-life trollops from it, so did she feel certain that, righteous or no, the absolute brutality of those murders would surely condemn the perpetrator to hell.

No, she thought, pushing her suspicions aside. If she had done the murders, surely God couldn't hold her accountable if she didn't remember. And besides, if she had done anything violent during her blackouts, it was really more John's fault than hers. If he hadn't been out whoring, she wouldn't have to drink and search him out, and then she wouldn't be left to wonder like this.

Her logic pleased her, and she resolved to question herself no further on the subject. She nodded her head sharply, as though to punctuate her decision, and, smoothing her skirt, made herself busy once more. And, as she went to and fro about the room, the song that she had sang earlier rose to her lips. "But while life does remain, in memoriam I'll retain/This small violet that I plucked from Mother's grave."

It was a popular song, yes, sung by many all over London. But it was also the last song that anyone had ever heard Mary Kelly sing, just before she was silenced forever by the Ripper's cruel blade. Of course, no one heard Martha's singing, and Martha herself put the matter from her mind, and resolved to think of John and his whores no more.

Her resolve lasted for nearly a year, as she quietly struggled to make ends meet without the benefit of John's income and was therefore too busy and distracted to spare much thought to John and his doings. She still partook of the bottle, yes, but never so much as to forget herself. Her fortitude was shaken, however, when a chance encounter with Emily stirred up her latent anger and sent her, reeling, back to the bottle. Emily had, for the most part, avoided Martha since their last meeting, and generally felt uneasy at the mere thought of her. But time had dulled her anxieties and, as the weeks and months went on and still the murderer did not strike, Emily began to think that perhaps she had overreacted in having suspected Martha of being capable of such atrocities.

So it was that when Martha hailed Emily on the street one Tuesday afternoon, Emily stopped to chat amiably with her one-time friend. And, as the women talked, Emily found herself unable to keep to herself the latest bit of gossip that she had: namely, that John had taken up with a woman named Alice.

Martha, who had thought herself well rid of John and better off without him, felt the news like a physical blow. Her belly felt as though she had swallowed a bucket full of hungry worms, nasty slimy things that chewed and gnawed as they fed on her insides. She realized that she had thought all along that John would come crawling back to her, begging for her forgiveness. But now, this Alice woman would ruin it all! She felt a hot flush of rage creep up her neck to color her cheeks as she considered the audacity of this woman who dared to take what was rightfully hers.

Emily watched as Martha's countenance changed, and quickly remembered what it was that she had feared so about her. The darting eyes, the twitching hands, the snarling lips: these were the signs of a madwoman. Hastily, Emily made her excuses and hurried away up the street, glancing back nervously as Martha stomped off to the nearest tavern to purchase a bottle of gin.

Within the hour, as the sun set and darkness overtook the East End, Martha had consumed enough of the gin to be quite drunk and not entirely in command of her faculties. She knew only that she was in pain, enraged; she knew further that the source of this pain and rage was this woman named Alice. Therefore, she set out to find her, in order to assuage her emotions.

As she didn't know exactly who Alice was, Martha determined that her best chance of finding her would be to find John. She called at the lodging house where she had heard that he stayed recently, but found that he was out and that no one knew where he had got to this evening. So she began to wander about Whitechapel, drinking her bottle and asking passers-by if they had seen him, and if they knew of Alice. No one could, or would, tell her anything, however, and so she continued to wander, drinking and becoming ever angrier as she grew frustrated in her search.

Eventually, Martha found herself on Pinchin Street, a particularly run-down street that ran beneath the railroad. As she approached Back Church Lane, she passed beside the stone arches that supported the train tracks. There, leaning against the stone, was a man. Good-looking, too well dressed for this neighborhood at this time of night, he doffed his hat to her and smiled. His blue eyes crinkled charmingly at the corners, and his blond mustache framed his full lips to their best advantage. Despite herself, Martha felt herself flush, and she giggled like a schoolgirl at his greeting.

"Hullo," she said shyly, batting her eyes in a ludicrously drunken attempt at flirting.

"Hullo, pretty lady," he said. "What's a pretty creature such as yourself doing wandering about alone at this time of night?"

"Oh, you know, I can take care of myself," she replied, trying hard not to slur her words. She found herself attracted to this handsome stranger, and thought that perhaps, with his help, she could forget all about John for a time. So she smiled as coquettishly as she was able, and licked her lips seductively. "But if you're worried for me, you could walk me home."

The man simply continued to look at her, his eyes taking in her body that had gone a bit soft, her teeth that had gone a bit yellow, her once-pretty face that had gone a bit haggard. She tittered and fluttered nervously under his close regard, and he laughed at her discomfiture before his smile turned into an ironic smirk.

Martha paused, uncertain. It suddenly seemed to her that that smirk was familiar, that she had seen it before. But where? Her drunken mind was slow to recollect.

The man moved forward, and he took her by the arm. "I'd be happy to walk with you," he said, as his fingers gripped her flesh somewhat too tightly, causing needles of pain to break through her drink-fogged thoughts.

"You was with Polly that night!" she burst out, suddenly remembering where she had seen the man. "Wasn't you?"

He pulled her to face him, holding her closely, his mouth only inches from hers.

"Guilty, my dear," he said. "Does this bother you?"

Martha thought for a moment. On the one hand, she was revolted by the thought of another man who partook of the whores of Whitechapel. But, on the other hand, it would feel good to take something that had once been Polly's, just as Polly had once taken something that had belonged to her. And the man's presence was commanding. Her body responded eagerly to the scent of him, so close to her, and to the feel of his mustache tickling against her lips. So Martha tilted her head back to invite the stranger to kiss her.

As she did so, too late did her mind process what she should have seen in an instant. Because, yes, this was the man who had been with Polly. He had been with Polly on the night that she was murdered, and now this same man held Martha closely in his embrace.

She stiffened and pulled back. "Who are you?" she asked, hoping that there would be a reasonable explanation for this terrible coincidence. "Where are you from?"

"I'm Jack, my sweet," he said, laughing, as a predatory glint came into his eyes. He opened his coat, and pulled a wickedly sharp blade from within it. "And I'm from Hell, my dear. I'm from Hell."

The Ripper Legacy
John Moralee

———

"God!" Emily said. "Is that clock accurate?"

"Yeah," Nick answered breathlessly, running his hands over her naked thighs. "Why?"

"I'm sorry." Emily reluctantly pulled away from him, rushing to the short skirt and lacy underwear she had stripped off and dropped on the carpet of Nick's office. She started dressing quickly. "My husband's doing a Ripper lecture tonight. I can't miss it."

Nick groaned. "Just another ten minutes, Ems. He won't care if you're not there. Come back over here, you naughty girl."

"I can't," she said. "I promised I'd be there."

Nick strode over to her and kissed her neck, his hand caressing her hips, tugging at her skirt, easing it down her legs. He whispered in her ear. "But I want you *now*."

Emily was very tempted to stay, but she was already half-dressed and feeling guilty for having an affair with her boss. It was such a cliché. "No. I can't." She gently slapped his hands away from her skirt. "I have to go. We have this weekend thing planned."

Nick stepped back. He looked annoyed.

"Go then," he said.

She hurried out of his office to the lift, where she adjusted her skirt and buttoned her blouse up to her neck as the lift descended to the underground parking level.

Emily drove out of the exit and travelled out of London to the Wetherley Hotel. The hotel was a country manor, which had been modernised into a three-star hotel by its owners. She collected her room key from the reception, dumped her bags in her room, then went searching for the conference room. It was easy to find because a life-sized Jack the Ripper figure stood beside the doors. The cardboard cut-out character was wearing a top hat and black cape – with a knife in one hand and a Gladstone bag in the other. It was creepily realistic. The Ripper's malevolent dark eyes stared at her like he wanted her to be his next victim. Her husband normally kept it at home in the garage, where it scared her every time she saw it. She felt like punching it as she walked by.

Aaron's stupid lecture had started at eight, but it was half past eight when she sneaked into the conference room.

Emily discovered only a dozen other members of the Ripper Society had bothered to show up for her Aaron's lecture. They included just one new member – a shabbily dressed bearded man wearing a black anorak. There had been over three hundred active members at the beginning, when Aaron created the society while a student at Oxford, but most had dropped out after a few years, leaving only the hard-core Ripperologists by the society's tenth year.

That evening her husband was dressed in his best suit and tie, standing behind a lectern with a map of London circa 1888 projected behind him on a large screen. Emily hoped Aaron would not be upset by her late arrival when she sat next to Kyra, the only other young woman in the group, but Aaron cast his disapproving eyes over her before continuing a heated argument with a heavily tattooed member called Gary, who wore a black leather jacket and aviator sunglasses indoors. Gary was a writer of Ripper horror stories. Unlike her husband, Gary didn't attend their meetings because he wanted to solve the murders. He came to get new ideas for his short stories and novels.

Emily mouthed "sorry" to her husband as she took off her jacket and made herself comfortable, but Aaron didn't see her apologising. He was shaking his head at something Gary had said.

Emily whispered to Kyra, "What are they arguing about?"

"Gary mentioned Lewis Carroll."

Aaron was a serious Ripperologist. He would not have liked that. He was glaring at Gary. "You are so wrong it isn't even funny. Lewis Carroll was a *joke* suspect. He wasn't even in London when some of the murders happened. A much more credible suspect is Charles Allen Cross, the subject of my lecture tonight."

Gary rolled his eyes. "Oh, come on! You don't seriously think he did it, do you? He's a boring nobody!"

"He's not a boring nobody. He's a credible suspect. Can I continue or do you want to interrupt some more?"

Gary shrugged. "Whatever."

Aaron looked around at the other members of the Ripper Society, his focus stopping on Emily. She remembered his intensity and passion quickening her heart, but she did not feel that way any longer. All she saw was his obsession with the Ripper ruining their relationship. For ten years it had been all he had been interested in after leaving university. He wrote books on the Ripper, ran a website and internet forum, organised monthly Ripper Society meetings, and blogged about it every day. Aaron spent more time researching the Ripper than he did with her. She was not in love with him any more, but he had not even noticed. At least Nick noticed her.

Emily watched her husband turn to point at the screen while pressing a key on his laptop. A section of the map enlarged to show Whitechapel in 1888. "Like I was saying before Gary *rudely* interrupted, Charles Allen Cross was here on Buck's Row, actually standing over the body of the second Ripper victim, when he was seen by another man. That witness – Robert Paul – would have definitely described Cross to the police as a suspect if Cross had not claimed to have just found the body. Cross said that he had just got there and seen nobody else around, but the body was still warm . . . so how did he not see or hear the killer leaving? There is only one simple explanation. Cross was Jack the Ripper."

"That's *too* simple," Gary said. "In my opinion, Cross was just what he claimed to be – an innocent witness. What does everyone else think?"

More people agreed with Gary than Aaron, clearly annoying Aaron, who had expected his argument to win greater support. Emily felt sorry for her husband. She had known he had spent weeks working on that night's lecture.

"Please consider the evidence!" Aaron said. "Occam's razor states the simplest solution is—"

"Dead boring!" another member interrupted. That was a platinum blonde woman in her mid-forties called Glenda. Glenda wore sexy clothes like Marilyn Monroe, showing off her large fake breasts, but she had a greater resemblance to the murderous Myra Hindley. "We don't want Jack to be some boring ordinary man. That's not interesting. I want it to be a conspiracy involving the Royal Family and the government. That's *exciting*!"

"What I'm saying might not be exciting," Aaron said, "but I'm after the truth."

"The truth?" Gary said, doing an obvious Jack Nicholson impression from *A Few Good Men*. "You can't handle the truth!"

His comment received laughs from some and disdainful looks from others. Not even remotely amused, Aaron slammed his fist on the lectern. "Listen to me! The evidence against Cross is strong. He lied to the police. He knew the area well because he worked nearby. His job as a cart driver made him practically invisible. He wore an apron and delivered meat for a slaughterhouse, so nobody would even think twice about seeing him with blood on his clothes. He could have done it, people! I've done a computer simulation of each murder that—"

Gary stood up and yawned. "I'm tired of this subject. We're all here to have a good weekend, right? Are we going to the bar or what, guys?"

Glenda jumped up, her breasts jiggling. "The bar!"

More people stood up.

That ended Aaron's lecture early as several people followed Gary towards the doors. Kyra stayed behind with Emily, but only until the room was almost empty. "Well, I might as well join them. Emily, you coming?"

"I'll be along soon," she said.

The lecture abandoned, nobody had a reason to stay. Everyone remaining headed to the bar, leaving Emily alone with her furious husband. She walked over to Aaron as he closed his laptop and put away his research material in a black briefcase. He was muttering something as she gently put her hands on his shoulders and rubbed his tight, tense muscles. "Don't get so upset about Gary. He's an idiot."

"But I'm right about Cross," he said. "He is a good suspect. Gary should admit I'm right. I hate that man. He doesn't come to talk seriously about the Ripper. He just comes to socialise and mock my attempts at being a professional investigator of the facts."

"Forget him," Emily said. "I was interested in what you said. Now let's go and join the others for a drink, OK?"

Aaron sighed. "Fine. Just don't expect me to be nice to Gary. He can go to hell." He slammed his briefcase shut. "By the way, why were you so late? Everything would have been a lot better if you'd been there on time. Was it your boss again, keeping you late at the office?"

"I left work at seven, but there was a traffic jam," she said, the lie flowing smoothly from her lips while she rubbed her wedding ring. "Being late wasn't my fault. There was an accident or something. Now, forget about what Gary said so we can have a good weekend."

In the hotel bar Emily and Aaron joined a group at a table where everyone was discussing the 'Dear Boss' letters. Those letters had been the first ones to give the Whitechapel Murderer the catchier nickname Jack the Ripper. Some people thought they were a hoax written by a journalist to reignite interest in the story, but the identity of the writer had never been resolved, deepening the mystery. The newbie in the black anorak had a lot of questions.

"Where's Gary?" Aaron mumbled to Emily.

"Uh – way over there."

Wisely, Gary was sitting at another table far away, drinking beers and flirting with Glenda. It looked as though the members had split into two groups according to how they had reacted to Gary's suggestion. The pro-Gary faction were laughing and having a good time – making Emily a little jealous because they were enjoying themselves. They were clearly not talking scholarly about Jack the Ripper, like the pro-Aaron group.

There had been a time when Emily had been just as obsessed with the Ripper as Aaron. Aged thirteen, she had done some homework for her Social Studies class which involved drawing a family tree. Using a genealogy website, she had discovered that she was related to the Ripper's fifth victim, Mary Jane Kelly. That fact had led to a keen interest in all things Ripper-related. At university she had joined Aaron's Ripper Society because she wanted to learn more. Aaron had been fascinated by her link to the Ripper, treating her like a celebrity. She had loved his attention. Emily remembered spending long nights with him in the university library researching Victorian London. After a long study session, they used to sneak into the stacks to kiss and make love. Now she could hardly remember the last time her husband had shown any sexual interest in her. Right then he was showing more interest in answering the newbie's questions.

"I'm a little confused," the newbie was saying. "What exactly are the canonical murders I've heard people mentioning?"

"Most experts believe just five murders can be attributed to Jack the Ripper because they match his MO of strangling, throat-cutting and dismembering his victims. They were Polly Nichols, Anne Chapman, Elizabeth Stride, Catherine Eddowes and Mary Jane Kelly. They are the so-called canonical murders. There were several more murders in Whitechapel that could be Ripper kills, but they don't match the same MO. Martha Tabram, for example, was stabbed multiple times, but she wasn't strangled first. There was also Rose Mylett and Lizzie Davies. They . . ."

Emily soon became bored by the conversation at her table because she had heard it all before. She stopped listening, choosing instead to focus on getting drunk with Kyra, who had been her best friend since they shared a room at Oxford. Kyra had joined the Ripper Society to support Emily, but over the years Kyra had developed an expert's knowledge in the subject. Kyra was a freelance journalist and Ripperologist, but she didn't talk about the Ripper endlessly. She only talked about that subject if asked. Emily appreciated that. They moved away to another table so they could chat about what they'd been doing since they last met in person.

"I haven't done much," Emily said. She nearly added: "Apart from having an affair." But she didn't say it. "You still seeing that guy – the TV presenter?"

"No," Kyra said. "He went back to his wife."

"I'm sorry."

"Don't be. He was a jerk. He never intended to leave her. He was a liar." Kyra emptied her glass of wine. "God, I wish I could find a good man. I'm sick of dating losers. You are so lucky, Emily."

"I am?"

"Absolutely. You're married to a man you love."

Emily sighed. "Lucky me."

Kyra frowned. "Hey – you look sad. What's up?"

"Our sex life is non-existent."

"Oh. But you two used to be all over each other."

"I know," Emily said. "These days we hardly do *anything* together. I'm always working and he's always researching. Hell, Kyra – you probably spend more time with him than I do because you share his interest in the Ripper. Frankly, I'm sick of hearing about the Ripper. He's like a third person in our marriage."

"Are you crying?"

"A little," she admitted, wiping her tears away before anyone else noticed. "God, Kyra, I've done something bad."

"What?"

The next words out of her mouth would have never escaped if she had not been drinking so much wine. "I've been having an affair."

Kyra looked stunned. "Wow." She lowered her voice. "How long?"

"Four months."

"With whom?"

"This guy at the office. Nick. My boss. He's married too. We started flirting one day and then it just sort of happened."

"Does Aaron know?"

"Of course not. You're not going to say something, are you?"

Kyra shook her head. "I'd never do that. God. What are you going to do?"

"I don't know. Maybe a divorce?" She felt a sob in her throat, which she had to suppress. "I don't like thinking about it. I need another drink. I'm not yet drunk enough to enjoy myself. I need another glass of wine immediately."

"I'll get it," Kyra said.

Emily stayed in the bar until midnight. The bar stayed open for another couple of hours, but she was embarrassingly slurring her words and did not want to stay up that late. She said good night to Kyra before approaching the table where her husband was still talking to the bearded newbie in the black anorak. "I'm going to bed, Aaron. Are you coming with me?"

"Uh – no. Just want to discuss something a bit longer."

Emily didn't bother kissing him. What would be the point? She staggered towards the lift in the reception area, where she saw Glenda waiting alone with a bottle of champagne. The door to the first lift opened after about a minute of awkward silence. They entered it together. Glenda pressed for the fourth floor. "Which floor are you on?"

"Uh – four."

"That's me, too. I guess we're all on the same floor because we booked at the same time."

"Guess so."

That was the end of their conversation. The lift opened on to a long red-carpeted corridor, which had doors to the left and right. Emily's room was number 404, which was to the left. Glenda exited and turned right. "Good night, Emily."

"'Night."

Emily reached her room and struggled to find the key in her hand-bag. It took her a long time to locate it even though it had a plastic fob attached. She fumbled the key into the lock and opened her door, pausing to look into the darkness inside the suite, which had twin beds instead of a double because her husband liked to sleep on his own.

A giggle down the corridor made her turn her head to see Glenda disappearing into a room. "Got the champers," Glenda said before the door closed. Emily was envious. Glenda wasn't going to sleep alone. Emily stumbled over to her bed and slumped down on it, lonely and angry, seriously thinking of sexting Nick, but Nick would be at home with his wife and kids. Calling him now would be a very dumb move. Feeling very sorry for herself, Emily stripped off her clothes and crawled into her single bed. She sobbed into her pillows until she slipped into unconsciousness.

"Emily . . . Emily . . ."

"What?"

"Time to wake up."

"Urgh. What's the time?"

"Six-thirty."

"Six-thirty?" She opened her eyes and saw her husband was already shaved and dressed. "I was sleeping. Why the hell did you wake me?"

"Breakfast's between seven and eight-thirty. It's best to be down before everyone else."

"Why?"

"It's buffet style. All the bacon and eggs will be freshly cooked if we get there early."

"Please don't talk about food. I feel sick."

"Hangover?"

"Yes. From hell."

"*From Hell*! That's the title of a Ripper film starring Johnny Depp!"

Emily could not believe he had brought up the Ripper before she had got out of bed or even woken up properly. A new record. "Go down on your own. Let me sleep a little longer."

"Come on. I gave you half an hour to get ready. I'll turn on the shower and make some tea."

She tried going back to sleep, but the sound of the shower running made it hard. Hearing the kettle boiling made it impossible. Confronted by a hot cup of tea that smelled vilely of clotted UHT milk, her stomach flipped and she rushed to the toilet just in time.

Aaron came to the doorway. "You OK, hon?"

"No, but you got me awake. Happy now?"

"You sound mad with me, but being awake is better than sleeping through a breakfast we've already paid for."

"Not to me it isn't." Her stomach couldn't cope with a big breakfast. But she was fully awake now. By seven she was ready to leave their suite for a very light breakfast – maybe some dry toast and fruit – so she followed Aaron into the corridor. They walked to the lift in silence. Aaron pressed the button. She pressed it too once, twice, three times.

"That won't speed it up," he said.

"Oh, shut up."

"What did I do?"

She sighed. "Let's just get down for breakfast. I'm not in the mood for talking to you this early in the morning."

The lift was coming up to their floor. Upon arriving, the door opened slowly, revealing a dark figure inside – with a knife.

It was Jack the Ripper.

"Jesus!" Emily cried out. It took her a second to realise it was the cardboard cut-out. "What the hell, Aaron? That's not funny! You scared me."

"I didn't put it there," he said. "I bet it was Gary. I should have a stern word with him."

"Forget him," Emily said. "Let's just go down now."

They squeezed into the lift with Jack the Ripper between them. Emily pressed G for the ground floor. The lift descended silently, almost like it was not moving. After a minute it reached the ground floor. Emily stepped out in the deserted reception while her husband lifted up his cardboard Ripper and carried it out. He stood holding it outside the closed, locked doors of the dining room.

Emily glared at him.

"What?" he said innocently.

"You are not bringing that thing with us for breakfast. The staff will think you are a nutter."

"OK. I'll put Jack back outside the conference room," he said, leaving her standing alone.

She waited impatiently until Aaron returned. They stood waiting for another ten minutes. Emily paced. "This is ridiculous. We obviously came down too early."

"Not according to my watch. They should have opened up by now. Where is everyone?"

"Are you sure you have the time right?"

"Yes," he said. He walked over to the reception desk. "I'll get someone."

He rang the bell for service, but nobody appeared. Emily was bored of standing around waiting for a breakfast she didn't even want. "I'm going back to our room."

"I'll stay here."

"Whatever. You can get me when they eventually open the dining room." She stomped off towards the lift.

The fourth floor was deathly quiet when she walked back to her room. On the way, she noticed several doors were ajar, which seemed strange because nobody had come down for breakfast. Maybe there were no guests in those rooms? She stopped at Kyra's room. Her door was ajar too, so she knocked and called her name.

There was no reply, but her knock pushed the door inwards, revealing darkness. The curtains were closed. "Kyra?" Emily identified the shapes of the TV, wardrobe and bed. The bed was occupied and, for a moment, Emily believed her friend was sleeping – but something was wrong. As her eyes adjusted to the gloom, a tightness gripped her chest so she could not even scream.

Someone had sliced Kyra's neck open to the bone. One of Kyra's internal organs – a kidney or her liver – had been draped on her shoulder. More organs had been removed and left in a heap on her butchered abdomen.

Emily stared at her in shock and disbelief. Her best friend was lying in a pool of dark blood, very, very dead.

Emily staggered backwards into the corridor, trying to shout for help, but she felt as though her own throat had been cut because she could make no sounds. She gasped for breath, looking up and down the empty corridor, afraid the killer would suddenly appear. A thought hit her like a powerful blow. Call the police! Her phone was in her bag. Her bag was in her room. She had the key on her, but she was terrified of unlocking the door in case the killer was in there, waiting for her.

A noise made her look towards the lift. There was a light on. The lift was coming up. Who was inside? Was it Aaron? She hoped it was, but what if it was the killer?

She ran up to a door that was slightly open and slipped into another dark bedroom. There was a male dead body on the bed with its throat cut, but she didn't scream because she was more frightened by the unknown person coming up in the lift. Any noise would give away her hiding place. She closed the door the way she had found it and listened as the lift stopped. She thought of hiding in the room somewhere, but what if her movements made a noise? No – she was frozen behind the door. Listening as someone stepped out of the lift. The soft carpet made their footfalls almost silent. Was it the killer? She peered through the gap as the person walked in her direction. A shadow passed.

She saw it was Aaron. Relief poured through her in a warm wave as she opened the door, making her husband jump when she whispered his name. He turned around, frowning. "Nobody showed up at the reception. What are you doing in Henry's room?"

"Hiding," she said. "Aaron, someone's killing everyone."

"What?"

"Look."

She stepped aside so he could see beyond her into the room. Aaron studied the crime scene like he was used to seeing dead bodies in hotel rooms. "My God! His wounds are like the Ripper's first victim."

"Kyra's dead too," she said. "I think someone's been in every room, leaving the doors ajar after killing the people inside. W-what are we going to do?"

"We'll get the police." Aaron patted his pockets. "Damn. I left my phone in our room. Do you have yours?"

"No. It's also there."

"OK – let's get our phones and call the police."

"What if the killer is waiting in our room?"

"I don't know," he said. "You want to risk it or just get out of here?"

"Out of here," she said.

"Lift or stairs?"

"Not the lift. We'd be trapped."

"The stairs then."

"OK," she said.

Just then she heard a door opening down the corridor. They both stared as a woman appeared wearing a hotel bathrobe, last night's clothes bundled in her hands. It was Glenda. She grinned nervously. "Oh, hi. You caught me doing the 'walk of shame'!"

"You're OK?" Emily said.

"Yeah," Glenda said. "Why wouldn't I be?"

"Everyone's dead – except you and us."

"What are you talking about?"

"They've been murdered in their sleep," Aaron said. "Their throats were cut – like Jack the Ripper's victims."

Glenda should have been shocked, but she continued walking towards them. "That's a sick joke, Aaron."

"I'm not joking." He opened the door of Kyra's suite. "Look if you don't believe me."

Finally, Glenda accepted what they were saying. "She's dead. Really dead. Have you called the police?"

"Not yet," Aaron said. "We left our phones in our room. Do you have yours?"

Glenda nodded. "Here. You report it. I can't even think of the name of the hotel. My head's spinning. I can't believe everyone's dead. I'd better tell Gary."

Aaron made the call while Glenda went back to the room to get Gary. Gary came out half dressed, wearing only his jeans and socks. Even though he had been told everyone was dead, Gary had to have a look for himself in several rooms. "They've all been butchered. Wow. It's like the Ripper's alive again."

He almost sounded excited.

Cool and collected, Aaron reported the murders while Emily looked up and down the corridor, fearing the killer would come back. She felt safer with four of them still alive, but none of them had a weapon until Gary went back to his room and brought back a mini fire extinguisher.

Aaron ended his call. "The police are coming right now. They should be here in fifteen minutes."

Gary swore. "Fifteen minutes? We could all be dead by then. Let's get out of here *now*. Come on, Glenda. Let's go."

He hurried to the lift with Glenda following him. Emily and Aaron warned them to come back, but they didn't listen. Gary reached the lift with Glenda right behind him. As soon as Gary pressed the button, the door opened. Gary stepped in, but Glenda was reluctant.

"What if the killer's downstairs, Gary?"

"Listen to me," Emily said. "We can't go down in the lift. It's too predictable. We have to get out another way."

Glenda nodded in agreement. "Any ideas?"

"The stairs?" Aaron suggested.

Gary stepped out of the lift. "You lead the way."

"No," Emily said. "The stairs go to the same place – the reception area. We need to think of something better. I know! The fire exit. It leads directly outside, down the side of the building."

There was a sign pointing in the direction of the nearest fire exit – around a corner to their left. Emily and Aaron led the way down the corridor until the exit was in view. There was a metal bar across the exit to be pushed only in emergencies. This situation definitely constituted an emergency. Emily and Aaron pushed the bar together and opened the door, stepping out into the cold, fresh air, triggering an alarm. Emily looked down at the car park below. In the distance she could see flashing lights on the road leading to the hotel. She hurried down the stairway, holding her husband's hand.

Just one police vehicle showed up in response to the 999 call, until the full extent of the situation was understood by the authorities. Soon after, the hotel was surrounded by police vehicles and ambulances. A paramedic checked Emily for shock at the scene. Her blood pressure was high, but not dangerously high. She wanted to go home, but a forensics officer had to examine her before letting her leave.

The massacre at the hotel was the biggest story on the news all week, although the police didn't release many details at first. The total dead was estimated at over eighty by the media, but the police would not confirm that figure – 'until we do a complete investigation'. A few days passed before a detective visited Emily and Aaron to give them an update. Eighty-four people had been killed. They included all of the staff and most of the guests.

"It appears the killer started with the staff on duty during the night. They had their throats cut. Then the killer used the spare keys to go room to room murdering everyone in their beds. They were all killed very quickly so they could not wake the other guests. The survivors had one thing in common, which probably saved your lives. You were not sleeping alone. We believe the killer did not risk attacking you because the other person in the room might have woken up during the attack."

"Do you have a suspect?" Aaron said.

The detective nodded. "There was one guest unaccounted for among the dead and survivors. This man."

The detective showed them a photograph of a bearded man. "Do you recognise this man?"

"Yes," Aaron said. "He was a new member."

"We didn't find his body," the detective said. "His name is Eric Casavian. We found some things at his home address that make us believe he was the man responsible."

Emily was curious. "What sort of things?"

"I can't go into details," the detective said. "I'll just say his internet history is quite disturbingly violent. He had a collection of over ten thousand horror movies. He recently joined your society, Aaron?"

Aaron nodded. "That's right."

"What can you tell me about him?"

"Not much. We only met at the conference. We had a long conversation about Jack the Ripper on the night of the . . . massacre. I explained to him what the canonical murders were. He didn't seem to think that five murders was a lot, considering how infamous the Ripper has become. He knew a lot about other serial killers like Ted Bundy. Do you think he murdered everyone just to outdo the real Ripper?"

"I don't know his motive," the detective said, "but what you've told me is helpful."

"Do you think you'll catch him?"

"We just don't know."

As one of the survivors, Emily was the focus of a great deal of media attention in the weeks that followed. At first she was portrayed as a brave survivor, but then a tabloid exposed her affair with Nick. Twitter trolls launched a merciless attack on her – many users somehow blaming her for the massacre – but that didn't hurt as much as Aaron's reaction. He moved out of their home.

She didn't lose her job because of her affair, but she was transferred to another department where she never saw Nick. For months she spent most of her time in her office working late because she hated going back to an empty house. She didn't know if she wanted to stay married to

Aaron, but she hated the hurt she had caused him. Working hard was something to distract her from the mess she had made of her life.

She spent much time using her office computer, visiting internet forums, curious to see what people were thinking about the murders. Most people thought Eric Casavian had done them to become as famous as the real Jack the Ripper. Others believed he was just a psycho. A small group believed Eric Casavian was not the killer, but another victim, as yet undiscovered. Some believed Casavian's body had been dismembered and his head taken away by the real killer to fool the police into thinking he had done it, but that theory had no grounding in the evidence. None of the body parts had DNA matching the DNA evidence collected from Eric Casavian's flat in Camden. In the darkest parts of the internet, wild theories spread like school gossip as thousands of people speculated about the identity of the murderer. One group suspected Gary because he had used the murders as publicity to sell his latest novel. Aaron had benefited from the publicity in a perverse way, too. His website had received five thousand new subscribers and his Twitter account had gained one hundred and seventy thousand new followers. He had also been invited to be a guest speaker at a convention of Ripperologists held in Las Vegas. He had become a celebrity. Was that a possible motive for the murders? Fame?

There was no evidence to prove it, but a leaked police report did make Emily wonder about her husband. The murder weapon used to kill everyone had been a sixteen-inch knife taken from the hotel's kitchen. If Eric Casavian had been the killer and he had planned the murders ahead of time, why did he not bring his own murder weapon?

The answer to that question haunted her mind.

For weeks she had been avoiding Nick, but she encountered him one evening when they had to share the lift going down to the underground car park. It was an awkwardly silent ride down. The underground parking area was dark and smelled of petrol fumes. Most employees of Waterman-Cooper had left hours ago, so just a handful of cars remained in the cavernous space. A weak strip of lights in the middle provided light, leaving most of the empty spaces in gloom. Emily hated parking underground because it reminded her of the dark streets of Whitechapel where Jack the Ripper had stalked his victims. Nick broke the silence as they walked towards their cars.

"I'm getting divorced."

"Oh. I'm sorry."

"Thanks. How are you and Aaron?"

"We're separated."

He nodded. "You want to get back with him?"

"I honestly don't know."

"What are you doing tonight?"

"I'm going to the gym. Taking self-defence lessons. I've been frightened ever since the murders happened."

"That's sensible." Nick stopped at his car. "Well, have a good night."

"You too," she said, walking on. She waved at Nick's black BMW when it drove by, heading for the exit. Then she was alone. Emily had become frightened of being alone anywhere, so she hurried towards her car. Her high heels echoed in the cavernous space, making her extremely aware of the silence all around her. She increased her speed, feeling her heart thudding as she approached her parking space in the darkest corner. She had her key ready when she slowed down to look around, checking nobody was following her. She feared Jack the Ripper would be hiding behind a concrete pillar, waiting to leap out to strangle her. She saw nobody. There was an electronic beep when her car unlocked, but she didn't get in straight away. A quick look into the back proved to her that nobody was hiding inside before she risked entering the vehicle. Once inside, she locked herself in, breathing a sigh of relief. She was safe. At least there was no Jack the Ripper in her car today.

Just then the phone in her bag vibrated, startling her, almost giving her a heart attack. She swore to herself before taking the phone out to look at the screen. One new text message from Nick.

I missed you.

Emily hesitated before texting back.

Missed you too.

They went for a drink a few days later.

One night she was alone in her office when she thought she heard a door banging down the hallway. Since the massacre, every little unexplained sound made her nervous, so she opened her door and looked down the dark hallway. It was deserted.

"Hello?" she called out. "Who's there?"

Nobody answered, but she had heard a door *bang*. Someone was there. Was it a late-night cleaner? Or was the murderer coming back to kill her? She walked down the hallway armed with a letter opener. She had her smartphone in her other hand ready to call 999 if there was anyone there, but she checked each office and found them deserted.

Probably a noise on another floor.

Probably.

There was another noise.

Ding.

The lift doors opened.

Nick was inside.

"I got your text," he said.

"What text?"

"You sent me a text asking me to come up."

"No, I didn't."

"Then—"

It was his last word.

Like in a nightmare, a black-caped figure appeared from behind a partition and stepped behind Nick, slicing his throat twice, opening his carotid artery, spraying his blood. Nick choked on his blood as he fell on to his knees. The killer stood behind Nick as he bled out. Nick struggled to close the savage wound, his eyes imploring Emily to help him.

She wanted to save Nick's life, but the Ripper would kill her if she moved forward. She had to call the police instead. She pressed 'send', but nothing happened. She looked at the smartphone and realised it was the same model as her own smartphone, but it wasn't hers. It was not connected to any network. It was dead. It must have been swapped when she was out of her office.

Jack the Ripper stepped around Nick's body, holding a Gladstone bag, his face hidden under a top hat, his long, sharp knife dripping blood.

Emily saw his beard and thought for a second it was Eric Casavian, until she realised it was just a disguise, because the eyes behind the disguise were all too familiar.

"Glenda?"

"Hello, Emily."

"Why are you doing this?"

"Why? Jack the Ripper is the most famous serial killer of all time – for only killing five people. I've always wanted to do something like that, to leave my mark on history. Everyone is talking about me and tonight's murders will just add to my notoriety."

"You maniac. You killed those people to become *notorious*?"

"Not just notorious – a legend. The secret of becoming a legend is creating an unsolvable crime, a mystery that is so horrific the world remembers it long after I'm gone. I decided to create a new legend. A new Ripper. I planned every aspect for months so I could provide myself with an alibi and a mysterious missing suspect. Gary provided the perfect alibi by drinking my drugged champagne. Getting rid of Eric Casavian's body was technically much harder. I needed to get his body out of the hotel and transport it in a van to a place where nobody would find it. That was hard to do on my own, but it was worth it. So far, my plan has been a spectacular success. Tonight your tragic death will add to my legend."

"You're insane, Glenda."

"No – I'm famous and infamous." Glenda laughed as she advanced on her. "Today's a special day, Emily. You'd know that if you cared about the Ripper as much as I do. It's the ninth of November – the anniversary of Mary Jane Kelly's death. Imagine what the police will think when they find you butchered just like her. How tragic! They'll think Eric Casavian came back for you. You will be his final victim before he disappears forever, leaving just his DNA at the scene."

Emily turned and ran for her office.

Glenda chased her down the hall.

Emily sprinted.

The door looked so far away.

Run, run, run.

Emily made it to the door a second before Glenda, hearing behind her the swish of a knife.

Thirty seconds later, a window shattered on the fortieth floor of the Waterman-Cooper building. A woman tumbled out, battered and bruised, screaming as she plunged towards the ground. She was wearing a black cape and flapped her arms like a bat, but it didn't help her fly.

Blue Serge
Martin Edwards

"Congratulations, Inspector!"

Walter Dew glanced over his shoulder. Tall and broad-shouldered, like a major in mufti, he failed at first to see who had called out to him. He was about to walk away down the Strand when he noticed a hunch-backed shrimp of a fellow waving his hand. The shrimp was enveloped in a woollen coat that had seen better days, presumably whilst owned by someone who was not four inches and three stone too small for it.

"Thank you. I regard the jury's verdict on the matter of compensation as no more than common justice."

This was the precisely the statement he had delivered outside the doors of the court following announcement of the decision in the case of *Dew* v. *Edward Lloyd (Limited)*. He was about to continue on his way, but something in the tiny black eyes gave him pause. Was the man a reporter? Even by the shabby standards of the fourth estate, he was unkempt. The straggly hair was unwashed, his stubbly jaw was in need of a shave, and he stank to high Heaven of ale and cheap tobacco.

"An Englishman's good name is his most precious possession, is it not, Inspector?"

This had been proved beyond doubt in the King's Bench Division of the High Court, not twenty minutes earlier. The publishers of the *Daily Chronicle* had already given a fulsome apology for defaming him, but now they had been ordered to pay him the sum of four hundred pounds. An excellent day's work.

Walter lifted his hat. "Indeed it is. Good day to you."

"Please, Inspector, hear me out." The shrimp might look like a scoundrel, but his voice and confidence suggested an educated man. Probably he had fallen on hard times due to an excessive fondness for drink. Walter had met many of this type during twenty-eight years in the force. He had scant sympathy for them. A man must learn how to master his weaknesses. "You are enjoying a first-class run. Last year you chased the cellar murderer across the high seas, before bringing him back to face justice in England. Now you have mounted a triumphant defence of your reputation in open court. Your traducers have been humbled."

Walter had not lost his detective's sixth sense. More was to come, he was sure. A note of caution entered his voice as he said, "That is true."

The man's crooked teeth gleamed in the pale March sunlight. "How d'you fancy making it a hat-trick of successes?"

"You will need to speak more plainly, sir."

"Inspector, it is perfectly straightforward. You are the most famous detective in the land, perhaps in the whole world. The man who caught Crippen. The court heard this morning that you have received rewards and recognitions of your services to the Metropolitan Police on no fewer than one hundred and thirty occasions. Such an outstanding record of achievement . . ."

"I was merely doing my job."

"And it is the job of a remarkable detective! Modest as ever, at the height of your fame, you chose to retire and to pursue other interests. Yet, surely, one disappointment remains, an irksome thorn in your flesh."

"What do you mean?"

"I refer, of course, to that dreadful business in Whitechapel. The one capital case that you were never able to solve."

Walter glared at the pestilential fellow. "I was no more than a young whippersnapper at the time. A detective constable, still finding my feet. My superiors were in charge of the investigation."

"Ah, yes. Chief Inspector Moore, Inspector Abberline and Inspector Andrews."

"You have a good memory," Walter said.

"I have made a special study of the case, Inspector. You don't mind if I call you Inspector? I noticed that your barrister was quick to remind the court of your former rank. But the reputations of Abberline and company never recovered from their failure. You caught Crippen, but Jack the Ripper escaped justice."

Walter waved away the flattery with a movement of his beefy right hand. "They were honest men, doing their best."

"It wasn't enough." The little black eyes danced. "Whereas now you have the chance to set matters right. To help solve the mystery once and for all."

"You talk in riddles, sir. Surely you do not suggest that you know who was responsible for the Whitechapel killings?"

"I do more than suggest it. I am sure of my facts."

"Then I advise you to contact Scotland Yard forthwith. You will understand that I no longer have an official connection with the police."

"Exactly. You told the court that you undertake private inquiries."

"That is correct. Though these days I am equally glad to spend time with my wife and children, and in my garden. As for my clients, they are all alive and kicking. The business in Whitechapel was almost a quarter of century ago."

"Nevertheless, I am in a position to put a proposal to you that will be very much to your advantage."

"Sir, I have lost count of the number of individuals who believed that they knew the name of Jack the Ripper. If you have new evidence, it should go before the proper authorities."

The little man gave an apologetic cough. "Inspector, I fear matters are not quite so simple. My previous encounters with the law have been much less happy than your own. Your stock could not be any higher. For my part, I was locked up in Pentonville until ten days ago."

Walter gave the man a hard stare. "I should have guessed as much."

The crooked smile returned. "Give me the chance, and I can be your partner in crime. No, don't walk away, please hear me out. We can collaborate to mutual benefit."

"Out of the question, sir." Walter made an airy gesture, as if swatting a fly. "Now, if you'll excuse me . . ."

"Do not be hasty, I beg you. Spare me an hour of your time, that's all I ask." He leaned towards Walter, although he lacked the inches to hiss directly into the taller man's ear. "*Jack the Ripper was Francis Tumblety!*"

"You are deceiving yourself," Walter said flatly.

"Please, give me a chance to explain." The shrimp paused. "The story is quite astonishing. I had it on the authority of Mary Jane Kelly's dearest friend."

"The Ripper's last victim?" Walter paused. "There was a girl, yes. Remind me of her name."

"Lizzie Albrook. At the time the outrages were committed, she was a slip of a thing. Nineteen, perhaps, or twenty."

"Lizzie Albrook, that is correct. She spoke to the newspapers," Walter said slowly. "After Marie Kelly was murdered."

"That's right, sir. But she didn't tell all that she knew."

Walter frowned. "Very well. I can give you one hour. Not a second more."

Within ten minutes, the two men were huddled over a table at the back of an ABC tea room. On the way, they had exchanged barely a dozen words as they dodged between cabs clattering over the cobblestones. Walter's stride was long, and his companion panted in the effort to keep up. Twice, the little fellow lingered outside a tavern door, but Walter kept on walking. He knew better than to be seen drinking ale in the company of a recent inmate of Pentonville. The ABC was unlikely to be frequented by one of his former colleagues.

At the counter, Walter had ordered a cup of tea for himself, but the other man seemed ravenous, and asked for three rounds of toast made from aerated graham bread, spread thickly with best butter, together with a fat slab of carrot cake. Walter paid, earning a grateful smile from the pretty girl taking the money when he told her to keep the change. Once upon a time, he had counted the pennies, but those days were now a distant memory. Four hundred pounds! The proceeds from his latest libel claim more than doubled his annual pension from the Yard at a stroke. To say nothing of the reparations made by the *Pall Mall Gazette*, the *Evening Standard* and *Westminster*. Nine separate actions prior to today, each resulting in a famous victory. His earnings as the most eminent private detective in England were in the nature of a bonus. He was not yet fifty years old, but from now on, he could pick and choose what he did.

The other tables in the tea room were predominantly occupied by women; the ABC was a safe haven for unescorted members of the fair sex. Glancing at a slender redhead in the queue at the counter, Walter was pleased to see that tight-lacing had not quite gone out of fashion. The death of an ABC waitress not long before had provoked controversy about the dangers of devotion to fashionably tiny waists, but Walter suspected that the girl's demise was more likely to be due to a weak heart than excessively tight corsets.

"You have the advantage over me," Walter said. "I do not know your name."

"I go by several names," the shrimp said, "but there is no point in bluffing a detective, is there? Especially one so eminent as former Inspector Dew of the CID. I was born Francis Rooney, and in my younger days I worked as a clerk in chambers in the Middle Temple. You see, we have something in common. You were employed in a solicitor's office in your youth, were you not?"

"I soon got fed up with it."

"Whereas I have always found the law fascinating," Rooney said. "Alas! A series of misfortunes concerning petty cash brought my career to a calamitous end. We are much of an age, you and I, and yet my life has followed a very different trajectory from yours. Bad luck has driven me down to the depths, while you have risen to giddy heights. Even when the newspapers misrepresented your conduct in the Crippen case, you contrived to turn it to your advantage. "

"I was the victim of actionable defamation," Walter snapped. "Accordingly, I found it necessary to take action."

"Oh, I implied no criticism, Inspector. The reports that you made unauthorised disclosures about Crippen were outrageously untrue, as the newspapers in question later admitted. You kept every confidence; you are quite the oyster. A man of rare determination, too. The apologies were fulsome, but you insisted on pursuing litigation to the bitter end. From long experience of courts of law, both of us know that many a plaintiff has come unstuck through an ill-judged libel suit. But you had no fear, and you emerged vindicated. Learned counsel for the *Daily Chronicle* made much of the fact that you had suffered no actual harm, and took care to remind the jury of your taste for seeking financial redress, but to no avail. He accused your barrister of seeking to inflame the jury – and to my ears, candidly, that had a ring of truth, but no matter. The jury was minded to punish his client, and to reward a loyal and long-serving public servant."

Walter drummed his fingers impatiently on the wooden tabletop. "Shall we get to the point, Mr Rooney?"

"Ah, yes, please excuse me. A lifetime's fascination with the law sometimes makes me a dullard. Let us speak of those dreadful crimes committed almost twenty-five years ago. As it happens, at the time I was lodging in Dorset Street. A stone's throw, you will recall, from where the last victim met her dreadful end."

Walter took a sip of tea. During his time in "H" Division, he had known that dismal maze of streets like the back of his hand. Whitechapel, Spitalfields and Shoreditch were his hunting ground, an area unsurpassed in the British Isles for vice and villainy, even before the Ripper began his bloody work.

"There was a common lodging house in Dorset Street, as I recall. The woman you mentioned, Albrook, lived there."

Rooney sank his crooked teeth into a slice of toast. "Well remembered, Inspector."

"Every detective depends upon his memory. Those were the days before the council was required to regulate lodging houses, and it was our miserable duty to make sure the occupants vacated the premises until the end of the afternoon. As if criminals and prostitutes did not have the wit to find somewhere to ply their trade during hours of daylight."

"My sentiments exactly. Lizzie was a fine young woman, albeit a member of the unfortunate class. She yearned to make a better life for herself. So, I am sure, did her wretched friend Mary Jane."

Walter shifted in his chair. "Marie Kelly was the Ripper's sixth victim, not the first. I don't see how . . ."

"Patience, my dear inspector. All will become clear in due course. But I must correct you. Tumblety did not kill six times. No doubt you will assure me that Emma Smith was the first woman the Ripper killed."

"That is my belief."

"In fact, she was violated and robbed by the old Nichol gang. They meant to punish her for trespassing on their girls' pitches, but what they did to her went beyond the pale. Before she died of her injuries, she said as much." Rooney was talking with his mouth full, an unappetising sight. Walter was glad he had not bought anything to eat. "The Ripper worked alone, and never in thoroughfares as frequented as Osborne Street. He did what he had to do in dark alleys and sinister courts. No, Inspector, Francis Tumblety did not kill Emma Smith. He was Jack the Ripper. *Ergo*, Emma Smith was not among Jack's victims. "

Walter shrugged. "Nobody was charged. The truth about the crime cannot be proved, I admit. As for your insistence on the guilt of this fellow Tumblety, you are misinformed. Witnesses who saw the Ripper spoke of a shorter, younger man. Tumblety was tall, with a flourishing moustache, and older than I am now."

"Pah!" Rooney bit savagely into his toast. "Eye witness testimony is notoriously fallible. The descriptions given to the police led precisely nowhere."

"Some evidence, nevertheless, is preferable to none. How can you substantiate what you say? "

"Patience, Inspector. The case against Tumblety may appear circumstantial, but it is strong. Did not Inspector Andrews travel to the United States with a view to tracing him?"

Grudgingly, Walter nodded. "The populace was baying for an arrest, the press was poisoning people's minds against us on the ground of our supposed incompetence. In such circumstances, who can blame the detective who clutches at a straw?"

"Andrews was not alone. Chief Inspector Littlechild reckoned Tumblety was Jack, and for good cause."

"Littlechild was in charge of the Special Irish Branch, and kept at arm's length from the investigation. Tell me, though, how do you come to know Tumblety's name? After so many false leads, we were under strict instructions not to disclose it to the world at large while our inquiries continued."

"Small wonder, given that he was at one time in police custody, and yet he managed to slip through the fingers of Scotland Yard, and out of the country."

Walter exhaled. "You are very well informed."

"I have taken care to make sure of my facts." Rooney smirked. "The Ripper had already caused your superiors deep and lasting embarrassment. If it were known that he had been allowed to escape, and live to a ripe old age on the other side of the Atlantic Ocean . . ."

"You failed to answer my question, Mr Rooney."

"Forgive me." A little laugh. "I have often been questioned by police officers, and old habits die hard. My story is so simple, I am sure you have already guessed it. During his brief sojourn in London in 1888, Tumblety rented a room in the lodging house at Dorset Street. It was not his principal address, but he found it . . . convenient."

"He was an acquaintance of yours?"

"I spoke to him half a dozen times at most. It intrigued me that he was not lacking in money, yet prepared to rent a room in a hellhole at four pence a night. Despite calling himself a doctor, he was no better than a quack. Of course, he was a degenerate. Night after night there was a procession of young ruffians to his room, and I doubt they were seeking medical advice."

"Indulging in unnatural behaviour is vile enough, but scarcely on the same level of depravity as murdering and mutilating unfortunates. It does not make him Jack the Ripper."

"Lizzie was afraid of Tumblety. She told me he was dangerous."

"Nor does a character given by a woman of the streets."

"Lizzie and I were friends, Chief Inspector. I became her trusted confidant."

"Is that so?"

"Now, Inspector, I ask you to trust me too." Rooney leaned across the table. "Tumblety hated whores. In his younger days in America, he had suffered grievously at their hands. Moreover, he had a record of criminality and violence. He boasted of it to one of his young bedmates, whose tastes in matters of the flesh were not confined to his own sex. The ruffian recounted this to Lizzie, and she in turn told me."

"Third-hand gossip," Walter said. "Purest hearsay."

Rooney glanced quickly from side to side to make sure that no one could hear him. "You have not heard the most dreadful thing Lizzie told me. Tumblety gave the ruffian a key to his room. Lizzie borrowed it, and sneaked inside when the Yank was out."

"To see what she could steal?"

"It is not a crime to be curious, thank God." Rooney lowered his voice to a whisper. "In a cupboard, hidden behind his clothes, Tumblety kept a set of glass jars. Inspector, they were crammed with women's matrices."

Walter wrinkled his nose. "The fruit of some anatomical experiments, perhaps. As you say, the man was some sort of doctor."

"What sort of doctor takes his own little museum exhibits of female innards to a place such as Dorset Street? I picture him gloating over his trophies at night, while his latest young man was fast asleep. Tumblety put his knowledge of surgery to use in the darkest corners of Whitechapel, Inspector, depend upon it."

With an elaborate sigh, Walter took his watch from his pocket. "I have to leave shortly, Mr Rooney."

"I am grateful for your patience, sir. I am sorry to have rambled, but it is seldom that I have the pleasure of such an attentive listener. The company in Pentonville holds little appeal for a man such as myself. I have resolved to enjoy better days and, with your help, I can."

Walter stood up. "That hour is nearly up. I confess to finding our conversation intriguing, but I am afraid I cannot help you. My business is in the here and now. There is no sense in raking through dead ashes, and no profit, either. May I bid you good afternoon?"

"Wait!" The little man scrambled to his feet, almost choking on his last piece of carrot cake. "I am sure we can work together to mutual benefit. I have told only half the tale. We must meet again to discuss the matter further."

"I am sorry, Mr Rooney!"

"May I assure you, Inspector, that you will not regret it. I am offering you the chance of a lifetime." He drew breath. "We must talk again soon. I want to recount the full story of Lizzie Albrook, Tumblety . . . and Blue Serge."

At half past five on the following Friday evening, Samuel Rooney halted outside a house in Perivale Lane. Carved into one of the gate pillars was its name, "The Nook". The wind's bite was cruel, and the sun had long since vanished, but Rooney's heart leaped with anticipation of his second meeting with Walter Dew. He'd anticipated this conversation with so much relish. As he walked up the gravel path, he swayed slightly; this was not so much due to the wintry blast as to a couple of pleasant hours spent in a hostelry in town, fortifying himself for his next encounter with the man who caught Crippen. Scarcely able to contain his excitement, he rapped imperiously on the freshly painted door. It came as a surprise to find his summons answered in person by Walter Dew.

"Marvellous to see you again, Inspector! Mind you, I had presumed that these days you would employ a maid to welcome your guests!"

Walter gave a complacent smile as he shook his visitor's cold hand. "We have engaged a young woman to help my good lady, as it happens, but she is spending the weekend with her parents in Ruislip. Anyway, it's a bitter evening. Come on in, before you catch your death."

Taking his guest's coat, Walter ushered him into the front parlour, where the curtains were drawn, and a cheerful fire blazed in an inglenook fireplace. All the furniture was solid mahogany, and a tall cast-iron plant with the glossiest of green leaves occupied one corner. A half-full china teacup stood on the sideboard, together with a teapot, a milk jug and an empty cup. Rooney pulled his chair closer to the flames, as Walter enquired if he would join him in a cup of Darjeeling, or if he preferred something stronger.

"A drop of Scotch would be most welcome on a night like this, thank you." Rooney sniggered. "My, my, this is all very cosy, I must say."

"We moved here from Wandsworth a few weeks ago, and there is plenty of work to be done. Painting, decorating, out in the garden." Walter took a decanter and a crystal tumbler from the cabinet. "But the children are growing up, and Mrs Dew is an excellent housekeeper. We live in a modest way, but thankfully we find ourselves comfortably placed."

"I should say so, after all your triumphs in the law courts." Rooney inhaled the aroma of his whisky. "Splendid, splendid. You won't have had much change out of two hundred guineas for a place like this!"

"We are very fortunate," Walter said. "But you did not come out to Greenford to talk about our new house. What is all this about Lizzie Albrook and the American, Tumblety? Be warned, I am sceptical by nature."

Rooney cleared his throat. "Tumblety was disgusted by the goings-on he witnessed in Dorset Street. He told Lizzie so. She liked to maintain the fiction that she was an innocent, and she believed that was what saved her life. He did not mistreat her, but she fancied that, apart from his indulgences with boys, Tumblety was not immune to the temptations of women. Lizzie reckoned he was one of Martha Tabram's clients, but something went wrong between them. You and I are men of the world, Inspector, we can guess what it was. Tumblety lost his temper, killed Martha – and found he enjoyed it."

"And what of his four subsequent victims?"

"Three subsequent victims," Rooney corrected. "It was much the same story with Annie Chapman, Mary Ann Nichols, and Catherine Eddowes."

Walter pursed his lips. "If Lizzie Albrook suspected Tumblety, why did she remain silent?"

"She does not possess the sharpest mind, and it was not until long after the death of her friend Mary Jane that she began to make sense of what had happened."

"Ah yes, the Kelly girl. She was the final victim."

"Not so, Inspector." Rooney wagged a nicotine-stained finger. "That is my point. On the day Mary Jane was murdered, Francis Tumblety was in police custody."

Walter shook his head. "There we must disagree. You piqued my interest when we met, and I have spent some time checking the facts of the case. Tumblety was arrested on the seventh of November, on suspicion of unnatural offences, but thereafter released on bail. After that, he skipped to Boulogne, and then fled back on a steamer to America, using an assumed name."

"He was not released from custody until the sixteenth of the month," Rooney said. "Mary Jane Kelly was slaughtered on the ninth."

"Can you be sure?"

"I am positive." Rooney drained his glass. "I assure you, Inspector, I too have checked. Your colleagues scrabbled around for hard evidence to connect him with the Ripper's crimes while he was on a holding charge, but their efforts were confounded by the grant of bail, and sloppiness thereafter allowed Tumblety to slip the net. A shocking display of incompetence."

"I cannot be held responsible for that. But, if what you say is true, how do you explain Marie's death? That was the most savage of all the killings. The work of a madman, assuredly."

"If you desired to select a hiding place for a leaf," Rooney murmured, "where would you choose? A forest, surely. My belief is that Mary Jane was murdered by a man who used the Ripper killings to conceal his own crime. He had plenty of time to do his worst that night."

"An extraordinary theory! I never heard anyone at the Yard suggest anything of the sort."

Walter poured himself another cup of tea, and motioned towards the decanter. Rooney needed no second invitation, and helped himself to another generous measure.

"It was a clever plan, Inspector, that's why. Consider for a moment, and anyone can perceive the logic. Mary Jane was much younger and prettier than the Ripper's victims. She was uncouth when in drink, but otherwise a delightful companion. Lizzie was very fond of her. They shared each other's secrets, and Mary Jane told Lizzie that she had formed an attachment with a young man."

"Nothing very secret about that," Walter grunted.

"Oh, but there was. You see, he was a respectable young fellow, hard-working and ambitious. For him, Mary Jane was the most unsuitable lover anyone could possibly imagine."

"He could have taken her away from that miserable existence in Dorset Street."

"No doubt he tried, in the early days, but infatuation never lasts, Inspector. He started to regret the liaison at much the same time as Mary Jane tired of his refusal to allow her to flaunt him on her arm. That was impossible, since he had neglected to inform her that he was already married. She threatened him with exposure and, from a hint she dropped to Lizzie, it seems she also pretended to be with child. To no avail. He was determined to break with her, and that made her angry, and bent upon revenge. Hell hath no fury, et cetera."

"Stuff and nonsense," Walter said. "Marie was a good-natured soul. I used to come across her on my beat, parading around Flower and Dean Street and Whitechapel Road with two or three others of her kind."

"You knew her very well, didn't you, Inspector?" Rooney leaned forward in his chair. His voice was unsteady, and pitched a little higher than usual. Never mind if the inspector's wife overheard. It was time to cut to the chase. "You often visited her room in Miller's Court, next door to the chandler's shop."

Walter said quietly, "Do you have the brass neck, Mr Rooney, to come to my home, accept my hospitality, and then accuse me – a retired chief inspector of unsullied reputation – of the foulest murder any man could conceive?"

Rooney stretched lazily in his armchair, and stifled a yawn. "That's about the size of it. You had a pet name for her, didn't you – Marie? And she called you Blue Serge. Of course, in all the mayhem after her death, nobody dreamed that she had not succumbed to the same fate as poor Eddowes and the others. It was a perfect crime."

"Your theory is preposterous, sir."

"You were the first man on the scene at Miller's Court. How very convenient. You had arranged everything so carefully to cover your tracks. And it worked a treat. This was the latest and most heinous of the Ripper's foul deeds. Why would anybody suspect an upstanding young police constable? Lizzie didn't, that's for sure. Not for a long time, anyway. She'd caught sight of you once, you know, when she came to call on Mary Jane. You were leaving in a tearing hurry, tucking your shirt into your trousers, if I remember right."

"Pure invention, it reminds me of something out of an old penny dreadful," Walter said calmly. "If Lizzie Albrook has told you this, and persuaded you to part with money in return, you are more of a fool than I took you for."

"She never had a penny from me," Rooney muttered. "Not all the years we've known each other. Good times and bad, though most of 'em bad. We've both spent more time inside than out. Now we're older and wiser, we just needed a spot of cash to see us to a decent old age."

"Is that it?" Walter demanded. "You have the temerity to come here with this farrago, and try to blackmail a decent man into paying for your booze?"

Rooney put a trembling finger to his lips. "Hush! We don't want Mrs Dew or the children to hear, do we? And you needn't come over all innocent. I know you bought Lizzie off."

Walter stared at him. "What are you talking about?"

"She came to visit me in Pentonville. I hadn't seen her for a long while. My last stretch was a heavy one – if the judge had had his way, he'd have locked me up, and thrown away the key. But Lizzie's a decent sort. She told me everything."

Rooney paused, and Walter said coolly, "Go on with this fairy tale."

"She'd seen your picture in a newspaper. All to do with Crippen, of course. The price of fame, eh? Despite the time that had gone by, she'd have recognised you anywhere. Just fancy, the man who caught Crippen turned out to be Blue Serge. The man who broke Mary Jane Kelly's heart, just before she died. Even back then, Lizzie couldn't help wondering whether there was more to her pal's death than met the eye. We talked about it at the time. Mary Jane had told her you were ruthless, especially when anyone crossed you. I suppose the way you pursued old Crippen across the high seas proved the truth of that, eh?" He mopped his brow. "But the word around Dorset Street was that Tumblety was the Ripper and, as you well know, there were plenty of other blokes in the frame. I asked Lizzie to do a bit of digging around in the past. She still had one or two friends in the force, and I wanted her to find out about Tumblety's bail. When she came back with a progress report, she said she'd been thinking it over. What if you'd done something to Mary Jane, and then disguised it as the Ripper's handiwork? Only thing is, she couldn't believe a copper would ever do such a terrible thing. The girl wasn't just killed and mutilated, was she? She was flayed to the bone."

"Nobody would believe anything of the sort," Walter said. "Wild nonsense cooked up by a harlot and a drunken criminal? I've shown how to deal with folk who besmirch my good name, and the press are a hundred times more powerful than a pipsqueak like you."

"Don't . . . count on it," Rooney said slowly. "Lizzie put the squeeze on you good and proper while I was in Pentonville, don't tell me she didn't. Ever since she was a kid, she's dreamed of spending time in France, like someone born into a noble family. That's where she's living it up right now . . . at your expense."

"What makes you so sure?"

"She . . . she . . . sent me a postcard."

Rooney coughed violently. Struggling for breath, he half rose to his feet. Walter waited until his visitor collapsed back on to the armchair, panting desperately.

"What did this postcard say?" he asked. "*It worked a treat. He paid up like a lamb. Wish you were here.* All this on the back of a scene of St Malo?"

Rooney's eyes rolled in horror. "That was . . . you?" he said in a croaky whisper.

Walter nodded. "Lizzie overreached herself. The downfall of so many of her class, need I say more? She should have kept her mouth shut. It was a sorry business, but people have always underestimated me. I can't think why. Her body washed up near Tilbury, I believe, but she wasn't in any state to be identified."

"You wouldn't . . ."

"You've spent a lifetime going wrong, Rooney, and that isn't about to change. Good whisky? Had you chosen brandy or gin, or even tea, the result would have been the same. I enjoyed my conversations with that little prisoner of mine, as we sailed back across the Atlantic on board the *Megantic*. He taught me a good deal about poisons."

Rooney made a horrid gurgling sound.

"And don't get any bright ideas about calling out for help. Mrs Dew isn't next door. She has taken the children with her to her sister's in Brighton. It's just as well. The garden's a wilderness, and I fancy I have a lot of digging to do this weekend."

Author's Note

My principal sources for this story have been *I Caught Crippen* by Walter Dew, *The Lodger: the Arrest and Escape of Jack the Ripper* by Stewart Evans and Paul Gainey, *Walter Dew: the Man who Caught Crippen* by Nicholas Connell, and *The Mammoth Book of Jack the Ripper*, edited by Maxim Jakubowski and Nathan Braund. Evans and Gainey argue that

Francis Tumblety was "the Batty Street lodger" familiar to Ripperologists, but acknowledge that "it is possible that he also had other lodgings in London". There is some uncertainty about when, precisely, during 1911 Walter Dew moved to "The Nook", but Connell notes that the house was "where he spent much of his time gardening". The idea that Walter Dew anticipated by almost half a century one of Agatha Christie's most diabolic murder plots appeals to me, but even though Walter is not, thankfully, able to sue for libel from beyond the grave, I should make it clear that this story is entirely the product of my imagination. I do not doubt that he was a decent man, and to my mind the case that Tumblety was the Ripper is, at best, not proven. At least this story provides a theoretically possible answer to the question posed by Jakubowski and Braund: "if Tumblety was the Whitechapel Murderer, who did him an enormous favour by copying and exceeding his previous crimes by flaying Mary Jane Kelly to the bone *while Tumblety was still in police custody?*"

The Simple Procedure
Paul A. Freeman

———

One frigid night in the late autumn of 1888, my slumber was disturbed by one of those noxious London fogs that so often plague our great city. The sulphurous fumes infiltrated every nook and cranny of my bedchamber, making further sleep impossible.

Whilst tossing and turning beneath the blankets, I noticed a light showing under the door. So I rose from bed, secured my dressing gown and entered the sitting room. I found my friend Sherlock Holmes ensconced in an armchair with a thoughtful air about him. Lying on the floor in front of him were a pile of newspapers and a copy of *The Medical Journal*, which he had evidently been poring over.

Looking about the room, I also observed that on the breakfast table Holmes had laid out the surgical instruments I often carry with me when undertaking private medical consultations. The tools of my trade – everything from stethoscope to scalpels – had apparently become objects of his scrutiny.

"A case?" I asked nonchalantly.

"Research," the great sleuth evasively replied. He fixed me with a curious gaze. "Do sit down, Doctor. There's a matter I wish to discuss with you."

My inquisitiveness piqued, I did as bidden and lowered myself into the armchair opposite him.

Holmes leaned forward, picked up several copies of the *London Gazette* he had previously been perusing and passed them to me. They were dated from two years ago, and their pages were yellow with age.

As I read the leading story of each edition, my eyes narrowed. The front-page articles chronicled the exploits of a vicious killer who had preyed on women of ill repute in the slum areas of Kabul, Afghanistan. I remembered the case well from my time in the medical corps overseas. At that juncture in my army career, stationed in the Afghan capital, I was called out on more than one occasion to pronounce death on the elusive murderer's handiwork.

"A terrible business," I said, recalling the murders as though they were yesterday. "The sadistic perpetrator of these horrible crimes was nicknamed 'Strangling Stan' on account of the initial method he employed of dispatching his victims." Elucidating further, I explained: "When the killer began his campaign of terror, his modus operandi was strangulation. As time passed though, he became more confident and invented more colourful ways of dealing with the poor women who ended up in his clutches."

"Did the authorities suspect anyone?" asked Holmes.

I shook my head. "The North-west Frontier of neighbouring Pakistan had just risen up against British imperialism. The army therefore had more pressing commitments than the fate of a few ladies of the night from Kabul's notorious red-light districts. However, because these areas of the city serviced the needs of morally weak British servicemen, it was believed that the culprit was most likely a soldier of Her Majesty's army. I fear that is as near as we'll ever come to identifying a suspect."

Holmes took back the pile of yellowed newspapers and flipped through them until he came to the final, inconclusive episode of the mysterious "Strangling Stan" case. "The gentleman stopped killing rather abruptly," Holmes noted.

"Indeed he did. And no wonder! Shortly after the fifth murdered woman was discovered, Pashdoon tribesmen swept down through the Khyber Pass, picking off our cavalry and infantrymen as they went. The fighting was often hand to hand, the casualty rate horrendous. And, as you know, Holmes, I myself was wounded in the arm during the heat of battle. As for Strangling Stan, he never struck again, so it was naturally assumed he was killed during those days of desperate conflict."

"Quite so," said Holmes, regarding me closely. His hawk-like countenance then took on a curiously stern expression, as though he had set his mind on some course of action he would not be deflected from.

Searching through the pile of newspapers on the ground, he located several more editions of the *London Gazette*. They appeared somewhat newer than those detailing that morbid sideshow of Strangling Stan from the Afghan War.

The front pages of these particular newspapers concerned another infamous killer, one who was presently stalking the streets of our very own metropolis and whom the British press had christened "Jack the Ripper".

"This murderer is terrorising the immorally occupied ladies of Whitechapel, and also employs strangulation as a means of subduing his victims," Holmes informed me. "Last week Inspector Lestrade consulted with me on the case. It appears that although Jack the Ripper is noted primarily for his use of bladed implements, there is little blood at the crime scenes. This indicates that just like Strangling Stan, the Ripper initially strangles his victims."

For some reason, my friend's words had a profound effect on me, causing the hairs on the back of my neck to stand up. "Have you devised a theory?" I asked.

Holmes rose from his chair. He paced up and down the sitting room, clenching and unclenching his hands behind his back. "You mentioned that in Afghanistan Strangling Stan became gradually more colourful in his killing technique. How so?"

"He grew adept at using a knife on his victims, just as this Jack the Ripper fellow has done."

"Or perhaps he was naturally adept with a knife from the outset, Watson – on account of his profession. Have you ever considered that?"

I shifted uncomfortably in my chair, aware that Holmes was at last coming to the crux of the matter.

"From my detailed examination of the body of the Ripper's last victim, Mary Kelly," said Holmes, "I believe that the perpetrator of the Kabul killings and the perpetrator of the Whitechapel murders are one and the same person. I also believe him to be a medical man – just as you yourself are a medical man, Watson."

Imagining that my friend's insinuation was some ill-conceived joke, I let out a burst of nervous laughter. Then, realising he was in earnest, I said, "This is preposterous, Holmes!"

"Not at all. Just think back to the Pashdoon uprising in Afghanistan. You said yourself it was assumed that Strangling Stan died in the fighting, thus ending the persecution of Kabul's fallen women. However, it is equally feasible that the killer had picked up a debilitating war wound which prevented him from continuing his murder spree."

Without thinking, I looked down at my arm. Still not fully recovered from a bone-shattering bullet injury, the weakened limb throbbed dully.

"I've had my suspicions about you for some time, Doctor," continued Holmes, "even before Inspector Lestrade asked me to aid him in the Ripper investigation. In fact, I've suspected you ever since the night of Mary Kelly's death when you told me you had a private medical consultation in Wembley."

"But I did have a consultation that night," I said emphatically.

"That's what your conscience wishes you to believe," Holmes explained. "I watched you leaving our apartments from the sitting room window. The hansom cab you boarded set off in an easterly direction, not a westerly direction as would be expected if you were heading for Wembley. Besides this, I also recall that you had private medical consultations on the nights of every other Whitechapel murder."

There seemed little point in arguing against my friend's deductive skills, for he was invariably correct in his assertions. And anyhow, now that he had accused me of being a psychotic killer, recollections of my murderous nocturnal activities began crowding my consciousness – memories too horrible to contemplate.

"What do you propose to do?" I enquired, resigned to whatever fate Holmes had in mind for me.

"The London constabulary has proven singularly ineffective in apprehending Jack the Ripper," Holmes said. "So perhaps their incompetence makes them undeserving of your apprehension."

He returned to his vacant armchair and sat down. Then, leaning forward, he picked up the copy of *The Medical Journal*, which was lying on the floor. With his free hand he made a sweeping gesture towards my surgical tools, which he had so carefully arranged on the breakfast table. "Earlier in the evening," he said, "I was reading an article by Doctor Shauffen of Berne University. The professor has pioneered a simple procedure to remove that part of the brain which encourages psychotic behaviour such as that to which you are so apparently prone. It's a simple enough operation, Watson. So if you'd allow me . . .?"

Jack's Back
Vanessa de Sade

———

1

Daisy first danced naked in the peepshow on the evening of her thirteenth birthday, exactly ten years since the last Ripper murder.

Shivering in the dark, she could see the shadowy outlines of men's heads beyond the row of darkened porthole windows, hear their coarse laughter and the tipsy giggles of the girls who were out there with them; then suddenly there was a hush and an intake of breath as the gas jets flared and she was revealed in all her undraped glory, her skinny waif-like body undulating slowly to the haunting gramophone record that Claudine had selected, her flawless white skin an icy blue in the magnesium-white glare. A proper pin-drop silence, in fact, Claudine later described it to the girls that night as they all sat round the kitchen table, Daisy glowing in the warmth of their adulation and a little drunk from the left-over champagne that they had smuggled downstairs for her birthday party.

And she had wanted to test the water and disrobe slowly, peel her garments painstakingly from her reed-like body like layers of superfluous skin, but Claudine had advised against it, said that it was hard to strip to music, especially when you were nervous, and the likelihood of tripping and its subsequent humiliation was also not to be discounted. And so she had undressed in the tiny anteroom behind the peepshow, shivering in the cold draught, her trembling hand in Claudine's, waiting breathlessly – heart thudding in her mouth – for her moment in the lights.

And, of course, she had always known that this day would come, and, truthfully, if the old madam upstairs had had her way she would have been doing this much sooner, too, *and* being taken upstairs to the plusher bedrooms by the gentlemen as well. But Claudine had refused to allow it, and, now that the old madam had taken almost permanently to her chamber and no longer perambulated amongst the gentlemen in the salon like a good shepherd surveying her flock in the abattoir ring, the running of the house was left almost solely to Claudine, and Claudine had decreed that no one was to lay a finger on Daisy before her fourteenth birthday, and so that was that. Though there were rumours of a waiting list after tonight's show, and that would surely please the old dame upstairs in her mountain of pillows.

Daisy had only met her once, the day after Claudine had brought her to the house, given her a bath with scented soap and bought her the first new dress of all her life. She was ten then, but already tall and gangly for her years with hair the colour of fresh straw and eyes like ice-blue lapis. And the shadowy room had smelled of the strange aromatic herbs that Claudine ground in a mortar down in the kitchen when one of the girls came knocking on her door late in the night. And, at first, as her eyes adapted to the gloom, she had thought that they were playing a joke on her, and that there was no one in the bed, but then she had discerned the outlines of a pale face on the pillow like an indentation of a grandma already eaten by the wolf, the skin translucent like the fine membrane of an onion, the skull beneath clearly visible in the half-light of that awful chamber.

"Come closer, girl," the ancient woman had whispered, her voice the cancerous whisper of a dying banshee. "Stand in the light, where I can see you."

And so she had stood like the good girl she was as the madam's thin spidery hand ran up and down her, reading her contours like a blind woman reads the lumps and bumps of an old Bible printed in brail. And though she had really wanted to shudder, she had stood stock still and endured, and later Claudine had taken her in her arms and kissed her forehead with pride, well pleased that her protégée had met with her superior's approval in that terrible room.

And, of course, everybody in the house loved Claudine and would do anything for her, girls fighting amongst themselves to be permitted to launder her Titian-blue taffeta frocks and fine Parisian silk under-wear, though it was only very special gentlemen who Claudine visited the rooms of these days. And she would always come back to her own bed in the small hours of those dark nights, her scent a medley of strange animal aromas that disquieted and yet somehow aroused Daisy, her hair smelling of cologne and cigar smoke and her breath sweet with cognac; though sometimes she would sob and hold the younger girl like a mother holds her child and murmur strange-sounding French words that Daisy couldn't understand.

In fact, there was much that Daisy did not understand about the world which she inhabited, though she knew of the things that men did to women and of the other things that men did only to women who lived in houses such as these. Not that Claudine permitted any such "nonsense" here, as she called it, and gentlemen who had a penchant for "the more brutal side of love" were firmly shown the door by the massive Louis – another of Claudine's waifs and strays – who could tear a man in two with his bare hands but was a soul so gentle that even a sad ballad portrayed in crudely coloured magic lantern slides could reduce him to tears.

And, of course, when the gas lamps sputtered and the nights were slow and dark, all the girls still whispered about the ever-present spectre of Jack, and how lucky the old madam's girls were to have this roof over their heads and protection of Louis against the likes of him out there in the cold corpse-kiss caress of the river fogs that engulfed the labyrinth of lanes and alleyways beyond their richly curtained windows.

"Has Jack really gone?" she had asked Claudine one watery spring morning as the sun streaked in the mottled panes of the kitchen windows and she peeled potatoes for the cook, paring the thin skin so finely with a glinting knife blade that it was almost transparent as it floated like gossamer to her feet.

"Jack? What do you know of Jack?" Claudine had asked guardedly, her soft grey eyes uncharacteristically narrow.

"Why everyone knows Jack," she replied precociously, as though she had read of it in some book somewhere. "He's the Whitechapel revenger, the working girls' avenger, the hand that grabs you in the foggy dark. He'll slice your quivering belly, from your chin down to your nellie, and cut you up and leave you in the park . . ."

But instead of laughing at her skipping rhyme, Claudine seemed to clutch at the kitchen table for support and spoke in a tight disapproving whisper. "Where did you learn that? You must never repeat that, not in this house, not anywhere in these streets, is that clear? *Never* again . . ."

And, to Daisy's astonishment, she stumbled from the room and clattered unsteadily upstairs, her face white and her body trembling.

2

It was, perhaps, not strictly true to say that *all* the girls loved Claudine, for as any good girl knows, where there is expensive ointment there is always a fly, and the particular *Diptera* in this happy unction was a gaunt-faced redhead known as Clara, who cared nothing for Claudine or the little Frenchwoman's way of running the house, and openly petitioned the dying woman in the soft feather bed upstairs on a regular basis to have her removed.

Clara was a woman of uncertain years, and though she herself would admit to five and thirty when pressed, popular consensus put her closer to a half-century and peered closely at her flame-coloured locks for telltale signs of grey beneath the liberally applied henna. A lone raven amongst a flock of blue jays, she favoured formal dresses of stiff taffetas in rainy slate greys, her attire the sole stroke of Puritanism amidst a sartorial palette otherwise resembling the gaudy plumes of a bird of paradise; the rustle of her many petticoats the Calvinist whispering of dead leaves on a cemetery path amidst the drunken frivolity of the unruly salon.

For, if she was to be believed, Clara had graced the boards of every major opera house of western Europe, her large alabaster bosom quivering to the reverberating melodies of Mozart and Verdi on vast flower-strewn stages from Paris to Milan, sipping champagne from her own slippers with crowned heads and American millionaires alike until some scandal so dark that it was only ever whispered about even in a house of ill repute such as this had flung her from her lofty perch and – literally – on to the streets, where she surely would have perished had not the old madam seen some potential in the haughty beggar who had pounded on her door demanding succour.

Though what it was that endeared her to the male callers remained a mystery, for her manner was brusque and her demeanour sullen, and yet she mounted the stairs with gentleman after gentleman each night. Some said it was the accommodating capacity of her opera singer's throat that was her fortune, but most plumped for the possibility that there was some inexplicable male gene that fired up like a libidinous *aurora borealis* when faced with the possibility of bedding one's old nanny or governess.

Be that as it may, Clara, for whatever reason, was a favourite and a high earner, and, as such, expected to have some say in the decision-making process of the house. She therefore resented bitterly the attachment between the cancerous Sleeping Beauty upstairs and the diminutive Claudine; so it was no surprise that it was she who burst – uninvited – into Daisy's birthday party that night like an outraged fairy excluded from the christening of a royal favourite and proceeded to spit and scream like a fishwife and generally dispel the mirth of the occasion.

Later, however, when questioned by Carmody, all the girls agreed that there had been friction between the two women for years, but that it seemed to have come to a head the previous night when they had clashed over the child, Daisy, and the loss of income the house had occasioned by Claudine's refusal to have her broken in and bedded that very evening.

All, likewise, agreed that Clara had stormed out into the night in search of gin and a sympathetic ear, and it had been supposed that she had taken herself and her indignation to a nearby tavern known ironically as the Jolly Sailor, where the austere landlady and she maintained a relationship that was as close to friendship as creatures of their ilk could ever aspire to. Claudine, meanwhile, had decamped to her room and not been seen until the next morning, when she had declined offers of assistance with her laundry and had been seen casting away a blood-stained garment when the dust cart had come slowly down their narrow street, bringing with it the news of the previous night's bloody slaying.

For Clara, it seems, had never made it to the hostelry of her grim-faced companion, and had been found in a pool of her own blood under the first grey-streaked skies of an uncertain dawn, her body sliced open from chin to navel. And, though the dour policeman refused to speculate on the fate of this dead whore, tongues were already wagging and all of Whitechapel was abuzz with the news that Jack was back.

3

Carmody, the dour police inspector, kept them both waiting at the scrubbed kitchen table for nearly an hour before he finally joined them. He was a heavily built, no-nonsense sort of man of perhaps five and forty, with short-cropped hair showing some signs of grey at the temples and eyes the colour of lead shot, and, with his investigation – such as it was – now completed, all he required was a confession so that the matter would be signed and sealed.

He questioned them both relentlessly, determined to obtain the admission of guilt that he sought before teatime so that he could declare the case closed and excise the word "Jack" from the yellow journalism of the broadsheet writers, but both the Frenchwoman and the girl remained stubborn in the face of his bullying and, eventually, he was reduced to calling upon his minions and merely having Claudine transported to the cells to await trial at some unspecified date.

And, in the normal course of events, that would have been the end of our tale, for there was no one to mourn the loss of this particular lady of the night, and, even as her body lay cold and white upon a slab at Bow Street, Carmody mused, two score or more fresh girls would be taking to the streets for the first time to ply a trade so old that it pre-dated history. Plus, though he had failed in his customary practice of obtaining a confession before making an arrest, he had a villain in custody, and a foreigner at that, and, though not ideal – a jealous lover or crazed suitor would make better headlines – the pretty little French prostitute would appease the tabloid hacks who had already begun to sing their old songs about the return of Jack. In fact, Carmody thought, inspired, on his way home he would send a message to the station to arrange for a sketch artist to visit her in her cell so that there would be a face to hate in tomorrow morning's papers.

Carmody grinned, pleased with himself, and motioned to the landlord for a valedictory glass of stout. The night was bitter outside and yet another fog had blown in from the river, and he dreaded even the short trudge home to his lodgings. But the publican's meagre fire had already burned low and the dishes from the policeman's evening meal were cold and congealing, and he knew that he could no longer postpone the inevitable. Downing his drink, he rose reluctantly to depart.

"Take care out on them streets, Mister Carmody," the landlord called after him, as he wrapped his great coat around his shoulders. "There'll be all sorts abroad in that fog on a night like this . . ."

Carmody snorted in exasperation. More blasted Jack references. Why did they always rear their ugly heads every time some street-corner doxy went and got her throat cut? "There is no such person as Jack," he bellowed to the room as he stormed bad-temperedly out of the door.

It was the last sentence that anyone ever heard him say.

They released Claudine late the following morning while reporters impatiently pounded the gossiping streets of Whitechapel, everyone desperate to finally view the murder site where Carmody's eviscerated remains had been discovered in the small hours, especially the blood-spattered wall behind him which bore the two stark words that all of London was mouthing:

Jack's back.

4

Claudine still had the letter.

> *My dearest sister,*
>
> *I know that it is many years since we last communicated and I know that harsh words have passed between us and things have been said and words used that should never have passed from the lips of one human to another, let alone between two sisters who have shared the same womb and suckled at the same nipple.*
>
> *But, though I would like to beg of you to let bygones be bygones, I know that the wrongs I have done you can never be expunged and must hang upon my soul until I am called to meet my maker and be judged, but I would ask you, my dear sister, for the sake of our poor dead mother and one who is innocent in all this, to show some modicum of mercy and grant me one single boon before I depart these city streets.*
>
> *For, without affectation, I must report that my physician advises that I have only days, if not hours, left among my peers, and would beg and beseech you to have mercy upon my only child, my Daisy. My beautiful angelic girl with your golden locks and her father's eyes . . .*
>
> *Please, do not let my poor baby be an orphan in this cold city. Take her to your bosom and love her as I do. Do this, if not for me, then for her and for the love that we once shared between us.*
>
> *Please, Sister, take my child and love her as your own.*
>
> *Your most beloved twin,*
>
> *Françoise*

Daisy was sitting on the bed in their room when Claudine returned to mop up the blood, white-faced but dry-eyed. She did not run to embrace her guardian as the other had expected, but sat where she was, eyeing her intently with eyes like Mexican sapphires. She had taken her hair up, accentuating her long white swan's neck, and in the late-morning light her tresses shone like carelessly polished platinum, her countenance suddenly that of a grown woman and not the child she had been before the events of these last two fateful nights.

"I danced naked again last night when you weren't here," she said by way of greeting. "But there was nary a soul to watch and the other girls played cards with each other in the salon until nearly dawn, but no customers came our way. Why is that, do you think?"

"For fear of Jack, I suppose," Claudine replied, unfastening her wrap and letting it slide carelessly to the floor. "The streets, they tell me, were deserted."

"And what do you know of Jack?" the girl asked pointedly. "And, more importantly, am I he? Did I kill those poor people, Claudine?"

Claudine sighed and shook her head. She suddenly felt very weary and desired nothing more that to get out of her clothes and wash the stench of Newgate from her body and hair.

"Draw me a bath," she whispered to Daisy, starting to undress. "Draw me a bath and I'll tell you a story . . ."

"I was not always as I am now," she began, letting the heat of the water seep into her tired bones and bring her solace. "My sister and I came from a respectable, if bourgeois, home in the Paris suburbs. Our father was a tax inspector; our mother had been a piano teacher before she married. We had a maid and a cook, and my father dreamed of owning a motor car. We were popular and my sister had many suitors though no proposals. I, on the other hand, had only one beau – an English military doctor, a brilliant surgeon, and madly in love with me. In fact, the banns had already been called and our marriage was being planned, when our parents decided on a day trip to Toulon . . ."

"My grandparents?"

"Yes, your poor grandparents. You know what happened. There was a terrible railway accident that day and they did not return. Françoise remained calm, but I was distraught when I heard the news and became quite hysterical, screaming and crying until the locum doctor, who had been summoned, prescribed heavy doses of laudanum and I passed into a fog for many weeks. Indeed, it was thought that I would never recover and it was not until I was moved to the hospital where a new doctor disagreed with the original diagnosis that I regained my health, eventually becoming well enough to return home.

"But what a surprise awaited me on my return. I found that in my absence my sister was now married. *And to my fiancé.* Distraught again, I asked how they could both have deceived me so and she replied, as calm as a piebald mare, 'Why, Françoise, whatever are you talking about, you know that Jack and I have been engaged for many months, it was only natural that I should lean on him and speed up our marriage in the light of the terrible tragedy that has befallen our poor family. Why, indeed, who do you suppose has paid all your medical bills these last months as you lay raving on your fever bed?"

"She . . . She pretended to be you to steal your fiancé? But how?"

"We were twins, we looked and dressed alike. In all the confusion, it was easy for her to tell the doctors that she was I and I was she, and she removed herself to his house after the accident so that there were not even our parents' old servants to spy out her deception."

"But what of he? Could he not tell?"

Claudine laughed without humour. "He was a young Englishman in love with a beautiful French girl he hardly knew. That was all he cared about. And, even if any doubts had crossed his mind, why would he reject his pretty and loving wife for the raving lunatic screaming in her hospital bed?"

"And, he, he was my father?"

Claudine nodded.

"And his name was Jack? Claudine, are you saying that my father is a monster?"

But the older woman merely shook her head again and sighed, not meeting Daisy's eyes.

"Then what, Claudine? I must have the whole truth . . ."

"I was furious and I wanted to unmask her, to tell her brand-new husband just exactly what sort of creature he had married, but her belly was already round and swollen with you inside her and I did not have the heart, for I loved you even then, even before you had crossed the mortal threshold into this world. So I resolved to go away and make my life elsewhere, but I had no home and no fortune, everything I had was tied to them and, believe me, I contemplated taking my own life many times during those dark days.

"But then I remembered that I had an aunt in England, a shady figure that my mother rarely spoke of and my father went silent at the mention of her name. But, what was I to do? I had no one else, save a sister who smiled too brightly and an ex-suitor too blind to see what was in front of him, so I wrote a letter to an English address in our mother's old pocketbook. This address, in fact . . ."

"Then the old woman upstairs, she is . . .?"

"Your great-aunt. She took me in and trained me in the ways of men, showed me how to become a favourite with the gentlemen, though, in truth, I despised every last man jack of them.

"In the meantime, your parents, also, had returned to London and, though they did not acknowledge me and I was not permitted to visit their lavish Highgate home, I would watch them walking with you on Sundays in the park. You were such a pretty child. And so I wished that you were mine—"

"But I cannot remember my father, and my mother's house was poor and squalid," Daisy interrupted. "I did not know the feel of silk or clean linen until you brought me here and made me your ward."

Claudine laughed again. "Ah, the vagaries of fate." She sighed. "Your father, though a brilliant man, was also cursed with many vices, playing at cards being paramount amongst them. At first luck favoured him, but when he left Paris and took up practice in this city, his fortunes abruptly turned and he began to sustain heavy losses. And with the bad luck came heavier drinking and . . . Other things . . ."

She faltered and Daisy looked coldly at her.

"You mean, he took to buying the love of women such as you and I? It is no surprise, Claudine, after all, the gentlemen who come here night after night all have other families and other lives. Why should my father have differed?"

Claudine nodded. "Girls talk, and I had heard rumours that he was abroad in Whitechapel for many weeks before I finally came upon him in the salon here one night when the fog was thick. I do not think he saw me, but it was about then that the killings began."

"Then it *was* he!" Daisy exclaimed.

"No," Claudine said very softly. "It was not he . . ."

"Then who?"

"She had changed her name and her personality once before. This time her mind was disturbed and she knew not what she did. She only knew that he was visiting the houses of ill repute when he should have been at home with her, and when the bailiffs came and she was alone, well, something snapped. They left her nothing save the tools of his trade, and so she went out into the night with his surgeon's knives and sought her revenge on the women he had betrayed her with . . ."

Claudine was crying now, but Daisy insisted on ploughing on. "But the killings ceased these ten years past, and I was with her for many years before her death, how can this be, Claudine?"

"Your father, though he had no money, still had some influence. She was treated in a sanatorium and they eventually pronounced her fit. She returned to the humble home he had set up for you both. He was a good man and as honourable as circumstances would permit, and he tried hard to atone for the crimes he suspected that she had committed, but his health was failing him and the house was cold and damp, and that winter particularly cold. The poor man did not see the grudging spring which finally came—"

"But I am still confused," Daisy persisted. "For my mother is dead and yet the killings have recommenced, and there are connections to us with both victims. Who is Jack, Claudine?"

Claudine had risen from her tub and dried herself while they talked, and she dressed quickly now and took Daisy by the hand.

"Once I show you this, life can never be as it was," she whispered. "Are you sure you would not rather let sleeping dogs lie?"

But Daisy shook her head. "I have come too far already," she said quietly. "I must know the whole truth."

The room in the cellar was pleasantly furnished and the early afternoon sun streamed through the barred windows making dancing patterns on the plumped cushions of the plush sofa. Colourful embroideries of playful dogs and cats lined the papered walls, and a soft rug dulled the sound of their footfalls as they entered.

A small woman in a nurse's uniform ushered them in coldly, her face half obliterated by a hastily applied bandage, her arms covered in scratches and bite marks.

"Twice?" Claudine said by way of greeting. "You let her get out twice?"

"What can I say, Miss Claudine," the woman replied. "She's as cunning as a fox and she's getting too strong for me. And the girls will talk in her hearing, so that when she hears things that upset her it's the very devil to keep her calm."

Claudine nodded. "We shall have to rethink. But where is she now?"

"In her bedroom, she won't let anyone but you go near her when she"s like this . . ."

The adjoining room, in stark contrast to the sunny sitting room, was dark and smelled like an abattoir. Daisy caught her breath and faltered, standing rooted to the spot on the transom.

"I don't think I want to see this after all, Claudine," she whispered, but her guardian held her hand and drew her firmly into that awful place.

"You wanted to know the secret of Jack, and now it is before you. You thought your mother was dead, but it is not so. Three years ago, when she felt her mind was deserting her, she wrote to me and sought my assistance in the last vestiges of her sanity, so that you would not be left destitute. Mainly, she is calm and we keep her in comfort here, but she still cares for deeply you, and for me, and when she feels we are threatened she tries to protect us."

"No, I do not want to see, Claudine," Daisy cried, sobbing now, but the other held her firm, and, as if her bouquet resurrected some distant memory in her, the hunched figure on the bed slowly looked up and smiled lopsidedly.

"Why good day, my dear," the crouched woman whispered in a strange deep voice, her dishevelled countenance still bloody and her eyes wild. "It is high time that we met. My name is Jack. I am your father . . ."

A Mote of Black Memory
Josh Reynolds

For Fritz Leiber and Robert Bloch

"De Castries, of course, had it by the right end with his seminal tract," Bidwell said, as he scratched his chalk across the brick wall of the courtyard. He'd been at it for twenty minutes, according to the pocket watch in Goode's hand. "Megapolisomancy is mostly occult theory, but a keen-eyed student can follow the paths between the paragraphs, so to speak. Amongst all the anti-Semitism and metageometry there are a few kernels of solid, reliable fact in the old fraud's theories."

"Such as?" Goode asked, as he snapped the pocket watch closed and slipped it back into the pocket of his frayed and faded waistcoat. He looked around nervously. Posters for Smith's crisps and Blue Band margarine warred for wall space in the courtyard with advertisements for Levy and Frank's Licensed Caterers and a number of gaudy ads for hosiery. From an open window somewhere above, a record player spat Clarence and Spencer Williams' "Royal Garden Blues" into the night. Voices rose and fell, bouncing from building to building in an off-putting fashion.

For those of a sensitive disposition, the East End of London was a sump of bad, black thoughts and evil emanations, even now, in the year of our Lord 1920. It had been such since the day the Saxons had begun to drain the marshy ground just outside the walls of the City of London to lay its foundations. It had always been a place of chaos, unearthly influence, madness and death. Even now, with most of the slums a thing of the past thanks to a recent flurry of rebuilding, a strange pall hung over the area, fogging the senses and loosening the morals of those who dwelt there. Or so it felt to Goode, who pulled the edges of his coat tighter about himself. *I want to go home*, he thought morosely.

"Cities, my dear fellow, are *aware*. Oh, not as we understand awareness, but it's there all the same. In every brick and every cobble, memories are contained. Moments in time, trapped like insects in amber. London *remembers*, Goode. It knows all. It sees all, through the eyes of its inhabitants. Every person in this pile is a part of a vast network; they – *we* – make up London's mind. What we see, what happens to us, London remembers. But until we learn how to listen, we cannot share in its accumulated wisdom." Bidwell stepped back and examined the marks he'd made. "London hoards its secrets jealously, Goode. It holds them close, hiding them in rumour, hearsay and folk tale. But, we shall prise them forth."

To Goode, the marks looked like nothing so much as a mass of numerical gibberish, but he knew his companion well enough by now to know that to venture such an opinion would be unappreciated at best and foolhardy at worst. Bidwell had a temper. It was one of the reasons he had been unceremoniously booted out of the Society for Psychical Research two years before. "You've figured it out then? How to listen, I mean?" he said. The quicker Bidwell got to the point, the quicker Goode could go home.

Not that home was much better than here, but it least it wasn't in Whitechapel. The West End wasn't much cleaner, but the ambiance was more to Goode's taste. Why he'd let Bidwell talk him into coming out, on a night like this, he didn't know.

Only you do, so stop lying to yourself, he thought. He owed Bidwell. Not as much as he once had, but even so a debt was a debt. And Goode always paid his debts. It was easier that way, on the mind and soul. He looked up, at the boarded windows above, and the sagging slates of the nearby rooftops. He could hear stray dogs snuffling close by, and rats scampering through the rubbish that choked the gutters. *Who in their right mind would want to hear what a place like Whitechapel had to say?*

Bidwell sniffed. "Obviously. Otherwise we would not now be standing in the East End at the wrong end of midnight, now would we?" He looked at Goode. "How are you feeling?" He tapped the side of his head. "Everything shipshape in the old melon?"

Goode frowned and rubbed his head. "If you thought otherwise, would I be here?"

"Now now, no need to be snippy, old thing. I'm just checking that your receptors are at peak sensitivity, what?" Bidwell said. He bounced the chalk on his palm. "Don't want to have another incident, do we? Not like that business in Shaftesbury Avenue, eh?"

Goode swallowed and looked away. "No," he said. *Don't think about it*, he thought, *don't, don't, don't.* Let the past keep itself to itself. Goode had enough problems in the here and now. And one of those problems was looking at him expectantly.

"So, I'll ask again . . . how's the grey matter?" Bidwell was smiling, but it didn't quite reach his eyes.

Goode sighed and shivered beneath his pea coat. "It's fine," he said. *After this, we're done*, he thought. He would never say it out loud. Bidwell might disagree, and he didn't know what he'd do then. It wasn't just that Bidwell was bigger than he was, although that was part of it. Bidwell was stronger in other ways.

"That's good to hear, Goode." Bidwell laughed. "I say, 'good', 'Goode' . . . ain't that a corker?" He stuffed the chalk into the pocket of his checked waistcoat and shook his head. "Any time you're ready."

"Ready for what?" Goode said. "You still haven't said why you've dragged me out here. Only that you needed my . . . my sensitivity." He nearly choked on the word. That was what the members of the Society for Psychical Research called it. He had a mind like a sponge, capable of soaking up all sorts of things, from all sorts of places. Most of them unpleasant. He looked around. "Why here, of all places? You know what places like this do to me." He ran his hands through his thinning hair. "How they make me feel . . ."

"Oh buck up, Goode. We all must make sacrifices in the name of science," Bidwell said. "And that is why I brought you here tonight. Science. Proof incontrovertible that de Castries' methodology was not flawed, that the city around us is a repository of human experience and history, more so than any dusty book or yellowing newspaper. You, my friend, are a trowel and now I shall use you to dig."

"Dig for what?" Goode demanded, letting a hint of exasperation creep into his voice.

"The past," Bidwell said. He gestured to the ground. "The Apaches of North America consider the past to be a well-worn trail. But it is an invisible one, for all those who remember it are mortal, and prone to – well – dying. Thus, the past-trail must be marked, with stories, songs, place names. Wisdom, they say, sits in places. Place-memory, as my former compatriots in the Society would say." He smiled. "There are many stories about this place, layered over one another like clay over stone. But one story stands head and shoulders above them all . . ."

Goode felt a chill. "No," he murmured, drawing the word out. Bidwell chuckled.

"Oh come now, old man. We've seen worse, haven't we? Besides, trauma anchors a memory better than anything. And what was he, but a living trauma?"

"I am not going diving in the spiritual sea, to hunt for Jack the Ripper," Goode said. He shook his head. "No, I won't do it." Ghosts were bad enough, as he'd learned at Shaftesbury Avenue – *don't think about it!* – but the ghost of a murderer?

"You will, I think," Bidwell said. "Besides, it will be easy. Whoever he was, he's buried in a shroud of ink and rumour. Every story, every bawdy song, they all crystallize about him, about the idea of him, holding him in place." Bidwell laughed and tapped the side of his head. "Those stories, Goode, were what started my line of inquiry. There were so many – some whispered that the Ripper was preventing a horror unlike any other, sacrificing the few for the many. Others said that he was possessed by some terrible power, a god of razors and sharp things, which demanded blood sacrifice." He laughed. "But the tales that most tweaked my ear were those that said the Ripper was a student of the occult, and had found the formula for immortality in the gin-soaked guts of back-alley comfort women."

"Bidwell . . ." Goode said, pleadingly.

Bidwell shook his head. "As I said, stories. And they did not end with the murders, no. Even now, new stories sprout like mushrooms. Jack is all things to all men, a monster for all seasons. All the fears of the city made manifest. Oh yes, the past is well fertilized here, Goode. And we shall reap its bounty."

"What are we even looking for?" Goode protested.

"I thought I'd made that obvious." Bidwell sniffed. "The truth, man. The ur-story. With my formulae, and your sensitivity, we shall peel back the layers of this onion, to reveal the core truth. With that in hand, we shall have proof of my theorems. Imagine it, Goode, imagine all that we can learn, all of the great secrets of London, there for the taking. We shall be voyagers in the sea of history, overthrowing old certainties and abolishing the lies of established wisdom." He made a fist. "London guards its secrets, but we shall slay the dragon and loot the hoard!"

"Very pretty," Goode said.

"Is that a hint of acid in your voice, Goode? I hope you're not thinking of backing out," Bidwell said, softly. There was a tincture of menace to his words and, for a moment, Goode wondered what the other man would say if he said yes. Bidwell had a temper, yes, but even he wouldn't attempt to force Goode to use his gift, surely.

He hesitated, considering, remembering Shaftesbury Avenue. With a sigh, he shook his head. "Step back, please," he said, in resignation. "I must have space, and quiet."

Bidwell smiled like a gleeful child. "Wonderful. I knew I could count on you, old man," he said, as he stepped back, hands behind his back.

Carefully, Goode emptied his mind, shooing out stray thoughts and idle whimsies. It required complete concentration to open his inner eye. The "spirit-eye", as his fellows in the Society called it. To peer through it was to peer into the unfettered spaces between one world and the next, and a slip in his concentration could have painful, if not disastrous consequences. He pressed his fingertips together in front of his face and relaxed the rest of his body, focusing all of his tension into his stiffened fingers.

He closed his eyes, and sucked in several deep, cleansing breaths. He felt the telltale pulse in his head, like the contraction of some dormant organ, and felt a vibration shudder through him as his third eye blinked blearily, and then focused on the world before it. Everything became soft at the edges and more vibrant as his senses expanded to fill the void left by his thoughts and physical sight.

Little by little, the hues of the world around him – the greys and blacks and browns of the courtyard, the deep blues and purples of the night – all blended and flowed into one another like watercolours. Everything became porous and gossamer and through his inner eye he could see the dim shapes of past moments flickering about like moths circling a flame – the after-images of the *ka* of those who'd passed through this place burned dully, like spots on his retinas. The Ka, or Odic Force, as Baron Von Reichenbach referred to it, was a force that permeated all living things, to greater or lesser degrees. But, more than that, the Ka was a psychic footprint. Where it passed, it left a trail, marking the history of its owner. *Memories of people*, Goode thought. Some were brighter than others, and some guttered like matches in a breeze. Bidwell's burned steadily – he was fat with the stuff of life, was Bidwell.

Goode swept his gaze over the courtyard, looking for something, anything, to give Bidwell. Some scrap of black memory, anchored to these stones, just to satisfy his hunger for knowledge. But, as he looked, he noticed a pall hanging over everything. For an instant, he was put in mind of what a hare must feel, as the fox closes in. Was it just the East End, making him feel this way? Or something else – Bidwell's theorems, perhaps, causing some strange resonance in the psychical plane.

A whiff of sensation caught his attention and he turned. There was something else in the courtyard, something dark. He found his gaze drawn to a corner, where something huddled. He made a strangled sound, and heard Bidwell say, "What is it?"

Goode said nothing. The huddled shape was just that – it wasn't a body, as such, but more the impression of a body. The absence of a life, a vague smudge where a human soul might once have been, the fading ashes of Ka. And it was not alone. Something else, reminiscent of oil spreading across water in a hundred different directions, rose up around it, as if his attentions, or perhaps Bidwell's theorems, had stirred it up.

Goode's heart sped up, rattling his ribs like a bird in a cage. The air around the spreading darkness looked almost infected, and he felt sick, staring at the pulsing un-colours that shone through the cracks in the world. The darkness spilled upwards, pouring into the shape of . . . something. It was long and lean and angled wrong, not like a body, but a shadow, a reflection in distorted glass.

It paused, looming over the huddled shape. It glanced over one shoulder. Eyes like raw, red wounds met his from across the courtyard, only they were bigger than the courtyard, bigger even than stars and staring right at him. There was no face that went with those terrible eyes, merely an odour of urgency and alien eagerness. A panting, hungry musk pawed at his ka idly and sent shivers of revulsion through him. He heard, or perhaps felt, a querulous grunt that seemed to echo through the hollow spaces of him, and then it turned.

From the crown of the old-fashioned top hat to the surprisingly pristine spats, the apparition that faced Goode was every inch the bloodthirsty Victorian bogeyman that Bidwell had made him find. Though no one had ever really seen Saucy Jack, everyone knew what he looked like regardless. A long cloak hung from its shoulders and its hands were hidden beneath white cotton gloves, just like a proper gentleman. But there was nothing gentlemanly about the leer on its face – that face, oh God, *that face* – or the inhuman hunger that burned in its eyes.

It was every artist's rendering and heated witness account come bounding to life, like a tiger out of the tall grass. The air around Goode stank of blood and pain. The cloak rustled, as if in an unfelt wind, and the shadowy edges of it seemed to grab the walls and it *stretched* towards him, swallowing the light as it came.

Goode took a step back. He had seen such things before, though never with such clarity. *Bidwell's formulae*, he realized. The metageometry of the infamous de Castries, chalked on the walls, manipulating the flow of the city, focusing what was diffuse into concentrated form. They had not revealed the truth, or perhaps they had, and, like a wound growing gangrenous, fiction had become fact. Regardless, the Ripper was here and it was not a man, it was an absence of humanity. "Bidwell . . ." Goode whispered.

"What is it?" Bidwell asked, voice harsh with eagerness. "What do you see? Describe it to me, man!" Goode's mouth was dry, and he couldn't work up the spit to answer. The world quivered at the edges, like the pages of a book caught in a strong wind. The sounds and smells of the East End, as it had been, when the flesh and blood primogenitor of the idealized and nightmarish facade coming towards him had stalked through cobbled cul-de-sacs. Like birds rising before the approach of a cat, the sound of carriage wheels and the stink of smog and poverty struck Goode's senses like hammer blows.

The discordant sounds and images were nothing more than the lashing of its tail, the padding of its paws through the tall grass, but no less potent for all that. *Wisdom sits in places*, he thought. But what horrible wisdom was this, which lurked in an East End courtyard? He shoved his hands out in a useless gesture of warding. "N-no, go away," he whined. "Go away, stop looking at me, *go away* . . ."

It watched him, head cocked, grin impossibly wide. It was an animal's grin, displaying not so much cheerfulness as allowing for the proper appreciation of the number and length of the displayer's teeth. *I am here*, it seemed to say. *You came looking and here I am*. Goode fought to control his breathing. It wasn't real, couldn't be real. It was just a memory, a mote of black memory, caught in the weft of history, but he could hear the click of its shoes on the cobbles and the hiss of its breath as it sauntered towards him out of the collective psyche of the past. No man had ever breathed like that.

But the Ripper wasn't a man. Not any more. London only knew what its inhabitants knew, what the people who made up its vast, heaving mind knew and what they knew was that no man could have done what the Ripper did, and so the Ripper *was not a man*. Goode wanted to scream, but the sound died in his throat. Bidwell was speaking rapidly, shaking him, trying to catch his attention, but he couldn't, *didn't dare*, look away.

In the watery quiver of the air around the thing, Goode could see gaslight streets and crawling fog. A London that-was, or never-was, depending how literally you took Dickens and Conan Doyle. Where the shadow of the Ripper stretched, things warped and changed, becoming something out of Sax Rohmer. Not history as it had been, but how it was remembered by those who had survived it, even as Bidwell had said.

"What are you seeing, Goode? Is it him? Have you found him?" Bidwell said, more loudly now, almost shouting. "What does he look like?"

Goode shook his head. "Not . . . not him," he croaked, trying to look away, but unable. The Ripper stalked closer, wavering like a mirage, sometimes there, sometimes not, but drawing steadily closer. A demented *flaneur*, straight from Baudelaire's darkest scribbling. The blade in its hand became a butcher's knife, a scalpel, an Athame, the gleam of steel fading to the dull grey of stone or obsidian, before shimmering silver anew. "It's not him," he moaned, digging at his eyes with the heels of his palms.

Bidwell caught his shoulder. "Tell me what you see, man," he barked. "You see something – what is it? *Who* is it?"

"It's nothing," Goode repeated. He said it again and again, chanting the word like a mantra, hoping that if he said it enough, the Ripper would simply burst like a soap bubble and vanish. He felt cold, and his skin was clammy. His heart thudded in his chest, and the gaps between the paving cobbles at his feet ran red. He could hear someone moaning, and thought that it was him. The cries spiralled up, drawn in the Ripper's wake like feathers sifted from the flapping wings of a seabird.

The Ripper opened its mouth, revealing a cavernous red maw of jagged teeth. Its shape bent at right angles, stretching to fill the limits of his vision. Its cloak flapped around it like the wings of a flock of ravens, its face a foggy nothing, pierced through by hell-bright eyes and that too-wide smile, a smile wide enough and deep enough to swallow London itself. Fingers like meat hooks tore through the dark places of Goode's soul, and teeth snapped together with greedy aplomb.

He would be eaten alive, from inside out. He wouldn't leave a ghost behind when he died, because the Ripper was going to eat that first and hollow him out. Goode thrashed, trying to free himself from its gaze, but the trap only tightened and a moan escaped his lips. He staggered beneath the weight of its attentions.

The Ripper was all around him, filling the courtyard. It was the courtyard, and the East End and perhaps the city itself, and every pain and indignation its inhabitants had endured. *London remembers*, Goode thought and giggled. He felt hands on him, shaking him, but he ignored them.

The knife shot forward and all of the air whooshed out of him. There was a dull ache in his belly, where the blade had entered, and he felt – *blade whistling as it carved a red loop across quivering flesh* – ill. He felt hot and cold – *eyes like lamps swept over his face as a smile like a crescent moon stretched wide over a featureless expanse of nightmare shadow* – and exhausted.

There was something in his head, like an itch he couldn't scratch. Out of the corner of his eye, under the surface of his thoughts, he could see – *blood, spattering across brick* – things and hear – *a man screamed, high and shrill, as a shark's grin was reflected in his bulging eyes* – voices and he tried to thrust the heels of his hands into his eyes, to rub out the images that sprang unbidden into his mind, but he couldn't.

He – *red, painting the air in a curlicue* – closed his eyes and – *the Athame whistled, nearly separating a head from a neck* – gasped out prayers. He curled up, gagging as the hot, sour taste of blood filled his mouth. He heard a whimper, and his eyes peeled open, to see Bidwell, on the ground. Bidwell, torn from his flesh by his – *the Ripper's* – hands. Goode saw that his hands were all red, and he wanted to scream but he couldn't.

The Ripper's grin stretched wider and wider, so that its head seemed ready to split in two as it gazed down at him. *I feed London, and London feeds me*, something whispered, deep in Goode's mind. Stories begetting stories. The Ripper was the East End, and the East End was the Ripper. That was the truth of it, two names, inextricably linked. *This is what I am, now. This is what I have always been, and will be, as long as these stones live. This is my temple, and I am god, as Mithras, Bacchus and a hundred others before me.*

I am London, and London is me, and my secrets are not for you.

Goode stared up at it, waiting. The Ripper's grin was a slice of pearly white across the black, as, with a tip of its tall hat, it turned away, back into the black past from which it had come. He heard its footsteps fade, taking with it the clamour of London-that-was.

Goode closed his eyes, and began to cry.

Catch Me When You Can . . .
M. Christian

. . . on the floor of the coffin room on Brick Lane, hot copper in her nose, cheek against splintered boards, red syrup crawling past her left eye, agony with each breath – and not many more to take . . .

Mamaí at the stove, porridge in a pot – a boiling of oats – giving her a ghostly veil of steam, hiding the blooms of her cheek; Dadaí at the table, bottle as always there – as much as the cap on his head – both drooping already, even before the first peak of sun, the beginning cries of early sheep . . .

A kiss by a cairn, the youngest McKesson boy chasing her down – as much as captured as surrendered – and trapping her with laughter, she yielding with giggles. Chill biting her cheek, a crisp plume with each sound from he and she till stifled with a touch of lips, to part with a rush of thick, cold morning smoke . . .

The percussive pop of her hand against Bradan's tiny face, the screaming that had ground glass into her brain rocketing with the baby's skyrocket from colic to true fright and real pain. The meaty weight, the thundering burst of Dadaí in answer, Bridget to the floor . . . Bridget to the floor and red syrup from out her nose, from the socket the tooth had been knocked from . . . cries of Mamaí with the cries of Bradan with Dadaí's gin-slurred roars . . .

Laughter by another cairn, the piled stones too set in their ancient ways to but she tried anyway, lifting the gritty, moss-slick over her head to smash in the bones and brains of the same McKesson boy who had fogged the world with that kiss, but who then hooted at the missing tooth in her smile . . . the stone falling short, a mocking dark smack into the soaked field . . .

"Anyone seen . . . what's 'er name . . . the potato girl . . . the new one? You know the one I mean . . . stands about so, got this darkish hair, you know? Red, like, but not red *red* . . . seems she was hereabouts then she weren't," Dolly said, pausing only to silently halfway down her glass of gin.

"The Cullen girl, you mean? The one used to hang on Old Jack?" Anne answered, swirling the thick dregs in the bottom of her own clipped glass, paying more attention to the balance of another against having enough for a four-penny coffin that night.

"Nah, not that daft piece o' shite. Didn't ya hear me, I said she's got red hair . . . like this, but not like this but much darker," Dolly said, plucking at the ribbon on Mary's hat.

"Get off it," the other woman said, jerking her head away and taking the ribbon and the hat with it. "We ain't seen no red but not *red* haired girl."

"But she was just about . . . you must have seen her . . ."

"They comes and they goes," Anne moaned, pushing her chair back with her decision to get another glass and just walk the night away. "You knows that. Only reason I know you sad creature 'tis we drink this sorry shit every bloody night."

"Suppose," Dolly said, finishing her own drink. "Must a' moved on or something. Tell ya, though, she did have the nicest hair . . . or was I thinkin' of the other one, the one with the tooth . . ."

That sister with the broom handle, more foggy breaths from the unlit stove in the corner. What was whispered to her hadn't been all that funny, the words half heard, less than half understood, but the laugh had come anyway . . . just as the sister paused, a wheezing gap in her coughing and gasping reading from the Bible. Hands on the table, peaked in tight fear, then cracked from vigorous wood brought down in insulted fury. The right hand, the second and third fingers, ached with spoken and, later, only wincing pain, for months after, and never worked the right way after . . .

A bloom of red and white in the mud, the screams and cries from that side of the street – and the side she'd been standing on – the cutting shrillness trapped in her mind as much as the sight of the horse hoof transforming the toppling drunk's head into crimson jelly and shattered bits of yellowed porcelain. Days past, and in her first station, standing and waiting for her first train, the shriek of the engine bringing tea and scones up and out on to the sooty stones of the platform . . .

The spotted boy, the tall one hanging around with the MacAteers that summer: they all full of rude sounds and clumsy hands, bluster and tripping over their own feet . . . but he was the same but not as much, a shit-smelling flower in a pile of shit. His sounds just as rude, his hands just as clumsy, his bluster just as grating, his feet just as lumbering . . . but he didn't laugh at where the tooth had been . . .

Split open and roaring, her cries ringing back off cold stones – the fast taps of a hole in the roof letting in a stream of water. The woman, one of the Rahillys, her hands shaking, pulled and poked beneath a blanket scratchy with wool and lice. When her own tears finally stopped and his did, the Rahilly woman put him in a broken-handled basket for her mother to take away . . .

"I'm sick of hearing it, I am," Flaherty said, flopping down another sack of wheat.

"Well, ya don't have to be listening then do ya," Dolski answered, adding his own to the stack. "Not like you have to say anything."

"Sees as I have to watch yer bleedin' backside go up and down the bloody ladder all day might as well listen to what comes out the other end." Flaherty grabbed the middle rungs and began to pull himself up.

"Just saying that I ain't see her for going on two weeks now. Not natural's all I's sayin'." Dolski waited for the other man to get higher up before following behind.

"Works a' wisdom, ol' salt. They comes and they goes. You just be lucky to have seen 'er when she was abouts. Take her memories and move on, I say," Flaherty said.

"Aye, yer right," Dolski said. "Just she had the sweetest li'l smile, she did. Tooth missing but in a nice way, you know?"

"I *don't* know and if you don't shut up about 'er yer gonna be missing yer own. Shut it and help with the next . . ."

A gap, a hole, a vacancy . . . the sailor's hat was there, a threadbare knit bird's nest stitched with multicolored coarse threads, like an old sweater had been pulled apart and fed into its weave; his breath was there, curling of her eyebrows, a tumbling in her stomach; his voice was there, like rocks tumbling in a loose barrel rolling down a steep hill . . . but the rest was gone. And the shadow, the looming iron was still there: the great riveted wall of the ship rising far above the docks, the alarm of its whistle making her bones shake even when she was elbow-to cheek with everyone else within it . . .

It was like a light, a spark struck before the fire took: bright and singing. She'd laughed, giggling so loud that a dustman turned to look at where the ringing sound had come from on such a heavy, dark morning. In her hand, a rough skin, but when she pulled and twisted the thing had ripped, spraying her face with sticky juice. She ate the whole thing, beginning in front of the cart and ending with swallowing the last of the peel in the moldy pitch of an alley on her way back to the dusty flop and the ferocious old woman she owed two days' rent to but was finally able to pay . . . trying to remember only the sweet meat and juice but – unbidden – the coins and the hands that had dropped them at her feet when he was done came with the bright surprise of the orange . . .

His name . . . no idea, but she called him Paul only because she always liked the name. When she allowed herself to think back to that tiny stone room, she sometimes wondered if that's what he'd been named, and what his life was like. But this other, the one she watched move bags of something up and down a ladder, she called him Paul as well. He was like so many she saw, a man of two arms and two legs going about his business. But there was also a difference to him, one that always made her stand on the street across and watch him while pretending not to watch him. Once, when a wobble-wheeled carriage had clamored down the street, forcing her off the cobblestones before the maddened driver could nearly crush her under his uneven wheels, she'd found herself close enough to speak . . . but she hadn't, pretending not to feel him approach, instead feigning interest in anywhere but there . . . and, that night, the snores and screams in the flop weren't what kept her awake . . .

He asked her name. So many others had, of course, but always with an air of gambit, to move themselves closer or to get her legs apart. The gentleman asked, with his words, his tone, she felt that he was actually interested her person. And when she replied, he asked a further question: to which she answered – and with it coming, of all things, a warmth to her cheeks – that yes that was where she hailed. It was not like people of his kind did not pass, or even descend to the shitty streets: it was not even her first . . . but this one, the gentleman who asked, was different. And when the third question arrived, Bridget still did not equate him with the others for whom her name, where she was from and if she had a residence were only preliminaries for the exchange of services. Fortune, she blessed herself with the response to his third question, was hers: a room on Brick Lane, which was shared but was hers for the night . . .

In the room, the lamp lit, his bag on the floor, and Bridget allowed herself the generosity of a smile and, heart fluttering in her chest, a question of her own, to which he did not say anything and instead reached out to stroke her cheek with a black-gloved hand . . .

. . . *on the floor of the coffin room on Brick Lane, hot copper in her nose, cheek against splintered boards, red syrup crawling past her left eye, agony with each breath – and not many more to take* . . .

. . . the final drops of her life spilling, a final tear mixing, a final thought: that somewhere she be in memories of others . . .

The weight of standing in silence forced Detective Inspector Walter Andrews to finally speak: "Such a business."

Detective Inspector Frederick Abberline nodded. The glow of a cold London morning was just beginning to reveal the chimneys and stacks of the city's horizon.

"Five of them . . . bloody hell," Andrews said, and without knowing what else to say repeated himself: "Bloody hell . . ."

"Maybe," Abberline said, looking across the street at a gang moving what looked like sacks of grain up and down a precarious ladder.

"What do you mean?"

Abberline breathed into his gloved hands then rubbed them quickly together for extra warmth. "That we know of."

"Christ," Andrews said. "You think there are others?"

After taking a minute to respond, Abberline nodded as he did: "More than likely. Probably more than a few other poor souls not lucky enough to get noticed."

"Poor blighters."

"Dying," Abberline said, "is one thing . . . being forgotten . . . well—" he looked out at the city "—that must be hell itself."

Ripper Familias
Terry Davis and Patrick Jones

————

10 April 1912

Three generations of Kingsford men boarded the RMS *Titanic* on a crystalline April morning. John, the patriarch – who insisted that he was a physician and demanded to be called Dr Kingsford – had been released from Bedlam Royal Hospital, the infamous asylum for the mentally ill, the day before. His son Will called him Father; his grandson Reggie called him Grandfather John. No diminutive endearments – no Dad, Pops or Grandpa for the Kingsford men. It was Reggie's first time on an ocean liner and the first time he ever set eyes on his grandfather; for all three, it was their last day in England.

Earlier, as they stood outside the Bedlam gates, Reggie hoped it was the last time he would endure the sight of Grandfather John's rotten teeth. They were not only the same color as the rusted iron bars of Bedlam's gate, they had chipped and broken into points reminiscent of the rusty spears that composed the fence surrounding the six-hundred-year-old edifice. Reggie wanted to like his grandfather, and he was resolved to triumph over his sometimes impatient and even unkind nature and kill Grandfather John with kindness.

"Reginald, help me with my bag." Most of their bags resided in the ship's cargo area, but Grandfather insisted a small black leather bag he'd purchased the night before needed to stay with him. His right hand shook so much that it was hard for him to carry it for a long time.

"Happy to help!" Reggie shouted.

"Good to know," Grandfather said. "I might need your help even more on this voyage."

"Anything you need." His grandfather's smile, ugly as it was, still brightened the morning.

The wizened old man struggled on his cane in the crush of men, women and children walking up the gangplank. The Kingsfords stood in the middle of the queue, the waiting line of one thousand three hundred people who had booked passage on the *Titanic's* maiden voyage. Boarding the ship among this many people was an ordeal.

"Don't worry, Grandfather John," Reggie said. "I'll hold on to you." The years in Bedlam had taken a heavy toll. The old man looked like a wraith in his black trousers and black cape.

"What a nice son you've raised, Will," the old man said to Reggie's father. "He will be a much stronger and courageous son than the one I raised."

Will let the insult pass, as he had others earlier in the day. Reggie thought Grandfather John would have been ecstatic to be out of that awful dark place and free under the sun and the blue sky among other free people with happy faces and voices raised on this day replete with color, the fragrance of the sea and the pull of the outgoing tide toward a new world full to the gunwales of new chances. Instead, he seemed angry.

The three reached the top of the gangplank, stepped on to the Boat Deck and followed a crewman's directions to the stairway to C Deck, three decks below, and their second-class cabin. Ahead of them, a bevy of young women and girls in great high spirits lined the rail in the space between two of the ship's twenty wooden lifeboats, which hung from divats – cranes that lowered them to the water. It seemed to Reggie that the lifeboats *framed* the girls like a painting, the title of which might be *High Hopes*. They were laughing and pointing westward and proclaiming visions of the Statue of Liberty.

"New York will be like London," the grandfather snarled. "Full of harlots." He lowered his voice when he bent to Reggie, but the vicious tone remained. "Look at them, Reginald. They are vile and sinful. They will go to hell."

Reggie looked. Nothing about them seemed to him vile, sinful or hell-bent. The rush of people swept the Kingsfords toward the young women. The only quality that Reggie thought anyone might judge risqué about them was they wore too much make-up for girls their age. As he passed, Reggie was stricken by their fragrance. He struggled against the current of people to remain in their aura, but he carried on. Reggie looked back at an older girl whose red hair contrasted so boldly against her white dress that she seemed to glow. She seemed to be looking at him, too. He waved at her briefly before his grandfather jerked his hand down. Reggie looked down and saw his grandfather's gnarled left hand around his forearm. It was like being caught in the claws of a bird of prey.

"You like her?" Grandfather John asked. "Don't bother. Women like that are vile."

"No," he replied with a shrug. This was a lie as colossal as the ship. Reggie liked that she smiled at him, and he liked girls in general; he hated that they didn't like him. The girls at school teased him because he was short, and they called him a daddy's boy because his father walked him to and from school. Yes, there were girls who didn't tease him and who were even friendly at times, but he was afraid to take the chance of talking to them. Something thick and dark in him wanted to hate girls and to hate his father, too. Yet, how could he blame his father for wanting to protect him from the pains of the world? The man had lost his wife to tuberculosis and his father to madness, of course he wanted to protect his son. But still Reggie hated his father, who seemed at times to love his drink more than his son. Reggie didn't understand why the best part of him couldn't prevent this worst part from rising up out of the dark fissure where it lived in his thoughts. He reflected upon these things in the tumult of fellow passengers, and saw in his mind the spikes that made up Bedlam's gate.

As they approached the stairway that would take them down into the ship, Reggie's grandfather spoke again, "The world is full of harlots and—"

This time his father interrupted. "That's enough, Father," Will snapped and shook his head in revulsion. Reggie noticed his grandfather exhibited a similar curled lip expression of disgust, although his was directed at the glowing red-haired girl.

*　　*　　*

"Don't let him out of your sight tonight," Will whispered to Reggie as they sat at the dinner table. Maybe tired of his father's insults, Will had walked briskly with Reggie, leaving Grandfather John steps behind, but in sight.

"Why do we have to watch him?" Reggie whispered back. Before his father could answer, a rare sound shocked their ears: Grandfather John, laughing loud and long.

Reggie turned to see his grandfather twirling his cape like a loquacious raven among the passengers entering the dining area. The bilious old man, who had spoken of the young women with such viciousness earlier, seemed empty of bile and unburdened of years. He led a laughing party of women to the dinner table.

"Why, ladies, I'd love to tell you about my skills with a scalpel," Grandfather John crooned as he held out chairs for the women at the dinner table. "But sadly, my career as a surgeon ended too soon, so just a few tales." Reggie stared at his grandfather in amazement as he spoke nonstop through the first two courses, telling tales as tall as the ship itself. Only when the entrée was served, did he pause and let others speak.

The old charmer poked Reggie with his shaking right hand; then with his left he held his steak knife and pointed with it across the crowded dining room. There was the red-haired girl. He dipped his head to Reggie and whispered, "She's chasing you."

Reggie blushed; his face as red as the rare steak the waiter sat in front of his grandfather. Grandfather John smiled broadly as he steadied his right hand to pick up his fork, held the steak with it and sliced open the meat. The red blood gushed on to the white plate. "This reminds me of an operation," his grandfather began another story.

Why was he telling stories and why didn't his father stop him? The Kingsfords were butchers. His father made a good living, and Reggie apprenticed in his shop.

Grandfather John raised his fork. "I developed this shaky hand," he said. "It could still make an incision, but not perform the full operation."

He lowered the fork then, raised the knife toward the red roses in the center of the table and held it steady as the table itself. "I believe I've become proficient enough with my other hand, however, to return to work in America."

He leaned forward, manoeuvered the knife in the manner of an orchestra conductor with his baton, then cut the stem of one of the roses with a turn of hand. He set the knife beside his plate, picked up the rose, flourished it as though he were toasting the table, then sat back. He gestured with the rose to the older woman to Reggie's right, then handed it to Reggie. "Reginald, be a gentleman," he commanded, "and pass this to the good lady." Reggie did as he was told. The woman smiled and Reggie blushed again.

Reggie listened to his grandfather's stories and felt disloyal for not believing a single one. He knew little about the man. His father had only told him about his grandfather in the past year. When Will had been just a few years older than Reggie, back in the summer of 1888, Grandfather John's wife died. Just a few months later, Will had told Reggie, on a busy morning at the shop before Christmas, John reached across the counter and sliced a woman's face. He was jailed and before long declared insane. As he listened to his grandfather speak, he marveled at how easily the man told lie after lie. He would have felt guilty, but believed the harmless tales hurt no one. Unlike the whiskey Reggie watched his father, like most nights, down with increasing ease and speed.

11 April 1912

Reggie woke to the sight of his father asleep on a chair set against the cabin door. "Wake up, Father," he whispered from his top bunk. He needed to get out the door and to the WC down the hall. Unlike first class, second-class passengers had only a chamber pot – which Reggie hated – and a basin. Will opened his blood-shot eyes, clutched his head as though in pain, then wrenched forth a great yawn that filled the room with the smell of whiskey. "Why did you sleep in a chair?"

"I told you, Reginald," his father replied. "Your grandfather can't wander out at night, this is the only way—"

Reggie interrupted. "Let him sleep with me. I'll make sure he doesn't leave the cabin."

Will rubbed his forehead again, then frowned. He set his jaw in a look Reggie had grown accustomed to since his mother died. The look said his father didn't trust him. "I can do it," he said. The frown grew darker. "Please, Father, I'm fourteen. I can do things."

Will looked at Reggie's grandfather asleep in the bottom bunk, then up at Reggie again. "That's what I'm afraid of."

On his way back from the WC, Reggie met the red-haired girl. She wore a red dress brighter than her hair. Over it she wore a thick black sweater. It was spring in London, but it was icy winter in the North Atlantic. "Good morning, fine sir," the girl said, then bowed. She had an Irish accent.

Reggie stumbled to reply. He didn't understand how Grandfather John could say mean things about women, but then at the table charm them so. He couldn't say anything to girls. He didn't know how.

"Cat got your tongue, sir?"

Reggie had no reply. He couldn't meet her eyes. "I don't feel well," he said. He felt as though all the air had left his lungs. Feeling weak, he clutched the railing in the hallway.

The girl put her right hand on Reggie's left. "Seasick?"

Reggie nodded rather than outright telling a lie. It was the waves of her red hair not the waves of the blue sea.

"I can't wait to get off this wretched boat," she said.

"It's beautiful, the finest luxury liner in the world," Reggie replied. "I didn't want to leave England, but if I had to, I was at least doing it on an historic voyage."

"Perhaps for those in first class or you in second. But, fine sir, it is not so for those of us in steerage," she said. "We're packed tighter than the sardines served for dinner last night. And we're so close to the engines, it's surely as hot as the gates of Hell."

"I saw you in the second-class dining room last night," Reggie said. "How did—"

"A lady never tells," she said. "But I'll just say I have a friend on the crew who owed me a favor."

Reggie wondered what kind of favor it was, but before he could ask he felt a hand on his shoulder and heard a voice. "And Hell is exactly where a strumpet such as you belongs." He turned to see his grandfather with his father a few steps behind.

Reggie turned back to the girl and opened his mouth to apologize. But he could not give voice to his humiliation before she tugged her sweater around her and fled.

"She'll be back," Grandfather said. "They always come back until . . ." His face took on a distant smile.

"Until?" Reggie asked, but Grandfather John didn't answer. Instead, he laughed like he'd told a joke. Nothing seemed funny, except the feeling in Reggie's stomach. But this time it wasn't the sea making him sick; it was the sound of his grandfather's laughter

After dinner, where Grandfather John charmed everyone again – except Will, who showed more interest in his drink – the Kingsfords ventured to the ballroom and took chairs along the wall. Reggie didn't know how to dance, and his grandfather was in no condition to waltz around with his cane. Will, however, was having a high ol' time thanks to the generous amount of whiskey he'd consumed.

"Your father should be ashamed," Grandfather John said. His voice was heavy, dark, tired.

"He's having a good time," Reggie said. "He's not done that much since Mother died."

The old man's face went lax and his voice fell. "When was that, six months ago?" he asked.

Reggie nodded. "The TB took her on the fifth of October," he replied.

"I was locked up for over twenty years thanks to your father. How many turns around Bedlam's ballroom do you think I waltzed in that time?" Anger brought back the old man's bravado.

"But, Grandfather, Father said that you were locked away because you killed a woman in your butcher shop."

"I didn't kill that woman in the shop, I gave her an early Christmas present," Grandfather John said. For the first time, Reggie thought he heard something like sadness in the tattered voice. "She'd been plain when she came in that morning. After my blade did its work, she was more attractive when they dragged her out."

The music stopped and applause burst through the room. Grandfather John leaned to Reggie. "But what I should have done was split her skull with my cleaver," he said, as calmly as if he were discussing the weather. From the ballroom, applause still filled the air. From Grandfather John, there was nothing but roaring laughter. Even though the room was warmed by the dancing bodies, Reggie felt a chill rattle his bones, matched by a conflicting fire in his blood. He was disgusted. He was curious. He wanted details.

12 April 1912

After breakfast, Reggie and his grandfather walked slowly around their deck – C Deck it was called, or the Shelter Deck. Unlike his words to the red-haired girl, Grandfather John spoke pleasantly with every person they encountered; he was most gracious with the younger women. One young woman, wearing a white hat with a brim nearly as round as a lifebuoy, found him particularly charming. She stopped when he addressed her. "Fine lady," he said. He reached for her hand, and she let him take it. He bent forward, gave the hand a dignified kiss, and straightened. "My name is John, but my friends call me Jack." He gave a modest bow, and the two Kingsford men walked on.

Jack? Reggie thought. They had walked only a few steps when the old man told the young man he was weary. Reggie looked for a place to sit, and then he saw a sign that said LIBRARY, and he raced ahead. He had wanted to bring some of his books, but his father said they could take only absolute essentials to America. He reminded Reggie that America had books, too. But Reggie was worried that America might not have his beloved Sherlock Holmes. He waited at the door for his grandfather and took his arm.

Reggie led John to an armchair, then joined the people inspecting the books in the glass cases. He was forced to stifle a joyful whoop when he caught sight of the *Memoirs of Sherlock Holmes*. He loved the story "The Final Problem." Of all the scenes in all his Holmes books, Reggie's favorite was the last scene where Holmes, after pursuing his nemesis Professor Moriarty to Switzerland, falls to his death in the Reichenbach Falls while locked in mortal combat with the arch-villain.

Reggie asked his grandfather if he wanted a book, but the old fellow was asleep. How this old man could wander off and hurt anyone, or even himself, was beyond Reggie. Now that's a mystery even Holmes couldn't solve, he thought. He returned to the cases and found more detective stories; then he awakened his grandfather. "We should get back," he said. "Father will be wondering where we've been."

The old man grunted. "Your father treats us like children," he said. "Are you a child, Reginald?" Reggie shook his head vigorously. "Neither am I. Why should we let your father tell us where we can go and what we can do? I propose an alliance between us. A secret alliance. You help me; I help you."

He extended his hand and his young ally gladly took it. With no brothers, no mates on the voyage, Reggie didn't want to be alone. An alliance sounded to him like a grand adventure. He slid a chair across the thick carpet and set it beside his grandfather's. The old man seemed revitalized. He patted Reggie on the back. "We've just met," he said with a smile. "Yet I sense you're just like me – unlike your father."

"Father has been sad a lot since Mother died," Reggie said.

The old man's face went slack. His good cheer was gone. "Dying is the only good thing that harlot ever did," he hissed.

Reggie was both hurt and astonished, but he had the presence of mind to whisper, "Why would you say that about my mother?"

Grandfather John lowered his voice, too. "You're young, Reginald," he replied. "You don't understand women like I do. You knew that woman as your mother. I knew her as the woman who stole my son. I wanted him to follow in my footsteps, but he wasn't like me at all."

Reggie didn't understand. "But he became a butcher, *too*." He said it in the rhythm of a question.

The old man cracked his cane against the floor, and people stared again. "Your father was never the man I was. He could have been great; instead he was a disappointment. But you won't disappoint me, will you? When the time comes, you will make me proud. I know it."

"I'd like to. Just give me a chance," was Reggie's whispered reply.

Grandfather laughed. He didn't mind the stares. "I plan to do just that."

The newly allied Kingsfords exited the library arm in arm. The ease that Reggie now felt with Grandfather John warmed him a little against the cold. But the old man tugged his cape tighter around him.

At dinner, Grandfather John charmed the ladies again, and the men laughed at his jokes. Will mostly drank his dinner. Reggie only spoke when one of the women mentioned she also had been to the library. He mentioned the fine mystery books there.

"Balderdash and rubbish those books are," his grandfather interjected.

"How so, good sir?" one of the men at the table asked.

"In books, the police are heroes, when in reality they are fools." Reggie's grandfather looked around the table for support, but he was alone in this opinion. The other men soon joined in defending the police, but Grandfather John would not stop. Even as the waiter placed his meal before him, he continued his assault. "Not only could they not catch a criminal, I doubt they could even catch a cold."

The women's laughter upset the men even more. Reggie liked his mystery books, but even though he'd only known his grandfather a few days, he wanted to love the strange old man even more. My grandfather has asked me for an alliance, Reggie said to himself. So it is time that I provide him with an ally.

"Sad to say, I believe it is true," Reggie said to the group in the most adult language he could muster. "While I do like to read these books, they are, after all, just stories. Grandfather is quite right about the real police, I believe."

A man with great gray mutton chop whiskers spoke from across the table. "Young man, how can you say such a thing? Scotland Yard is the finest force in the world."

Grandfather John pointed his steak knife at the man. "Then why did they never catch him?"

"Catch who, good sir?"

"The one who murdered those women in Whitechapel. Jack the Ripper they called him."

The table erupted in conversation about Jack the Ripper with everyone participating except Reggie, his father and grandfather. Will appeared distracted. Reggie knew little about the infamous murderer. Grandfather John had lived in London at the time, but he said nothing. He cut his steak in tiny pieces and ate with a look of total satisfaction.

Grandfather and grandson returned late to the cabin and turned down Will's invitation to go to the ballroom with him. Reggie felt that their refusal was a cementing of their alliance. They walked around the ship – again arm in arm – to the very bottom deck where Reggie asked a steward if he would show them the boilers. At first the steward resisted, but Reggie found within him a guile he had never realized he possessed and talked the man into it. Grandfather John was proud, and Reggie was proud to have an adult look upon him with pride rather than disappointment for a change.

"We saw the ship!" Reggie said to his father when he and Grandfather John returned to the cabin. "It was grand fun!"

"I told you to be back in case there was a lifeboat drill," his father said.

Reggie held up the ship's newspaper, which he'd also found in the library. "The lifeboat drill is Sunday morning, the fourteenth," he said. "And it's a silly waste of time."

Will shook his head angrily. "Reginald, I do not like your tone."

"And, Father," Reggie shouted, "I do not like yours!"

Will looked surprised. Reggie had never stood against him before. But then, Reggie never had an ally before.

"Young man, listen—"

Grandfather John finally spoke. "Then treat him like one."

"Like one what?" Will replied.

"You say he is a young man, yet you treat him like a child," Grandfather John continued. "You do the same to me. If you want your son to grow up to be a man, then treat him like one!"

Will said nothing. He stared at his father as if he were a stranger not a relative, then twisted his upper body as though he were in pain.

Grandfather John pointed at the chair. "There we have it. Sitting in a hard chair guarding against us leaving, as though we were criminals. I was locked away for a long time by the foolish police and the corrupt doctors. I shan't be locked away any more, let alone by my own son."

Before his father could answer, Reggie spoke. "Where could we go? What could we do?"

Will continued his silence. Grandfather John changed clothes and readied himself for bed. Reggie noticed on his grandfather's right arm was a tattoo in red ink of a five-sided object. He tried not to stare at the pentagram that had been carved into John's arm.

"Good night, good sirs," John said, then lay down in the bottom bunk. Reggie started up to the top, but his grandfather reached out and gripped his ankle. "Reginald, you will sleep with me. Your father can decide if he wants to rest his hurt back in a chair and not treat you like a man, or if he wants to sleep in the top bunk and show you the respect you deserve."

Reggie climbed into bed with his grandfather as his father crawled into the top bunk, still dressed. Before long, Reggie heard his father snoring.

"Are you awake?" Reggie whispered to Grandfather.

"Yes, Reginald, yes, I am."

"Thank you for taking my side."

"Anything for you, Reginald," Grandfather John said.

"Anything for you, Grandfather," Reggie whispered.

Before he drifted off to sleep, he heard his grandfather whisper, "We shall see. We shall see."

13 April 1912

Will shook Reggie awake. "Where is he?" he growled.

Reggie looked at the empty space next to him.

"I thought he was still asleep, so I left for the water closet," Will said. "I locked the door. I didn't think he'd be able to open it."

Reggie sat up. "His right hand is weak, but his left hand still seems strong."

"I knew this would happen if I didn't guard the door," Will said.

"This wasn't my fault, Father," Reggie said. "I did my part. It was you who failed."

"Get dressed! We need to find him now!" Will shouted.

As they left the room, Reggie saw that his grandfather's black bag was missing, too. He and Will searched the Boat Deck, then he suggested they split up. Will fought the idea, but Reggie fought back. "Don't you trust me?" he said. "Why? Do you think I'll get into trouble?"

His father took a deep breath. "I think trouble finds you. Just like before Christmas."

"She started it," Reggie shot back. But his father looked as unconvinced as he had then. Reggie had been expelled from school for a short time. He contended that it had not been his fault. "A nasty girl," he said, "told one of the masters that I'd tried to kiss her. It wasn't true, but they believed her." Grandfather is right about some girls, Reggie thought. He imagined he had a cleaver in his hand. He felt the weight. He saw the face of the nasty girl who'd told on him for trying to kiss her.

"I want to trust you, Son," Will said. "But it's hard because of your grandfather. I don't want you to turn out like him. I want you to be a good person and do the right thing."

"I will, Father, I will." Reggie's father hugged him for the first time in what seemed to Reggie like forever, and then they went their separate ways.

The lower Reggie went in the ship, the fewer people he encountered. In spite of the cold on the Boat and Shelter Decks, people were more comfortable there than in the terrible heat closer to the ship's enormous coal-fired furnaces. No wonder the Irish girl had said it was hot as the gates of Hell. He was about to return to the cabin when he heard a girl screaming. It was the most terrifying sound he had ever heard. He asked himself what a man would do? It was the world's easiest question. Answer: a man would help. He was more afraid than he had ever imagined it was possible to be afraid, but he followed the awful sound to a stairway door. It changed before he reached the door. It wasn't screaming; it was *gargling* now. He kept running, but the gargling sounds stopped before he reached the door. He felt as though the silence would crush him, but he grabbed the iron door handle and wrenched it open. A man in a black cape held the red-haired girl against the white wall with one arm and with the other worked a butcher knife in her middle. Her neck was cut almost in two. Her head lay on her shoulder. Something white held her head to her body. She was bloody from her displaced chin to her knees. Even as a butcher's apprentice, Reggie had never seen this volume of blood.

Reggie didn't see his grandfather's face, but he didn't need to. The old man turned and hissed through his rotten teeth. "Finish it." Reggie went weak. He moved his feet to try to remain standing, but he slipped in the blood. He scrambled to his knees.

His grandfather let the girl's body slide down the bloody wall to the floor, bent to Reggie and extended the knife. A garland of intestine hung over it. His grandfather dipped the knife and the intestine fell to the floor. It made a splat in the crushing silence. "Reginald, you said you'd do *anything* to help me." He held the neck of Reggie's jacket and pulled him across the floor until his knees stopped their slide against the girl's legs. Reggie slid easily through the oily blood, but still his grandfather's strength astonished him. The old man knelt, took Reggie's hand, wrapped his fingers around the wooden handle of the knife and held both his hands over Reggie's with that astonishing strength. He guided the knife down over the ripped bloody dress below the girl's torn stomach. He lifted the dress with the knife tip and exposed her. He let go his hands, so now Reggie himself held the knife.

"This is how we finish them, Reginald," the old man said. "First we rid the world of them, and then we rid them of their vile woman-ness. The first is the hardest, but you'll find over time it gets easier and easier. You'll do fine. You're just like me."

The dark enormity of the thing he was partaking in finally settled over Reggie. He let go the knife and gasped for breath. He crumpled on to the bloody floor. He could not breathe, and he knew he did not deserve to breathe. "Grandfather John . . ."

The old man bent to the boy's ear. "Don't doubt yourself, my boy. The first is the hardest. And no need to call me John any more. We're friends and allies now, so you can call me Jack."

Enough clean white cloth was left in the girl's dress for Jack to wipe the blood from his face and hands and from Reggie's. He stood the boy up against the wall and slapped his face hard enough to arouse him, but still with affection. He unclipped his cape, dropped it over the body and told Reggie to pick her up. The red-haired girl's body was the heaviest thing Reggie ever carried. Jack carried his black bag with the knife in it. They passed a chute in the wall, the cover of which said REFUSE ONLY. "Dump her here," Jack said.

Reggie hesitated.

"Her blood is on your hands, Reginald," Jack said. "I'm an old man, and I'm finding myself again. Trust me. You don't want to be locked up for the rest of your life. You want to stay free. There's much that I could teach you."

Terror pushed Reggie a small step toward courage. "I don't want to learn—"

Jack laughed. "Do it, Reginald."

Reggie knew he had no choice but to do the wrong thing. He steadied the body on his shoulder and lifted the cover with his free hand. The opening was just big enough.

The blood on their dark clothes could have been any liquid, and the few people they encountered on the stairs paid their appearance no mind. "Quite a voyage so far," was Jack's greeting to one and all. Will was on the Boat Deck looking for his father, so he wasn't there when they returned. They changed clothes, and Jack sent Reggie to the refuse chute on their deck with them.

14 April 1912

Will woke Reggie early for the lifeboat drill, but it was canceled. Reggie was glad; he wanted to stay in bed and pretend it all had been a nightmare rather than his life. He claimed sickness and stayed in bed all day. Will insisted that he join him and his grandfather for dinner. Reggie and his grandfather shared a terrible secret. The boy sat in horror of his own flesh and blood. But the old man from whom he inherited his blood continued to delight everyone. Even more than the deed his grandfather had committed, his words – "You're just like me" – terrified Reggie to the depths of his soul.

A steward visited the table and described the sights they would see when the ship drew closer to the North American shore. He described the beauty of the port of New York where *Titanic* would dock on the fifteenth. Reggie didn't doubt that everyone would be happy to leave the ship after a week at sea, but he knew that no one could want to leave more desperately than he did. Once they arrived, he would tell his father.

"One last thing I need to ask all of you," the steward said. "A young Irish girl has gone missing. Bright-red hair. The captain wants to know if anyone has seen her."

No one at the table spoke, a strange silence hung over them.

"Poor thing," Reggie's grandfather said, shaking his head from side to side, but it still didn't conceal the small smile it looked like he was trying to suppress.

As talk turned to the missing girl, Jack reached under the table, grabbed Reggie's hand, leaned to him and whispered, "You didn't finish. It was not a full meal, and I've been too hungry for too long." He let go Reggie's hand, leaned away and asked if he understood. Reggie didn't look at him. What Reggie understood was that not even the freezing North Atlantic was colder than the blood pounding in his veins. His grandfather leaned in again then and poked Reggie's chest with his bony right index finger. Reggie looked up. He couldn't help staring at the blood dried under his grandfather's fingernail. His eyes followed that hideous finger as it moved to direct his attention to a girl at the next table. He remembered having seen her on deck and having smiled at her white hat with the brim as big around as a bicycle tire. Reggie remembered smiling, but he didn't smile now.

Will had drunk too much and fallen asleep with his clothes on. Here in their cabin on C Deck his snoring was louder than the ship's engines. Reggie was awake but pretending to sleep when his grandfather struggled out of bed. Reggie lunged and grabbed a spindly old leg. There was not a way he would allow that man out the door. Jack didn't say a word, nor did he try to fight. Reggie knew the leg was going nowhere, but he wasn't paying attention to the lethal hands. And then, in the dim nightlight, he saw that they were in the black bag. Then the light caught the knife blade above his father's chest.

"A strange harlot or your father?" his grandfather hissed. "You decide, Reginald."

Reggie let go his grandfather's leg. He was so afraid that he stumbled getting to his feet and putting on his pants. He felt the old man's excitement and heard it in his rapid wheezing breath. His grandfather exited the cabin first, then Reggie stepped out and shut the door. Not a sound rose through Will's snoring. The old man was so high on the hunt that Reggie had to hurry to catch up to him. "Maybe she's in the ballroom, should we look there?"

Reggie stumbled for an answer. *What would a man do?* Reggie asked himself as he followed, reasoning maybe he could still stop his grandfather's murderous rage. They heard the music before they reached the ballroom. It was lovely, and Reggie asked himself how anything could touch him so in this new world to which his grandfather Jack had introduced him. It was warm and bright inside. There she was, across the room, leaning against the wall with two other girls. She stood out with wearing that white hat.

The old man nodded toward her and looked up at the ballroom's grand wall clock. "It's nearly midnight," he said. "I should be tired, but I'm not. I'm alive again. I've waited this long, what's a few—"

Three bells sounded and, seconds later, the ship rocked one time. It made Reggie think of hitting a curb on his bicycle. Everyone standing was knocked to the floor, and even the seated people spilled from their chairs. The more physically able passengers gained their feet and ran for the door. Grandfather Jack lay in the doorway.

"Help me up, Reginald, please," his grandfather begged. It sounded like the bark of a small dog. Reggie reached down, held both his grandfather's arms, planted his feet as a fulcrum, bent at the waist and levered the old man to his feet.

Reggie supported his grandfather and fought against the current of people raging through the corridor and upstairs to the boat deck. He wanted to get back to the cabin and wake his father, but he couldn't do it with the old man in tow. Nor could he have done it alone. There were too many people energized by fear for their lives. His grandfather found the energy to break from Reggie's hold and turn to let the flow of people carry him along. Reggie turned and followed. Sometimes the force of larger people was so great and the pack of them so dense that Reggie was lifted off the stairs.

He popped on to the deck like a cork from a champagne bottle, so many of which had been emptied that evening and previous by the people in whom conviviality was lost to terror or deadly seriousness as they waited for seats in one of the lifeboats crewmen lowered from their divats.

"Women and children first!" a ship's officer called.

Some men, but by no means all, tried to fight their way on to the boats, but the crew and the more courageous men fought to keep them out. Only one or two old men found seats.

Reggie watched as women, including the white hat girl and her two friends, climbed onboard the lifeboat in front of him. All of them were crying.

A man in a uniform behind encouraged Reggie to board the boat. "Children too."

Reggie spoke softly under the chaos around him. "I'm not a child. I am—"

Reggie stopped when he heard his grandfather cry out in pain. Reggie turned and saw he'd let his cane fall to the deck. "Someone help that old man!" a voice yelled.

Reggie watched his grandfather reach up with his good hand shaking as though it were palsied. "Help me, help me, please," he whined. Two men helped him stand. He clutched the arm of the crewman who had helped the girls into the boat. "I pray to Heaven there's room for one skinny old man?" he bleated.

Reggie knew if his grandfather boarded with the women, it would not be a lifeboat, but a death boat. Before the crewman could help Jack into the boat, the pathetic old man bent with the dexterity of an acrobat and grabbed his bag and his cane.

Reggie watched his grandfather's eyes glare at the girls on the boat. Pushing aside bigger men around him, Reggie tackled his grandfather like a rugger, knocked the bag out of his hand and wrapped his legs in what he meant to be a death grip.

"What are you doing?" one of the men who had helped his grandfather yelled. He knelt and pulled at Reggie's arms, but Reggie locked on.

The other man kicked him in the ribs again and again. Reggie let his grandfather go, rolled away through the thatch of legs and fought to his feet. He winced when he took a breath. Before he could take another, he was alone there with his grandfather, who stood over him blocking the night sky, as everyone had run further toward the bow where another boat was being lowered.

"You're hurt, Reginald. Let your old Grandfather John help you." The old man worked to his knees, held the rail with both hands and stood. He put his weaker arm around Reggie's waist and reached for the cane, which lay next to Reggie with his other.

"Give me my cane and I'll guide you to another lifeboat. Let your grandfather save you, my boy." Reggie released the cane into his grandfather's hand. The old man stepped away then. Even if Reggie hadn't been hurt he would not have been able to avoid the blow. It came too fast. The cane cracked him above the eye and split the flesh. He was afraid he wouldn't be able to keep his feet. He was dazed, but he had the presence of mind to fall into his grandfather. Reggie held him in a desperate embrace as his eye filled with blood. It ran down his face on to his neck.

"Let me go, boy," the old man hissed. Reggie's cheek lay against the old man's neck. He was afraid the old man's rotten breath would finish him, but he clung tighter.

The old man struggled, but Reggie held his arms so he couldn't hit him again. "What are you doing, boy? Let go of me!"

The old man hauled him along the rail with a strength that felt to Reggie almost supernatural. With his arms still tight around the old man, Reggie was able to grab the rail in both hands and hold him there. "Let go! Obey me. You are my grandson and—"

"I'm not your grandson. I'm nothing like you, Jack." Reggie stared into his eyes, and then ripped open the right sleeve of the old man's shirt. Reggie pressed down on five-sided tattoo, one slice for each of the women butchered in Whitechapel.

A ship's officer shouted, "There's room for the lad in the next boat!" But Reggie held his ground even as he felt the ship sinking into the ocean. Like Holmes with Professor Moriarty, Reggie would sacrifice his own life to kill off an evil menace.

"Hurry," the ship's officer shouted. "There's little room left!"

With blood running down his forehead into his mouth, Reggie struggled to breathe, to keep his grandfather from escaping and to find courage he never knew he had.

"Let him go!" It was Reggie's father. Will ripped his son's arms from around his own father. Grandfather John fell to the ground.

"The boy must hurry!" the ship's officer yelled.

"Go, Son!" Will shouted.

The pain in Reggie's chest almost knocked him out as the officer held him tight against his hip and hauled him to the boat. He looked back once. His father was holding his grandfather by the collar and dragging him like a half-beef toward the submerged stern. The old man looked to be crying out for help, but all Reggie heard were the voices of the people waiting for seats in the lifeboat, and faintly, calmer voices singing "Nearer My God to Thee".

He was lifted and passed by many hands into the lifeboat where other hands received him and set him in the only space remaining. Before they reached the water, a woman speaking a language he didn't know wrapped him in a blanket. When they reached the water, the crew manning the boat began to row away from the ship.

All around him people prayed, but Reggie thought not of God, but of the Devil that was his grandfather John – or was he Jack the Ripper – who now rested at the bottom of the deep-blue sea, his first step toward the fiery furnaces of hell where he belonged.

Kosher
Michael Gregorio

Author's note

I have been collecting Victorian photographs for many years. Positive images on metal or glass plates (so-called "hard" images, i.e., daguerreotypes, ambrotypes and ferrotypes) became a rarity as cheap paper photographs conquered the market in the 1860s and 1870s. Each "hard" image was unique, as there was no negative involved, and no copy could be made except by re-photographing the original plate.

I have always been fascinated by these rare one-off efforts, especially those that were sometimes made in the street by wandering photographers. What was so important about the occasion that it merited a photograph? Often, too, the photograph itself poses another enigma: what exactly was the occasion?

One day in 1994 I found an unusual ferrotype – a cheap photographic process made by spreading a silver halide emulsion on a sheet of tin – in an East London street market. It was in poor condition, almost beyond redemption, but the image was just about visible. I was entranced and puzzled, so I bought it. I checked my catalogue this morning and noted that I had paid the princely sum of £5 for it.

Cheap though it was, and battered as it is, the image made an impression on me which has never diminished, for reasons which I will explain in the course of this story.

The question I asked myself was this: why would three young butchers pose with their tools of slaughter for a wandering street photographer? What "special event" were they celebrating? It was probably made in 1888, or shortly afterwards.

Many men had known them girls, but one man stole their lives away.

I was living in Castle Alley in those days, just off Aldgate High Street, right in the middle of the doings, so to speak.

You've no idea what it was like down our way lest you'd been living there for a bit. Whitechapel's a regular cesspit and no two ways about it, full of Irish navvies, factory hands, weaving girls, half-day labourers, immigrants, con men, drifters, all the scum that London's busting with these days. Apart from the foreigners – Jews like me, for the most part – they've up from the country most of them, plus trainloads of scruffs scarpering from Birmingham and the towns in the north, what with the iron and cotton industries being shot. And what are they all going to do in London? It's obvious, isn't it? If they can't find work, they turn to betting on street corners. Find-the-lady, a dick's game. They get themselves in debt, of course, and then they need to go out thieving.

That's what a chap does, anyway.

But if you've got a fanny between your legs, there's easier ways of making a bit of cash to scrape by on, the coves you find down our way after dark. They're even making a joke about it these days, we've gone that far down the road to "perdition" as the Sally Army soldiers call it. They don't know what they're on about, that lot. You can't preach God and sobriety to girls like them. They don't give a karzy. They just get on with business, which is blooming now that things are settling down again.

But let me tell you about it – the joke, I mean.

The other night, before stopping off for a swill at the Middlesex, me and the lads were strolling west on Aldgate High, stopping now and then to chat with girls we knew, or to look at the pictures in the photographers' cards – you know, them big glass display cases they hang outside their workrooms, showing off the best of what they've done, likenesses they've taken, or ones they've nicked off some other snapper.

I do like looking at the rows of pictures, but you can't stop long for all the yattering the callers blast you with. "Step inside, gents – tintype gem cards, six for a bob. Split the cost three ways if there's three of you. Fourpence each, two likenesses apiece. Or one for a miserly threepenny bit!" It's enough to drive you mad. And there's loads of them all over the place. They stand in the doorways, hawking for customers, while you're looking at the pictures in their cards. Often enough, you end with one of them shouting in one ear while another one's giving it his best down your other lughole. Then it's time to move on. I don't waste my money on pictures as a rule . . .

Where was I? Oh yes, the joke.

So, there we were in Aldgate High, parked outside this photographer's gaff, looking at the likenesses in his card. It was me that stopped them – Charlie and Georgie, two mates that work with me down Feigenbaum's yard – 'cause I saw that they wasn't just the usual pictures you see. The "usual" is all these boring faces – Tom, Dick and his brother, Bert – all with the same wing collar, tie and sanctified smirk on their horrible gobs. This set of pictures was different altogether. They were laid out in a sequence, telling a story, one after the other, like you see in picture books. There's this pretty young girl being courted first, getting wed, then getting bored, next thing this young tumbler's climbing out of the front window while her hubby's turning the key in the front door. The last one really caught my eye, though – the joke I was telling you about. The same girl, standing outside a different door, under a big sign that gives the game away. You can't see all the sign, but you know what it says, you've seen them signs a million times before round here. It should say "Warehouse", but the only bit you see is "Ware", and that's where she's standing. Standing still, as any street girl knows, is against the law. Malingering with intent, as the peelers call it. Well, it's obvious to anyone, innit? What's happened, I mean. You've lost your husband, you've lost your home and your name – there's only one place left for you to go. If you're a girl, that is.

That was Mary Jane Kelly's story, more or less.

She was living with a bloke called Joe – a brick-maker, skilled labourer, something similar – when I first met her. A good-looking lass she was, long hair hanging down over her shoulders, sometimes red, sometimes ginger, depending on how long ago she'd had it hennaed. Strong drink was Mary's problem. A pint of rum, a pint of port, it didn't matter. Give her a pint, she'd drink it straight down, tell you her name was Emma, Ginny or something else, then tell you to bring her another one quick. Strong drink would make her laugh a bit, then scream and shout, kicking up a rumpus all over the place. Even with her mates. Even with a working man like me who might have paid a shilling or two for a night of it.

If you ask me, that was what done for her.

Him, and drink.

Drink the bar dry she could, and walk a straight line to the door. This Joe of hers – Joe Barrett, Barnett, something like that – had given her the push, told her to sling her bloody hook, get lost, and not come back no more. Mary Jane was out on the street, she was, all on her own, except for her mates on the game.

The game was all she had by then, of course, though she'd been out on the streets a dozen times before by her own admission. It always started with a fella, she said. She'd hook him, wed him, shack up with him – her husband had died down a coal mine, I seem to recall, though she might have been spinning me one – then, next thing, she'd be out on her ear, walking the streets at dead of night, dying of thirst, looking for any old cove to buy her a pint of something, give her sixpence and a mattress to sleep on.

I've let her share my mattress more than once, I must admit, but she wasn't up to much. Drink does that to a girl. It takes the fire out of her. And things got worse when the killing started down the East End. She knew them all did Mary Jane – the dead ones, like – friends of hers, she said, but maybe it was just a clever way of getting a chap interested, then squeezing a drink out of him. It was funny really – well, not funny at all – and some poor girl had to pay the price to put an end to it, I suppose. It started as a lark when we saw her there that night. We were down the Alma one Friday, same as every Friday, me and the boys, straight out of the yard with pay in our pockets – me, Charlie and Georgie – when Mary Jane came rolling in through the door. She was high as a kestrel, but most of them are on a Friday. Who ain't on a roll when there's *gelt* about? We had the next day off, it being the Shabbat, so every Friday night, we had a few, and, being bachelor boys, a few led to a good few more.

Next thing, in comes Mary Jane, showing off her bare tits to some man who must have given her the eye a trice too long. Two minutes later, she's sitting on his knee with a pint of mother's comfort in her fist and her tongue halfway down his throat.

"She's gonna cop it," Charlie said behind his hand. "I'd bet me wages on it."

There'd already been four by then, and we'd known all of them, at least by sight.

Hang on, though. Let me get this thing straight.

I'm no great storyteller, as you've probably realised, so maybe I'd better start by telling you a bit about us before I goes any further. Charlie, Georgie and Harry, that's me. Them's the names we use when we go out rollicking on Friday nights – Saturdays, we've got other things to do, the synagogue for one, and Sunday's a working day – but they aren't the names we were born with. We work for Abel Feigenbaum down Spitalfields, remember, and there ain't no mistaking a name like Feigenbaum's. We're kosher butchers, all three of us. Well, kosher slaughterers really. Abraham, Efraim and Israel – that's me – but everyone down the *chevrot* and the synagogue calls me Izzy. We're careful not to use our real names when we're out on the town after what he wrote on the wall that time. What was it he said when he killed the second or the third one? No, hang on, it was the night he killed the two of them together inside an hour, one straight after the other. "The Juwes are the men that will not be blamed for nothing," he wrote, or so the peelers said.

It was that *Juwes* that got me.

Nobody could spell it out like that. Why use five letters when four's enough? And why go and get one wrong? It's easier to write Jews than *Juwes*, unless you're up to something, of course, like fooling old Bill, and getting poor innocents like us into trouble. There were loads of us down the East End, more and more of us pouring in from Russia, Poland and Germany, docking down on the Thames near Tower Bridge, looking for a bit of peace. They don't like us lot over there, you know, though London wasn't much more welcoming if you drifted out of the East End. Me and Efy came over together in 1883, and Abraham was Efy's cousin. Abe was working for Feigenbaum and he got us in as well.

Jews? Ruskies? Poles? Them girls don't care where you come from, and that's the truth. They don't care where you're going, either. All they care about are the shillings and pence, and what they can buy with them.

Abel Feigenbaum's a kosher butcher. You know, ritual slaughtering. Things used to be strict back in the old country, but here in London, well, they've stretched the rules a bit. Feigenbaum's a *schochet* and we're his helpers. He watches over the killing, makes sure we don't take any shortcuts. Abe's got his pole and his lanyard, which is like a noose. He catches the animal, leads it into the yard, holds it steady, pulling tighter on the lanyard 'til it falls down on its knees and starts to lose consciousness, then I go to work with my knife. I slit its throat and open its belly, empty out the unclean innards, then I grab a big wooden spatula and sweep the blood and the guts into the drains. Then me and Abe help Efy lift the carcase up on to the block and Efy quarters it with his cleaver. The cow, bull or sheep doesn't know what's hit it. It's there and gone in the space of twenty seconds. The animals make a lot of noise coming in – some lads say they smell the blood – but once the lanyard's on, that's the end of it. Efy keeps on chopping, sectioning the meat, then the edible pieces go into the shed for ritual *triebering*. We don't have anything to do with that. It's Abel Feigenbaum's job to strip off the forbidden fat and remove the veins. After that, the meat's hung up to drain out all the blood. Then it gets washed – soaked in warm water for an hour – then, finally, it gets salted.

Kosher!

Feigenbaum wasn't out with us that night, of course. It was no ritual slaughtering. There was no ritual *triebering*, either. This was a different sort of butchering job altogether. When Mary Jane and her beau decide to leave the Alma, Abe says, "Quick, lads, let's follow them. Just in case."

"In case of what?" says I.

"Don't play dumb," he says, "you know what I'm on about. I'd stake my wages on it. He's gonna do her."

"You think that's him?" says Efy.

"Why not?" says Abe. "It could be anyone, the peelers are saying."

"The pub's full of blokes," I threw in. "We can't follow them all, can we?"

"We can follow her, though," Abe says, draining his beer. "It'll be a laugh if nothing else, see what Mary Jane gets up to. As if we didn't know!"

We trailed them through the streets as far as Miller's Court, which is halfway up Dorset Street, where Mary Jane and the fella went into a room on the ground floor. It must have been her room, I suppose – the papers said so afterwards – though she didn't have no key. She pushed her hand in through a broken window next to the door, then opened it from the inside.

"Give them a couple of minutes," Abe says, "then we'll check him out."

A few minutes came and went, then Abe crept up beneath the window and glanced in through the broken glass. "That was bloody quick," he says, coming back. "The cove was already pulling up his pants."

The words were hardly out of his mouth when the door flew open and out came the customer. He looked left, then right, then he bolted out of the court and into Dorset Street. And right behind him, Mary Jane was at the door. "Fucking sixpence?" she screamed. "A measly fucking six pence?" She slammed the door hard, and more glass fell out of the window.

Me and Efy grinned. "Hand over your wages, Abe," I said. "You lost the bet."

He wasn't having it. "The night's yet young," he said. "I'll tell you what I'll do, I'll buy you both a beer."

We spent the next few hours in the Queen's Head. The Shabbat starts on Friday night, but this is London, not the New Jerusalem, which was what we called Bialystok when we were living there. In Whitechapel, we start the Shabbat first thing on Saturday morning and we carry on till nightfall. Sometimes Friday night we don't go to bed at all, Saturday being a day of rest and abstemiousness. If you know your way around the East End, there's always some place open where you can get a drink or grab a bite to eat. And that's what we did; the idea of following Mary Jane around had lost its shine by then.

We had a last drink in the Britannia in the early hours of the morning, then we rolled out on to Dorset Street, getting ready to go home. It was as we were walking past Miller's Court that something happened. Abe heard a shout – or said he did – and he dashed inside the court to see what was going on.

"Bloody peeping Tom," says I. "He wants to see what that girl's up to."

I hadn't finished speaking when Abe comes running out. "Fuck me!" he says, and he threw up onto the pavement. "It's him. It's *him*."

If he hadn't been sick, I wouldn't have believed him. I'd have thought he was taking the piss. But soon as we stepped inside the court, I knew that something wasn't right. Mary Jane's window was lit up bright, though covered with a sheet or something. There was an orange glow like flames inside the room. I opened my mouth and I would have shouted "Fire!" but Efy pulled back from the windowpane, and said. "It *is* him. It's Jack the bloody Ripper! He's more of a butcher than us lot. He's killed her and gutted her."

We heard the lifting of the latch and the door opened.

What were we to do?

Follow him, try to catch him?

That was not what happened. As a man stepped out of Miller's Court, Abe pulled the lanyard loose from his belt and threw it over the bastard's head. "Give him one, Izzy," he hissed, and that's what I done. I pulled my knife out of its sheath, and I jabbed it in his guts. He tried to go down, but Abe held him up by the rope. "The throat," he muttered, and so I slit his throat. He was dead by then, so Abe let him fall on the pavement and he used the lanyard to drag the body back inside Miller's Court. There was light from the fire in Mary Jane's room – not much, as I said before, but enough to do what had to be done. I ripped him open, turned him over, and all the offal, blood and guts came tumbling out. Efy used his cleaver to open a grid, and me and Abe used our boots to push the mess down the drain. While we were busy doing that, Efy had his head off, then chopped him up into bits with his cleaver. The meat went down the drain as well. It was all done and dusted in three minutes flat, then we got out of there as quick as we could.

No one ever suspected what had happened. They never asked us any questions. Why should they? He'd always got away with it before. They'd think he'd got away with it this time, too. There was just one question ringing through our minds.

"Who the fuck was he?" Abe said, as they left me at the corner of Castle Alley.

None of us knew, and none of us would ever know.

There was only one thing I was certain of.

"He won't be sending us no letter from Hell now, will he?"

It was five days later, Wednesday lunchtime, when this man came wandering down by Feigenbaum's yard in Spitalfields. He was touting for business and we'd finished up for the day more or less. We'd been slaughtering sheep since six o'clock that morning, and the boss had told us to go and get something to eat. So, there we were, three butchers heading for the Ten Bells, each one with the tools of his trade in his hand. Pole and lanyard, knife and cleaver. We never leave our tackle lying around for fear they'll get nicked.

"Hey, lads," this photograph fella calls out, stopping his handcart. "You wanna picture took?"

"Why would we want a picture?" Abe says back at him.

"You might be celebrating something," the man says, quick and sharp.

Well, we looked at one another, and Efy smiled.

"Let's celebrate," he says. Then he says, "How much?"

"A tintype? Sixpence. One shillin' with a nice brass frame. Go on, it's only fourpence each, or I'll do you three for two bob."

"Just one'll do," Abe said. "For ninepence. With a frame."

"You're on," the photographer said, as he slopped some stuff on a sheet of tin, then slipped it into his camera.

Threepence each to celebrate the death of Jack the Ripper.

It was cheap at the price.

Boiling Point
Alex Howard

———

It was in a box at the Alhambra in Leicester Square where we had met to see Charles Morton's latest review, featuring diverse new acts, and I was watching the comedic antics of Little Titch doing his Big Boot Dance when the idea came to me. I turned to my companion whispering, 'Ruby, I have a plan.'

Ruby had been strangely quiet all evening. Even when the young soubrette Marie Lloyd had sung 'The Boy I Love is Up in the Gallery', the look of worried concentration had not left those dark, attractive features.

I felt slightly hurt that my plan should have aroused so little curiosity in my companion's breast. I am not the kind of man who naturally hatched plans in the way a hen might eggs. Far from it. The Chinnor family, of which I am the eldest scion, has many qualities but intellect, alas, is not one of them.

The review ended with a resounding chorus of 'Down at the Old Bull and Bush' and Ruby and I emerged into the chilly air of Leicester Square. It was a marvel, lit by the new development of electric light. It was thronged with a wonderful assortment of people of every type, colour and estate drawn from all over the Empire: native Londoners, swags and idlers, wearing loud check suits, importuning the flower girls huddled in their shawls against the cold, and not, I fear, desirous of purchasing the first of the early daffodils up from the West Country, some grave Mohammadans, sturdy yeomen from the shires and costermongers. All human life was there. I purchased a pennyworth of fried fish from a woman selling from a barrow and ate the hot, steaming morsels of codling as we wended our way through the streets southwards to Pall Mall and my club.

We passed through the imposing doors of the Reform Club, the porter greeting us with a cheery, 'Good evening, Sir Robert.' The title (I am a baronet) was one of the many things left to me by my now sadly deceased pater, together with the Chinnor physique (like Papa I stand six foot four in my stockinged feet) and I have inherited the family strength. He also bequeathed me the family title, a manor house, land in the Chilterns and staggering debts, the strain of which I strongly believe killed him in an untimely fashion.

Ruby and I made our way to the dining room. Old Jenkins, the servant in charge of seating, led us to my usual table and handed us the bill of fare.

'Very pleasant it is to see you, Sir Robert,' he remarked. ' And you too, Mr Silberstein,' he said to Ruby. My companion smiled politely,

'I have changed my family name to honour my English roots, Jenkins,' he said. ' I am now Mr Silverstone.'

'Very good, sir,' said Jenkins gravely. He withdrew while we studied the menu.

I shook my head at Ruby. 'Still convinced that there will be trouble with Germany, Ben?' I chaffed him. The idea seemed preposterous. My own mother, Frederica, was Bavarian, and the new emperor, Wilhelm II, was, of course, a grandson of our own dear queen. My tone was light, but Ruby is a wise old owl and I have never known him be wrong on any issue of substance.

'I fear so,' was my companion's reply. 'But come, Robert, let us talk of brighter things, your eye is almost healed.'

I touched my left eye ruefully. I had boxed for the university, a sport I still keep in trim with and I recently had the honour to go ten rounds in a Gentlemen versus Players contest with the battling Cornishman Bob Fitzsimmons. I managed six rounds with the celebrated pugilist and I fancy I made the champion blink a couple of times with my right before I succumbed to his famous solar plexus punch. I am pleased to say Mr Fitzsimmons was every inch the gentleman, despite his humble origins, unlike the foul creature that now walked into the Reform dining club.

They say 'noblesse oblige' and in my experience it usually does, but every so often a malign Providence introduces a snake into the garden, although even to compare the most venomous of serpents to this particular sportsman is to traduce the scaly race. Lord Ravenscraig may have been born into the nobility but he was one of the basest of creatures it is my misfortune to have met.

He came over to our table.

'Bless me, Sir Robert Chinnor, I haven't seen you since varsity days.' Nature had bestowed upon this most evil of men a pleasant, open face, but if you looked closely the warning signs were there: a thin-lipped cruel mouth with a significant downturn at the corners, like a shark's, and cold, pale eyes. He had an ill-favoured companion with him, bald, fat-featured and coarse-looking.

'I saw you fight the Freckled Wonder at the Clapton Boxing Club, my, but the claret did flow.'

Ravenscraig had been sent down after a scandal involving the daughter of a college servant. They say he had forced himself upon the unfortunate maid and so used her that she had lost the faculty of reason and had to be confined in a hospice. I was dismayed to see him in my club.

'Standards must be slipping if the Reform allows you entrance to these premises.'

For a second the mask of good manners fell from his face and I could see a glimpse of the beast within, then his features composed themselves and he said, 'I dine with Gregory here, and friends of the Home Secretary, Sir Robert, but I fear our conversation may be too elevated, a trifle too epicene for your lowbrow tastes. However, allow me to thank you for your martial performance with Fitzsimmons, I won two hundred guineas on a wager that he would best you before the eighth. I bid you good evening.'

They turned and, as they did so, Ruby said in his cultured, clear tones, 'Emma, Martha and Mary Ann . . . who will be next, Lord Ravenscraig?'

I saw his back stiffen, then he stalked away, accompanied by the squat figure of his companion.

That was the first time I heard those poor wretches' names. Now, of course, they are all too sadly familiar as the initial victims of the man then known as Leather Apron and now, as Jack the Ripper.

In the dining room of the club, as we ate our dinner – mock turtle soup and the famous '*côtelettes à la* Reform' – Ruby described to me the police investigation that was being conducted by those human blood-hounds of Scotland Yard – Inspector Abberline and Dr Robert Anderson. With marvellous knowledge of the innermost workings of our police force, which have made them the envy of the civilised world, he expounded upon the deaths of these forlorn and despised women.

'But surely,' I expostulated, 'Mr Henry Matthews will not allow such ravages to go unchecked?'

Ruby's response to my mention of the Home Secretary was one of measured pessimism.

In the light of the gloom induced by my companion's preoccupation with the case of the Spitalfields Terror, my own news, that I intended to open a restaurant rather like Kettner's or Rules or Simpson's, seemed trivial. For a man of my totem, such a course was a bold departure, but when your ship is about to hit the reef, desperate measures are called for. And I desperately needed money.

Ruby, bless him, with the sagacity of his race, long schooled in the vicissitudes of the world, nodded and said, 'Well, I had better help you get some experience. I can get you a position in a commercial kitchen so you get some knowledge of what to look for in a chef when you hire one in your own establishment.'

As we clinked glasses to celebrate, Ravenscraig's companion lurched drunkenly up to us.

'Still drinking with that filthy Hebe, are you, Chinnor?' he growled at me as he passed by, evidently making for the privy. I rose and followed him, ignoring Ruby's restraining hand. As we entered the Reform Club's sanctum sanctorum, Pawley, the aged club guardian of the cloaca discreetly absented himself.

As the man busied himself with his trousers, his back to me, I coughed discreetly, he turned and stared at me and I let him have it. A straight right fist to his nose. He was no Bob Fitzsimmons and my blow rendered him half insensible. His nose cascaded with blood and his knees buckled. He slid down the marble panel of Mr Thomas Crapper's newly invented gentlemen's standing urinal. His capacious bottom rested in the fragrant contents of the trough and then, with a hiss like a serpentine Niagara, *Crapper's Valveless Siphonic Water Mechanism*, as the legend said on the tank above us, voided several gallons of water over his expensive Savile Row tailoring. As I left the facilities, I winked and tipped Pawley half a crown.

'Very treacherous, those marble floors can be, sir,' said the aged sportsman. 'I'd best fish the young gentleman out.'

I returned to our table and Ruby and I left the club.

Two weeks later, I had settled down into the harsh, pressurised regime of the kitchens at the newly opened Langham Hotel in Regent Street. The hotel was the last word in opulence and was a temple to modernity, with its courtyard and entrance ablaze with the new electric lights that will soon banish forever the Stygian gloom of London. But all the talk was of the latest outrage that had befallen poor Annie Chapman, and the ghastly manner in which her body had been despoiled.

Down in the vast, gloomy kitchen, an overheated inferno where we toiled like slaves, the conversation was of little else.

I was employed as a *casserolier* and assistant to the *potagiste* or chef in charge of soups of which we made half a dozen daily. My duties consisted mainly of peeling, washing and blanching and boiling endless quantities of vegetables and preparing enormous amounts of stock for the broths and sauces. This was partly because it was a job suitable for the unskilled, as I was, and partly because I was the only person in the kitchen strong enough to be able to lift the gigantic cauldrons used for the stocks on to the tops of one of the many stoves in the kitchen. There had been an enormous African employed by the kitchen for this purpose, but he had been lured away by a travelling circus as a strong man and he was now earning a pretty penny and some fame as the 'Black Hercules'.

In the joshing manner of kitchens I had acquired the nickname because of this as the 'White Hercules' and, because of my title and background, 'Sir Hercules' or variants thereof. My accent marked me as a toff in the eyes of the kitchen staff who were on the whole a likeable bunch of rough diamonds.

There was one exception – Albert Joseph Fierny, the meat man. His job was to cut up the carcasses of the cows, pigs and sheep that arrived from Smithfield every morning and to prepare the offal in a general way for the more exacting preparations of the chefs. He was tall and cadaverous, balding, with bushy Dundreary whiskers. By the end of his shift these would be drooping and stained with blood. He wore a long leather apron to protect his body from any mischance with the razor-like knives he employed.

Fierny, a violent man, was highly unpopular in the kitchen, only tolerated because he could do his sanguinary job with efficiency and speed rather than finesse. After two weeks of vegetables, I was sent to work with him. I had spent a great deal of time on Highland shoots stalking wild deer and had been instructed by Lord Ross's head ghillie in the art of the gralloch (and anyone who has had the privilege to attend one of his Lordship's drives, beats or stalks will know what a rare privilege that is!) so my ability with a boning knife made the meat preparation section a place where I could shine. But I suspect that the real reason M. Jean-Claude, the chef, had put me there was that my size, strength and ability with my fists meant I was the only person in the kitchen not afraid of Fierny.

One Tuesday, at the end of September, Fierny was in a state of odd excitement. Usually taciturn in the extreme – another reason nobody liked to work with him – he was almost garrulous.

'You finished them rabbits yet?' He gave his mirthless, truncated laugh. 'Lovely little, bloomin' conies . . . Nice to make a tippet for a dolly-mop eh ? Bet you've had a few little dolly-mops eh, your lordship, bet you've dabbed a few in yer time.' He picked up a rabbit and, casually, with savage skill, brought his cleaver down on its neck.

'Bet this is what you'd like to do to a Judy, eh!' By now I think he was speaking more to himself than me, as he busied himself with his knife, his apron slick with blood, his horribly bushy side whiskers drooping with sweat. He rambled away about prostitutes and how filthy they were, but how they lured men siren-like to their syphilitic dooms and how behind it all lay the evil genius of the Jew, the filthy Yid, as he put it, with their plans to lay waste to the virility of the English.

I worked silently alongside this unpleasant Bedlamite, uneasily aware of his obvious relish in violence accompanied by the razor-sharp implements that surrounded us. I was also aware that the other chefs – some thirty of us in this enormous subterranean kitchen with its high-vaulted ceilings and banks of coke-fuelled stoves, red hot, and the noise of men shouting and the clanging of pots like a version of Hades – were all giving us a wide berth.

After a while his profanity-filled muttering became part of the background noise and I ceased to notice it until he said something, more to himself than to me, that grabbed my attention with as much force as if he had seized me by the throat. 'By God, when Lord Ravenscraig tells Jack to do his bidding tonight, then the claret will flow and those filthy Yids will know the meaning of the word retribution and much good their d***ed shekels will do!'

Fierny and I finished our shifts at 6 p.m., having toiled the day away since 6 a.m. I had resolved to follow the man to see if I could discover the link between Fierny and Ravenscraig. I could do nothing to disguise my height, but I relied upon the great press of people in the street to help conceal my presence.

The great thoroughfare of Regent Street was a heaving mass of people from all walks of life, omnibuses, carts and hackney cabs. I followed the thin, hunched shoulders of my quarry through the streets of Soho, past the painted faces of the dolly-mops and Judies, even the occasional Molly boy.

Fierny disappeared through the door of a public house of the kind they call a flash-house, a disreputable establishment. Its windows overlooking Wardour Street were frosted, but only partially, and, drawing myself up to my full height, I was able to see inside. There, to my excitement, I saw Fierny engaged in conversation with the man I'd seen at the Reform, Ravenscraig's companion, the one I'd left sprawled in the urine-filled gutter of the most modern addition to waste water management. I was pleased to see I'd blackened both his eyes.

Wardour Street was beginning to empty now with the approach of dusk heralding nightfall. I realised that following Fierny and the other man would prove a severe problem. I was cudgelling my brains when a young guttersnipe, dressed in rags, came up to me.

'Spare a fadge, guv'nor?' he asked hopefully. His features were pinched with poverty and he was tiny. I guessed that stale bread and sugar had been his diet since he could eat. Truly the lot of the London poor is a hard one. In his arms was a quart pot; I assumed his father had sent him to this establishment to purchase ale. I asked him and he confirmed my guess.

'There's a gent in there, a toff, talking to a tall, bald cove. Lend an ear, young man, if you can and tell me what they're saying and there'll be a whole penny for you, not just a farthing,' I said.

He nodded, gave me a confident grin and disappeared inside. A costermonger had set up opposite and was frying morsels of fish for the passers-by to eat as they made their way along the narrow street. The boy rejoined me, breathless, clutching his now full jug.

'How many of you are there back home, my boy?' I asked the urchin.

'We're six, sir,' he replied. 'Ma, Pa and my three sisters,'

I crossed the road and ordered fish for six from the Italian seller; the boy's eyes widened. While the cook fried our fish, I asked, 'Well?'

'They was talking about someone they would meet at the Seven Bells near Berners Street. A geezer with a name like a bird like what they have in the Tower, that's all I heard. The bruiser, the whiskery one, was getting fair excited and the toff shut him up sharpish.'

I nodded. 'You did well, my lad.' I gave him the fish, paid the hawker and handed sixpence to the child. His eyes widened. 'A tanner,' he gasped and took the coin. Then he did a curious thing. He slipped his battered shoe off and tucked the coin into a much-darned grimy sock before replacing his shoe. 'Pa's a lushington,' he said' 'When 'e clocks someone's given me food he'll finger me for any moolah. He ain't gonna find this, sir, this is for me and me sisters.'

Then he saluted me with an odd solemnity and disappeared into one of the grimy alleyways that ran off Wardour Street.

I carried on up the road to Oxford Street and hailed a two-wheeler. I climbed into the cab.

'Berners Street, cabbie,' I commanded, 'Spitalfields.'

The hansom cab driver touched his hat with his whip and we lurched off eastwards into the gathering night.

As we trundled along New Oxford Street and crossed into Holborn, the shadows lengthened as night fell. The buildings grew shabbier and meaner in sharp contrast to the West End and I was becoming increasingly aware of what our former Prime Minister Disraeli had called the Two Nations, rich and poor. I paid the cabbie off and he turned his vehicle around with barely disguised relief and I made for the Seven Bells public house.

I entered the saloon bar and purchased a pint of porter. I looked at the clientele around me in the fug of beer fumes and smoke from pipes and cheap cigars, working men and a sprinkling of women. Not the kind of place I would have associated with Ravenscraig. At the back of the pub was a staircase guarded by a couple of bruisers whose battered features suggested they were ex-pugs. I walked towards them and they barred my way.

'Private function, guv,' said the more senior of the two, placing a minatory hand on my chest.

I drew myself up to my full height. 'I am Lord Naphill,' I said in my most intimidating tones, 'and I am a close personal friend of Lord Ravenscraig. He will not be best pleased when he knows you have blocked my path. I bid you let me pass.'

They looked at each other in some confusion. They were not to know Naphill was a solitary hypochondriac who had not left home for nigh on forty years. Nor did they wish to cross Lord Ravenscraig, a man of such violent temper that an alienist might consider him criminally insane.

'Sorry, your lordship, up you go.'

I stalked by them, haughty as a cat, praying that I would not encounter Fierny. At the top of the stairs was a large rectangular room, filled with maybe two hundred men, of all walks of life from the rough-hewn labourer to the silk top-hatted banker, and, on a small stage, Ravenscraig and Gregory, the man I had met at the Reform. Fierny was in sight too, standing in the wings with two other men.

Above the stage was a banner with a lion and a unicorn and a slogan, *The True Knights of the Just*. Ravenscraig introduced Marius Gregory and the audience cheered. I stayed for about ten minutes as Fierny and the other two men were passing through the throng with hats, soliciting donations. I judged it wise to leave before Fierny recognised me.

Gregory's speech was a rant about Jews and Freemasons, nothing original, nothing that would ordinarily have filled a parlour, let alone a room this size, but these were not ordinary times. The savage murders of Jack the Ripper had inflamed the minds of the ordinary man and the crowd was in an ugly mood.

As I left the room, I heard Gregory's voice declaim, '. . . and heed my words, we shall see yet more vile crimes from the baby-killing Hebrews, yea before the week is out !'

I exited down the stairs and the two pugs were still on duty, together with a third man whose waxed moustaches, billycock hat and loud check suit proclaimed him no gentleman.

'Are you off so soon, my lord?' asked Waxed Moustaches with an air of insolence.

'My business is quite concluded,' I said coldly. 'I bid you gentlemen good night.'

I strode out of the pub and lengthened my stride down Berners Street. The night was black as pitch, the darkness tangible. I stepped over a dead dog and walked around a mound of decaying vegetables that had been dumped by some wretch of a barrow boy. The road and neighbourhood were wreathed in Stygian gloom and smoke from the overcrowded tenements added to the blackness. The air was oppressively foetid too from poor sanitation and what smelled like the effluvia of tanneries and glue factories. The roads had not been adequately cleaned of horse manure and, once or twice, I felt my heels skid on rotting matter unseen but not unnoticed underfoot. I rounded a corner and realised that I was hopelessly lost.

In the distance I could see a single street light burning and I headed towards its welcome radiance. It was then that I became aware I was being pursued.

There were three of them. Their forms were indistinct in the darkness but the central one had a bullseye lantern and I could see in its glow he was flanked by an accomplice on either side. Lantern Man had some kind of knife in his other hand. I saw the blade of the shiv gleam in the reflected light of the lantern. The other two were armed with cudgels.

I am no coward, and it was a decision that pained me, but in the face of these overwhelming odds I decided to show them a clean pair of heels. I had played in the rugger team for Blackheath once or twice and I knew I had a fair turn of speed that my pursuers could not hope to emulate. I looked away from them towards the far street light and then my heart sank. From either side of the street ahead two more figures appeared.

I was caught in a trap.

I turned back to the three men. They were now but a few feet away. They were the men from the pub. Waxed Moustaches was the man with the knife and the lantern.

'Well, if it isn't Lord Naphill. Looking good, your lordship, for a ninety-year-old, ain't we? Wot a pity for you the landlord has a copy of

Burke's Peerage.' His voice changed from a bantering chaff to a snarl of command. 'Come on, boys, up and at 'im.'

I tensed myself, ready to spring, then the ruffian to the left let fly a cry of pain and an oath I cannot repeat here and staggered, dropping his cudgel, clapping his hands to his face, shouting, 'My d****d eye, I am blinded.'

I had no time to ponder this. I had wrapped my overcoat around my left arm and, as Waxed Moustaches thrust his knife at me, I used the fabric as a makeshift shield. The blade caught in the heavy cloth and I felt its tip sear into the flesh of my forearm, but I was able to bring my right fist scything down into the side of my opponent's head. My knuckles made contact with his temple and all the weight of my seventeen stone was behind it. He dropped, insensible, to the floor.

Then I felt an almighty blow to the back of my head. I had sensed the movement and rolled forward, raising my shoulder so the muscle connecting it to my neck took most of the force, but I was stunned and dark spots swam around my vision like a kaleidoscope. The brute's cudgel must have been loaded with lead. I fell backwards to the ground next to the insensible Waxed Moustaches. My assailant raised his arms over his head, holding the stick with its metal-filled handle high above him, and I waited for the crashing descent, which would smash my skull to a pulp.

The blow never fell. There was a movement behind him and a sickening thud. His legs folded and he keeled over on top of me, his face pressed against mine so I could feel the sandpaper texture of his ill-shaven cheeks against mine and smell the rum on his breath and the rank sweat of his labourer's body. I felt momentarily as if I were a maiden that this coarse fellow had tried to force himself upon. I heaved him off me and took the hand of the man who had saved me, his features hidden behind a scarf. He pulled me to my feet and I looked down the street for the other two who had disappeared, obviously deciding to flee.

'Thank you,' I gasped. He pulled aside the scarf and I stared at the well-known visage of Ruby.

'Quick, Robert,' he gasped, 'speed is of the essence, the others will be on us in a trice.' Following my friend, we melted away into the darkness.

Thirty minutes later, I was sitting in the enormous library of my friend's house. It was a former Huguenot mansion in Spitalfields. The Huguenots, notable lacemakers from France, had fallen on terrible times of hard poverty since technological advances of our modern times had made their weaving skills redundant.

I sipped the excellent brandy that Ruby had given me as a restorative and listened as my friend expounded on Ravenscraig.

'Marius Gregory is Lord Ravenscraig's dupe, his cat's paw. He believes utterly in the nonsense he promulgates, which makes him such an effective speaker. Ravenscraig wants nothing more than to engineer a wave of popular feeling against the Jews.'

'Why?' I asked.

'Have you not noticed the influx of my people from lands such as Poland? And Russia? They are fleeing persecution, the pogrom. We are a wandering people. We have been that way since the Temple was destroyed by the Romans under Augustus. Since Hadrian butchered six hundred thousand of us.' He sighed. 'One day we will have a homeland, but that day is far off. Ravenscraig wants to create a climate whereby he can drive us out of London and buy our property and businesses cheaply in a fire sale. He has established a war chest of mortgage arrangements and loans specifically for this purpose. His mobs, organised as the True Knights of the Just, are ready to burn, loot and pillage the homes and businesses of the hundred wealthiest Jews in London. They await a signal.'

My blood ran cold at Ravenscraig's evil scheme striking at the very heart of our civilisation.

'Jack the Ripper is to be the catalyst. Tonight, two women are destined to die, another in November and then in December one more. Then the finale, a member of the aristocracy, a woman in line to the throne is to be the victim, then the bloodbath begins.'

'We must stop it,' I cried. 'For God's sake, Ruby, we can save those two women tonight.'

He shook his head. 'They are doomed.' He sighed. 'We can do nothing for them. They have been chosen already, we know not where or when. We can try to save November's chosen sacrifice, but already your friend is abroad and busy about his business.'

'My friend?' I was puzzled.

He nodded. 'Albert Fierny is the man known as Jack the Ripper.'

The morning shift at the Langham was terrible. Fierny was all smiles today; he had the air of a man who had done a good evening's work. He greeted me affably. Either Wax Moustaches had not passed on a description of the impostor of the night before or possibly he was still insensible. I had hit him very hard indeed and it could have destroyed some part of his wits. As I cut cows' carcasses into fillets, sirloins, skirt, brisket, all the usual cuts that would appear on the menu in their multifarious forms, I constantly stole glances at Fierny.

As I dropped the kidneys from the beast into a china container, I saw a strange expression cross my companion's face.

'Like kidneys do you, your lordship?'

'I do indeed, but only encased in a pie with beef,' I replied. Ruby had been insistent on my remaining on good terms with the man so as to glean any information.

Ruby – only I called him that. Ruben was his proper name. I shook my head in wonder. He had always been a dark horse. We had met at school, where I had given a couple of young bully boys a sound thrashing with my fists for tormenting him for his race. We had become firm friends and I was always in admiration of his matchless intellect whereas I was a complete duffer. He had gone to Cambridge, I to Oxford, and our friendship strengthened. Ruby had bailed me out over Papa's debts, and now he had saved my life. It was he who had shot the pug in the eye with a new-fangled airgun, blinding the brute, and it was his life preserver that had felled the other. He had found me the position at the Langham because he, through his circle of informants, had heard about Fierny's involvement with Ravenscraig and suspected the worst. He had wanted me in there as his eyes and ears, but then events had moved faster than he had anticipated.

Fierny put his hand in his leather apron pocket and produced something wrapped in a screw of waxed paper. He was staring raptly at the bowl of kidneys next to me. We had a small stove in our section of the kitchen and he put a pan on it and added some dripping. I gestured at the kidneys.

'You may help yourself to one,' I said, 'M. le Chef will not notice.'

He gave a curious smirk. 'I brought me own.' He unwrapped the kidney – it looked small, deformed and unhealthy. I wondered what beast it had come from – a pig I guessed. Fierny lightly fried it – it smelled faintly of urine and blood – and then speared it with his knife and ate it rapturously, his eyes half closed, his head tilted backwards to better savour the taste. A trickle of sanguinary juices ran down his chin and cheeks into the black of his wiry whiskers.

Later that day, as I was walking back to my new digs near Portland Place, very close to the Langham, I saw the headline. I tossed the vendor a coin and read more: 'Ghastly Murders' and underneath 'Dreadful Mutilation'.

As I read further, my eyes alighted on the ghastly fate that had befallen Catherine Eddowes and the mystery of the provenance of Fierny's breakfast became clear.

I recalled the beastly joy on the man's face as he had devoured the morsel. My stomach rebelled and I was heartily sick in an alleyway near my temporary home.

October had come and gone. Christmas and the end of my contract at the Langham's kitchen were both in sight. I had been promoted at work and was a junior chef on the grill section, turning the beefsteaks and the lamb and pork chops previously prepared by Fierny.

Ruby had cast a net around Fierny as fine as the one spun by Hephaestus to catch Ares *in flagrante*. The killer resided in a shared room in a flop-house off Hanway Street at the end of Oxford Street. An agent of Ruby's stayed there too. Fierny drank himself into oblivion every night in a public house nearby – the potboy was in Ruby's pocket. I monitored him at work. There had been no communication with the man that any of us could ascertain until the end of October.

Then, one morning, a waiter threaded his way through the kitchen with a letter for Fierny. I saw him tuck it into the pocket of his apron. A while later, when Fierny was called away to inspect a delivery, I hurried over to where he had flung his apron. I put my hand in the pocket and drew out the missive and perused it before replacing it.

'So what did it say?' asked Ruby. We were in my digs, discussing the day's events. The card was a signal, for another killing. His tone was languid but his tense posture betrayed his keenness.

'It said nothing,' I said, bitterly.

'Come,' said Ruby, 'some kind of cipher then.'

I shook my head and described it. A penny postcard, the numbers 9.11 and some strange drawings like a child would make, a windmill, a stick man and a stick figure blindfolded holding a scales in one hand.

I drew them on a piece of paper for Ruby.

'Come, come, this isn't so dusty,' he said. 'Use your mind, Robbie, what is the date today?'

'The eighth of November,'

'And a day hence, it will be the ninth – 9.11 – does not that seem plausible?'

'Indeed,' I said, brightening a little. 'But where?'

Ruby has a queer, intuitive mind whereas mine is woefully slow. 'The card, what was on the obverse side, the picture side?'

'The giant figure from Cerne Abbas wielding a club,' I said.

He nodded. 'And where is Cerne Abbas?' He answered his own question. 'Dorset.' He took a piece of paper, folded it carefully and tore it into five neat strips. He picked a pen up, dipped it in an ink bottle and wrote 'Nov.9' on one strip. 'Dorset' followed on another. 'A man in a windmill,' he mused.

'A miller?' I suggested

'Excellent,' he said, writing this down too. 'And as for this?'

'The Old Bailey,' I ventured. 'The Scales of Justice?'

He nodded. 'A court.' He wrote this down on the fourth and 'street' on the fifth paper strip. He laid them out. 'So, either Miller Street, Dorset Court or Miller's Court Dorset Street. Have you a Gazetteer?'

I did and we hastily perused it. 'By Harry,' I said, 'there is a Dorset Street in Spitalfields.'

'Then come,' my companion said, 'there is no time to lose.'

'But surely,' I said, 'we have a day ahead of us.'

Ruby looked at me. 'The ninth begins at midnight.'

So it was that the night found us in Spitalfields. The air was cold and foul with the smell of drains and cheap sea coal. Ruby was armed with a revolver and I had his life preserver, an eighteen-inch piece of flexible whalebone surmounted with a ball of lead. We found the court known as Miller's, a sad, dreary place very ill lit. The only illumination was that of candles or the flickering of fires through grimy windows curtained with rags.

There was no obvious place of concealment. There were over a score of dwellings in front of us around the court and the windows rose upwards into the malodorous night where any kind of devilry could be happening. But we could scarcely linger in full view of anyone walking into the court. We returned to the street, selected a doorway that commanded a fair view of the entrance to the court and concealed ourselves in its Stygian shadows.

There was a church clock nearby that tolled the hours and I guess it was 2 a.m. before we spotted our prey. Hitherto, we had observed the sad denizens of the street, harlots and their drunken clients. One in particular caught my attention – a dark-haired lass steering a ginger-haired man. She was drunk and singing 'The Boy I Love' and it recalled to me with unimaginable pathos the night at the music hall that Ruby and I had spent together. It felt so long ago now.

I watched exhausted workmen stumbling home from the pub, worn-out nags with terrible sores from their harnesses plodding along the grimy road, hooves clacking on the cobbles. Several times I saw the heartening sight of a bobby on his beat, but, as he passed, the night and darkness closed in again, inexorable, threatening and concealing.

Then we saw him. Fierny and the ginger-haired man. I knew then that the girl, so animated and gay, would now be dead. I felt a hot rage rise in me. We had failed, and failed dismally.

He removed his derby and then his hair. It was a wig. Gregory, for it was he, looked at Fierny with an expression of fear and hatred. Fierny by contrast looked exalted. He carried a small Gladstone bag.

They passed within two yards of us and I heard Gregory say, 'By God, you are the very Devil, Fierny.'

Fierny glared at Gregory, who was white and shaking. 'Shut yer blasted yap before someone notices.'

I brought my loaded cane out, but Ruby stayed my hand. 'They are but the servants, we need the master.'

We left the darkness of our lair and followed the pair of them at a distance. The night that was so treacherous, now served us well. We wended our way through the rough streets and alleyways of the east of London in our nightmarish pursuit. This was a London I had never seen, the squalor and filth indescribable. Huge rats ran across the road from dark, filthy tenements. Twice Ruby had to show his revolver at men drinking by the light of a brazier, footpads of the worst kind. I marvelled at my friend's knowledge of this underworld.

Then I could sense the mighty river, the Thames. I could smell it before I saw the ships, the stench of the effluvia that poured into its troubled waters and the dockland smells of tar and cordage, rotting fish and damp from the nets and the sails.

We rounded a corner and there was the dock with its jibs, booms and gangplanks ready to welcome the next day's merchantmen, brigs and barges. Moored against it were a selection of craft and, in splendid isolation, at the end of a pontoon, a forty-foot steam yacht, her sleek, expensive lines redolent of speed and money, like a thoroughbred stallion among packhorses. There was light in the sky – the city light of London reflected from low cloud – and I could see smoke issuing from her funnel.

'Ravenscraig's yacht,' whispered Ruby, 'the *Ganymede*. If they board that they have escaped.'

Our quarries were picking their way carefully along the edge of the dock. All manner of obstacles were there – large bollards for the mooring hawsers of the barges, fishermen's nets spread out to dry or for repair, crates and boxes and vast coils of rope.

They were fifty yards ahead of us, with fifty yards to go before the pontoon where the *Ganymede* was moored. Ruby produced his revolver. I doubted at that distance he would be able to hit the great mass of one of the huge cranes by the side of the river let alone a man. That gave me an idea and I hastily whispered it to Ruby. In all truth, it was our only chance.

From one of the cranes, a six-inch rope ran diagonally down from on high to the other side of the *Ganymede*, passing close by the stern of the ship, and fastened to a stanchion on the dock. I took my pocketknife and cut a piece of rope from one of the coils on the dock and clambered up the ladder of the crane as fast as I could. I stood on its gantry and looked down. Far below, I could see the two men laboriously picking their way along the dockside.

I slung my length of rope over the hawser, gripping both ends with my hands.

Ruby observed I was ready. He stood on a crate. 'FIERNY!!!' he bellowed. Fierny stopped and looked back. Ruby raised his revolver and fired. God knows where the shot went but it made a loud bang. Fierny raised himself to his full height and shook his fist defiantly. I noticed figures of the yacht's crew swiftly casting off.

I leaped off the crane, clutching the rope on either side, as it slid with terrible swiftness down the cable. Like a child on a zip wire, I hurtled down towards them at amazing speed.

Gregory was my target. The rope passed about five feet above his head and I shot down the rope, silently and unobserved. Their attention was on Ruby. They were unaware of me. Something must have alerted Gregory, for he looked round in time to see my boots as they drove into his chest. It checked my momentum, the force of which slammed Gregory off the dock and into the noisome filth of the river.

I relinquished my hold on the rope and then Fierny was on me. I was unarmed, but not so my adversary. He had a life preserver like the one I had left behind with Ruby and he swung it at me with all his might. I dodged the blow. It hit a packing case and its lead-tipped head smashed the timber to matchwood. With his backhand, he swung it at my head and I ducked, feeling its tip ruffle my hair. He raised the weapon up to bring it down on me.

The mind is a queer thing. I had a sudden vision – Bob Fitzsimmons, the great boxer whom I had been gifted the privilege to fight, had floored me with his trademark punch and, while I recovered after our bout, he did me the honour of showing me how it was done.

The solar plexus punch. It was this I hit Fierny with – an uppercut under the heart, driven by all my desperation, all my hatred of Fierny the woman murderer and every ounce of my seventeen stone. It lifted him off his feet and he crashed insensible to the floor.

I heard footsteps on the planks. It was Ruby. Down below, in the water, we could see Gregory striking for the *Ganymede*. In the stern, leaning over the rail, smoking a cigar, was the unmistakeable face of Ravenscraig.

'Help, my lord,' called Gregory.

Ravenscraig flicked his cigar up and it described a glowing arc as it spun into the river. He called a command and the *Ganymede* went into reverse. We saw Gregory's face fill with horror as the yacht backed towards him, and then he disappeared into the boiling wash as his body met the propellers of the *Ganymede*. Then she turned, and made her way down the Thames.

I opened Fierny's Gladstone bag, which lay beside him. There were the bloodied tools of his night's work and the souvenirs of his hideous crimes, too horrible to enumerate or describe.

Ruby and I looked at each other. Would justice best be served by allowing Fierny the notoriety and ever-lasting fame of being known as Leather Apron or Jack the Ripper? Or, would it be more fitting for the great river to carry and dispose of his body in secret, flushed away like the rest of the city's sewage?

We took an arm each and dropped the unconscious creature into the waters, watching as he floated away, face down.

'*Requiescat in pace*,' said Ruby. We turned and walked away.

Oh Have You Seen the Devil?
Stephen Dedman

———

"I reckon he's dead," said Kate, cheerfully.

The journalist managed not to wince, but he stared into his glass to hide his sour expression and wondered whether he should risk drawing attention to himself by contradicting her. Fortunately, Michael broke the silence by asking, "How would we know? Nobody knows who he is. Or was, if he *is* dead."

"Well, the jacks ain't caught him, that's one thing certain," said Bill. "They couldn't track a bleedin' elephant through a snowdrift, much less through all this bloody fog."

There was a murmuring of assent at this; September had been unusually foggy, even by the standards of the East End, and the police were not much loved by the clientele of the Ten Bells.

"Maybe *he's* a jack," suggested Esme.

"A Jack Tar, more like," said Jenny. "That's why he's been quiet. His ship's bin out to sea, but next time it's in port . . ." She drew a finger across her throat.

"I reckon he's a Jew, like that Lipski," said Maggie. "No Christian would—"

The door opened to admit another shabbily dressed woman and the sound of the church bells, and Michael shook his head as she weaved towards the bar.

"Right-o," said the landlord. "Those of yous got homes to go to, go there. The rest of you, clear out anyway."

"One drink, Johnny?" the new arrival mumbled. Her Swedish accent, slightly marred by her missing teeth, was thick enough to tell Michael that if she wasn't quite drunk, she was well within spitting distance of it.

"You got any push?"

She looked around, then pointed at Michael. "He'll pay."

"Hell, I will," said Michael, shooting her a look as poisonous as the cheap gin. "Sounds like you've had enough already, Liz – more'n enough. You comin' with me?"

"You can't send us out in that," Esme whined. "'E might be out there, waiting for one of us."

The landlord snorted, and the man they called Mr Memory shook his head. "He's never done it on a Monday night. Only Friday or Saturday. Nor when it was foggy, neither."

"Don't mean he won't," said Jenny, uncertainly.

Mr Memory eked out a living as a sideshow freak at Tom Norman's penny gaff show with his ability to memorize and reel back long strings of numbers or other words – a popular joke at the Ten Bells was that he drank to forget – but his tendency to see patterns everywhere meant that he was less reliable as a prophet.

The crowd stared at him for a moment, until Michael asked, with mock politeness, "You know when he'll do it again, then?"

"A Friday or Saturday, or maybe Sunday; Friday, Saturday, Sunday, it's a pattern. And it'll probably be the end of the month, like it was when he killed Polly Nichols. It'll be this weekend, if it's not foggy."

Everyone stared, a few of the women gasped, the journalist made a note on his cuff, and Bill nearly choked on his gin. As far as anyone could tell, Mr Memory utterly lacked a sense of humour and had never told a joke, drunk or sober. Michael was the first to ask the question on everyone's mind. "D'you know who he is, then?"

Mr Memory blinked. "No. Do you?"

This started most of the drinkers in the pub laughing. "I wish I did," said Michael. "I could do with a hundred quid." He glared at his common-law wife again, then emptied his glass and walked towards the door.

"Couldn't we all," said the landlord. "Righto, everybody, you heard the bloody bells, so clear out."

Sluggishly, the drinkers obeyed. "'We have heard the chimes at midnight, Master Shallow',' Mr Memory muttered, as he disappeared into the fog.

The journalist sighed, and headed home.

Michael rolled over in his bed and glared at the snoring woman next to him. He'd known she'd been a whore when he'd let her move in, and had never held that against her, but far too often she'd disappeared with whatever money was in their rooms, and sometimes anything she could carry easily that she could pawn or sell, staying drunk until all the money was gone. Not that he was a saint in that regard, either – he'd done three days for being drunk and disorderly back in July – but sometimes she didn't leave him enough to pay the rent, or took something he'd managed to steal from the docks. She always came back – she seemed to like him better than any other man, at least while she was reasonably sober, though less than she liked gin or rum – but he was fairly sure she'd added injury to insult by giving him the pox after one of these jaunts, too.

He turned his back on her and, before falling asleep, made a mental note to lock her in and to take all his money with him when he left, as well as his best hat and coat, his new razor and his clasp knife.

The editor looked up as the journalist walked in, and grunted, "Mornin', Bulling. Any luck?"

Thomas Bulling, still more than slightly hungover, shook his head. "No new evidence at the inquest. Nothing from my friends at the Yard. I talked to Le Queux, and he said he hasn't heard a bloody thing either, nor have Springfield or Hands; they're even starting to run out of theories that're worth printing. And I went 'round the pubs in Whitechapel and Spitalfields, like you asked, and folks are saying Leather Apron's dead – either that, or he's skipped town, probably on some cattle boat, or been locked up in Colney Hatch. It's been two weeks, two weekends, and nobody's found a clue, much less a body."

"Not in Whitechapel, leastways. Some woman's been killed and ripped up near Gateshead; they've sent Dr Phillips up there to look at the body, just in case. Maybe he *has* moved on."

"Want me to go up there?"

"No, go back to the inquest. Did they say anything about the doctor who was paying for quims or whatever?"

Bulling shrugged. "They don't think he's the killer, just the boy who buys the beef, but the killer might be working for him. But since nobody knows his name or where he lives, just that he's American, that's not a lot of good. But I've got an idea that might help . . ."

"If it involves killing some poor whore, I don't want to know about it."

"Nothing so crude. What if we` published a letter from this Whitechapel Murderer?"

"How do you propose—" The editor blinked, then grinned. "Have you got it?"

"Not yet, but give me a minute . . . and some red ink . . ."

The editor handed him an old Waverley pen. "It'll help sell some papers, anyway. And who knows, maybe it'll inspire the *real* killer to write a letter that gives the bobbies a clue."

"Good point."

"And see if you can come up with a better name than 'Leather Apron' or 'Whitechapel Murderer' while you're at it."

"Already done," said Bulling. "What do you think of 'Jack the Ripper'?"

Michael returned home from the docks to find Liz gone and the padlock he'd put on the door tossed on to the sagging straw-filled mattress. The cow must have had a key, he thought sourly, as he searched the squalid little room to see what she'd taken with her. While all of her clothes were gone, at least she hadn't stolen his other coat, not that a pawnshop would give her much for that. Even if she'd saved some money of her own from sewing or cleaning or from begging from her church, it probably wasn't enough to stay drunk on for more than a week – two at the outside – and she'd be back. She'd always come back before.

The chief constable looked at the facsimile, and snorted. "'I keep on hearing the police have caught me but they wont fix me just yet.' No wonder Bulling says he treated it as a joke. He's probably laughing fit to burst."

"Shall I file it with the other one, sir?" asked his clerk.

"No, send it to Abberline, just in case. All the newspapers will have it by now, and they'll probably print it, and if this lunatic *does* strike again, they'll ask why we ignored it." He looked at the accompanying note again. "Tell Abberline that it's bound to be a fake, not that he won't work that out himself."

"How do we know?"

"*If* the real murderer decided to write a letter, which I very much doubt, he might send it to us, or he might send it to a newspaper, but he wouldn't send it to the Central News Agency. Only a journalist would think to do that. Bulling most likely wrote it himself – no, *don't* write that down: we've no proof. Is Dr Phillips back from Gateshead yet?"

"Michael! Michael Kidney!"

Michael spun around, not quite overbalancing. The fog had lifted, but it had started raining heavily and water was dripping from the brim of his hat, so it took him a moment to recognize the driver of the laden cart as Bill, another regular at the Ten Bells. He waved, and was about to continue on his way to the pub when Bill called, "You still looking for your missus?"

He hadn't been, but it occurred to him that it would be reassuring to know where she was. "Have you seen her?"

"I think so. It looked like her, any road. D'you know the Queen's Head, on Commercial Street?"

"Yeah." He knew most of the pubs in and around Whitechapel, but that one was memorable because Liz had been arrested there for drunk and disorderly a few months before.

"She was just leaving, with another woman. Heading north. I waved at 'em, but I had a load to deliver so I couldn't stop."

"When was this?"

"I dunno. Ten minutes ago, maybe. Likely she won't be far away."

"'Ere! Gummy Amy! That's Leather Apron gettin' 'round you!"

Liz stopped kissing the well-dressed man she'd met in the Bricklayer's Arms, just long enough to look around and notice two labourers standing on the footpath nearby, clearly intent on seeking refuge from the heavy rain inside the relative warmth of the alehouse. She stuck her tongue out at them, showing the gums that had earned her one of her nicknames, but pulled her escort out of the doorway far enough to let the two men squeeze past. The man she'd been kissing raised his sandy eyebrows at the accusation, but he looked more amused than outraged; he glanced across the street and, with a faintly murmured, "Shall we?", led her across the road towards Berner Street.

Forty minutes later, another workman saw her in the doorway to number sixty-three, kissing a sailor in a black cutaway coat, and heard the sailor comment, "You would say anything but your prayers."

Shortly after half past twelve, she was seen outside the International Working Man's Educational Club with yet another man – first by Police Constable William Smith, and then by Michael Kidney, who ran towards her with an expression of such utter fury that Liz's prospective client quickly retreated along the street. Liz spun around to face her lover, who grabbed her by the shoulders and snapped, "You're coming home now."

"No," she replied. "Not tonight; some other time."

She tried to wriggle out of his grasp, and staggered backwards through the gateway into Dutfield Yard, screaming softly as she fell on to the slippery cobblestones. Michael glanced back into the street, and saw a Jewish-looking man watching him; he yelled, "Lipski!" and the man fled, not slowing until he'd reached the shelter of the nearby rail-way arch. Another man, emerging from the Bricklayer's Arms, also took fright and headed in the same direction. Michael smiled, and strode towards Liz, who scrambled back into the shadowy yard.

"You don't get to tell me what to do," she said. "I got more'n 'nough for the doss house, still, and I'll come back when I want, if I want. I met a man tonight, a real swell; he said my mouth was bang up to the elephant, best thing he'd ever stuck his pogo in. He gave me a whole shilling and bought me gin and a rose too and—"

"What d'you want fuckin' flowers for? Fuckin' flowers is for fuckin' funerals." He reached for her wet tangled hair with his left hand and tried to pull her to her feet. She struggled until she'd slipped out of his grasp, then turned away from him and tried to pick herself up off the cobblestones. He grabbed at her again in the near-darkness, grasping the check silk scarf tied around her neck and twisting it. Liz clawed at the makeshift garrote, gasping as it began to choke her, but Michael was too drunk and too angry to notice. She fumbled in her pocket, hoping for something she could use as a weapon, but found nothing more dangerous than a comb, a pencil stub, or a spoon. Her fist closed around a small bag of cachous as she blacked out for the last time.

Michael continued to tighten the noose for nearly a minute after she'd stopped moving, before the realization of just what he'd done slowly cut through the alcoholic fog in his skull. He let her fall, then turned the body over and stared at her. He slapped her face twice, hoping for a reaction, some sign of life, then tried to think.

Mr Memory had said that the Whitechapel murderer would strike again that weekend, end of the month, if it wasn't too foggy. Well, here it was Saturday night, maybe even Sunday morning, raining too heavily for fog, and Michael hadn't heard of any other attacks yet – and that was the sort of news that travelled fast. So, if he could make this look like Leather Apron's work, maybe the jacks would blame the murderer instead of him.

Michael blinked, remembering that he still had his clasp knife in his pocket, then drew a deep breath, knelt by Liz's head, and tried to remember what he'd heard about the murders of Polly Nichols and

Annie Chapman. He knew that their throats had been cut, and that Dark Annie had also been butchered, but he couldn't recall any of the details of her mutilations. He opened his knife and hacked at her throat, trying not to weep, then froze at the sound of a horse and cart approaching. He hastily backed into a corner away from the passageway into the yard, glad that his clothes were mostly black enough to blend in with the soot-caked walls in the near-darkness, black enough to conceal the bloodstains on his sleeves. He waited silently, and bit his lip as he heard the horse shy.

The carter probed the darkness with his buggy-whip, crying something in a foreign language as the tip of the shaft poked Liz's lifeless body. Michael held his breath as the man grunted something in a foreign language, then climbed down from the cart. Michael raised his knife in case the man came any closer, then nearly sighed aloud with relief when, after a moment peering into the darkness, the man turned on his heel and walked towards the door of the International Working Man's Educational Club. Michael dropped his knife into his pocket and hastily slipped out of the yard, heading south and turning the corner into Fairclough Street before slowing his pace to something approximating normal.

Inspector Abberline glared across the mortuary table at Dr Phillips, and repeated the question. "Do you really think we have *two* lunatics running around ripping up women in Whitechapel?"

George Bagster Phillips refrained from pointing out that Catherine Eddowes, the night's second victim, had actually been murdered in the City of London, not in Whitechapel: he knew that Abberline was well aware of that, and was fuming because this placed it in the jurisdiction of the City Police, not the Met. This had enabled the commissioner, Sir Charles Warren, to personally destroy what might have been a vital clue – some graffiti found near a public handbasin where the murderer had left part of Eddowes's apron. "It's possible, but that's not what I said," Phillips replied patiently. "There are similarities, but there are also differences. This woman, Elizabeth Stride, was also drunk and believed to be a prostitute, as were the other victims, and died either from strangulation or from having her throat cut, either of which would have silenced her. But she wasn't mutilated like Eddowes or Chapman—"

"The killer may have been interrupted," Abberline interjected. "The man who found her, Diemschutz, said her body was still warm. Nichols wasn't mutilated, either, and neither was Tabram."

"It's certainly possible that he was interrupted. I don't know whether whoever stabbed Martha Tabram also slashed the others – the attacks do seem to be getting worse – but I don't think it likely."

"I disagree."

Phillips shrugged. "All I can say for sure is that Annie Chapman was killed and mutilated with a blade that was at least six inches long, narrow, and very sharp; Nichols and Eddowes were killed with the same knife, or at least one very similar. Tabram was stabbed with something larger, possibly a sword bayonet, as well as something as small as a penknife. And Stride's throat was cut with a blade that was rather blunt, probably less than six inches long but an inch wide, with a rounded or bevelled tip. That could have been done by anyone, with or without any anatomical knowledge, in just a few seconds. So if it *was* the same killer, he acquired a much more suitable knife some time in the forty-five minutes between the two attacks."

Abberline looked sour. "The papers are already calling it a double event, and calling Stride the fifth victim, counting Tabram and Emma Smith. And we received a postcard from 'Jack the Ripper' yesterday, taking credit for both; it'll be in the papers tomorrow, along with the letter we received the day *before* the murders."

"Do you think either is from the killer?"

"More likely they're both from a journalist who doesn't know any more about the killer than we do. Of course, everyone has a theory. Stride's common-law husband, Kidney, came into Leman Street yesterday, full up to the knocker, saying that he could catch the killer if he was in charge of the case, but when they questioned him, he couldn't actually tell them a damn thing." He stared at the body on the table. "Why does he do it? I could almost understand if he was an ordinary sadist, but all of the women were already dead when he mutilated them, weren't they?"

"Apart from the cut throats – maybe – yes, I'm sure they were."

"So why does someone cut up women's bodies that are already dead? Present company excepted, of course," he added hastily.

Dr Phillips was silent for a moment. "Maybe it's not about pain. He doesn't hide the bodies, he knows they'll be found; maybe it's about the way they're displayed. Maybe it's all about fear. Maybe he just wants people to be afraid."

Three weeks later, Michael was back in the Ten Bells doing his best to drown his sorrows, when he thought he heard his name. He looked up, and saw that the landlord was reading from a newspaper. "What was that?" he asked, as clearly as he could.

"The Ripper sent Mr Lusk, the cove from the Vigilance Committee, a letter and half a kidney," the landlord repeated. "He said he'd taken it from his last victim, and ate the other half."

"Catherine Eddowes," said Thomas Bulling, reclaiming his paper. "The Ripper *did* take one of her kidneys." Mr Memory nodded his agreement.

"Bloody hell," said Esme. "What sort of nutter takes a bloody kidney as a keepsake?"

"Maybe he was signing his work," said Bill, who was sitting opposite Michael. "Maybe Kidney's his name."

Michael, white-faced, tried to lurch to his feet, then held on to the table to steady himself. "You saying I'm the Ripper?"

Bill held up his hands in a placatory gesture. "Nobody's saying that. You can't be the only bloody Kidney in London."

"They usually travel in pairs," said Bulling.

There were some subdued chuckles at this, but most of the pub's clients, atypically silent, waited to see whether a fight was about to erupt. Michael stared at the carter, then sat down again. "I spoke to the jacks. They know it wasn't me."

"I know," said Bill. "It was just a joke."

"Not very bloody funny."

"A bad joke," Bill conceded. "I know you're not the Ripper. I know."

Michael grunted, and looked Bill in the face, still wanting to erase that faint smile with one good punch . . . and then, in what was either a flash of drunken delusion or horrible sudden clarity, he realized *how* Bill knew.

I know it wasn't you, the smile seemed to be saying, *but I also know that you killed Long Liz. That's why I took the other whore's kidney – I thought it would lead the jacks to you, but they're too bloody stupid to pick up a clue, even one as obvious as that. But whether they think you did the others or not, you can't prove I had anything to do with it and they can still hang you for Long Liz, so I wouldn't go talking to the jacks again or trying to claim any rewards if I was you.*

Michael stared helplessly as Bill finished his beer and walked out of the pub. The Ripper stopped briefly to exchange a few words with the once-pretty redhead standing outside, then vanished into the thick October fog.

Flowers of the Chapel
Sarah Morrison

———

Lizzie tried her hardest to be both quick and silent as she hurried over the cobbles. She had, so far, managed to dodge around the worst of the muck whilst maintaining a vigilant watch for puddles. The telltale glint of moonlight from their surface the only indication that one lay before her in the darkness. She hadn't intended to be out alone at this time of night, not with all the current trouble. It wasn't safe for a girl like her. She sighed. If she had but been born one of those fine ladies, with their carriages and their protective husbands, she would be asleep in soft, thick blankets by now, dreaming of pretty dresses and cakes. No such indulgence for her. An orphan, raised to womanhood on the streets, only had one option for making a few bob. Walking the alleys of Whitechapel as the virtuous slumbered constituted her existence. By lifting her skirts for gentlemen who tossed a couple of coins her way afterwards, it meant she was worth something to Charlie; and, if you mattered to Charlie, you had a dry place to sleep and something to eat, at least once a day.

She risked soaking a foot and surrendered to the urge to glance over her shoulder as she scurried along the narrow alleyway. Few souls, innocent or otherwise, were out of bed at this hour, so as not to burn tallow they could scarce afford. The gloom behind her could have harboured rogues, footpads or even Queen Victoria herself for all that Lizzie could see. She pressed her lips together in determination and concentrated on the route that lay ahead. All she had to do was reach the Ten Bells and she would be safe. Well, as safe as she could be when Charlie found out that her work-fellow, Kate, had gone off walking with some gentleman who had offered to pay for her favours with half a bottle of gin instead of copper. Lizzie was dreading delivering the bad news. It wasn't her fault. She could have no easier stopped Kate than she could the hands turning on the clock tower, but Charlie would have other ideas. She knew that Kate would be in for it when she sobered up and returned, but until that time, it would be Lizzie that suffered the brunt of his anger. Although, it wasn't the first time he'd hit her and it wouldn't be the last. Resigned, she gave a mental shrug and focused on her goal.

The alley was beginning to open up into a wider street. A light mist was brewing, preparing to smother the whole of London in a dense, early-morning fog. Lizzie could still see the outline of the Ten Bells pub through the haze and a steady, yellow light in one of the downstairs windows told her that Charlie was waiting up for her and Kate to bring him the night's earnings. Free of the oppressive murk of the alleyway, she stood for moment to catch her breath and shore up her courage. She no longer felt the presence, real or imagined, of the Whitechapel Ripper pursuing her. Both of her feet were wet and cold and she flexed her toes inside the worn leather to warm them. Tomorrow, when Charlie came to her full of chagrin and a piece of boiled sugar hidden in his hand, she would tell him she needed new shoes. He would bluster and complain, but he'd get her what she wanted. They wouldn't be new, of course, but they'd be better than the scraps of nag-hide held together with string that she was using at the moment. He'd wrest them from some helpless dolly-mop he held under his sway and give her Lizzie's cast-offs in replacement. His street girls had more need for a good pair of shoes than some amateur who only entertained a gentleman when she was down on her luck. She closed her eyes and imagined how it would feel to walk the streets without the chill of the cobbles seeping through the bottom of her stockings. She began to close the gap between her and the public house, her anxiety growing with every step.

The interior of the Ten Bells was clouded in darkness, but years of familiarity had taught her how to navigate by touch past the rough, wooden tables and chairs and along the length of the bar with the ornate tile design decorating the wall behind it. A door led to the back rooms and she knew this was where she would find Charlie. He kept an office in the Bells and used it as a meeting point for his girls and as a place for them to solicit men when the coppers were cleaning up the streets. It occurred to her that he had not bothered to call them all in to work from this haven, away from the threat of Jack the Ripper. The air was full of the aroma of spilled ale and stale bodies, but she took a deep breath to steady herself and gripped the doorknob. Charlie was asleep on a straight-backed chair with his long legs stretched out in front of him, crossed at the ankle. His arms were folded and his head had fallen on to his chest. By his left elbow was a writing desk, on it a single candlestick holding the lit taper that she had seen shining through the window. Lizzie chose her steps with care as she picked her way across the creaky floorboards until she was close enough to touch him. She reached down into the front of her dress and pulled out a handful of coins, her earnings for the night. Being wary not to let them jingle, she placed the contents of her fist on to the table and began to make the tentative return journey to the lounge.

Before she had taken more than three steps, Charlie spoke. 'I see your takings, but where's Kate's?'

Lizzie turned and had the presence of mind to arrange her mouth into a disarming smile first. He had pushed himself upright and was staring at her from under heavy brows with narrowed eyes. Despite his menacing demeanour, he really was handsome. All the girls said so. Well, the new girls did, anyway. After a few years under his protection the thrashings wore the sheen off his appeal until the fascination he once held became diminished to a resentful attraction. It was rumoured that he shared the bed of a high-society lady. If the story was true, Lizzie wondered if it was just a business arrangement and he charged her for his services, or whether she was as smitten with him as the rest of the female population of Whitechapel. Either way, Charlie would make sure he got his hands on a portion of her coin.

She tried to inject a cheerful note into her tone. 'She'll be in later, never fear. You know what she's like, flighty and all. She's probably not thought to ask for the time since she went out.'

Charlie used his index finger to count the coins on the desk. 'So, you walked home on your own then?'

Lizzie nodded and felt her insides clench as he stood up.

'I thought I said no one was to be out on their own? I can't afford to go losing Judies to this Ripper.' He shrugged with one shoulder. 'It was no matter to me when he took one of Old Harlow's girls, though.' He chuckled. 'It just left more business out there for you lot.'

'I'm sorry, Charlie, I was careful, I really was.'

Charlie moved towards her at a deliberate pace. 'Careful, was you?'

Lizzie nodded again, cursing her luck that he didn't just stay asleep and let her slip out.

In one swift movement, he was behind her, his forearm around her neck. She was unable to move her head but she didn't need to look down to know that the pain pricking into her belly was caused by the tip of a knife. She screamed, but Charlie only responded by increasing the pressure on her windpipe until she choked into silence. Tears rolled from her eyes. She had known she was in for a beating, but she never thought he would go as far as killing her for her disobedience.

He spoke into her ear in a low hiss and she knew he was taking pleasure in her fear. 'What if Jack had come at you like this?' He pressed the knife harder into her side for emphasis. 'Could you have beat him off?'

He moved his arm an inch to allow her to croak out, 'No.'

With one final dig with the blade, he released his hold and spun her away from him. Her legs collapsed beneath her and she tumbled to the floor, hands flying to massage her throat. She kept her eyes averted from his and waited for the knife to bite into her flesh. The makings of a rueful smile pulled at the corner of her mouth. At least she would see her mother again.

'Go on,' said Charlie, 'get back to the lodgings. I don't want to see you until tomorrow.'

She dared to look up at him. The knife had been sheathed in some hidden place about his person and, without paying her any further heed, he poured himself a glass of brandy. She scrabbled to her feet and ran past him into the comforting still of the pub, slamming closed the door behind her. She leaned over the bar and cradled her head in her arms. It was several minutes before the sobs subsided and she felt strong enough to walk. Still in the dark, she felt along the sticky wooden surface she had been resting on until she came to a heap of used glasses stacked in piles of five or six. One by one, she lifted each glass and dipped her fingers inside, then, with urgent movements, gulped down any liquid she could find.

The next day Lizzie woke to the sound of muted voices. The dregs of gin had helped her into a deep sleep, something she was finding harder and harder to achieve without the medicinal properties of alcohol. She sat on the edge of her cot, one of four in the room, and began to pin her hair in place. It was early evening and she still had a few hours before she would be expected to start work. This was one of Charlie's houses. He called it 'lodgings' for the girls he ran. He slept in the attic and entry was barred to all except by invitation. After finishing her hair and fixing her dress, loosened for sleep the night before, she opened the door into the hallway and listened. The sounds were coming from the room opposite hers. She pressed her ear to the wood for a moment before turning the handle and entering. Two girls were sitting on either side of a cot, with a third lying smothered in blankets, a wet flannel covering her face. Lizzie had no need to ask who it was.

'How is she?' she said to one of the girls.

It was Mary who answered. 'As well as can be expected.' She pointed to the other girl. 'Me and Alice here have been looking after her.'

The other girl nodded in agreement.

Lizzie walked towards the cot and in a soft voice said, 'Kate?'

Without replying, Kate's hand reached up and pulled down the wet cloth. It wasn't as bad as Lizzie had feared. She had two black eyes and a split lip, but her nose was intact and after a week she wouldn't look half as bad. However, Lizzie knew from experience that Charlie tended to go easy on the face. A girl that looked done in never got as many requests as a fresh-faced one. It was Kate's body that would have suffered. With its perpetual covering of petticoats and skirts, no one would ever see the bruises she bore underneath. Only she would know the full extent of her injuries and prudence dictated she hid her pain well lest she invite more abuse from Charlie for not attending to her duties.

'Oh, Kate,' said Lizzie with tenderness and reached for her hand.

'I'm sorry, Lizzie.'

'Now, don't you be silly,' said Lizzie. 'What are you sorry for?'

'He had at you too, didn't he?'

Lizzie turned her face from side to side to display her unmarked skin and poked the fingers of the hand not holding Kate's into her torso to show she was free of bruises. 'He didn't touch me. Just shouted a bit and then fell down dead drunk.'

Kate's face brightened. 'Really? Oh, I'm so relieved.'

Mary caught Lizzie's eye and gave her a doubtful look.

'Anyway, I'm still sorry,' said Kate. 'If I hadn't gone off with Gaslight John then neither of us would've got into trouble.'

'Why did you go, Kate? You know he wants coin at the end of the night. If you take payment in gin, Charlie's not just going to be satisfied by getting drunk off the fumes when you get home and breathe on him.'

'I know that and it was silly, but I just wanted to have some fun. John's nice to me.' Her face became coy under the bruises. 'He says I'm beautiful and that he'll marry me one day.'

Lizzie gave Kate's hand a gentle squeeze. 'Men don't get wed to girls like us, Kate.'

Kate's expression became downcast and she reached for the cooling cloth. 'I think I'd better rest for a bit now.'

Mary helped her position the flannel over her face again and then followed Lizzie into the hallway.

Once they had closed the door again, Mary said, 'That was nonsense what you told poor Kate.'

Lizzie frowned. 'What nonsense?'

'About Charlie giving you a pat on your behind and sending you on your way when you come home without your charge.'

Irritated at having to discuss her ordeal, Lizzie asked, 'Why, what did he tell you?'

'He didn't tell me nothing, but you screaming like a good'n when you went in with your takings told me plenty. He might not have marked you, but he scared you well enough, didn't he?'

Lizzie stepped closer to Mary and lowered her voice. 'Keep that away from Kate's ears. She's suffered enough today, let's not add to her grief.'

Mary nodded and left, leaving Lizzie standing alone in the hallway.

She turned and went back to her own room, intending on spending a little time looking at her Bible. She couldn't read it, but she liked to gaze at the images printed around the first letter of each page. When she reached her cot, she noticed the boiled sweet on her pillow and knew that Charlie had left it. She had no compunction against accepting such delicious appeasements, even from someone who had wronged her as much as Charlie had. She stuffed it into her mouth and slumped down on the edge of the cot as the intensity of the unfamiliar sweetness flooded her senses.

'You make that last now.'

She jumped at the sound of Charlie's voice. He was lying on the cot behind the door with his hands cushioning his head.

'Have you come here to carve me up with that shiv, then?' She eyed him with suspicion.

He laughed, all traces of the threatening bully now vanished. 'Would I come bearing gifts, if I was just going to top you?'

Lizzie hesitated. She had only seen the sweet. Did he have something else for her?

Charlie swung his legs off the cot and walked over to her. 'I think these are yours.' He reached under the frame of her own cot and pulled out a pair of boots.

All fear fled her mind and she grabbed the boots from his hand. She unlaced one of her own ragged shoes and slipped her foot into the new one. The feeling of the firm upper and the intact sole under her foot was exquisite. She beamed at him. 'They're a bit big, but I can pack them out with rag.' There were some small signs of wear, but whoever these had belonged to had not had much of a chance to wear them before Charlie had taken them. The leather was supple and well stitched. She wondered if he'd taken them from his fancy woman.

'Where did you get them?' she asked.

With an expression of gentle admonishment he said, 'Now, you know better than to ask questions like that.' He picked up her old shoes and turned in the doorway before he left. 'You go out with Mary tonight,' he said, 'and make sure you stay together. These are dangerous times we live in.'

'I will, Charlie,' said Lizzie, who was admiring her new boots and dreaming about striding through puddles as though they didn't exist.

Later that evening, after her meal of stewed vegetables and an apple, she went upstairs to find Mary. She checked her own room first and, making sure the other occupants didn't see her, she unwrapped the remnants of the sweet she had hidden under her pillow and popped it in her mouth. If she was careful she could make it last all the way to the end of the alleyway. It turned out that Mary had also received instruction from Charlie about the night's activities and Lizzie heard her calling her name from downstairs. She followed the sound and together they ventured into the night.

'It's getting colder,' said Mary, tugging her shawl tighter around her shoulders.

Lizzie was still crammed with excitement about her boots and, once they had passed the Ten Bells and began heading towards one of their regular positions under a lamp post, at the end of the alleyway, she stuck out one foot to show off her new acquisition to her companion.

'Blimey,' said Mary, bending to touch the leather. 'Such good quality too.'

'Look at the stitching,' said Lizzie, 'there'll be no water getting inside these darlings.'

Accustomed to Charlie's habit of placating his victimised employees with handouts, Mary said, 'Well, whatever Charlie did to you, it was worth it.'

Feeling brighter than she had in a long time, Lizzie said with a smile, 'Perhaps if you rile him up, he'll bring you something afterwards, too.'

'I'm quite happy with my lot, thank you.'

They were about to occupy their regular place when Mary grabbed Lizzie's arm and pointed. 'Look, that's Old Man Harlow's girls in our spot.'

Squaring her shoulders, Lizzie marched towards the women with Mary in tow. 'Hey now, you couple of dolly-mops, it's time to move on.'

One of the women answered her with mock apology. 'Oh, I'm sorry. Is this your place?' She turned to her friend. 'We did wonder what that lingering smell was, didn't we, Helen?'

Mary stepped forward. 'If I was you, I'd start walking, in that direction.' She gestured to the other end of the alley. 'It would be a shame for my friend to get her new boots all mucked up with your blood.'

Lizzie lifted her dress and stuck out an obliging foot. She was surprised by the response.

'Where did you get them boots?' said the first girl, her eyes fixated on Lizzie's foot.

Her friend, Helen, ducked down and examined the boot. She looked up at the other girl and said, 'They're hers all right, Doll.'

Doll used her head to indicate the boots. 'You'd better tell us where you got them.'

Mary replied, 'What's it to you anyway?'

'I'll tell you what it is to us. They belong to Clara Caudy. She's one of Harlow's girls and he's been spitting feathers because he bought her those boots and now she hasn't been seen since last night. Now you turn up, wearing what's hers, so you need to have a good reason why.'

Lizzie snorted. 'She's probably done a runner and sold the boots for a few coppers.'

Doll shrugged. 'Then they belong to Harlow, so take them off.'

Lizzie may have been intimidated by Charlie, but even odds like this meant she had no problem with throwing her weight around. 'Make me,' she said, stepping towards the other woman. Mary, following her lead, shadowed her back.

Helen took one quick step forwards and then, head down, retreated behind her friend when it became apparent that her advance had no effect. Together, she and Doll backed away into the night, shouts of how Harlow would come for his property emanating from the darkness. After watching them leave, Lizzie turned and gripped on to Mary's arm. 'I have to tell Charlie. He needs to get ready if Old Man Harlow is coming round with his boys.'

Mary nodded and gave her a light push in the direction they had come. 'You go, I'll stay here. One of us had better bring in some coin or we'll both be for in for a thrashing. Boots or no boots, I don't want him doing to me whatever it was he did to you.'

For the second night in a row, Lizzie found herself making the same hurried journey home. Preoccupied with the urgency of the situation, she forgot about her new-found protection against puddles and skipped around them as she always did. Once at the lodgings, she searched the rooms calling for Charlie as she went. It was too early for him to be in his office at the Ten Bells, and she expected to find him lounging around. She was gratified to see Kate up and about and related to her the story of the boots and the impending threat of Old Man Harlow. Kate agreed with Lizzie's hypothesis about how Clara probably sold the boots to raise enough money to get out of town. It wasn't unheard of. Girls sometimes escaped the life and managed to either trick a man into becoming their husband, or ran away to family in the country, if they would have them.

After it became clear that Charlie was not in the building, they came to the conclusion that he must, indeed, be at the Bells. Keen to get back into his good books by helping to deliver the news that a rival ponce and his cronies were on the march, Kate insisted on accompanying Lizzie. However, a further search at the pub proved fruitless and an exasperated Lizzie could only assume that Charlie was off entertaining his fine lady somewhere.

'Harlow will burn Charlie's place down if we don't do something,' said Kate chewing a fingernail.

Lizzie nodded. 'Maybe there's a bill, or a chit or something for the boots. If we show that to Harlow then he'll have to believe that Clara sold the boots and that Charlie bought them fair and square.' The truth was that Harlow may call off the attack if he got proof that Charlie was an innocent party in the transaction, but he would still want the boots back. He would offer Charlie a few coppers to help him save face, but, to avoid an all-out war, Charlie would have to hand them over. She looked down at the one beautiful thing she had ever owned and tried to commit their image to memory before they were gone forever.

'But Charlie's not here to ask,' said Kate, breaking her rêverie.

Lizzie met her eyes with a steady gaze. 'We're going to have to go into the attic.'

Kate recoiled. 'No, Lizzie. Imagine if he found us, or someone told him.'

Lizzie put a hand on Kate's shoulder and squeezed it. 'You wait in the kitchen, I'll go and check on my own.'

Kate sighed. 'No, I left you before and it turned out bad for both of us. I'm not leaving you again.'

Lizzie smiled. 'Then I suppose we'll be able to do the search in half the time.'

Kate returned her smile and they set off again for the lodgings.

The place was empty when they returned. It was well into the night and the girls were all out working. Lizzie and Kate climbed the flights of stairs to the top floor, calling out Charlie's name as they went.

Neither of them wanted to breach the sanctity of the attic and they hoped they would find him before they had to. They stood together in front of the door.

'Have you been in here before?' asked Lizzie.

'No, have you?'

'Once or twice,' said Lizzie, recalling the few times that Charlie had summoned her for his entertainment. 'The bed is on the left and there's some cupboards on the right.'

'You take the cupboards and I'll search around the bed,' said Kate. 'We have to be fast, Lizzie.'

She nodded. 'We will be.'

Lizzie gripped the door handle and for several seconds made no move to turn it. After murmured encouragement from Kate, she opened the door. Kate headed towards the bed while Lizzie hurried towards a wardrobe and opened it. In it were a few of Charlie's clothes that she recognised and a number of items of female clothing that she didn't. Why would he have women's clothes in his bedroom? She rummaged in the pockets and felt all along the bottom of the cupboard, but there were no slips of paper. Nothing to prove the boots had been bought as part of a legitimate sale. She called over her shoulder to Kate to see if she had any better luck and received no reply. Lizzie turned round and started as she found the other woman in front of her. Without warning, Kate hit her hard in the stomach. The blow caused Lizzie to stagger back until she thumped against the doors of the wardrobe she had just been searching. Breathless and confused, she wondered how such a frail girl could muster the strength for such a devastating punch. She felt the scratch of the bare wooden floor beneath her hands as she slid down the furniture. Kate stood before her, her face expressionless. What had made Kate angry enough to hit her and why was she finding it such a struggle to stand up? Her hand fluttered to her abdomen and, when she encountered cold metal, she understood. It had been a knife in Kate's hand. 'Why?' she managed to gasp.

'He said it was only me that he had brought up here.' Kate's voice was calm and conversational. The severity of what she had done seemed to escape her. 'When you said you'd been here too, I had to change that. Make it so that I was the only one.'

Lizzie was having difficulty keeping her eyes open. 'You love Charlie.' It was a statement, not a question.

'Yes, and he loves me.'

Lizzie began a laugh but gasped when even those slight movements magnified the intensity of the pain. 'But what about Gaslight John?'

Kate smiled. 'Gaslight John isn't real. That was a special code between me and Charlie. If I said I'd been with John, then Charlie knew I'd been a bit of bad girl. He'd go and tidy up the mess I'd made and take anything worth keeping.'

'Clara Caudy?'

'Yes, Lizzie.' Kate's face was earnest. 'I did her in for you. She was parading around with her swanky boots in the alley and I knew yours were all old and leaking. I waited until you was busy with a gentleman then I followed her and used my knife on her. Charlie came later and collected her things and took her off somewhere.'

'But your face?'

Kate's tone became defensive. 'He had to make it look like he'd been angry with me. In a way, he was. He said I was a lunatic for doing what I did, but he still took their shoes and their clothes and helped me get clean. We laughed so much about this Jack the Ripper tale.' She cast her eyes down and a small smile played on her lips. 'Sometimes he called me Jill the Ripper. I called us Mr and Mrs Ripper. Quietly though, so he wouldn't hear.'

Lizzie let out a sob.

'Don't cry, Lizzie,' said Kate, kneeling beside her. She reached out to stroke her hair. 'You're my friend. I'm not going to carve you up like I did those other girls.' Her eyes drifted to the knife still protruding from Lizzie's stomach. 'It won't be long now.'

The pain was beginning to subside and Lizzie found that she was shivering. She remembered how she felt when she thought Charlie was going to kill her and she embraced the thought of being reunited with her mother again. It would be a comfort to leave this world and find herself waking in loving arms.

A shriek from Kate shocked her back to reality and she cried out in agony as Kate's body fell on to her outstretched legs. Behind her stood Charlie, in his hand, covered in Kate's blood, the knife he had threatened Lizzie with two days earlier.

He dropped to his knees and clutched her hand. 'Lizzie, dear Lizzie. I never wanted this to happen to you. Kate was worried you were my favourite, see? Even though she did it for you, she still got jealous when I gave the boots to you.'

Her own voice seemed to come from far away as she said, 'Kate was Jack the Ripper.'

Charlie gave a short laugh. 'There is no Jack the Ripper, just a poor girl, touched by the moon. She hacked them up for fun, I think. Sometimes because she thought they made eyes at me.' He laughed. 'I played my part though, I suppose. Laid a couple of the bodies out to be found, after I'd took anything off them worth having, that is. I know a fellow at the Central News Agency, told me some fool has taken to writing letters, pretending to be Jack. I know it wasn't Kate, she couldn't read.'

'Why make us go out in pairs, if there was no real danger?'

Charlie shrugged. 'I had hoped she would find it harder to partake of her little habit had she a minder to ditch beforehand. Seems she found a way, well enough.'

He reached over and, at first, Lizzie thought he was running his fingers through the dead Kate's hair in a gesture of tenderness. Then, to her disgust, he cut off one of her ears and dropped it on the floor next to the body. He looked over at Lizzie and, registering the horror on her face, he offered an explanation. 'The letter, it said something about slicing off an ear. I think it's fitting that the coppers will come cooing and ahhing over poor Kate's body, saying what a sorry dupe she was, when she was the Ripper all along.'

He looked into Lizzie's eyes. 'Mary knows about the boots, doesn't she?'

Lizzie made no reply. She was beginning to feel cold again and she would have sworn she heard her mother's voice.

Charlie stood up, walked to the bed and pulled a sack out from underneath. It had reddish-brown stains on it. He rolled Kate off Lizzie's legs and pushed her lifeless feet into the sack, continuing to work until the sack covered her from sight.

The last thing Lizzie was conscious of before the darkness took her was the sensation of Charlie tugging at the laces on her boots and the words, 'You'll be Kate's last victim, but not Jack's.'

The Roebuck Cabal
Martin Gately

If you'd seen the windows of the upper storey of the Roebuck Public House anytime before its demolition in 1995, you might've thought that they had been painted black at the time of the London Blitz as part of air raid precautions. Or perhaps you'd have guessed that their appearance had something to do with the tradition of the "lock-in" – when favoured customers remained illicitly in the pub receiving beer after the end of licensing hours. Of course, it had nothing to do with the Blitz or the 1915 changes to licensing laws. The real reason was that a group of men who wanted to be very sure of their own privacy periodically met in the upstairs function room. They met as frequently as once a month during the earlier part of 1890, but as the years went by the meetings became infrequent and irregular.

Walter Randall was a huge, burly man, who worked as a Billingsgate porter. He'd been rendered deaf during a childhood illness. When the secret meetings at the Roebuck took place he was paid to sit on the steps that led to the upstairs room armed with a cudgel. As far as any of us know, no intruder ever even attempted to get past him. The men in the room came from a variety of different backgrounds: inevitably, they were policemen, private detectives, doctors, lawyers and journalists. And one would've thought that a hostelry in the West End might've suited them better. However, the down-at-heel Whitechapel pub had not been chosen at random. Its location was everything. Whitechapel changes slowly, and even during the final meetings of the Roebuck Cabal during the spring and early summer of 1920, the locality was scarcely any different from how it had been in the autumn of 1888.

The attendees came to the Roebuck from all over London, and one doctor from as far afield as Edinburgh. But some were locals. The man who travelled the least distance was Rabbi Abraham Coriell, who resided in the Waterlow Buildings in nearby Bethnal Green. Coriell had a great intellect and, perhaps even more importantly, an infallible memory regarding the history of London in general, and Whitechapel in particular. He also had good relations with the Christian clergy in the parish and ensured that they too were co-opted on to the Cabal.

It was not a coincidence that whenever the Cabal met, a free boxing match, fair or other entertainment had been laid on for the local residents. This was necessary to minimize any suspicions that might be aroused by the men's comings and goings. There were a few occasions when the Cabal's activities could not be restricted to the meeting room. Over the years there were several timed walks to test certain theories. But these were undertaken by just one or two members discreetly using stopwatches. Of course, there were some questions in 1892 when the artist Sickert joined the Cabal. Several of his paintings, fortunately wrapped tightly in canvas, were carried up to the room – and there they remained for nearly two decades. The landlord had been forced to say to one over-curious onlooker who had observed the delivery of the paintings that some form of private art auction was taking place in that upstairs room.

More curious than the delivery of the paintings was the requirement of the Cabal for an elephant's foot umbrella stand. This was placed in the centre of the room during meetings, for the men did not sit at a table, but rather on chairs up against the walls. The significance of the umbrella stand was that all the members of the Cabal carried the precise same type of walking stick: an ebony stick capped with the figure of a hooded monk. This served to both identify themselves on arrival and as a means to tally votes following a resolution by the group. The members cast votes by placing their sticks in the umbrella stand – inverted to indicate disagreement with a resolution. Under the group's unwritten constitution, there was an expectation that the voting be unanimous in order for the resolution to be acted upon. Sometimes the Cabal wanted simply a blackboard in the corner of the room; other times highly detailed maps of Whitechapel; on other occasions bound volumes of newspapers seemed to have been mysteriously liberated from the British Library under the authority of these men. One man who was not formally a member of the group attended meetings in 1918. That was McDaniel, a senior keeper of genealogical records at Somerset House.

You will recall that I told you that the Cabal met only twice during 1920. It did not cease its function due to a gradual loss of interest in the events of 1888. The work of the Cabal reached a conclusion: a climax. So, as it turned out, there was little need for further meetings as a result of the final and deadly determination at the penultimate meeting; the details of which are reconstructed for you below, commencing with the opening address to the assemblage from the retired Scotland Yard man, Abberline:

"Gentlemen, we have considered long and hard the case against the suspect Montague Druitt. I hope that we can now agree that it is almost entirely circumstantial. Yes, he may have studied anatomy before he became a pupil barrister, but we have found no definite proof. There is nothing to connect him to the murders except his disappearance while they were taking place. The fact that his cousin Lionel may have worked at a general practice surgery in the Minories, and that the Minories as an address is mentioned in just one of the many thousands of letters purported to have been written by the killer, is neither here nor there . . . it does not connect him to crime and it would not convict him in a court of law. And we must operate to the same standards we would expect from an Old Bailey jury. Unlike a jury, we have the luxury of being able to direct the investigation, to explore new lines of inquiry these long years after the murders. Shall we now put the innocence or guilt of Montague John Druitt to our final vote?"

"You neglected to mention the Goulston Street message," began Dr Bell. "Members of this esteemed body should not forget the message or the means by which it was written. The deliberate misspelling of the word 'Jews' – rendered as J-U-W-E-S could be an attempt by Druitt to exonerate himself. No teacher would ever make an error over so simple a word . . . he attempts to lay a trail that leads suspicion away from an educated man. Yet, who but a teacher always carries chalk? Who but a teacher could write swiftly and very legibly with that same chalk? Aye, I grant you that it is circumstantial, but it is heavily suggestive."

"One more thing," said the young American detective, Harry Dickson. "There is the uncanny resemblance between Druitt and the Duke of Clarence. Now, I've seen identical twins that were more different. We've long since eliminated the Duke of Clarence as a suspect, but can we be sure that they never swopped places? If Druitt took the Duke's place at some Highland function . . . then we potentially have His Grace running around the East End ripping whores."

"We cannot go in circles," said Dr Llewellyn. "Such arguments were put forward and sensibly dismissed long before Mr Dickson was admitted to this group. I would urge him to greater study of our previously recorded resolutions in the archive."

Suitably chastened, young Dickson crumpled slightly from the bearded doctor's reprimand.

"Then may I call you to a vote? Indicate in the usual way if you believe that Montague John Druitt is guilty of the Whitechapel murders beyond all reasonable doubt," said Abberline.

There was the expected shuffling of chairs and clearing of throats as the men got up and placed their walking sticks in the elephant's foot umbrella stand. Abberline could see that no man was left with his stick, but he went through the nominal ritual of counting all thirteen. They had viewed the evidence as merely circumstantial and unanimously found Druitt "not guilty" as indicated by placing their walking sticks into the umbrella stand upside down.

"Thank you, gentlemen," continued Abberline. "We must now make our final deliberations in relation to the dossier on Charles Allen Lechmere, prepared by Dr Llewellyn and disseminated to you at our last meeting. Lechmere was a carman for Pickfords – he handled meat and might therefore be found wearing bloodstained clothes as a matter of routine. Every one of the murders took place along his route to work or a minor variation thereof, and at times when he was going on to his shift. Naturally, his job required him to be skilled with a knife. But, most damningly of all, he is the only man to have been found alone with the body of one of the victims. Moreover, he lied about his name at the coroner's inquest. That is the action of a man who feared discovery."

"Mister Chairman," said Rabbi Coriell, "the weight of evidence against this man is particularly strong. It beggars belief that he was not viewed with greater suspicion at the time. But I think we all know the reason . . . the police, the public and the press were not looking for an ordinary man, they were looking for a monster. His very ordinariness allowed him to slip the net. His discovery with the corpse of Polly Nichols takes his candidacy beyond the realm of circumstantial evidence. Every fact fits him like a glove. But now, what of it? These long years we have sought the truth. And now we have most likely found it. The intellect is satisfied. Who does it serve to drag the name of his family into the dirt?"

"What is known perhaps only to Dr Llewellyn and myself is that Lechmere isn't deceased. He is alive and well and living in retirement in Bethnal Green in a large house on the edge of Victoria Park. After he left Pickfords, he set up his own dairy produce and meat delivery business. The venture did well, so Lechmere is respectable and comfortably off," said Abberline.

"That puts a very different complexion on it," said Dr Oxley, speaking for the first time this evening. "Then this is no longer a purely academic exercise. We have a live suspect to interrogate. Perhaps he could be brought here to be questioned and confronted with the evidence. He may confess to this extra-judicial Cabal."

"That is not the course of action that I would advise," said Dr Lewellyn. "Mr Sickert, please bring forward the Miller's Court Triptychs."

Without ceremony, Sickert placed the two paintings on easels so that they could be displayed more easily. The paintings were both mounted in hinged wooden frames that could be folded out; essentially each picture had a smaller additional picture attached on both the left and right sides. The two "triptychs" when viewed together showed a three hundred and sixty-degree view of the room where Mary Kelly had been found murdered. The image was derived from meticulous research. Sickert had spoken to every man who had entered the room while Kelly's remains had been in situ, and spent weeks studying and extrapolating from the scene-of-crime photo. The Cabal had commissioned the painting from Sickert and viewed it on numerous occasions. Nevertheless, the vivid and bloody images retained their power to shock the viewer to the core. The total physical destruction of a human being had perhaps never before been captured in such horrifying detail. The excised heart . . . the mutilated breasts . . . the draped intestines . . . it was almost too much for the mind of a sane man to process.

"Gentlemen, we have viewed Mr Sickert's painting of the final murder scene many times before," said Dr Llewellyn. "And you will recall that I have previously pointed out what is conspicuously missing from this painting. Not due to omission by the artist, but rather because it was absent from the murder scene itself. It is my firmest belief that this trophy will still be in the possession of the Whitechapel Murderer even after all these years. If Charles Lechmere's property can be searched and the trophy found, it will be incontrovertible proof of his guilt and he should face summary execution by the Cabal's Sergeants-at-Arms. I immediately propose a resolution that Lechmere's home should be searched and, if the proof is found, his death should follow without further ado."

This resolution was formally seconded and agreed upon. But Abberline had more that he wanted to say.

"Members of this esteemed assemblage will know that young Mr Dickson and myself are the duly elected Sergeants-at-Arms and so the duty falls to us. We will take revolvers for protection and for threatening him with, if necessary. But death will come via the syringe of lethal poison supplied by Professor Van Dusen. I have, I must confess, taken the unprecedented step of anticipating your resolution. I have arranged for Lechmere's wife to receive a telegram indicating that her sister in Northumberland is gravely ill. Lechmere will therefore be alone in the house tonight. Tomorrow is Friday, and he is in the habit of walking to the Salmon and Ball public house at lunchtime. That will give us approximately an hour and a half in which to search the property before he returns. I hope that will be long enough."

Harry Dickson's mouth widened into his usual self-confident grin. Yet trepidation formed like a knot of ice in Abberline's gut. He could not shake off the feeling that even at seventy-six years of age, the killer would be unpredictable and dangerous. What had happened inside Mary Kelly's room was a glimpse inside Lechmere's charnel house of a mind. It was tempting to ask him why he'd stopped, as there were different opinions on that here in the Roebuck's upstairs room. Dr Oxley maintained that the Whitechapel Murderer did not cease, and that Frances Cole and Eunice Lang were just two of his further victims.

The following day at fifteen minutes past twelve, Abberline was loitering halfway down Driffield Street lighting his pipe. Lechmere came out of his front gate, wearing a long grey coat and black soft felt brimmed hat. His beard was almost completely white and his posture was upright. He set off for the pub, having paid no attention at all to his would-be executioner. When Lechmere was almost out of sight, Abberline trotted around to the back of the row of large terraced houses into the alleyways that ran along the modest rear gardens. Dickson saw Abberline approaching and opened the back garden gate, which was set in a tall privet hedge. Within seconds, he was forcing the back door with a steel jemmy.

Abberline looked disapprovingly at Dickson's handiwork.

"Don't worry. Assuming we find the trophy, we can make it look as if he lost his keys and forced the lock himself. No one will be any the wiser," said Dickson.

"We'll start in the master bedroom. Anything that anyone wants to hide they keep close to where they sleep. That's where we'll find the trophy," said Abberline.

The pair of detectives padded up the stairs and along the landing. The bedroom door was open with the double bed amateurishly made by Lechmere in his wife's absence. By the window was a dressing table festooned with cheap costume jewellery. There was also a robust-looking oak wardrobe and a couple of bedside tables.

"Probably not the dressing table . . . that looks like the wife's territory," said Abberline.

"Good Lord! Look at this," said Dickson.

Hung on the wall in the corner of the room was an original oil painting in a gilt frame – about eighteen inches by twelve. The subject was a foggy street in Whitechapel with a menacing man in a tall hat walking towards a street corner on which stood a lone woman. A tiny metal plaque on the frame bore the legend *Autumn of Fear*. And the painting itself was signed by Walter Sickert.

"Sickert's painted loads of pictures that allude to our murders and the murder in Camden Town. Of itself it proves nothing. Lots of people like them. There's no accounting for taste."

"How might Dr Bell put it – it's *suggestive*, right?" insisted Dickson.

"Just start looking through the wardrobe, and keep your wits about you, we've no idea what it will be in – if anything – or quite what it will look like after all this time," said Abberline, who was beginning to doubt that Dickson would've cut the mustard as a Scotland detective as opposed to being one of that gaggle of Marylebone dilettantes, the best of whom had retired just as the Great War was kicking off.

Dickson opened the wardrobe and then took out his notebook and pencil. Like most of those trained in the art of illicit searching, he wanted to make a record of how everything looked before he commenced disturbing it so that he could replace it exactly as it had been. A few swift pencil strokes and a handful of notes sufficed for this purpose. He started taking out the old shoeboxes, loose ties and unwanted coat hangers that had accumulated at the bottom of the closet. While at the same time, Abberline went to work on the contents of the bedside table drawers. They continued in silence for almost twenty minutes. When Abberline was engaged in the task of carefully returning everything to the final drawer, there was a gasp from Dickson which bespoke both surprise and 'Eureka!'

"This could be it," said the American. He held in his hand something like a small jam jar. The glass of the jar had long ago been painted matt black – though in some places it was starting to flake off. The metal lid had been crimped at the edges so that it would be impossible to remove no matter how hard it was twisted.

"Let me see it," ordered Abberline. The old Scotland Yard man felt uncharacteristically nervous as the jar was passed to him. He took out his pocketknife and started to scrape at the paint. He dragged the blade along the surface of the glass again and again – it was obvious that it had been painted black more than once. After a minute or so, his work had created an uneven transparent window in the jar's coating. Bobbing in the formaldehyde was an approximately four-month-old human foetus. It would've been Mary Kelly's baby had it lived. Its tiny arms were flung wide, as if anticipating the mother's embrace that it could never know.

"We've got him," said a pale-faced Dickson.

Abberline just nodded. He could not take his eyes off the contents of the jar. His mind had been transported back to room thirteen at Miller's Court. This was what had been missing from that accursed place. Stolen by the killer from Mary Kelly's womb, it had been a memento too precious to leave behind, too precious to send to the police with another letter (unlike Eddowe's ginny kidney). Abberline wondered if Lechmere occasionally scraped off the paint himself so that he could admire his handiwork. If so, the killer was even more of a sub-human ghoul than Abberline had always believed.

"And what the devil is goin' on here?" demanded Lechmere from the bedroom doorway.

Abberline and Dickson both had to suppress the urge to physically attack Lechmere. Having done so, they simultaneously tugged their revolvers from concealed shoulder holsters.

"Get onto the bed, Lechmere," said Abberline.

"I don't know what this is about, but I know how to protect myself. I still have my knife!" he cried.

"Yes, I'll bet you have," said Abberline.

No sooner had the stubby knife been drawn from his pocket than Dickson slammed the barrel of his Webley down hard on Lechmere's wrist, dashing the blade on to the bedside rug. Abberline then grabbed Lechmere by the collar and pulled him with considerable force towards the bed. Dickson drew his left arm back to punch the old man in the face, but Abberline stopped him.

"No! Don't mark him . . . it needs to look like natural causes," said Abberline.

Upon hearing that, all of the colour drained from Lechmere's countenance. He realized that he faced his executioners.

"There are sovereigns under the floorboards at the end of the bed. Just take 'em and let me live," begged Lechmere.

"You hear that, Harry?" said Abberline. "He thinks we're here for his money."

Abberline picked up the jam jar from where he had dropped it after Lechmere entered.

"We know who you are and who you killed. This is the ultimate proof. Who else would have this in a jar?" asked Abberline.

"What is it? I've never seen it before," said Lechmere.

"Then take a bloody good look because it'll be one of the last things you ever see," said Abberline.

"A dead baby in a preserve pot . . . a picture of a whore about to be murdered on your bedroom wall . . . why don't you just confess? You know you're not leaving this room alive," said Dickson, as he removed the leather syringe case from inside his jacket.

"That Sickert painting was a gift to my wife from her employer . . . wait a minute you can't think that I'm—" and before he could finish, Dickson jabbed him in the calf with the syringe.

Lechmere's expression of shock eroded into mere disbelief before finally relaxing into peaceful acceptance as the poison took hold.

"I can't believe that it's finally over. Justice is done, even though it has not been seen to be done. The women are avenged," said Abberline, tears forming in his reddened eyes.

Like automatons, they carefully removed Lechmere's shoes and put them neatly by the side of the bed, and then replaced every single item back in the wardrobe apart from the jar and the knife; these they took with them. His keys they dropped into a nearby drainage grate.

It was almost a month later when the Cabal convened again. The jar and the knife were handed round for all the members to examine. As was a copy of the *Hackney Gazette* with Lechmere's death notice.

Dr Bell looked at the knife carefully for some time, placing the short blade against the flat of his hand and then passed the weapon to Colonel Openshaw.

"It seems incredible that our purpose has finally been served and we can dissolve this assemblage for the last time, with the mantle of contentment upon us," said Dr Bell.

"Not without some proper celebration, Benjamin," drawled Van Dusen, as he reached for the brandy bottle, filled a crystal bloom and pressed it into the Scotsman's hand. "Your father would, I think, be very proud of what we have achieved. His work – his life – was a beacon of inspiration to all those working in the fields of detection and forensic science. But what I think he would be most proud of is our sheer doggedness in continuing this quest, year after year, when all hope seemed to be gone and reason told us that the trail was now impossible to follow. We collectively reviewed the evidence and tested supposition until the answer presented itself. Now we can rest easy. We are the men who caught Jack the—"

"Quiet, my friend," interrupted Dr Llewellyn. "We have vowed never to use that vile sobriquet here, and we should not violate our traditions even at our final meeting. But I am much troubled since the execution of Lechmere. It is with some diffidence that I must raise this final matter with the Cabal." And, with that, Llewellyn stood up and took the place normally occupied by Abberline when he was chairing meetings, for the rightful chairman was duly occupied lighting a cigar.

"Gentlemen, it seems to me that the progeny of Lechmere are legion. There are seven children who have already produced numerous grandchildren. Within the next few years there will be great-grandchildren. His bloodline will be carried forward by an army. London will be awash with his tainted seed within three generations. Our understanding of heredity is still in its infancy, but we know that diseases such as haemophilia are passed down through families . . . can we take the chance that a creature like Lechmere will not emerge within that family at some point in the future?" asked Llewellyn.

"And what of it, sir?" asked Dickson. "We can surely do nothing about crimes that might be committed by men as yet unborn. What would you have us do?"

"You would doubtless do something about an overgrown tree branch that threatened to damage the eaves of your house, or about an infestation of rats in your cellar. This is no different. We could nip in the bud what might one day be a plague upon us. We congratulate ourselves on the execution of Lechmere, and yet we give him the last laugh if we allow his very essence to survive via his descendants. We must stymie the pseudo-immortality that he has achieved by simply breeding."

"You want us to become like Herod. I will take no part in it," said Abberline.

"No, not like Herod, because this enterprise is just. Where is the justice for Mary Kelly's babe – for the life it was never allowed to live while Lechmere's sirelings breed like maggots in a corpse? Yes, I would risk becoming a new Herod to wipe out the Devil's Spawn. We are not the monsters; we are not the animals. I suggest that we employ a gradual programme of covert humane euthanasia against the male members of the family over a period of fifteen or twenty years. And to limit the growth of the family we could take the opportunity to secretly sterilize the women whenever they undergo any sort of surgical procedure in hospital. Many of us are doctors. I say it can be done," said Llewellyn.

"Perhaps there is something to this, Abberline," said Dr Bell. "After all, we surely cannot allow the Whitechapel Murderer any sort of victory even in death."

"I propose that members of this assemblage do not engage in action against the wider Lechmere family. Do I have a seconder?" asked Abberline.

"No, sir. You do not," said Llewellyn. "The Roebuck Cabal has run its course and been more successful than any of us could have imagined. The time for resolutions is past. The terms of reference of this group are clear – we existed only to solve the mystery of the identity of the Whitechapel Murderer . . . and, of course, to bring him to justice if possible. I acknowledge wholeheartedly that the extreme and distasteful line of action I have proposed is unlikely to meet with the unanimous approval of all members. But I have never been a great believer in being subject to the 'tyranny of the majority' – the requirement here is for a new assemblage of like-minded people who are prepared to assist in the eradication of the Lechmeres."

Abberline glared at Llewellyn while he ground out his cigar in the cheap tin ashtray by his side.

"Now, who is with me?" asked Llewellyn.

There was a murmuration of assent from at least five of the thirteen members, which amounted to a death sentence for the Lechmeres.

"This is an area where we can be guided by scripture with confidence," began Rabbi Coriell. "For it is written that the iniquity of the fathers shall be visited unto the third and fourth generations. Our activities in this regard cast us as the agents of God's will."

Abberline was tempted to storm out of the Roebuck, but he didn't want his departure to be misconstrued as petulance rather than disgust. He was also curious about what precisely was being birthed here.

Sickert rose from his place and began to address the Cabal.

"Gentlemen, it seems to me that our work in solving the murders could, unlikely though it may seem, be replicated by someone else. And if that were the case, it is possible that the trail could lead back to us. Previously that might have been of no great import. But if we are to embark on the full-scale euthanasia of an entire family tree, we do not want to get 'caught in the act'. I very strongly recommend that we do our best to muddy the waters and create a smokescreen that makes it all but impossible for an investigator to pick his way through the facts. In the imagination of the public, the murderer is often thought to be some high-ranking doctor ... and we have looked at such figures and discounted them. But our knowledge of these suspects may serve a purpose; one of colossal misdirection. For it is now in our interests to point the finger as far away as possible from Charles Allen Lechmere. I will make it my business to seed half-truths and anecdotes, which, over time, will take on the aspect of facts – to the uninitiated. If the populace want a doctor to be the Whitechapel Murderer, then I will give them Gull or Spivey. And no one will ever be able to say differently," said the artist.

"That is an excellent idea, sir," commended Van Dusen.

Gradually, the atmosphere in that smoke-filled upper room turned back into one of celebration. After four more brandies to cloud his reasoning, even Abberline was starting to think of Lechmere's clan as little more than cockroaches. Around midnight, Dr Llewellyn began making his excuses, and also made a promise that the first meeting of the new Cabal would be in some salubrious West End venue. On the stairs, he bade farewell to Walter Randall and then headed out into the night.

Llewellyn had heard rumours that Old Bailey judges sometimes suffered from involuntary ejaculations when pronouncing the death sentence in court, and now he could understand why. He had found himself in a state of considerable arousal when the Cabal agreed to wiping out the Lechmeres. He was too old now to prey on the whores of Whitechapel, but getting the do-gooders of the assemblage to kill vicariously on his behalf was the next best thing to going on a killing spree himself. Doubtless his priapism would not abate until he roughly took his housekeeper when he arrived home. He had instructed her to wait up. He was seldom able to reach a climax without thinking back to the murders – and to the events in the little room at Miller's Court in particular.

Llewellyn had found in Lechmere the perfect scapegoat. Possibly he would never have heard of him had not his wife come to work at his surgery as a nurse. A chance conversation revealed her husband's involvement in the Nichols inquest and, from that point on, he considered ways of using Lechmere to frustrate, or end, the Cabal's investigations. Still friendly with Mrs Lechmere, he had planted the jar in her husband's wardrobe only the week before its discovery while she hurried to bring in the washing during a cloudburst. It had been achingly painful to let his prize possession go. Leaving nothing to chance, on that Friday, Llewellyn had arrived at the Salmon and Ball pub half an hour after Lechmere and told him that he had just visited a patient in Driffield Street and seen two suspicious characters loitering near his house. That was sufficient for the rambunctious Lechmere to go and investigate, to go to his death.

He was perhaps the most obvious suspect, and yet the Cabal had never thought for one moment that he might be Jack the Ripper. Llewellyn reached into his pocket. Yes, the jar was still there. No one had seen him take it.

A Small Band of Dedicated Men
Andrew Lane

————

The backhand blow caught Francis Thompson across his face, knocking him out of his seat. His cheek and his forehead slammed against the floor, sending a wave of sick pain through him. He lay there for a moment, head throbbing and the tiles cool against his cheek, but a hand caught him beneath his shoulder and pulled him upright again. He was thrust back into the wooden chair. It rocked under his weight, almost sending him toppling backwards to the floor again before he could grab hold of the table to steady himself.

'Admit it,' the sergeant shouted in his ear, 'you knew both Mary Nichols *and* Annie Chapman! You'd lain with them in their filthy whore beds!'

'I didn't know Annie Chapman,' he said, tasting blood in his mouth. His lip was split, and stinging. 'Mary Nichols, yes. I'd . . . I'd been with her on a few occasions, but not Annie Chapman. I never even met her, to my certain knowledge.'

The sergeant walked back around to the other side of the table. 'You trained as a doctor,' he challenged, placing his hands flat on the wood and leaning forward. 'But you're a poet now, or so you say. I don't know much about literature, sonny, but I'm pretty sure a poet don't earn as much as a doctor could, no matter how fancy their words are. How is it you can afford any woman – even one as cheap as Mary?' He scowled. 'Is that what happened – did you try and take that which she offered but then found you couldn't pay, so you sliced her open to stop her from asking?'

'I . . . I wasn't eating,' Thompson muttered. He couldn't look up from the table to meet the sergeant's scathing gaze. 'I managed to scrape together a few pennies from a poem I sold. Mary was very . . . accommodating.'

'Yes, I'm told you were spending all your money on opium down on the Limehouse Causeway. That takes away a man's appetite, and his means to pay to slake it.'

'Not *all* my money,' he said quietly. 'Not all the time. Just when . . . when things got too much for me.'

'Things?'

'Life.'

'Ah.' The sergeant pushed himself away from the table, sneering. 'The things that the rest of us poor mortals have to deal with. I s'pose those with a more *poetic* sensibility need something to lean on.'

Thompson glanced up at the policeman, feeling a flush of anger overriding the throbbing in his head. 'Yes,' he said, 'but judging by your nose and cheeks you're more of a gin man I'd say.'

This time the blow crashed upwards, smashing his teeth together. He thought he could feel fragments of enamel sharp against the inside of his lips.

'You cut Mary's throat twice, so deep that her head almost fell off when we picked her up, and then sliced her belly nine or ten times. Why'd you do that then? Something you learned at your medical school, was it?'

Thompson felt the bile rise in his throat. He could see, in his mind's eye, the way the wounds would have looked. He'd spent long enough at medical school for that, at least. Mary hadn't been a pretty woman, or indeed a clean one, but he'd lain with her on more than one occasion and she'd been kind to him, even when he couldn't pay her.

The sergeant clenched his fist again, drawing it back for a punch, but the door to the room opened and a constable entered. He drew the sergeant aside. Thompson closed his eyes, savouring the chance to breathe properly for a moment, but he could hear them speak.

'Inspector Abberline says you'd best let 'im go,' the constable whispered.

'Why?' the sergeant countered angrily. 'What's Abberline know 'bout this cove that we don't?'

''E knows you got five blokes locked up in 'ere, all for the same murders, an' you're working your way down the line until you get one of 'em to confess. 'E says that's not the way things are done.'

The sergeant turned to glare at Thompson. 'Well *you* can let him out,' he snarled, 'because I ain't going to bother myself with it. I'm going to see Abberline about this. How does he expect us to catch this murderer if he ties our hands in the questioning of suspects?'

It took an hour for the right paperwork to be signed, and then Thompson was ejected out on to the Whitechapel streets without any apology. He staggered off towards his lodgings – a room above a stable with gaps in the roof through which rain came in, and a single bed that bowed under his weight so much that he could feel the floor through the thin mattress – avoiding the horse dung and the occasional dead dog or cat left along the sides of the road.

Three men were standing outside the stable as he approached. They were dressed better than most in that area, although their clothes still would not have gained them entrance into any reputable London restaurant. As soon as they saw he was heading for the stable, they converged on him, pulling notebooks and pencils from their pockets. Their voices struck his ear in a babble.

'Mr Thompson? Are you indeed Leather Apron, as they say?'

'Why did the police release you from their custody, Mr Thompson?'

'Did you kill Emma Smith and Martha Tabram as well as Marie Nichols and Annie Chapman?'

He pushed his way past them roughly and went through the stable to the stairs at the back, which led to his room. They followed him to the foot of the stairs, asking questions all the way and not leaving any time for answers even if he had wanted to give any, but he shut and bolted the door in their faces and stumbled up the stairs. Glancing out through the cracked glass of the window, he could see them standing in the street, looking up to see if he was still there.

He lay on his bed as the sunlight gradually faded and the pain in his head withdrew. Normal sleep eluded him. He craved a deeper sleep, one that he knew could be found a walk away, in a room lined with rotting timbers and illuminated by flickering candles if only he had the means to pay for it. The trouble was that he was out of cash, and the opium dens of Limehouse didn't extend credit or swap drug-induced visions for medical expertise. Their idea of getting medical attention for a customer in one of their dens was to carry them out and throw them into the street – or into the Thames.

It was dark outside when he heard the sound of wheels on cobbles, the jingling of reins and the snickering of a horse outside. He didn't react – carriages were infrequent where he lived in Spitalfields, but not unknown – but when he could still hear the sounds the horse was making half an hour later he went to the window. It wasn't so much to assuage any curiosity he had: it was more that he wanted a distraction from the gnawing in his insides, and the visions of Mary's ripped body that kept tormenting his mind.

A black two-wheeler was sat outside. The stables were closed, so the carriage's driver wasn't waiting to get a horse shod. He was sitting on top, muffled up in an overcoat and staring down the street. The journalists appeared to have disappeared – probably to the nearest pub.

Eventually, Thompson went down to see what the driver wanted.

He looked down from his seat. 'Mr Thompson?'

A small bud of unease started to grow in his stomach. 'Yes?'

'Mr *Francis* Thompson?'

'Yes?'

He nodded. 'I been told to take you somewhere. I been told to tell you that it's not for the police, an' it's not for the papers. I also been told to tell you that you'll hear somethin' to your advantage at the end of the journey.'

'Where are we going?' Thompson asked.

'Brixton,' the man said. 'I been told to bring you back afterwards.'

'After *what*?'

'I ain't been told that.'

Eventually, it *was* curiosity that pushed Thompson into climbing into the two-wheeler.

The journey took them along the Limehouse Causeway to Tower Bridge, then across the Thames and through Southwark. Thompson watched as people, animals and buildings passed by in a series of dream-like and nightmarish firelit tableaux.

Finally, they drove up a gravelled driveway towards a small house set into its own grounds. The driver waited as Thompson got out warily. The front door was open and, after a few minutes of waiting, he walked through it into a well-appointed hall. No servants were around. That was probably for the good – Thompson's current state placed him even further down the social scale than the servants, and there would have been some awkward moments.

The door to the dining room was open, and there were sounds of movement and voices from inside. He walked across the hall and entered.

The dining table was clear, apart from several decanters, some crystal glasses and a gasogene. Eight men were standing in small groups, looking awkward. Judging by their clothing, they crossed several different classes within London society. Most of them had bruises on their faces, and one or two had torn knuckles.

Thompson stared at the men in the room. They, in turn, stared back at him. Noticing that they all held drinks, Thompson steeled himself and then crossed the room to the table and took a glass. As he was pouring what smelled like brandy from one of the decanters, he heard someone in the doorway.

'Gentlemen, we are quorate, I believe. Please take your seats.'

The man who had entered was tall, finely featured, with black hair that was drawn severely to either side from a central parting. He moved to the head of the table as everyone sat, apart from a massively built and roughly dressed man with a huge moustache, which hid his lower face. The big man took a step forward and said, in a thickly accented voice: 'What is this? Why are we here?'

The tall newcomer gestured to the last remaining seat. 'Please, join us and I will explain.'

The moustached man hesitated, looked around the group for support, and then reluctantly sat down when he found none.

'My name is Montague Druitt,' the newcomer announced, sitting. 'I am a barrister, well known in this city, and this is my house. Welcome, one and all.' Glancing around the table, he continued: 'Unlike many in my profession, who make a virtue out of speaking at length, I will cut to the nub of the matter. We have, all of us here, been accused recently of being the notorious killer known to the press and in the streets as "Leather Apron". Moreover, and more importantly, none of us *are* Leather Apron. There may be some around this table who are capable of, or who have even committed, crimes of various sorts, both in this country and abroad, but none of you are guilty of recently murdering prostitutes in London. I know this because I have seen your police files and I have made various enquiries of my own over the past weeks.'

Like all of the others around the table, Thompson stared at the other faces in surprise. Had any of these men been in adjoining cells to his, earlier in the day, he wondered. Had *they* been beaten up, as he had been? Their bruises suggested that they had.

'Allow me to make introductions,' Druitt said. Looking to the bearded man on his left, he went on: 'John Piser; you are, I believe, a bootmaker from Poland. Your nickname, unfortunately, is "Leather Apron", which certainly hasn't helped your case.'

His gaze moved on to the next man: the one with the huge moustache. 'Ludwig Schloski; you were born Seweryn Klosowski. Polish, again, but a barber rather than a bootmaker.'

The next man was barely in his twenties: a clean-shaven and nervous youth. 'Thomas Cutbush: a medical student. You have what can only be described as an ambivalent attitude towards women.'

Cutbush blushed, and looked down at the table.

Sitting beside Cutbush was a man with bad skin and staring eyes. 'Michael Ostrog,' Druitt said. 'You also claim to have trained as a doctor, although I have found no evidence to back that up. You are Russian, for certain, and a confidence trickster and thief by repute.'

Ostrog started to climb to his feet, but then slumped back as Druitt stared him down.

Next to Ostrog was a thuggish, low-browed fellow who stared at the table and occasionally glanced around, as if he could hear other voices somewhere. 'Aaron Kosminsky, a Polish Jew like Mr Piser and Mr Klosowski, and a barber like Mr Klosowski. Interesting, how Judaism, Poland and hairdressing keep coming up in connection with these murders.'

Thompson himself was sitting at the end of the table, beside Kosminsky, and it seemed almost like a dream when Druitt turned to look at him and said: 'Francis Thompson, a medical student like Mr Cutbush, but with an unhealthy liking for opium, which has destroyed your career. You have written some poetry, which has been described as "promising", although I find nothing admirable in it.'

Druitt's gaze moved on. The man on Thompson's left was small, rat-featured, with decent clothes and a moustache that extended well beyond the borders of his face. 'Francis Tumblety – you were born in Ireland but lived for many years in America. You describe yourself as a "herb doctor", but it is generally accepted that you are, like Mr Ostrog, a confidence trickster.'

Tumblety opened his mouth to object, but Druitt turned smoothly to the other side of the table. 'Richard Mansfield,' he said, cutting Tumblety off and looking at an ordinary-looking man with wire-rimmed glasses on a length of ribbon. 'Born in Germany, you have made a career for yourself here in England as an actor.' He smiled. 'I actually saw you in the dual roles of Doctor Jekyll and Mr Hyde in the sensational drama by Robert Louis Stevenson.'

Mansfield nodded, smiling dreamily.

Druitt glanced to his right, to a stocky man who had finished his brandy and was looking at the decanters. 'And finally we have Joseph Barnett, a fish porter.' He leaned back in his chair. 'We have something in common, gentlemen. Mud has been thrown at us, and it will stick. If Leather Apron's true identity is never determined then our names will be indelibly linked with the murders that have already occurred, and with those murders that have *yet* to occur. We will forever be in the shadow of Leather Apron – our friends will leave us, women will refuse to spend time with us, and people will call after us in the street and throw eggs and human refuse at our doorways. There is, I'm afraid, only one way to stop this from happening. *We* must catch Leather Apron.'

Ostrog and Kosminsky started laughing, while Piser and Klosowski sniggered. Thompson glanced across at the other medical student – Cutbush? – who looked back and shrugged weakly.

Mansfield, the actor, took his glasses off languidly and started to polish them with a handkerchief. 'Accepting everything you say, Mr Druitt, surely the best thing is to wait until the police apprehend the killer. That, after all, is their job.'

Druitt was about to answer when Francis Tumblety slapped his hand on the table. 'The police?' he said. His voice held an American twang. 'They ain't going to do anything. The fact that they've accused all of us, and others, tells us that. They ain't got a clue and they never will!'

'My proposal,' Druitt went on, 'for what it is worth, is that we form teams and we patrol the area around Whitechapel and Spitalfields every night between, say, midnight and five o'clock. There are ten of us – if we go out in pairs then we can make up five teams. We look for anyone suspicious – anyone who seems to be following a working girl, or who has blood on their clothes without good explanation, or who looks out of place.'

Thompson surprised himself by speaking up. 'Didn't I read that there are vigilante groups already walking the streets, looking for Leather Apron? Won't we just be duplicating their efforts?'

Druitt nodded. 'A fair point, Mr Thompson. A man named George Lusk, a builder and decorator by trade, *has* set up the Whitechapel Vigilance Committee, mainly because the work of Leather Apron is keeping people out of the east of this city and depriving business of custom. His men patrol the streets at night, yes, but they are innocents abroad. They don't know what they are looking for, and they don't know what to do if they find it. They are more for show and bluster than for any practical purpose.' He looked around the table, meeting every man's eye. 'We know those streets better than they do, and we have a much more personal reason to identify Leather Apron. We can succeed where they will undoubtedly fail.'

Ostrog stared at Druitt, a sneer on his face. 'You know those streets, do you? You, with your fine house and your fine brandy. What do *you* know of these places, where we live and work?'

Druitt looked away, towards the fireplace. 'Oh, I have spent . . . many hours . . . in the East End of London, looking for . . . companionship of the female variety,' he said softly. 'I knew both Emma Smith and Martha Tabram – not well, but intimately, you might say. I have as much reason as you to want Leather Apron identified, and I believe I have as much knowledge of the locality as you do.'

It was the young medical student, Cutbush, who broke the silence that followed by asking: 'Why in pairs? Why not individually? We could cover more ground that way.'

Barnett, the stocky fish porter on Druitt's right, stood up and walked around the table to the decanters. 'I'll refresh myself, if you don't mind, Mr Druitt.' As he poured himself another brandy, he went on: 'The answer is obvious, even if I do say so. We're suspects already. If any one of us is found wandering the streets of Whitechapel after midnight and identified, then the game is up for us. We'll be strung up on a lamp post quicker than you can say "boiled mutton".' He passed the brandy decanter to Kosminsky, who was sitting nearest. 'Going in pairs means each man can provide assurance for the other – and nobody yet has suggested that Leather Apron is two men, or three men, or a gang.'

'Exactly,' Druitt said. He met everyone's gaze. 'The Whitechapel Vigilance Committee will fail, because they are motivated by business concerns and by fear. We will succeed because we are motivated by self-preservation, which is the strongest and most basic of drives.'

Aaron Kosminsky, who had said nothing up to that point, looked up from the table. 'What,' he said in a deep and broadly accented voice, 'is in it for us? Apart from this self-preservation you value so highly?' He swigged from the brandy decanter, wiped his lips and passed it to Thompson, who immediately passed it on to Tumblety.

'A shilling a night,' Druitt said. 'Non-negotiable.'

'With a bonus for whichever team catches Leather Apron,' the actor, Richard Mansfield added softly.

Druitt nodded. 'Agreed.'

The subsequent discussion went on for an hour, but nothing of substance was exposed that had not already been brought to the table. Eventually, every argument for and against Druitt's proposal having been hunted down and dealt with, they all agreed to join in. Druitt produced a schedule for who would patrol where, and with whom. Maps were brought out and spread across the table with the streets, alleys, public houses and opium dens that should be checked regularly marked. Each team was represented by lines of a different colour, and the lines crossed each other at regular intervals at places where the teams would stop for a while to compare notes. There were also type-written lists for everyone with the names – well, nicknames such as Saucy Mary and Fruity Tess – of the various whores, hundreds of them in the area, who should also be checked to make sure they were alive and safe. The teams would change composition every night, to keep them fresh, and they would both start and end their patrols at the Prospect of Whitby tavern, where a late dinner would be provided before they started and an early breakfast when they finished.

'Gentlemen,' Druitt said eventually, 'I believe we have covered all the salient points. There are carriages waiting outside to take you back to the places you live. I shall see you tomorrow night, at one hour to midnight, at the Prospect of Whitby.'

The next night, Thompson arrived at the tavern to find everyone else already there, and drinking. He had thought that at least one person would drop out, but obviously the lure of Druitt's money was stronger than the unspoken risks. As they occupied the balcony that ran along the back of the tavern, looking out on to the oily black waters of the

Thames, they all boasted of how they would catch Leather Apron, and what they would do to him *when* they had caught him.

'I hear,' Mansfield said, moving up to where Thompson stood, 'that a letter was received by a man at the Central News Agency. It is supposed to have come from Leather Apron, although my information is that he signed the letter "Jack the Ripper". The men who run the agency are debating whether to pass it on to the police or keep it for its publicity value.'

'"Jack the Ripper"?' Thompson repeated. 'I really don't think that will replace "Leather Apron" in the minds of the public. Not at all.'

Thompson's first partner was Tumblety, the American herbalist. Their patrol around the darker areas of the city was marked by plenty of fights, some window smashing, various pickpocketing offences and two suspicious fires, but nothing else. The next night he was with the actor, Mansfield, but again nothing transpired. They saw the competing patrols organised by the Whitechapel Vigilance Committee, but the fact that there were two of them together – four if they were meeting at one of the points where their patrols crossed – seemed to rule them out as suspects. They nodded at the committee patrols, and moved on. The mood of the city on both nights was strange – scared, yes, but also heightened. People seemed to Thompson to be in search of stronger pleasures, and quicker ones, than previously. It was as if they were poised on the edge of something, waiting for an event to happen but also dreading its occurrence.

He still felt the tidal pull of the opium dens, the ache of need deep in his stomach and the itch of desire in his brain, but he was able to resist – even with Druitt's shillings in his pocket. It was as if the importance of the task at hand had given him a purpose that he had lacked before. Or so he told himself.

During the days, when he wasn't sleeping, he was scribbling furiously, producing poem after poem that stacked up on sheets of paper beside his desk. When he reread them later he discovered that they were darker, more serious than the opium-influenced visions and dreams that he had previously written about. They had an intensity that he had never managed before.

The third night Thompson spent walking the East End of London with Michael Ostrog. Where Tumblety and Mansfield were chatty companions, Ostrog was sullen and uncommunicative. He hardly said three words to Thompson as they patrolled.

At just after one o'clock in the morning, based on the chiming of Big Ben, they both heard whistles and shouts from nearby. Thompson glanced at Ostrog. 'I know it's off our route,' he said, 'but we should check it out.'

Ostrog nodded, and together they ran towards the commotion.

A crowd was gathering in Spitalfields, in Berners Street. A building opposite was lit up, and Thompson could see the painted sign above its door – THE INTERNATIONAL WORKING MEN'S EDUCATIONAL CLUB. Montague Druitt and Aaron Kosminsky were standing at the edge of the agitated crowd. When he saw them, Druitt beckoned them over.

'What's going on?' Thompson asked breathlessly.

'Messrs Cutbush and Mansfield saw a woman being dragged into the yard over there,' Druitt said. His expression was thunderous.

'That's Old John Dutfield's Yard,' Kosminsky muttered.

'When they went to investigate, they found the woman with her throat in the process of being cut. The killer ran off. They are in pursuit, and there's a driver of a horse and cart in the yard now who's busy claiming the credit.' Druitt made a growling noise in the back of his throat. 'Too late! We were too late by moments!'

'At least we can all account for each other's movements,' Thompson pointed out. 'That's something, surely?'

Druitt nodded. 'It is, but I would prefer more. I would prefer us to be able to catch this man in the act, so that we can *prove* our innocence to the world.'

'Who is the girl?' Ostrog asked – more words than he had exchanged with Thompson during the whole of their patrol.

'The word is she was known locally as "Long Liz".' Druitt gazed into Dutfield's Yard. 'I wonder,' he mused, 'if I could get in there to have a look at the body.' Seeing Thompson's frown, he added quickly: 'In case there is any evidence on the body, or left behind in the yard. The killer did run off in a hurry. This may be the break we need.'

'We're not the police,' Thompson pointed out. 'If there is evidence, then they should examine it, not us.'

'You're right, of course.' But Druitt still gazed into the yard for a while, an expression on his face that Thompson had difficulty in reading.

It was near sunrise when they all gathered together again at the Prospect of Whitby. The sky in the east was a watery blue colour, with wisps of cloud, and there were plates of bacon, sausages and oysters provided for breakfast, along with strong beer. Thomas Cutbush and Richard Mansfield were the last back, and they both sank most of a pint of porter each before they could give a coherent report.

'Did you catch him, or even *see* him?' Druitt demanded.

Mansfield shook his head. 'No,' he said, 'but there's been another death.'

Druitt's face was shocked. 'Another? On the same *night*?'

Thomas Cutbush's face was white, and his hands shook as he held the tankard. 'We stopped him doing what he wanted,' the medical student said. 'So he found someone else. You don't want to know what was done to her, you really don't.'

'Her face . . .' Mansfield muttered. 'Dear God, her poor face . . .'

Druitt walked to the balcony and looked out over the waters of the Thames, glittering coldly now in the light of the rising sun. 'Tell me,' he said quietly. 'I need to know every last detail.'

By the time Mansfield had finished his tale, Cutbush and the fish porter, Barnett, had been sick into the river, and Thompson wasn't feeling too well himself. The oysters were sitting uneasily in his stomach. Word had come in from new arrivals to the tavern that the dead woman was one Kate Eddowes – a whore, like the others.

They went home despondent. Thompson stood at the door of the stables, one hand on the wood, and thought about wandering off to find one of his favourite haunts: a place where a small man in long robes with a pigtail hanging down his back would heat up a ball of opium resin until it started to smoke, and then allow Thompson to sit and inhale the vapours for hours that would stretch until they seemed like centuries. Twice he pulled his hand from the door, but his feet wouldn't move. Eventually, he pushed the door open and went to bed. Maybe, he thought bitterly, the hours of walking and the regular meals were doing him some good.

The next night the ten of them met again. They were all more despondent than they had been on previous nights, and with good reason. They had failed to catch their man.

Thompson was paired with Montague Druitt on that night's patrol. Druitt seemed disturbed: thrashing the black malacca cane he carried through the air as they walked, as if he was attacking invisible assailants. When he spoke it was in terse snatches. Of all Thompson's partners, he was the one who made Thompson the most nervous.

There was no murder that night – well, not one that involved a whore and a knife and which couldn't immediately be blamed on a drunken punter or angry pimp. Nor was there a murder the next night, or the night after that. The group still met together every night, driven by Druitt's insistence and his apparently inexhaustible supply of money, but the reason for their gathering seemed more and more remote. This wasn't a calling any more – it was a job.

'This is a success, not a failure!' Druitt cried one morning, as the sun was rising and they were eating their breakfasts on the balcony of the Prospect of Whitby – an area they had effectively annexed as their own.

'Leather Apron is still out there,' Barnett observed.

'But he's not killed anyone for a week now,' Druitt countered. 'He knows we're out there, every night, looking for him. He has gone to ground.'

'And, like any wild animal, he will re-emerge from his den when he gets hungry enough.' Richard Mansfield removed his glasses and polished them thoughtfully. 'Whether that is tomorrow, or next week, or next month, Leather Apron will be back.'

'Unless he is dead,' Michael Ostrog pointed out. 'Or in prison for something else. Or maybe a crewman on a ship, heading for God knows where.'

The whole of October went past, and a week of November as well, before Leather Apron struck again. Thompson hadn't habituated an opium den for all of that time, and the miles of walking every night was getting him fitter and fitter. With Druitt's shillings in his pocket, he had moved to better accommodation, and his poetry was flowing from his mind like water from a fountain. He had also struck up friendships with the actor, Richard Mansfield, and the medical student, Thomas Cutbush. The three of them had started spending time together outside their regular patrols – taking lunch, and even visiting early shows in the music halls.

It was the night of 9 November, and Thompson was walking with the strange, twitchy Polish barber, Aaron Kosminsky. The streets of Whitechapel and Spitalfields were as familiar to him now as anywhere. He knew each street, each alley, each yard and each tavern. The various whores and doxies would wave to him as he went past, knowing that he was there for their safety. The Whitechapel Vigilance Committee had stopped their patrols after a fortnight, given that they all had jobs to go to, but Druitt's men went on.

It was that sheer familiarity that almost allowed Leather Apron to escape them. Thompson had seen so many women being escorted into back alleys by well-dressed men – and intervened many times, to curses and threats – that another one nearly passed him by. It was only when they were on Dorset Street, for the second time that night, that Kosminsky's head twitched, as if he could hear something.

'Screaming,' he said. 'Woman, screaming.'

'I can't hear anything.'

Kosminsky glanced at him. 'I hear many things that other people cannot. Including woman screaming.'

Reluctantly, Thompson followed Kosminsky into an alleyway that ran off Dorset Street and gave access to Miller's Court – a small enclosed space with several doors leading off it. There was a stench of decay and human waste hovering in the air, so thick that it was almost visible. Thompson felt as if they were wading through it to get to the open door on the far side.

'You – stop!' Kosminsky yelled, then cried out as a man in a dark blue coat and a cap pushed violently past him. Kosminsky staggered sideways, and Thompson saw that his sleeve had been slashed through, and blood was seeping into the cloth: black in the moonlight. The man waved a bloodied knife at Thompson, who stepped back rapidly to let him pass. Kosminsky snarled and ran in pursuit despite his injury, shoving Thompson out of the way. Thompson nearly fell backwards into the room from which the man had run. He turned to see if whoever was inside needed help. One look sent a fountain of stomach acid up into the back of his throat.

Illuminated by a fierce fire in the grate, the woman in the tiny and incredibly hot room had been . . . disassembled. Taken apart. Scooped out. Apart from her arms and legs, which were relatively intact apart from splashed and spurted blood, she had been *emptied*. Everything that had been inside her was now outside, and her face had been slashed in so many directions and so many times that it was just raw meat. In the flickering firelight, the room looked like someone had thrown a bucket of red paint into it from the doorway.

There was nothing he could do for her. Apart from catch the man who had killed her.

He turned and ran after Kosminsky, swallowing the bitter bile that was flooding his mouth.

The chase took them through twisty alleys and empty streets, their footsteps and their ragged breaths echoing from crumbling brick walls. They shouted for help, but their cries were absorbed by the heavy night air. Mist drifted in off the Thames like cobwebs floating in the air. Thompson's heart was hammering in his chest. Kosminsky ran with no grace, bouncing off corners and forcing himself through gaps in walls. Thompson kept catching glimpses of their quarry over Kosminsky's shoulder: the man was quick footed, nimble, and he obviously knew the area well judging by the way he never entered any cul-de-sacs and found ways around houses – and sometimes *through* the empty and dilapidated ones – that Thompson had never been aware of.

But they cornered him on a quayside overlooking the Thames. Stairs led down to the creaking wood from the street, but the far end was blocked by a pile of crates and bales. There was no way out.

The man stopped and turned, the knife still in his hand. 'Stay back!' he shouted. His voice was accented, just like Kosminsky's, Piser's and Koslowski's were. Now that Thompson could see him more clearly, he realised that the man was wearing a pea coat, like sailors did.

Kosminsky was standing in front of him, blocking his escape. 'What is your name?' he asked.

'You're Polish?' Leather Apron asked, wide-eyed. 'Like me?' He was barely in his twenties, and fair-haired. His eyes were a pale blue. He looked to Thompson as if he only had to shave every other day.

'Nothing like you,' Kosminsky said. 'Your name?'

'Smaceck,' the man replied. 'Tomas Smaceck.'

'A sailor?'

He nodded, swallowing.

'And the women?' Kosminsky pressed. 'Why?'

'Because they are diseased!'

'You caught a disease from them?'

Smaceck nodded, embarrassed. 'How can I marry my girlfriend now?' he cried. 'How can I explain to her that I caught this filthy disease from a syphilitic whore? They deserved it, for what they gave me!'

'You won't have to explain,' Kosminsky said. He stepped forward. Smaceck swung at him wildly with the knife, but the Polish barber caught his hand, twisted it, and then hit Smaceck hard on the side of his head. The sailor fell sideways, eyes rolling up in his head thanks to Kosminsky's blow. His foot caught on the wooden edge running along the side of the quay. He fell, gracelessly, splashing into the water.

He never surfaced.

Thompson and Kosminsky stood there for perhaps half an hour, waiting, but there was no sign of him. He had sunk beyond their reach, beyond anybody's reach.

Back at the Prospect of Whitby, and out of earshot of any other customers, Thompson explained haltingly to the others what had occurred. Kosminsky just sat there, staring at his feet and occasionally reacting to some noise that nobody else could hear.

Druitt was surprisingly calm. 'We should have brought him to justice,' he said, gazing out across the waters of the Thames, 'but at least no more bodies will be discovered. If the ten of us are seen around, conducting our daily business, while all the time no more murders occur, then we will stop being suspects. The police will turn their attention to people who died, or went to prison, or shipped out abroad, or had some other reason for stopping the killing. I think that we are safe.' He frowned, and glanced at Thompson. 'What did you say his name was?'

'Smaceck,' Thompson said. 'Tomas Smaceck.'

'And the girl who died tonight – what was her name?'

This time it was Piser who answered. 'The constable I talked with said that she was an Irish girl named—' he thought for a moment '— Mary Kelly.'

Druitt thought for a moment, then closed his eyes in realisation. 'Yes,' he whispered, 'of course!'

'Of course *what*?' Thompson stared at Druitt, who was shaking his head. He looked at the others on the balcony. 'Of course *what*?'

Richard Mansfield had a newspaper in front of him – an early edition. He was busy scribbling something in the margins of the paper. 'The names!' he said, and shook his head. 'How could we have known?'

Thompson couldn't see it. 'Known *what*?'

Mansfield turned the newspaper around so that Thompson could see what he had been writing. He had listed all the names of the murdered whores, one above the other, and underlined particular letters in their names:

Emma Elizabeth <u>S</u>mith
<u>M</u>artha Tabram
Mary <u>A</u>nn Nichols
Annie <u>C</u>hapman
<u>E</u>lizabeth Stride
<u>C</u>atherine Eddowes
Mary Jane <u>K</u>elly

'He was spelling out his own name, using *their* names,' Mansfield said, amazed. 'A pattern that meant something only to him.'

Thompson stared at the writing on the newspaper. 'And would he have stopped?' he asked, amazed. 'Was this it? Would he have finished with Mary Kelly and never killed again?'

Mansfield shrugged. 'Who knows? He was obviously badly damaged in the head. Maybe it was the syphilis, maybe something hereditary. We will never find out.'

The meeting broke up soon after that. Nobody seemed to want to talk about what had happened, and nobody wanted to go to the police. It was all over, and not in a way that any of them had predicted, or wanted. But, as they left the tavern, Montague Druitt got them all to reach into a leather purse that he was carrying. It was their last payment – a guinea this time, rather than a shilling.

Thompson tucked his guinea safely into a pocket and moved to leave, but when he heard Druitt say something behind him, he turned around. Michael Ostrog was standing in front of Druitt, towering over him in fact, and holding up his coin. He seemed to be asking something about it, and Druitt was explaining. Thompson shrugged, and turned to go. It wasn't any of his business.

It was three nights later that the black carriage appeared outside Thompson's new rooms. He heard the whinnying of the horse, and the clinking of the reins, and went to the window to check. *Surely this is all over*, he thought. *We stopped the murders, and we stopped Leather Apron. What else is there?*

Eventually, of course, he put on his coat, walked downstairs and entered the carriage.

It rumbled and rattled through night streets that seemed, somehow, safer now than they had before. There was still crime and death there, and even evil, but the satanic pall of horror that had been cast over the city was gone. Thompson leaned back in his padded seat and smiled. He had been part of that. He had helped bring things to their end.

The carriage finished its journey around Mile End, rather than at Druitt's house in Brixton. Confused, Thompson got out. The night air was cold, and his breath frosted in front of his face. Ahead of him was a shack built on a patch of waste ground. A donkey grazed incuriously on the scabby grass around the shack.

The door was open. Thompson walked across to it.

The other nine men were inside. They were clustered on one side, all staring across to the other side with unreadable expressions on their faces. Thompson followed their gazes, feeling the questions piling up in his throat unable to get past the lump that was forming there.

A metal-framed bed was pushed up against the wall on the other side of the shack. On the bed was a girl: plump, red-haired, freckled, naked. She had been . . . spread out. The flesh between her fingers had been carefully sliced through down to the wrists and pulled apart. The flesh between her toes had been sliced through to the ankles and similarly pulled apart. Her hands and feet looked like splayed red spiders. Her attacker hadn't finished with the extremities however: the ulnae and radii of her forearms and the tibiae and fibulae of her lower legs had also been separated with a sharp knife, and the bones pulled apart until they were almost at right angles. Her chest had been opened up and the ribs spread wide in a starburst. Her jaw had been broken apart at the chin and pulled wide. She looked . . . barely human.

There was a roaring in Thomson's ears, and a feeling of pins and needles in his hands and his feet. His brain felt as if someone had wrapped it in cotton bandages soaked in some anaesthetic chemical.

Montague Druitt stepped forward from where he was standing in the middle of the group. He was holding a leather sack.

'Ostrog's work,' he said, smiling. 'A creditable first attempt. He used to be a surgeon in Russia – did I mention that? He killed several women there – the first was accidental, during an illegal abortion, but the others were very deliberate. In fact, several of our little group have secrets in our pasts – either things we've done or things we've thought about doing. Mr Piser and Mr Cutbush have made several minor assaults on prostitutes in the past, for instance, while Mr Klosowski has poisoned at least one woman that I know of. The others? Well, let's say that insanity runs in several families – including mine.' He held the leather bag out towards Thompson. 'Please, take one. Everybody else has.' He turned to Ostrog. 'Burn this hovel down,' he said. 'Leave no trace.' Turning back to Thompson he confided: 'That was Smaceck's biggest mistake. That, and killing to a pattern.'

Driven more by habit than anything else, Thompson reached into the bag. He didn't take his eyes off the wreckage that had once been a red-headed, freckled girl. His fingers closed on a coin, and he automatically pulled it out.

It was a guinea, but it had been painted black.

Everyone else was holding a guinea as well, he noticed, but theirs all glittered metallically.

'Ah, it's your turn next,' Druitt said gently. He reached out and took Thompson by the arm. 'Astonish us.'

Dear Boss
Nic Martin

Tom Bulling had always heard it said that the dead looked peaceful, but he had never found it to be true. *Empty* was the adjective he would use; or *still*. There is a stillness to the recently dead, an emptiness, that the deepest sleeper cannot match.

There wasn't much peace to be found in the features of the woman lying before him. Her eyes unfocused, lids half closed, lips parted from her final breath; she looked almost punch-drunk. The great gash where her throat should be told the tale well enough: it was the expression of a woman in great pain, fainting away as her life gushed out in front of her. Tom felt his stomach turn over as he realised that the last thing those eyes had seen had been her own death, her own murder. Gouts of blood and the face of her killer. Her final thought must have been the knowledge that she was dying. *Fear* was all Tom saw written across her face. Not peace. A bottomless, endless fear. Had her killer had any soothing words for her as she drowned in blood? Unlikely. Was there a colder, crueller death, than to die in terror and pain whilst another stands by and admires their handiwork? This was not murder but butcher's work.

Butcher's work; that's good. Tom scratched a note in his notebook.

"So is that what did it?" Tom traced a line across his neck with his finger.

"More than likely," the attendant said. "Although it was more like . . ." The attendant traced a line across his neck and then again, left to right each time.

"He slit her throat twice?"

"One is little more than a nick compared to the second. Damn near took her head off with the second one. And then there's this."

He pulled back the sheet that kept what dignity she had left. Tom blanched and took a step back, as much from the revealing of the woman's sex as the knife wounds on her abdomen, the doctor's clean, precise incisions contrasting with the jagged cuts of the murderer.

"Good God."

"First body, is it?" The attendant chuckled, folding his arms.

"No, but this is the first murdered woman I've seen. And I had not expected her to be in this way . . . arrayed."

"Ah, a prude, eh?"

"Hardly," snorted Tom. "Not much of a virtue in my line of work, but still, she looks so . . . vulnerable, I suppose." It was strange and sad seeing the woman like this, as naked as the day she was born. Someone must have held her and loved her once. As a babe, as an adult too, perhaps. And now here she lay, cold and naked and alone in death. Her skin pale, nipples stiffened as if by the cold in the room. Tom averted his eyes. Only Susannah had he ever seen so intimately; his few other dalliances being hasty fumbles with skirts hitched up but never removed. Was there somebody missing her tonight?

"I don't think the whore'll mind none. She's used to gents copping an eyeful, I'm sure."

"Definitely a prostitute, then?" Tom scratched another note. "What can you tell me about her?"

"Now you're asking," the attendant said, sucking in his breath. "Like I said, she's a brass, five foot. Still working on a name."

Tom cocked his head to look at her. Her face was delicate looking, with high cheekbones, and framed by brown hair flecked with grey. There were creases around her eyes and mouth. Not an ugly woman, as far as East End prostitutes went, but no *Venus de Milo* either.

"About the deed itself?"

"Not an awful lot to say. She was last seen around half two in the morning. The body was found in Buck's Row about an hour later, throat cut ear to ear. Then, as you can see, he seems to have made a good attempt at opening her belly up. Actually, first we knew about that was when we got her undressed on the slab here and found her guts half hanging out."

Tom grimaced with the bitter taste of bile that crept into his mouth. The attendant smirked to himself but didn't comment. Instead, he pointed at the livid wound snaking through the milky-white flesh of her belly.

"First this deep gash here on her left, then another four, here on her right. Any one of these would be enough to kill, but it was her neck that probably done her in. The villain used a long knife, fairly sharp. Left-handed as well."

Tom scribbled it all down, verbatim. It made a good excuse to look away from the woman, her sleepy face and shredded belly. He tapped his teeth with his pencil, thinking.

"So he cut her throat and then opened her up? Why?"

"Why stab someone thirty times when once would be enough?" the man countered. "Some maniac goes into a frenzy, don't realise what he's done."

Perhaps, Tom conceded, but it felt wrong.

"Who found her? Do you know?"

"You'll have to speak to one of your boys in J Division about all that."

Tom nodded. Shouldn't be too hard. Thanks to his late brother John, he had connections all over the force.

"And she plied her trade just before she died?"

"Actually, no. Whoever killed her didn't fuck her first."

Interesting. Unprintable, but interesting. "Is that unusual?"

The attendant pivoted his hand, *sometimes-yes-sometimes-no*. "It depends. Sometimes they're raped first then killed. Sometimes they're killed because it's cheaper to hand over a knife than a threepenny bit. Seen enough?"

Tom nodded and put his notebook away inside his jacket before thrusting his hands deep into his trouser pockets to warm them while the attendant pulled the sheet back over the woman. Even now at the tail end of summer, the mortuary was as cold as a midwinter's night and the chemical smell was beginning to nauseate.

"I asked you to let me know about anything unusual and you deliver me a dead prostitute," Tom said. "That doesn't strike me as exactly 'out of the ordinary' these days?"

"Not even one hacked up like her?"

"Even then."

The attendant crossed to the door, cracked it open, peeked out. Closed it again. When he spoke, his voice had dropped to a whisper. "What if I was to tell you she wasn't the first like this to cross my table?"

Tom Bulling felt a chill run through him that had nothing to do with the temperature of the mortuary.

"I'm listening," he said quietly.

"What we need," said Bartholomew Webb through the billowing cloud of cigar smoke, "is a really good murder. Something to get the blood pumping, what?"

Tom ran his finger around the inside of his over-starched collar. His "Sunday best", as Susannah had called it, rarely had much occasion to be worn these days, even on Sundays. He must have been a lighter man the last time he had worn this attire, for now it seemed as if it had been tailored from a hundred grasping hands, each seeking to strangle and squeeze the life out of him.

The invitation to come to the Press Club had arrived out of the blue the day before, Moore calling Tom into his office just as he was preparing to leave for the day. He had promised Susannah that he would at least try to be home before nine o'clock for once. She had understood the hours that came with being a newspaper man when they married, but that didn't stop the reality of it being lonely and miserable for her.

"Yes, boss?"

Moore had motioned him to a seat and shut the door behind them. "You've got a dinner jacket and all that, somewhere, I take it?" he said, sitting down on his side of the large, cluttered desk.

"Somewhere, boss. I'm sure Susannah can lay her hands on it. Can't say it gets much use these days. What's the occasion?"

Moore intertwined his fingers, leaned forward. "How do you fancy taking supper at the Press Club tomorrow?"

Holy shit.

Tom took a moment to swallow, clear his throat. Run the words Moore had just said through his head, make sure he had heard them correctly. "The Press Club, boss?"

The Press Club. Fleet Street's own gentleman's club. Members only. Invitations rarer than hens' teeth. Where the air is the rarefied oxygen breathed by editors, publishers, the great and the good. Entering the Press Club was like passing through the gates of Heaven, only far more exclusive.

"Yes," Moore had said, leaning back in his chair. "It seems as though you've come to the attention of Bartholomew Webb and he'd rather like a word."

"A murder, sir?" Tom ventured now.

"Yes, and a damn good one, too. Something to really capture the imagination, sell papers, what? What do you think, sonny? Think you can turn one up for us?"

Moore leaned forward in his seat, looked Tom in the eyes. "Bartholomew has been very impressed with your ability to turn up stories, Tom."

"He has, b—Charles?" His mind spinning over the abrupt turns in conversation, Tom forgot his instructions that here in the Press Club everyone was on first name terms – although Webb was self-important enough to still require an arse-licking from an underling.

"He has, Tom. He was particularly impressed by the story you turned in about the business on Cleveland Street."

"Couldn't print a word of it, of course," Webb interrupted.

"No," agreed Moore. "But it showed . . . resourcefulness."

The story had been passed on to him by a friend on the force whose job it was to rough up the wrong kind of prostitute – in this case the kind that gets itself in trouble with certain members of a certain British family. Tom hadn't really expected such an incendiary story to ever make it to print and he hadn't been disappointed. But, as he had hoped, it seemed to have gotten him noticed.

"Let me ask you, boy," Webb boomed, "what's your job with the Central News Agency? And, before you open your mouth, I don't mean the title Charles has given you. I mean what do you *do*?"

"Well, I suppose I report on current affairs," Tom ventured.

Webb brought his palm down on his side table with a slap loud enough to quieten the tables around them. "WRONG!"

"Sir?"

"Your job, our job, the job of everyone in this club, in every office up and down this street—" Webb waved a drunken arm about, nearly knocking the brandy at his elbow "—is to sell newspapers. Do you understand? Your job is to give us something that will make people buy our paper. If people don't buy papers, none of us eat. Do you see?"

"Yes, I think so."

"You see, Tom, we need a murder we can sell," Moore said quietly. "Something that can run and run . . ."

Tom dropped the dog-end on the street, crushed it out beneath his heel as he did up the buttons on his jacket. It had been a mild night but the sun had set a few hours ago and much of the warmth had bled away shortly after.

Another long night wallowing in the gutter after a long day in the office, then home for a few hours' kip. This was no way to start married life, or any way to start a family, come to that.

The dead prostitute was Polly Ann Nichols and, with a little goosing from Central News and some further editorialising from Webb, her death had shocked London. Tom had written up the murder as the third victim of a maniac terrorising Whitechapel, one sensational murder following on the heels of the last. Not that anyone – not even the family, let alone the community – had actually cared much about the last victim – a tart by the name of Martha Tabram – or the one before that, Emma Smith.

The specifics of Smith's slow death had been both gruesome and unusual enough to raise eyebrows but, depraved as it was, it was clear to Tom and all the policemen he spoke to that her death was nothing to do with the others. Nevertheless, on paper – or rather, *in* the papers – there was nothing to stop them linking all three and inventing a public outcry at the same time. Webb, for his part, relished any opportunity to stick the boot in to Warren, the heavy-handed, unpopular Metropolitan Police Commissioner, now guilty of ignoring bloody murder in the East End that would likely have been swiftly wrapped up had they occurred a few miles further west (or so *The Star* proclaimed).

The Nichols murder had been common knowledge in Whitechapel by breakfast, but within hours of the late editions linking the murders, the public had been whipped up into a frenzy and Buck's Row had become choked with people eager for a glimpse of where the bloody deed had been done.

Tom had walked around Whitechapel for the first time that night, finding the streets alive with talk, the tension in the air a palpable thing. Excitement too – murder was ever a spectator sport in London. But, as the night had worn on, the tension had grown noticeably tighter, the excitement curdling into fear. Tom was well acquainted with Whitechapel by night, the wheels of its seedy, prurient industry turning as much by dark as by day. And yet, come three o'clock in the morning, it was emptier than he had ever seen it, with only the most desperate and the drunk still wandering the streets. And, Tom noted, the most vulnerable. Easy pickings for any villain looking to do harm.

Tom returned the next night and the night after that, watching as the place returned to something like its usual self. Fear may keep people off the streets for a night or two, but poverty will bring them back before long.

A whole week of this now; a bloody waste of time. What was he expecting to find anyway? He'd already filed a write-up of his "patrols"; there was no need to be out here when he could be curled up in the warm beside Susannah.

"Cold for the time of year, ain't it, love?"

Tom started and turned around. A stocky, plain-faced woman, older than Tom by nearly a score, was stood behind him.

"How about I warm you up? What'd you say?"

Tom looked her up and down. One didn't come to Whitechapel for a tart's looks but, even so, the vulgar woman fell below even Tom's meagre standards. It didn't help that she was nearly old enough to be his mother.

"I say, not even if you paid me," Tom replied.

The woman spat a fat glob of phlegm into the dark by his feet and went back into the night, hurling a few choice curses after her.

Tom lit another cigarette, sucked on it until it burned down to his fingers and then headed off in the same direction. He headed up Wilkes Street, turned on Princet Street and into the dark, stinking mouth of Edward Street, little more than a squalid, stinking passage that led on to Hanbury Street.

He was just about to turn on to Brick Lane when he stopped. From somewhere came the flutter of fabric and footsteps echoing away. Tom paused for a moment then carried on, his route taking him circuitously round to Commercial Street half an hour later.

Somewhere behind the dilapidated jumble of taverns, lodging houses, breweries and tenements, the sky was glowing with an eerie red fire that bathed the streets a deep, unsettling scarlet. Tom shivered and reflected again that a man needs more than four hours' sleep to chase the demons away.

From somewhere behind him a whistle blew, the shrill noise cutting through the pre-dawn stillness. Tom stopped mid-stride and cocked his ear. The whistle blew again, a desperate note filled with panic. His blood froze in his veins. It was coming from Hanbury Street.

Tom rushed in the direction of the sound, his feet slapping against the uneven stones. For a moment he couldn't find the source of the panicked whistling; the street was deserted, the whistling seeming to come from the air itself. He noticed a door beside him between a packing-case makers and a cat's-meat shop; it had been flung open, a narrow alley running between the terraced houses, light spilling from the far end. The whistle sounded again, close at hand. Tom dashed down it and out into a little yard beyond.

A woman lay stretched out on the cold cobbles, her stockinged legs drawn up, her feet pointed towards the alley. Her skirts had been pulled up and the killer had torn her open from her sex to her abdomen.

"Mother of God." The red sky wheeled overhead and Tom had to brace himself against the cold bricks to stop himself fainting.

The woman had been disembowelled; her entrails pulled out and draped over her shoulder.

Two men stood over the body: a policeman with curly red hair and a short little man in the soot-stained clothes of a cartman. Both their faces seemed entirely drained of colour. The policeman couldn't take his eyes from the corpse, while the cartman was weeping, his back to the body, his hat clutched tightly in his hands.

They had seemed entirely unaware of Tom's presence, but, at the sound of his scuffing feet, they both looked up.

"Who the fuck are you?" the policeman yelled.

Tom's eyes flicked from the woman's guts to her face. He frowned.

"I said, who the fuck are you?"

Tom pushed himself away from the wall and waved a conciliatory hand at the policeman. He staggered forward like a drunkard, eyes fixed on her face. As he got closer, Tom could see a deep gash across her neck that had all but taken her head off.

"I know her."

"You what?"

"I know her," Tom repeated. "I was talking to her a couple of hours ago."

Her face was swollen, her eyes bulging and her tongue pushed out between her teeth. But it was her.

Tom turned away and vomited, tears streaming down his cheeks.

*　　*　　*

It was full dark by the time Tom returned home. It had taken a good few hours to extricate himself from Scotland Yard's finest, time that would have been better spent at his desk. A liquid breakfast followed, and then a trip to the morgue.

Unsurprisingly, seeing the woman laid out hadn't banished the images of the bloody yard that intruded on Tom's vision every time he closed his eyes. If anything, being stripped and cleaned and placed under the too-bright electric light of the mortuary had made the savagery of the murder all the more apparent. *Ripped* was the word that came to mind, that found its way into the write-up he had submitted for the agency and telegraphed to newspaper offices up and down the country; *ripped* the word that seeped into each local paper's own reporting, trickling down to drawing rooms and breakfast tables the length and breadth of the country . . .

Tom felt sick to his stomach.

A drink had helped. A second had helped even more. The fifth not as much, and so he had abandoned it and finally stumbled home.

"You're home then?"

Tom had opened his front door with less dexterity than he'd meant to and it had banged loudly against the wall. He'd slammed it shut and sagged against it, exhausted. Susannah stood at the end of the hall, a dark silhouette against the soft light spilling out of the kitchen behind her.

"No, it's a fucking ghost," Tom slurred. In his head it had been a light-hearted remark, but from his mouth it sounded bitter and cruel. "Susy, I'm sorry."

"You're drunk."

Tom waved an arm and pushed himself up from the door. "'Mnot."

Susannah stepped aside as he sloped into the kitchen and watched as he pulled a chair out from the table and slumped into it. He rested his elbows against the tabletop and his head in his hands.

"You shouldn't joke about being a ghost. About being dead." Her voice was softer, but Tom still heard the edge to it. "You go out there, to that place, skulking around all night—"

"I don't skulk."

"Walking the same streets that this maniac who guts people like fish . . ."

Torn open from her sex to her abdomen . . .

". . . leaving me here on my own, day after day, night after night . . ."

A deep gash across her throat . . .

". . . you don't know all the things I've imagined, all the fears that find me when you leave me here on my own . . ."

Slender fingers squeezed his shoulder.

Tears ran down Tom's face, unbidden. He reached up, touched her hand, felt the warmth of the blood flowing through her veins.

". . . you don't know how lonely I've been . . ."

The smell of her . . .

Entrails pulled out . . .

"Tommy, you're crying?"

Tom stood, kissed her urgently. She made a noise, somewhere between surprise and anger and kissed him hungrily back. She sighed as he kissed her neck, her fingers fumbling as she undid his belt and drew him out.

Tom grunted at the feel of her fingers against his skin and spun them both around so the table was behind her. He pulled up her skirts as she freed herself from her undergarments, a dizzying sense of vertigo making his head swim.

He lifted her on to the table and she cried out, her hands gripping the edge of the table as she arched her back, exposing her throat. Tom looked down as her writhing hitched her skirts up higher, revealing pale skin and soft dark hair.

Ripped open from her sex to her stomach . . .

"Oh God . . ."

And Tom was done. He pulled himself away, stumbled to the back door, flung it wide and vomited his guts up in the yard, his trousers still round his ankles. Doubled over, he braced himself against the wall with one hand and let the strings of saliva and bile hang from his lips and drip down into the dirt. He turned his head to look at his wife, lying out on their table. She looked back at him through lazy, half-lidded eyes, seeing but unseeing as she finished the work he had started.

The rich, bitter smell of roasting coffee seemed to do little but sharpen the edges of Tom's hangover and intensify the acidic tang lingering at the back of his throat. He glanced down into the thick black liquid cooling in front of him and saw a man he barely recognised gaze balefully back with vacant, haggard eyes.

Tom had woken that morning from the same black dream, the paper on his desk crusted to his face as he jerked awake. Moore had not been impressed. Moore never was.

There hadn't been a murder in weeks. Sales were waning. Something had to be done.

At the start of all this, Thicke, Tom's contact on the force, had given him a suspect: a boot finisher called John Pizer, aka Leather Apron. Tom suspected some private vendetta between the men, but had typed it up anyway. Now that had run its course, Pizer arrested and exonerated, he needed something else. Moore wanted more. A suspect that couldn't be so easily discredited.

There was a perfectly good coffee house on Fleet Street, but Tom needed to get away from newspapermen and the fresh air of a long walk wouldn't hurt. His feet led him east, to a dingy little coffee house just off Commercial Street.

His brother John had died in a coffee house like this. He hadn't even been on duty at the time. He'd been sat having a cup of tea when a man walked in off the street, slashed the throat of the girl behind the counter and calmly walked back out. The girl had lived but John had been stabbed to death trying to apprehend him. You never know when your number's up. Tom knew a few Whitechapel tarts who could testify to that.

With a shake of his head, Tom pulled the items he'd purloined from the agency's withered old bookkeeper out of his pocket and placed them carefully in front of him. He took a sip of his coffee and nearly gagged at the bitterness. Glancing surreptitiously around – no one could see him; he'd sat in an alcove in the far corner for that very reason – Tom pulled a small bottle of gin out his pocket, poured a tot into his coffee and tasted it again. Much better.

Tom picked up his pen, dipped it in the bottle of red ink and set it to the paper.

Dear Boss,

Damn, he'd meant to put *Mister Moore* or some such. Only the boys at the agency called him "boss". Oh well, he only had the one sheet of paper.

I keep on hearing the police have caught me but they wont fix me just yet. I have laughed when they look so clever and talk about being on the right track.

Good. Whoever the killer was, he was bound to be pleased about the pig's ear the Yard were making of it. Now, let's get Pizer out the way, shall we?

That joke about Leather Apron gave me real fits. I am down on whores and I shant quit . . . Cutting? Tearing? No, there really was only one word that would do.

. . . ripping them till I do get buckled. Grand work the last job was.

Suddenly she's there again, hovering just beyond his vision. Torn open from her sex to her abdomen. Her warm guts steaming in the cool morning air. The stench of her shit. Tom knocked back half the gin in one swig. Sod the coffee.

I gave the lady no time to squeal.

Tom stopped to wipe his eyes, put the pen to the paper, took it away. Enough about the girl. Let's go back to childish taunts.

How can they catch me now. I love my work and want to start again. You will soon hear of me with my funny little games.

Tom stopped for a sip of coffee. A line of green ginger beer bottles ran across the top of the shelves behind the counter. Tom remembered a story John had told him about a butcher and amateur poison pen writer who had tried to write his letters using pig's blood kept in beer bottles. It had been at the back of Tom's mind when he had taken the red ink. It would be obvious the letter wasn't really written in blood, but it was still a macabre little touch.

Time to move it forward. Threats.

Tom pinched the bridge of his nose, his pulse pounding in his head. Come on, think like a murderer. You've seen his handiwork. Rippings and guttings. Cutting bits off. Give the punters what they want.

The next job I do I shall clip the ladys ears off and send to the police officers just for jolly. Well, that should do it.

And finally, to business. Tom's business.

Keep this letter back till I do a bit more work, then give it out straight. My knife's so nice and sharp I want to get to work right away if I get a chance. Good luck.

Yours truly . . .

Hmm. Tom tapped his pen against his teeth. "Leather Apron" was good. Whether it was Thicke who came up with that or not, Tom would never know. The name on his letter had to be evocative . . . memorable. Something from a penny dreadful.

Suddenly it dawned on him. The name should encapsulate who he was and what he did.

Jack the Ripper

What else could it be?

"Well, John," Tom muttered to the empty chair opposite, "you always complained I never put your name in print."

Tom had posted the letter on the Tuesday and instantly regretted it. He spent the next couple of days at the bottom of a bottle trying to forget it, or hoping it wouldn't be delivered.

It arrived Thursday morning, addressed to *The Boss*. The boy in the mailing room had sought Edgar out to see if he should take it directly to Moore or not.

Edgar had looked at the red spidery writing on the dog-eared envelope and torn it open. Tom watched from the corner of his eye, palms sweating.

Edgar's eyes ran back and forth across the paper, reached the bottom, turned over, flipped back, read it again. Then he burst out laughing.

Soon the letter had been passed round the whole office, boyish colleagues crowding eagerly round to read it.

Eventually it went to live in Edgar's desk. No one dared show it to Moore.

Sunday morning. Too early, even for him.

Tom swayed on his feet from more than just the cheap gin swimming through his veins. He'd had the dream again. The butchered girl lying on the cold cobbles, knees bent and no knickers as if offering herself, her gash torn open, entrails pulled out, obscene and intimate.

But somehow the nightmare had crawled out of his head and followed him to waking.

Tom gazed down at the soles of four leathery feet bared towards him, at the mottled, marbled skin of legs and thighs and two contrasting mounds of coarse, wiry hair. Tom struggled to look up any further.

The women were like grotesque opposites of each other.

The one on the left was pale but intact. Covered with a sheet she would almost look asleep, but, naked as she was, she looked cold and vulnerable and unmistakably dead. A familiar criss-cross of slashes across her neck were the only marks upon her, her skin pale and pristine.

The woman on the right had been torn apart.

The fiend had sliced her face open from the bridge of her nose deep down into her right jaw. He'd cut off the end of her nose, the stroke biting down through her lip and into the gum beneath. Both cheeks had been carved up and he'd tried to cut off her eyelids. No one could ever mistake her for sleeping.

He'd gutted her too, for good measure, and, like before, he'd placed some of the intestines over her shoulder. "The rest he cut off," the attendant snickered, "placed them carefully under her arm. Can you imagine?"

She'd been stabbed in the groin. The inside of her thighs had been slashed, her sex mutilated, her throat slit. None of this held Tom's attention.

"You won't believe this," the attendant said, not realising Tom wasn't listening. "It's not just her intestines he pulled out. He took a kidney and her womb too. Well, most of it anyway."

Words. Noise. Tom didn't hear. Instead, he pointed.

"Her ear," Tom stammered. Dizzy, as if he were at the very edge of a cliff face, the ground crumbling beneath him.

"He clipped it off."

Tom slumped down in his chair. Most of the desks were empty this early on a Sunday, the news of the double murder yet to reach the boys. Give it an hour or two and the place would be noisier than ever. The story would miss the papers that day but there was much to do for the early editions tomorrow.

Two murders in one night. It looked like Tom's letter hadn't been needed after all – this would reignite the public's ghoulish fascination like nothing else. The fiend had done his work for him.

Tom pulled open his drawer for a quick spot of "hair of the dog". He gazed at the cluttered contents and instead pulled out the little bottle of ink, a pen and a blank postcard.

He didn't stop and think; he didn't dare.

He just wrote.

I was not codding dear old Boss when I gave you the tip, you'll hear about Saucy Jacky's work tomorrow double event this time number one

squealed a bit couldn't finish straight off. ha not the time to get ears for
police. Thanks for keeping last letter back till I got to work again.
    Jack the Ripper

Tom looked down at the postcard, a feeling of nausea turning his stomach that for once had nothing to do with gin or dead prostitutes. This
sickness was his alone.

By the time Tom had got back from mailing the postcard, Edgar was at
his desk, hammering excitedly at his keyboard. A shadow moved behind
the glass of the boss's office.

"Hey, Bulling!" Edgar waved to Tom. "You hear about our friend
Jack?" The boys had all adopted the name amongst themselves.

Tom nodded wearily. "I've just come from the mortuary. I need to
see the letter again, Egg. You still have it?"

Edgar nodded slowly, a frown creasing his large, flat forehead.
"Yeah. Why?"

"Just show it to me, will you?" Tom snapped.

Edgar gave Tom a dirty look – he didn't like being ordered about.
Still, he pulled open his drawer and removed the letter.

Tom snatched it from Edgar's meaty fingers and pretended to read
it. "My God," he muttered.

Edgar frowned. "What? What is it?"

Tom flicked his attention up from the letter. "We need to show this
to Moore," he said, looking Edgar in the eye.

"What?" The man spluttered, spraying Tom with spit. "Have you
lost your wits? You know what he'll say if we bring him rot like this!"

"Edgar, listen to me. One of the tarts. She was missing an ear."

Moore turned the letter over, finished reading it. Again. By Tom's count
he had read it through five times.

Finally, he put it carefully down on his desk and rested his splayed
fingertips on top.

"What is it?" he asked mildly.

"A letter, boss," Edgar said.

"I can see that," Moore replied. "Why are you showing it to me?"

Tom waved a hand in front of Edgar to stop him speaking.

"It came in on Thursday, boss. Obviously we thought it was just a practical joker, but then the murders last night . . . Boss, one of the girls, she had her ear cut off."

Moore didn't say anything. He just sat staring at Tom. Tom had the uncomfortable feeling he was taking the measure of him.

Eventually, Moore turned his attention to Edgar. "Would you mind giving Mr Bulling and I a moment, please, Edgar?"

Edgar blinked twice as though he didn't quite understand, and then forced himself up. "Of course, boss," he muttered. The door creaked quietly behind him.

Moore leaned forward, pinning Tom with his pale blue stare. Time itself seemed to stand still.

"Tell me the truth, Tom," Moore said at last, his voice a soft rasp. "The letter's a hoax."

Tom licked his lips, mouth suddenly dry. "I don't know, boss. Probably." He met Moore's eyes. "But it's a story."

"It's a few inches. At best." He leaned back again in his chair. The atmosphere seemed to lift. Tom knew he'd reached a decision.

"Write it up," Moore said. "But make it clear we think it's a hoax. The police will have to see it, of course. And if they find whoever wrote it, he's on his own. Understand?"

Tom made himself look mildly confused. "Of course."

Moore nodded. Tom was dismissed.

He was halfway out the door when Moore called after him.

"The thing with accountants, Tom, is that they take stock of everything. Literally. Like the pot of red ink that went missing last week. Keep an eye out for it, will you?"

*   *   *

The next day's papers were a sensation. News of the murder of Elizabeth Stride and Catherine Eddowes had seeped out by word of mouth in pubs and dining rooms across the East End and beyond. A shocked public clamoured for all the gory details.

And now the monster had the name. The two dead women had been identified, their names printed with the sad, squalid details of their lives and deaths.

But there were only three words on everyone's lips.

Jack the Ripper.

The days swept past in a blur of cheap booze and dirty work, turning up witnesses, suspects, friends and experts. Tom kept himself moving, kept running. The sad, hollow women were always waiting for him, standing in the darkness, opening themselves up, spilling themselves out, their cold fingers whispering at the back of his neck. He worked and drank to exhaustion, falling into a dreamless sleep that kept their accusing looks at bay. Awoke at his desk and started again.

The dying warmth of autumn bled into a chill, wet winter. London awoke each dawning day to no news of further "rippings" but it didn't matter, the story had a life of its own now. More letters from other hoaxers appeared; one even contained a human kidney, marked "From Hell". How Tom wished he'd thought of that.

The flames of interest burned ever brighter as the calendar turned to November. No news was news itself. Where was the fiend, the butcher, this so-called Ripper? Where had he fled to? Why hadn't the Yard caught him? What good were they anyway? The press knew more about the Ripper than the police ever had.

Tom stood naked in the bathroom, dragging the razor carefully down his face, the blade rasping against his skin as he shaved away five days' worth of growth. He finished, shut the blade and looked down at himself. His ribs stuck out from his chest, his stomach was a stretched sack of skin. Images of Catherine Eddowes flooded through him, her stomach concave where her insides had been scooped out.

Tom dressed for warmth. The bitter winter winds were blowing and a man could catch his death on the streets of Whitechapel.

The sheets in the bedroom still smelled of Susannah. Sometimes he breathed her in and wept. He had slept downstairs last night, curled up on the too-hard settee. He preferred sleeping at his desk.

Tom's hands were shaking; he took a medicinal nip of gin and, properly fortified, set out for his nightly patrol.

The cold air bit mercilessly at Tom's face so that entering the suffocating heat of the pub felt like being lovingly smothered with a warm pillow.

"Usual please, Mike."

Mike jerked a hairy thumb at the table by the hearth. "It's sat over there."

"I'm sorry?" Tom asked, blinking. The world always seemed a few steps ahead of him and he was constantly running to catch up.

"Gentleman over there ordered it for you."

Tom followed the landlord's gesture. A man was sitting reading a paper at the table by the fire. Two pints sat on the table in front of him: one half drunk, the other set in front of the empty chair opposite.

"Who is he?"

"No idea," Mike said, stalking off to serve someone else.

It was probably just someone wanting to do a little business. Well, a drink's a drink.

Tom took a seat, raised his pint to the stranger. "My thanks for the drink, friend."

The man folded up his paper with a sigh.

Tom frowned. "Do I know you?"

The man didn't reply. There was something terribly wrong about his eyes. Tom wanted to leave but felt rooted to the spot; held there by the force of the man's stare.

"So, you're the man who speaks with my voice?"

"I'm s-sorry?" Tom stuttered.

"I tried writing my own letter. Even sent a present. Didn't work. Wasn't the same. Still, I'm not a professional like you." The man took a sip of his beer, sucked the foam from his thin moustache. "I've got me other skills."

Tom could feel his heart beating painfully in his chest. Felt the skin prickle at the back of his neck. He wanted to look round for Edgar, sniggering. "This is a wind up?"

"I reads the paper, asks myself much the same," the man said. "Hear your wife's moved out to Miller's Court, Mr Bulling. Tut-tut. You should know how to treat a woman." His eyes glistened in the firelight.

"Think maybe I pays her a visit." The man stood, drained his pint, shrugged on his coat. "Look for me there in the morning, Mr Bulling. I'll have a present all wrapped up and waiting."

He made to walk past Tom, but stopped and rested his hand on his shoulder. "I've been so wondering about you, Mr Bulling," the man sighed. "But now that we've met it's all so disappointing. But then you probably feel the same, I shouldn't wonder."

The hand squeezed his shoulder and withdrew. Tom didn't turn, didn't watch the man leave. It took time for his hand to stop shaking enough to lift his pint. For a long time he just sat staring at the glass. And then he gulped it down and ordered another.

Dawn broke late in the warrens of Whitechapel. Tom awoke, curled up in the gutter, cold dirty, vomit-crusted.

Footsteps and rushing. A rippling of excitement. Words that cut through the alcohol fog like a hurricane, a jolt of electricity in his veins.

Ripper. Murder.

Tom forced himself to his feet, lurched into the hurrying throng, let himself be carried by the tide. He knew, deep in his guts, where they were taking him.

The whole of the East End seemed to be out on the streets this morning, gushing from their holes to collect here, a great, fetid pool of humanity. Tom had never seen so many people in one place at one time. But here they were, all trying to cram themselves into Miller's Court, all wanting to be part of the story.

The boys of J Division were struggling to turn back the tide. Tom knew one of them, a sergeant called Boynes; he forced his way forward, slipped the man all the money he had in his pocket and, with a nod and a sly look, was allowed through, to much hullabaloo behind.

Tom dashed through, crying, whimpering, calling Susannah's name. A breadcrumb trail in blue led him to the door of number thirteen.

Led him to a scene from Hell.

The air was thick with the cloying smell of blood; there was an acrid tang behind it like something burnt. A group of men, Scotland Yard's finest no doubt, huddled round the bed in the far corner, complexions pale, hats in hand. Tom pushed his way through.

A wet, faceless lump of meat lay inside out on the bed, blood saturating the sheets, pooling on the dusty floor beneath. Arms and legs, bone white on scarlet, and a lump of gristle where a head should be were the only clues that this had ever been a woman.

Tom looked at the familiar tatters of clothing, the sodden mop of hair. He must have screamed; suddenly the men were yelling and he was being pulled backwards by two stout constables. He screamed and kicked, crying his wife's name over and over until his throat felt like fire.

The constables let him go at the entrance to Miller's Court, the crowd beyond too thick to put him out on the street proper. Tom kept calling Susannah's name anyway, pointlessly, until a pair of eyes in the crowd snatched his attention.

He stood, looking at the man, saw the garb he was wearing. Wheels turned in his head and suddenly Tom saw it all clearly for the first time: why the murders all took place at weekends; why the gaps between rippings, longer and longer each time.

Tom stared, open-mouthed.

The man smirked, dipped his hat to Tom and strode away through the crowd.

Tom shouted, pointed, begged people to stop him as he fought his own way through the suffocating mob. Nobody listened, they just shoved him back, another raving drunk. They'd heard it all before.

Tom sat shaking, shaking enough to make the chair rattle. There was a sour smell in the little office; distantly Tom realised he was probably the source.

Complicated emotions flickered across Moore's face: anger; revulsion; regret; pity. He was letting Tom go. Pizer was suing everyone who had defamed him and all the papers were pointing their finger at the agency. Worse, the police knew where the "Dear Boss" letter had come from. Moore had enough connections to spare Tom from prosecution, but protection came at a price.

More to the point, Tom could barely string five words together.

None of it mattered.

"Boss, I know who the Ripper is. I know who killed my wife."

Moore sat back, recoiling from the sour smell of Tom's breath. "Tom," he said kindly, "your wife isn't dead. It was just some poor tart. Go home. Clean yourself up, dry out and go find Susannah."

"No, you're wrong, wrong. I've found two witnesses, see. Two—" Tom held up two fingers "—who *swear* they saw Kelly at ten o'clock the morning after. That's hours after she should be dead."

"Tom, please. Go home."

Moore stood and held the door open. Tom opened his mouth to protest, then stopped. Fine, he'd come back with more proof. Moore wasn't stupid and the Ripper still sold papers. If he gave him proof, Moore would print it. He'd have to.

Winter gives way to spring; spring turns to summer; summer fades to autumn; autumn frosts to winter. Again, and again and again. A new century dawns. The Ripper passes into history.

A figure shambles through Whitechapel, cursing at the walking tours wandering around Hanbury Street and Miller's Court. He's no longer welcome at the Ten Bells – they don't take well to people harassing the tourists there.

The man heads west, tatty shoes slapping against cobbles. Long fingernails pick at scabs, scratch at fleas.

He stumbles into Fleet Street, dives into the flowing river of men going hither and thither. He catches glimpses of familiar faces, calls out to them, though their names are lost to him.

Wait, here's one now . . .

"Edgar! How are you old chap? Have I got a story for you? I know who the Whitechapel murderer was! What a scoop! I can tell you all about the Ripper! Edgar?"

Oh well.

"Wallace! Wallace, old chap! Stop a moment. Have I got a story for you . . .?"

His Last Victim
K. G. Anderson

"Hoy there, pretty Judy!"

Puryear snickered as I took a turn about the hall, swishing my skirts. I came to a stop beside the burly plain-clothes man and smacked him on the arm with a worn kid glove. "That's 'Inspector Judy' to you, Sergeant."

General laughter.

"Starritt, it'll be the devil getting you back into uniform," came a growl from the back.

Like most of the men in the drafty muster hall at Scotland Yard, I was dressed tonight for undercover work. That said, I was the only member of Central Investigations wearing an actual dress: an elaborately flounced deep blue silk with padded bustle and a tattered petticoat peeking out beneath the hem. A brown wool jacket with worn velvet trim at the wrists completed my ensemble. Not the latest London fashion for autumn of 1888, but, then, Whitechapel was hardly Kensington.

And Whitechapel was where we'd be going.

When Inspector Abberline strode through the door, he pretended to ignore the wolf whistles my costume was attracting.

"For the grace of God," the inspector muttered, as I hurried past him to a front-row seat. I belatedly thought to totter a bit in my high-heeled boots, demonstrating an unfamiliarity with ladies' garb that only I knew to be an affectation.

More than three dozen constables and plain clothes men from the CID and H Division were crowded into the hall for Abberline's briefing. Some sat on chairs or perched on battered desks. A few latecomers, hastily shoving pipes and tobacco into jacket pockets, stood against the walls.

Abberline consulted a sheaf papers on the table beside him. He appeared in no hurry to begin. Then, abruptly, he straightened up and smacked a copy of *The Times* on the table. I saw the word "Ripper" in the broadsheet's banner headline.

"I can't say I fully approve of what we're about to do," the inspector began, glancing over at me. "But, gentlemen, we find that our backs are to the wall."

Abberline paced as he talked, occasionally gesturing toward the large map of Whitechapel behind him. I found it hard not to fidget. We'd heard much of this before.

What the press called the "Ripper" investigation had been tossed back and forth between the Metropolitan Police Whitechapel CID and Central Office at Scotland Yard as if it were a hot potato. And plenty of fingers were getting singed. They'd put a chief inspector from Scotland Yard over Abberline to "coordinate" the inquiry. Gents from the Whitechapel Vigilance Committee were bumbling around in the streets with some private detectives they'd hired. Add to this a pack of baying journalists, led by scoundrel named Bulling. There were even rumors that Sherlock Holmes, the consulting detective, had taken an interest in the case.

You couldn't help but feel sorry for Abberline, by all accounts a career desk man. Tonight, he stood pale but determined before us and attempted to rally the troops.

"This madman has been at work since August," he was saying. "He's claimed at least five victims and now taunts us through the press as 'Saucy Jack.' When I met with Sir Charles today, I assured him that we could stop this depraved scoundrel and restore the reputation of Scotland Yard."

A general nodding of heads and muttering of affirmatives. Abberline stopped pacing, surveyed the room, and gave a short nod. He muttered a few words to Inspector Lashley and left the hall.

Voices rose, then died back as Lashley, a grizzled old-timer, lumbered to the front and rapped the table for order.

"You heard the inspector," he said. "We'll nab this Ripper fellow — even if it takes sending out one of our finest as a ladybird."

Laughter rippled through the room and less elegant sobriquets for my role were offered.

We'd already spent five weeks on the streets disguised as gamblers, drunkards, and con men – in short, precisely the types who'd be expected to be roaming Whitechapel, scene of the Ripper murders, in the wee hours. I'd been playing the role of an inebriated toff. Last week, as we returned before dawn to change back into our own clothes, someone joked that we should set out a woman as bait for the killer.

All eyes turned to me: slim, clean-shaven, and at five feet, five inches, one of the smallest men on the force.

I'd shrugged and allowed that I'd be willing to give it a try. I'd borrow an outfit from my landlady. I didn't feel it necessary to mention that I was already in possession of a lovely chignon wig.

Now here I stood in my get-up. The dark wig was topped by a suitably cheap and garish hat Puryear had borrowed from his aunt, a shopkeeper at the Baker Street Bazaar. Liberal applications of rouge and pearl powder completed my disguise.

"They don't much care if we catch this fiend or kill him," Lashley said. "Our job, lads, is to get Jack off the street and out of the newspapers."

He brandished the copy of *The Times* Abberline had left behind.

"'Gripped By Fear,' that's what they're saying." Lashley tossed the broadsheet back on the table. "Well, they've got that much right. Aren't any of those judies wanting to meet this Ripper. They've taken to going about their business in pairs. Which means that a lone woman – our Inspector Starritt – will be mighty tempting."

Turning to the wall map, Lashley took us through the evening's plan. Nineteen men in plain clothes would stroll the streets and keep an eye on the pubs, gin houses, and street corners. Ten uniformed constables would make their customary rounds. Everyone would be on the lookout for me – they all turned to mark my costume – as I walked a route that criss-crossed Commercial Road. Whenever possible, I'd be discreetly tailed by two of the undercover men.

On our way to the armory, Puryear fell in beside me. "What madman could resist you, darling?" he said, giving me a wink.

I laughed, but stared straight ahead and quickened my pace. I wondered how much Puryear knew of my life outside working hours. After all, his brother, a member of my dressing club, was the friend who'd told me about the opening with Scotland Yard five years ago. No time to worry about that now. I had plenty to occupy my thoughts.

These days we were going on duty armed to the teeth. Tonight, I tucked a regulation Webley pistol into my beaded reticule and a silver whistle into my jacket sleeve. A six-inch knife went inside a special leather sheath sewn into the bodice of my gown, giving an unpleasant new meaning to the word "cleavage". God knows, we'd seen enough cleaving recently.

Despite this arsenal, I had no plans to go hand-to-hand against the Ripper, by all evidence a man of unusual strength and savage determination. The expectation was that I'd lure him to attack, sound the alarm, and leave his capture to my comrades.

For the past two days, I'd been conducting quite literal dress rehearsals to get a feel for Whitechapel from a streetwalker's point of view. No question but that my feminine costume was believable; at dusk last night, I had already been followed by prospective trade. But, more importantly, I'd gotten to know the working women who gathered at the Blue Dog, a gin shop with a reputation for cheap drink and a warm hearth. Any resentment the women might have had about a new girl working their streets was muted by their fear of the Ripper. They'd known his victims, and immediately set about telling me the grisly stories.

Martha Turner (or Tabram, depending on who you asked) had led a client into a tenement in George's Yard for a four-penny quick one only to be stabbed thirty-nine times.

"Two different blades he used," said a young Irish girl in a tatty pink dress.

Later that month, Mary Nichols had been found on Buck's Row with her throat cut open.

"Still warm, she was, when the constables got there," came a voice from the back of the room. The speaker, a blowzy older woman, shuddered and turned back to her tumbler of gin.

The Ripper's next victim had been "Dark Annie" Chapman. Many of the women knew her from Crossingham's on Dorset Street where she'd done crochet work and paid eight pence a night for a shared bed. Short of a few pennies for the room, Annie had gone out late to turn a trick. She never returned. Her body was found the next morning in the backyard of a Hanbury Street tenement – minus the innards.

The latest had been the double murder. "Long Liz" Stride was found with her throat cut near Dutfield's Yard. While the police rushed to the scene, the Ripper was just around the corner at Mitre Square, dispatching Catherine Eddowes. "Kate" was discovered in a pool of blood, skirts pulled up to her waist.

"Killed her right under their noses," someone behind me said softly. "Much good them coppers do."

I turned to see a statuesque young woman I judged to be in her late twenties. She introduced herself as "Ginger Mary." She dandled a little boy, feisty as a terrier pup, on her knee, introducing him as "my nevvy, Beau." She even treated him to a sip of gin.

To my surprise, many of the judies brought their children with them to the Blue Dog in the afternoons. The little ones would be dropped off with friends or family before work began in the evening. Despite their fascination with the gory details of the Ripper murders, most of the women had returned to working the fog-shrouded streets. Quite simply, they needed the money.

When I enquired today about a place to doss down, Ginger Mary suggested that I pay for a share of a bed in her rented room on Miller's Court. I didn't let on that I knew the place, which was often described as the most dangerous street in London. As we approached the grim tenement, I recognized it as the very rooming house where Jack's first victim had put up for a while. I'd interviewed the tight-lipped landlady, a Mrs McCarthy, early in the investigation but today she showed no signs of recognizing me, in day dress and bonnet, as a copper. I paid for a week's lodging and told Mary I was going round to my cousin's to pick up my bag and would be back later that night.

I returned just before nine, dressed for the evening and carrying a small carpet bag containing a towel and some toiletries. Ginger Mary sat at a small table in the shabby, much-painted room, using a mirror propped against the wall to apply her rouge. She indicated that I should put my bag under the sagging bed.

"About the rules," she said, squinting at her reflection and fussing with a pale blue hair ribbon as she talked. "They say we can't bring a gent in the room. But if you have one wants his privacy, they'll look t'other way. It might cost you a tuppence, at most."

My red-haired roommate was, at a distance, a handsome woman. But she was missing an eyetooth and her breath was acrid with gin. I tried to imagine how drunk or desperate a man would have to be to select her for a bit of fun, but my imagination (which I've been told is quite lively) flagged at the challenge.

When Ginger Mary had finished her toilet we strolled out together along Dorset Street. It was now quite dark, and sounds of carriages and an evening crowd could be heard in the distance. At the corner of Crispin, we passed two raucous drunks, whom I recognized as officers Thompson and Varner. Varner honored us with an exaggerated bow that got him a perfunctory offer from Mary.

When he turned her down, a shadow crossed her face.

"Pity," she said. "He seemed a nice one."

I coughed and nodded.

"I need some business, or else it's back to Cardiff," she said, confirming the Welsh background I'd suspected.

"You'd be safer there," I said.

She shrugged. We walked on in silence for a while.

"I knew two of the girls killed by him – that Ripper fellow," Mary said. "One of them a ways over there."

She pointed north toward Hanbury Street where Annie Chapman had been killed.

"But not to worry. Everyone says he's moved on to Gateshead now." That rumor had been in the papers.

Mary brightened as we approached McCarty's.

"A bit of gin might warm us. And there's often a good sort in there that'll buy you a drink."

When I declined, she hurried into the pub, leaving me alone on the streets.

I'd dressed often as a woman, but I went out in public only in a discreet manner, taking a cab to and from private parties, usually in the company of another "dressed" friend. You know the arrangement: two young gentlewomen on their way to a private dinner.

Finding myself out alone at night, dressed, in a part of town as decadent as Whitechapel, was both stimulating and disturbing. I enjoy playing the part of a demure society woman; it had never occurred to me to dress as a prostitute. And a woman alone on the grimy streets of Whitechapel at night could be nothing but. For years I'd prided myself on the ability to pass so well that no one noticed anything out of the usual as I tripped up the stairs to a friend's home. Now there was no possibility of going unnoticed; men with eyes bright with drink and drugs examined me frankly and the slow smiles on their lips told me that they saw me as woman.

I was at first amused to note that I responded in character. I found myself swaying along the narrow streets, returning their smiles and indulging in a broad flirtation.

"They'll have you on the boards at the Old Vic, Starritt," mumbled a drunk (I recognized him as Inspector Crosby) as he stumbled past me.

"Damn you."

My husky voice was, as always, the weak point of my disguise.

We were well into November and the evening was cold. My wool and velvet jacket, though lined, was flimsier than I'd thought. I observed others of my new profession clutching thick woolen shawls around their shoulders and wished I'd thought to bring one. Tomorrow night, I told myself. Unless, of course, we caught the Ripper tonight. I shivered again, and it wasn't all the weather.

By mid-evening, Whitechapel had the air of an unnaturally late-season country fair. People crowded past on Commercial Road: couples arm in arm, groups of young gentlemen headed for the gambling dens, pairs of confidence men who clearly knew their way about, and sometimes a lone man whose elaborately casual stroll and darting eyes marked him as a shopper for the local goods. Occasionally, a sharp glance alerted me to the presence one of my fellow officers. Once or twice, a particularly hard and appraising stare made me wonder if I might not be meeting the gaze of Mad Jack himself.

When I turned into any of the side streets, the crowds thinned and the city was surprisingly dark and silent. Street lights were few, and often the only light was from the open doorways of tenements where women gathered in twos and threes, and restless children could be heard playing on the steep stairways. All too often a pile of refuse against a wall would stir, revealing itself to be a human being. I'd see a hand reaching out, or hear the muffled rattle as a bottle fell against the cobblestones.

The evening wore on. Each time I crossed Commercial Road, the voices were harsher, the lighting more garish. My delicate, high-heeled walking boots were rapidly losing their charm. I stumbled over the cobblestone and cursed softly. It occurred to me that much more of this assignment might spoil my pleasure in dressing.

Men had favored me with flirtatious glances early in the evening but now one or two of them grabbed my arm – something I'd not expected. One gentleman proved particularly difficult to disengage. I caught only the flash of a silver tooth as he dragged me, protesting, toward a side street.

He was no doubt surprised to find his other arm grasped firmly by a constable who led him away.

Puryear appeared at my side. "Time to go in," he said in a low voice. "It's nearly two."

Although exhausted, I shook my head.

"I'm taking you in, miss," Puryear said, this time in a mock-official tone. I thought the better of it and went along.

The next night was more of the same, only worse. By now my boots were ruined – likely beyond help from the cobbler, and how could a lady explain this kind of wear?

I glanced at my wristlet watch and saw to my relief that it was close to midnight. I'd become vaguely aware of a man walking quietly behind me. I could only hope it was one of my colleagues – or the Ripper, closely followed by my backup.

I drifted down a side street, trying not to limp in the cursed footwear, and stopped to pose under a gaslight.

It was then, through a veil of fog, I caught sight of a woman I thought might be Ginger Mary. She was in negotiations with a slight, dark man in a well-tailored topcoat. I fiddled with my reticule, adjusted my hat, and continued to watch them. Sure enough, it was Mary. She took the fellow's arm, and they headed in the direction of our room at Miller's Court. On a hunch, I stepped out of the light and followed them, staying close to the buildings. As they passed beneath a street light, I saw that he carried a Gladstone bag. My heart jumped – we expected the Ripper to have just such a case for transporting the tools of his gruesome trade. When the fellow cast a look over his shoulder, I ducked into a foul-smelling doorway. A moment later, I stepped out into the street again, trying to drift along behind the couple. I hoped my tail was, in turn, following me. I glanced back several times, but saw no one. Thicker fog was rolling in from the river.

Now, oddly, there was another up ahead. A tall fellow dressed in the shabby garb of a laborer shambled along behind Mary and her John. I wracked my tired brain. Was he one of ours?

I slipped around the corner from Dorset Street just in time to see Mary and her customer opening the door of our doss and stepping in. The door closed behind them, and a moment later a light appeared in the window. The roughly dressed man following them walked past the door and vanished in the fog.

I stopped and looked around for my backup. Nothing we knew about the Ripper suggested that he took any intimacies with his victims, so I had to assume that if it were he, he'd be getting right down to business with his knives. I crept up to the door and listened. Nothing. The window was covered with a heavy blanket; all I could see at one edge was a sliver of flickering candlelight.

Still no sign of my backup. Apparently, I'd have to use the whistle to summon them. If the Ripper bolted, or came to the door, blade in hand, it would be up to me to hold him until the others arrived. Far from ideal, but the best plan I had.

I reached into my sleeve for the whistle, rummaging around in the lining and lace. Damn. I checked the other sleeve. Then the first one again.

Had I heard a moan from the room? Again I patted both sleeves: nothing. No whistle, no way to summon backup. Seconds were ticking by.

I reached for the Webley and was startled to find myself without a holster. But of course, the gun was in my reticule! I dug in the beaded bag, brought out the pistol, and braced myself to kick open the door and take on Mary's assailant.

I took a step back, and that's when he grabbed me from behind.

"Don't move."

His voice in my ear was crisp, the tone cultured – and oddly familiar. I struggled but found myself held tight. A knife at my throat stifled my instinct to shout.

"The man in there is the Ripper," the low voice said.

I held very still, aware of the sharp blade against my skin. "And I'm the police," I said in an equally low tone.

He withdrew the knife, spun me around by the shoulders, and peered into my face. "Damn."

Despite the diction, it was the man in workers' clothing.

I opened my mouth to call for help, but he clapped across it a damp cloth. I struggled, unable to avoid inhaling the perfumed ether. Soon I felt myself lowered to the cold, hard cobblestones. My hands and feet were numb. As I lay there, fighting the chemical, I could hear two men arguing in the doorway of the doss.

"We must go," I heard my assailant say. "Now."

"No, no," said the second voice, high-pitched and agitated. "I still have so much work to do."

"Your work's done, sir," said the first voice.

There was the sound of scuffling, then footsteps clattering past on the cobblestones by my head. Despite my efforts, blackness consumed me.

A constable found me a short while later, as I struggled to raise myself on my elbows.

He shrilled his whistle while I tried to speak.

"In there." My voice was a ragged croak. "The Ripper."

My skull felt as though it were about to split. I rolled on to my knees and got to my feet, cursing the high-heeled boots and the tangle of skirts and petticoats. Puryear and two others had arrived. They pushed open the door, peered inside, and emerged, pale. I heard one of them vomit. Someone whistled, again and again, for backup. I tottered over to the doorway.

"You don't want to look." Puryear threw out an arm to block my way.

I pushed past him.

What I saw in the doss was beyond anything I could have imagined.

You've seen the pictures from the files. Ginger Mary lay on her back, stripped naked, one leg bent at an angle. He'd gutted her, neck to thigh. I was told later that flesh and organs removed were found beneath the bed. But what I saw that morning was her face, slashed again and again until it was quite featureless. I hoped for a moment that it was another woman, but I recognized, surrounding the gore, her lovely ginger hair and the pale blue ribbon.

I didn't dare approach any closer. The floor was pooled with blood and marked with footprints I hoped would be saved as evidence.

While Puryear and the others roused the landlady and neighbors, I gathered my filthy skirts above my boots and limped back to the armory.

"Enter."

Abberline came from behind his desk and motioned me to a chair. The room looked like a banker's office, devoid of personality. The inspector sat down in a chair across from mine, looking as if he'd been up late closing the books. In a manner of speaking, he had.

"Inspector Starritt, I trust you have recovered from the injuries you sustained last week."

"Yes, sir. And I've submitted my report."

"I've read it."

Abberline stood without drama, and walked slowly to his window. It overlooked Whitehall Place, crowded with carriages and pedestrians in the dark winter afternoon. A fire burned in the hearth, but the large windows exposed the room to the chill winds.

I shivered, and told myself again that I wouldn't be giving up much in leaving the force.

"You omitted something from your report," Abberline said.

"Sir?"

"You recognized the man who attacked you."

I answered carefully. "Sir, I don't believe he was the Ripper."

"Indeed he wasn't," Abberline said. "I don't think you saw the Ripper. I think you saw—" He left the sentence hanging.

I shook my head. There was no way that I could explain how I recognized the man who'd gently but firmly rendered me unconscious.

Abberline's mouth twitched. Was it a grimace or a fleeting smile? "You saw someone who shares your . . . skill in disguises. I'm sure that's how you knew him."

With relief, I nodded. I could give him that much. I was leaving the police, after all. I believed Abberline was a fair man.

"This will go no further than my office," he said.

I gave in. "I'd seen him at parties. Dressed sometimes as a woman. Other times, he escorts other men who are dressed. I think it's a fascination of his . . . But, really, I don't know his name. Or why he'd be in league with Ripper."

"In league? Hardly." Abberline gave a dry laugh that ended in a cough. "Your compatriot caught the Ripper – yet another one of his services to the Empire."

Abberline leaned closer and lowered his voice. "Mad Jack turns out to be someone with powerful connections. Thanks to your friend's intervention, the 'Ripper' has been put away somewhere where he'll never walk the streets of London – or any other British city – again. Our work is done. And, as for your friend, he's been acknowledged, once more, in the highest circles."

Services to the Empire. Acknowledged in the highest circles. I was beginning to realize the identity of my fellow dresser.

Abberline continued, "Your own role in this case has been recognized, I believe, quite fairly?"

I nodded. "Yes, sir. Thank you, sir."

Abberline stood up, signaling the end of our interview. "My thanks to you as well, Inspector, and my very best wishes to you on your retirement."

I was married in June 1889 to Margaret, who knew and understood my interests and was, in fact, an amateur thespian and a superb costumier. We moved to Brighton, bought a small hotel, and soon became part of a social circle where there were dressing events perhaps once a fortnight.

It was at a private party there, perhaps a dozen years later, that I saw the man who'd caught Jack the Ripper. Of course, he was not wearing his trademark deerstalker hat and Inverness coat. He was dressed that night as a wealthy dowager, resplendent in a costume of black widow's weeds and jet that complemented his long jaw and severe features.

Our eyes met, and we nodded to each other from across the room. It went no further.

The Face of the Killer
Violet Addison and David N. Smith

———

The man stood at the bar had blood on his hands.

On any morning it would not be unusual for Tom to see the victims of the previous night's drunken fights still lying in the gutters, or the victors of such battles still staggering back to their dosshouse, all marked with blood. However, that morning the marketplace at the end of the road was bustling with rumours of another brutal murder, so any man covered in someone else's blood was not going to go unnoticed.

The stranger had entered the pub as soon it was open, only a few minutes after the landlady had opened the doors. The sky outside was still red with the light of dawn, as the stranger sat down beside Tom and they both ordered their first drinks of the day. The Prince Albert pub was warm and dry, so it was a good place to spend the day, and there was usually some good company to be found at the bar. Tom had hoped to find someone generous enough to buy him another drink, but the moment he saw the bloodstained stranger, he knew that he was not going to have any such luck that morning.

The stranger's hand shook as he passed over a single penny to the woman behind the bar.

Tom could not stop himself from staring at the red stains on the man's fingers and knuckles. There were lumps of congealing blood beneath his fingernails. The woman behind the bar looked at the stranger with obvious suspicion, but she still accepted his coin, as nobody in Whitechapel would ever turn away money.

Once the coin was safely in her apron pocket, she slipped away, hurrying across to the landlady to seek guidance on what to do with the sinister, bloodstained customer.

The agitated man, apparently oblivious to the stares he was drawing, raised his half-pint mug to his lips and drank; but, as he lifted his arm, his coat fell open, revealing a badly torn shirt and further splashes of blood around his neck.

The stranger looked as if he had been in a violent fight, but his skin was not cut or even scratched, so all of the blood must have come from his opponent. Nobody could have lost that much blood and walked away.

Tom stared at the man, uncertain what to do.

He did not feel inclined to confront a man who may well be a brutal murderer; he was far too sober for such an act of bravery. That kind of stupidity got people killed.

Instead, he focused on studying the man, so that he could at least give the police a description. He was around the same height as Tom, over forty years old, with a distinctive ginger moustache. He had a square chin, a small nose and short, sandy hair. There was, however, something abnormal about his features, they lacked the symmetry that Tom would expect to find in a face, its two halves not quite matching up.

It was a face he would remember for ever.

The stranger glanced at him, suddenly aware that he was being watched. His eyes nervously flitted around the room, noticing that the landlady and the woman who had served him were also now staring at him and whispering to each other.

He used his bloodstained left hand to pull the collar of his coat closed, suddenly self-conscious of his torn shirt and the red marks on his neck. He hurriedly finished the last of his beer. In the time it had taken the man to down his drink, Tom had barely touched his own. Tom was in no hurry, he was well practised in making a half pint last a morning. By contrast, the stranger suddenly appeared to be very keen to get away. He turned his back on the bar, leaving via the main door, glancing furtively around him as he stepped out on to the street.

The landlady, Mrs Fiddymont, no longer making any attempt to conceal her concerns, followed him outside. Tom glanced at his own mug, knowing that any decent man would follow and assist her, but he did not want to abandon his barely touched drink. He could not afford another one. He would have to be a fool to abandon it; unattended beer mugs had a habit of rapidly disappearing in any London pub.

A few minutes later, Mrs Fiddymont returned to the bar, breathless with excitement, saying she had dispatched a friend to follow the stranger. The whole bar, now rapidly filling, was soon speculating wildly about whether they had just had an encounter with the infamous Leather Apron, who had been terrorising their streets.

An hour later, they learned that the rumours of another murder were true. The body of another streetwalker had been discovered over on Hanbury Street, just on the other side of the market, only a short walk from where they were.

As a young carter gave them the horrific details, even the most excitable gossips of the audience became pale and silent. Much of the resulting conversation focused on one key detail, that the woman's throat had been slit in exactly the same manner as Polly Nichols, meaning it was undoubtedly the work of the same killer.

"Do we know who it was?" enquired Mrs Fiddymont, keen to learn as many details as she could about the murder. "Which woman?"

"Dark Annie," replied the carter, causing a smattering of gasps from around the pub. Many of the clientele knew her, as she only lived a few streets away and could regularly be found plying her trade on the busy thoroughfare of Commercial Street.

She had been a good woman, cursed with bad luck. She had often talked fondly of her eldest daughter, who had died at the age of twelve. It was the event that had brought her to ruin, her marriage being unable to withstand the loss, while she could only find solace in the numbness of drink. Her husband had continued to support her financially until he died, but after that there was only one way she could find to support herself.

Tom had shared a bed with her on at least two occasions, possibly three.

Mrs Fiddymont was already talking about going to the police, offering her eyewitness account of what she had seen, and they would doubtless be much more interested in the report of a respectable publican than they would in that of drunken vagrant like him. His testimony would not be needed. Tom downed the last of his drink and stood up. He left the pub and headed in the opposite direction to the killer, in the hope of picking up an afternoon of work from one of the stallholders.

As he walked down the busy street alongside Spitalfields market, he found himself confronted by a police handcart, being drawn along the cobbled road by a single officer. On its back was a single wooden coffin, its sides stained with blood.

In it, Tom was sure, was whatever remained of the body of Annie Chapman.

It was only at that moment that he realised the severity of what he had done.

He had sat and drank with her killer, only a short while after her death, while her blood had still been on her killer's hands. He had done nothing. He had not even spoken a word.

Tom suddenly had a deep desire to get another drink, to drown his guilt in an alcoholic stupor, but unfortunately there were no more coins in his pockets.

He could still picture the man's face.

His distinctive ginger moustache and mismatched features would make him easy to find. Tom looked around the marketplace, examining each and every one of the countless faces that were streaming past him.

He would find the killer.

It would be impossible for the police to find the culprit in Whitechapel, there were thousands of potential suspects in narrow streets and dark alleyways, but he had an advantage over them. He had seen the face of the killer.

Tom had never been a lucky man.

Misfortune had been his constant and faithful companion for as long as he could remember. He had lost what little money he had by lending it to a friend, who had since emigrated overseas without returning it, which had in turn led to his wife leaving him and taking up residence with another man. His philosophy for life had therefore become simple: if he had a penny in his pocket, it was best spent on a half pint of beer or on a few moments of pleasure with a streetwalker, before someone had the chance to take it away. Good fortune had to be seized, before it was stolen.

The idea that someone wanted to pay him to do a task he actually wanted to do seemed impossible to him, particularly when he could not see how they profited by it.

He stared sceptically at Samuel, the carter he had met on that fateful morning in the pub.

"They want to pay us to walk the streets?"

"They want to pay us to *patrol* the streets, we ain't streetwalkers!" Samuel grinned at him, laughing at his own joke. "Easiest money ever, right. All we have to do is walk about, and blow a whistle if we see anything."

It seemed too good to be true. He had wanted to go looking for the killer, but now someone actually wanted to pay him to search the streets.

They were on the far side of Whitechapel, far from dosshouses and unlit alleyways of the rookery, where a better class of society resided. They were still meeting in a pub, because it did not matter how high anyone climbed up the ladder of society, almost every working man still enjoyed a drink and the company of his peers. Samuel led him up the stairs of the Crown and knocked on the door of one of the private rooms.

"Come!" hollered a confident voice.

After removing their hats, they both shuffled through the door and found themselves standing before a trio of well-dressed businessmen. One of them, a fifty-year-old man with short greying hair and horseshoe-shaped moustache, rose from his chair.

"Good evening," he said, offering a handshake. "I am George Lusk, chairman of the Whitechapel Vigilance Committee. Your names?"

"Thomas Wright," he replied.

Mister Lusk shook his hand, apparently oblivious to the dirt on Tom's fingers.

"Samuel Grange," replied the carter, shaking the offered hand firmly.

One of the other men at the table wrote their names down in a ledger.

"You understand what we need you to do?" enquired Mister Lusk, stepping back to take measure of them, his eyes lingering for a moment on the worn-down soles of Tom's shoes.

Tom and Samuel both nodded.

"The police are not providing enough protection for the poor souls of Whitechapel, so we need good men like you to help stop this monster. Patrols start at midnight and continue until dawn. You will each receive a shilling in wage, a police whistle, a new pair of shoes and a long stick to assist you in your task. Does that sound like a satisfactory arrangement?"

"Yes, sir," Tom replied immediately, keen to make sure his enthusiasm was not in doubt.

"Then tell me, why, from all of our volunteers, should I employ you?"

"I've seen his face, sir." Tom knew it would get their attention. "I was in the Prince Albert when he came in, covered in blood, after he killed poor Annie."

"It's true, sir." Samuel nodded. "Mrs Fiddymont says Tom was sat right beside him, that's why I brought him to see you."

Lusk nodded thoughtfully, then reached into his pocket and handed each of them a shilling. It was enough to pay for a bed in a dosshouse and two pints of beer. It was more than a fair wage for a few hours of patrolling the street.

Lusk then reached beneath the table and collected a number of items from a box. The first was a pair of police whistles, which they hung around their necks. The second was a pair of shiny black shoes for each of them, which looked like they had never even been worn. The third was the stick, which was just over four foot long, equally capable of being used as a support while walking or a sturdy and reliable club. Tom was reasonably strong, so if he hit someone with it, he had no doubt they would be unlikely to get up before he delivered a second blow.

"What will you do if you find this monster?" asked Lusk, pushing the stick into his hand.

"I will whistle for the police," he lied. He was smart enough to know it was the answer that the respectable businessmen officially wanted to hear, but he knew that if he found the man that had slaughtered Annie then he had no intention of letting the police deal with the matter, not when he had a perfectly serviceable club in his hands.

"Good." Lusk nodded, apparently pleased with the answer, but he held Tom's gaze for a moment longer and nodded subtly, as if deep down he knew his true intentions and approved of them. "Let us find and deal with this monster before he kills again."

Tom left the room with a shilling in his pocket, new shoes on his feet and a weapon in his hand. He had a job that needed to be done.

The new shoes felt strange. Tom could no longer feel the uneven cobblestone beneath his feet. If he stood in a puddle of water, or any other effluent that ran through the streets of Whitechapel, his feet were no longer immediately soaked in it. The shoes had chafed a little on his first night's patrol, but now they fitted snuggly. The also drew him a certain amount of attention.

"Oo, look at 'em," gushed Long Liz, one of his neighbours, as he strode out of the front door of the dosshouse on to Flowers and Dean Street. "I bet they cost a penny or two."

"Perk of the job." He shrugged.

"They kind of make you look like an undercover policeman," she laughed. "The shoes always give 'em away!"

"I guess that's kind of what I am." He shrugged again, taking a swipe at an imaginary opponent with his club. "Unofficially."

"Us streetwalkers all feel safer already," she chuckled. "Don't we?"

Another of his neighbours, Kate Conway, glanced over.

"Forget reading a man's fortunes by looking at the lines on his palm," she said. "I can tell a man's fortune by looking at his shoes. And yours is looking better, Thomas Wright. Perhaps we won't end up like poor Polly Nichols, with you 'ere to defend us."

Tom nodded.

The woman she was referring to was the first victim, who had her throat slit, and while that murder had happened almost half a mile way, it still felt personal to all of them, as the woman herself had lived in a doss-house on their street. With Annie living only a short walk away, it was beginning to feel as if their neighbourhood was being specifically targeted by the killer, so, regardless of the shilling in his pocket, he would still have felt it was his responsibility to defend the people that lived there.

He marched to the end of the street, feeling a genuine thrill of purpose for the first time in many years, and hurried down Commercial Street to the doorstep of the Britannia. The pub was at the very corner of Dorset Road, where Annie had lived, so it had felt like an appropriate place for him and Samuel to start their patrol.

They shook hands and began the hunt.

Even at midnight, long after the trams had stopped running, Commercial Street was alive with activity. The pubs were still open, and outside the Ten Bells pub, they found Black Mary working her corner. The young woman, just twenty-five years old, had been working her patch for four years and was known to everyone. They crossed the road to talk to her, just to find out if she had seen anything suspicious in recent nights.

It was at that moment that Tom spotted the figure lurking on the other side of the road, on the edge of Spitalfields market. The man was loitering in the shadows, too far from the street lamp for Tom to be able to identify him properly, but he was carrying himself with the same nervous disposition as the bloodstained man he had encountered in the Prince Albert.

Leaving Samuel and Mary behind, Tom crossed the road, positioning himself between a pair of wagons that had been parked beside the market. It enabled him to conceal himself, while he studied the nervous figure more closely. As the man edged closer to the lamplight, Tom could discern a familiar coat, with a hat that was covering hair that was just the right length, but his face was still hidden in the darkness.

Tom could not contain himself any longer.

Even being unable to see his face, he was in little doubt that it was the man he had been hunting. The man's frame and mannerisms were just too distinctive for it to be anyone else.

Raising his stick, he strode out from between the wagons, moving rapidly towards him. He would have to be fast and brutal; if the man was carrying the knife he had used to commit the murders, then, given the chance, he would doubtless retaliate with lethal force.

His stick suddenly did not feel like much of a weapon for such a battle, yet he found himself continuing to advance, surprised by his own lack of fear. His hate had given him courage.

"You!" he hollered. "Stay where you are!"

The nervous figure froze, turning his head to look at Tom, his features moving into the lamplight. It was him. His small nose, ginger moustache and lopsided face were unmistakable.

Tom charged him, his stick raised, a ferrous yell spilling from his lips.

He struck the man across the side of head, knocking him to the ground. A knife fell, clattering on the cobbles. The man raised his hands defensively, but it did not stop Tom, who struck a second time.

The monster in front of him had murdered his friend and done unspeakably horrible things to her body, he had brutally killed another of their neighbours, and was responsible for who knew how many more horrendous crimes. He did not deserve to live. He deserved to die.

A police whistle sounded, echoing down the street.

Samuel rushed between them, not to help him, but to defend the killer. Tom almost struck him to the ground, but just held back, not quite able to bring himself to strike the young carter.

"It's him!" Tom seethed, anxious to recommence his attack, struggling to push his way past his friend, who was doing his best to restrain him.

"Calm down!" Samuel replied, pulling the stick from Tom's hand. "Let the police deal with him, or you'll be up on a murder charge yourself!"

Tom stepped back, his fist balled, trying to contain his anger.

He did not want the police to be involved. He wanted to kill the man himself. It would redeem him for sitting idly by when he had first encountered the monster.

Tom raised his fists, and was about to knock his friend out of the way, when the first policeman arrived, evidently responding to the whistle that Samuel had blown. The uniformed officer raised his oil lamp, looking warily at their faces, shoes and sticks. He then looked at the bloodied man on the floor, who had already risen up on to his knees, and was looking up at them with terror-filled eyes.

"That's the killer," Tom yelled. "I saw him covered in blood the morning Annie was murdered."

The police officer leaned closer to the man, studying him by the light of his oil lamp.

"Jacob Isenschmid?" the policeman enquired.

The man nodded mutely, wiping a trail of blood from his lip.

"We've been looking you." The officer smiled, grabbing the man and pulling him roughly to his feet. "We've got three or four other witnesses who've pointed the finger at you."

Tom backed away, as two other policemen rushed in, grabbing hold of the man.

Samuel stared at Tom with an open mouth. "You did it, Tom." The young man's voice was filled with awe. "You caught the killer!"

Another police whistle had been blown.

Tom trudged towards the sound of the whistle, his shoes now well worn in from three weeks circling the streets and alleyways of

Whitechapel. Since the arrest of Jacob Isenschmid, the murders had stopped, but there was still a wearying amount of disturbances to handle each night.

When Tom arrived in Dutfield's Yard, he was sure that it would be another false alarm, or just a regular drunken scuffle. He was quite confident that the killer was incarcerated, so he was not at all prepared for what awaited him.

He only realised his mistake when he saw the number of pale-looking police officers crowded around the body. The corpse lay in a darkened corner of the yard, her throat slit. Despite the lifeless eyes and splatters of blood, it was a face that Tom recognised.

"Long Liz," he muttered, knowing only his neighbour's street name.

Tom felt his stomach turn, knotting, as horror overwhelmed him.

"But," he rasped, more to himself than the police officers, "we arrested him."

One of the officers shrugged. "Guess we got the wrong man," he said. "They're saying there's another body in Mitre Square. They're saying he's killed two tonight."

Tom felt his world collapse.

Everything he had been sure was true had been wrong.

He turned away from the corpse, unable to continue looking at Liz's terrified eyes, and began hurrying towards Mitre Square.

The scene he found there was infinitely worse.

"Kate Conway." He barely dared breathe her name, as the woman in the corner of the square was hardly recognisable as the person he had once known. Her face had been obliterated almost beyond recognition. Her familiar green skirt had been lifted up around her waist, revealing that her abdomen that had been sliced open, her intestines removed and draped across her shoulder.

It was however not the gruesome horror of her body that caught his attention the most, but her feet. She was wearing a pair of her husband's old boots, presumably because she had long since pawned her own for rent money. A rip up the side of one boot had been neatly sewn up with red thread. They were old, second-hand and inappropriate, but they had still been mended and reused, given as much life as they could.

Tom looked down at the shoes on his own feet. The once shiny leather was faded and splashed with dirt. While he had been meandering through streets, confident the killer had been arrested, his soles had slowly been worn away.

Shoes and people were treated the same in Whitechapel, life wore them both away to nothing.

Tom was waiting at the door of the Prince Albert as Mrs Fiddymont unlocked the doors. As soon they were open, he stumbled inside and ordered a beer. He had nowhere to go and he had nothing to do, so he had come to the pub, in the hope that the beer would steal away the memory of his neighbours being slaughtered.

If he closed his eyes he could still picture Liz's terrified eyes and slit throat. Sometimes, even with his eyes open, he would sometimes picture the bloody ruins of Kate's face. Now, on the newspaper in front of him, printed in ink, was a mortuary photograph of a fifth victim. Black Mary. He had spoken to all three women on the night they had captured Jacob Isenschmid. Now they were all dead, despite his patrols.

He could not forget their faces while sober, so he drank, just as Annie had done after the death of her daughter. The beer tasted good.

Tom's eye lingered on the newspaper. He was not a particularly literate man, but he knew his basic letters, and understood what the headline meant. While the killer still had no face, he had acquired a new name. He was no longer Leather Apron, he was now Jack the Ripper. It was as if by naming their horror, it somehow made it easier to tolerate. Whoever he was during the day, or what he looked like, was irrelevant compared to the atrocities he had committed.

Another man shuffled into the pub, positioning himself at the bar beside Tom, and ordered a half pint of beer. It took Tom several moments to realise that he knew the man. His square chin, small nose and distinctive ginger moustache were unmistakable.

"Jacob Isenschmid." Tom muttered the name of the man that he had tried to kill. Jacob glanced at him, but there was no recognition in his eyes. "They let you go?"

"I didn't do anything wrong!" He shrugged away the simple explanation, despite the fact he must have spent weeks in confinement. "When Jack did in those other women, I was locked away, so they knew none of it was me."

"But you were in here, covered in blood."

"I'm a butcher." He shrugged again, pulling a knife from inside his coat and setting it down on the bar. "I like to make my own cuts from the meat that's on offer in the market. I repack it and sell it across town."

"But you were caught in the street at night."

"I like to be at the market at dawn, to get the best cuts, so sometimes I sleep on the street right by there." The man sank another mouthful of beer, and then turned to face Tom, apparently bemused that anyone would show so much interest in him. Jacob tapped the side of his head and smiled sadly. "Some days I don't always keep it together. Some days I am a little peculiar. The day I was here, covered in blood, my clothes a mess, was not a good day. Today is better."

Tom stared at the man, suddenly aware that he was talking mainly from one side of his mouth, as if the other side of his face was partly paralysed. It explained why his features looked lopsided. Tom had seen such illness before, and knew that it was always accompanied by oddness of behaviour, mania or outright madness. If he had taken just a moment to talk to the man on their first meeting, he would have known. It was not the face of a killer. It was the face of an ill man, barely able to cope with the world. Tom took a shilling from his pocket and bought the man a drink, because it was all he could do, he knew of no other way to put right what he had done wrong.

Tom looked down in shame, staring at his reflection in his beer. If Samuel had not held him back, Jacob would be dead, and the face in the reflection would have been the face of the killer. He closed his eyes, unable to look at himself.

He had let his hate rule him and it had almost cost a man his life.

There was no goodness to be found in the death of others.

Finishing his pint, Tom stood up and left the pub.

He walked past the market on way back to the dosshouse. As he did so, he examined hundreds of faces he passed, all desperately haggling for the resources they needed to stay alive. He knew, like him, that they were all capable of becoming killers, each and every one of them, but almost all had the strength not to succumb. However, in the hopeless alleyways of the rookery, where people sold their shoes and bodies just to survive, obliterating themselves with drink just to endure their miserable existence, was it any wonder that one of them had become a monster?

He considered himself lucky that he had not become another.

A Head for Murder
Keith Moray

───

4 August 1888, Cumberland Lodge, Windsor Great Park

It was the sort of day that made a person feel good to be alive.

The sun beat down from an almost cloudless cobalt sky as it had done for the past week. The cricket pitch, so carefully prepared and watered by Prince Christian of Schleswig-Holstein's gardener and his team of under-gardeners, had proven a near ideal playing surface. Now, in the closing stages of the game, there was a state of high excitement among the spectators watching from their deckchairs, the ladies shaded by parasols and the gentlemen by their cricket caps pulled down to protect their eyes from the dazzling sunlight.

It was not every day that one had the opportunity to play on a private cricket pitch within a couple of hundred yards of the magnificent red-stoned Cumberland Lodge, with its towers, crenellated walls and flag flying high. The flag, of course, made everyone aware that Her Majesty, Queen Victoria herself was staying with her eldest daughter, Princess Helena. It was highly likely that she would be observing from the great drawing room, for she had established an annual tradition of coming to Cumberland Lodge to watch her grandson's cricket eleven take on a visiting team. Two years before, she had watched them play and beat the Parsee Cricket Team, the final match of the Indian side's 1886 tour of England.

Prince Christian Victor's side this year was playing the Blackheath Cricket Club, which included several county players of note. Prince Christian Victor, the Princess Helena's eldest son, was twenty-one, a graduate of Magdalen College Oxford and latterly of the Royal Military College, Sandhurst. His passion for the game was considerable, as was his talent for the game, witnessed by the fact that he had captained the cricket team at both venerable institutions.

Also on the team, as he had been the past three years, was Prince Albert Victor, the Duke of Clarence, the second in line to the throne, after his father Albert Edward, the Prince of Wales.

The prince's team had been boosted by none other than Dr W. G. Grace, whose characteristic round-arm bowling method and fielding had dispatched many of the Blackheath men. At the start of the final innings it had been assumed that Prince Christian Victor's team would romp home to a significant victory, but the Blackheath team bowlers had found their form and it looked as if the tide could turn.

It was for just such an eventuality that W. G. Grace had been put in to bat in the middle of the order. Who better, the prince had reasoned, than the greatest batsman of his day to save the day. And indeed, although Grace was not on top form, his defensive play kept him in the game while he slowly notched up a middling score of runs. Not so fortunate were the other batsmen, who were picked off one by one until the last man was called to the wicket. This was none other than Prince Albert Victor, the Duke of Clarence and Avondale.

The bowler, Mr Montague John Druitt, a young barrister and part-time schoolmaster at George Valentine's Boarding School in Blackheath was a fine athlete. He had captained his college side at Oxford and was a fine sprinter, a wing three-quarter at rugby and champion at fives.

He was determined to make the four balls of the over count. He tossed the ball meditatively and stroked his neatly trimmed moustache with an elegant finger as he walked back to his mark, preparatory to bowling to the duke.

W. G. Grace, standing at the bowling end wicket, leaned his bulky sixteen stone frame on his bat and tugged at his prodigious black beard.

'Perhaps you ought to be a tad careful with the pace, Druitt. You don't want to be the man who injures the second in line to the throne, do you?'

Druitt noted the deadpan face and gave a thin smile, but without comment. Grace's gamesmanship was famous and he had no intention of being put off.

'And you might remember that his dear grandmother, Her Majesty the queen is probably watching.'

Druitt frowned, rubbed the ball on his whites and then went into his run. He was a right-handed overarm fast bowler. His action was smooth and graceful and the result was perfect. The ball hit the ground, bounced under the duke's attempted straight drive and crashed into the wickets, dislodging two and sending the bails flying.

'Owzat!' he cried exultantly, raising his arms above his head as the fielders ran towards him in celebratory mood.

He had the good grace to bow his head as a furious Duke of Clarence petulantly slammed his bat into the single remaining stump, which broke in two.

'Well bowled, Druitt,' said Grace, offering his hand. 'Although you've just made me lose ten pounds.'

He leaned closer, bending slightly from his great height and whispered conspiratorially, 'That is five pounds on the match and five pounds that the Duke wouldn't break his wicket.'

It was a tradition at the Cumberland Lodge cricket matches for the teams to go to the orangery for a smoke and a glass or two of cider before taking tea in the pavilion.

As ever, Prince Christian Victor was an amiable host. He was balding and looked older than his cousin the Duke of Clarence, who, at twenty-four years of age, was a handsome figure of a man with a good head of hair and a strong jaw.

W. G. Grace had already downed a pint of cider and was on his second, surrounded by players keen to talk to the sporting legend.

'Do you actually spend any time doctoring, Grace?' the duke asked.

Grace gave a gruff laugh. 'It is a testimony to my skills as a doctor that my patients are all so well they have little need of me, sir.'

Soon the cider loosened tongues, eased the inevitable constraints of social protocol that surrounded royalty and the players separated into little cliques. Montague Druitt found himself standing on the edge of the ring surrounding W. G. Grace. It included the two royal princes, the barrister and author Mr Ernest Bax, a viscount and a member of parliament.

The duke struck a light to a cigarette in his slim amber cigarette holder, then blew out the match. 'Did you all see that nonsense over a thousand women striking at Bryant & May the matchmakers? Disgusting, I call it.'

'Disgusting, sir?' Grace repeated. 'Why so?'

'Because they said they wanted equal pay with men. Ridiculous.'

'They are paid poorly, Cousin,' said Prince Christian Victor. 'Don't you think women should have the same rights as men?'

Ernest Bax, a stocky man in his early thirties, snorted derisively. 'Begging your pardon, sir, but I for one do not think so. I wrote a paper in the *Commonweal* a couple of years ago. I am concerned as a lawyer that women's rights have overtaken men's rights. All this feminism, as they call it, is part of an anti-man crusade. I can give you countless examples of the way the legal system is stacked heavily in favour of women to the detriment of the male sex.'

'Well said,' returned the duke. 'What do you think to that, Grace?'

'Well actually, sir, I confess to a soft spot for women,' the cricketer replied, with the merest hint of a wink, before taking a hefty swig of cider.

'And you, sir,' said the duke, turning to Montague Druitt. 'What is the opinion of my cricketing executioner?'

Caught slightly off guard and not expecting to be addressed directly by the duke, Montague Druitt looked blank for a moment. Then he recovered himself.

'I have to concur with my learned colleague, Mr Bax. I also am a barrister, you see, sir. I have been concerned about these matters since the Contagious Diseases Acts were repealed in 1886.'

'What's that? Was it about cattle or something, surely,' asked Prince Christian Victor.

'It was not, sir,' interjected W. G. Grace. 'As a doctor I know something of it. The Act was an effective defence against the spread of venereal disease.'

'Indeed,' went on Druitt, warming to the subject. 'They were a series of acts, designed to curb the spread of these diseases in the navy and the army. The first was passed in 1864 and then it was extended in 1866 and again in 1869. They gave police officers the right to stop and arrest any woman thought to be a common prostitute. They would then be taken to a station and examined by a doctor for any evidence of venereal disease. If found to be contagious they were then treated in a secure hospital until safe to be released.'

'And what if they refused to be examined?' Prince Christian Victor asked.

'They would be sent to prison and made to do hard labour for six months.'

'And why was it repealed?' the duke asked.

'The feminists said it infringed their rights,' Druitt replied. 'Now there is no curb on prostitution.'

Grace finished his cider. 'And as a result venereal disease is rife.' He laughed heartily. 'Why, I'd be willing to wager that the majority of men in this orangery have had the pox at some stage. It isn't pleasant, either. Trust me, I know. I'm a medical man.'

This time no one in the group was laughing.

'And on that note,' Prince Christian Victor added, 'I think it is time we all headed back to the pavilion and joined the ladies for tea.'

Friday, 9 November 1888
Whitechapel, London

It was the custom of Walter Beck, the duty inspector at the Commercial Street Police Station to drink a pot of tea at eleven o'clock each morning. A man of firm habits, he was smoking the charred old briar pipe that he had bought sixteen years previously with the first wage packet he had received after joining the force. On the other side of his desk sat young Detective Constable Walter Dew, a clean-shaven, dapper young fellow who had been nicknamed Blue Serge on account of the blue serge suit he habitually wore ever since he had joined H Division the year previously. He too was smoking a pipe, albeit a smaller variety containing a far less pungent tobacco than the inspector's.

After briefly discussing the current cases under investigation and their respective thoughts about the news that Sir Charles Warren, the Metropolitan Police Commissioner, had resigned the day before, they had inevitably turned their attention to the indirect cause of Sir Charles's resignation. Neither of the two had slept well for the past three months and both had lost weight. They were well aware of the general anxiety that had gripped the whole of the capital, but Whitechapel and Spitalfields in particular, ever since the murders had begun and Jack the Ripper had announced himself to the world.

A day did not pass without some lurid article in the *Pall Mall Gazette* or the *East London Observer* or any half-dozen other newspapers about the killer, his victims or the general incompetence of the police in catching him. All of this was greatly magnified by the killer himself, who had taken to sending badly spelled and poorly written letters to various newspapers. Indeed, it was from one of those letters that the newspapers had given him his macabre sobriquet.

Dew felt the accusations of incompetence were unjust, for despite the horror of the murders and all the blood at the scenes of the crimes, the Ripper had left barely any clues; certainly none that had produced any tangible leads. There were witness statements by the score and numerous supposed sightings of the Ripper, but few tallied with one another. Similarly, there were plenty of reports from the public as to the identity of the murderer, a great many of which Dew and his colleagues were able to determine arose out of petty feuds where folk had pointed the finger of suspicion at enemies. Yet every single possible lead had to be painstakingly followed up. Doctors, butchers, slaughter-men, leather workers and virtually anyone who used a cutting tool or instrument were potentially under suspicion. Dozens of officers made inquiries and searched common lodging houses, brothels and doctors' and dentists' surgeries. They checked the movements of several hundred suspects. Dew himself had interviewed seventy-six butchers and slaughtermen as well as a band of Greek gypsies, three cowboys from a travelling Wild West show and three insane medical students.

Every 'gentleman' that was spotted in Whitechapel had to be interviewed and checked up on, since few came to conduct business. Their interests generally seemed to be more carnal than fiscal.

Dew had personally also interviewed doctors, lawyers, several members of parliament and at least two celebrated artists, including Walter Sickert. He had even called upon George Robert Sims, the novelist and journalist who wrote articles about the Ripper for *The Referee* under the pen name of Dagonet. He had been pointed out by a coffee stallholder on Whitechapel Road, who had seen a portrait of him advertising his latest novel. The vendor had said that he was sure he was a man who had come to his stall with blood on his cuffs the day before the infamous double killing. As they chatted, he had remarked that there would be two more deaths soon. Fortunately for him, the novelist had witnesses who could substantiate his movements on that day.

Another visit had been to the Whitechapel Dispensary for the Poor on Aldgate Street to interview a Russian gynaecologist, Dr Alexander Pedachenko. A Russian tea importer had called at the Commercial Street station and suggested that he was a bad-tempered foreigner who despised women. Dew had found him to be neither bad-tempered nor obviously misogynistic. True, he had railed against the abolition of the Contagious Diseases Acts, but he justified his position because as a gynaecologist he had to deal with the aftermath of venereal disease among his patients. He had a successful Harley Street practice, but gave his time voluntarily to treat the poor of the East End in clinics in Whitechapel and Shoreditch. Dew reported it as another false lead.

Yet all of this had to be done as well as the usual work, for thieves, forgers and assorted bully boys and villains had not ceased their activities and their way of life just because of Jack the Ripper.

Like every other officer in the force, they both fervently hoped that the killing spree had come to an end. It had, after all, been over a month since the double murders of Elizabeth Stride and Catherine Eddowes on 30 September.

'Sir Charles has left us in a right state, Dew,' said Inspector Beck, finally.

'Any idea who will take over, sir?' Dew asked.

The inspector pursed his lips. 'Not sure, Dew. The only likely thing is that whoever it is, he'll not have much of a background in proper policing.'

A sudden commotion from the outer office was followed by the door being unceremoniously thrown open by a uniformed constable.

'Sorry, Inspector, Indian Harry's just come in with his boss, John McCarthy, the chandler of Dorset Street on his heels. The Ripper's struck again. He's carved up Mary Kelly in her room at thirteen Miller's Court. It's the worst one yet, by all accounts.'

16 November 1888

Detective Constable Walter Dew thought that he had a strong constitution, but the sight of the mutilated body of Mary Kelly, whom he and the other officers knew as Marie Kelly, a twenty-five-year-old buxom blonde with blue eyes, upset him badly. He felt nauseous for a week afterwards and found himself unable to sleep for more than an hour or two before he awoke drenched in perspiration from yet another nightmare. Passing a butcher's shop made him want to retch, for the sight of raw flesh conjured up the images that he had forced himself to endure and study in as dispassionate a manner as he could muster.

It seemed to have been a frenzied attack, albeit one that the examining doctors thought would have taken several hours to perform, conducted by the firelight from a fiercely stoked grate. The Ripper had disembowelled her, removed her face and laid her vital organs luridly about her eviscerated corpse on the blood-soaked bed. There was no sign of her heart and it was assumed that the Ripper had taken it with him.

Inspector Frederick Abberline, seconded from Scotland Yard, was, in Dew's opinion, one of the ablest detectives he had known. He looked up to him and respected his opinion. He was a portly man with thinning hair, mutton chop whiskers and a moustache. His secondment was welcomed by everyone in H Division, since he knew Whitchapel and Spitalfields like the back of his hand. Yet even Abberline had to admit that they were no closer to catching the killer this time than they had been when he had killed little Mary Nichols by the stable gates on Buck's Row on 31 August.

At a morning meeting of his detectives, he had spoken frankly, almost desperately it seemed to Dew, explaining that a stroke of luck was needed to lead them to the murderer.

'Quite honestly, men, I need you to follow any lead you can, no matter how slender. The population of London is panicking. The prime minister is raging like a bull, because so many upstanding and prominent citizens, including an important member of the Royal Family, have been accused of being the Ripper. Although she had not heard about the latter rumour, Her Majesty Queen Victoria is furious at the lack of progress and wants this monster to be caught no matter what.'

He sucked air between his lips and straightened his back before going on.

'All this being the case, as well as standard policing, that is interviewing, house-to-house enquiries and checking everyone coming and going, I want you all to think of any way that could lead to a breakthrough. You will all have heard about Robert Lees, the spiritualist medium who came offering his help last month?'

'Wasn't he turned away, Inspector?' asked Sergeant William Thick, who was known as Johnny Upright, on account of his stiff posture and no-nonsense approach to policing the East End.

'He was, twice in fact. But I have to say that two days ago I visited him myself, just in case he had got information of value. As it happened, he didn't. I think the man is a fraud.'

'What about other psychics, sir?' Thick queried.

'Officially, the answer is no,' replied Abberline. 'But, unofficially, in your own time, follow any line you can.'

Walter Dew had taken the inspector at his word, hence his attendance at a public lecture at the Egyptian Hall in Piccadilly that evening, when he would have preferred being at home with his wife Kate and their son little Willy.

Professor Henry Armstrong of the British Phreno-Mesmerism Institute held a public lecture every month at the famed Egyptian Hall. Dew had passed the building many times but never entered. It had a quasi-Egyptian façade with columns, statues of Egyptian gods and a sphinx. Inside, it had several galleries and a number of halls, which were available for rent for private lectures such as this.

Dew had read a little about phrenology and had heard that the professor's lectures were both enlightening and entertaining. He just wondered whether there was something in the science that could be of value in his search for the Ripper.

The lecture hall was almost full, but he managed to get a seat in the third row. While he waited for the curtain to rise, he looked around and assessed it to be a pretty mixed audience. There were people of all classes, both men and women. Some looked as though they were eager to hear a serious lecture, while others seemed to be in music hall mood. He wondered whether the professor would satisfy their differing expectations.

The curtains parted without fanfare to reveal a dapper man in a frock coat with a cravat and stiff collar. He was completely bald, although, as he stepped into the light of the gas jets, it was apparent that his head was shaven. A black goatee beard and moustache gave him a distinguished look, in keeping with his title.

'Good evening, ladies and gentlemen,' he said, his voice booming and brimming with confidence. 'Welcome to my little introduction to the wonderful science of phrenology.'

He pointed to a table upon which were several plaster casts of male and female heads, with coloured squares and circles covering the crowns, alongside a series of human skulls. Behind the table, on a large easel, was a diagram of a person's head with the same areas numbered and annotated.

Dew listened as the professor told them of how a Dr Franz Joseph Gall had developed the science of phrenology at the end of the eighteenth century. Using the chart and the various skulls and busts, he explained the basic premise that the brain was composed of a number of small organs, which he called faculties, each of which governed an area of the mind, or an emotion, talent or mental tendency. He explained how a skilled phrenologist could determine the exact character of a person by examining the pattern of lumps and bumps on the skull, because each of those lumps exactly mirrored the development or otherwise of the corresponding faculty underneath it. It all sounded completely plausible to Dew.

Then the professor called an assistant, who wheeled in a steam-driven magic lantern. Once it was set in operation, the lights were turned down and the professor projected a series of images of a number of subjects. With each one he listed their attributes or deficiencies, drawing gasps of amazement and murmurs of interest from the audience.

'And now, ladies and gentlemen, I move to the more macabre, so if any of you are of a sensitive nature, then please do feel free to leave right now.'

He waited a few moments, then smiled when no one moved.

'I said that, because now I am going to show you a few casts of heads and the corresponding death masks taken from a number of executed murderers. I want to demonstrate the predictive power of phrenology. I begin with the cast of the head of the body-snatching murderer, William Burke.'

Dew immediately sat up, his interest piqued.

*   *   *

When Dew reported back to Inspector Abberline the following day, he was pleased to see that his superior officer was initially intrigued. More so when Dew described how the professor had called for volunteers from the audience to demonstrate his technique of phreno-mesmerism.

'It was impressive, sir. After doing what he called a brief delineation, that is feeling their scalp all over, he proceeded to list things about the person's character. He told them their qualities, the things that they had potential for and the things that they weren't any use at, at all. He told one chap he had no sense of direction and the man replied that he even got lost on his way home from work. Well, then he waved a watch in front of him and sent him into a mesmeric trance. Then he started massaging a small area on his head, all the while telling him his sense of direction faculty was being improved. When he woke him up, he showed how it had improved by standing him up, getting him to close his eyes while he turned him round and round. He asked him to point to the north and he did it three times, each spot on.'

Dew then told him how he himself had called out a question at the end of the session, about whether he could predict if someone was a murderer.

'He said definitely, sir. He could demonstrate it just like he did on the magic lantern slides. He said that another phrenologist called Frederick Bridges, who died five years ago, had scientifically proved it by showing that a particular angle between the nose, ear canal and the brow, what he called the *phreno-metrical angle*, was always above a certain figure in murderers. He had measured these on a series of executed murderers, including Dr William Palmer, the Rugeley poisoner.'

Yet later that day, when they discussed the matter with the police surgeons, Drs Brown, Bond and Phillips, they all three denounced phrenology as utter balderdash.

Inspector Abberline thanked Dew for his input, but declined to waste police time on the matter.

'Keep thinking, Dew.'

Which is precisely what Dew intended to do.

31 December 1888

It had been a bleak Christmas in Whitechapel. Another murder victim, Rose Mylett, was found dead but unmutilated in Clarke's Yard. The totally different findings led Abberline and his team to conclude that she had not been a victim of the Ripper.

Then, at lunchtime on the Monday after Christmas, waterman Henry Winslade hauled the body of a well-dressed gentleman out of the Thames just off Thorneycroft's Works at Chiswick Mall. He called the police, who arranged the removal of the corpse to the local mortuary. There, Constable George Moulston had the unpleasant task of examining the badly decomposed body. He found four large stones in each pocket of the coat. He also found a pair of kid gloves, some loose cash, a gold watch with a spade guinea as a seal and a wallet containing visiting cards, two cheques for a considerable amount of money, a half-season rail ticket from Blackheath to London and a second-half return ticket from Hammersmith to Charing Cross, dated 1 December 1888.

From this, the police were able to determine that the deceased was Montague John Druitt, a barrister and schoolteacher from Blackheath. His brother was contacted and identified the body. He told them that he had not heard from him since the end of November and that he had gone to his rooms in mid-December and found a note that said: *'Since Friday I felt I was going to be like Mother, and the best thing for me was to die.'*

Subsequent enquiries revealed that their father had died shortly before, leaving a modest estate and that their mother was an inmate of the Brooke Mental Asylum in Clapton. All this was duly reported at the inquest, which was held at the Lamb Tapp Inn on Church Street by the coroner Dr Thomas Diplock on the following Wednesday. The verdict of the inquest was suicide while of unsound mind.

Arrangements were made by his brother for the funeral and burial at Wimborne Cemetery the following day.

Detective Constable Dew had been detailed by Inspector Abberline to follow up all leads of suicides and was fast on the trail. Upon questioning the brother and checking the route that Druitt would take from his rooms in Blackheath to visit his mother in the asylum, which he did on Friday or Saturdays, he would pass through Whitechapel. He also learned that the brother was deeply suspicious of his brother's behaviour and he discovered that Montague Druitt had been dismissed from his post as a schoolmaster at Blackheath, because of dubious morals.

'He was sexually insane!' the brother told him. 'He had never been what you might call normal and he was never well after he visited our mother.'

Dew suspected that he may have found the Ripper. Yet there was no tangible evidence. He was aware that it was merely surmise. Abberline's advice to keep thinking spurred him on and he took a hansom to see Professor Henry Armstrong at his home and consulting room in St Andrews Place.

He persuaded the phrenologist to travel with him to the mortuary before the coffin was taken to begin its hundred-mile journey to Wimborne in Dorset for the burial.

'I warn you the body is neither a pretty sight, nor a wholesome smell,' Dew said as the body was uncovered.

Professor Armstrong's face visibly paled and he looked as if he might gag.

'My question is simple,' said Dew. 'Can you tell me if this man had a head for murder?'

The professor's eyes widened. 'Are we talking about a common or garden murderer or someone more significant?'

'Entirely more significant, sir, but I cannot go into details. And this is, as I said, entirely confidential.'

'I understand, Mr Dew. My profession is bound by an ethical code, just as the medical profession is. Now let me see.'

And, having tied a large handkerchief about his mouth and nose, put on a pair of wire-framed spectacles, he leaned over the bloated, discoloured corpse and started to feel the contours of the skull. Then, with a set of calipers and an angle protractor, he made several measurements of the face.

Finally, he stood and pulled the handkerchief away. 'This man's head most definitely has murderous potential.'

Using the calipers, he illustrated the landmarks on the head. 'The phreno-metrical angle is greater than forty degrees. This is a universal finding in convicted murderers. I should note also that the moral faculties on the top of the head are flat, indicating a head of no moral standing. On the other hand, the animal faculties of amativeness, which is to do with sexual desires, and the neighbouring ones of secretiveness, are large at the back of the head. But, most importantly, the faculty of destructiveness behind the ear is huge. In essence, this is the head of a murderer, potentially a very brutal murderer, who would have been extremely adept in hiding his trail.'

'Thank you, Professor, you have pretty well confirmed my suspicions.'

Inspector Abberline listened to Dew's report on his investigations the next morning.

'Good work, Dew. The trouble is that this phrenology business fails to cut the muster with the doctors and, when it comes down to it, we have no firm evidence to link Montague Druitt to the murders. I'll report it all on to Sir Melville Macnaghten, the assistant chief constable, but I fear he will think the same.'

'So we can't make these suspicions known, sir?'

'Probably wisest not to. At least now we can probably relax the police presence in the area. Let some of the men have a rest. Then, in a year or so, when there are no more murders, we can officially close the case.'

22 January 1889

He skewered the last piece of bacon and dipped it in the last of the fried egg yolk before carefully placing it in his mouth and chewing precisely forty-six times. One chew for each faculty of the mind, it was one of the ways that he celebrated the power of the mind in general and the perfect functioning of his own remarkable brain.

He smiled as he glanced at *The Referee*, neatly folded and propped against his silver coffee pot so that he could read the regular column written by the novelist and journalist George R. Sims under his pen name of Dagonet. He knew the writer as both a client and a social acquaintance and his regular pieces about Jack the Ripper amused and interested him.

22 January 1899
There are bound to be various revelations concerning Jack the Ripper as the years go on. This time it is a vicar who heard his dying confession. I have no doubt a great many lunatics have said they were Jack the Ripper on their death beds. It is a good exit, and when the dramatic instinct is strong in a man he always wants an exit line, especially when he isn't coming on in the little play of 'Life' any more.

I don't want to interfere with this mild little Jack the Ripper boom that the newspapers are playing up in the absence of strawberries and butterflies and good exciting murders, but I don't quite see how the real Jack could have confessed, seeing that he committed suicide after the horrible mutilation of the woman in the house in Dorset-street, Spitalfields. The full details of that crime have never been published – they never could be. Jack, when he committed that crime, was in the last stage of the peculiar mania from which he suffered. He had become grotesque in his ideas as well as bloodthirsty. Almost immediately after this murder he drowned himself in the Thames. His name is perfectly well known to the police. If he hadn't committed suicide he would have been arrested.

'Well said, Dagonet. That will let the public think they are safe from Jolly Jack,' he said, as he lay down his knife and fork and dabbed his lips with his napkin. He drained his coffee cup and stood up.

'And thank you, Montague Druitt. It was quite fortuitous that you came along to see me for a phrenological delineation after your mother was incarcerated in the asylum.'

He recalled the interview so well. Druitt had been disturbed that his mother had gone mad and he had been sure that his own sexual proclivities with others of his sex would result in due course in him following her to the asylum. That was when Professor Armstrong had suggested treating him with phreno-mesmerism.

How fortunate that he was such a good subject. With little difficulty he planted suggestions into his mind that he should make visits to Whitechapel on his way to and from the asylum on Friday or Saturday nights. This he did, making sure that he was seen in the early hours in certain streets, all of which would eventually attract the attention of the Whitechapel Vigilance Committee. And it had been extremely useful when the good professor was busy with the actual carvings of the flesh, as he liked to think of his work.

And at the consultation after the professor had performed his pièce de résistance on the Kelly woman, he implanted the suggestion that he should firstly confess his nature to the headmaster at the school. This Druitt dutifully did and, as expected, he was dismissed and given a severance payment on the spot.

Then, under a further mesmeric trance, he implanted the suggestion that he should indeed commit suicide. He dictated the note with instructions that he should leave it in his rooms, then make the journey to the Thames, fill his pockets with stones and do away with himself.

A perfect false trail. The letters he had written and sent to the news-papers, especially the *Dear Boss* one, had been so amusing to do and had stirred the whole of London into a frenzy of panic.

He laughed when he thought how it all worked so perfectly, as if it was meant to happen. Even to the point of that dolt of a detective, Walter Dew, coming to his lecture and then seeking his opinion about Druitt's head.

'How easy it was to dupe the fool!'

He ran a hand over his shaven skull, admiring his own genius.

But now it is time to have a well-earned rest, he mused to himself as he rang the bell for the maid to clear his breakfast away.

In a few months he would go hunting again, but no more of the anatomical flesh carvings. He'd go back to decapitation and dismem-berment. He'd just leave the torso to give them something to think about. Just as he had done when he left that first headless body at the start of 1888 in the construction of the new building at Scotland Yard. How apt that had been, the so-called Whitehall Mystery. He had left his mark on their headquarters right from the start.

He was still laughing at the thought when Agnes the maid came in.

'You sound to be in a good mood, Professor Armstrong,' she said, as she began clearing the crockery on to a silver tray.

'Oh I am, Agnes. I am. It is a fine morning and a good day to be alive. Don't you think so?'

The Keys to the Door
William Meikle

———

The twelfth of November was the start of another foggy London weekend; the autumn of 1909 had many of them. This latest one was setting up to be one of the worst in memory and, despite my overcoat and hat, I still felt damp through by the time I arrived on Carnacki's doorstep in Chelsea. Our host himself seemed likewise affected by the seasonal damp, appearing listless and torpid, and far from his usual exuberant self.

He did, however, perk up considerably after supper and several stiffeners of brandy. By the time we were settled in our chairs in the parlor around a roaring fire, he seemed greatly improved and became much more animated as he began to regale us with his latest story.

"The weather tonight is jolly apt," he started. "For this is a tale that starts – and indeed ends – in fog. I cannot promise you an altogether happy ending – only an ending; one that old Lady London has been waiting on for quite some time.

"It begins, as all good tales do, with a knock on my door on Tuesday morning. I opened up to find two people there, as disparate a couple as you are ever likely to see.

"The girl took my eye first – she looked to be in her early twenties, and was dressed plainly, her skirt and petticoat being of the cheap variety often seen on street traders and the like. Her features were drawn to the point of giving her a haggard, starved look that almost, but did not quite, hide obvious signs of sleeplessness and, something else, something that looked very like raw terror. Her lips quivered, and I feared either tears or screams were imminent – I know not which would have bothered me the more.

"I looked away to avoid her obvious distress, and studied her companion. At first glance I took him for a retired bank manager. He wore a fine dark wool suit and overcoat, his fob chain was of impressive heft, his cane was silver tipped at top and bottom, and his mutton chop whiskers, although gray, were neatly trimmed and under control. It was only when I looked into his eyes that I knew the man – he had aged somewhat, but when I was much younger his face was in all the newspapers, and you chaps, like me, would have known him immediately.

"As I showed the strange couple inside out of the cold, I wondered what fate had brought Chief Inspector Fredrick Abberline, formerly of Scotland Yard, to my doorstep."

"I got the story out of him over a Scotch and cigar. It was not quite noon, but the combination of the girl's distress and the arrival of Abberline I had thought him to be somewhere on the Continent working for Pinkerton – had me in quite a funk, and I welcomed the stiffener as we sat around the fire in the library.

"Abberline did all the talking – the girl stared into the flames the whole time, as if trying to burn something from her sight. I was not at all sure I wanted to hear what was coming next as the inspector began.

"'You know who I am, Mr Carnacki,' he said. 'And I know you, at least by reputation. Normally, I will have no truck with any mumbo-jumbo, but the facts of this matter have led me to one, and only one, conclusion – you are the only man in the city who will understand, and the only one I know that I can ask for help.'

"Now that all sounded rather ominous to me, but as you chaps know, I cannot turn away a request for help – not from a retired Yard man – or a girl who looked to be at the end of her tether. I waved Abberline on, and he laid out a series of facts, as if he was at the Old Bailey, laying them out for a jury.

"'Firstly, my ward here is Mary Wilson, and today is her twenty-first birthday. I knew her mother, Ada – I interviewed her in Whitechapel in early '89. She had Mary with her, just a babe in arms, when she came to see me at the station. That day Ada told me a tale, of a night in March the year before. She had been taken advantage of in Mile End, forced at knifepoint, by a man wearing a long coat and a hat. This man had cut her, promising more of the same if she did not succumb to him. Poor Mary is the result of that night's unhappy union.

"'Now, Carnacki, you know the case I was working at the time, you know why I had talked to this woman. I never managed to link her to the Whitechapel murders, but I had a hunch, you see, and I have kept an eye on Ada, and the girl after Ada's passing, over the years since.

"'There has been little of note to report – until I received word this past March that Mary had been admitted to Bedlam – hysteria and mania, they said. Fortunately for Mary, it passed and she was eventually allowed home, but thereafter she started talking about the shadow, the creeping shadow that stalked her, and whispered vile things to her in her dreams.

"'Hysterical young ladies are not uncommon, as you know, Carnacki, and I thought little of it. Then, on the first of September, I received further word, that Mary tried to kill herself the day before, having been seeing visions of bloody death – death that involved knives, fog and darkness. It happened again on the eighth of the month, and I knew then that something right strange was happening. When there were two more incidents on the thirtieth I had to step in, for I had seen the pattern all too clearly.'

"'As have I,' I interrupted, with some degree of trepidation. 'This poor girl's attacks, whatever they are, are happening to coincide with the nights of the Ripper murders.'

"Abberline nodded.

"'And there's more, Carnacki. Tonight is the ninth of November – the twenty-first anniversary of the night Mary Kelly became Jack's last, and most bloody, victim.'"

"'I think you have come to the wrong place,' I replied. 'The doctors in Bedlam might be better able to serve your lass, for I see nothing here to which I can lend my expertise.'

"And despite being bally intrigued by the inspector's tale, I was sorely tempted to send them on their way. But Abberline begged my forgiveness, told me there was more to it than he had yet said, and promised to get to the heart of his tale in a more straightforward manner. Just as he said that I saw him stare at the skylight in the library. Whatever it was he had seen, it brought about an immediate attack of panic in the girl, and her mouth started to work – this time it was most definitely going to be screams.

"'It's in the fog, Carnacki,' Abberline said softly 'It is coming with the fog. Can't you feel it?'

"And, by Jove, I did indeed feel something: a certain coldness and dampness in the air. A shadow moved from under the library door. I felt a slight breeze that brought with it the unmistakable odor of spilled blood. The smell got stronger as I walked over and put my free hand on the door handle, and there was a scrape on the wood, followed by a distinct thud. I stepped back, taking my hand away. There was no repeat of the noises, but I had the distinct impression that there was something there on the other side, waiting. Thin fog drifted through the gap between the door and the floor and the temperature dropped markedly.

"Abberline shouted out. 'He's here. He has come for her. Save her, Carnacki. Save her soul.'

"At the sound of his voice the thudding started up again, and all of a sudden I knew exactly what it was – someone was plunging a knife – and a hefty one at that – time and time again into the wood on the other side of the door.

"I raised my voice in the chant of exorcism that has always served me well in tight spots such as these. '*Ri linn dioladh na beatha, Ri linn bruchdadh na falluis, Ri linn iobar na creadha, Ri linn dortadh na fala.*'

"The thudding got louder still, more insistent until I brought the chant to an end with the last shouted phrase of the ritual. '*Dhumna Ort!*'

"My voice mingled with a fading howl of frustrated rage that echoed around us for long seconds before silence fell once more.

"On opening the door, I was faced with some fine wisps of fog, already dissipating, and some deep gouges on my hardwood door, which I fear will be there for ever. You chaps can go and have a look at them later if you like – they are rather impressive, and will always serve me as another reminder that the ethereal planes are perfectly capable of manifesting in the physical given the right opportunity.

"'You did it. You sent it packing, Carnacki,' Abberline shouted, and you will never have seen a happier chap go sad so quickly as when I had to inform him of the reality of the situation.

"'I am afraid not,' I replied. 'I now know the nature of the thing. Your lass has caught the attention of something from the Outer Darkness, Abberline, and it might be some time yet before she is free of it. Fear not, I will help you. But first, I need the story – all of it, in the right order and with all the facts in place. And I need it now.'

"Abberline bade me join him again by the fire. He leaned over and, almost tenderly, lifted the material of her blouse to expose the girl's lower arm. There were five wounds in the flesh, scoured deep. Four had scabbed over, almost healed, but the fifth was as fresh as if it had been cut mere seconds before, oozing small beads of blood.

"'There's that,' Abberline said, as he gently pulled the girl's blouse back down. 'And there's the fact that today is the girl's twenty-first birthday. Today she comes of age – and I fear that it is not only her that reaches that milestone. She was conceived of blood, born out of bloody ritual – one that ended with Mary Kelly's death at the very moment, as far as I can ascertain, that Ada gave birth.

"'And, today, that ritual comes to final fruition. Today, Jack will be reborn into his reign of terror.'

"Now, all of that sounded somewhat bombastic to my ears, all the more so for coming from such a staunchly skeptical policeman. But I saw in his eyes that he believed every word of it, and I could not naysay him, for I only had to look at the fresh gouges in my door to see the evidence for myself."

"We spent the rest of the day in the library. Now that the sun was well over the yardarm, I fetched some ale up from the cellar and put fresh logs on the fire in the grate. I was to be thankful for both before the afternoon was done, for the theory that Abberline laid out chilled me to my marrow.

"'As a copper, I'm used to looking for patterns,' he said. 'And that's what we have here. It has long been suspected that the Ripper was following a crazed plan of his own devising, but what was never known was the desired outcome. I think that is what we are now seeing, Carnacki – whoever – or whatever – the Ripper is, the plan all along was to be reborn, here, now, on this night, through this girl.'

"It took me several seconds to digest, but, in the end, I was forced to agree with his logic. And I told him so.

"'As for what – I think you are right in not ascribing it to anything human, and right in coming to me for help. This is an old thing, a thing of the Outer Darkness – I have felt its like before. And what you call the ritual is its foothold, its way to stay rooted here on this plane.'

"'Old, you say?' Abberline replied. 'It has done this before?'

"'It would not surprise me.'

"'Nor me,' the inspector muttered and went quiet. He sat by the fire with the girl, smoking another of my cheroots and drinking my ale, while I set about preparing some protections for what I feared was to come.

"I will not bore you chaps with the details again – you have heard often enough of the efficacy of my electric pentacle. I set the colored valves up on the protective marquetry circle I have inscribed in the center of the floor in the library – a most fortuitous decision on my part, I am sure Arkwright will agree, although he berated me mightily over the expense of it at the time. After ensuring that the generator was feeding steady power to the system, I joined Abberline by the fire for another smoke and some ale.

"We talked for some time over inconsequential matters. He proved an excellent conversationalist, and we passed the time rather pleasantly in the circumstances. The girl was as quiet as ever – she had not yet spoken a word since her arrival.

"Just as I was thinking of preparing us something to eat to fortify us for the night ahead, the sound I had dreaded returned, shockingly loud in the quiet library. Something thudded, and I knew there was now a fresh gouge on the door outside.

"'You and the girl best get into the protections,' I said to Abberline. 'And be quick about it.'

"He was smart enough to do as he was bid without hesitation, taking the girl by the hand and leading her into the circle. I stepped in beside them, just in time as thin fog curled under the door and the temperature dropped again.

"The red valve of my pentacle flared and dimmed in a rhythmic beat. At first I presumed it was a problem with the supply from the generator, but as the blade thudded into the door again I realized that the valve was keeping perfect time with the blows. The beat was becoming more rapid by the minute, as if something was building up to a crescendo. The thudding increased in frequency, a frenzied attack on the door, the whole library echoing with the sound.

"'Do something, Carnacki,' Abberline said, and, at the sound of his voice, the door shook violently in the frame as something heavy launched itself, time after time, against the other side. The air smelled of blood again. I was starting to fear for the integrity of my library door as the noise reverberated around us as if we were inside a huge drum being played by a maniac.

"Then, as quickly as it had come, the attack faltered. I spotted why several seconds later as the light in the room improved markedly, thin evening sun coming in through the skylight. The fog had lifted and, with its passing, the threat, for the time being, had gone.

"Abberline was somewhat shaken by this latest experience. As for the girl, she seemed to be in a state of shock, and I got only a blank stare in reply when I asked if she was all right. I fetched the three chairs by the fireplace into the circle and had my guests sit while I went for some vitals to sustain us through what might be a long night.

"Abberline was not happy about being left alone in the library. 'But what if it returns?'

"I pointed at the skylight. 'If it gets foggy again, call out. I will be mere seconds away at all times.'

"As it turned out, Abberline's worries were baseless, and I was able to fetch some pork pies, cold meats and bread without any interruption. He took to the food with some gusto, clearing his plate rapidly, after which we sat and smoked in silence. The girl would not touch hers, merely sat, staring at the library door, as if resigned to whatever fate may befall her.

"Eventually, night fell around us. I left the circle to light some lamps. As I returned, I thought I heard something at the door, and turned in that direction – just as the door burst open and something huge and black barreled through. I had no time to react. It was on to me in the flash of an eye, and its weight threw me to the floor. I felt cold, damp breath on my cheeks and heard a sniff as it smelled at me. The weight lifted, and a howl of frustration echoed around the library. Something flashed in the light – silver and bright, and cold where it sliced through my shirt and into my belly. I felt blood flow. I screamed out, the only thing I could think of at that moment, the last syllables of the protective ritual that had worked earlier.

"'*Dhumna Ort! Dhumna Ort!*'

"The weight lifted, as if it had never been there, and a black shadow sped away from me, out of the door and off, the door slamming hard behind it in final punctuation to the attack.

"I felt at my waist. I was indeed cut, and bally sore, but it was a shallow wound, and could be temporarily patched by stuffing a handkerchief under my shirt. I would live. I dragged myself back inside the circle where a wide-eyed Abberline could do nothing but sit and stare in amazement."

Carnacki paused in his tale to knock out his pipe.

"I know you chaps will find it hard to believe that all of this was playing out in the room just yards from where you sit tonight, but I can assure you that every word is true. More than that, I can show you."

Carnacki unbuttoned his shirt at the waist and pulled it open. He was swathed in a bandage around his torso, one that was lightly dappled with red stains in places. He looked at me.

"Now you see the reason for me being off color, Dodgson. Do not fret – it hurt like blazes at the time, but is no worse than toothache now, and in a week I'll be right as rain. Worse things happen at sea. Besides, it is time to fill our glasses again, before I bring this tale to its conclusion."

We did as we were bid and recharged our drinks. Carnacki waited until we were settled again, with fresh smokes lit, before continuing.

"Abberline gaped at me for several minutes after I made my way back into the circle and sat, somewhat gingerly I can tell you, in my chair. My wound throbbed something fierce and felt damp near my waistband, but I wasn't about to leave the circle again any time soon – one silly mistake was all I was willing to allow myself.

"'It's the Ripper, isn't it?' Abberline said after a time, and I heard a quiver in his voice. 'It's the Ripper – and it has come for her.'

"'Well, it is certainly a ripper, of sorts,' I answered. 'But whether it is indeed the stuff of your obsession, your Jack of Whitechapel, is something we may never know. It may be that this thing from beyond is attached somehow to the girl for some other reason. It makes no never mind in either case – it is obviously here. And equally obviously, we shall have to deal with it.'

"'And how do we do that?' Abberline said grimly. 'It seems to hold the upper hand here.'

"'You came to me for a reason,' I replied. 'And I have my methods. Now that I know the nature of the thing, I will not be caught out so easily again. Just follow my lead, and do not leave the circle.'

"'I won't be leaving this chair, never mind the bally circle,' the inspector said, and managed a brave smile that gave me hope for his strength in the battle to come. I had a feeling we were going to need as much of it as we could muster.

"The next attack was not long in coming, but this time it was stealthy, and almost caught me by surprise. I smelled the odor again – I will never forget it now – copper, slightly rancid, as if it festered and rotted. Abberline threw me a look. He had smelled the same thing.

"'He is here,' he said, with an air of some despondency.

"Fog thickened by the door, as if curling through from the city outside, the gloom swallowing the light from my lamps and even causing a certain dimming of the pentacle's valves. The odor got stronger, and there came the sound of heavy breathing from beyond the door.

"I started to sing softly, the same Gaelic chant as before, but this time it had no immediate effect. The door swung open with a creak and fog rolled into the library. A shadow came with it, one that took shape, thickening and coalescing in dark clumps that merged and swelled until a tall black figure stood before us fully formed. The tall hat and black cloak it wore as clothing were little more than wispy shadows, but it had human form; it also carried a long, thin surgeon's knife in its right hand that looked most definitely solid. The Ripper raised his head. Red eyes blazed in the gloom as his gaze found us.

"I raised my voice again in the chant and motioned with a hand gesture that Abberline should join in. His singing was nervous and hesitant, but he added what he could. The Ripper paced outside the circle, but did not advance. Instead, it was I that took the initiative, stepping forward to the edge of the defenses and raising my voice to a shout.

"'*Dhumna Ort! Dhumna Ort!*'

"The Ripper did not back away. He laughed back at me, so loud that he set the old chandelier swinging, the noise reverberating through the whole house. I would not be surprised if he did not wake half of London.

"I dared not take my eyes from that blasted knife. The Ripper showed me the weapon, and another grotesque low laugh echoed around the library. Abberline shouted, I bellowed and stamped in time to my chant, but our efforts were not rewarded. The Ripper grew firmer, more solid than ever, even the hat and cape taking on solidity there in the fog. Drops of blood fell from the knife as it was raised in an attack. I braced myself to meet it.

"The Ripper hit the defensive circle, the red valve flared, bright as the sun, and the attacker fell away, whimpering as if he had just been kicked. Thick fog swirled just outside the defenses and the shadow slunk away into it, until not even a part of him could be seen.

"Abberline yelled in triumph, but it was short lived. More fog rolled in, wave after wave of it filling the room until the library shelves disappeared from view and we were left inside a dome of gray, protected by the defenses, but completely surrounded by a lowering gloom.

"Silence fell once more.

"The red valve pulsed and dimmed, pulsed and dimmed.

"Somewhere out in the fog the Ripper breathed in time.

"I do not know how long we sat there, lost in the fog. It certainly seemed like several hours, over the course of which Abberline grew increasingly agitated. The Ripper prowled around the circle all the while, sometimes breathing heavily, at others scratching the knife across the floorboards in a most menacing manner, and every time the girl so much as twitched it let out a rumbling laugh that sent ice shivering down my spine.

"'Dash it, Carnacki,' Abberline finally said, accompanied by another of those terrible laughs. 'Is there nothing you can do?'

"'I am open to suggestions,' I said. 'But I have found a wait-and-see approach often yields results in matters such as these.'

"'Matters such as these?' Abberline said with a harsh laugh. 'I suppose you have seen hundreds of cases of spectral Rippers? Are you the one that will not be blamed for nothing?'

"'What did you say?'

"I had him repeat it – and remembered, the strange particular phrases from the original case, writing on a wall that no one had ever made sense of. I was now thinking, of ritual, of blood, and of patterns.

"As Abberline spoke, the Ripper laughed again, long and hard, but this time I scarcely noted it, for the inspector had given me an idea – a damn fool idea, but an idea none the less.

"'Do you have a pocket knife on you?' I asked him, and at first he looked at me as if I might be deranged, for he did not see the purpose of the question.

" 'A small one, yes,' he replied finally.

" 'And do you trust me in this matter?'

" 'I would not have come if I was not ready to put my life in your hands, Carnacki.'

" 'Let us hope it does not come to that. I need you to cut the girl – we will need some blood, hopefully not too much of it. When I start chanting, I need you to pipe up too – doesn't matter what you say, as long as you make a noise. And, when I ask you to do something, you must do it, immediately, and without hesitation.'

"He had raw fear in his eyes at that, but he was a stout enough fellow at heart, for he took out a small knife, and nodded. 'Just say the word. Where shall I cut?'

" 'Across her palm should suffice – nothing that will require stitching or cause permanent damage. We need just enough to get his attention.'

"The Ripper laughed somewhere in the fog.

" 'I should say we have achieved that already,' Abberline said drolly.

" 'Then let us begin. Make the cut – remember, not too deep. But there must be blood, that is the important thing here.'

"I watched as he cut the girl – she did not even so much as flinch – and saw blood, too red, start to pool in the bowl of her palm. Out in the fog the Ripper sniffed, twice, the second closer than the first. He had found the scent, and taken the bait.

"I stepped forward to the edge of the protections. The Ripper came forward too, emerging out of the murk to stand just beyond the valves. His chest heaving, he breathed heavily, knife raised, ready to jump forward. The red eyes flared and dimmed; my red valve responded in kind.

"I raised my voice in chant again – Abberline had inadvertently told me what was required. This time my chant was the same words as before, but with the cadence subtly altered, matching the rhythm and flow of the words written on that Whitechapel wall these twenty-odd years passed. As with most rituals, the words themselves did not matter, it was the rhythm of the thing, and the intent with which they were said.

"'*Ri linn dioladh na beatha Ri linn bruchdadh na falluis.*'

"In my mind I heard my chant doubled with the original words.

"'*The Juwes are the ones that will not be blamed for nothing.*'

"I continued with the second phrase.

"'*Ri linn iobar na creadha, Ri linn dortadh na fala.*'

"I heard Abberline shouting along, nonsense words, but more than enough to get the Ripper's attention. The tall black figure turned from me to look at Abberline, tensed, and pounced, the knife raised high. He hit the defenses and the red valve flashed brightly. This time he did not back away, but came straight back into another attack.

"'The blood – sprinkle him with her blood,' I called.

"Abberline smeared the girl's blood from her palm into his – then surprised me by walking forward toward the edge of the circle. At the same instant as the Ripper hit the pentacle full on again, Abberline stepped completely out of the defenses.

"'I've got you now, you bastard,' the inspector said. 'I've finally got you.'

"He grabbed the Ripper hard at the shoulders, smearing blood where his hands touched. The Ripper howled, as if sprayed with a strong corrosive. The pentacle screeched. The Ripper howled again, and tried to pull away, but Abberline would not let go. The Ripper's knife flashed, twice, and I heard the old copper grunt in pain, but still he refused to release his grip.

"'You're not getting another one,' he shouted. 'Not on my watch.'

"As they grappled I raised my voice loud again, and behind me the girl, Mary, came out of her torpor and joined in.

"'*Ri linn dioladh na beatha, Ri linn bruchdadh na falluis.*

"'*Ri linn iobar na creadha, Ri linn dortadh na fala.*'

"The blackness of the Ripper seemed to swirl and melt, becoming insubstantial. I kept shouting, as loud as I was able. The girl stood and came to my side, and, like a priest delivering holy water, sprinkled her blood over Abberline and the Ripper in time with my voice.

" '*Ri linn dioladh na beatha, Ri linn bruchdadh na falluis.*

" '*Ri linn iobar na creadha, Ri linn dortadh na fala.*'

" 'That's for my mother, you bastard,' the girl shouted.

" '*Dhumna Ort!*' I called, bringing the ritual – both rituals – to a conclusion.

"The Ripper fell apart, shadows and dust that were eaten by a rising glow of deep red from the pentacle. The fog went with it, drawing away and out of the open library door. There came a single thud – one last knife stroke that hit only wood – then all was silent.

"The Ripper was gone."

Carnacki put down his glass and stood up, his tale done. Arkwright, as ever, had a question before we were shooed out into the night.

"So, this bally Ripper case – that is it done – it is finally done?"

Carnacki laughed bitterly. "I have no idea. It may never be done. Or it may not have been the Ripper at all. It may be that the thing I saw in my library merely came full blown from the febrile imagination of a young girl's mind, made solid by Abberline's obsession. Or it may be that we have indeed rid the land of an ages-old menace that will now never be able to return.

"There is only one thing I know for sure, and for me, that will suffice. He believes it, and I choose to believe it.

"Chief Inspector Abberline of the Yard finally got his man.

"Now, out you go," Carnacki said, and sent us on our way.

The fog still hung thick over the Embankment, and I walked swiftly, listening for any snuffles, any scrape of knife on stone. But none came, and I made my way safely, if rather uncomfortably, home.

It's All in the Genes
Cara Cooper

He said he thought bodies were often more beautiful dead than alive. It was when we were having lunch in the Victoria and Albert Museum. We were walking back past the marble statue of a Roman noblewoman.

'I think she's ugly,' I said. 'Look at those arms, they're as heavy as a man's.'

'Oh no, she's utterly beautiful.' He stopped to gaze at her. I gazed at him thinking much the same. He's tall with immaculate hair and soulful eyes, which just make me melt. 'She's alluring,' he went on, 'because she's sort of exposed. We can walk around her, look at her, stare at her. We can study every limb, every inch of her being and she can't flinch or turn away. She's there for anyone to enjoy and she always will be.'

I guess that's why he chose to study Forensics. Because he finds dead creatures to be like statues and more beguiling than their live counterparts. Jay is so clever, he has a sharp mind. Like a razor.

He took me to the specialist Forensics Unit at the Natural History Museum on our second date. It's where he studies. He told me, 'I spend so much of my time there, come with me and take a look.' We'd been to see a film at the Curzon Mayfair. Then walked through Hyde Park, which is magical at night. 'I'd like to show you, it's totally special, one of the secret places of London.' Other girls might think that was the weirdest second date ever but I didn't. I thought it was amazing. It was so different. Like him. He knows things other people don't. And he sees things normal people don't. It's almost like he can see inside you.

I visited the Natural History Museum as a child and the collection I love best is the gemstone gallery. Sapphire, jade, carnelian, watermelon tourmaline. Even the names of the stones are entrancing, conjuring up far away lands. Who wouldn't want to go to India, Burma, Tanzania. I hope one day to go to exotic places and have a man who'll buy me gems, adorn me with them. If only it could be Jay. Sometimes I see him looking at me as if he'd like to see me clothed in nothing but a string of pearls to match my pale skin, and with earrings of deep orange citrine to set off my fiery hair.

He grabbed my hand as we went up the stone steps, they were dingy this time of night, blending into the darkness. I felt secure with his fingers wrapped round mine. Jay has a pass and knows all the security guards. We went through the museum's staff entrance at the side, our footsteps echoing in the empty chasm of the great hall. Deserted, the massive space is reminiscent of a cathedral without a congregation. The museum's a Victorian building, all gothic arches and turrets, like a fairy-tale castle but not at all Disneyesque. It's in one of those turrets where the Forensic Unit is housed, way above London. It sits in the clouds like it's floating in its own private alien world. Especially after hours.

There was a silver coin moon in the sky, glinting through the casement windows. 'You're like Rapunzel up here in the tower with your long hair.' He smiled. I squinted as my eyes became accustomed to the gloom. Thin light spilt over Formica counters illuminating the area where they cut things up. It trickled into cabinets where weird things moved and squirmed, unsleeping even in the dead of night. 'Let's not switch on the light,' he said, stroking his angular fingers over the back of my hand, 'the moonlight sort of goes with this place. I come here when I can't sleep. I often don't sleep well, and I just look at all the stuff we've been working on during the day. I like the silence when the other students aren't around. It doesn't worry me to be on my own.' I felt honoured when he said that. Honoured he'd chosen to take me up there and I knew in that moment he'd never brought any of his other girl-friends there. To that eerie place.

He squeezed my fingers and I felt heat flood through my body as if I'd taken a shot of tequila straight to my veins. I was drunk with him, intoxicated. 'What's that noise?' I asked. There was a low buzzing, not like anything that comes from a machine. Then the odd tick. I looked frantically around, green eyes blinking in the half-light.

He laughed, a low purr that was incredibly sexy. 'Well, actually we're not alone.'

I felt suddenly scared. He moved closer. What did he mean? Were we on camera? There seem to be cameras everywhere nowadays. It was horrid to think some security guard might be spying on us, watching Jay's hand caress my shoulder, move down my back, circle round my waist. I wanted this moment to be ours, to be totally private. My hackles rose.

'What do you mean? Not alone?'

The buzzing grew louder, the ticking more insistent, as if something were tapping on glass. It was beginning to freak me out. The whole place was. But it excited me too. I like to be frightened. Fear is close to ecstasy, don't you think? The same pounding of your heart, the same quickness of breath, the same moistening of the palms. I began to focus through the dimness. I glimpsed giant jars full of yellow liquid lining the wall. Things floated in them, twisted, bits of bodily things. And there was a sickly scent in the air, an odd nasal concoction of chemicals and meaty animal odours. I was desperate to open the window. I felt suddenly faint.

'We're not alone, because we're with them.' He leaned down and placed his hand in the small of my back to beckon me down too. He peered into a glass tank, the moonlight shining directly into it and I saw something inside moving. Jay chuckled deep in his throat. He was enjoying our bodies touching, the intimacy of it. 'Don't worry,' he said. 'They can't get out.'

Flies, that's what it was, hundreds maybe thousands of blowflies. Some crashed their heads against the glass as they sensed us. Most were moving over an object that looked like a child's leg, without a foot. There were so many of them crawling, undulating en masse, that it appeared as if the limb itself was waking and twitching. As if the dead thing had somehow come to life and any moment might haul itself up and hobble out on its bony footless ankle.

'Ugh.' I recoiled and jumped back. He caught me and, in a moment, I was folded into his arms and his lips were searching out mine. Soft and silky, firm and insistent, sensual and hungry with passion. I didn't resist. I fell into his kiss. Don't be surprised, I'd been waiting for it all evening. My pulse raced so hard I could feel it tick-tock in my wrist. I would have collapsed if he hadn't held me up and, for the first time, I felt a thrill at the power of his arms, surprised at how muscular his body was under those baggy oversized shirts he wears. The moonlight shone on to my eyelids. They flickered and closed as I enjoyed surrendering to his hold, submitting to his domination. My breath came in shallow bursts as his hand stroked gently then closed over my throat guiding me further into him. A prisoner, I was pinioned in his embrace.

Then, in a moment, he was done.

He released me.

Like he wanted to save something for later.

I wanted more, so much more. It was the most exciting kiss I had ever had, sweet and sour in that unearthly place. No other boyfriend had ever kept me on the edge in the way Jay did. Funny thing is, he can turn on and off, just like that. Almost like he's two different people. One minute the fervent lover, the next a cold, detached practitioner of Forensic Science. The participant becomes the observer like a switch has been flicked in his brain. I suppose you have to be like that if you study what he's studying. If you let it get to you, you'd crack up. He examined the tank, as if he were a teacher lecturing a new student. 'They're bluebottles, *Calliphora Vomitoria*. Isn't that a disgusting name? It always makes me laugh. It sounds like some awful Roman goddess of nausea. We feed the flies on animal carcasses. The one they're on now is a leg of lamb. We measure their rate of reproduction and their life cycle. You can tell a helluva lot from the maggots and how long it takes them to hatch. They're extraordinary creatures, the tools of our trade. They can solve all sorts of mysteries, like whether a body has been moved since death. Or how long a carcass has been exposed above ground before burial. We're doing good work here; we help to fight crime. I feel we're providing a useful service to society. Lots of girls would shy away, would find them disgusting. I'm glad you haven't, Grace, you're different.'

It wasn't long after that night we became lovers. Fervent, energetic lovers. My friends envy me, he's just so darned good-looking. I see them thinking: how did Grace with her bee-sting breasts and her pale freckled skin, which turns pink the moment it hits the sun, hook a guy so gorgeous? The thing they don't understand is that *he* chooses. He chooses everything about his life and anything he wants, he takes. He always has done. I suppose that's what you get with men who come from wealthy families.

I learned a lot from Jay about so many things. He spends ages in the museums, he's like an encyclopedia. Not that I'm stupid. I study at the Royal College of Music, opposite the Albert Hall. I'm a pianist, and although music is good for the soul, I realise his chosen field might be considered a lot more useful to the world than mine.

I think the music thing is why he reckoned me to be good girl-friend material. His family are intellectual snobs. I learned that when he took me to lunch there for the first time. They have a superb house, in the back streets of the Boltons, a sought-after area, not flash or brash like Knightsbridge. One neighbour's a QC, the other's a plastic surgeon. They like to pretend they're not posh by slumming it. So their sprawling townhouse is messy with books and newspapers over every surface and no one ever seems to empty the dishwasher. You can barely find a place to put down a mug of tea, or a drink. It was drinks, of course, when we arrived, expensive claret poured by his father, who practises in the City. I wasn't listening that well. I was too enthralled with Jay's mother and her utterly beautiful jewellery. Understated, but dazzling to me who's never owned more than glass beads.

She was wearing a pair of orange drop earrings, which glistened every time she tilted her head. I couldn't keep my eyes off them. They looked dark, amber like autumn leaves against her greying hair. Until we went into the garden, out in the sunshine, where they caught on fire as if they'd been ignited with little flames. At one point, later in the evening, they started to annoy her – she kept on rubbing her lobes. She took them off and just chucked them in a corner amongst a load of unopened junk mail. So careless, I really worried about them getting lost. They must have cost a fortune.

I watched his mother more closely after that. I'd say she is the nervy sort, always on edge. She never sits still, is always up and about, and fiddles with everything. Her skirt, her hair, her jewellery. She habitually plays with the rings on her hands like they're worry beads. I see Jay's father's eyes constantly flick in her direction, as if he's expecting a pan of milk to boil over.

There was another relative there, a cousin up from the country. We were sitting over dessert – a chocolate and raspberry roulade. Jay's mother, Annabel, barely touched it. She eats like a bird. The cousin, Sarah I think her name was, was sharp and angular. She looked like a beady-eyed mouse with lots of dull-blonde hair. 'You know I've been doing our genealogy?'

'Yes,' said Benedict. That's Jay's father. 'Have you found we're related to royalty?'

'Not quite. Rather the opposite, I'm afraid. More like a serial killer.'

Annabel gasped. Jay's father laughed – he's much more relaxed than Annabel. He quaffed another gulp of wine. 'Really?'

'It looks like we're distantly related to Jack the Ripper. I don't know if you read in the papers recently, there's speculation that they've found conclusively who the Ripper was through DNA tests. A shawl turned up for auction, reputedly salvaged from one of the crime scenes. Blood on it has been attributed to one of the suspects, a Polish man whose descendants are around today. I've traced a connection to them. Anyway, we're distantly related.'

Jay sat up in his chair and looked animated for the first time that evening. Previously he'd been bored by his mother endlessly going on about her ailments. Now his interest had been sparked. 'How amazing. Do you think that sort of thing runs in the genes?'

'What, the Murder Gene you mean?' Benedict scoffed, spitting out a dribble of wine. 'I know I've felt like murdering the odd judge in my time, and some of my clients.' He'd had much too much, his speech beginning to slur.

Jay was deadly serious. 'Why shouldn't it? Other traits run in families. There are acting dynasties like the Redgraves and there are ruling dynasties like the Gandhis. Why shouldn't there be murdering dynasties?'

'Jay, stop. Don't talk about it, it's not nice.' Annabel looked even more uptight than normal. Like she wanted to run away from the confines of her rarefied existence.

That evening, as he said goodbye to me, Jay peered deep into my eyes like he was trying to see into my soul. 'Does it worry you, that you might be sleeping with someone whose blood is the same as Jack the Ripper's?'

'And that he studies Forensics, and skulks about in dark places in the moonlight and probably keeps weird things in his briefcase?' I tried to keep light-hearted. Nevertheless, the hairs stood up on the back of my neck at the thought of it.

I'd always been reluctant to have Jay meet my family, his is so cool and colourful in comparison. My mother, Theresa, lives in a small terraced house on the outskirts of South London. It's a world away from Jay's but he was the total gentleman when we visited. He said all sorts of nice things about Mum's homely lamb hotpot and her apple turnover and custard. I was hugely grateful to him. He seemed to be making a super-human effort to make her feel at ease. While I watched him making her laugh, being the consummate charmer, I almost expired with love for him. My heart was like a huge, great down-filled pillow that wanted to envelop him and hold him for ever. I'm so lucky. In that moment I made the decision to compose a piece of piano music for him, a priceless present from me to him. No other girl can give him that. I vowed to paint him wonderful pictures, write him poems, learn how to sew and make him things, personal gifts, lover's gifts to keep and treasure.

My mother always does a pot of tea after a meal. While she was off clattering with cups and jugs in the kitchen, getting out the special china she never normally uses, he noticed a photo on the mantelpiece. 'Your dad's not around, is he?'

'No, he went away when I was tiny. He didn't come back.'

'So this must be you with the long red hair in pigtails and the blue dress. But who's this?' He lifted up the photo and pointed to a pram.

'I had a younger sister. Zara. She died when she was a baby.'

'I'm sorry.'

'Don't worry, it was a long time ago. It was a cot death. We got over it, Mum and I. We supported each other. We're very close.'

After that, I might be imagining it, but Jay seemed even more attentive towards me. He's so sensitive, it's just like him to pick up on any emotions and respond to them. I thought I was so head over heels, I couldn't love him more, but after that day I did. I don't want to appear too needy, but there are times when I got desperate even when he was up there studying with all those bluebottles and horrid things. I don't love by halves, you see. The Royal College of Music is so close to the Natural History Museum, so I'd go down there at lunch-time, sit on a bench in the street, and eat my salad looking up at the window where he works. It helped me feel close to him. I started doing it in the evenings too.

We were walking round the Albert Memorial one day, arm in arm, looking at that huge monolith of a statue, thinking our own thoughts and saying nothing. Perfect companions can be happy together in silence. I was pondering on the amazing affection Victoria had for Albert and how extraordinary the memorial is as a monument to one woman's outpouring of emotion for a single man. If I were a queen, I'd have done the same for Jay. I hoped Jay was thinking something similar, he was so quiet.

'What are you thinking about?'

'I was just thinking how so many things round here were built at the same time Jack the Ripper was around. This memorial, the Albert Hall, the museums. The Ripper could have visited any one of them. My ancestor, my relation, could have stepped here. I could be walking in *his* footsteps. Isn't that amazing?'

'I guess so.' But I wished he'd been thinking of me. This Ripper thing was becoming an obsession.

The next day, Jay didn't phone me as usual in the morning. I missed my early fix of him, I was like an addict not getting her drugs. I phoned and texted and there was nothing. I went at lunch-time to the museum, worried there was something wrong. There was an ambulance and police cars at the entrance and they weren't letting people in. To say I panicked was an understatement. I was beside myself.

Finally, when I thought I would go insane, Jay phoned.

'Where have you been, I was worried sick.'

'Don't go crazy, Grace, something happened today. We came into the lab and one of the other students, a guy called Callum, was found dead.'

'Dead?'

'Yeah, stone cold. I went in with one of the other guys and there he was. He looked mind-blowing.'

'*Mind-blowing*, what do you mean? Jay, you do my head in sometimes. I've been so worried about you.'

'I was fine, don't fuss. But he did look extraordinary in death. His face was entirely free of troubles, at one with the world, like he'd found his rightful place.'

'What happened to him, how did he die?'

'Chemical poisoning they think, that's the rumour, although there'll be an inquest, of course. Callum liked to indulge in the odd illegal substance, and there are a lot of chemicals in the museum with all the research and stuff the academics do here. He used to drink a bit too. I once saw him slip a bottle of vodka out of the cupboard when he was working. I reckon he had a problem.'

'That's awful.'

'Yeah. They'll dissect him, probably, to find out what it was. When

I'm qualified in Forensics, I'll be doing just that. It's all about learning the truth, Grace, and you know what Keats said, "Beauty is truth, truth beauty." He was a Victorian too, just like the Ripper. Just like my famous ancestor.'

He was full of the Callum thing; that's all he talked about that evening.

He took me to Whitechapel once, the district where the Ripper killings took place. We went on one of those guided Ripper walks given by an actor in a top hat and a cape. Whitechapel was chilly and dark and it's an odd part of London. Tatty and run-down, it sits as incongruously as a tramp plonked on a bench next to a smart City insurance broker. The finance district is ultra smart with its chrome and glass then you turn a corner and there's Whitechapel all covered in litter and cheap market stalls. The area is still murky and at night there are echoes of the past with its dark doorways and shady past. 'It was easy in those days, Grace, to kill someone I mean. It's a lot more difficult now to get away with it. There are complications, you have to think more, you have to plan and you have to be lucky. But people do still, literally, get away with murder.'

I looked at him curiously. I never know what's going on in his head.

We often pop round to his parents and watch TV. The house is huge, they have three televisions so we can huddle away, just the two of us while his dad's working in the study and his mother's upstairs nursing one of her many migraines. Jay told me she went wandering the other night. Went off all on her own without telling anyone, just said she needed to be alone. Weird. 'She gets depression. She's done it before.'

While I was there though, Annabel surfaced and made herself some chamomile tea. Isn't it amazing how the skinniest pasty-looking people are always eating and drinking so-called healthy food? Annabel sat with us for a little while and I noticed she had on not just her citrine earrings, but a fabulous matching pendant. The light sparkled off the gems, reminding me of the ones in the museum. I'd love to try them on. They must have cost a fortune, but she doesn't care for them like she should. She said the pendant annoys her, it's too heavy and sometimes the chain breaks. Annabel doesn't know how lucky she is; she's a real glass-half-empty sort of person. I feel Jay bristle and stiffen while she's in the room. He's too loyal to say anything but I think she gets on his nerves. She said, 'I ran into Mrs Grammaticus today. Do you remember her, the mother of that poor boy you were at school with? He drowned on a school trip, Grace, it was truly awful for his mother.'

Jay sounded impatient, annoyed she'd disturbed us. 'Of course I remember her, Mum.'

'Her other boys are doing well – one's got a place at a hospital in Portsmouth, he'll be a qualified doctor this time next year. The other's going to be an architect, and the third's going into law like your father. It was a terrible tragedy though, her eldest son dying like that. I should never have got over it.'

'She had others to take his place, didn't she?' It might sound like Jay was uncaring but I think he was just exasperated by Annabel. Sometimes he can get quite uptight. I guess he's learned it from her. We learn everything from our parents, don't we? Later, when we were alone in his bedroom he finished off a whole bottle of wine single-handedly. He rarely drinks, but it was like he had something on his mind. Like he needed to share. He said, 'I do remember the Grammaticus boy very well. He used to steal.'

'What?'

'He'd steal money from our blazer pockets while we were having rowing practice on the river. He was a cheat too. A proper little criminal in the making. He stole a key to the cupboard where they kept the exam papers, copied the answers and passed with flying colours. No one ever found out except me. I caught him red-handed. He swore he'd beat me up if I let the secret out. I despised him. I taught him a lesson later though.'

'What sort of lesson?' We were curled up on his bed and it was like we were in a cocoon, all safe and sound where the rest of the world couldn't get us. It was just us two. I loved him more than I loved my own life and he knew it. I guess that's why he felt safe telling me, that and the drink. He knew I'd have done anything for him.

His voice was quite steady when he said it.

'I killed him.'

I stayed silent, didn't know what to say. I merely raised an eyebrow. He went on. 'He was being a little shit as usual. We were in Cornwall on this geography field trip, digging about, collecting stones and stuff at the bottom of the cliffs. We'd wandered away from the group. The Grammaticus boy had been standing on this large rock making fun of me. He said I was feeble because I wouldn't climb up there with him and play some stupid game. At first, I hadn't meant to kill him, I just got cross and threw this rock at him. It hit him in the eye and he fell. He was lying there on the sand and the tide changed – it does in Cornwall, really quickly. I saw it lick at his shoes. I could have saved him then. I'm really not sure if he was dead straight away. But he looked extraordinary with his eyes closed and his evil pug-nosed face all still. Suddenly, he couldn't hurt or aggravate me. His expressionless body was wonderful. Pale and blank and powerless. I just left him there. In fact, I deliberately circled away from where we'd been and joined the others from a different direction. It was a good ten minutes before they realised he was missing. By that time, he'd been washed out to sea. I've been wondering lately about that Ripper stuff. I might be a rein-carnation of my dearly departed relative, who knows?'

'Oh shut up, Jay, you're just drunk.' But, it was then I began to wonder about Jay's fellow student, Callum. I began to think about how well Jay understood all those chemicals. I imagined him sitting there once it was all done, looking at the dead body and thinking how beauti-ful it was. Longing to cut it up but resisting, leaving it till morning to turn up innocently with his fellow students to 'discover' the body.

Some people might think I was mad to stay with Jay, but I loved him, and love truly is blind. What's more, I never feared him. I wasn't with him long enough for that. I believe he loved me, he would never have done anything to hurt me.

Except for that day when I was going home past the Natural History Museum on the bus and I saw him come out with a girl. I was late; it was a Thursday. I'd stayed to do some practice. We'd stopped at the traffic lights and I was on the top deck. I could see him clearly, and her, and he was looking deep into her eyes. Just like he'd peered into mine. As I watched his hand creep around her waist, and he moved down to place his lips on hers, it was as if all the flies in that rotten tank he'd shown me had flown out of the museum window. It was like they'd swarmed through the window of the bus deliberately to find me. Like they'd migrated straight into my belly, and were squirming and churning and their maggots were eating my insides. I felt like throwing up the entire contents of my stomach. For I knew, there and then, that he'd taken her up there, to his 'secret' place. The bus pulled away. I missed my stop, of course, and I missed college the next day. Jay and I were due to have lunch and I even missed that. I told him I was ill.

He phoned me. We were due to go and stay with his parents that weekend, at their house in the country, in Dorset. I told him yes, I was still going, of course I did. I wanted to see how he treated me, how good an actor he was when he was two-timing me. I found out he was a very good actor, a superb one. He was attentive and kind and charming. Typical Jay. I let him touch me; I wasn't at all distant. I didn't want him to suspect I knew. But I decided I'd get my own back. It's amazing how quickly love can turn to hate. I can't stand it, you see, when people betray me, and they so often do, don't they? I don't know why I put my trust in anyone.

I learned that lesson when I was young, when my little sister Zara came along. I helped Mum to bathe her and change and feed her in the night. I was the best sister ever. But do you know how she repaid me? By stealing Mum's love, that's how. Gradually, I saw how Mum favoured her over me, with her blonde hair and her blue eyes ringed with those dark lashes. Even more so because she was delicate, some problem with her heart it was.

She had to go.

It was easy to creep into Zara's bedroom one night.

One of those really cold nights. Zara was a very docile baby, she rarely cried. Even if she had, Mum was taking sleeping pills then, it was just after Dad left. She'd go out like a light and I often got up in the night to see to Zara. I undressed her carefully. Babies find it very difficult to regulate their temperature and I watched Zara's lips turn blue. Then I put her clothes back on and wrapped her in a really thick blanket and watched her face go puce as she overheated. Then I took off the blanket and left her, just as I'd found her. The next morning the house was silent, so silent. Apart from Mum screaming. Zara had always been a weak baby, I just helped her out of this world. Of course it upset Mum and I felt bad about that, but she got over it, with my help. I was ever the dutiful daughter.

Dorset's lovely for a weekend, even with Jay the betrayer here. Him and his dad are going down to the pub in a bit. They'll be there till last orders. I'm staying here to keep his Mum company while we watch the tennis. Annabel's been twitchy the whole time we've been here. Personally, I think she's heading for some sort of breakdown. I can hear her pacing round upstairs. She said she had a headache, didn't want to watch TV. She's got those wonderful earrings on again and that superb pendant, the one I like so much. She told me today how she's always losing jewellery. How she once took off a sapphire ring when she washed her hands in the loos at John Lewis and, when she went back to find it, someone had stolen it. Well, they would, wouldn't they? Benedict was furious, and raised it whenever they had a row about how messy she was and how she didn't keep the house properly while he was out working till all hours.

I took her up a cup of peppermint tea and some sliced mango. I prepared it myself, to show I care. I sat on her bed and chatted. I knew how open to suggestion she could be. 'It's a lovely evening out there, Annabel, the air's really fresh. There's a fabulous sunset and the first stars are just appearing. You seem a bit restless. Why don't we go out for a walk? We could go down the pub and join the boys?' I knew she wouldn't want to; she hates pubs. All those glasses clashing, people jostling and laughing loudly. It upsets her equilibrium she says. 'No, no, I'm OK.' I could see she wanted to be alone, but at least I'd planted the seed. I remembered how Jay said she can wander off on occasions. Now all I had to do was wait.

I heard her creep out. I was listening for her while I watched the TV. She didn't want to offend me by not asking me to go with her. I got up, looked out of the window and waited until she'd turned the corner in the lane. Then I set off after her. The countryside round here is pitch black once you get off the beaten track. At times, it was difficult to follow her. I had to keep my wits about me, especially when she stumbled off the track and into the woods. But she was making enough noise even when I couldn't see her. She was in a dreadful state, poor Annabel, crashing around, running, falling over, crawling a bit. Then picking herself up, looking up at the stars and wringing her hands in that way she does. Actually, it was a kindness what I did next. It's horrid to see a depressed, anxious woman who's had enough of life carry on. All that wealth, all that money and fine houses in the town and the country don't necessarily make you happy. I could see she'd had enough. I followed her for ages, as she wandered in that demented way until finally the right time came.

It must have been an old chalk quarry, or maybe a bomb had dropped there in the war or something. I don't know. But what I do know is that it was a ruddy great hole in the ground and the edges of it were a sheer drop and all overgrown. It was perfect. I waited till she'd stopped, then I called out sharply to her.

'Annabel.'

She gave a little scream, more like a squeak really of surprise, and turned around. She didn't know it was me at first in the darkness. Poor thing was scared stiff. She looked like a madwoman, trembling and with her hair all over the place. 'Who is it?' she asked, her voice breaking with terror.

'It's only me.' I wanted to put her at ease. I needed to get close.

'Grace?'

'Yes. I was worried about you. What are you doing out here all on your own?'

Her mouth opened and closed. She looked like a fish. She was embarrassed, confused, annoyed at me invading her private moment of madness. 'Come on, let me take you home.' I reached my hand out in the darkness, as if I wanted to take her arm, but it was the chain with that lovely pendant I was aiming for. I always thought the chain was too thin for such a heavy gem. I grabbed it and it snapped off in my hand. I grabbed the gem quickly as it fell from her neck. The stone was warm in my hands, warm from her skinny chest. 'See,' I ticked her off, 'it's silly to be wandering here in the country all on your own. You'll lose stuff and Benedict will tell you off. Come on, let me help you. Let's go back.'

It was touch and go really, she looked like she wanted to run, like she couldn't make a decision whether to come with me or take off. It didn't matter either way really, I nearly had what I wanted. I stepped towards her. She was right on the edge of the drop. She held out her arm to me. She thought I was going to hold her hand. She gave me a little smile. I smiled back.

Then I thrust out my hand and shoved her. Hard. It was like toppling over a skittle with your little finger. Her scream pierced the darkness as she fell, fell, fell way down. It reminded me of a black bin bag hurtling down a rubbish chute. Then I heard the brambles and undergrowth swish and close over her and all was silent again.

I didn't hang around. I'd lost all sense of time, all I knew was it was very late. I needed to get back to the house and resume my place in front of the TV before Jay and Benedict got back from the pub. I ran back like all the demons in hell were after me. At one point I almost got lost, which would have been a disaster, but the one good thing about the country at night is that the villages stand out like beacons amongst those dark fields and woods. I simply headed towards the lights. When I got in, I hid the pendant in one of my socks and buried it deep in my bag. I was sorry about not getting the earrings but hey, it doesn't do to be greedy.

There was a search, of course, but they didn't find her at first. Not for weeks. I have to admit it was a difficult time for me. A worrying one.

Finally, they did find her body. It was assumed she'd sneaked off on one of her wanderings, and slipped over the edge. It was a hell of a drop. She'd broken her back. I heard Jay and Benedict talking about it all. Benedict was distraught; he really did love her. Jay mentioned the missing pendant and talked of climbing into the quarry to look for it. He's a cold-hearted bastard.

I'm so much better off without him. My new boyfriend's a banker. He has shedloads of money, we're off to Australia on holiday and he said he'd buy me one of those fire opals. I absolutely love those. And I love him; he's amazing. I'd do anything for him.

The only thing I miss about Jay is his intellect. I think he was right when he said he'd inherited the Ripper gene though. He's got it, for sure. We never see each other now and I never even wonder what he's doing. I congratulate myself on having moved on.

I went to see my father the other day, even though I hate going there. He'll never get out of prison, it was a life sentence he was given for what he did to those women. I study him when we're talking during those dismal visits. The place gives me the creeps. I always have to wash my hands three times afterwards and throw my clothes in the washing machine. It smells of boiled cabbage and sweat, like all institutions. I only do it as a kindness to Mum. It's too painful for her, so I go to see Dad and let her know how he's doing. I look at him, and think to myself, like father like daughter. Jay was right, the serial killer gene can run in families. The thing is, I'm more clever than Dad. More educated and . . . well, just more clever than him. He was stupid.

I'm different.

I know I'll never get caught.

A Child of the Darkness

Brett McBean

The boy pushed open the doors and entered the pub with an air of anticipation.

Hope was in short supply here in the East End of London, and what little did seep out of the poor and unfortunate denizens consisted mostly of pitiful desires for enough food to stave off the clawing hunger pains and enough work so they didn't have to stand in line at the dreaded workhouse. Still, as young Henry Morris made his way towards the bar, moving cautiously around the hazy forms of people drinking and laughing, slapping his wicker walking stick against the floor, he was hopeful. His belly was fluttering, and it wasn't simply through lack of anything to eat.

There was a large crowd at the bar. For a Thursday evening, the Princess Alice was busy, but then it was chilly outside and the cold always brought the people into the pubs, especially on nights like tonight, when the air was thin and the wind like ice.

Henry stopped behind the wall of drunken patrons. He wanted to squeeze his way to the counter, but feared getting crushed by the much bigger men and women.

"Excuse me," Henry said, his voice getting lost among the singing and the shouting. "Can I get through?"

Nobody was listening. The great mass of bodies remained as one. Henry raised his cane and waved it in the air in the hopes Mr Ferrar or one of the barmaids would see and realise he was here. "Mr Ferrar!" Henry cried, but his youthful voice was no match for the din inside the pub.

"Hey, lookit 'ere," one of the bodies said, catching sight of the waving cane. "John, I think the lad wants a drain."

Another body standing close by laughed. "What's your poison, Son? Jacky? Ale?"

Henry lowered and clenched his cane. Anticipation was starting to turn to frustration.

"No, I just want to speak with Arthur."

"You lookin' for a job, lad?" the first man said and then he snorted. "I dunno what use Art would 'ave with a blind boy. Do ye sing or dance?"

A friendly voice from behind: "Ah leave him be, Mickeldy Joe. He's a good lad."

Henry spun around in a blur of light and shade. He set his half-blind eyes on the short figure in front. "Sarah." He looked at her vaguely, flicking his eyes about as if he were still fully blind. In truth, he could see the roundness of her face, the way her hair was pulled back and the way her apron stretched over her ample body.

"You're in luck," the waitress said, answering Henry's question before he could ask. "He's 'ere."

Henry's grip on his cane tightened even more, but this time from excitement and even a small helping of fear. "He is?"

"Got in about 'alf an hour ago."

I knew it! Me belly don't lie!

"Where is he?" Henry asked, practically panting.

"Sitting at the table near the stairs."

Henry nodded. Smiled.

"You need 'elp gettin' there? Give me a minute to put down this tray and I'll let you borrow me arm."

A shake of his head. "I know me way around. Thanks anyway."

"Of course you do. But if ye need any 'elp, just let me know."

The muddled figure of Sarah moved away and Henry started towards the staircase.

He moved through the throng of revellers, tapping his cane, even though he no longer needed to, especially not in brightly lit places such as public houses. He was now able to make out shapes and distinguish between light and dark. He was even beginning to see what he assumed were colours, although only when they were particularly bold and he was standing close, and even then the colour was hazy. Still, it was a vast improvement over what he had known before: total blindness ever since he could remember. Blackness. Nothingness.

He waded through the fog of smoke, sweat and gin- and beer-soaked breath. It was muggy inside the pub, the fire must be blazing fiercely and the thick crowd didn't help matters. Or maybe it was just nerves making Henry's hands sweaty.

He walked past one of the long tables, where a group were bellowing out a song:

". . . met a cornet was in a regiment of dragoons . . . I gave 'im what he didn't like . . . and stole his silver spoons . . ."

Light of varying intensity flickered before his eyes while shapes of varying size rolled past.

Finally, he arrived at the table near the stairs. A small table, propped against the wall and away from the crowd. It was just the kind of spot Henry would have expected him to sit.

Henry stood there, throat suddenly stuffed with wool and mouth parched.

The hunched shape at the table was eating and, from the smell, Henry guessed the meal was potatoes and smoked haddock. A large pot of beer sat beside the plate, and on the other side, close to the wall, was a small parcel of some kind, wrapped with what looked like newspaper. Henry watched with his murky eyes as the figure took two mouthfuls of food before stopping. The man turned and looked at Henry.

"I ain't got anything to give ye. So go on, bugger off."

Henry swallowed the lump in his throat. "Are you Hutch?"

The man, whose voice was softer than Henry had imagined, though still coarse like leather, took a swill of ale. He grunted. "Like I said, I'm spent, I can't be giving anything to no beggar."

"I don't want money. What I want from you won't cost you a penny."

The man straightened. He heaved in and then breathed out a heavy sigh, adding the fresh stink of beer and fish to the stale pub air. "What do you want? What is this?"

Henry blinked. With the shadows of the stairs looming over the table, coupled with a wide-brimmed hat shielding half his face, Hutch's features were veiled; all Henry could see was the general spectre of darkness.

Henry drew in a breath, then he spoke. "I need you to kill again."

Henry saw a dark flash of movement, but he had neither the reflexes nor the understanding to move away in time. The hand struck Henry on his left cheek. It was only an open-handed slap, but there was still a lot of power behind the strike and Henry toppled backwards. He hit the floor, wicker cane leaping from his hand, mouth getting a taste of gin and sawdust.

The pain from the fall wasn't great, but his face stung. Around him some of the laughter dropped and he heard people muttering.

Almost as quickly as he had been hit, strong hands were gripping his ragged shirt and pulling him to his feet. Those same hands brushed his clothes and then Henry's walking stick was thrust back into his hand.

A dark shape drew in close and then the man Henry knew as Hutch spoke quietly into his right ear, hot breath tickling his pale skin.

"Meet me out the front of the Victoria Home. But give me ten minutes. Now go on, get."

Hutch sat back in his seat and continued eating and slurping at his beer.

Henry left his father to finish his meal in peace.

Compared to the warmth and brightness of the pub, Commercial Street was bitter and full of shadows. Despite the inclement weather, there were still people about. Costers and women alike were out selling their wares, although after the events of the past few months, there were fewer of the latter out on the streets.

Standing outside the towering lodging house, the smell of pipe smoke pungent in the night air, Henry continued watching the pub from across the road. Specifically, the luminous light glowing from the monstrous lamp that hung out the front like a miniature sun. Dark shapes entered the pub; dark shapes stepped out, sometimes two at a time.

Somewhere a fight was breaking out. Cries and shouts peppered the brisk autumn air: "Jest you 'it me, go on, try it!" "You'll git this rock on ye 'ead!"

The women were clearly drunk. Soon the shouting turned to shrieking and, shortly thereafter, things grew quiet.

Over by the Alice a man carrying a basket called out repeatedly, "Yarmouth herrings, three-a-penny!"

Still there was no sign of Hutch.

Henry cupped his hands over his mouth and blew, his breath mildly warmer than the frigid air. He moved up and down in a kind of jig, occasionally doing some squats, all in an effort to keep the blood circulating through his scrawny body.

Surely more than ten minutes had gone by.

Henry was about to walk back over to the pub, when a hand grabbed him by the shirt, a soft but dark voice said, "Come on," and, without warning, Henry found himself being dragged down Wentworth Street, away from the lights and bustle of the pub and Commercial Street.

Hutch had appeared out of nowhere, and it was unnerving. Henry prided himself on his extra-sensitive hearing. That, and his keen sense of smell. With no use of his eyes, his body had made up for it by developing his hearing and smell to far greater levels than anyone else he knew. He could tell, just by the sound of the shoes clapping against the flagstones, whether it was man, woman or policeman. But he hadn't heard Hutch coming; no sound of his boots, no breath puffing from his mouth.

The world grew darker and quieter as Hutch led Henry down the narrower street. His feet skipped along, trying to keep up, and his left hand held the string that was tied around his baggy pants for fear his worn trousers would drop down around his ankles.

Henry became blind again as he was pulled into a court, one of the many cramped dead ends where nary a speck of sunlight touched the whitewashed walls even during a summer's day. The smells of tobacco and fish were replaced by rotting garbage and the stench of sewer gas.

Henry was pushed against a wall that felt like a block of ice. An arm was pressed against his chest and then the tip of something cold and finely pointed was pressed against his throat.

"What's to stop me from slittin' ye throat right here and now," Hutch said, voice low and growly. "Huh? I don't care if ye blind."

"You can't," Henry puffed out. "You don't know who I am."

"Yes I do. Still won't stop me from stickin' this knife in ye."

Henry faltered at Hutch's admission, but the feel of metal pressing into his flesh quickly brought him back around. "But you won't. You don't kill family."

"What? Who says?"

"Or else you would 'ave killed me mother a long time ago. Instead, you kill those other women. Isn't that right?"

Hutch was silent, save only for the bull-like sound of air snorting in and out of his nostrils.

Close by a baby was crying. Somewhere further away a child was screaming.

The arm that was nearly crushing Henry's chest went away, as did the knife.

"Isn't that who you see when you slit their throats? Gertrude?"

A huff in the darkness. "What the hell do you know? You don't know nothin' about me."

"I know enough."

More silence.

"How did you find me?"

Hutch spoke quietly, and uncertainty had begun to creep into his voice. Henry could tell that his father wasn't tough. Strong, sure, and probably crazy, but he wasn't like those men who picked fights for the hell of it and who got tattoos and were thick-necked. No, Hutch had a shy way about him, almost nervous.

"I asked around. It's amazing how loose-lipped people are around cripples. All I knew about you was that you was a soldier and that you went by the name of Hutch. That's all me mother said of you. God knows I asked, but she got madder than hell whenever I brought you up."

"She was a wild one, that's for sure. Mean and blessed with a violent temper, she was. I was young when I was with Gertrude, young and foolish, and I soon grew tired of the old hag."

"Anyway, I've always been curious about you, been close to tryin' to find you a few times, but I figured, why? You slung it before I was born, so why should I care about you? But now I have a reason. So I asked around, and one day I ran into a fellow who told me he dossed with a bloke at the Victoria Home who goes by the name of Hutch, and who was an ex-soldier. So I went to the Victoria Home about three days ago and the deputy told me he ain't seen you in days. But he said you was a regular at the Alice, and so I've been checkin' in there for the past few days, hoping to find you. Now, I 'ave."

Henry, a little out of breath, stopped talking and swallowed. The air was thick and greasy and tasted like coke fumes and spoiled cabbage.

"So, how'd ye pick me so soon?" he asked once the silence grew as heavy as the stench around them. "You been checkin' up on me without my knowin'?"

That last part was spoken in jest, but a small part of him hoped it might actually be true.

"Nah, I slung out as soon as I learned Gertrude was with baby. But I knew who you was the moment I saw you standin' at the table. You look a lot like her: same puggish nose, same beady eyes. You still live in the Nichol?"

"Yus. Boundary Street."

"Christ, Son, what the hell do you want with me? I just got back from Romford and I'm worn out. State your business and then be off."

Henry licked his cracked lips. "I know who you are, what you've done."

A beat passed before Hutch spoke. "And you want money or else you'll go to the coppers, is that it? Kin or not, I'll still cut your throat if I have to. I don't take too kindly to threats."

"No, no, that's not it at all. Like I said, I want you to kill. I *need* you to kill again."

Hutch sighed. "You're as crazy as your mother. Why don't ye go home and forget ye ever saw me."

Henry heard footsteps clicking away. He jerked his head around, trying to find the arched entrance to the court; some patch a smidgen lighter than the darkness that swallowed up this court. "You're leaving?" he breathed. "No, you can't leave."

"I can, and I will. Just keep ye mouth shut, or else. Ain't nobody gonna believe a blind beggar boy anyhow. I'll let you live because you're me kin, but I'm giving you just one chance. I find out ye blabbed, I'll come for you. Just remember the feel of the knife against your throat if ye ever feel your lips gettin' too loose."

Henry reached out with his cane, swinging it around in the darkness. "No, please, you can't go. You owe me."

The footsteps stopped. Barking laughter was choked out. "Owe you? I don't owe you nothin'."

"You left me with that woman. You left, knowing how mad and mean she was. Do you know how I became blind? I wasn't born this way."

"What do I care? Smallpox, I suppose."

"She beats me. If I don't bring 'ome any gilt or somethin' to eat, she lashes out. I do the best I can. I'm good at makin' things with me hands, especially wicker. This old clown taught me 'ow years ago, and so I sometimes sell wicker chairs and baskets. I made this walking stick with me own two 'ands. I beg when I 'ave to. Sometimes I sell matches and street ballads in pubs, mostly in the Alice and Ringers, the landlords there are nice people. But Christ, I can only do so much."

"What does she do? Still a scrubber?"

"Occasionally, when the work comes in. But 'alf the time she's outta work. She drinks like a fish."

"She always did like the taste of gin."

"She tried to kill me when I was still inside her. Did ye know that? She tells me all the time, how she drank like a sailor in the 'ope of stopping her from 'aving the baby. It didn't work, which only made her madder. She often cries about 'ow she doesn't want to live, about 'ow she'll get DT and kill herself in a fit of madness. She gets those fits a lot. I think she was 'aving one the day she almost killed me and turned me blind. I was three or so, so I don't 'ave any memory, but mother tells me about it when she's worse for drink, and the neighbours fill in the rest. It was one evening, I was cryin' worse than usual, work was scarce and so was food and drink. Gertrude was in one of her moods and, in a fit of anger, she grabbed an old rag that was stoppin' the wind from blowin' through a hole in the window and stuffed it down me throat. When that didn't stop the cryin', she dragged me over to the door and started bangin' me head against it. She hit so 'ard that Mrs Collins from next door came in to see what was makin' such a racket. By the time the coppers came, I was out of it and bleedin' from the head. Days later, when I finally woke, I was blind. Been that way for the better part of ten years. You know the craziest thing about the whole sorry story? I wasn't taken from Gertrude's care. She was reprimanded, given two weeks in the house, but once she was out, I was given straight back to her. I was blinded, me body scarred for life, and what did me mother get for almost killin' her only child? Bleeding fingers from pickin' oakum."

Henry felt water splash his cheeks, and for a moment he thought it had started raining. But he soon realised his eyes were leaking, so he rubbed them dry.

"I'm sorry for what 'appened. But what's this got to do with me?"

Hutch sounded weary and muddled. "I don't blame you for my going blind, even though you're partly responsible for bringing me into this accursed world. But, you are responsible for makin' me see again."

"Huh?"

"Ever since I can remember I've been praying to God to give me back me sight. Not for food or for money, or even for you to come back to me and Mum. No, me only wish was to see again. Well, that wish has started to come true. And it's all because of you. Now, I need you to finish what you started."

Light, cautious steps clacked closer to Henry.

The smell of beer and fish grew stronger in Henry's nostrils.

"What are you talkin' about?"

"Me whole world used to be darkness. All I had was me smell, hearing and touch. But since August I've begun to see. All I can call it is a miracle. I don't question it, all I know is it's 'appening and I need it to keep on 'appening 'til I can see like you do."

"You say you're not completely blind? Prove it."

"Why?"

"I've asked around, too. Many years ago, I was curious. Blind they told me. Cripes, a cripple for a son. So how am I to believe ye? You could be a liar, too, for all I know."

"I'm no liar. But how can I prove it? I can only 'alf see at the best of times, and it's blacker than coal in 'ere."

"You saw me in the pub. 'Ave I got a moustache, a beard, or nothin'?"

"I don't know," Henry said, "I couldn't see you very well in the pub. But I do know you're wearing an 'at."

"So do most men."

"Yours has a large brim, like a wideawake. And I did notice that you ain't overly tall, but you do 'ave broad shoulders. Oh, and you got with ye a parcel, small and wrapped with paper."

Silence.

Then: "Lord lumme, so it's true." Hutch made a clicking noise with his throat. "So you need me to do what exactly?"

"Like I said, kill again. It all started with that one you did in George Yard early August. I didn't know what was 'appening at first. But on that mornin', while people were talkin' about the 'orrible stabbing murder of the whore, I started getting a funny tingling feelin' in me eyes. Behind, too, like there was fleas jumpin' around in there. The strange feelin' stayed that way 'til three weeks later. When I awoke that Friday mornin', the tingling had lessened, but instead of the usual blackness I was seeing somethin' else. I still couldn't see, exactly, but I knew somethin' had changed. I guess you could say it was like lookin' at an overcast day with a grey sheet over your face. But really, it was the first bit of light hitting me eyes since I 'ad lost me sight more than ten years ago. I couldn't believe it. I didn't know what to do or think. Could it be? I wondered. Was me wish comin' true and me eyesight comin' back?"

"Did you say anythin' to Gertrude?"

"No. I couldn't even begin to think how I'd find the words to tell her. So," Henry continued, "I didn't connect me slowly returnin' vision with the murders. At least, not 'til the third one, Annie."

Hutch emitted a strange shuddering sound at the mention of the woman's name, like a dog being scratched behind the ears.

"When I woke up that mornin', a week after starting to see a grey haze, and I saw blurry shapes, I actually shrieked with joy. No longer was I lost in a fog. I could make out people and objects. I couldn't see any details, and light was still very 'azy, but it was an improvement. And then I 'eard the cries of the paper boys: 'Whitechapel terror! Another ghastly murder in the East End!' I thought back to the other times there was a change in me sight, and . . ."

The sound of someone coughing coming closer. As the man staggered past, great wet coughs rattled his body and it was the sound of death spluttering into the cold November night.

Henry waited until the old man had passed down the street before continuing, speaking at a lower volume. "I realised they were connected. Somehow, every time the Whitechapel Murderer struck, me sight got better. It was then that I remembered a dream I'd 'ad, the night before the first murder. It was of you. Well, not you, exactly, but a man I knew to be me father. He stood before me with a knife. He slashed at me eyes, and that's when I awoke, eyes full of a strange tingling feelin'. Remembering that dream made up me mind that me father and the man they were now callin' Leather Apron were one and the same, and that we were connected. After you did two in one night, I awoke to a most startlin' scene: I could see some details of things up close. The patterns on the wallpaper in our room – some kind of flower – and the clothes Gertrude was wearing: white apron and a dirty green dress. I could even see her face, although some of the finer details were still 'azy. In the light of the day, up close, I could see, how did you describe it, her puggish nose and her beady eyes. Of course, she didn't know I could 'alf see, and I wasn't about to tell her, and every time I got close she told me to piss off and go earn us some dinner. I didn't care that she treated me badly. I was so 'appy that me sight was comin' back.

"So, I waited. I worked out that the longest time between murders was around three weeks, sometimes it was only one, and so I waited breathlessly after the night of the twin murders for a week to pass. Nothin'. I waited two more weeks. Me eyesight remained the same. And the papers started runnin' out of stories to print. I started gettin' worried. This couldn't be it. There had to be more. I was 'appy I could at least partially see, but I wanted to see fully. When it passed the five week mark, I knew I 'ad to find you. I needed to tell you me story, beg you to kill again. One more is all it will take, I'm sure of it. So please, can the Ripper strike once more?"

Hutch remained quiet for a long time; long enough for Henry to worry that his father had slipped away while Henry was talking, unnoticed, in that disturbingly silent way.

"I don't know if he can."

This time when Hutch spoke, he sounded different: his voice was still soft, but it had turned deeper and more even, with a fiery undertone. Behind his half-alive eyes, Henry saw the image of embers smouldering in a fireplace.

It was then, standing in the pitch blackness amid the raw, choking stench of the dead end, the frosty air less cutting and more like a hovering cloud, that he remembered he was in close quarters with a brutal murderer. It wasn't just his long-absent father, the one Henry had been seeking in the hopes of restoring his sight to its fullest capacity. No, he was also a killer. A man who had so far butchered five women. A man who had a darkness in him that Henry, even when he was fully blind, couldn't begin to comprehend.

"Sure you can," Henry said, voice wavering. "You've done it before. You can do it again."

"It's too risky. There are more police than ever out on the streets. Some have even taken to wearing women's clothes in order to catch me. Also, the whores stay mostly off the streets, and when they do step out they travel in pairs. It ain't like it was before. It's harder to find a good prospect."

"You 'ave to try. Please. I 'aven't asked ye for anythin' in all these years. I need to see properly. I want to see what the sky looks like and the rain, people's faces and what they look like when they laugh and cry. I was given a rose the other day by a flower-seller, some lady who felt sorry for the poor blind beggar. She told me it was yellow, like the sun. At the moment when I look at it it's murky, like muddy water. I want to see the rose in all its colour. Can you do that for me?"

"Boy, you ain't missin' much. This whole stinkin' place is made up of two colours: black and grey."

"What about red?" Henry ventured to ask, even though at present colours were more of an abstraction than a reality.

"Yes, red," Hutch said with a sigh. "A colour too seldom seen. Still, why do you want to lay your eyes on all the misery and ugliness? Ask me, you're better off stayin' blind."

Henry felt his shoulders drop and he puffed out a solemn breath. "So you won't do it for me?"

A pause. The sound of a hand ruffling through a pocket. "I didn't say that."

Coins fell to the ground, their tinkling echoing through the court.

"You had anything to eat lately?"

Henry instinctively touched a hand to his sunken belly. "Just the snot out of me nose."

"Get yourself some food. And then go home." Hutch sniffed the air. "It's gonna rain later."

Henry hadn't noticed, but now he thought about it, there was the tangy smell of impending rain in the air, along with the stench of the poor.

He heard the sound of his father walking away. This time, Henry was alert and ready and he reached out and clasped his bony fingers on

Hutch's arm. There was a good deal of muscle underneath the heavy coat.

"Wait, before you go, can I feel your face? It's still the best way for me to see what you look like."

Henry felt a quiver pass through Hutch's arm, which then passed on to Henry and reverberated through his body.

"You don't wanna see what I look like. Best I stay in the darkness. It's better for both of us that way."

A calloused hand gripped Henry and his hand was pulled away.

The Ripper walked out of the court and Henry stood there listening to the footsteps as they faded away. Then he got down on his hands and knees and started scrounging around for the coins.

When Henry opened his eyes that Friday morning, he knew right away.

His father had done it.

Jack the Ripper had struck again.

Sure he felt a twinge of sadness for the dead woman, but in a world overflowing with pain and heartache, where death was close at hand for a great many, Henry included, he couldn't summon much feelings of guilt or remorse for her.

Henry sat up. He rubbed his eyes, dislodging the build-up of sleep and grime collected in the corners. He blinked and then widened his gaze. His view was dim, although, for the first time since he could remember, it wasn't because of his poor eyesight. It was early and the rain was still coming down, so the room was dusky. Even so, Henry could see better than he ever had.

He looked down at his mother, who was sleeping the sleep of the drunken. Her snoring rattled the bottles on the floor and her sour gin breath added to the musty aroma that came from two bodies caged in a tiny, airless room all night. She was on her back, the ratty blanket pulled up to her chin. Henry edged closer, as close as he could stand before the stink of her breath made him queasy.

Her skin had a lot of lines, especially on her forehead and around her mouth and eyes. She had a plump face, yet, even in sleep, it was hard. Henry had never seen a face scowling, but he'd heard people talk about it and he was certain that's the expression he was looking at.

Hers wasn't an attractive face, and Henry wondered was he just as ugly? Hutch had said they looked alike, so was Henry's face this pinched, this wrinkled and locked in a constant grimace?

The room was icy, there was a smell of dampness, and, as Henry threw off the cover and hopped out of bed, a deep, bone-seizing shiver coursed through him. With hands shaking, he slipped his old boots over his equally aged socks, the holes in both matching up with stunning accuracy.

He reached for his cane, lying like a faithful dog on the floor beside the bed, but stopped. He shook his head and managed a quivering smile.

He no longer needed help walking. His eyes probably needed time to fully adjust, but he was sure he had almost total vision, and, as he stood up and made his way over to the fireplace, a thought jumped into his head, one that filled him with momentary chills that went deeper than the morning air: *It must've been a particularly brutal murder for me eyesight to come so good.*

The fire was in a pitiful state, the flames barely licking the coal, so Henry turned his eyes and saw a sack of what he took to be coke. He grabbed a few handfuls and tossed the coke into the hearth, which left his hands dusted with grey. The fire soon grew and, as warmth and fresh light spread into the room, Henry remained squatting by the fireplace and watched with awe the way the flames curled and seemed to wave at him, and at the sparks that popped like magic.

With the room a little brighter, he straightened and got his first proper look at the hovel he had called home for fourteen years.

He first noticed the pile of turnip tops and onion stalks near the fireplace. Given to them by the coke vendor as extra fuel, the offcuts had been retained by Gertrude as a last resort, in case neither of them was able to get anything better to eat. Looking down at the sad, limp leaves and the pale, slimy stalks, Henry couldn't fathom putting such garbage in his mouth. They smelled bad enough, but they looked worse. Luckily, he'd bought a slice of currant cake from a coffee stall last night, thanks to his father's meagre generosity, and had promptly gobbled it all down, so his belly was at least half full this morning, as opposed to its usual empty state, so he wouldn't need to chew on garbage that not even the dogs would want to touch.

Turning around, he surveyed the room. Over the past few months he had begun to see various blobs that he knew were the few pieces of furniture his mother owned, and then more distinct shapes as his sight continued to improve. Now, in the gloom of the wet morning light, he could make out the chair with the one broken leg and the way it leaned against the wall like a drunk on a Saturday night; the cheap chest of drawers beside it and the way the wood was warped from years of neglect; the skeletal chairs and the rickety table in the middle of the room, its corners chipped and the wooden surface stained and empty except for a half-melted candle; the sorry-looking couch with armrests as bare as a naked behind and the coverlets frayed; the bed with the thin mattress that was as dirty as the blanket was old and worn; the iron bedstead that was bent and knobbly like an old man's back; and a small chest, the wood scuffed and the hinges rusty. He knew he and his mother owned very little pieces of furniture, but to finally see them with his eyes, the scant items seemed even more pathetic.

He noticed how low the ceiling dipped, even with his short stature he could almost touch it without having to stand on the tips of his toes, and the layer of soot and grime on the walls appeared even thicker than when he could only half see the world.

With a new-found confidence, Henry walked over to the window, moving past the table and chairs with ease, a smile never far from his face. With his mother still asleep and the heat from the fire starting to eat some of the chill in the room, he stood by the window and ran a finger down the glass. The coating of grime was oily and, by the time he reached the bottom sill, the tip of his finger was hidden inside a black clump. He looked at the long streak he had made. The contrast between the grimy window and the strip of clear glass that cut down the middle fascinated him and he stood gazing at it for a good while. It was only when he heard a dog barking and he snapped out of his daze that he realised he could see rain falling outside through the narrow clearing, which prompted him to find a rag and wipe the rest of the muck away. He cleaned the glass as best he could, but the window remained streaked with greasy dirt, although it was at least better than it was before. He looked out and watched with wonder at the falling rain.

The instant the rain stopped, about an hour later, Henry headed outside.

He opened the door slowly, he didn't want to wake Gertrude, but even so the hinges squeaked. His mother stirred, but she remained asleep.

He walked the short distance along the ground-level passage of the two-storey brick building, found the street door open, and stepped outside.

It was overcast, the spread of clouds greatly diluting the sun's light, but, even so, Henry had to squint. To his eyes it was like a sparkling summer's day. Shielding his eyes with an arm, he moved on to the street. The flags were slick with water and grime. Soon he was able to take his arm away and, while the morning light was still glaring, it didn't nearly blind him.

He looked down the long, narrow street and saw a seemingly never-ending stretch of brick cottages, their chimneys throwing black smoke into the grey sky. With the rain stopped, doors and windows began to open and faces as hard and scowling as his mother's started to emerge.

Henry stood on the street and, over the next few hours, watched the goings-on with a mixture of fascination and, occasionally, confusion. He was like an invisible person, the people who lived on his street knew him simply as the blind boy, and they mostly ignored him, which suited him fine.

He watched some kids jump in puddles far down the street, marvelling at how small they looked (it was going to take some time to fully grasp perspective and distance); he watched a pale, sickly woman cradling a crying baby, its wailing not easing even when the mother put the infant to her breast; he watched a man stumble out of one of the buildings and bring up the night's excess; he watched plump rats nibbling at the garbage scraps on the street and some kids chase the rats away; later, the same kids chased a dog who had sniffed out the fish and meat bones that were scattered in the gutters; he watched women standing about in doorways, chatting, and men lolling about smoking pipes and cigarettes; he watched a group of young boys and girls catch a cat and proceed to string it up by its tail to a pump handle and, with the cat screeching and clawing at the air, the children, faces smudged with dirt, hair tangled and clothes torn and ragged, beat the creature with sticks, their giggles and taunts mingling with the cat's piercing cries; he watched the same group later make mud pies by scooping up the wet dirt with old oyster shells, the dead cat still hanging and drawing flies nearby; at some point Henry's mother finally woke and, shuffling past, she mumbled to him about going for some ale, scarcely glancing at him and not noticing he wasn't holding his walking stick; some time around mid-morning, the sun trying its hardest to break through, but only managing a peek, a small girl with arms the size of matchsticks and hair looking like it had been washed with ash, spotted a pair of old boots near Henry, and he watched as she picked up the shoes, the soles of which were nearly coming all the way off, making them look like two dogs panting, and slipped them over her grubby bare feet. Then, with a nod and a smile, she skipped away, somehow not stumbling and falling to the ground, even though the broken boots were far too big for her.

Watching all of this and more, Henry remembered what Hutch had said about how this place was made up of only two colours. Henry was beginning to see he was right. Black and grey dominated all he could see. Even women's white aprons and the red brick of the cottages had been painted with the same ashen shade as the sky and the flagstones.

Suddenly, Henry remembered.

He drew in a breath as he thought: *Me flower!*

He left the street and entered his building, still feeling strange walking without his cane clutched in his hand. Inside his room, he stepped over to the rose. The single stem was sitting in water in an old teacup, the flower slumped against the wall, unable to stand upright in the shallow excuse for a vase. Carefully, Henry took hold of the rose and lifted it to his face. In the gloom, the petals were a dull yellow. So he headed back outside.

By the time he returned to the street, a wave of intense chattering was passing between the people, preoccupying their worlds and momentarily taking them from their mundane existence.

As the gossiping continued (he heard bits and pieces of those close by, ". . . worse one yet, they sa . . ."; ". . . butchered her in her room . . ."; ". . . cut her up like some pig at the market . . ."), Henry looked at his rose in the hazy light of day. He didn't know if it was the colour of the sun – Henry hadn't yet seen the blazing fireball in the sky – but it was breathtaking all the same. It reminded him of the glowing lamplight outside the Alice, only better. The shape of the rose was a sight to behold, petals like swirling flames, but the colour held Henry's gaze as if it was the strongest magnet on earth. Amid the suffocating dullness and harshness of a world made of bricks, stone and misery, the yellow of the rose was like a single star shining in a black sky.

A shadow moved past, stopped, and then spoke. "'Ave ye heard? The Ripper's killed again!"

The sudden intrusion caused Henry to jolt. His fingers slipped and one of them caught on a thorn. A moment of sharp pain sliced at his index finger and a coldness sluiced through his body.

The shadow moved away and Henry raised the cut finger.

"Yes, I know," Henry said, squeezing his index finger with his thumb and watching as blood rolled out, the colour rich and looking like a red raindrop, "isn't it wonderful?"

My Name is Jack . . .
Andrew Darlington

Sometimes things happen for no real reason. Sometimes things happen with no apparent motive.

I died in Sevastopol. In freezing blood-red rain that chills the soul. In black mud that sucks your boot heels down to Hades. The mind-cracking horror mixed in with bone-weary fatigue. And that's when the shell's banshee screech brings the explosion of an incandescent sun that trembles the very ground beneath. The breath punched out of me. The blazing heat of it scalding me, as if the very sulphur-spewing gates of hell have opened up. All the world grows dark. I don't remember what came next. Only that it hurts. Only that my mind recoils from it as though brushing white-hot coals.

My name is Jack. Jack Harlan.

I pace the warrens at the mouth of the passageway linking Miller's Court to Dorset Street. Along the lodging flophouse fronts, the stalls and street vendors, beyond the wet clothes drip-dripping dismally from washing-lines strung across the alley. There, I can see the 'Blue Coat Boy' where the prozzies, pinch-pricks and razor-toting hoodlums congregate. Bony rascals, trickster peddlers and cheeky black-hearted rogues. But the promise of cheap ale is luring. Even its rich aroma promises a few hours of delirious blindness. There's a woman's laughter coming from an overhead window, carrying an uncertain edge.

The moon is reflected in the brackish gutter tide. One moon. Just one. The flagstones smell of stale piss. I was hunting Yellow. So close I catch its sniff. But who, in this human zoo, is Yellow? Watching her bustle by. Could it be her? She must be mid-twenties. Her long, none-too-clean red hair, cascading over a maroon shawl. Her stained white apron worn over a dark dress of coarse material that drapes to her boots. So close I can feel the warm pulse on my thigh. I feel drunk. I know drunk. It's an inner climate I'm used to. Pausing momentarily, distracted to note the man on the corner, a surly Negro, his boot heel overhanging the kerb, as though looking for someone who is looking for a fight. He wears a waistcoat and gold cufflinks, as a token attempt at respectability.

My attention shifts back to the filthy alley. My mistake. He fells me with the effortless swiftness of a powerful beast. Silence crashes back stunning the world. Darkness. Yet it's more than darkness. It extends inwards. Into my soul. Touching the poison that resides there. Where there's nothing that is not tainted. Nothing that is not stained by this evil. Not everything has to mean something.

I'm in a powder-white living room with a gilded piano and floral-patterned wallpaper. 'Good day to you, sir.' The lady with the American accent pours Indian tea into a bone-china tea service. Her smile gives every impression of being carefully composed. 'You will take tea? I apologise for the means employed to bring about our introduction. But you are Red, and we have urgencies in common that override etiquette.'

'This is less than an introduction. I've been here before.'

'You will please address me as Mrs Ryneveld. Mrs Lorelie Ryneveld. I am a widow, sir, but my late husband left me well provided for, sufficient to journey here from Alabama with two of my trusted . . . servants, to lease this fine property, and implement the modifications I require. So please don't adopt that huffy tone with me, Mr Harlan.'

'No, I mean no offence, merely that this place is familiar to me. I know you.'

'That's not difficult to explain. Our lives overlap. You sometimes catch glimpses of my memories. I see something of yours. We, and three others.'

It is uncomfortably warm. As I stand with my back to the blazing log fire in the grate, she appraises me up and down. I must present a figure by no means easy on the eye. Barely passable. She's critically itemizing me all the way from my untidy auburn centre-parting and side whiskers, the black necktie fastened with a horseshoe stickpin, to the long dark coat trimmed with astrakhan. But my cuffs are dirty, and my shoes are laced up wrong. More scarecrow than man.

This setback inflames my fretful temper. 'I was hunting Yellow. I was so ruddy close.'

'Yet now you are closer still. Take a look.'

The pulse on my thigh. I hesitate.

'Check your status,' she insists. 'Don't worry, I've hardly lived to this age without a passing familiarity with a gentleman's wedding tackle.'

'I don't doubt that for a moment, madam. But you've not seen mine.' Nevertheless, I haul the hem of my shirt up, unbuckle my belt, and lower my pants sufficiently. The red blister is now aligned with the dull glow of an adjacent orange one. As I watch, she mirrors my actions. Pulls her blouse up with feminine delicacy, inching the top of her skirt down as if for a lover. I watch with skin-crawling fascination.

'It seems we've been touched by the same fingers.' The same red and orange blisters aligned on her shapely white thigh. I stare for as long as I dare, before tearing my attention away.

'You see the need for my actions? "Richard of York Gave Battle", you understand. Red. Orange. Yellow. Green. Blue. The spectrum. A sequence recognizable to any sentience with eyes to see. So there are five of us. We are drawn together by a hypnotic compulsion, as iron filings are drawn by magnetic lines of force. Yet we must never all meet. For we are up against vast forces beyond our understanding. But now we are two. That doubles our strength. Tell me your tale.'

With the slight flush of mutual embarrassment passed, I slump low onto the embroidered chaise longue, aware of the smell of my own sweat. 'Perhaps you can explain, lady, because I certainly can't. My name is Jack Harlan. A grenadier, during the siege of Sevastopol. I was wounded. They told me the wound was mortal. That I would not survive.'

'Do you have memories of that time? The war for Crimea was thirty years ago. Yet you look no older than thirty years.'

'You think I'm unaware of these absurdities? Of course I know this. I live with it every day. There are no memories, but I have dreams. I have nightmares.' They begin with a sky of three splintery moons.

'And the wound that killed you. You bear the scars?'

'No. There's no scar. My healing has left no trace of my wounds. Only the row of five blisters. Although at first I used my blade to try to gouge them out. I cut and cut. Repeatedly. To no avail. The only scars I bear are those left by my own knife.'

She nods in grim agreement. 'You are Red. Which means you must have been the first. That explains the temporal discontinuity.'

'So who is doing this to me? To us. Who is responsible?'

'They belong to a species that has been known, at one time or another, as parasite, ghoul, leech, vampyre.'

'You're asking me to believe we're compromised by a variety of gnomes or elves?'

'Perhaps vocabulary has no words sufficient to express what I mean. But I suspect that, despite your denial, you know as well as I do what I mean. Meanwhile, there are other, more human agencies involved too. Follow me.'

Her image, in a panelling of mirrors, paces beside us across the landing. One reflection slithering into the next. Until she indicates a tripod-mounted telescope pointing out of the window. 'Our presence here has not gone unnoticed. For I am being observed. See here.'

At first it was difficult for my eyes to adjust. I turn the focus. There was a high wall, and the street beyond.

'The Chinese, you mean?'

'There are opium dens in Limehouse.'

'I was close to Yellow. I know that. Had your agencies not abducted me, I would have had Yellow.'

She nods. 'We must return to Whitechapel. We shall find Yellow together.'

I don't go looking for trouble, but somehow it always seems to find me out . . .

*   *   *

There was nothing about that crisp September morning to hint that it was to be one of the crucial days in London's long history. We stand within an arbour set into the ornamental wall of her gardens to the rear of the house. A flow of water trickles over mossy stones into the pond below where the shadowy shapes of fish dart and flick between lily pads.

'They are beings of great evil?' Some of my normal composure regained.

'I don't consider them to be such, no. I think of them as gardeners of the celestial realm. And a dutiful gardener must make choices. To prune certain flora from his flowerbed in order to allow others to flourish.'

'And we are being pruned?'

Mrs Lorelie Ryneveld inclines her head, as if in agreement, yet her wide lips are pinched by indecision. 'What we need is a beginning. A fingernail inserted beneath the veneer, with which to strip the cover away, exposing the diabolical machinations beneath. There are five of us. Five separate components of the same infernal device. Drawn together by an implanted hypnotic compulsion. So what happens when the five of us stand together in the same room?'

We are an explosive device, primed to detonate. When shall we ride that secret track to the unknown future? When is that moment of extinction, when it all ends?

I am a soldier weary of killing. I have seen the vileness in the hearts of men. I've had my fill of death. Each forgotten battle in every time-lost war across our ten-thousand year history has been pointlessly futile. Yet it shapes every detail of our world, the geography of maps, the racial make-up of nations, the cultural spread of faiths, languages and values. The death of every foot soldier made a difference. Without that, the world would not be the same place. Has all this so painful ascent from barbarism been for nothing? Has it been judged and found wanting? Must it be wiped clean as if we're nothing more than a virulent disease? And yet, witnessing the human quagmire of Spitalfields, the accusation seems not entirely without foundation. Are we to be the agents of that great cleansing . . .?

The soldier whose choice it is not to fight. Isn't that a contradiction? I just want this deadness inside me to abate. And it will only go away when the truth is revealed.

I'm lost beneath the sheer weight and gravity of the city. A tremor of apprehension shivers its way through me. Footfall clack-clack-clacking on stone paving. A dog barking, as though it's ensnared in pain. The soot-grimed buildings of this midnight sinkhole of destitution loom on all sides. Down the holes of concealing shadow where whores service their clients. Where they spread their legs. Or where they crouch to give mouth in narrow passageways. Each tart trapped in her own dreary hell of gin and filth. The air roiling as dense as silt on the Thames riverbed. Here, all that is normally forbidden is abnormally released and realized.

'Polly Nichols. She's a strumpet.' Short in stature, little more than five foot, aged forties-ish, her brown hair already greying. A wide-brimmed hat with a feather jauntily angled on her head, her cheeks flushed with gin. A bright kerchief at her neck, focusing attention on her fleshy cleavage, plump beneath her wrinkled gown.

'She's no better than she should be.'

God Almighty, what a strange expression. To what goodness should she aspire? I've seen squalor and poverty. I know to what ends it compels folk. I slept in the foul warrens of Istanbul, working my way back across the Black Sea, seeking passage to Venice. I saw them begging by exhibiting their deformed and freak-birth kin, I saw them drooling in the relentless sun, and shudder at the horror of it. I know to what extremes desperation drives. I don't blame this drunken whore for her human failings. Meanwhile, the wait scrapes away at my nerves.

We follow her. She stops on the corner of Osborn Street, where it cuts away by a Whitechapel Road slop-shop. She talks with another slattern. Her wild gestures show evidence of alcoholic lubrication.

Then we lose her. But guided by the warm pulse. Close. Getting closer. A low brick wall, Buck's Row.

Of course, there are sounds. The street itself is breathing, contracting and expanding like lungs.

'She's dead.' When next we find her, her throat is slit twice from left to right.

'Can we be sure she was Yellow?'

'Check her thigh. We must be certain.'

I rip her gown up. Her underwear is gone. 'There are no blisters, nothing.'

'But she's dead. In death they may fade. Use your razor, discover what they've planted inside her.'

'No. I can't do that.'

'We must, hurry, while we have time. We – all of us – have something planted within us. A device of some kind. Find it in her, and we'll know what we're dealing with. Do it, do it now.' She kicks her Gladstone bag forward.

I steel my mind to ice. I've seen worse on the battlefield. I've seen worse in field hospitals. I've heard them scream. I hear it still. I close her dead eyes, so she can't see. Polly Nichols does not scream. There's only a wheezing of escaping foulness as I make one deep jagged incision across the abdomen. Nothing but subcutaneous fat and internal organs. I make several more openings, and three or four similar cuts to the right side at least six to eight inches long, my blade cleaving violently downwards. A rich welling of blood. A coil of intestines. But no device. Nothing that does not belong. That was how I must have appeared after the shell-burst took me. That was how they found me sprawled and shattered in the mud. How they took me into the field hospital. Or what I assumed to be the field hospital.

'Enough. We were wrong. Mistaken. It was not her.'

'It must be. We both experienced Yellow. You can't deny that.'

'Maybe we just saw through the eyes of Yellow, and this was his victim? It's too late now. We get the hell out. No more.'

*   *   *

Within the hour, I was back gazing out the window over the darkness of her stone-walled rear garden. A night that is now too quiet. A distant street lamp shimmers in the branches of the elm, and the elm throws fidgety shadows across the house. I watch the fingers of shadow play. I'm fretful and impatient to crawl clear of this oozing slice of absurdity that makes all of my life, and everything I understand to be true, into a colossal sham. My being swallowed by unlovely and unthinkably ancient forces that pirouette between the stars. In the passing eddies of time, this silence has meaning. In moments such as this, precaution becomes an abstraction. In this vision there are three splintery moons, within the incandescent gleam-stung shower of the Milky Way slanting off to a seemingly infinite distance, like a waterfall without beginning or end.

Days drift by. We become reconciled to each other. Her, and her two loyal silent menservants, Joseph and Thomas. They it were who abducted me and brought me here. I accept that such a recourse was necessary. I sleep in the guest bedroom. Once shaved and bathed, I become almost presentable. I feel a part of human discourse for the first time in what seems like years.

'I returned to London and it was changed. It was no longer my home. My parents were dead. To my regiment I was also dead, killed in action. There was no one left to recognize or welcome me. Nothing left but the foulness that burns within me. Nothing to distract from the compulsion to seek out the others I glimpse in shafts of dream. It seems a strange thing to say, something I should never admit, but meeting you – even under such heinous circumstances – has saved me. Before we met I had nothing. Now, despite everything, I have hope. Thank you for giving me that chance of a better life. I haven't always expressed my gratitude.'

A week has passed. It is dark. The hours well before dawn. My sheets are moist with sweat. It's always hot. She has a furnace roaring in the cellars below, attempting to replicate her home climate. The floor-boards creak. Was there a knocking on the front door? Or more likely a magpie scrattling across the roof? Shocked awake in my bed in crawling terror. Annie Chapman is being butchered. Her intestines ripped out and thrown over each of her shoulders. Her uterus slashed away. The violence is so sudden and so vivid an intrusion I collapse on to the floor retching. Once the terror is gone, I lie there breathing in desperate gasps as sweat cools across my skin. My inner thigh pulsing. Yellow. Yellow.

Lorelie is standing at the door in a long white gown. Her face is aghast.

I crawl back to sit on the edge of the bed. 'You saw it too?' Despite the receding shock waves convulsing me I'm not unaware of the feminine curves outlined by the simple white nightgown. The red blister is not the only source of warmth emanating from my groin.

'We are linked. It's a beacon connecting us. Such violent intensity reaches out.'

'We were wrong before. It wasn't the woman who was Yellow. Yellow is the monster who killed her.'

'Why would he do that?'

'There are two possible reasons. Because he was looking for the same thing we were looking for. The trigger, the device. The other reason is even worse. That he saw what we did to Polly Nichols, and he enjoyed it – after all, he sees what we see.'

There is silence between us as we breakfast. She's stronger than I am. Is there a space missing in the timeline of her life, a discontinuity? Something to do with the American war between the States, what she calls 'the war of northern aggression'. Something to do with slavery. Sometimes I see her in a crowd in a city I've never been to. I glimpse cotton fields. The whip. A city put to the torch. A slow-moving river that is sometimes the Mississippi, and at other times the Ganges. I crossed France sleeping on the bare earth beneath rogue stars, dreaming other people's dreams. Oft fearing I'd lost my mind. Perhaps I had, and this is all a symptom of our collective insanity. These are things not designed for the human mind to measure. There is nothing within knowledge to construct from, no rational foundation to build upon. To know it, we must see and feel and touch and taste it. Does she know what it is to die? I fear to ask.

'There are five of us,' she says at length. 'We are but two. There is Yellow. And there are two others we have yet to meet. But be sure of this. We experienced the shock of that murder. So they must feel that same intensity. That is what we share.'

I follow her across the landing, following her image in the mirrors. She indicates the tripod-mounted telescope pointing out of the window. 'He is there now, watching us. He must be the means of our introduction.'

My eye to the lens again. Yes, he is there on the street corner opposite. My decision made. As usual, one level of my mind has been furiously digesting, working harder than it has for a very long time, while the surface churns in seeming confusion. This is war. War against the fates that hunt us down. I leave through the kitchen, by the rear garden arch. Out into a narrow passage. I circle around, right, then right again. I halt on the thoroughfare. Yes, I can see the encircling wall. Up one, two flights. Count the windows. There is the glint of the telescope behind the glass pane. Then across, to the cobbled pavement facing it. He is there, standing as though casually, without obvious purpose. But he has been there, holding his vigilance now for a week. Maybe more. I adopt a similar pose. Stroll unhurriedly in his direction. Three children, two boys and a girl, chase each other past us, their laughter leaving a glittering trail. A horse-drawn omnibus clatters by. I halt beside him. He barely glances at me, his attention fixed on the house set back from the street opposite. He wears a cap pulled low over strands of lank black hair, a shapeless sack of an upper garment. He is Chinese.

I am a soldier. I know combat. I move quickly, seizing him and twisting him around, his arm forced up behind his back to breaking point, my arm tight around his scrawny neck. He twists and turns, but he is slight, he lacks my strength. I have the advantage. 'Hush, you understand my words. I'm not here to rob you. We have business with your master. It is time we met. You will help us bring that about. Or I swear I'll crack your damned spine . . .'

He leads, grudgingly. I follow closely. It seems he's acquiesced. He shows no resistance and makes no attempt to break free as it begins drizzling relentlessly. We tramp from Whitechapel to Limehouse. I thought I was used to trudging, I've trudged halfway across Europe. But my pace is sagging by the time we reach the high wharves lining the north side of the Thames. We reach a misty passageway between high warehouses, a murky place of cutthroats and rogues called Upper Swandam Lane, and splash through gathering puddles to approach an opening set between a steam laundry and a gin house. We pass down a tunnel of sandstone steps, their centres worn low by the repetitive pacing of slurred feet. He fumbles the latch by the buttery glow of an oil lantern recessed into the wall above the arched door, disturbing a nest of scuttling spiders.

We step into the long, low cellar of an opium den, its furthest extent lost in a drifting haze heavy with narcotic, and terraced with wood-frame bunks resembling the inner deck of some accursed convict hulk. But the low throb on my thigh is strengthening. Through the gloom I catch chilling glimpses of bodies slumped in horrible torpor, hollow-cheeked and haggard. A few Orientals. Most not, but their wretched-ness uniting class and race, their shoulders bowed, their knees bent, heads thrown back, with here and there dark, apathetic eyeballs moving behind closed lids. It's a grotto of dream, a nightmare print by Gustave Doré of Dante's circles of hell. Some, it seems, seek oblivion in gin, or absinthe, others come here. Alike in their luring vice. Small roseate glimmers of light glow on low wicks out of the black shadows and the dull humid warmth, fluctuating like the pulse of stars, as bullets of brown poison absorb in the bubbling bowls of hookahs and long-ridged white water pipes. Hallucinations dance and shimmer at the edge of vision. Isolated lotus-eaters slump in silence, while low mutters of conversation ebb and flow in tides around them. It's like eavesdropping on the high-pitched chirrup of insects, unless the opium fragrance is already tilting my perceptions? Perhaps wherever they are is a better place? Perhaps I need go no further? The stupefying air grows somehow denser. All I need do is inhale . . .

My guide leads me down the narrow gallery between the double row of laudanum dreamers, holding my breath to avoid the toxic drug fumes, glancing about wildly. He'd been my captive. My hostage. Increasingly, I feel the tables turning. This was a mistake. What heart of darkness have I been drawn into? I should never have allowed him to bring me here, into his realm. I'm exposed, vulnerable. A true hero wouldn't hesitate, he would stride into the midst of his foes singing his last hurrah. I'm not that man. I'm on the point of turning and getting the hell out. He guides me, shoving as though to emphasize the shift in our status. A wooden structure of five steps takes me up into an alcove. How far it extends I'm unable to tell because it's divided off by a bead curtain. The grip on my arm indicates me to halt, and holds me there.

A low voice whispers. The words fall quite distinctly. 'We could kill you now. Tell me why we should not kill you?' A woman's voice, accented.

I strain to see, but detect nothing beyond shapes. 'Because you are Green. Because our lives are linked, and things are getting way beyond our control. We need to talk. We must meet face to face on neutral ground. More than just our lives depend on us. The lives of others too.' My head thumps with opium echoes. Like a slow heart attack. I'd thought I was beyond fear, apparently I'm not.

Laughter without humour. 'You came here alone. We respect that. So you may leave without harm. We shall do as you suggest. We know where you are, we will come to you. We will talk together, the four of us. Red, Orange, Green and Blue . . .'

'You know where to find Yellow?'

'We sense the presence of Yellow. We see through the eyes of Yellow, just as we see through you. But no. Yellow is out there. And Yellow is insane, in a place beyond reason . . .'

*　　*　　*

Tangles of brambles in an unkempt corner of her garden. Fruit ripening from deepening red to shining black beads. If we all die, who will there be to eat the berries? Will they just rot away to moist pulp? In my bleakest moments I'd considered suicide. The river would take me, and end it all. That would resolve the dilemma. Or maybe that's too easy a solution. Those who judged us must have factored that in. It needs two to be eradicated to defuse the doom that hangs o'er us. That's why they'd not killed me in the opium den. I'd gambled on them guessing that too. Calculated, and come through.

September closes. Two more savage murders. Long Liz Stride and Kate Eddowes spread like smashed fly-crawled rag dolls. The popular press creates a delicious contagion of panic. 'Each policeman regards himself as a small, but vital link in the administration of justice, but George Lusk of the Whitechapel Vigilance Committee seems helpless to stop Leather Apron.' Time passes. Through the telescope we see the observer is still there. He watches us. We watch him.

The sound of a disturbance at the front entrance. Joseph and Thomas admit two visitors. We wait in the powder-white living room with the gilded piano and floral-patterned wallpaper. The room in which my first interview had taken place. I watch as they're ushered in. This is Green and Blue? A darkly shimmering woman and a tall bearded man. A Chinese lady who smokes a cigarette through a long holder, and a Sikh armed with a cricket bat? Standing with their backs to the blazing fire, these are the figures I'd glimpsed behind the bead curtain?

'Welcome,' says Lorelie. 'We realize words are inadequate, but you're welcome anyway.'

'I am Madam Mei,' she announces.

I note each detail with military precision, my eyes wide with more than seeing. As though appraising targets. Not just looking, but observing that she wears a full-length Manchu gown embroidered with grapes, with broad horseshoe cuffs and a neckline of contrasting threads. She's an ornate doll in a silver filigree headdress inlaid with pearls and tassels. But with a sense of powerful intelligence.

Lorelie looks questioning at the man.

'Adarshpal.' He bows slightly. He wears a white kurta over pyjama leggings. He brandishes the bat. 'Weapons are suspect. I would not be allowed to bear weapons here. So I carry the clicky-ba. By wielding this I've already put four men in the infirmary. It makes a most effective skull-crusher.'

'Is it safe for us to be together like this?'

'We have yet to integrate Yellow. What is within us will only activate with all five together. We are safe.' Her prominent ornamented finger-nails were arching.

'And what is it within us? What happens when all five assemble? Do you know?'

'The words are beyond me. But they have shown me, yes. A burst of toxic light that will reduce us all to vapour. Every human being in the world. Every man, woman and child. Leaving nothing behind but the beasts of the field, the birds of the sky, the fish of the sea. Things that squirm, slither, crawl and burrow.'

'Which the greater sin, the squalid murders of the Ripper, or this clean precise extermination? Mary Shelley wrote of this. Or something very like this, in a romance called *The Last Man*. Yet I am less assured than you. There must be more to it than that. This has got to be more than merely notice of execution. If they possess such awesome power they could have done this straight away. Why the delay? Surely they are allowing us space for choice. I prefer to believe this to be a test designed to determine our collective worth. If we can work together to resolve this, work through from cause to effect using logic and reason over our more base instincts. It's imperative we talk about this.'

'Wrong. The dialogue has already taken place. It's finished. This is no time to debate the essential nature of mankind.'

'I disagree. There has never been a more appropriate time.'

'You overestimate our potential. There are, at best, three or four dozen intellectuals alive in the world at any given time. Maybe they would be capable of interpreting this. But us, we can't rationalize our way out. No, there's another way. A simpler way. We can end this now.' Madame Mei gestures with her white hand. The door behind her opens. Three armed men file in. They must have forced their way in past Joseph and Thomas. The first two carry big knives, with long, cruel blades. The third wields a meat cleaver.

Mrs Lorelie Ryneveld's mouth forms a thin line. 'So be it.' She moves a single step to the left. Plunges an ornamented lever. As the blast-screen drops, the detonation is stunning. The incandescence hurls me back. The heat of it scalding me, as if the very sulphur-spewing gates of hell itself have opened up beneath them, to devour them. The shrieking momentary pain of their deaths rams a paralysing knife through my brain. Sprawled across the carpet, I pull myself up on one elbow. It feels like my head's been wrung out like a tavern slop-rag. The other half of the room has gone. A guttering ruin of flame. They are extinguished.

'This is the simpler way' she said softly. 'Cleansed by fire, not of my choosing. I'd have preferred another way. But they left no alternative.'

'You had this prepared? You had this terrible fate premeditated?'

'The first moment we met, you stood where they stood. At any moment if your replies had not pleased me . . . yes, it could have ended then. But I stayed my hand.'

'For that, Lorelie, and for so much else, I thank you. So what happens now?'

'Yellow is still out there. And he, or she, has developed a powerful taste for blood. Our work is not yet done . . .'

He paces the warrens at the mouth of the passageway linking Miller's Court to Dorset Street. So close I catch the sniff of Yellow. He's watching her bustle by. Her stained white apron over a dark dress of coarse material that drapes to her boots. She is Mary Ann Nichols. He sees her through my eyes, because she is in my memory. Sometimes things happen for no real reason. Sometimes they hang upon the most tenuous of connections.

An Anatomically Inspired Tale
Betsy van Die

The pursuit of the unusual for her cabinet of curiosities had taken Anna all over the world. Although she was a fine artist and anatomical illustrator by profession, her occasional sale of a painting or medical illustration was not enough to sustain her insatiable passion for collecting. Anna acquired a couple of small pieces when she was still in high school, a few years after the tragic death of her dear father. After thirty years of treasure hunting, she had amassed an impressive Wunderkammer collection. A trust-fund child, by the time she was nearing forty-five, Anna had depleted a large portion of the fortune her wealthy father left her. So it was with this harsh reality staring her in the face that Anna decided to open her collection to the public with an admission fee that would help offset costs. Although she had more than 1,200 oddities in her possession, Anna's obsessive nature pushed her to always want more. Now that she had several investors for the museum, Anna felt compelled to find a few exceptionally rare relics before the scheduled grand opening.

Anna's reputation as a collector was well known, but she drew the line when she was offered the skeleton, preserved genitals and brain of the famous Hottentot Venus (Sarah Baartman) in 1987, more than a decade after the Musée de l'Homme in Paris removed them from public display. The price was too high and she did not like the exploitation and humiliation the South African woman had been subjected to during her lifetime, as well as after her death. She regretted her decision and tried contacting the museum a few years later, only to be told that the remains were no longer for sale.

The most macabre pieces in Anna's collection were reminiscent of her favorite Roald Dahl short story, 'Skin', about a Russian tattoo parlor owner named Drioli who had a tattoo of his wife Josie on his back created by his famous painter friend Chaim Soutine. The punchline was that the highly varnished tattoo ended up displayed in the gallery Drioli worked at in his old age – a painting with a huge price tag. In Anna's real-life scenario, a notorious serial murderer had requested preservation of the intricate tattoos from his chest and back in an iron-clad will that was upheld after he was put to death. His widow kept the two tattoos for years but eventually needed money, selling them to an underground dealer who knew Anna.

Anna's collection included ephemera of all types—from antique quack medical devices to freak-of-nature animal specimens preserved in jars, as well as large taxidermy mounts. She had two shrunken heads, acquired at an auction in the early 1980s, several extraordinary skulls and a few early pieces obtained directly from Gunther von Hagen before he mastered the process of plastination. Anna met Gunther for the first time in 1988 at a small exposition of plastinated organs in a hall in Pforzheim, Germany. She was one of fourteen thousand people who attended this expo in a two-week period, which inevitably led to Gunther's remarkable Body Worlds shows, the first of which was held in Japan in 1995. Anna and Gunther developed a long-term friendship and he gave her five cast-offs for her collection.

Anna's obsessions went beyond collecting anatomical and medical curiosities. She was also quite the fan of crime mysteries and, as such, was determined to acquire a few unusual crime-related oddities to highlight at the museum. In addition to the tattoos, she had obtained a unique skull from an anatomical museum that was paring down its collection. This skull had the nefarious provenance of a convicted serial killer imprisoned at Alcatraz – the guy was an intellectual eccentric by all accounts, and had generously bestowed his brain to medical science upon his death.

She had read forty or so books on Jack the Ripper and had lived in London during the mid-1980s for eight months. In fact, like so many others, she had retraced the places the depraved serial killer had butchered his victims, methodically documenting each site for a project that never materialized. She did this herself, rather than going on one of those ubiquitous commercial tours.

During the time she lived in London, as well as on half a dozen subsequent trips, Anna always visited the markets. On one occasion around 1996, she wandered off the beaten path a little at the Portobello Road market and discovered a dimly lit indoor stall that was selling illegal goods – there were two leopards, elephant tusks, a black rhino, a white tiger, and several other animals that were endangered. An unsavory guy standing in a dark corner leered at her and she hightailed it out of there, fighting her way through the crowds outside. Her travels and near escapes with death were more than enough fodder to fill the pages of not one, but two novels, but for some reason this encounter really spooked her. Although Anna had quite a few animals in her collection, none of them were procured illegally.

Remembering some of the unusual items she had uncovered at London markets in the past, Anna decided that would be the first stop on a six-week treasure hunt to obtain those few spectacular pieces for the museum's grand opening. Old Spitalfields and Brick Lane markets were two of her favorite haunts, but she had heard that of late, unique antique finds were far and few between. On this occasion, neither one of these excursions turned up anything unusual, but, just as she was about to leave Old Spitafields, an adorable elderly gent named Arthur whom she had chatted to at length earlier in the day, said, "Stick around past closing – I have a special something bespoken for you, luv."

Anna replied, "I've been left, right, and centre and found nothing, but sure, I'll wait if this piece has not been nicked." Anna had discovered years earlier that taking on the vernacular of her surroundings worked in her favor. There were more than a few times that she thought doing so persuaded grumpy old antique dealers and stubborn collectors to cough up trade secrets and part with marvelous pieces.

So it was on this Sunday, 14 May, in the year 2006, that Anna was about to learn a deep, dark secret that would put her museum on the map. Arthur beckoned for Anna to come closer to his stall as he was closing up, and said in a hushed tone, "If you are game, I would like to meet you at the Pride of Spitalfields in thirty minutes – I don't want anyone to see us going in there together."

Although Anna was a little taken aback, she sensed something in Arthur that was genuine and decided to trust him. "Sure, you're on, Arthur. I'll meet you there, but a lass going into a pub by herself – I cannot promise I won't be spoken for if you're late!"

True to his word, about thirty minutes later, Arthur walked into the pub with a little leather satchel under his arm. He proceeded to tell her a story that sounded like something out of a fictional novel, but he told it with such seriousness and an eye for detail that she believed every word.

It turned out that Arthur was a great-grandson of the renowned British physician, Sir James Risdon Bennett, who served as president of the Royal College of Physicians from 1876 to 1881. "My granddad died in December 1891 and since there were six children that survived out of nine, there are a few relatives scattered here and there. It turns out that I am the only one with an interest in history and antiques. In fact, some of my bloody relatives have the nerve to call me the junk man."

Anna laughed because she had experienced similar bias from her relatives, but with decidedly stronger words due to the nature of her collectibles. "I know what you mean, Arthur. I have been called far worse than a junk woman, and a lot of people think I'm dodgy for what I collect."

Arthur continued, "I discovered that Dr Percy John Clark lived at twenty-two Margaret Street, Cavendish Square, and my granddad was his neighbor and close confidant. As you may know, Percy was assistant to Dr George Bagster Phillips, the divisional police surgeon during the infamous years when the Jack the Ripper murders rocked the East End. As such, he inspected several of the bodies and was privy to much of the same pathological information about all the murder victims as his boss, although he is not very well known. The poor chap doesn't even have a Wikipedia page. Dr Phillips lived at two Spital Square and, when he died suddenly in 1897, Percy took up residence there until the building was demolished.

"You know something, we are a few blocks away from where these two distinguished chaps lived, although the building was torn down in 1928. Eh, nobody seems to care anything about history nowadays – all the modern office building and residences that have gone up here in this area and all over London. But I suppose that's the case in big cities in the States too."

Anna let out a sigh, "Yes, I am a bit of an expert on the history of New York City, and I'm always grumbling about old, quaint buildings being knocked down to make way for yet another unattractive high-rise! But let's get back to the matter at hand, please continue with your story, Arthur."

"I'll cut to the chase now and why I asked you to meet me here. Percy was only in his mid-twenties at the time of the murders and, from what I can surmise, my granddad, who was long retired from active practice, was fond of mentoring young physicians. But what I am about to show you has far more intriguing historical implications than that."

Anna watched Arthur meticulously lay out a soft silk cloth on the table before setting down a thick leather book with an ornate, hand-tooled cover. Arthur said, "This diary belonged to my granddad and I inherited it in the oddest fashion. About twenty years ago, a long-lost relative who had moved to the States was given this diary by an ex-flame who was an antique dealer. The antique dealer knew of Sara's connection to Sir James Risdon Bennett and when he spotted it at the Brimfield flea market, he immediately thought of her, thinking he might rekindle the flame. Well, Sara had no interest in the dealer or the diary and she was one of the few relatives who didn't belittle me for my trade. It's hard to believe, but after I read this diary cover to cover, I have no doubt that nobody else took the time to do the same."

By now, Arthur had become rather animated and Anna could hardly wait to hear what secrets would unfold as Arthur turned the yellowed pages. All sorts of thoughts swirled through her head and she could barely contain her excitement. For her, the hunt for an elusive treasure was often the most thrilling part of being a collector. She was hoping that the treasure she was seeking for her museum opening was hidden within those age-patinated pages.

The diary had about five-hundred pages and was brittle with age, although remarkably intact. Arthur mentioned that, out of necessity, he had to make an entrusted linguistics professor friend privy to this secret. Some of the clinical language and antiquated terms were difficult for him to interpret. That friend had confirmed the authenticity of the diary based on age and examples of the famed physician's handwriting housed in the archives at the Royal College of Physicians. He helped Arthur by translating some of the clinical jargon into more understandable language, which he had in a separate little notebook in the satchel. More than 220 of the pages detailed discussion between Arthur's granddad and Percy Clark during the height of the Jack the Ripper murders.

Leafing through the diary together, Arthur and Anna marveled at page after page. Anna was visualizing the two physicians sitting in the elder gentlemen's study, discussing theories about the murders down to every gruesome detail – similar to what was in the inquest and autopsy reports. Sir Bennett noted a discussion he had with Percy that alludes to the misguided opinion of Coroner Wynne Edwin Baxter after the murder of Annie Chapman on 8 September 1888. This entry was dated 12 September, which was two days after the start of the official inquest.

There is no doubt in both of our minds that it is rubbish that the murderer is a person with medical knowledge. And further, Percy and I are in agreement that there was nothing of a professional nature about these wounds, the bodies were simply slashed about from head to foot. There is no indication that this maniac had a strong compulsion to steal organs, although the disappearance of this poor woman's uterus is a mystery.

"Since you said you are very well read on Jack the Ripper, Anna, are you aware of the theory that the organs were taken from some of the victims to sell for medical purposes?"

"Yes, I believe that theory was debunked almost immediately by many medical experts, but I've always wondered what became of those organs and if Jack the Ripper or some other criminal took them."

Arthur continued, "Well, my granddad and Percy concurred that the 'American' theory, as my granddad called it, was daft and the next entry in the diary goes into far more detail about this subject."

Even if it should transpire that in the case of the Mitre Square victim the uterus was missing, I should not be disposed to favour what I may call the American theory in the slightest degree, and I must confess that it was with considerable surprise that I noticed in certain newspapers a disposition to readily accept the theory which Wynne Baxter had concocted surrounding the earlier murder of Annie Chapman, regarding her uterus being removed. Percy and I agree that if any person wanted a number of uterus specimens, and was possessed of surgical skills, that he would undertake this himself rather than employ an agent to do so. No love of gain could possibly induce a sane man to commit such horrific atrocities. And further, perfect uterine specimens can be obtained at medical institutions either in England or America for legitimate purposes. The Royal College has such specimens for teaching purposes, and Percy and I do not understand how this theory would be given any credence whatsoever. Nevertheless, we both wonder what became of the Annie Chapman uterus since it was not found with the body or in close proximity.

Further on, as Arthur was pointing out a longer passage dated 1 October 1888, Anna experienced a strong feeling of déjà vu. After wracking her brain, she realized she was remembering a paragraph in one of the books she had read on Jack the Ripper. Sir Bennett had been quoted in the press shortly after Elizabeth Stride and Catherine Eddowes were murdered in the very early morning hours of 30

September 1888. Anna said, "Given that the press expected a rapid response even back then, I bet your granddad didn't have much time to prepare a statement. Perhaps he was briefed by Percy before being interviewed by the reporter and wrote this down in preparation for that."

My impression is that the miscreant is a homicidal maniac. He has a specific delusion, and that delusion is erotic. Of course we have at this moment very little evidence indeed, in fact I may say no evidence at all, to the state of the man's mind except so far as suggested by the character of the injuries which he has inflicted on his victims. I repeat that my impression is that he is suffering under an erotic delusion, but it may be that he is a religious fanatic. It is possible that he is labouring under the delusion that he has mandate from the Almighty to purge the world of prostitutes, and in the prosecution of his mad theory he has determined upon a crusade against the unfortunates of London, whom he seeks to mutilate by deprivation of the uterus. There are, on the other hand, a number of theories which might be speculated upon as to the particular form that his mania takes: but insomuch as we have no knowledge of the man himself, but only of the characteristics which surround the commission of his crimes wherewith to guide us, I come to the conclusion that his delusion has reference to matters of a sexual character.

Arthur took a couple of small papers out of his satchel and showed them to Anna. "This, my dear, is an added bonus to what I am sure you'll agree is already a spectacular piece of history. The real icing on the cake, however, is what is revealed in these documents. These papers were sewn into a secret compartment in the back inside cover of the diary, along with a key. Upon closer inspection, it was obvious that these were written in Percy's hand and I'm thinking he gave them to my granddad for safekeeping. I did some research and found out that Percy did indeed keep papers, correspondence and photos regarding the major cases he was involved in, and apparently he showed a few to the London *Observer* in the lone press interview he did in May 1910. Nobody has any idea what became of that ephemera. What is known is that in 1925, at the age of sixty-one, Percy emigrated to America with his wife Eveline and twelve-year-old daughter Mary. And he obviously returned to England because records show he died in Chertsey, Surrey in January 1942."

Arthur rose from the table and said, "You know what, Anna, I cannot tell you the rest of this tale here at the pub. I live just a few blocks away—would you mind coming to my flat?"

The two had been talking for well over two hours and it was now pitch dark outside.

"Well, all right, Arthur, since you've been so gracious to share this diary with me, I'm game, let's go."

When they arrived at the flat, Arthur had to disarm the alarm system and unlock what seemed like an extraordinary number of door locks.

"Wow, Arthur, I thought the Crown jewels were housed in the Tower of London!"

Arthur laughed, but then with a more serious tone said, "You can make fun of me, Anna, but you will understand in a very short time why the security is necessitated."

"This is a very nice flat, Arthur—you have amassed a beautiful collection of art pottery, which is why I'm guessing you have such security. I don't know much about this area of collecting, but these look like museum-quality heirlooms."

"Yes, I have a weak spot especially for Moorcraft, Ruskin and Della Robbia – you won't find ol' Arthur going for mundane Wedgwood or Royal Doulton, I can tell you that, luv. You know I want to be remembered as a man of unusual and discerning tastes – so in my will I have bequeathed my entire pottery collection to the Museum of London, after being turned down by the British Museum. They have promised to house my collection in a special wing with a bronze plaque. My dear mum would be so proud, God bless her soul."

Arthur chuckled. "Just like you, I go for the unique, although I certainly don't share your fascination for those medical oddities. Which brings me to why I brought you here. To be honest, it's about more than those papers, although they hold important clues to what I am about to reveal. You had better sit down, Anna – this tale is going to knock your socks off!"

Arthur went into the adjoining room briefly and, when he returned, he said, "Let's pick up where we left off at the pub. The papers that were concealed in the diary have never been seen by another living soul – remember, I found them before sharing the diary with my professor mate. Quite frankly, the contents scared the living daylights out of me and I wasn't quite sure what to do with them. Although the following text is public knowledge, it sent shivers down my spine. As you may recall, George Bagster Phillips presented testimony at the inquest of the brutal murder of Mary Jane Kelly. There is a copy of that taped to one of Percy's papers, dated 14 November 1888, nearly a week after what was the most horrendous of all the slayings."

The mutilated remains of a female were lying two-thirds over towards the edge of the bedstead nearest the door. She had only her chemise on, or some underlinen garment. I am sure that the body had been removed subsequent to the injury which caused her death from that side of the bedstead that was nearest the wooden partition, because of the large quantity of blood under the bedstead and the saturated condition of the sheet and the paillasse at the corner nearest the partition.

The blood was produced by the severance of the carotid artery, which was the cause of death. The injury was inflicted while the deceased was lying at the right side of the bedstead.

Arthur said, "Anna, take a look now at what Percy wrote and read it out loud if you will please."

Two days after the horrific murder of Mary Jane Kelly, a petty criminal we used as an occasional informant came up to me on the street when I was off duty. Malcolm had been locked up a handful of times for pickpocketing and street cons, and, although he had a reputation as a liar, some of his tales panned out. He said he had information about the missing organs of Annie Chapman and Catherine Eddowes, but could not reveal his source. When I threatened to have him locked up on suspicion of being the killer, he broke down, sobbing hysterically. What a sight that Malcom was – he fancied himself a smooth con man and here he was crying like a baby. Apparently, he had been loitering in the area after a nearby con and, although he did not witness the murder at Mitre Square, he saw a shadowy figure approach and labour over the body, leaving with a cloth bag. He could not see the face of the cloaked perpetrator, but, unknown to him, the bloke caught a glimpse of him as he momentarily stepped out of the darkness of Church Passage.

A few days later he was grabbed in a dark courtyard and threatened with his life if he mentioned anything about what he saw in Mitre Square. In fact, his attacker said, "I'll see to it that you are butchered, with all your parts cut out, just like those dirty slags." Malcolm got a glimpse of his attacker's face and recognized him as a thug who had at one time worked at the Whitechapel mortuary. He was sacked after being caught red-handed in the act of stealing jewellery and other personal effects from corpses.

When prodded, Malcolm admitted that he did not go to the police because he feared he would be named the killer. I shared this information with Dr Bennett and he said he would put out feelers with some of his colleagues at the Royal College of

Physicians. I implored him not to share any of the information I had told him – although it went against every fibre of my professional training, I had to protect Malcolm from what would surely be his grisly demise. And, I am ashamed to say, if the organs suddenly turned up, it would make the police look quite inept.

Anna said excitedly, "It looks like the text about the case ended abruptly at that point, so how did this mystery play out, Arthur?"

"I found a brief entry dated sixteenth of November that corroborates having a discussion with Percy about the informant, but Malcolm is not mentioned by name. In any case, it looks like it took months of sleuthing on Granddad's part, but this entry from the fourteenth of March 1889 reveals shocking, but historically important details about the missing organs."

I tried in vain for several months to get answers from my contacts, but nobody wanted to talk. Finally, received an urgent message on 6 March to pay a visit to the Royal College. I was brought down to the sub cellar, where they generally keep specimens that are deemed unfit for medical teaching. In a small locked back room, they uncovered two uteruses, properly preserved in medical jars with formaldehyde. It was clear that whomever perpetrated this crime knew something about preserving specimens. Just the same, one of the technicians put them in more archival jars to be safe. Upon closer examination, evidence of hasty removal and hack marks matched the coroner reports on Annie Chapman and Catherine Eddowes.

Two mysterious deliveries were made to the back cellar door of the Royal College of Physicians – the first was discovered when a clerk went out for a cig in the early hours of 9 September 1888, and the second when a night watchman stepped out at dawn on 1 October 1888. There was no demand of money, which further dispelled the trite American theory that the organs were stolen to sell for medical purposes. However, there were grisly notes left both times that read, "Report this to the police and your wives and daughters will be my next victims." My theory is that Jack the Ripper paid this bloke for the repugnant act of stealing and delivering the organs to play out his sick, deranged fantasy.

The staff at the Royal College said they thought about calling the police but decided it was too risky if the notes were more than a hoax. I understood why nobody came forward and wholeheartedly concurred, although deep down I felt like we gave in to a lunatic's threats and justice had been betrayed. But the public was already so outraged by what they saw as ineptitude on the part of the police for not finding the Whitechapel killer. All these months later, it would look horrible to come forward with this ghastly secret and, of course, Percy's well-being and career were foremost on my mind.

I was well respected at the Royal College and the burden of responsibility fell on my shoulders as to how to handle this delicate situation. After disclosing my findings to Percy, we agreed that the missing uteruses must remain a secret. Perhaps if they had reported it right away, this would not be the case, but there was far too much at risk at this point to do anything. So I returned to the sub cellar on 12 March with my solicitor, a locksmith friend of mine, and a small safe. We had papers drawn up that legally made the remains mine, stating that the room and safe must remain sealed for at least 100 years after my death. After that, if somebody had the resolve to locate the key, my diary, and the safe combination, they could pursue transferring the legal rights and claim the remains. But the informant's name had to remain a mystery forever, per Percy's request.

"Good Lord, Arthur, I can barely believe my ears. How did you keep this a secret all these years?"

"Well, I have to tell you that I've had many a sleepless night wondering what to do about this. And let's go back to what I told you in the pub – Sara sent me the diary in September 1986 and I did not discover the hidden papers for a few weeks. Then that professor mate was away on a sabbatical in South Africa so I had to wait until January 1987 to share the diary with him. He had it verified by March 1987 and, upon returning it to me, he mentioned noticing something amiss about the inside back cover. I played dumb, saying, 'Sorry, chap, I was so thrilled by this find that I really hadn't noticed the odd seam.' He didn't question me further, but after I read the diary cover to cover, I was on a mad hunt for the combination to the safe and decided to open the secret compartment where I had found Percy's papers and the key. Somehow I had missed a cryptic message written faintly in ink."

Whitechapel, add two to the month and day of the first, add ten to the second, and add twenty to the double.

"It wasn't hard to figure out that Granddad was referring to the murder victims and that these numbers were the safe combination. Look at the paper here where I sorted out this simple logic, Anna."

(Mary Ann Nichols 8/31 = 39 plus 2 = 41); (Annie Chapman 9/8 = 17 plus 10 = 27); (Double murders of Elizabeth Stride and Catherine Eddowes 9/30 plus 20 = 59).

At this point, Anna jumped up from the sofa and seemed a little over-wrought, because she realized that the physical treasure in this incredible story might be within reach. "Oh my God, Arthur, you cannot keep me in suspense another moment – do you have the safe here in your flat?"

"Anna, if I told you yes, would you let me finish the story?"

Anna jumped up and down like a child before calming down. "I'm sorry, Arthur, you have to understand how fantastically important this find is to me – forgive me for my daft behavior."

Arthur beckoned her to sit back down and patted her on the shoulder like a child. "No worries, luv, it will be just another few minutes and then ol' Arthur will reveal the hidden treasure.

"So let's back up again to when my professor mate had the diary verified in March 1987. Remember, my granddad stated that a hundred years had to pass before something could be done about this situation. If you recall, he died in December 1891, so what an agonizing three years and nine months that was for me, I tell you! In January 1992, I made a few calls in preparation for what I knew was not going to be a slam dunk, as you Americans say. Through my solicitor, an appointment was made to visit the CEO of the Royal College. Naturally, I had the diary, key and safe combination with me when we were ushered into the office on the morning of the twenty-seventh of January 1992.

"The CEO was unaware of this secret, but upon having the historian check the sealed archives of my granddad, found the written agreement. It turned out that the sub-cellar room had been forgotten to history and was actually blocked by years of discarded clutter. We couldn't access the room that day, but a week later my solicitor received a call and we made an appointment for the eleventh of February at noon."

"Oh my, Arthur, I bet you could cut the air with a knife that day down in the sub cellar!"

"Well, yes. At one point I became light-headed and had to sit down on a little bench down there. After recovering, I handed the key to the director of security and, sure enough, the lock opened with a loud creak. The little room was clearly untouched, as evidenced by more than a century of thick cobwebs. The safe was in a corner and they let me do the honors of trying the combination. When the two jars were uncovered, everybody in the room let out such loud exclamations that they must have heard us throughout the upstairs quarters! And the dreadful notes were also in the safe, enclosed in an envelope with my granddad's seal. My solicitor had no trouble getting the Royal College to uphold granddad's wishes, so yours truly was suddenly the new owner of this deep, dark gruesome secret."

Arthur went into the kitchen and came back with crisps, Double Gloucester cheese, a box of Carr's crackers and two shot glasses. "Anna, it is way past dinner and we haven't eaten a thing. Let's toast this occasion with a spot of my best Scotch and eat a little snack. Cheers, my dear!"

After twenty-five minutes or so, Arthur jumped up rather spryly for an older gent and beckoned Anna to a little locked closet in the hallway. His hand was shaking as he opened the lock and this time it was Anna's turn to nearly faint.

The two hammered out a deal, which Anna felt was too generous of Arthur. All he wanted was £1,500, which would more than cover a gorgeous, scarce Ruskin vase he had been eyeing. He also asked for a bronze plaque to be installed at Anna's museum, stating that he had donated the Jack the Ripper artifacts. He seemed tickled pink to know that he would have two plaques – one at the Museum of London and another in New York City at Anna's museum. Of course there were some legalities to iron out and, on Anna's part, a lot of red tape to finagle before having the specimens shipped legally to the States.

At the museum grand opening gala on 15 September, hundreds of people attended as well as a flock of reporters, including Anna's best friend, who was a longtime correspondent at the Associated Press. A few days later, Arthur was sitting in his living room reading the *Guardian* and this headline was music to his ears:

GRAND OPENING OF SIR ARTHUR WUNDERKAMMER MUSEUM IN NYC
UNCOVERS SPECTACULAR NEW ARTIFACTS IN JACK THE RIPPER CASE!

The Ballad of Kate Eddowes
David Bishop

———

In October 1888, the City of London Police headquarters could be found on Old Jewry, a red-brick building tucked behind the main street and facing a small courtyard. When Thomas Conway approached it for the second time in as many weeks, the light was already fading. He glanced up at the darkening sky as he took off his hat, before he stuffed it into his coat pocket, smoothed his hair and went inside.

Conway gave his name to the sergeant at the desk, then waited on a narrow wooden bench until his name was called. The City Police kept him waiting for nearly two hours. As he sat there, watching uniformed constables come and go, sharing his seat with drunks, thieves and whores, Conway reflected on the last time he'd been here. The police had wanted to see him as soon as Kate was killed, but he'd stayed in hiding. He had been worried, and not just because he feared they might try to pin the blame on him. Now, a week later, he was too scared to stay away. He breathed deeply and watched as the outside grew dark, a halo of light pooling ever larger around the heavy wooden doors.

Eventually, a short, solid man appeared and waved Conway through the door. This was Detective Baxter Hunt, whom Conway had met on his previous visit. He was wearing a dark suit, gold watch chain glittering across a hard-looking stomach. He was also completely bald and, as Conway followed him down, he watched the light shine off the top of his bare head. Hunt led Conway into a room at the back of the building, the same one he had been interviewed in a week before. It was small and dim, a gas lamp on one wall and a high window that gave a view of damp brickwork and little else.

The room was already occupied. Another man in a suit sat at the table facing the door. He was taller than the first, with a thin face cut in half by the luxuriant moustache that obscured his mouth. A pipe stuck out of it, smoke curling lazily up to the ceiling. On the table in front of him was a bottle, half empty. A glass, also empty, stood close by it. Hunt closed the door behind them, then took up his position in front of it.

Conway knew the man sitting at the table as Detective Sergeant John Mitchell. He pulled out the chair on his side and started to sit down, before looking up at Mitchell who nodded. Conway continued moving, settling himself into his seat. Mitchell glanced at Hunt, who pulled a face, then he returned his attention to Conway.

'You told me everything last week,' Mitchell said. It wasn't a question, just a statement of fact. His voice was low, quieter than his appearance would have suggested. Mitchell was a man used to not having to shout. He had other people to do that for him. 'You told me you hadn't spoken to Kate Eddowes in years.'

Conway shrugged unevenly. 'I've been thinking about some of the things you said.'

Mitchell raised his eyebrows as if to say, *So?*

'You told me she was killed because she was a whore—'

'Which she was,' said Hunt from behind Conway. 'Why else would she be there, all alone on Mitre Square at one o'clock in the morning?' Mitchell gave him a glance.

'That made me think,' continued Conway. 'That, plus the state he left her in.'

'Her and the rest,' spoke Hunt again. 'Like a fucking abattoir.'

'Detective,' said Mitchell, this time without looking at Hunt. Again his voice was low, but Hunt got the message. He made another face but kept quiet.

'I had an idea.'

Mitchell sat back in his chair, and laughed. But the sound that came out of his mouth was bitter, and there was no joy in it. 'Listen, Conway, I'm up to my tits in theories. Every lunatic from Belfast to Newcastle, Birmingham to Manchester has a tale to tell about Jack the Ripper.'

'This isn't about him, it's about Kate. And I owe her.'

Mitchell reached for the bottle and poured a measure into his glass. He swirled it around then chucked it down his throat and grimaced.

'What's your point, Conway?' Mitchell asked. Then his eyes widened as the other man began singing.

'*Oh come all you feeling Christians, give ear to my tale—*'

Mitchell looked up at Hunt who rolled his eyes, then back at Conway. 'Have you been drinking?'

Conway's voice died away. 'My pledge is sound,' he said, eyes wandering towards the bottle.

Mitchell shook his head. 'You're wasting my time. Detective,' he said to Hunt, 'show Paddy O'Reilly here the door.'

'There's only one way you'll catch him,' Conway said, feeling Hunt move behind him.

'And what would you know about police work?' Hunt hissed into his ear.

'You need to know about them,' said Conway. 'About Kate. They're more than just dead whores.'

'As if,' said Hunt, grabbing the back of Conway's coat and pulling him up. 'Now get out and get up.'

Conway looked at Mitchell. 'You'll never catch him. You've no chance unless you see him for what he is, and what he took away. You look like a man who knows about loss.'

Mitchell's eyes flicked up at Conway, before they went back to his glass. He rolled it from side to side in a meaty palm, before putting it lightly down on the table. 'Put him down, Detective,' Mitchell said quietly. Hunt reluctantly let go of Conway, then returned to his place by the door, straightening his waistcoat. 'Go on then,' Mitchell said. 'I haven't got all night.'

Conway nodded, holding his gaze. Then he sat back in his chair and started talking.

'*You ought be there. He's family.*'

Kate nodded, and looked out at the darkness that surrounded them on the lonely road. It wouldn't be light for another couple of hours. They were surrounded by fields, somewhere near Dunston. At least another hour before they would reach Stafford.

'I hardly knew him,' said Kate, her voice drifting away on the wind. 'Second cousin, no closer than that.'

'It doesn't matter,' Tom said. 'Blood's blood.'

Kate pulled her woollen hat down over her ears. The quiet that surrounded them was total, the only sound that of their feet dragging on the rough gravel. Tom had brought a lantern, but he hadn't kept it lit. They could follow the road, and the moon was half out so there was plenty of light to walk by. But the cold – it took Kate's breath away.

They'd left the previous evening, managing to hitch a lift as far as Coven. The rest of the journey had been on foot. Earlier they'd found a barn, snatching a couple of hours' sleep and a warming fuck before Kate forced them back out on the road.

'There's money to be made,' she'd said, buttoning Tom's trousers and running a soft hand over his crotch. 'We leave it too late, our chances are as dead as our Kit.'

'Everyone loves a good murder,' Tom said, watching Kate pull up her stockings and bending her knees to squirm her way back into them. She brushed loose flakes of straw from her back, and shook out her skirt. 'Some people have violence running through them, like a red river. That will never change.'

Afterwards they'd come reluctantly back out into the January night. Kate pulled her shawl closer to her, glad she'd not had to bring Catherine. She would have cried all the way, tired and hungry.

Kate's flushed face gradually drained of colour, and the cold and tiredness seeped back in her bones. She wanted to curl up, her eyes shutting as her step on the road became slower and heavier. A couple of times she opened them with a start, convinced she could hear voices, children's voices.

'Catherine?' she called out weakly. She turned her head towards them and they fell away.

'All right, Chick?' asked Tom, squeezing her arm.

Kate shook her head to try to clear it. 'Tired. I just want to be there.'

'Soon. I'll buy you breakfast when we arrive, wake you up.'

'And a drink,' Kate groaned. 'To keep out the cold.'

They kept walking, and then Tom started singing. It was the ballad they had written together, the one they were planning to sell. The one about the

hanging. Eventually, Kate joined in and, as their voices grew louder, they
tried to outdo each other, until Kate pushed Tom in the side and he pushed
her back, and they fell on to the road in a heap, laughing in the dark.

'Doesn't seem right,' said Kate after the sound had died away.

'Too late now,' said Tom, and he pulled her up. They carried on walking
and didn't sing again.

'We travelled all over. I promised her once I'd show her India. But we
never got that far.' Conway could hear the scratch of a pencil behind
him, as Hunt wrote in a notebook.

'How lovely,' the detective said in a sarcastic voice. *Scratch-scratch-*
scratch.

Conway reached into his pocket and pulled out a pipe, pressing
tobacco down into it and lighting a march with his thumb to get it
burning. 'She was nineteen, maybe twenty,' he said between puffs.
'Beautiful, but with the devil in her, you know? Beautiful.'

'All the nice girls love a soldier,' said Hunt. 'Mind you, so do the
whores.'

'We met in Birmingham,' said Conway, glancing over his shoulder at
Detective Hunt.

'Fascinating,' said Mitchell. He rapped impatiently on the table
with one fist.

'She was living with her uncle, an ex-boxer,' said Conway. 'No bloody
good, face like a smashed potato. She was aching to get away, I could
tell. We hit it off straight away. All this was before the drink took her.'

'Disgraceful habit. In a woman,' said Mitchell, glancing at the bottle.

Conway kept quiet, but everything he wanted to say was in his eyes.
You're not the one to talk tonight, Sergeant.

By the time they reached the edge of Stafford, a line of grey light showed
along the horizon. They'd walked through the night, and fell into the first pub
they found open. It was busy, considering how early it was, people from all
over come to watch the show.

Tom looked on as Kate destroyed a pint of beer, nodding at the barman for another one before starting on a chunk of pale, flabby bread.

'I need that singing voice in fine form,' he said, rubbing his eyes.

'Exactly,' said Kate, her mouth full and her head now pleasantly light. 'I'm wetting my whistle.'

'I did that already,' said Tom with a dirty laugh.

Kate elbowed him in the stomach and he used the opportunity to grab at her breast, pulling her close and breathing in her smell. He kissed her neck and she pushed him away, picking up the fresh pot of beer and taking a healthy swig.

After they'd finished breakfast, they walked towards the town gaol. Outside it the wooden platform had already been built, the empty noose swinging gaily in the breeze. Two boys were trying to grab it, jumping up and down on the trap-door, which shook beneath them. An ugly-looking man with a flat nose and a beard told them to piss off, and chased the boys until they ran away laughing.

Tom and Kate weaved their way through the crowd, which was already large even that early in the morning. Tom had said they needed to find a good spot, somewhere close to the gallows where they could be seen when the mob wanted their souvenirs. A little something to prove they were there when they hanged Robinson.

Kate had learned the poem by heart as she always did, and she knew it was a good one. Tom was so talented, that was what had drawn her to him. That's what came of being Irish, Kate supposed. He'd seen the world, almost been killed in the mutiny. Lucky to escape with his life, just as she'd been lucky to find him.

By eight o'clock, over a thousand people had gathered. Kate and Tom found a space towards the front on a small rise, brown paper parcels at their feet. They waited and, as the clock struck eight, the door to the gaol opened and Robinson was led out. Kate felt dizzy as she saw him. He'd changed – they'd never been close, but my how he'd changed since August. How much weight he'd lost and how grey he looked. A ghost already.

His neck was still wrapped in a tight white bandage that seemed to make it grow longer, covering the scars from when he'd tried to cut his own throat.

His head was erect at the top of it. Kate noticed that his feet were bare, and wondered where his shoes were.

All around them the crowd shouted and hissed. A couple of them called out Harriet's name, and Robinson looked up, earning more jeers. Kate watched him climb the scaffold. Smith was already up there – Kate recognised him as a man from Dudley who normally worked in the cattle market, a man who had gained a reputation for delivering a quick death. Then the priest blessed Robinson and asked him if he had anything else to say. The noise from the crowd dropped suddenly, and Robinson looked around him as if he'd woken from a dream only to find it still happening around him.

Smith took his silence as an agreement to continue, and he stepped forward to place the rope around Robinson's neck, tightening it to keep it in place. Robinson lifted a hand to feel the rough cord and, as he did so, a light seemed to come back into his eyes. Kate held her breath, watching. Then Smith began to pull the hood over Robinson's head. Just as it dropped down over his eyes, he cried out 'Lord Jesus, have mercy on my spirit!' He continued talking, but the hood muffled his words.

Smith fussily made sure Robinson's head was covered, and then in a quick motion stepped back and released the bolt that held the trapdoor. Robinson dropped through it, then there was a whistle and a thump and a high crack. The crowd watched in silence, and then shouts started up as Robinson began to kick his legs, trying to get a purchase on thin air.

Concern clouded Smith's face. He leaped off the scaffold and ducked under it, jumping up to grab Robinson by the thighs and hang on to him, dragging him down. He pulled with all his strength – Kate remembered seeing him do something similar at the market, him and two other men pulling a runaway cow down on to the ground to stop it moving. Smith's meaty forearms bulged and he clung to Robinson until he also stopped struggling, the two of them swinging slightly. Finally, Robinson's legs stopped shaking and Smith dropped down, wiping sweat from his forehead with the back of one hairy arm.

The movement seemed to break the spell and the crowd began to murmur once more, before pockets of cheering and shouts sprang up all around the scaffold. Kate felt tears in her eyes; then she felt a nudge on her thigh, and looked around to see Tom breaking open one of the packages. He handed her a sheaf of papers. Then he took his own and waved it in the air, starting to shout out. 'The Ballad of poor Robinson, only a ha'penny, a true and terrible story of bloody murder, only a ha'penny, cheaper than the price that young man just paid!'

'She had a beautiful voice,' said Conway. 'She could have sold them on her own, just by singing.'

'And look at all the good it did her,' said Hunt. 'And you. Business must've really boomed.'

'Maybe you can write a song about her next,' said Mitchell. 'Then she'll be famous for, what? Five minutes?'

'I haven't written anything decent since I left her.'

'What was she, your muse?' asked Mitchell.

'She deserves a longer legacy than that,' Conway said, ignoring him. 'More than I can give her.'

'I'd say you gave her plenty,' said Hunt, walking round the table to stand beside Mitchell. 'Two lovely black eyes,' he sang, his voice throaty and full.

'That wasn't me,' said Conway, before falling silent. Mitchell watched the look in Conway's eyes change. 'That was years ago. She drank, she got violent—'

'Self-defence, was it?' laughed Hunt.

'It was never that bad.'

Mitchell pursed his lips. 'Says the wife-beater.'

'We never married.'

The two detectives laughed. 'Well, that makes all the difference. Not only a Mick, but one with a whole tribe of bastards at his feet,' said Mitchell.

'And a whore for a—well, if she wasn't your wife what would you call her?' asked Hunt.

Conway bared his teeth, forming the words with angry precision. 'Kate. I called her Kate,' he said.

*   *   *

Tom winked at her and, as Kate began to sing, the tears flowed fully now. They streamed down her face as she sang the ballad, and Tom took the money and handed out the broadsheets. Kate hardly looked at her customers, her gaze instead fixed on the pitiful bundle that Smith was cutting down from the scaffold. Kate could hardly believe there was a man inside it, it looked so small. She watched as they carried the body into the prison, the enormous wooden gate shutting behind them. Kate's voice rose as they disappeared, then she stopped and began the ballad over again.

'Come all you feeling Christians/Give ear unto my tale,/It's for a cruel murder/I was hung at Stafford gaol.'

Within an hour nearly all the broadsheets were gone. Tom wrapped his arm around Kate and kissed her cheek. 'You should cry more often, chick. I've never seen them sold so fast.'

Kate wiped her eyes with a handkerchief that Tom gave her.

'He may be dead, but he's famous now,' he said. 'No one will forget your Kit. That has to be worth something, right?'

'Not the sort of fame I want,' said Kate. She leaned close to Tom, and they walked together to the pub where he bought her a beer. Later, half drunk and cuddling up to one another, she whispered in his ear, 'Will you write a song about me one day, Tom?'

'I'm not sure I'm up to it,' he said, stroking her hair. 'What could I say that would match this moment of bliss?'

Kate gave him a light slap on the leg with an open hand, laughing. 'You Irish are all the same.'

Tom grinned back, and emptied his glass. 'Come on, let's find a bed for the night.' He put his arm around her, and they disappeared into the cold January dark.

'I've had enough,' said Mitchell. The bottle on the table was empty, and the backs of his legs ached from the hard wooden chair he'd been sitting on.

'I've told you everything,' said Conway, half turning in his seat. 'You needed to know what she was like. You needed to care. The way you talked about her before, it was like you murdered her again. But now you know who she was, maybe you'll treat her with more dignity.'

Mitchell shook his head. 'You waited out there, for two hours, to tell us a bloody fairy story? Happily ever after?'

Conway contemplated his pipe 'For too long, it's been all about Jack the bloody Ripper. That's all I've heard, all you're interested in. Who is he, where will he strike next? But Jack's not the real story. Those women were real – Kate, she was real too. And they deserve better.'

Mitchell looked up at the ceiling, sadly it seemed to Conway, before taking a deep breath. Then he looked over his shoulder at Hunt. 'Detective, if you please.' Hunt didn't need telling twice. His squat body moved lightly around the table, grabbing Conway as he was rising to his feet. Hunt turned him round and pushed forward, pinning Conway to the table. A hand on the back of his head kept it there.

'You really have tried my patience, you stupid Mick cunt,' Conway heard Hunt say. Then he felt a blow to the lower part of his back, then another. His vision blurred, and then came back into focus. He felt himself be rolled over so that he was lying on his back, feet dangling just off the floor.

Hunt had taken his jacket off and was in the process of rolling up his sleeves. 'You lot just don't learn, do you?' Conway could see a tattoo on Hunt's right forearm, something that looked like a pair of compasses. He was just wondering what it meant when Hunt descended on him and he felt a jab to the stomach. There were several more and he lost count, red flashes across his eyes. Conway coughed, his body shaking with pain. Then Hunt stopped and Conway lay on the table giving a throaty moan.

Finally, the punches stopped. Conway could hear someone breathing heavily. As the breathing slowed, he opened his eyes in time to see Hunt standing over him, upside down. Hunt leered then brought a heavy wooden truncheon down hard on to Conway's face. Conway screamed, and felt bone crunch and snap. There were two more sharp blows, then the shadow standing over him moved back. Conway rolled onto his side and coughed, tasting blood in his mouth.

Then he heard a voice very close to his ear. Hunt. 'Now, take your dirty Mick arse and leave my station,' he said quietly.

Conway lifted himself gingerly from the table. Every move ached, but he managed to get up. He walked painfully to the door. 'Good luck catching him, Sergeant.'

'Don't you fucking worry about that,' said Hunt. 'We found you, didn't we?' He opened the door and stood to one side, allowing Conway to weave his way through. He held his smashed face in one hand, the other pushed deep into one pocket of his coat. He glanced back at Mitchell, who was standing on the other side of the table.

'And what if there is no Jack the Ripper?' Conway asked, the words slurred with blood.

'Enough,' said Hunt. 'Get out before I beat you again.'

Conway looked at him, then back at Mitchell. Then touched his hat with his free hand, and left.

Hunt led him back along the dingy corridor, and into the entrance hall. Despite Conway's appearance, the uniformed policeman at the desk threw nothing more than a glance his way. He carried on writing, the scratch of the nib the only sounds that Conway noticed. Hunt held the door open and Conway stumbled out into the night, glad of both the darkness and the cool air.

Through the door Conway heard Hunt's muffled voice. 'Waste of fucking time, Constable, that's what that was.'

Conway shook his head, and gave a weak bloodied smile. *Not to me* he thought, massaging his jaw where it hurt. That wasn't the first beating he'd taken on Kate's account. His tale had been told and Hunt and Mitchell had heard it, even if they didn't realise what it was. Conway looked up at the sky way above him, pale wisps of cloud drifting across it. Then he put his hat back on and walked painfully towards the lights of the main street, singing a low song as he went:

'*Oh come all you feeling Christians, give ear to my tale . . .*'

They All Love Jack
Nick Sweet

———

I saw her making her way along Brady Street. The clock of Whitechapel Church had just struck three. Nobody about at this hour but whores and mischief-makers. Coppers, too, of course, but it's easy enough to dodge them.

It was clear to me from the way she moved that she was the worse for drink, but I wasn't about to complain. On the contrary, her state of inebriation suited my ends perfectly. She was petite and had a fresh look about her, in her nice new bonnet.

I caught up with her. 'Nice girl like you shouldn't be out on her own,' I said.

'Get away with you,' she laughed. 'How'd a gentleman like you fancy a little company?'

'Don't tell me a pretty girl like you hasn't earned her doss money for the night yet?'

'Earned it and spent it three times already.'

I scarcely needed to ask her what she had spent it on.

She grinned in a way that was no doubt supposed to be charming, but I merely found her dull and stupid. She was perfect for what I had in mind.

'Knee-trembler'll cost you fourpence,' she said.

I assented and she took my arm as we continued down the street. We passed a large board school and the road narrowed. The towering warehouses cast shadows that were scarcely disturbed by the single lamp. Rather a respectable little street in the bustle and light of day, it seemed dank and gloomy at this time of night.

We came to some stables, and I stopped by the gates and took her by the hand. 'This'll do as well as anywhere,' I said. Better than most places, in fact, I thought. Of course she had no idea of what lay in store for her. The little trick that I had up my sleeve.

She reached a hand down below, but I wasted no time and went straight for her throat. She didn't have time to scream. Strangling her was a simple business and didn't take long. Then, as the body fell to my feet, I took out my nice new shiny knife and slashed her throat clean through to the vertebrae.

The following morning I recorded the event in my diary:

I have shown all that I mean business; the pleasure was far better than I had imagined. The whore was only too willing to do her business. I recall all and it thrills me. There was no scream when I cut. I was more than vexed when the head would not come off. I believe I will need more strength next time. I struck deep into her. I regret I never had my cane, it would have been a delight to have rammed it hard into her. The bitch opened like a ripe peach. I have decided next time I will rip all out. My medicine will give me strength and the thought of the whore and her whoring master will spur me on no end.

I attended the inquest at the Whitechapel Working Lads Institute, along with all the others that thronged to hear news of the murder. A Dr Llewellyn, who practised at a surgery in Whitechapel Road, was called to examine the body. He reported a jagged wound on the left side of the abdomen, running to two or three inches in length and so deep that the tissues had been cut through, along with several incisions across the abdomen and more cuts running down the victim's right side.

Nothing for me to worry about at all.

Another entry in the diary:

The wait to read about my triumph seemed long, although it was not . . . They have all written well. The next time they will have a great deal more to write, of that I have no doubt . . . I will remain calm and show no interest in my deed, if anyone should mention it so, but I will laugh inside, oh how I will laugh.

In the church I sing sacred hymns and reflect on my dark deeds. The reporter in the *Star* has come up with a theory. Claims to have interviewed fifty women in a period of three hours and has hit on the wonderful idea that a man known locally as 'Leather Apron' is the killer. All working out marvellously for me, of course.

Couldn't make it up if I wanted to.

On further investigation, I discover that this Leather Apron chap turns out to be a boot finisher whose real name is John Pizer, a Polish Jew. The East End is eager for blood, and the smell of anti-semitism is in the air.

Meanwhile, a theatrical version of Stevenson's *Dr Jekyll and Mr Hyde* is thrilling audiences in the West End. I shouldn't be surprised if the play's success didn't redound to me in some way. Perhaps I should write to the author and demand a share of his royalties. Have him send them to my address at . . . But no, perhaps that would not be such a clever idea. You think I am stupid, but I am not. Nor am I mad, although my brother is . . . But more of that later.

Time to make another entry in the diary:

I will not allow too much time to pass before my next. Indeed, I need to repeat my pleasure as soon as possible. The whoring master can have her with pleasure and I shall have my pleasure with my thoughts and deeds. I will be clever. I will not call on Michael on my next visit. My brothers would be horrified if they knew, particularly Edwin, after all did he not say I was one of the most gentlest men he had ever encountered. I hope he is enjoying the fruits of America . . . Unlike I for do I not have a sour fruit . . .

The gentle man with gentle thoughts will strike again soon. I have never felt better, in fact, I am taking more than ever and I feel the strength building up within my. The head will come off next time, also the whore's hands. Shall I leave them in the various places about Whitechapel? Hunt the head and hands instead of the thimble. <u>Ha ha</u>. Maybe I will take some part away with me to see if it does taste like fresh fried bacon . . .

*   *   *

And another entry:

If Michael can succeed in rhyming verse then I can do better, a great deal better. He shall not outdo me. Think, you fool, think. I curse Michael for being so clever. I shall outdo him. I will see to that. A funny little rhyme *shall* come forth. Like this one for instance:

> One dirty whore was looking for some gain
> Another dirty whore was looking for the same.

I am taking more all of the time. If I leave off taking it for a single day, the suffering I undergo is quite unbearable. I am sure that I am quite mad. I must and will strike again.

I have struck again. This time in Hanbury Street. Once again I failed to get the head off, but I ripped her stomach open and threw her intestines over her left shoulder; then I tore out her uterus and part of her abdomen.

My brother is up in Liverpool with his Florie. He is taking his pills, or I am taking them for him. Make of that what you will. His Florie is cheating on him, and I can make something of that. Oh yes, I can make something of that. Just you wait and see.

The East End is in a right rumpus, I must say. Seem to have stirred things up in that part of the world with my little tricks. Group of businessmen down that way have formed the Whitechapel Vigilance Committee. Fat lot of good it'll do them, too. Naturally, I am no East-ender, for I will not play my funny little games on my own doorstep. *Ha ha.*

Have to laugh, what with all this talk about it being a Jew behind the killings. The Leather Apron. Not that the good people of the East End are bigoted, mind you; it's just that they fail to see how an Englishman could possibly be responsible for such abominations. I am beginning to think this bigotry of the common man is an uncommonly appealing quality, and one to be greatly encouraged, if you understand me. *Ha ha.*

I shall write them a little clue.

Here goes:

May comes and goes
In the dark of the night
he kisses the whores
The jews and the doctors
Will get all the blame
but it's only May
playing his dirty game.

Do I need to spell it out for them?
May as in *May*brick.

I have struck again, twice. Double for my money. *Ha ha*. My third was Elizabeth Stride, my fourth Catharine Eddowes.

Time for another diary entry:
To my astonishment I cannot believe I have not been caught. My heart felt as if it had left my body. Within my fright I imagined my heart bounding along the street with I in desperation following it. I would have dearly loved to have cut the head of the damned horse off and stuff it as far as it would go down the whore's throat. I had no time to rip the bitch wide, I curse my bad luck. I believe the thrill of being caught excited me more than cutting the whore herself. As I write, I find it impossible to believe he did not see me, in my estimation I was less than a few feet from him. The fool panicked, it is what saved me. My satisfaction was far from complete, damn the bastard. I cursed him and cursed him, but I was clever, they could not outdo me. No one ever will.
I ripped her stomach and tore out her internal organs. Then I left my calling card on her face: M.

Laughed myself silly when I read it today in the first edition of the *Daily News*:

Dear Boss,

I keep on hearing the police have caught me but they wont fix me just yet. I have laughed when they look so clever and talk about being on the *right* track. That joke about Leather Apron gave me real fits. I am down on whores and shant quit ripping them till I do get buckled. Grand work the last job was. I gave the lady no time to squeal. How can they catch me now. I love my work and want to start again. You will soon hear of me with my funny little games. I saved some of the proper *red* stuff in a ginger beer bottle over the last job to write with but it went thick like glue and I cant use it. Red ink is fit enough I hope. _Ha. Ha._ The next job I do I shall clip the ladys ears off and send to the police officers just for jolly wouldn't you. Keep this letter back till I do a bit more work, then give it out straight. My knife's so nice and sharp I want to get to work right away if I get a chance. Good luck.

And I signed it, giving myself the trade name of 'Jack the Ripper' before I added a couple of postcripts:

Don't mind me giving the trade name.

Wasn't good enough to post this before I got all the red ink off my hands curse it. No luck yet. They say I'm a doctor now. _Ha ha_.

And the text of the card I sent written in red crayon appeared in the 1 p.m. edition of the *Star* on 1 October:

I was not codding dear old Boss when I gave you the tip, you'll hear about Saucy Jacky's work tomorrow double event this time number one squealed a bit couldn't finish straight off. Had not the time to get ears for police. Thanks for keeping last letter back till I got to work again.

Jack the Ripper

The fall guy is up in Liverpool with his beloved Florie who's playing him false. He's taking more pills than ever, which plays right into my hands. Florie does, too. She's a very handy kind of girl, I find, is our Florie. Not that she knows it, mind you.

I'm going to have her kill him in the end, whether she likes it or not. Arsenic will do the trick. Arsenic'll trip over clever Jim. Leave it in a bottle near the sickbed. Won't be long now. He's already dying of the stuff. Dying for it even as he dies of or because of it, poor blighter. Won't mind, I'm sure, if he goes to the grave with all of my crimes on his head. They're his crimes, the way I see it, because I'm doing all this for him. For him and Florie. So he can confess and she can put him out of his misery. That way I can get shot of both of them in one fell swoop.

Once he's so sick he can't move, it'll just be a case of getting the will rewritten with myself named as sole executor. Then Jack dies of the poison, Florie goes to the gallows and I inherit the house and all of his money. Nobody will be too bothered to see the back of Saucy Jack when he takes a trip. On the contrary . . .

I think I'll strike once more, just to put the icing on the cake. This time I'll really go to town, so they'll never forget Jack. Jack or James. Jack for James, I should say. May as in Maybrick will be playing his dirty game some more. And all the while he'll be up in Liverpool taking the blame. You have to admit my plan is perfect. More than clever enough to hoodwink that fool Abberline. He thinks he's so clever it's pitiful.

And I carry on with my songs, my sacred songs. I am the talented brother. The one who can do no wrong. I am the toast of the nation. I am to be pitied about my brother. Or I will be, come the day when they find the diary. His diary that I'm writing for him, even though he doesn't know it. I shall lock it up in his desk. That way it will look like he tried to conceal it.

I have to laugh when I think of the merry dance I'm leading that fool Abberline. And the beauty of it is that the dance is set to go on forever. There will be no end to the fun. Why, it will continue when we are all dead and buried. I shall even lead future generations up the garden path. I am a genius, though I say it myself. You have to be a genius to do what I've done and pull it off.

Of course nobody would dispute that. For the nation has it that I am indeed a genius. It's just that they do not realize the full extent of my talents . . . They credit me with the songs I have written, songs that I have seen performed at the Royal Albert Hall before Queen Victoria herself. Oh yes, they credit me so far, but no further. And in that way they are unjust, for they do not even begin to guess what I am truly capable of.

As clever Jack for James would have it in his diary that isn't his:

They give much of the credit that is my jew to the juwes. *Ha ha*. The juwes and the doctors. You have to laugh.

I will show them one more time, and then I will retire gracefully.

Because it is to be the last time, I will leave them something to remember me by. This time I will really go to town in the heart of London's East End. Let the fools of Scotland Yard try to stop me if they can and let the Devil take the hindmost.

Speaking of the Devil, sometimes I wonder if I am that individual. If I am he, or he is I. Who knows, maybe I really am mad and not merely pretending. Maybe I am madder than my brother James, or clever Jim, will appear to be in the diary I am writing for him. Maybe it is the pills. Maybe it is my genius. Maybe the most heinous evil and the celestial harmonies found in my music are wed in some hideous marriage of heaven and hell in my dark soul. William Blake would have loved to meet me. He would have written poetic masterpieces in homage to my works. Not that I could give a monkey's. My fame will tower over that of a thousand William Blakes. William Blake can kiss my arse while I let rip. *Ha ha*.

But I digress, and there is work to do . . .

Turns out a man by the name of Hutchinson reckons he saw me at work. Had to laugh when I learned of how he told them I was of a dark and 'foreign' appearance. Perhaps I am the Leather Apron!

One thing Hutchinson did get right, though: he says the man he saw wore a black tie with a horseshoe pin. Pictures of me wearing the very same horseshoe pin have appeared in magazines running articles whose purport has been to eulogize my musical talents. You may have seen me in one of them yourself. But of course nobody will draw a connection. Why should they, when Hutchinson, the damned fool, seems to think I am a foreigner?

Once again I have the wonderful bigotry of the local people to be thankful for. All down to their not being educated, of course. Wonderful thing, if you ask me, having the plebs go without an education. For, as any true gentleman knows, a little knowledge is a dangerous thing, and therefore it naturally follows that educating the masses would be certain to destroy the moral fabric of the nation. Why if the day ever comes when they start to give the whores and their whoremasters an education, then it will be time for me to go and live in the Congo.

I have nothing against Jews; it is whores I have had it in for. Or rather, it is whores that James has had it in for. Clever Jim's down on them because his wife Florie's cheating on him. She's playing the whore with her whoremaster, as the diary would have it. So James has taken it upon himself to have it out with a few of the good ladies who work the streets of the East End, would you believe. Abberline will fall for it like a pack of cards when he finds the diary. Just you wait and see.

I shall enjoy having the use of my brother's house. Rather a grand affair it is, too. Of course it's true that I'm already rather well set up in my place in Regent's Park, but one can never have too many properties. Indeed, the desire for acquisition lies at the heart of what it means to be respectable, does it not? After all, as everyone knows, the gentleman who has failed to acquire sufficient wealth soon finds himself ceasing to be a gentleman. Even the whores and their whoremasters know that much. Just as they know that the truly genteel are those who take a whip when dealing with the poor.

Anyway, neither James nor Florie will miss either their house or their money where they're going.

I should like to say they are going to a better place, even though I sincerely doubt that . . .

Hutchinson's words:

They both then came past me and the man hung down his head, with his hat over his eyes . . . I stepped down and looked him in the face. He looked at me stern. She said all right, my dear, come along you *will* be comfortable. They both went into Dorset Street. I followed them. They both stood at the corner of the court for about three minutes. He said something to her. He then placed his arm on her shoulder and gave her a kiss. She said she had lost her handkerchief. They then went up Miller's Court together. I then went up the Court to see if I could see them but I could not. I stood there for about three-quarters of an hour, to see if they came out. They did not, so at 3 a.m. I went away.

She cried 'murder' at one point, but nobody heard the little squealer. Not surprising, I suppose, because it would have been around four in the morning. And in that area I'm sure they are used to such performances. Then I really went to work on her. I sang quietly, under my breath, as I went about it. You can imagine the song, I'm sure? That's right: 'They All Love Jack'. One of my very own masterpieces, of course. Sang it to audiences all over Europe.

'I know how to show a nice gentleman like you a good time,' she said.

I doubt that, I thought. Or rather, I didn't doubt it. Only I was quite sure that what *she* meant by 'a nice time' was rather different from what *I* had in mind. When she asked me my name, I hardly knew what to tell her. Should I tell her I was Stephen Adams? Or Michael Maybrick? Or perhaps I was James. Or else I was Jack . . .

I went to Leipzig in 1865 and studied keyboard and harmony there, before later deciding to train as a baritone in Milan with Gaetano Nava. They had no idea I was going to turn out to be Jack. And when I appeared with great success in Mendelssohn's *Elijah* in London, back in 1869, they had no idea of who I was, or who I was to become, either. No more idea than that fool Abberline.

Of course I didn't become Stephen Adams until the early 1870s, and it was as him that I sang my own compositions. My sea song 'Nancy Lee' sold more than a hundred thousand copies in two years. I did well with a number of other songs, too; sentimental and romantic ones like 'Your Dear Brown Eyes' and 'Children of the City', and sacred songs like 'Holy City'. But there's never any doubt in my mind as to which one is my own personal favourite. You and I know it's 'They All Love Jack'.

I toured the United States in 1884. Old Sherlock Holmes was right – or perhaps I mean his creator, Conan Doyle – when he advised the good gentlemen of the Yard to investigate an American connection . . . Conan Doyle was no fool, but mercifully he was out of the way writing his books. As for Holmes, he was, I have reason to believe, being kept rather busy by a fellow by the name of Moriarty. A professor, no less. Some sort of evil genius. *Another* one. My soul mate, perhaps. Indeed, there are times when I sometimes wonder whether I am he . . . that is to say, whether I am the evil Professor Moriarty, or whether he is I.

You have to be a genius to kill the way I did. I sang to her as I worked. Not that she heard me, because she was long gone by then. 'They All Love Jack' . . . Oh and how true it is turning out to be.

They cannot say I haven't left them enough clues. I have been fair with them. Is it my fault if they are such dolts? Am I to be blamed if Abberline has fewer brains than a mongrel bitch in season?

After all, there's the business with the horseshoe pin. And then there's the title of my favourite song – written, of course, by none other than yours truly.

But they didn't cotton on.

I feel I'm worthy of my brother's house and money if the bastards at Scotland Yard are so stupid, don't you?

But there is more to it than that, much more. I am not so low as to be motivated merely by greed of gain. Far from it, for aesthetic souls such as mine are driven by higher aims. While low types follow the scent of lucre to the exclusion of all else, artists such as I long to achieve more complex ends. Lucre has its attractions, I shall not deny it; but there are desires for sensations of a more pressing kind, rhapsodies of heart and mind, euphorias of the spirit that are the true preserve of the artist; delights which are to be known only by the man of genius.

I do not suppose any of it would have happened had Sally not slept with Father. I saw them together, you see; spied on them through the keyhole. I was only nine years old at the time, but that was old enough for me to know that what they were doing was wrong. James never found out about it, and I was too frightened to tell him, not least because I derived a certain guilty pleasure from watching them.

Sally caught me spying on her with Father one day, and she came to me the following afternoon. I was a filthy monkey, she said, and it was high time I took a bath. Then, when I was in the tub, she began to scrub me all over, paying particular attention to my penis, testicles and anus, which she handled and washed with loving care. Then she leaned over the side of the tub, and took my penis in her mouth . . .

After that, Sally would pay me regular visits. She would often take my penis – her 'favourite little man', as she described it – in her mouth and suck and lick it. On other occasions, she would kiss and lick my bottom. Or else she would sit down on my face and tell me to wash her privates with my tongue. I knew that what we were doing was wrong, but somehow my awareness of this only added to my excitement and made me want to continue with my sinful ways all the more . . .

Then one afternoon Mother bade me come to Sally's room, at the back of the house, at a time when Father was out with my two brothers on an trip to the West End, and what I found there I shall never forget.

Murder was clearly not enough for Mother, for her rage knew no limits. So it must have been, anyway, for poor Sally was no longer to be recognized. Mother had slit the poor girl's throat, before proceeding to rip her up. Sally's internal organs were strewn about the room, and I had to take care to avoid stepping on a kidney here or a breast there; the sack that had been the poor girl's uterus was on one side and the bloody muscle that was her heart on the other . . .

Mother was laughing in a way I had never seen anyone laugh before.

'But what have you done, Mother?' I began to remonstrate with her, once I found I had regained the power of speech, of which I had been temporarily deprived by the truly horrific nature of the spectacle before me.

'I think that's rather a redundant question, Michael, don't you?' She giggled. 'Question is *why* I've done it, I should think . . . But then you and I know the answer to that, don't we?'

The penny dropped like a lead weight banging in my head.

'The filthy whore had it coming to her after what she was doing to you and Father,' she said. 'Yes, I saw the way she corrupted you both.' She giggled again. 'What, did you think I wouldn't find out?'

'But even so, Mother, you—'

'Don't you *even so* me, my lad,' she hissed. 'The whore came into my home and did the Devil's work, and for that she had to pay. So it fell to me to be the one to present her with the bill; and I was equal to the task, as you can see . . . Oh yes, I'm down on whores, my lad.'

Mother forced me to make a full confession of the evil deeds I had enacted with Sally; and then, 'as payment' for my sins, she forced me to take up the knife and cut what was left of our benighted governess into small pieces.

I sobbed as I worked, but, as has always been my way, my tears did not prevent me from getting the job done. And when Sally had been reduced to parts that were small enough to go into a sack, I was then given the job of going and disposing of 'the rubbish', to use Mother's term.

Over the days that followed, Mother served up Sally's kidneys, liver and heart for the five of us to eat at dinner in a stew. Of course Father and my two brothers, James and Edwin, were blissfuly ignorant of the fact that it was Sally's internal organs they were eating, and, as for me, well, as you can understand, I was not about to let them in on what had come to pass, for I felt as though Mother and I were in cahoots, given how I'd helped her to cut up and then dispose of the body. Strange thoughts were passing through my young mind, and it was as though I had come to understand Mother and approve of what she had done, in a complicated sort of way, even as I continued to love Sally and cherish her memory . . .

When Father began to wonder as to Sally's whereabouts the following morning, Mother showed him a letter she had 'discovered in Sally's room'. The letter, which Mother had of course written in her best imitation of Sally's hand, told of how our greatly beloved and much-hated governess had decided to depart England's shores for America post-haste. She loved us all far too much to take her leave of us in person, for she hated emotional farewells, and so it was with a heavy heart and some misgivings that she'd decided upon using a letter as the form in which to say goodbye . . .

You could say that these experiences from my childhood have left their mark on me. Indeed, I am sure a psychiatrist would argue that all of the business I underwent with Sally – and that Sally underwent with me and my parents – must have something to do with my lust for killing whores . . . For you see, I am something of a mother's boy, and, just like Mother, I am very down on whores. But be that as it may, I am as I am, and it is for the dullards of the Yard to get off their arses and catch me if they can. Don't you agree?

Time for another diary entry to record what happened with this last one:

I really got carried away this time. I left nothing of the bitch, nothing. I placed it all over the room, time was on my hands, like the other whore, I cut off the bitch's nose, all of it this time. I left nothing of her face to remember her by . . . I thought it a joke when I cut her breasts off, kissed them for a while. The taste of blood was sweet, the pleasure was overwhelming, will have to do it again. It thrilled me so. Left them on the table with the other stuff. Thought they belonged there. They wanted a slaughterman so I stripped what I could, laughed while I was doing so, like the other bitches she ripped like a ripe peach.

*　　　*　　　*

Afterwards, I wondered if I'd really done all that. Or had it all been a marvellous dream? A fantastic fantasy?

But no, not according to the *Pall Mall Gazette* anyway, which called my latest little performance a 'Story of unparalleled atrocity'; if I may quote: 'The breasts had also been cleanly cut off and placed on the table which was by the side of the bed . . . the kidneys and heart had also been removed from the body and placed by the side of the breasts.'

Similar reports appeared in *The Times* and the *Star*.

Another one for the diary:

One of these days I will take the head away with me, I will boil it and serve it up for my supper.

key	rip
flee	initial
hat	
handkerchief	whoremaster
whim	look to the whore
mother	light
father	fire

with the key I did flee
I had the key
the clothes I burnt
along with the hat
the hat I did burn
for light I did yearn
for the sake of the whoring mother
and I thought of the whoring mother . . .
a handkerchief red
led to the bed
and I thought of the whoring mother . . .

*   *   *

The 'whoring mother' is of course Florie, my brother James's wife. My brother is me. He is Jack. I am Stephen Adams, the famous composer. I am the genius. My brother is dying in Liverpool. It will not be long now. The poison pills are working their magic. He is a jolly fool. He will go down in history. His repute will outlive mine, I fear. All cheer to him! I must not envy him his success as he envies me mine.

Did you notice how he is ignorant of the fact that it's the music I write and not the lyrics. One of the small deliberate errors I included in the diary, just to fool them. It's become something of a work of art, the way I've written it. At times I practically wax poetic. I shall out-versify Tennyson. Except that it is not me writing but my brother James. Me writing as him, that's to say. He will fool people in years to come. Fool them without even knowing he's doing it, for mine is an artful act of ventriloquism. I do violence to language, even to the point of using bad grammar and spelling words wrongly here and there to achieve my effects. For clever Jim's a man of business, and he never really allowed his masters to educate him.

I will make detectives of the literary critics and literary critics of the detectives. And I am not just talking about dolts like Abberline, for my legacy will tie the brains of the country in knots. It will have the aesthetes of Camden and Hampstead running to Scotland Yard, and the plods of the Yard running to Camden and Hampstead. I shall be laughing from beyond the grave for all eternity.

An initial here and an initial there
will tell of the whoring mother
I left it there for the fools but they never find it. Left it in the front
for all eyes to see. Shall I write and tell them? That amuses me.
She reminded me of the whore. So young unlike I.

Do you remark the violence of my grammar with that 'unlike *I*'? My brother James always was a dreadful philistine. A dolt like him would never hurt a fly. He lacks the imagination for the work. An initial here . . . Do I have to write a full confession?

M
wrote it loud and clear on her face. There for all to see.
wrote it on the wall above the bed, too.
M
M on wall
Wall=brick
M on wall=M on brick
M for May
Its only May playing his dirty game
Maybrick
M for Michael, too
F next to it
Florie Maybrick
Florie and her clever Jim for a husband, James or
Jack
I wrote it all there for them to see if they wanted to see it.
How many clues do they need?

Letter M it's true
along with M ha ha
will catch clever Jim.
Am I insane?
No, James is.
One whore no good
decided Sir Jim strike another
I showed no fright and indeed no light
damn it, the tin box was empty . . .
sweet sugar and tea
could have paid my small fee
but instead I did flee
and by way showed my glee
by eating cold kidney for supper
bastard

Abberline
bonnett
hides all
clue
clever
will tell you more . . .
Sir Jim trip over
fear
have it near
redeem it near
case
post-haste
he believes I will trip over
but I have no fear
I cannot redeem it here . . .
am I not a clever fellow

Do they expect me to write it all down in a story and post it to the Yard?

Goulston Street.

PC Alfred Long passed by that way earlier and saw nothing.

They do not see clever Sir Jim's for a tripping over. He is up in Liverpool taking his pills. He is slowly going crazy. Or I am doing it for him. I am a man of many parts.

Punch: The jews and the doctors will get the blame.

Packs a punch.

The Juwes are the men who will not be blamed for nothing.

I had to laugh they have me down as left handed doctor, a slaughter man and a Jew. Very well, if they are to insist I am a Jew then a Jew I shall be.

I am a man of all nations and all seasons. I am politic to the very end. The worms will gnaw my secrets.

My funny Jewish joke.

October the first, my name's birthday.

I will bring Ripperology to the masses.

My legacy will light up the East End like an opium pipe.

Clues, I shall sprinkle them all over.

I had forgotten how many Jewish friends I have. My revenge is on whores not Jews.

I am taking my revenge on the whore F who goes to her whoremaster.

Or is it all a tricky plot to make Sir Jim trip over?

Jack for Jim. Jack for James, my brother. M for Maybrick. M for Michael, too.

Cane for Cain. Me. Fratricide by proxy.

Time has passed. James is dead and Florie faces the noose.

I have inherited James's house and his money. The nation loves me, as it should. Because They All Love Jack. But sometimes my conscience troubles me. I cannot live without my medicine. I am afraid to go to sleep for fear of my nightmares reoccuring. I see thousands of people chasing me, with Abberline in front dangling a rope. I am tired and I fear the city of whores has become too dangerous for me to make a return.

James's children, who are now in my care, constantly ask what I shall be buying them for Christmas; they all shy away when I tell them a shiny knife not unlike Jack the Ripper's in order that I cut their tongues for peace and quiet.

I do believe I may be going mad. I may be going the way of James, who was not really mad at all, of course, although I created him that way in my own image. *Ha ha*. I have never harmed the children, but I do take great delight in scaring them so.

I fear I may have gone too far with that last one. I am cold. Curse the bastard for making me rip. I keep seeing blood pouring from the bitches. The nightmares are hideous. I cannot stop myself from wanting to eat more. God help me. Damn you. No one will stop me. God be damned. She meant me no special harm, after all. I will pray for the women I have slaughtered. Perhaps I should top myself. I could not cut like my last, visions of her flooded back to me as I struck. I tried to quash all thoughts of love. I left her for dead that I know. It did not amuse me. There was no thrill. There was no pleasure as I squeezed. God forgive me for the deeds I committed on Kelly. No heart no heart.

Sally, I have never stopped loving you.
Oh, Sally my love, what have I done?

Question is, whether I shall be able to stop. The last time still disturbs me, but, be that as it may, I am sure the urge will return before too long. But another thought holds me back: if I resume my naughty games in the East End then I will ruin everything, now that my brother James (alias Jack the Ripper) Maybrick has gone to a better world.

If I am drawn to strike again it will have to be during one of my foreign tours . . . How fortunate it is that my career as a musician and composer requires me to travel! The world is not just my oyster, it's a veritable sea full of oysters, and I have a free hand.

Perhaps another tour of America might be on the cards, for it is high time that the good people on the other side of the Atlantic became better acquainted with the songs and works of Michael Maybrick. I'll have them singing my music note for note. I'll teach them to love Jack all right!

Monkeys
Steve Rasnic Tem

———

All of a sudden it were morning, and Maude couldn't hear herself think what with all the rattling carriages going about. She swore some days all that metal on stone shook the nerves right out of her, and she had to scream inside her head to rid herself of the sound. Most mornings she weren't up to dick. She needed breakfast and a drink, but mostly a drink. Drink enough and you didn't think too much about the state of your belly.

Polly offered her some bow-wow mutton and the little she had left from her pint. Maude thought she'd have to spit that foul mutton out but knew she shouldn't, lest she pass out in the street. Besides, Polly were her chuckaboo, and Maude didn't want to be rude. Polly'd talk your ear off, a real church bell, but if Maude weren't too drunk she liked to listen. She didn't have nobody else to talk to these days, and Polly was kind. Yesterday, she give Maude a bag o' mystery right from her pocket and Maude was grateful to eat it. She learned a lot about goings on in the Chapel from dear sweet Polly. And she trusted what Polly told her. She knew Polly wouldn't sell her no dog.

"You best watch yourself, sweetie," Polly said after their eating was done. "The Ripper got another Judy last night. Mary Kelly, 'member her? We used to see her at the Queen's Head. They say he butchered her like a pig. Tore up every sweet piece."

"Oh, Polly. Folks is always throwing the hatchet. You shouldn't believe everything you hear." But, even as she spoke, Maude believed every last word.

Maude needed fortification, so she searched the place till she found Old Charlie, who always seemed to have a bottle on him by whatever means. It didn't take much cuddling to get him to give it up. That, and a quick peek at her crinkum-crankum. Still, she didn't want to cheat him, so she gave him a little of her quail pipe. Then he played some with her kettledrums till he passed out again.

By the time Maude got outside the doss she was surely half-rats, and on her way to being tight as a boiled owl. It were a fine start to her day. There was a small crowd a few steps down. One of them foreigners had his self an ape. No, a monkey. Maude seen one before, not that long ago. Oh, he'd done all manner of tricks, that one. He wore a little red military hat – he was quite the gentleman, bowing to all the whores. Then later she reckoned he'd had too much to drink, and went after their faces. Now the coppers muscled them out, if they saw them, them and all them other animal acts. Most of them foreigners with their singing dogs and dancing monkeys and painted pigs. Some mores had canaries doing clever things, some mores had mice.

She didn't blame the monkey because of the drink. Only a put would give an animal a drink, not to mention it were a sad waste of liquor. But she knew the feeling – more than once she'd felt like tearing a face off after a drink or three. Not that it stopped her from drinking. She reckoned it wouldn't a monkey neither, once it got a proper taste.

But she liked them monkey acts well enough. This one here didn't have no liquor – she reckoned the word got around that it weren't the best idea. But the way it eyed her bottle – she tried to keep it hid. This one's clothes was plain, no better'n one of them street arabs, really. 'Course she still didn't get too close because of them big yellow teeth, but also because both the monkey and the foreigner handling him stank like shite. But oh how that little monkey could dance, and he'd play fight with you with his little wooden sword!

Shame the way the coppers would chase them out. He weren't out to cause no trouble – he was like an artist or something. He could make her smile, and that was no common feat these days. You'd think the coppers would have better things to do with their efforts, what with the Ripper about and all.

They got all kinds of entertainers coming through the chapel, men what would dress up and do some foolishness for a coin or two. Most of them weren't no real acts, not like you'd get in the music hall if you could afford it, but good enough for a minute or two she reckoned, just to distract you from whatever vile circumstance you was in.

Yesterday, on the corner she saw a Billy Barrow in his cocked hat and red feather, wearing some kind of a soldier's coat. The day before there was this old gent in a painted face in three or four ladies' dresses (she reckoned because of the cold). He sang songs in a high-pitched geezer's voice, and in one or two he weren't too bad.

Not that all them performers was welcome, as far as she was concerned. Last month there were a feller in a devil's suit dancing and following her around, sniffing at her. No joke – whenever he got close enough to her she'd hear him sniffing and smelling her so hard it was like he wanted to suck her right inside. Of course she'd been drinking so maybe the poor feller was just sick with the crud and couldn't help his sniffing. Or maybe – him dressed up like a devil and all – he weren't there at all. Or maybe, it being the chapel, he were the real Devil his self, there to give her a personal invite to Hell.

The shouting came at her like a bunch of broken church bells. Here come them raggedy boys again, them street arabs. They was more of a bother than the flies or the rats, and almost as many, buzzing in her ear, running over her shoes. They was like a whole tribe of monkeys, them boys, but worse. And the ones that was sick or lame, or been beat too bad, they'd just lie around in the corners of the alleys all day, touching on each other for comfort. It were a sad thing to watch.

"Hey you old dolly-mop!" one of them little cheeky bastards shouted as he came running by, and slapped her on the nancy. She swung around and tried to kick the ape, and nigh near dropped her bottle. You couldn't feel sad for them monkeys long, now could you, what with the pranks they pulled. "I ain't exactly amateur!" she shouted. It were the only thing she could think of to say. She didn't follow. That bunch looked eager for mafficking, so she stayed clear.

Not that it were their fault, she reminded herself. Anywhere you got lots of whoring, you got lots of them street arabs as a result. One begets the other – the ones what got nowheres else to go, homeless and barefoot. Half of them died before they were old enough to stand proper. And those were the lucky ones.

And they weren't all that scared of Jack, not that she could tell. "Watch out! I be the Ripper!" one of them shouted, and the rest went running away giggling like hens.

She looked sadly at her empty bottle. She didn't remember finishing it. After a while drinking was like breathing. Whoever thought about how much air they breathed? Whoever made it their business to count? Maude knew she oughtna drink so much. It got her into some terrible scrapes sometimes. That was how she met her last husband, weren't it? Ran into him in the pub. He could be right handsome, had a door knocker of a beard. A bit of a gal-sneaker and too much of a tot-hunter, but he could say some awful pretty words. Said he couldn't help his self, he were a man who loved a bit o' jam. He always wore a nice coat, and a pair of gas-pipes showing off what he had to offer a gal. But sometimes he'd hit Maude in the sauce box or up on the face and she'd cop a mouse, and that would hurt her earning for a time, although most of her customers weren't that particular, long as she showed them a good backside.

She heard a shout and looked down the lane, saw them monkeys go batty-fang on an old man. She wanted to be bricky about it but she was too scared about what they might do to her. She didn't stay around to watch.

The rest of the day she went walking and scrounging, more walking than scrounging because times was hard and the competition were fierce. She'd never been good at either begging or thieving. What she was good at was best done in the dark, without folks looking on. Even in the Chapel folks could be modest at times.

She guessed that was one thing she had in common with the Ripper. Plying her trade in the dark. She still had a little bit of shame in her. Did he?

She knew that Mary Nichols. She got hers late August, or maybe September. Annie Chapman was September for sure – Maude seen her walking around the day afore. It happened that fast, like the Ripper was the Lord's very judgement. That slapped her a bit. There was always clergymen around, ministering to unfortunates such as herself. Could one of them holy men be the Ripper, delivering God's own last judgement?

Last winter they lost Annie Millwood and Ada Wilson. 'Course nobody knew about the Ripper then. Maybe he done them, too. Maybe he'd been doing whores long as she'd been alive, and before. She'd never trusted them churchmen – never would. She'd heard tales from other whores about the things they liked to do in the dark what weren't no joke. The question was, why wasn't God doing something about it, unless like everybody else in London he'd given up on them poor Chapel folk.

She cut through a court and stumbled over a couple of them street arabs, lying together on the side of the lane. They looked like nothing but a pile of rags until they started moving and panting. She hated to see it, children shouldn't be up to such doings, but times being what they were children was doing everything adults did, including all manner of crimes and evilness, including murder. So what's a little adult comfort when the young ones were suffering, long as it was for each other and not for some nonce? Where was the harm? Maude would have to let God sort that one out.

A bunch of them monkeys come running down the lane then and near knocked her down. She couldn't see their faces but she reckoned they was just more of that same bunch. They was everywheres today, and either their faces was too dirty to see what they looked like, or they had them rags wrapped round their heads like foreigners. It were spooky to look at, like somebody's sorry bit of laundry decided to run off by itself.

Some lucky soul was cooking fish somewheres. It made her mouth water so bad she had to walk away from there otherwise she might start bawling. She was hungry almost always, but it got far worse when there was cooking nearby. But sometimes just looking at a bit of shoe leather reminded her of what meat used to taste like.

She ran into another of them street monkeys all wrapped up in his rags and trying to sleep. She kicked at it as she walked by, and it groaned. She felt ashamed about it later, but them arabs had scared her right enough, and she'd been drinking.

She reckoned for most of them that street life seemed better than working the factories making matchboxes, or sweeping the way for the rich to cross the road. Sometimes them folk would pay you, sometimes not, but it were always humiliating, weren't it? Least she thought so.

There was always kids dying in the chapel. Some deserving it more than others, she reckoned, just like adults. She couldn't do nothing about it anyways. It was hard enough keeping herself alive, much less some youngster.

At least she'd never shite one out herself. She was proud of that. 'Course maybe she had no choice in the business. Maybe God wouldn't allow it. Still, some whores she'd known turned their babies out at night so they could conduct business in the room. Let them children wander alone into all kinds of darkness. Least she'd never done that. She'd rather be a sack maker than do that to her own flesh and blood.

Especially what with the Ripper about. He cut that Eddowes woman up like a cow hanging in the market they said. She supposed any little boy'd be safe, but them girls, some of them girls looked older than they ought to. Some of them young girls might be just to Jack's tastes.

Them children in the Chapel – they didn't have no chance.

Still, nothing Maude could do about it. Any soul living up in a doss on Flower and Dean Street had their own troubles to worry about. Fourpence got you a coffin to sleep in, but most nights she ended up leaning on a rope. It were a blessing she was tired all the time. She reckoned she could sleep just about anywheres if she could just shut her eyes. If she had a walnut in her pocket least she'd have something to eat, but most nights she had nothing. Maybe some night she'd sleep so well they couldn't wake her up in the morning, and wouldn't that be a blessing?

It were getting dim now, the world closing its eyes 'cause it didn't want to see too clear the goings on down in the Chapel. Time to make her rounds, stand outside the pubs till some gent showed some interest.

She run her identical routine every night, so she hoped the Ripper weren't watching her, 'cause if he did he'd know exactly where she'd be. She'd go through most of them every night: the Queen's Head, the Ten Bells, the Horn of Plenty, the Britannia, the Alma and the King Stores. Then a quick walk around Saint Botolph's Church to throw off the coppers afore trying another. There were whores making that round trip of Saint Botolph's all night ever night. What did the coppers think they was all doing, praying?

The bell at Christ Church rang, and she heard one of them criers in the distance selling whatever – she couldn't afford nothing anyway. Other than them few sounds the world suddenly looked empty and heartless, and quiet as death. Maybe she'd died. She could only hope. What was sure though was she'd lost some time. That's what come of drinking all day. You lost pieces. Which tweren't so bad.

She'd go stand outside the Queen's Head. Some gent would set her up good and proper – all she could drink, if she picked him right, and yet she'd still make sure she was up for walking away. She'd make sure he was very arf'arf'an'arf himself, cause he wouldn't be up for doing much. Later maybe she'd tell him they'd been up to all kinds of nasty business – she'd rub up against him plenty so he wouldn't know the difference. Not that she particularly wanted to cheat a customer, but some nights her lady bits was just all wore out from plying the trade. Some nights she just had to let them things rest.

She didn't like them shadows over there, or them over there neither. The dangerous thing about the drink were that it made her skittish, and kicked up her imaginings. Some nights she saw the Ripper everywhere, in many a gent's face, or in the shadows where probably no one be at all. Nobody really knew what he looked like, but you'd hear descriptions of him just the same. Some said he was pale, but then there was those who swore he was swarthy. Some said he had hair all over his face, more like an animal than any kind of proper human being. But others said he just had a slight moustache, or none. Lots of folk said he wore this long black coat, but more than a few said it were red (which she doubted, less that was because of all the blood he'd spilled). A lot of folk claimed he was a foreigner, but anything going bad in the Chapel they most always blamed them foreigners. He could a been a right famous gentleman, maybe even a banker. Maybe even a royal. No one knew. But every moving shadow seemed like it might be him, or every bloke leaving a pub, was that a knife he was hiding? Or she'd see some gent acting right skilamalink, and she'd think he must be the Ripper for sure.

Maude figured it were twixt four and five, and she couldn't see nothing much 'cept shapes and shadows and a little bit of yellow cast by the lamps, the sky being so black and the shadows blacker still. She'd pass a lamp and she'd see the black bits floating in the air, and she didn't like to think about it, but course that's what they all breathed – a little bit of air, a little bit of sky, and a whole lot of black bits floating down into you and gumming up your lungs. Good thing most died young, she reckoned, otherwise they'd grow old enough to fill up with black bits, burying them from the inside out.

At least the Chapel looked better in the dark, 'cause it couldn't look no worse now, could it? She couldn't understand what held some of them buildings up, less it were the filth caked on them bricks. Tens and hundreds of years probably, with never a good wash. 'Course you couldn't keep clean in a city like this, less you was one of the rich folk what could afford a hot bath and new clothes.

A couple of them raggedy boys come screeching past, stinking of monkey. Scared the piss out of her. She'd shout at them but she could force nary a sound out of her mouth. She wished she had Polly here with her. That old gal would tell them monkeys a thing or three.

She'd had too much to drink that day, she reckoned. Or maybe she hadn't had enough. Maybe she was just about due. She felt all wobbly.

They was a big pile of rags in the middle of the lane. She kicked at it, but this time the rags didn't move, and made nary a sound, so either they *was* rags, or they was dead. But she didn't feel much like checking.

That brick wall in front of her was crumbling, and all drippy. She stumbled then, and fell against it. And found that weren't no brick crumbling off, but somebody's innards stuck to it and peeling off, and them dark coppery drips must be redder than red. She turned and barked up some sick, and looked at them rags again, 'cept now she knew they weren't no rags, or at least they didn't use to be. Used to be some poor whore, but all she was now was some ripped-up rags.

The stench was something awful, which was saying something, given she'd lived in a slaughterhouse and a sewer most of her sorry unnatural life.

She heard him running on the stones, or maybe it was them children. There were too many steps. Too many sounds. She heard a child's pitiful crying, then realized it was herself making them sounds.

Maybe she'd just start running. Maybe she'd run down to Aldgate and Leman – she knew a few folks there. But it were dark, and what if there was nobody about she could trust?

Maude started running anyway. She could think of nothing else to do. But she kept running into them piles of rags. There was stinking piles of rags just about everywhere in the dark lane.

She went up to one, and she didn't kick it. She just nudged it ever so carefully with her shoe.

That's when them skinny monkeys leaped up, climbing over each other, climbing up to the height of a very tall man. And she couldn't tell amid their stink and their screaming if they was the real trained monkeys or them half-starved poor street arab babes she sometimes felt sorry for.

But what surprised her was how they had them tiny knives hidden in their scrawny little hands. And how they knew just how to cut, and where.

Knowledge of Medicine
Erin M. Kennemer

The only thing I could possibly do was walk. All the coaches had been put up, and I was not inclined to beg a ride from the departing Dr Digby. I kept to Whitechapel Road, though the passing of the late-night carriages spattered mud over my frock.

"You smell like fish, love," came a voice from Cavell Street.

I didn't respond. I had my apron and cap on, as clear a sign that I was a nurse as I could give without holding a banner.

The man who had so rudely addressed me stepped from the adjoining road. "You free tonight?"

"I'm not a woman of that persuasion." I picked up my step, taking a wide berth around him.

"Plenty more women here." He splayed his hands wide. "Jus' watch your step. Even a good girl can run afoul of a man's sword."

I shook my head, disgusted. He was at my back now, which was better and worse. Cold tickles traced up my spine, but I resisted the urge to look back. He was right. There were plenty more women on the streets, in back alleys and dark rooms. He didn't need to harass a nurse on her way home.

A hand grabbed my arm and whirled me around. The air went out of me as I was thrown hard against the stone wall of the county court. Before I could let out a cry, a hand went to my mouth. The face in front of me was smeared with rouge, and her long red hair was done in a loose braid. I shoved her off, brushing at the dirt her hands left behind.

In a hushed voice, my sister said, "Sorry to scare you, but you mustn't walk home this way."

"I'm half to my grave with fatigue, Mary Kelly. What are you up to?"

"This innt a time for you to ignore me." Mary stepped back, her eyes dark pools. "A doxy's run afoul of some bastards."

I turned away from her, listening hard. "And you're just going to hide out here?"

She stepped in front of me again, hands on her dainty hips. "You and me both."

"I'm going to fetch a copper."

She narrowed her eyes at me. "I don't expect he'll have much time for the likes of me. I'll let you sort it."

She stepped into the alcove in front of the county court. I sighed at her cowardice, but supposed it was for the best. She didn't blend as well as I did with gentler folk. I had to walk back as far as the hospital to find a patrol. By the time we returned, Mary had fled her hiding space, and the streets were eerily silent.

"I'm not interested in buying, if that's why you brought me down here," said the tall man in his ill-fitting uniform. His eyes were small and watery. The moon washed out his complexion entirely so that he looked like a wraith.

"A woman has been attacked."

"Did she mention where, or was it just a general sort of discussion?" His eyes danced, clearly amused by himself.

"I think it was this way." I was acutely aware that the gentleman beside me was only one man. The law still commanded respect in the daylight, but the night belonged to the bastards, the women, and the Devil.

Flickering light down Osbourn Street caught my eye. Faint crying spurred me into a run. My sister knelt on the stones, holding a woman's hand. She was laid out on her back, her clothes in tatters. Mary stroked the woman's hair and muttered comforts that were softer than the sobs that wracked her.

"Well?" The copper strolled in my wake.

"Who did this to you, dear?" I asked.

"There were two—" Sobs cut her off. "Or three. One was fresh-faced. Couldn't have been more than fifteen. I screamed for them to stop . . ."

"To think this could happen to a fine woman such as yourself," the copper said.

I turned, horrified. The copper dared to look bored, rocking back on his heels and looking everywhere but at the sobbing woman.

"She was attacked. Nothing else should matter. 'The police are the public, and the public are the police.'" Even quoting Minister Peel left him unaffected.

Mary had fallen deadly silent. Trouble. The woman on the ground drew in a breath and cried anew.

"Turn off the waterworks," the copper said. "If a child steals a sweet, you'd ask me to look the other way. Why such hysterics over a theft of service?"

Mary grabbed the tattered fabric that covered the woman's privates and pulled it back with a bloody flourish. The copper screamed and stepped back. I looked down in morbid fascination at the wreck that had been left of her loins.

"We have to get her to hospital. Now."

"I agree with you, Miss Kelly." Constable Dashard, the policeman from the night before, swayed uncomfortably at the edge of Emma's hospital bed. "I'm afraid they'd all need to see it for themselves before they'd feel the way I do."

"March them here, then!" I fought the tears that threatened to turn my passion into a woman's hysterics. "Let them see the lifeless mess that remains of Emma Elizabeth Smith. She died in my arms, you know. Crying for her mother. Do you know what those 'boys' did to her? They raped her until she bled and shoved a cricket bat into her until her internal organs burst from the trauma. Is that still 'theft of services', Constable?"

"You're yelling at the wrong man, Miss Kelly. I only came down here to pay my respects and let you know a report has been filed."

"But what are they doing about it?"

"You're lucky there was even a report. The first reaction I got was . . ." Constable Dashard trailed off, his head dipping in contrition.

"Similar to how you acted last night," I finished.

He nodded.

"Leave off him, Ester Kelly. You'll get nowhere with him or those like him." Mary sat in a small chair, pointed slightly away from the bed that held Emma's corpse. She'd arranged the covers so that Emma looked gentle and fair, her hair brushed and washed. It was probably the cleanest she'd been in years. The horror under the covers was well concealed.

The constable murmured goodbye, then turned and left. I sighed and went to join her as we waited for the attendants to collect Emma's body.

"With a report filed, maybe the violence will decrease." I crouched beside her, the white apron of my uniform stretching over my knees.

"Women go missing all the time. What good did we do? Now I know her name and face. She had a family once. Maybe she was happy."

I flashed back to the long night before. At intervals, she'd told us her name and made us repeat it. It was the only thing she could bequeath, and we, her only family, two sympathetic strangers. Now if we could only get the coppers to see Emma Elizabeth Smith and not "female victim".

"The brutality changed one man's mind. Perhaps others will hear, and someone will finally do something about the men that prey upon . . . you."

"I'm a prostitute, Emma. You're not going to get anyone to care about me. Men are as hard in the heart as they are in the trousers. It's bad enough you're here now. You've some reputation to protect."

"I do work here."

"That work doesn't include talking to me."

"Quite so." Folds of blue linen blocked my view of the surrounding beds, but I felt secure in our anonymity. My sister was a dear soul, but it would mean my job if I were connected with the world's oldest profession. And then, I supposed, I would become part of it.

I squeezed Mary's hand and stepped away. I had to tidy my appearance and clear my head. There was no shortage of those in need of employment, and I could not risk being tardy.

I didn't see Mary for months after Emma's death, but I did notice the shift in how the women who worked the streets behaved. Fear ruled the night, but desperation kept them out. I was no different. Hunger kept me at work long after I became afraid of the men on the streets. Dr Digby took me on as his personal assistant, but I knew where his true interests lay. Never mind that I was as cold to his advances as I could be without employing the use of a weapon.

I was fleeing one such attempt when I saw Mary, white as a sheet, headed up Whitechapel Street toward me. The look upon her face made me glad it was still daytime. I waved, painfully aware of our close resemblance and the cut of her dress.

"Fifteen," she said.

I closed the gap between us. She led us to the small alcove in front of the county court, and a shiver went up my spine.

"Fifteen disappearances since Emma."

"God Almighty." I fanned myself, suddenly aware of the August heat. "How do you know they aren't moving on?"

"That's the question, isn't it? I know their names, fifteen girls are gone now without so much as a goodbye. And they didn't leave, Ester. They're just gone."

"Calm down, Mary. Do you know for a fact they were killed?"

"That's just it, Ester! No one cares to find out. And since no one's been caught, the men are bolder. Those with darker desires are taking solace in our flesh." She leaned in, her breath against my ear. "Martha Tabram. You'll find her in your morgue."

The mortuary was cooler than the street, but beads of sweat gathered around the nape of my neck. I'd talked my way in using Dr Digby's name.

The attendant had given me wax to plug my nose, but I left it off. Martha was newly dead, and the stench had not settled upon her yet.

Her face was round and swollen. I wondered if she had looked so puffy in life, or if that was from the beating she'd taken. They hadn't dressed her yet. I wondered if the coroner had even examined her.

I lifted the sheet, feeling it stick against the fluids of her body. Chopped meat. She'd been stabbed so many times, I couldn't tell one wound from another. The largest hole was on her breast, two fingers wide, at least. I replaced the sheet.

She was older than my sister, worn. In the lines of her face I saw the inevitable. Would Mary end up this way, laid out and grieved by none?

By me. She'd be grieved by me. A tear came unbidden. This shell was not my family, but it had been a person, and I felt the sorrow for what else she might have been.

Fascination gripped me, and I couldn't resist lifting the sheet one more time. I could feel the attendant's eyes on me, but I was transfixed. Someone had transformed Martha from a person with hopes and dreams into a crudely carved Sunday roast. Person to beast. I stepped back, taking a breath. How could I turn her back into a woman? The brutality of this murder would get attention, but would it change anything?

I met with Mary that night, and we waited for the papers to tell the tale of poor Martha Tabram. Her inquest was splashed across the pages in vivid detail. Firstly stabbed by a bayonet or dagger, then mutilated by a penknife; all of the papers agreed on the broad details and varied only in their embellishments.

On the streets, people spoke of her as "the poor woman". Even the finer folks gossiped about her with voices tinged with pity. The murder was a spectacular success in catching attention. Now there was public outcry for action, but I knew it would not last.

The days after, the horror was fresh, and Martha was still pitiable. As people had time to reflect upon her profession, they began to care less. "Well, you know these things can happen when one lowers oneself," and "no real danger to God-fearing Brits" became the death knell for the cause.

That was until Mary found the next body.

"It's a horror, right enough," said Mary, bending over and breathing hard. The small workroom was cramped, and I wished for fresh air. Privacy was key, however.

On the ground between us was a slight woman. Her hair was dark and plastered against her face with drying blood. Her eyes were open, her mouth slack, as if she were perpetually screaming for help.

I pulled a small dagger from my apron and set it on the ground. Kneeling, I donned a pair of gloves I'd nicked from the hospital. I stared at the faint smattering of blood droplets across my smock. Were they from the woman, or from my long day assisting Dr Digby? Did it matter?

I picked up the knife and poised over the woman's stomach. Mary hadn't spoken since we'd dragged her in here. I didn't need help, and I'd told Mary so, yet still she leaned against the door, stalwart.

"No one can hurt her any more," I said, as much to myself as to Mary.

The knife slid in so easily. So little blood, too. When Dr Digby made a cut, I always had so much to clean. This, though, was pure. I could see the layers of skin giving way to the fat and finally muscle. What blood there was oozed around the knife and dribbled in rivulets along her waist. I needed to make it messier.

I tried a few cuts around her abdomen, but Mary's retching made me stop. "Please leave if it's going to bother you that much." Though I had to admit that my own gorge was rising.

"How are we making what some murderer did better with this?" I could tell that she didn't want me to answer, so I waited for her to continue. "Look at her face. He knocked her teeth out before he did her. He cut her neck so deep it liked to trim her hair. Isn't it horrible enough?"

I looked at the woman's face, really looked. She was a sad thing, thin enough to pass for younger than she was. She'd already started to bruise when she died. "It's an ugly bit of work, I'll grant you, but so was Emma. They forgot her. They even forgot Martha. We won't let them forget this one." I needed Mary's help to drag the body back to streets.

"Foul. Evil."

"Talk is cheap. We knew this wouldn't be fun."

I took another stab, this time putting force behind it. I hit a rib bone, and my knife slipped farther than I'd intended. The resulting gash was a horrid stroke of red against her pale skin.

Mary gasped. "Are you sure you're not having fun?"

I narrowed my eyes and saw the panic in her face. It seemed better to say nothing. I was not having fun, but I couldn't quit now.

"They called her Polly, I'm told," said Mrs Golding. Her sanguine smile made my skin crawl. "You know, the Nichols girl? I do hope they catch the killer."

Mrs Golding had come into my care for exhaustion, which kept me away from Dr Digby's more pressing cases. However, time with Mrs Golding proved to be less than a respite. Her constant stream of gossip on Leather Apron was beginning to wear thin.

"Oh, and Ester, did you read – do you read? Anyway, did you read that this might not be the killer's first victim? Apparently, women of ill repute have been dying in droves. Be careful on your walk home, dear. Not to imply! I mean, really, all of us women have cause for concern."

I smiled vaguely as I finished tidying the room. "Anything else for you, Mrs Golding?"

"You don't talk much, do you, dear? I have a sister who is phlegmatic. Just be a love and keep an eye out for my husband. He should be visiting soon."

"Of course." I left the room feeling a rush of energy. Her thinly veiled insults had eventually led to what I was praying for. The victim was a woman. All women should be afraid. It was rich old women like

Mrs Golding who could start the wave of change. Let her poor husband come and get an earful about Polly the prostitute. And let him take that earful and give it to Scotland Yard.

Just one week, and already a fire was burning in Whitechapel. I just needed to stoke it a little more.

An insistent hand shook me awake. I struck out in a panic only to find my sister staring back at me. "Come quietly, and bring your knife."

Mary led me to a lodging house and then beyond to a small yard, and there *she* was. I didn't know her name and may never have, but hers was a face I had seen on a walk or at the market. I looked at Mary, terrified that this woman was a friend of hers.

She seemed to sense my unease and shook her head. "Talk is cheap."

I was suddenly aware of how exposed we were. Here with the body and a knife in my hand, I could be blamed for it. All of it.

This woman was slit across the neck just as Polly had been. A damp handkerchief was stuck in the blood as if someone had tried to sop it up. I wondered if the same man had done it. If there was a God in Heaven, my actions would get him caught. Two slit throats might not be connected, but two mutilations?

It was hard to get close; her arms were spread wide, and her legs were drawn up, feet resting on the ground. I pushed her knees outwards, a most undignified pose, and Mary shifted. She was about to see much worse.

First, I moved the right arm across the breast so I could lean over her. I'd practiced this next part in my head over and over. It was like a procedure Dr Digby had performed for hysteria. I felt sure I could replicate it as well as him.

I was just a medical student practicing on a cadaver, I told myself as I pulled back her clothes and set to carving out her uterus. I wasn't expected to put her back together again, so I simply pulled out the bits in the way and scattered them about. Her intestines ended up thrown over her shoulders like a macabre scarf.

Mary wandered off before I finished. I was almost smiling as I stored part of the uterus in my sleeping cap. I began to wipe my knife on the grass when the woman's face stopped me. Her tongue protruded between her front teeth, and her lips were curled back. She hadn't looked that way when I arrived.

My blood froze. She was looking at me. I fumbled for her throat to take a pulse, but she was mangled, could not have survived. My mind and the dim light were playing tricks. I stood, examining the scene. Nothing of mine remained. I needed to find a bin to toss in the uterus, clean my hands, and my part in the tale would be hidden.

Mary appeared from around the building, practically running. She grabbed me, spinning me around and taking me with her. I almost dropped the cap and its dirty secret.

"I saw him, Ester, and he saw me."

It took for ever to calm Mary down after Annie Chapman. The newspapers were no help.

"He saw me, Ester," she kept repeating.

"You saw a man. He was no one."

"I know it was him, deep down in my core. And look at this description Mrs Elizabeth Long gave to police. 'Shabby-genteel in appearance. Dark of complexion. Wearing a deerstalker hat.'" She gestured at the news clipping. "This is the man I saw."

"So you keep saying. Killer or not, he wouldn't know you from one-hundred paces, and besides, what interest would he have in some stray woman wandering in the early morning?"

"We're outing him! We're taking his loosely connected murders and knitting them together. He would see us dead before that."

I pursed my mouth. I'd thought the same thing. "We started this venture because of how casually men were dispatching the women of Whitechapel. That is still our root problem, not catching a killer."

"Why shouldn't we?"

"So what do you suggest?"

"So far, he's only killed prostitutes. I doubt he's only done the two we found. Maybe he did Martha, too, maybe even Emma. Maybe there are more outside of Whitechapel. We can find them, take the evidence to the police."

"Maybe some who aren't prostitutes?" I bit my lip. It could help our cause, but if we went after the man and not just the victims, we could find that the hunters could easily become the hunted.

"I say we enlist the other girls. More eyes to find him. We may be able to deliver him to the commissioner himself. In pieces, I say."

Did she really think I could cut up a live person? It was one thing to do work for the cause, quite another to contemplate killing on my own. Still, Mary's idea would help us at least find bodies before the coppers, but it might also expose my role to the women on the streets. I didn't care for anything that might hang the murders on my shoulders.

We settled on telling the other women that we had the ear of Scotland Yard and to report anything suspicious to us. We didn't have much luck at finding any killers. Mary's friend Frida took a vicious beating from a gang of men, but they didn't finish her off. By the time we got there it was long over, and all I could do was tend her wounds and sit up with her. It put a fog in my mind, feeling so helpless. I began to walk around in a stupor, my life knitted into a gray haze.

"Miss Kelly, please don't dawdle. I need the scalpel." Dr Digby gave me a soft kick to the behind, and I hopped to attend to him.

I was thinking about the murders again. Previously, my nights on the streets and my life at the hospital were two separate things, but lack of sleep meant they bled into one another. I handed him the scalpel.

He used steady and even pressure as he cut into the flesh of his patient, so intoxicated by morphine she was unresponsive. I stepped forward and watched the blood welling from her. He noticed my stare and snapped a finger toward the rags.

I began sopping up the blood, but I couldn't pretend I was not fascinated.

"You're a different sort of woman." He dried his brow against his sleeve.

"Doctor?"

"Have you heard that they think Leather Apron may have knowledge of medicine?"

My stomach fell out of me. The room began to spin. He continued his work without speaking. As the silence stretched, I said, "I hadn't heard that."

"He may be an educated man with a strong moral objection to prostitution. I wonder how long until his tastes shift upward." Applying pressure to the wound, the doctor looked back at me, his stare heavy with meaning. "Sutures, Miss Kelly."

I readied the needle and offered it to him, but he shook his head.

"Step over here. I'll hold the wound closed and you stitch her up."

I pushed the needle in, as I had seen him do so many times. It gave me the oddest rush, more intense than what I was used to with the prostitutes.

"That's perfect." He placed his bloody hand against my waist, standing close. I wondered what he might know.

"Done." I tied the last stitch and admired my work. It was as good as he could have done, and he must have known it.

"Good enough. But what a careless oaf I've been. I've gotten blood on your dress. Perhaps you'd better take it off."

I blanched. An orderly entered the room before I was forced to react. Dr Digby directed him to take the patient to her room and turned his attention on me.

"You walk home most nights, don't you? Given these murders, you must ride in my carriage. This monster may not know the difference between a woman of quality such as yourself and a common trollop."

"Quite kind, Doctor, but I prefer my walks. I keep to Whitechapel Street and haven't been bothered."

"Nonsense. Meet me in an hour. And change before you do. I shan't have people talking of a bloody woman in my carriage!" He laughed and headed for the door.

I worked quickly on cleaning the surgical room. If I could be done before he was ready to leave, I could slip past him. I didn't think he'd dare criticize me for it, as the invitation itself was unseemly.

I heeded the warning call of a passing coach and hugged the wall beside me. Mud splattered across my sorry clothes, hiding the bloody handprint left by Dr Digby in a thin film of filth. I was beyond caring about such a trifle. My speed at finishing the clean-up in the operating room had led to extra tasks, and Dr Digby had departed with nary a word. His chivalry extended only as far as convenience, it seemed. That was just as well. I didn't want to be alone with his wandering hands. I also feared that he might question me about the mad killer. What could he know? Mary's idea of asking the other women for help had left me so exposed.

"They tell me you know the truth of Christ, our Lord?" said a furtive voice behind me.

I turned to face a blushing trollop, no older than fifteen. "Let me tell you of our Savior," I answered back.

She nodded and ducked into the alley beside the workhouse. I wasn't particularly fond of the charade Mary had contrived, but it protected my reputation well enough. I could always explain away why I spoke with so many prostitutes.

"Another girl's gone missing, love."

"When?"

"I'm not sure. I was having a laugh with a gent on Hound Switch and noticed a bit of blood along the wall of the chandler's. I left off the lad and went to have a look. Sure enough, I found this." She presented me with a small embroidered clutch. It was of fine design but well worn.

"I don't understand."

"This belonged to Nell the Tooth. I haven't seen her in two or three days. This thing was about her only possession; she wouldn't just leave it."

"Have you asked around for her?"

"No sign of her anywhere. Even her cot at the rooming house was cleared out. When I asked around, no one could remember seeing her pack up."

"Quite the mystery." I was losing hope that this led to another body. I was too far behind the trail.

"So, you'll tell them? You'll tell Scotland Yard?"

I looked into her eyes and rounded down my estimation of her age. It would be a miracle if she were fourteen. "I will. Please, take care of yourself. Don't go out at night without someone with you."

She laughed. "I always have someone with me at night. Do you?" With that, she walked off.

The street had gone pitch black. With a shudder, I headed back to Whitechapel. The night air was cool and sent shivers down my arms. My clothes were still wet with mud from the coach. I tried to distract myself with thoughts of supper but succeeded in only remembering the destroyed meat of Martha Tabram. Nothing was better for the women on the streets. Not enough had been done. If I wrote a letter, as the killer, and sent it to the Central News Agency, it might force regular patrols in the area. My sister's job would be harder, but the men who preyed on her kind would think twice before brutalizing her. First, I'd need a name. Something macabre, some terrifying monster, a moniker that would set all of London alight.

"Dear Boss," I whispered as I walked. A good start.

Jack the Ripper, a dark dream of mine, lived on the pages of the tabloids. Dr Digby took to calling himself "Ripper" in the surgical room. I took his lightness as evidence that he didn't know my dark secret, and that he was a complete ass.

There were patrols on the street now, so I slept with the ease of the unburdened. On the night of the thirtieth, three days after my literary foray, pounding on my door roused me from a deep slumber. It was the dead of night. I threw on a dressing gown and peered out through a crack in the door. Mary shifted from foot to foot, her face a study in fear. I beckoned her inside.

"I saw him again." She paced in a circle, clutching her head. She wore a fetching blue dress, nicer than I knew she could afford. I would have asked, but she grabbed my shoulder. "His eyes were brown, rimmed in red. His face was unshaven and marred by lesions. He had devilish claws, Ester. I saw him kill her, and he saw me watching."

"What's happened?"

"I was on North Street with a few other women. They went right, but I headed on. There was a wet sound. It was the same man from before. I tried to hide, but he saw me. I heard him looking for me, but I managed to duck into a storage shed."

"How long ago?" I asked as I dressed. I grabbed my nurse's apron in case there was blood.

"You aren't thinking of going there?"

"If it is just one man, then we can stop him."

"I'm afraid, Ester. Please."

I looked back at her, one hand on the door, the other putting my knife in my apron pocket. "We're so close. Stay here, Mary."

I practically ran toward North Street.

If he'd seen my sister, he'd try to find her.

I wouldn't rest until every pair of eyes in London were focused on Whitechapel, and everyone knew what a monster he was.

I needn't have worried about finding the body. A crowd had already gathered around it. Their lanterns blinked in the darkness from across the street. I stayed to the shadows, cursing my luck.

"Look at the face. At the ear," said a familiar voice. Constable Dashard.

"Still, don't look half as bad as the rest of Jack's girls," said another copper.

I slipped away and studied the street. Perhaps the killer had left evidence of himself. Perhaps his dark soul had left an imprint.

I kept my head down on the walk home, knife at the ready but concealed within the folds of my apron. By the time I made it back to Mitre Square, I was exhausted. I stepped around the corner, headed to my flat. A large pile of something rested on the stoop. As I approached, I recognized the form of a woman. I dashed forward, my palms slick with sweat. Was it Mary? As I reached the body, I stifled a scream.

She was on her back, her head turned toward the door. Her throat was monstrously cut. I could see the bones of her spine through the wound. Wrapped just below it was a handkerchief, like the one on the previous victim. The intestines had been pulled out and thrown over the shoulder. I flashed back to the woman whose uterus I had removed. This one had been done in much the same way, but the cuts were jagged. One arm was by her side, but the other was pointed at my door, a piece of paper sat gently on her palm.

I stepped over the grisly remains, grabbing the letter and letting myself in the door. It snapped shut behind me. Shock ruled me as I opened the folded note. Mary slept on my bed, oblivious to the scene scant feet away.

She called herself Nothing, so I made her Something. I was Nothing, and you made me Jack.

Silently, I slipped off my dress and put on my robe. I sat on the foot of my bed, careful not to wake Mary. I couldn't be the one to discover the body. I couldn't be drawn into the investigation. I would have to wait for the knock on my door or the scream of the poor soul who found her next.

Like a stone rolling downhill, I had lost control of Jack the Ripper. Mary was shaken when the police questioned us about Catherine Eddowes, the poor woman on my stoop. It took days to convince her to leave my room, but I felt she was safest elsewhere, and she finally agreed. I was the focus of his rage, not her.

I resigned to terminate my nocturnal activities, but it did not stop the evolution of Jack. Letters I didn't write appeared in the paper.

People talked about the "Double Event". Dr Digby joked about cutting off nurses' ears. I could feel Jack's rage crawling over my back. Despite the tone of his note, the ferocity of Catherine's mutilation made it clear; he loathed the light I had cast him in.

And it just kept shining. I accepted rides from Digby each evening, falling victim to his "accidental" groping and lascivious stares, but at least I was safe.

Then came the gifts. Little pieces of women, mostly ears, wrapped in white paper and left on my doorstep. I considered quitting my job and moving, but something told me he would follow.

On 17 October, I received a letter with my daily gift. I had been leaving the abominations unopened, but fear urged me to read the missive.

Dear Boss,
    Didn't know you still had a sister.

Dr Digby led me to his carriage as usual, the cold November wind rushing us. It was late to be leaving, but a patient had taken a turn for the worse, and we had stayed on hand until half past midnight. I settled inside, braced for our inevitable scuffle. Instead of sitting beside me, he took the seat across and stared hard out of the window, barely moving.

"Mrs Wilshire is recovering well," I said, uncomfortable in the silence.

He said nothing. The carriage started down Whitechapel. My heart thudded, and my mouth went dry. I was almost surprised at my reaction. So long I had thought of the doctor as a philanderer and clod, but sitting in silence, he transformed into something else.

I studied his face, his red-rimmed eyes, picturing him unshaven and covered in lesions. In the darkness, such an affliction would be easy to imitate with a little make-up. The silence stretched.

He tapped one hand against his knee. The body on my stoop hadn't been eviscerated by a practiced hand. Yet a feeling of dread continued to crush my chest.

"A police officer stopped by the hospital today." He kept his eyes just above mine, so I felt like he was seeing all of me without seeing me at all. "He asked about you. Told me you had a sister."

My heart froze. The handwriting on the note hadn't looked like Digby's, but that could be faked. "Did he?"

"You never told me. He said that Jack had killed her."

I couldn't hold in a gasp. The carriage seemed to tilt sideways. If my sister was dead, why had no one told me? How had he found her?

"I've made those terrible jokes. I've said those terrible things to you. I'm so sorry."

The carriage halted in front of my house, and I jumped out. I ran straight for Mary's place in Miller's Court. It was dusk, so the streets were still emptying of people who were quite disturbed by my mad dash. I didn't care. I slammed into Mary's door, fighting with the handle. It gave way, and I fell inside.

Mary stood by her bed, one candle in her hand, only half dressed. She looked alarmed, but unharmed. I stumbled back, shocked.

"I thought you was the Devil hisself. What are you doing here?"

"Someone told me you were dead."

I spotted the man in the corner of the room, looking as bright as an apple. He rushed for his trousers as I stared, fumbling to put them on.

"You owe me!" Mary said.

He didn't answer, put his head down, and pushed past me out the door.

"I'm fine, Ester. The place is crawling with coppers. Just stay away from me, and I'll be fine."

I stepped back and bit my lip. She closed the door in my face. I turned toward home.

I ducked into a pub on the way home. I hadn't had a drink in years, but my head needed the sorting only alcohol could manage.

I got a spot of food and drank a few pints before laying my head on the table. My face must have told the whole story; no one bothered me until closing.

A young man with deep laugh lines sauntered over and clapped me on the shoulder. He stank of ale and body odor.

"Did you get away from the man who was chasing you?" He spoke with the fine lilt of an Irishman.

"What?" I asked without lifting my head.

"When you dashed through the street here earlier. I thought your hair must be on fire, or that man was after you."

"I . . . just felt like running. What man?"

"The one following you. Let me know if you need someone to walk you home, darling. I'm partial to redheads."

I sat up, mind blurry with drink. Who would have been chasing me?

Cold poured down my spine. Jack had known where I lived, but not where Mary lived. He'd followed her when she'd seen him the second time and found my place. I'd stayed clear of hers since the presents started. But then I'd thought she was dead, so I ran to her, I ran . . .

Oh, God. Mary.

The Monster's Leather Apron
Adrian Ludens

———

The moment Edward completed work on his fifth artistic endeavor he sensed the wheels of fate beginning to turn. Ginger, she'd called herself, though he doubted that had been her real name. What a filthy, ignorant wretch she'd been at the start. Like the others, she'd been an unwieldy hunk of sculptor's clay, rough and unfinished. He'd carved with his blades until he found her true essence. No masterpiece, he had to admit, but a vast improvement and a strong artistic effort given the resources available at his disposal.

And yet a mounting sense of dread compelled him to flee Whitechapel in the black of night, while her blood still soaked into the straw mattress where she lay. He'd stowed away in the back of a peddler's creaking wagon. He couldn't afford to be seen. Not that he feared recognition; published eyewitness accounts varied. He'd wanted to escape notice because he'd kept his leather apron and knives with him when he'd fled. He could not bear to leave them behind.

Edward smiled in the darkness. Scotland Yard, and the insufferable Abberline, had attempted to place him under surveillance. Though his name had not yet made the papers or the latest edition of *Puck*, Edward felt the noose closing around him. Abberline, Moore and the others would doubtless be enraged to find that their quarry had escaped. How far would their pursuit extend? When, Edward wondered, could he stop running? A nagging, yet comforting idea came to him. *Perhaps there will be others who feel compelled to act as I do, others who will take up my work.* Edward contemplated this as the wagon he rode in reached the outskirts of London with the first gray light of dawn.

The fugitive fought the needling panic that came with the approaching sun. He scanned the empty streets, unfamiliar with this borough's layout. Edward spotted a small shed and leaped from the still-moving wagon. His boots scraped the cobblestone but he kept his feet beneath him and ran. The unwitting peddler never looked back. Edward could see a frumpy woman inside her shop. The enticing aromas of meat pies and fresh bread invaded his flaring nostrils as he ran. Edward glanced around then stole into the dank confines of the shed. He crouched behind a stack of crates, sending a trio of rats scurrying for the corners.

Ensconced in darkness, Edward tucked his knees under his chin and contemplated his situation as morning broke. Despite the cramped quarters and preternatural knowledge that he'd be discovered soon if he didn't leave London, he managed to doze. He'd rested for an hour before he received unwanted attention.

"What are you doing in there? And who the devil are you?"

Edward sat up, his mouth parched, pupils contracting from the invading light. The sunshine turned the figure into a black silhouette blocking his only means of escape.

"Why are you in my shed?" The figure's strong Cockney accent was shrill, grating.

"A trio of unsavory characters beat me and robbed me on Wapping High Street. I remember one of them had a cudgel." The lie came easy. Edward pressed a hand to his temple and shaded his eyes as if in pain. In truth, he covertly examined his inquisitor, who seemed to be alone.

The woman – whom Edward was certain he'd seen in the bakery window – seemed nonplussed. "Wapping High Street, you say? Then why did they dump you here?"

"I don't know, ma'am. I don't even know where I am."

"Blackwall. Near the docks." The wood creaked beneath the woman's shifting feet. "You can't stay here."

Edward nodded, winced, and said, "I think my kneecap's dislocated. Will you help me stand?"

The woman sighed but moved toward him, skirts rustling against crates. She bent and held out an arm.

Edward took it, twisted it, and drove the woman face first into the shed's wall. He maneuvered behind her and snapped the woman's neck. He staggered to the door and pulled it nearly closed, allowing only the thinnest line of sunshine to reach the interior. Edward crawled back to the woman and withdrew a blade from his leather apron. It felt comforting to touch. So would the woman's inner workings – once he had arranged them just so. But he paused, reflecting. This would not do. He could not leave a trail. Lips pressed together in a tight line, Edward fought against, and resisted, the nearly unbearable compulsion to use the woman as his canvas of flesh. Sighing, he put his knife away.

Edward stood and eased up to the crack in the door. He closed one eye and surveyed the street. Horse-drawn wagons passed in either direction; nearly all were filled with goods. Here and there, a carriage held occupants, but most of the traffic seemed to be commerce-related. Edward thought of the docks, now within walking distance. Did he have enough money for passage across the ocean? He believed so. Perhaps he could pick up work along the way. Edward slipped from the shed and strolled with his hands in his pockets, his treasured knives rolled up in his leather apron tucked in the crook of one arm. He decided upon a destination as he walked to the docks.

Ten years later and half a world away, Edward still fled fears of detection and incarceration. He also fled his own reckless urges. Edward had traveled in a restless zigzag across America in a fruitless attempt at leaving suspicion of his previous crimes – and tempting new flesh canvases for his blades – behind him. He sought only solitude.

Edward had taken notice of the newspaper reports detailing the discovery of gold in the Klondike region of the Yukon. This region appealed to him. There, he thought, he could avoid the slatternly women who too often caused him unbearable temptation. And with no small amount of luck and a great deal of hard work, Edward might return reinvented, a wealthy man.

This morning, however, Edward lay silent, listening to the sounds of betrayal.

"Hurry up and get the other dogs harnessed. The more ground between him and us when he wakes the better."

"It doesn't bother you to leave him?"

"Edward's a monster. I won't be the one to stop him, but I won't be around when they hang him, either. They might want to string us up just because we're with him." The man grunted with exertion as he hefted something onto one of the sleds. "Besides, once we're home, won't half of the gold spend a lot nicer than a third?"

Though the other man did not respond, Edward knew his Klondike prospecting partners meant to abandon him, to leave him starving, feverish and alone against the elements.

He lay in his tent, wakened by their stealthy movements as they broke camp. His partners, Sheldon Winslow and Morgan Lynch, expected him to die – and soon. Edward meant to prove them wrong.

He'd paired up with Sheldon in Portland at the start of the trek north. They'd met Morgan in the Alaskan port city of Skagway. The trio formed an alliance, marrying their fortunes, literal and figurative. The prospecting and survival supplies, the food and rations, the cold-weather clothing, the purchase of good sled dogs, and a hundred other expenses they hadn't counted on had depleted their existing funds. Yet they'd been lucky. Edward and his partners had been among the first to stake a claim on the newly christened Eldorado Creek, and had mined more gold than those earlier arrivals who worked claims on the famous Bonanza Creek. Most of the other fortune seekers found nothing at all, save for frostbite on the Yukon Trail and syphilis in Dawson City's brothels.

Because of the brothels, Edward came face to face with what he loved and loathed most. He should have known. Wherever men and money were found, there too would flocks of soiled doves congregate, feeding off the men like parasites. Poisoning the men with disease and insanity. These women needed reshaping. Edward knew he was the perfect man for the work. No one else had his experience, his pedigree.

And so he'd removed his leather apron from where he had kept it hidden deep in his pack. The blades sang to him as he picked each one up in turn, examining them for sharpness. One artistic endeavor led to another, and soon he had equaled his Whitechapel output.

Recently, Edward had been battling a fever. Now his prospecting partners meant to take advantage of his situation, meant to leave him behind.

The pounding headaches, the burning throat and the muscle stiffness he could bear, and had. Fever dreams plagued him at night, but he'd felt sure recovery was imminent. It had now become obvious that his partners disagreed.

Edward regretted last night's outburst. They'd just crossed the Yukon River. Fort Yukon lay behind them; Dawson City lay ahead. The trip south across the river had seemed endless – to Edward. His illness, apart from taking a toll on his body, had begun to take a toll on his mind. Every few minutes, he felt convinced that he could hear the river's ice cracking beneath their feet. He fought the waves of panic, letting the dogs find their way. At last they set up camp on the other side, nestled amongst the spruce timberland. Sheldon and Morgan had wanted to go on, but Edward insisted on stopping. Once the tents were pitched, he had crawled inside his, legs dragging, body shaking with exhaustion.

When Sheldon brought in strips of bacon on a tin plate for him some time later, Edward mistook the food for strips of human skin. "You're supposed to leave those whores to ME!" he shouted. "It's my blades that cleanse, not yours!"

Sheldon had withdrawn from Edward's tent, thin-lipped and glowering.

Edward's sleep had been plagued by fever dreams and jumbled recollections. He had started awake, only to find he'd left one nightmare to enter another. The sounds of their furtive movements drifted into his dark tent. He lay there hearing so much, but seeing so little.

Now, driven by equal parts fear and fury, Edward finally threw off the clinging blankets and crawled toward the tent opening. He tried to shout through the walls of his tent, but his throat only made a dry clicking. One of the dogs whined. One of the men grunted as he lifted something heavy. The sounds all had a muffled quality, as if already fading from memory. He tried to call out but all that escaped his mouth was a cracked whisper. He fumbled in the darkness for the opening of the tent.

"Mush!" Morgan's voice commanded. The sound of one of the sleds began to diminish as it moved away from camp and found the trail. Edward heard more whining. He wondered if it came from Iluq. The squat, gray malamute with the missing tail had always preferred him to the other men. Perhaps Iluq would be his ally now, refusing to budge until Edward had joined them. He felt a flicker of hope.

A whip-crack pierced the air, extinguishing Edward's short-lived optimism. The jingling of leather traces were enough to convince him that the second sled had joined the first in their exodus of betrayal. He still had his knives, always kept them close at hand in their leather apron. If they came back now, Edward vowed to slice them both open out of spite. Take a blade across their throats and another across their bellies. Let their steaming entrails flash-freeze in the sub-zero conditions. And all that gold! That, too, provided Edward with incentive to survive.

He fumbled with the tent flap and winced at the burst of frigid wind that slapped his face when he pushed it through the opening. The air felt so cold it burned. He hadn't appreciated the comparative warmth of the interior of his tent until now.

No clouds floated in the Arctic sky, yet no sun shone either. Except for the spruce trees, the world seemed to exist in shades of gray. Steeling himself against the cold, Edward crawled on his elbows the rest of the way through the tent opening.

"Morgan! Sheldon!" This time he had mustered a feeble cry, but nothing that could be considered an actual shout. He spat in disgust and his saliva cracked before it hit the snow. He realized that meant it was colder than fifty degrees below zero.

The sled tracks led down a deep ravine. Edward scanned the landscape on the other side and caught a flash of movement in the trees.

The sleds were now on the opposite side of the ravine, only about fifty yards away as the crow flew, but it would be much farther if he intended to catch them by following the trail. One sled burst through a copse of trees, the other followed a moment later. Tendrils of icy fog moved between the spruce branches above the sleds like wraiths haunting the woods. The dogs strained in their traces. The men were hunched shapes draped over the backs of the sleds. Edward opened his mouth to curse at them but the words froze on his lips.

An enormous gray figure moved along the trail from the opposite direction. Larger than even a Kodiak bear standing on its hindquarters, it moved like a predator scenting for prey.

The creature and the sleds seemed on a collision course. Couldn't the dogs sense it? Edward rubbed his eyes and looked again. The giant presence had disappeared.

Maybe he was wrong, maybe this was like the imaginary flesh-strips on the plate. He'd tried to convince himself that his fever had broken, but what he thought he had seen was impossible. He blinked and the towering creature returned. Edward could only stare with dread and fascination at the ominous shape that seemed to swirl and shift as he watched. The dogs and sleds moved ever closer, seemingly oblivious to the obstruction.

The miasmatic shape lunged forward with an abruptness that shocked the watching man. Nugget, a sleek husky and the lead dog on the first sled, jerked into mid-air. The other dogs collided with each other and then rose off the trail. Morgan had tumbled into a snow bank and Edward could hear him cursing. Sheldon's sled had been lagging far enough behind to avoid a pile-up and he had halted his team on the trail. Sheldon did not, however, rush to aid his trail mate as he rose to his feet. Instead, he stood apparently transfixed. Edward couldn't blame him.

The abomination held Nugget high in the air, level with the highest treetops. The other dogs hung in their traces. Edward watched them strain and thrash, some nipping at each other in frustration and fear.

Nugget, however, did not move. Edward decided the animal was already dead.

Whatever force had halted the progress of the first sled now jerked the team so high that the sled itself lifted off the ground. The barking and howling from so many fine malamutes and huskies made Edward's skin crawl. Then the creature cracked the entire team through the air like a whip. The sled's packed gear exploded over the trail. Swallowed in the enormous grip of the abomination, Nugget became an unrecognizable pulp of gray and red. Edward watched Morgan blunder through the snow, kicking up small white clouds as he neared Sheldon's sled. The creature tore each dog apart in a spray of red, voraciously disemboweling and devouring every member of the team.

Edward ground his teeth in impotent rage when he recognized Iluq's turn had come. What a horrible way to treat a fine animal! He closed his eyes and welcomed the solace of the darkness. When he looked again, the trail across the ravine stood empty. He groaned and buried his face in his horse-hide mittens. Had it all been a convincing hallucination? A twisted manifestation of the vengeance he desired? Or the retribution he deserved?

A guttural bellow brought Edward's head back up, eyes avidly on the trail. The abomination, he saw, had reappeared, apparently finished with the dogs and now reaching a smoky arm toward Morgan's fleeing figure.

The creature seized Morgan and began to fold him in ways that a man's body should not bend. Morgan's scream choked off into silence and Edward heard the report of a shot from Sheldon's rifle echo across the ravine.

The gunshot had little or no effect, as far as Edward could tell. Sheldon's tangled and panicked dogs tried to flee in every direction and went nowhere. As Sheldon reloaded, the creature tore Morgan's brawny frame apart like a child plucking petals from a wildflower. Arms and legs were stripped of their flesh and then cast aside. They flew in great arcs over the spruce trees at the monster's whim. Edward realized he could never match that level of carnage, even in his finest hour. The creature roared again, a blood-curdling mixture of triumph and rage. A black dot flew across the gray sky and, for a brief instant, Edward mistook it for a fleeing bird until it drew close enough for him to recognize. Morgan's severed head crashed through several branches, ricocheted off of a tree trunk, and rolled to a stop a few yards from Edward's tent. He gaped at the brutalized visage of his former partner and was surprised at his own arousal. Not of a sexual sort, although he felt himself becoming fully erect. No, this was different. This was a joie de vivre, akin to what he felt when carving the prostitutes. Death reinforcing his love of life.

Sheldon shrieked in terror from across the ravine but Edward didn't bother to look. The creature took its time with Sheldon. Edward heard the man's cries as he crouched, deep in thought.

The creature appeared to have been following the sled trail. If it continued on its present course it would be on top of him in minutes. Terror at the prospect of spending his last moments being mauled and tortured at the hands of a sadistic supernatural demon gripped him. He cursed his former partners. They'd left him. He still had his blades, but what could they do against such powerful might? He had no means of escape, and even if the monster somehow missed him, how long could he survive in fifty-degree-below-zero conditions without food or supplies?

Edward let the thought go. He glanced across the ravine. No dogs or men, just parts scattered over the snow-covered ground, a previously blank canvas now awash in spatters of red. He closed his eyes, counted to five and looked again. This time he saw only a serene landscape of spruce trees and snow. Edward blinked and the carnage returned. He glimpsed a towering mass of swirling gray gliding along the trail. Spruce branches on either side bent to accommodate its girth.

Edward crawled into his tent, deciding it would be his sanctuary until death came.

"Our father in Heaven, hollow is thy name," he croaked aloud. "Now I lay me down to sleep in a frozen tomb, dark and deep." He closed his eyes. Strange how cosy his hiding spot now felt. After all he'd witnessed, he decided death itself wouldn't be so bad as long as he met it on his own terms. Could he freeze to death before the creature overtook him? Edward considered stripping naked and laying outside on the snow, but couldn't summon the strength he needed to execute his plan.

He concentrated on the drifting sensation that now buoyed him, curled in his murky womb. A womb or a tomb? Perhaps they were one and the same.

He drew his knees up to his chest. He felt safe. I'm surrounded by white, yet I see only darkness. Edward smiled at the gentle incongruity.

"What are you doing in there?"

Edward struggled into a sitting position, his mouth parched and his pupils contracting from the invading light. Someone held the tent flap open. The sunshine turned the figure standing before him into a black silhouette. A sickening sense of déjà vu swept over him. For one moment Edward thought himself back in the shed beside the bakery in Blackwall – the past ten years a dream. Then he realized the truth. A wiry, dark-skinned man crouched, looking into the tent.

No sound of breaking branches or inhuman roars came to his ears.

He glanced back at the newcomer – an Inuit. He seemed to be melting, his substance fluid. Edward's mouth went dry. He shook his head, as if willing his mind into coherent thought.

"Sick. Fever," he rasped. "Need help."

Then he collapsed again and allowed himself to be cradled in darkness.

His companion seemed to fade in and out of sight as he told the tale of a vicious and violent demon named Kigatilik. When the apparent shaman referenced the "Claw People," his gnarled hands twisted into hideous pincers. He said he had once encountered a pair of prospectors lying naked in the snow, entwined in each other's arms, and frozen stiff. These stories and more replayed themselves with feverish repetition on a stage in Edward's mind. He tried to tell the strange man to stop but couldn't find the words. The faces and forms of his victims interspersed themselves in the scenes of mythological depravity and carnage. Blood-soaked figures contrasted with endless white mountains in Edward's nightmares. Had the demon, Kigatilik, wreaked this havoc?

"No, Edward," said a pulpy red maw that once anchored a face. "Not Kigatilik, but *you*."

Edward awoke from this most recent dream with a start. It had felt more like a visitation. Like the long-ago Sunday school story of Paul on the road to Damascus, the scales had fallen from his eyes. He'd been going about it all wrong. But the great god Kigatilik had come to him, had demonstrated for him.

"My god has taught me how to pray," Edward marveled.

"You're awake. Good."

Edward recognized the speaker but tensed when he realized he didn't know where his leather apron and knives were. Without them he felt naked, exposed.

"Who are you?" Edward asked the stranger.

The old man sat down across from him. Between them a campfire blazed. "I am Sawaya, a Yupik shaman."

"What do you want?" Edward's eyes darted around, taking in his surroundings. He'd been moved, he saw. His location had changed. And the absence of his knives troubled him.

"Have no fear," the older man said. "If I wanted to kill you, I would have already done so, using a ceremonial ivory-bladed knife given to me by Tagish, one of the tribe's hunters in exchange for healing his sick child."

"Or you could have bored me to death with another story like that one."

The shaman leveled his gaze on Edward. "I have kept you warm and safe as you thrashed and sweated. The stars have appeared and danced their dance in the sky five times, and I have watched over you. The caribou hide blanket you have curled under I have brought for you. I hunted to keep you fed; not a simple task since you scared away most of the wildlife with your ravings."

Sawaya rose and approached him. The old man fingered his carved-stone orca amulet with one hand and withdrew an ivory blade with the other. He crouched beside Edward, brandishing the weapon.

"Better put that thing away," Edward hissed. "Or I'll take it – and the entire arm holding it – as a souvenir."

The Yupik paused, considering. Then he sheathed the weapon. "You do not understand. I act as a go-between, serving my people, the Yupik, and the spirits of the sea animals."

"What do you want me for, a ritual sacrifice?" Edward felt his lips pulling into a humorless smirk. "I'll never let it happen. I've walked away from much worse."

"No. I dragged you away from worse. That is the truth. I mean you no harm. That also is the truth."

"How is it that you speak English?"

"I interact with those in the white people's village."

"Dawson City?" The words were out of his mouth before he could stop them. Edward winced; he didn't know if his description had made the rounds.

"Yes. The place you have fled."

An icicle of fear slid down Edward's spine. "How do you know that?"

"I've been watching you since you arrived. The first time you arrived," the old man said pointedly. "I witnessed your violent actions toward the woman on that first night and toward the others on nights that followed. I hope my silence, despite my knowledge, has helped build the level of trust between us."

"You saw the things I did. And yet you sought me out. You said you wanted to test me. Why?"

"I consult dreams. I listen to the spirits. I often know more about people than they themselves know."

"If you're trying to get me to pay you for your silence, your minutes are numbered, old man."

"You radiate a power unlike anything I have experienced. The only word I can use to describe it is *otherness*. You wish to feed your dark instincts."

"I fought against them," Edward admitted. "But then . . ."

"You had a vision," Sawaya finished.

Edward nodded.

"You saw Kigatilik."

Edward remained silent.

"Few see him. Fewer still see him and live. This is why I believe you can help me." Sawaya knelt and stirred the campfire with a stick. "There's someone else nearby who would interest you."

The shaman had piqued his interest. "Tell me."

"He is powerful, like you," the shaman said. "Mumetaq is the largest and strongest of our tribe. He towers over all others by two heads. But he attacks his own people. He was once a man, now he is a monster."

Edward felt his nostrils flare, his eyes narrow. He couldn't tell if he felt insulted or intrigued. A mix of both, perhaps. "Why is he like me?"

The shaman flushed. "Alike, yet different."

"Where?"

"He wanders, but can often be found near the seal camps. It's where he preys, where he eats."

"He kills seals? That is of no concern to me. You've wasted enough of my time." Edward cast the caribou pelt aside and stood.

The Yupik raised both hands in a warding gesture. "Mumetaq kills members of his own tribe. He eats them. He eats *us*." Sawaya grimaced. "He went hunting but returned possessed by the demon spirit we call the Wendigo. The transformation was instant, his hunger relentless. I tried everything I could to heal him. Nothing worked."

"And this Mumetaq; he still terrorizes your tribe?"

"Yes. He is a monster, with the strength of a polar bear. He does not protect us, does not honor our ways. Only a monster attacks, kills, and eats his people."

"Why tell me?"

"You can save our dwindling tribe." The Yupik clutched his orca amulet. "You alone have the expertise needed to do the job. I'm asking you to spare me and kill him instead. Consider it a challenge."

Edward grinned. "First, you will return to me my leather apron and knives. Next, you will lead me to your cannibal giant, old man. And then you will leave us alone."

Coming to him for help would prove to be the worst mistake the Yupik shaman had ever made. Of this Edward felt sure. He sneered at the old fool's sincerity as he tracked his quarry. He had to give the old man credit, however, for the herb-infused stew he'd prepared for him. Edward had wolfed it down and his fever had broken. He felt like a new man as he took a deliberate step into Mumetaq's field of vision.

The giant lunged and swiped at him with polar bear-like ferocity. Edward dove into the sparse scrub cover provided by the tundra. His attacker lumbered toward him but Edward darted out of harm's way.

Edward studied the other man's enraged visage. Bulbous tumors pushed out from his head in every direction. This was certainly the murderous outcast, Mumetaq. The shaman had described him well. His arms were enormous, his fists like limestone blocks. His sinewy legs looked like they could carry him a hundred miles before tiring. The giant focused on Edward, bellowed, and charged.

Knowing he faced imminent danger, Edward reached into his leather apron and withdrew six blades, three wedged between the fingers of each hand.

Mumetaq's brutish eyes widened. The big man slowed, stopped, and then drew back, not out of fear but apparent reverence. Edward gave his first convert a beatific smile. He flicked the blades, quick and effortless, and saw how the mad cannibal admired how they reflected the starlight.

Edward had decided to serve his own purposes by not complying with the shaman's instructions. He offered Mumetaq his largest knife. The other man received it and an immediate change came over him. The perpetual look of rage drained from the big man's face. A look of malicious glee replaced it. The Yupik outcast sat down and looked at Edward, eyes agleam.

Edward flicked his wrist. He mimed approaching someone and slitting their throat, their chest. He showed the giant cannibal how to carve a body, and the important role the blades played. Edward pointed at himself. Then he pointed at Mumetaq, who now trembled with excitement. Edward pointed in the direction of the mining camp.

The giant grinned. A slaver of drool from his mouth caught the starlight. Edward realized the cannibal was literally hungry for action. Come to think of it, Edward thought, he could go for a bite, himself. A special variation of steak tartare perhaps. Or fresh tongue. Why be afraid to try new things? He turned and began walking across the tundra back toward Dawson City. Mumetaq rose to his feet and followed.

Gladys Beasely, bundled against the night's bitter chill, marched along the all but deserted road on the edge of Dawson City. She'd been out late, speaking with other like-minded citizens about cleaning up the town's vices: the gambling, the dance hall girls, the drinking. Someone had inferred that some of the dance hall girls did more for the miners than just dance. For Gladys, that had been the last straw. She meant to confront these women of ill repute immediately, and either drive them from town or compel them to kneel and pray for forgiveness. She'd learned of the location of one of the largest brothels from a red-faced man, who had quickly clarified that he'd overheard some other men talking about it, but had never visited the location himself.

Gladys knocked on the door of the establishment but no one answered. She vowed not to give up. She hammered on the door. Still no one came. "I know you're in there!" she called. Her skin prickled with anger. When they opened the door she'd be ready with the word and the wrath of God. She gazed at the door. Nothing happened.

Then she heard approaching footsteps. They rounded the corner of the building. Gladys flushed and turned to face the street, ready to explain. Two men, obscured by the night, approached. One towered over the other. Something hovering near the smaller man's midsection glinted in the starlight.

"On your way out, ma'am? I know this place," the shorter man said, "and I must say it is an affront to your better nature which, I've no doubt, lies hidden deeply within. Fortuitously, I am just the man to help you find it."

Gladys's knees threatened to buckle. She found herself unable to speak, unable to breathe. The giant savage intimidated, yes, but the shorter man with the English accent infused her with deep, penetrating dread. His eyes glittered maniacal, monstrous. He wore, she saw, a leather apron. In each hand he held two menacing blades. He twirled the knives with ease and tossed them each aloft in turn, like a juggler at a carnival. It was quite a feat. One, she realized belatedly, that she'd never have the chance to see again.

Gladys fell to her knees on the frigid, muddy ground. Movement had become impossible. She gazed straight ahead as they approached, until all she saw was the monster's leather apron.

Bluebeard's Wife
Catherine Lundoff

He walked away briskly, shedding his blood-soaked gloves as he went. They vanished into his medical bag to be disposed of later. Unlike the implements in the bag, there would be no washing the stains from them. Such was the price of performing a grim duty for the public good. He permitted himself a small, self-satisfied smile at the thought; it was a price that he was more than willing to pay.

On him had fallen the task of purifying his little portion of the Empire. He would do it proudly and skillfully, as any gentleman worth the name would. He would cleanse its alleyways and streets of the kind of filth that pervaded it. Filth that threatened even the sanctity of his own home. But no more. He had seen to that. Adele would have no more need to taint herself by association with creatures like the one he had just disposed of. The idea that his wife, the one he had chosen for her superior nature and refinement, would disobey him and stoop to such depths, sickened him.

Screams from the alleys behind shook him free from his thoughts and he gave a sly smile as a couple of drovers ran past him, heading back the way he had come. They would see his handiwork and they would know that a new predator had come to roam these noisome thoroughfares. And they would tell others, spreading word of his deed until the human trash feared to pollute the city's streets with their disgusting presence.

He walked on into the fog, his strides swift but not nervous, not at all. For what had he to be concerned about? He was a respectable surgeon, returning home from his hospital. There were always murders in Whitechapel, after all. It could have nothing to do with him, nothing at all. The knowledge was intoxicating.

The newspaper headlines screamed from the breakfast table, and he smiled at them before folding the paper over so that Adele would not see them. The articles were full of gossip and speculation and barely controlled terror over his deed, and it pleased him immensely to see those things, to feel the ripple of fear on the streets, and to know that he was responsible for it.

Adele was chattering now, some nonsense about a group of charitable ladies and some scheme for training some of the worthy urban poor in domestic service. He let her words wash over him until it was difficult to distinguish one from the other. If Adele had a child of her own, there would be an end to all this foolishness, but, as yet, her womb had not quickened. He would have to brew another tonic for her and try again. He gave her a sidelong glance, imagining her as she lay still and pale as a corpse in his bed and felt a sharp pang of lust.

From the other side of the table, he could feel her withdraw, her flesh cringing from his thoughts as if she could read them. That pleased him even more: a truly moral woman would never welcome a man's touch. Such a woman was the angel of a man's household, not like the decadent filth he had cleansed the other night.

There was a clatter from the grate as the new maid dropped the poker, then as quickly retrieved it with a scared look and a mumbled apology. He gave her a fierce glare, trying and failing to recognize her. When had his wife brought on a new servant? Why had she not informed him? In any case, whoever she was and wherever she had come from, she was too clumsy to serve in his household. "Out." He pointed at the door, his meaning clear, and the girl ran, sobbing.

Soon, Adele was sobbing too and he stalked out of the house and hailed a cab to return to the hospital, leaving all the wretched noise behind him. Here was quiet, for the moment. Here, too, was blood in plenty, and death, but none of it his to own, his to taste and savor. He stalked the corridors, frustration and rage driving his pace like a coachman's whip.

It was not enough, had never been enough. He knew that now. He needed more.

That craving drove him to Whitechapel again to roam its filthy streets and byways the very next night. Yet something of his desire must have shown in his face and the creatures that haunted the darker ways cringed away from him, vanishing into doorways and taverns when they caught his eye. He snarled at yet another empty street and slipped into a quiet tavern to wait, to bide his time. His prey would grow less wary as the night passed and the foulness of bad liquor would blind their minds to their terror.

Shortly before dawn, he returned to prowl the streets in the thickening fog, looking for the right prey, the right place, but without success. Thwarted and angry, he wandered until sunrise before he stalked home and threw himself into his bed. Then, an early telegram from the hospital called him back, and back again the next day, filling his days with an exhausted stupor that left little time for him to hunt at night.

It was just as the furor began to die down that his opportunity came again. And this time, he discovered new pleasures. The very surgical skills that enabled him to save lives at the hospital could be employed to new ends, namely, seeking the source of the impurities within the second slattern he cleansed from the streets. This beast was as far beneath him as the rats that scurried through the alleys so why not use this opportunity to advance his learning?

It fascinated him, did this experiment, and left him with a burning enthusiasm for discovery. If he could find the source of moral decay in a specific organ, something that drove such beasts to disgrace themselves, it would be the pinnacle of his medical career. He imagined the queen knighting him for his services as he stripped off the blood-soaked apron he was wearing and dropped it into a pipe that led to the river. That grimy waterway could wash it clean or send it out to sea: it mattered not. What signified was that he had found a use for his new obsession, one that would lead to his own personal glory.

That ambition sent him out to the darkened streets of Whitechapel whenever he could leave his home or hospital without undue notice.

Discovery, power, and bloodlust, these elements mixed together to propel him forward like fuel for a steam engine.

At first, he was careless of his safety and it was only through the rawest of cunning that he was preserved against the Metropolitan Police and the denizens of the very streets he attempted to wash free of their sins. But he soon realized that a man of middle years, impoverished yet genteel, walking the soot-smeared cobbles would be assumed by passers-by and by the slatterns themselves to be an ideal client. And, more importantly, common enough to be forgettable. He modified his dress to blend in with the crowds before and after his experiments, one more fallen "gentleman" amongst many.

Descriptions given by the police and the newspapers varied widely as a result. He found that he had to fight the temptation to read of his exploits in print, then correct the very writers who brought fame to his deeds. Vanity was a vice that he had admonished Adele about from time to time, and now he was tempted to indulge it himself. It was true then that corruption spread like a contagion, a disease infecting even those with the purest of motives. He would have to be on his guard and he vowed as much to himself, as he did his best to ignore the cries on the street from the filthy urchins hawking their papers.

For a time, he wondered if he might find other roots of corruption in their young bodies too, but he soon dismissed the idea. It was their mothers who should have cured them, their mothers whose purity should have shone as a beacon to guide their way up from the gutters. He must continue to address the sickness at its source and he would do so if he had to cut down every trull in Whitechapel. A grim satisfaction filled him with the thought.

The response grew so much louder each time they found one of his experiments that he could not help but pay attention to the hue and cry. When some fool claimed credit for his deeds and dubbed himself, or was dubbed, he never bothered to determine which, such epithets as "Leather Apron" and "Jack the Ripper," he dismissed the impulse to correct them all. His day of glory would come when his experiments were complete and he could display his results before Her Majesty. Until then, such petty prizes as personal renown were not for him.

So occupied were his thoughts with all this, that at first he failed to notice that Adele had employed a new housemaid – a tall, rough girl, perhaps from one of her former charities. But hard as he pressed, she would tell him only that the girl was their cook's cousin, newly up from the country. Since the girl often vanished when he was at home, and came only when summoned, he nearly forgot about her as quickly as he noticed her.

Adele, too, seemed more inclined to disappear whenever he was at home, vanishing into the kitchen with questions for the cook or into her bedroom with headaches. It began to irk him, this submissive, silent vanishing. True, he had his work and his experiments to return to, but his wife should be at his side when he was at home, soothing his brow and encouraging his efforts.

In a fit of madness, he nearly thought to find Adele and tell her all, that she might appreciate his labors better. But to trust to a woman's silence was the height of foolhardiness and he soon dismissed the notion. Instead, he realized that he had been too lenient, too permissive. A wife needed a firm hand.

That evening, he came home and waited quietly for her in the sitting room, allowing no sounds to announce his presence. When she returned from wherever she had gone and the front door closed behind her, he emerged and seized her arm. She let out a small scream. "Where have you been, my dear?" She trembled in his grasp and he felt his vision go red around the edges, as it did whenever he approached one of the creatures in the alleys and byways. Was this then an indication that Adele, too, was more corrupt then he realized?

"Please, please forgive me. My aunt is . . . ill and I thought you still at the hospital. I was late because I was nursing her. Oh, please, no!" This last cry was louder than the rest as he reached for the strap he kept on a hook by the door. It was somewhat stiff from disuse and he vowed that he'd apply it to that slattern of a maid for poor housekeeping when he was done with Adele.

The leather snapped across Adele's shoulders and she shocked him with a sharp scream. In a moment, the maid, cook and coachman spilled into the hallway. The latter was the first to have the decorum to look embarrassed and turn away, as well he might for interrupting a husband in what was his right. But the cook was made of denser stuff and her cry was dash of old water on his mood. "We thought the Ripper himself was here! And Gladys has gone and cut her hand proper, she was so startled. We didn't know you was home, sir." She bobbed a curtsy at him as he glared at her.

With his fury redirected, his grip on Adele loosened and she slipped free, stepping away from him. She seized the maid's hand. "Oh, such a lot of blood!" Her voice choked on the words and he found himself studying the maid's hand clinically. It was wrapped in a bloody rag but some of the stains appeared to be dry already, as if the wound were an old one, perhaps reopened.

But no matter, this tableau forced a change in his plans unless he intended to dismiss the entire household staff at once. It was plain that they were reluctant to take themselves off unless Adele went with them, as if he was some barbaric Eastern potentate on the brink of beating his wife to death. He snarled and shot a glare at Adele to remind her that he would reprimand her when he returned. Then he turned, seized his coat and his bag and flung the door open with a flourish before vanishing into the foggy street.

He excelled in his experiments that night, leaving limbs and organs where they were most likely to be found. If his wife and servants feared the Ripper now, let their fears increase tenfold when they heard of this, as long as it brought obedience with their terror. He felt a strange laughter growing inside him at the thought and had to mask it in a coughing fit to maintain his disguise intact.

Yet once that impulse had passed and he had disposed of his old bloodstained coat, he felt strangely calm and weary. His steps led him to his cot at the hospital rather than to his own bed from habit rather than intent. Spent from his fury and his exertions, he cleaned his tools and changed the rest of his garments before falling into a deep and dreamless sleep.

When he did return home, the house was clean and quiet. Adele sat by the fire doing some mending, a closed book on the table beside her. He did not trouble himself as to what the text might be as it was a prayer book or a Bible, no doubt. Something suitable for his wife's reading. Instead, he took its presence as an indication that she had remained home to wait for him and greet him, just as she should.

A distant part of his mind considered completing the punishment he had begun the night before, but in his new-found calm, it seemed unnecessary. Instead, he kissed Adele on the cheek and watched approvingly as she cast her eyes down and bowed her head. If she shrunk away a bit at his touch, so much the better. Her shoulders were covered with a shawl, and he didn't doubt that it also covered a welt or two, as a reminder. That would suffice, for a time.

The maid slipped in, silent as a cat, bearing a cup of tea. One of her hands was bandaged but he noticed that she had full use of it. She curtsied politely to him and he sent her out to fetch tea for him as well. Her swift return gave him pause, as if she had anticipated his command. Or wanted to prevent him from being alone with his wife.

Was Adele foolish enough to form an alliance against him with her social inferiors? He watched them closely, looking for a signal or a sign between them as long as the maid was in the room. But he noticed nothing suspicious, not yet. He determined that he would need to watch his wife more closely, pass more time at home.

It was a pity, in its way, this strange new calm. He had always enjoyed listening to Adele beg him for leniency. Her family had not approved of the match, not at first, and he well remembered the series of petty humiliations he endured as an impoverished young medical student before he could claim her as his own. Perhaps he would find an infraction of his rules in the next day or two so that he might remind her once again that he was her master. Perhaps that might even supplement his new-found pleasures for a time.

But even as he held the thought close, he realized that it was no longer enough. His experiments had given him something new, something greater. What was the power to merely hurt or wound when he held power over life and death? Satisfying himself with a few bloody welts on his wife's body paled by comparison. It was a minor pleasure, like that of using her in other ways as he saw fit, and it would simply no longer do.

He gave another moment of consideration to conducting his experiments at home and seeing what corruption he might discover in Adele, the maid and that imbecile of a cook whose name he had never bothered to commit to his memory. But then, would not he himself be implicated in their failings? Was not any corruption they might possess within them something to be laid at his door as their master? It was a realization to give him pause. No, it was better to content himself with those who had no connection to him; he was less likely to blind himself to their crimes that way.

With that decision fixed, he joined his wife at supper. Even the unexpected appearance of forgotten guests was insufficient to ruffle his new-found tranquility. The meal was adequate, the conversation somewhat less so, but it was respectable. This was what the queen would expect when he was presented to her. She valued respectability above all else, and a surgeon with a record of successful medical service to the Crown and impeccable morals was likely to be made a knight by Her Majesty's own hand. That thought filled his mind as he endured the company of his guests – a pompous but well-connected colleague and his wife.

When they left, he was too exhausted to go out hunting or to go to Adele's chamber. Instead, he retired to an evening of study until he fell into a dreamless sleep, as near to death as any living man might know. The maid's entrance the next morning roused him to a warm cup of tea, hot water for washing and a fire in the grate. Those comforts pleased him the more by having been rare when the previous maid had been in his employment and he unbent enough to wish her a good morning.

The girl looked up, startled as a fawn, and met his gaze for an instant, before dropping her eyes and bolting after a brief obeisance. There had been something familiar in that face, something he had seen recently, but the memory eluded him as to where and when. Did she resemble someone he had encountered? But where and when? He could not recall and, after some minutes, his time for reflection evaporated. He had his patients to visit and they were of far greater importance than some chit of maid who might resemble someone else.

Yet, the interaction lingered in his mind, making him remember his earlier plan to punish her for interrupting him. He would have to find a punishment suitable enough for such disobedience, and a crime that justified it. Appearances must be maintained and he was not a hard master, merely a stern one. He washed and shaved, donning his clothing with a certain pleased satisfaction. Corruption would find no foothold in his castle.

But the hospital beckoned and he could brook no more delay. Once there, he found far more than he had bargained for in the way of labors requiring his attention and he was in no humor to discipline either maid or wife on his return that night or the next. Still less did he have energy to hunt.

On the next night, however, he found his steps leading him back to the noxious streets of the stews, and there he found suitable prey. He accompanied the creature to her den and took her there, carving his knife into her flesh deeper than the others who had preceded her. He examined each piece of her that he removed, expecting them to give him some sign, some portent of what lay within that had twisted and burned away all the purity that should have been there. He carved until he was spent, still failing to find what he sought. Wherever the corruption lay, it was beyond his powers to determine it, at least on this occasion.

The thought weighed heavily on his mind and slowed his steps even as he took the usual precautions and disposed of his outer clothing in a sewer. He considered returning to the hospital to clean his instruments but in his despair at failing once more, he changed his mind. Let the maid clean them at home; she would not know that the blood had not come from his patients. After all, in a manner of speaking, it had. His experiments would enable him to treat his patients, once he understood what was truly wrong with them.

Frustration and weariness drove him home to his bed, after he deposited his bag at the kitchen door. The maid would find it in the morning and clean it without additional instruction from him. If not, Adele could correct her. His wife must learn to train the domestic staff properly or do the work herself.

He fell asleep with a grim smile on his face at the picture. He would never permit such an aberration of respectability in actuality, but it might be useful to indicate that he was considering it. The music of Adele's remembered pleadings on other occasions lulled him toward sleep. He wondered if she would beg as prettily to avoid scrubbing the grates, and promised himself that he would find out soon before he yielded to his weariness.

This time, when morning came, he woke as the maid closed the door behind her with a quiet thump. He shaved and dressed and went downstairs to join his wife for breakfast. Adele was very, very pale and her hands trembled as she poured his tea and pulled his toast from the fire. "Are you ill, my dear?" He asked the question solicitously, as he had heard others ask it. He so seldom asked it himself that he was not surprised to see her start.

"I . . . I have a bit of a headache, that's all." Her voice shook a little with her words, but she did not ask for his permission to leave the room and he did not volunteer it. She would no doubt recover swiftly enough when he desired it. He intended to desire it, quite soon, in fact.

Adele placed her cup on the table, and her trembling fingers dislodged a newspaper and a book, which fell to the floor. They both stared down at the headlines that screamed some nonsense about "the Ripper" and for an instant he thought they had discovered his most recent experiment. But it was far too soon for that to have been found, so perhaps it was one of his imitators or one of his earlier efforts.

Whatever it was, the sight of the paper was enough to make Adele close her eyes and shudder. He studied her through narrowed eyes. Did she suspect him of these deeds? Had the maid spoken of the contents of his medical bag? That would be unfortunate; she would almost certainly fail to understand the importance of his work. While she could not bring the minions of the police to his door, she might create other obstacles to his work. And that could not be permitted. He trembled with rage at the thought.

The maid chose that moment to enter with the tea and kippers and he remembered that in order to control Adele's tongue, he would have to rid himself of the servants as well. But this was too soon, too early! He was unprepared, even his instruments were not to hand. He could not kill both of them with his bare hands, not without raising an alarm. He must plan and to do that he needed to control himself.

Something shifted in the atmosphere of the room. He surprised a surreptitious glance from maid to mistress, but nothing more. They made a happy, respectable domestic picture, at least on the surface.

Adele reached over and dropped a lump of sugar into his teacup as the maid knelt and picked up both the book and the newspaper. He sipped his tea and stared at her bent head, willing her to look up, willing his brain to remember why she was familiar to him. She stubbornly looked away, rescuing the burning toast from the grate instead and placing it on a plate. Adele cleared her throat and the maid knocked over a vase of flowers on one of the tables when she rose.

He cleared his throat at this act of seemingly deliberate clumsiness. There would be punishments to go around today for disturbing his peace, as well as to destroy whatever alliance his wife and his maid were forming. He drained his tea and smacked the cup down on the saucer as the maid stammered an apology and tried to use her apron to mop up the spill. He lurched to his feet, intending to seize her and beat her then and there for insolence and incompetence. Another strap lay near to hand in a drawer, he had only to stretch out his hand to reach it.

But the room shifted and he was unaccountably lying on the carpeted floor at Adele's feet. She drew them back and, as she moved, he could see that the book she had dropped was one of his medical texts. What the deuce was she doing with that? She was nowhere near clever enough to understand it. A paroxysm of pain shook him and he convulsed, twisting away from his wife and knocking over another small table.

"Should I fetch someone?" the maid asked, her voice distant. He squinted up at her face through the red haze that filled his vision. Why didn't the stupid girl go and fetch a doctor? He might die if this continued.

Her face loomed above him, eyes wide with fright, and he remembered another face like it from a fortnight or more before. One of his experiments had looked at him in the same way, with those same eyes, but without that small, pleased smile. He tried to shout, to tell Adele that this viper in their nest was killing him.

But he could not form the words and another wave of pain washed over him, sending him writhing across the carpet. He was surrendering to it, losing all control. Why was no one fetching a doctor?

Adele's voice came to his ears from far away, "Not yet. He may yet recover. I want to be sure of him before we fetch anyone." Their faces hung before his eyes for an instant, maid and mistress, pale, terrified and resolute. They glowed white, those faces, as his vision faded to black. Like angels of the house, with no trace of corruption that he could see. But he knew it was there. He wanted to slice them open and discover it, but it was too late. They had tricked him into looking outside when the very devil lay within. He choked on his rage as the world disintegrated around him.

Signed Confession
Martin Feekins

"This is the twentieth century, Aaron Rothman, women will not be subjugated."

"I don't want to subjugate you, Jemina."

"I think it had better be Miss Abrams, at least for now."

Jemina knew she was being cruel, but Aaron deserved it.

"As you wish . . . Miss Abrams."

They were washing dishes at the Soup Kitchen for the Jewish Poor in Butler Street. Jemina had no doubt Aaron volunteered at the kitchen only because she did so. His interest in her had been obvious since he began his apprenticeship at her father's tailor's shop. Jemina's nursing studies meant she was not often at the shop, but it was clear not only to her but to her father and mother that Aaron contrived to arrive early and leave late in the hope of seeing her. Volunteering at the kitchen allowed him to spend time with her without offending her parents. Jemina was pleased by the attention, but not flattered. That would have been a response from an earlier age.

"It's 1910, Mr Rothman – just the sound of it is futuristic – and yet you still believe women should not be given the vote."

"That isn't what I said. I said it was an important decision and should be considered carefully."

"By men, no doubt. We each work in this soup kitchen, we each see the need in the people who come here, the injustice of it. We each have opinions about what should be done."

"I know what you're going to say."

"But only you have a vote that might actually make a difference."

"Yes, but—"

"But you're frightened of giving women a voice."

"No danger of you not having a voice."

It was a whisper, but Jemina caught it. Calmly, she removed her apron and folded it over the back of a chair. She retrieved her winter coat from its hook and slipped it on.

"Jemina—"

"In the interests of equal rights, I am going home and you can finish the work here, work that can be done equally well by a man as by a woman."

"But, Jemina, Miss Abrams, I should walk you home, I promised your father. And I want to, of course."

Jemina started for the door. "So the men have decided that I need a man to look after me. Is that correct? I think we both know where I stand on that."

She opened the door and stepped through.

"Jemina, you're being—"

Aaron stopped himself as Jemina turned to glare. They both knew the sentence could end several ways, but none of them would be good for Aaron. Jemina closed the door on him.

She knew she was being unfair, but his comments about the vote for women angered and disappointed her. She liked him, but any man who wanted to court her would have to support her views on that topic.

She had put Aaron in a difficult position. If he came after her, he would incur her wrath. If he didn't, he would risk incurring her father's wrath, and perhaps feel less of a man, though Jemina saw the latter as a valuable lesson. She wasn't sure which course she would prefer him to take.

In the meantime, she could find her way safely home alone. It was a short walk to Wentworth Street and the evening was not yet especially late. Across the country, women were fighting for the cause, some making huge sacrifices. So far, all she had done was talk. Making this small stand was the least she could do.

Still, the night was cold and dark and did not invite her in. Jemina had spent her twenty-two years on these streets and considered all of this part of the East End her home, but tonight the red-brick alley walls corralled her, the shadows carried a threat and the street lights a warning. The heels of her boots were too loud on the flags. Their click-clack grew more rapid as she unconsciously stepped up her pace. Her glance darted from one shadowed corner to another.

She cursed Aaron and her father and all men for making her feel vulnerable. She would not be afraid simply because she was alone. She slowed her pace and fixed her gaze ahead.

At that moment, the attacker detached himself from the shadows. Had her sense of foreboding been a warning? If so, it was too little to save her from the first sweep of his knife. The blade sliced across her stomach. Before he could strike again she grabbed with both hands the wrist below the fist that held the knife and pushed it away. She was surprised by her success. The attacker pushed back, but she held him at bay. She kicked his shin at the moment he grabbed her hair, pulling her head back, and they performed a clumsy pirouette in the shadows. Jemina knew her strength would carry her only so far. Defeat seemed a matter of time. Her attacker's face spun in and out of the street light as they danced, giving her a sense of age, grey skin worn and lined, and eyes sunken in darkness even in the light.

She missed her footing at the top of a short flight of stone steps and they fell together. Stone struck an elbow, a knee, an ankle. The blade struck again, too, high in her shoulder, but fear and panic fuelled her and she twisted the weapon to stab her attacker even as they crashed through a door at the foot of the steps and continued their tumble down a second flight.

Jemina flew free of her attacker, but had no memory of hitting the floor.

She opened her eyes to pain and confusion. She had most likely been unconscious for only a few seconds, but could not judge with certainty.

She was badly hurt. Blood seeped through her clothes at the waist. The wound stung, but she thought it was not deep. The thick winter coat had protected her from the worst of the blow. Her shoulder ached, and she knew that ache would worsen and the muscles would stiffen. But these things were not her chief concern. Her right leg was broken. She didn't need to see it clearly to know that below the knee it was bent at an unnatural angle. The pain made her nauseous and she was shivering. She knew enough about shock to know she could not afford to succumb to it.

Her surroundings were dark, but the smells of soap and vegetables told her she was in the basement kitchen of one of the terrace homes that backed on to the alley. The room was warm. She could hear the rumble of the furnace. Perhaps a family was at home above her, but no one had arrived to investigate the noise she and her attacker had made.

The attacker. He was here with her, of that she could be certain. Had she hurt him? She thought so. Dare she hope the fall had killed him?

The exterior door to the basement closed with a solid click. Jemina's head snapped towards the sound. Her vision was adjusting to the gloom and she made out his shape. He was huddled on the stairs. His breathing was laboured. She heard it over the furnace's grumble and under the roar of her blood in her ears. As he brought his breathing under control he was no doubt searching her out. Did he still have his knife? It seemed wise to assume so. And who was he? Jemina was surprised at how little that seemed to matter.

She tried to keep her own breathing slow and shallow, so as not to give herself away. She was on the opposite side of the room, up against a wall, so might not be easy to spot. The furnace was between them. Beside it was a coal and wood store and behind it a laundry area, including a set of laundry slides through which she had crashed. One of the broken wooden slats was wedged between her and the wall, digging into the small of her back, though the pain it caused was negligible beside the screaming agony in her leg. She tried to straighten the leg, but the message sent to her muscles brought only more pain. She bit her lip to stay silent and tasted the sour metal of blood.

Perhaps she should shout for help, but the lack of noise from above and the risk of pinpointing herself for her adversary kept her quiet.

He was on the move, pushing himself to his feet and leaning against the wall for support. A sharp breath suggested the effort cost him, but slowly he descended. Clearly, she or the fall had hurt him, but he had the advantage over her in that he could still move. To her left were steps to a door that must lead to the rest of the house. To her right were two stores, probably for groceries and laundry. One offered escape, the other a hiding place, but she doubted she could drag herself to either.

He reached the foot of the stairs and disappeared. Jemina hoped for a moment that he had fallen, but knew the truth was that he had ducked out of sight on the other side of the island formed by the furnace, fuel store and laundry.

The man had all the advantages. He had movement, most likely he had a weapon and he could come at her from one of two directions. She could only wait and hold onto her pain to stay conscious. Even as that thought formed, she berated herself. If that was really all she could do, she should be ashamed.

He came at her from the right, rising up like a dark ghost behind the shirts and trousers that hung crookedly from the broken laundry slides. Jemina was relying on those slides to save her, because the three-foot slat that had been wedged behind her back was now in her hands, held beside her shattered leg.

His movements were unsteady, but not enough to stop him reaching her, and her eyes had adjusted enough to leave her in no doubt that he retained his knife, blade held ready for a slicing stroke.

"Stop," she said.

He checked himself. Perhaps he had thought her already dead, but he didn't halt his advance for more than a moment. Jemina had not expected he would. The word was more for her than him, a signal to gather her strength for what might be her final act.

She lifted the wooden stake at her side with both hands, ignoring the pull on the wounds at her shoulder and stomach, and thrust the jagged end upwards. There was resistance as it struck his abdomen and she feared the wood would simply snap or be brushed aside, but the resistance lasted only a fraction of a second before the attacker's momentum carried him forward and the splintered wood pierced clothing and skin. Jemina pictured a spoon breaking the surface of cold custard before sinking into the soft yellow beneath.

The man howled. He teetered and Jemina braced herself for the impact of his weight falling on her. His free hand reached out to steady him, but came down on the hot surface of the furnace. He wrenched it away and staggered backwards, dropping the knife in his shock. It hit Jemina's damaged leg. She cried out, but clung to the slat, which did now snap. The attacker stumbled backwards and fell heavily.

Jemina's rapid, rasping breathing matched her attacker's. She stared into the gloom, expecting his dark shape to rise again. When it didn't immediately do so, she took her eyes off him long enough to locate the knife. It had bounced across her legs and lay a few feet to her left. She stretched with the remaining length of the slat, but the knife was a couple of inches out of reach. Her leg screamed with the slight movement the stretch forced from it. She daren't push it any further for fear of passing out.

The man now lay barely six feet from her. His ragged breathing calmed a little, but he made no effort yet to renew his attack. Could he see the knife from his prone position? There was nothing to lose by assuming he couldn't.

"I have the knife now," said Jemina, "and you know I'm not afraid to use it. I would suggest that, if you are able to move, your best course of action would be to leave now."

The splutter from her right might have been laughter. The shape making it shifted and Jemina gripped the slat more tightly, but he only pushed himself a little further back and more upright so he could lean against what Jemina thought was the grocery store. He grunted with each movement. They now sat at ninety degrees to each other, about seven feet apart.

"Go while you can," said Jemina.

The laughter was stronger and crueller, but it ended in a prolonged and clearly painful coughing fit. Jemina took some small joy in that, though she knew it was a false pleasure. Her situation was desperate. Would it have been different if she had not lost her temper with Aaron, if she had swallowed her pride and allowed him to walk her home? Almost certainly. Had she had a man to protect her, this man would most likely have targeted some other vulnerable woman. That made her angry and anger felt powerful. She would not have this man laughing at her.

"Who do you think you are?" she said.

The beginning of another laugh was cut short by more coughing. He took a few moments to compose himself, then found his voice.

"Who am I? That is the question to be answered here tonight, and you are very much a part of that answer. You will be my true signed confession."

It was an old voice. Once it might have been commanding, but now held only an echo of that tone.

"But that answer isn't for you, it's for posterity. Instead, let me tell you what I know about you. First, you do not have the knife. It's still on the floor. I'm used to seeing in the dark. Second, if you could leave you would have done so, rather than urging me to do so. Therefore, you are immobile. Therefore, you are dead. I will make you what I need you to be. And, my dear, you would be remiss to assume I carry only one knife."

What he said was indisputable, infuriatingly so.

"I am not your dear," said Jemina.

If he did come for her, she would lunge for the dropped knife and attempt to defend herself, because at that point, regardless of the pain or any further damage, she would have nothing left to lose.

She could not judge how long she had been in the basement. Already it felt like this was the world she inhabited, but in reality it could have been no more than three minutes. How long would it take Aaron to come after her, to realise she had not arrived home and for him and her father to begin searching? Not long, she hoped, but perhaps too long. She would have to rely on herself if she was to survive this.

In the meantime, there could be merit in keeping her attacker talking, both in the hope of rescue and of devising a plan to save herself. And there were things in what he had said that begged questions.

"What do you mean, I will be your signed confession?"

"My dear, that really is not something with which you need concern yourself."

"No! I hear that all the time, from men. It is no longer acceptable in the world and it is certainly not acceptable in whatever hell I currently inhabit. If I am to die in this basement, I will have answers."

The speech exhausted her, but she found again her anger helped to sustain her.

Her adversary's slow handclap filled the silence that followed her outburst.

"Bravo, my dear. There is something to be said for hearing the prey try to assert its individuality. It's a richness I've unwittingly denied myself in the past. It's all pretence, of course. We all know that all Eves are one."

A woman-hater. Well, that was familiar territory.

"So, you hate women. You're hardly alone in that. You've just chosen a method of subjugation at which even most men would balk."

"Perhaps I simply show them the way."

"The way of the coward. The way of men who are afraid to address women as equals."

Was that what Aaron had been trying to do? she wondered. Had he been trying to engage her on the complexities of the argument? Perhaps, though only men believed the issue was complex. Women knew it was simplicity itself: they were equal.

Her accusation of cowardice seemed to have silenced her adversary, but the victory brought little comfort, though if he was talking he was less likely to be acting.

Jemina's right leg answered a renewed demand for movement with fresh pain and she was still losing blood with no way to staunch the flow. Her strength was pooling around her on the tiled floor and she was becoming light-headed. Would this be decided by who had a greater will to survive or would they both drift quietly into oblivion? Speaking at least gave her a focus.

"Sulking, are you? Don't like to be called a coward? Doesn't fit with how you see yourself. You're a warrior, perhaps an avenging angel. You call us Eve. Are we temptresses, threatening to defile your purity? Who tempted you? Your mother, your sister, a lover who rejected you? Tell me how you justify yourself, you pathetic little man."

With a bellow, the dark shape surged up and forward. Jemina flinched and winced at the pain her reaction brought. She raised her meagre weapon, the broken slat. But as quickly as the shape rose, it subsided.

"You are all whores." His voice surprised her with its quiet calm. "I will kill you, but on my terms. I don't dance to a whore's tune."

"No woman chooses to be a whore. Men make them that."

"I unmake them, as I'll unmake you."

"You've done this before."

"Oh, my dear, in my pocket are precise details of exactly where and when I have done this before. That confession will be discovered with your body. Your body will confirm the truth of the confession."

Jemina couldn't deny to herself that she was afraid, though if she left there alive she would admit it to no one else. Aaron wouldn't hear it from her lips.

"Then I return to my original question," she said. "Who are you?"

"You know who I am, my dear. My name is written across the years, at least, my nom de guerre. My true name is written in here."

Jemina assumed the fluttering sound was him tapping the pocket holding his confession. In the silence that followed, the penny dropped. Jemina understood who this man thought he was.

"You claim to be him."

"It's no idle claim. I am him."

"I imagine many have confessed. Why should you be believed?"

"I will be believed with your help, my dear. You are the final page of the confession I will sign. You and the details in my pocket—" again the fluttering tap "—details no one else could know, will be entirely persuasive."

"I was born on the night of his first murder," said Jemina. "That is not a shared anniversary I relish, but that was twenty-two years ago. If you are him, why have you kept quiet for so long?"

His laughter was mean and spiteful and Jemina was glad when it ended in a wet, gurgling cough.

"Believe me, my dear, I have been busy. London isn't the only hellhole lousy with Eves. Serpents have entered the garden across the world."

Every word from this man's lips strengthened Jemina's determination to survive. But her body was stiffening, not only around her various wounds, but everywhere it had been battered by the fall down the steps. Another attempt to ease her broken leg failed, but she was able to shuffle sideways, bringing her inches closer to the knife.

"Why reveal yourself now?" she said. "No, wait. You're dying, aren't you? And not from any wound I inflicted. What is it? Cancer? Your heart?"

No answer came in the pause she left.

"It doesn't matter. It's something fatal and imminent. You want them to know who you are, don't you? Who wants to be immortalised? Do you think you'll be viewed as a hero? God knows, perhaps there are quarters where you would be.

"If you confess now, you think you'll be dead before you can stand trial. Or perhaps you plan to flee, perhaps you think you'll disappear into the night and die uncaught."

Still there was no answer, and Jemina realised too late that she become distracted by her thoughts. Her adversary rose faster than she believed he could and charged towards her. He hadn't lied about having a second knife. It shone in his fist.

Jemina lunged for the fallen knife. Pain shot the length of her spine and slammed into her head. She cried out as the room grew dimmer around her, but her hand closed on the weapon. She twisted her body to face her attacker, yelling at the pain and to cling to consciousness, and pointed the blade towards him.

He landed on her heavily, straddling her, and swatted her hand that held the knife. The weapon flew from her grasp, landing so far away that it might as well have been in another room.

In one hand he raised his knife and with the other he held her down. Her body was all pain now, and all that pain was caused by this man, who believed his will trumped hers. The pain made her angrier and stronger than ever.

The broken laundry slat still lay by her side. She grabbed it and swung it in an arc towards the hand that held the knife. Its splintered end struck the attacker's wrist. He cried out and dropped the weapon. They both reached for it, but Jemina knew she would not get there first.

Then she felt his muscles tense. His legs clenched around hers, he reared backwards, his right hand grasped his left arm.

"You're dying," said Jemina. She knew she would not be proud of her words later, but anger outweighed restraint. "But I'll live, and I will make it my mission to ensure that your name is not remembered."

He reached an open hand towards her. Was it a final attack or an appeal for help? A word was squeezed from his clenched lips. It might have been "please", it might have been "Eve".

"No," said Jemina. She pushed the broken slat against his chest and slowly he toppled from her and thudded to the floor. He did not move. The only sound was her own breath.

Jemina felt sick with pain. She wanted only to close her eyes, but there was one more thing she must do before she died. She dragged herself to the fallen body. She could not tell what further damage the action might do to her, but the pain had reached a crescendo and she could feel no worse.

She rummaged inside his coat and pulled out a manila envelope addressed to Scotland Yard. Reaching up, she pulled a shirt from the damaged laundry rack before making the tortuous crawl to the furnace door. Wrapping the shirt around her right hand, she pulled open the door. By the light of the furnace, she opened the envelope. Within were several pages filled with small, precise handwriting. She scanned it: names, dates, descriptions.

The name at the foot of the final page, beneath the signature, meant nothing to her, nor would it ever.

Other names meant much more: Mary Ann Nichols, who died on the day Jemina was born, Annie Chapman, Elizabeth Stride, Catherine Eddowes, Mary Jane Kelly.

His victims deserved to be remembered, but he was so much less than them. She would not allow him his immortality. He would forever be a nameless monster.

She fed the pages and the envelope into the fire.

Now, she could die here.

She was awoken by Aaron repeating her name and gently shaking her shoulder. A figure in the shadows behind him startled her.

"Who is that?"

"She lives here. They arrived home, saw the damage to their basement door and found you. I ran into her husband as he was on his way to fetch the police. Are you all right?"

"My right leg is broken and I have at least two stab wounds. Help me up."

"You shouldn't move."

"Who's the nurse? I want to be out of here. Support me."

Aaron put Jemina's arm around his shoulder and eased her up on her good foot. She winced at the pain, but nothing more.

"Jemina, please forgive me. I should never have let you go off alone."

"You didn't let me. You really will have to learn that."

"I will. What happened here?"

"I think I made a stand."

The woman stood aside to let Jemina step past the dead man. He was unremarkable. On the street, he wouldn't have warranted a second glance.

"Do you know who he is?" asked Aaron.

"Just an old monster."

Jemina didn't know how she was going to make it up the stairs, but she knew she would.

Autumn of Terror
C. L. Raven

"She didn't get the chance to squeal."

I struck her jaw, slipped my fingers around her neck and silenced her outside the stable yard. Laying her on the ground, I slit her throat twice. The second incision was eight inches long and deep enough to ensure her screams could not betray me. As her blood abandoned her body for the gutter, I gouged her abdomen. Once on the left, four times on the right and several lacerations across.

Murders were nothing new in Whitechapel, but this one would spawn a legend that would never die.

I rose; the demon within sated with the sacrifice. Scarlet tears trickled off my long bladed knife as I scrutinised her ruined body.

The crowd applauded tentatively. I bowed, cleaned my knife with a cloth and climbed onto the mini stepladder I always carried. Being five foot seven was great for exploring caves, but not so great for leading tours.

"Mary Ann Nichols, known to everyone as Polly, died on 31 August 1888, beginning the Autumn of Terror. Having been in and out of the Lambeth workhouse for years, she sold her body to pay for a bed in the dosshouse. She'd raised the money three times, but drank it. Impoverished prostitutes like Polly were worth two or three pence a time – the same as a large glass of gin. A tragic life with a tragic end. An end that would bring her everlasting fame. Had she not fallen prey to Jack the Ripper, she would've been yet another forgotten name in London's sordid past.

"Buck's Row no longer exists. It's now Durward Street. In 1888, the Brown and Eagle Wool warehouse, Essex Wharf and Schenider's Cap Factory were across the road from Brown's stable yard where Polly died. A board school was on one side and cottages for better paid tradesmen lined the other. I killed her almost below Mrs Emma Green's cottage window and, despite being a light sleeper, Mrs Green heard nothing. Fear renders people deaf and blind. Or erases their memory. Visibility in Whitechapel was abysmal. In certain places, it was too dark to see your hand before your face, let alone a murderer creeping up behind you. Even the gas lamps were scared to venture into the alleyways that snaked through London like blackened veins through the devil's dark heart. A hellacious paradise for monsters to hide."

My captivated guests' modern clothes would look out of place in Jack's era. Today, dressed as Jack, I was the one who looked out of place. The group was as fascinated and horrified now as Whitechapel's residents had been then. London had changed, times had changed, but murder always drew a crowd.

"PC John Thain and Sergeant Kerby passed Buck's Row at 3.15 a.m. Neither of them saw anything. At 3.40 a.m., Charles Cross found Polly on his way to work and called another man, Robert Paul over. She was still alive. Not wishing to be late, they lowered her skirts to preserve her dignity and told PC Jonas Mitzen. By the time he arrived, PC John Neil had discovered her and summoned Thain. Polly was dead. Lowering her skirts may have restored her dignity but it couldn't restore her life."

I hopped off my ladder as the group photographed the area and Polly Nichols' body. Her vacant grey eyes stared through me into the other realm. A realm crawling with the shadows of the lost.

"Was she Jack the Ripper's first victim?" a man asked.

"First *official* victim. Other women are rumoured to be my victims, but the centuries' old dust that shrouds the past ensures they'll never prove anything. They cannot rouse me from my grave and question me. Martha Tabram, who was killed on the seventh of August, is suspected to be a member of my elite club. At nearly midnight, she accompanied a private into George Yard for intercourse. At 3.30 a.m., her body was discovered on the first-floor landing, but the witness mistook it for a homeless person. The alarm wasn't raised until 4.45. She suffered thirty-nine stab wounds including five to her left lung, two to her right, one to the heart, five to the liver, two to the spleen and six to the stomach. The 'Ripper's' target areas." I indicated on my body as I listed each wound. "The wounds were caused by a penknife, not the long blade I favoured. Maybe I was perfecting my craft." I winked. "The sternum wound was believed to be caused by a bayonet or dagger. There were similarities between this murder and Annie Millwood's attack on February twenty-fifth. A man with a clasp knife stabbed her legs and lower torso. She survived."

"Do you believe he killed before?"

"The skill I demonstrated is born from practise. Killers rarely begin with mutilation. We progress as we become more comfortable with murder and find what we enjoy. Like when you take up dancing. You sample the foxtrot, waltz, tap or even zumba, before realising you're better suited to crochet."

When all the photos had been taken, I smiled. "Shall I introduce you to my next victim?"

I led the group away, checking over my shoulder for stragglers. Polly Nichols faded until she was only a memory. Seconds later, she rose again to act out her final scenes for eternity. It wasn't just Jack's legacy that never truly died.

We walked through the darkened streets. If I closed my eyes, I could resurrect the Whitechapel of 1888. Though, thankfully, not the stench.

"I didn't kill again for nine days. But when I did, I made Polly Nichols' murder look merciful."

I stopped at 29 Hanbury Street. Annie emerged from behind the mortal veil. A man stumbled back, swearing. "Witnesses heard Annie Chapman talking to a man in the backyard. Half an hour before her body was discovered, the neighbour at number 27 heard her say 'No!'"

Annie lifted her black skirt and two petticoats, revealing red and black striped woollen stockings and inviting me to use her body. I would. But not the way she'd imagined. I grabbed her chin and strangled her before she could speak her last words. Fear tainted her bulging eyes as she stared into Death's soul. I eased her to the ground and slit her throat. Her scream slithered out with her blood.

"Blood on the fence post fourteen inches away indicated she was lying down when her throat was cut, so most of the blood pooled on the ground, rather than spraying me. Even in Whitechapel, you don't wish to walk the streets soaked in blood. I was smart. I knew how to evade capture. And this was before *CSI* taught murderers how to manipulate forensic evidence."

"This tour's very violent," one woman remarked to her friend as I made two cuts beside Annie's spine. "Not like the one last night."

I'd been on all of the tours. The guides knew the case well and had opposing theories about his identity. But they were merely facts recited on Whitechapel's bloody stage. None of them could resurrect Jack the Ripper's horrible history like I could. My Autumn of Terror Tour was controversial but memorable. Like the other guides, I knew who he was. But I would take my secret to the grave.

"He's pretending to be Jack the Ripper; it has to be violent. It says he re-enacts the crimes."

"I didn't think it would be this brutal."

I glanced over my shoulder. "The title 'Ripper' wasn't bestowed upon me because I smothered people in their sleep. Murder looks different in real life to on a page. Vivid descriptions can't compare to the rancid smell of a gutted stomach, or the metallic tang of freshly spilled blood. The life fading in their eyes that were once windows to their souls but are now just pretty mirrors."

I rolled Annie on to her back and opened her abdomen. Someone vomited as I swiftly severed the intestines and placed them on Annie's shoulder.

"I'm never eating sausages again," a man moaned. How many other guests turned vegetarian following my tour? How many stuck to it?

A thud disturbed me from removing the uterus. A woman sprawled on the floor. That was the problem with audiences – they missed the best parts. Removing the upper part of the vagina caused a man to faint, and cutting away two thirds of the bladder turned the rest of the group into various shades of sickbay green. It's fortunate public executions were abolished – half the crowd would pass out. I should hire a doctor for my tours. Or buy an ambulance.

"Annie's missing organs were never found."

"What happened to them?" a woman asked.

I lowered my voice, leaning closer. "Maybe I cooked them for my supper." I licked my lips. One person laughed. "Maybe I sold them to the baker for his kidney pies, forcing the people of Whitechapel to feast upon their neighbours. Maybe I was building Frankenstein's bride and needed some vital parts. People yearn to discover my motivation, my identity, but they don't *really* want the answers. The mystery makes it thrilling. Doctor George Bagster Phillips, who performed the post-mortem, believed this work could only be performed by an expert with anatomical knowledge. He said he couldn't have achieved it in fifteen minutes, and had he been careful, it would've taken him an hour. Half an hour elapsed between the neighbour hearing Annie shout and her body being discovered. The 'ripper' label is unfair. I didn't rip my victims like a slaughterer; I dissected them like a surgeon."

I placed Annie's left arm across her left breast, positioned her feet on the ground and spread her legs.

"How could anyone do that to another person?" a woman asked.

"It's no different from a butcher slaughtering an animal."

"These are *people*."

"Life is life, no matter which body it's torn from. Some men enjoy watching football, some enjoy fixing cars. Others find pleasure in mutilating women."

"This isn't a hobby."

"Just because there's no magazine subscription for it, doesn't mean it's not a hobby." I wiped the blade. "There wasn't much in the way of entertainment then. The internet hadn't been invented. People interacted with each other more." I tucked the cloth and knife in my coat. "Shall we continue?"

Nobody wanted to stay. Enjoying the history lesson was difficult with a corpse spoiling the view. Some guests lingered to take pictures.

"Would you mind posing by the body?" a young woman asked.

"My pleasure." I pretended to remove Annie's ovaries. "You've caught me red-handed, exposed the monster behind the mask. You could get a book deal."

She laughed. I enjoyed having guests with a twisted sense of humour.

"The bodies are so lifelike."

"It's hard selling a nightmare using mannequins, or organs that resemble soft toys. Jack the Ripper's become a twisted fairy tale. I wish to remind people of his reality."

"It's like we're watching the real murders."

I winked. "You are." I stood and faced the group. "On to my next victim, Elizabeth Stride. Originally from Sweden, she moved to London in 1866. I knew nothing about these women when I murdered them. Google knows them better than I ever did."

I roused the fainters then led everyone to Berner Street, now renamed Henriques Street. Elizabeth emerged from the shadows and accompanied me. "Like Polly and Annie, Liz was known for being drunk. On the night she died, she was seen in the company of numerous men around Berner Street. One had a billycock hat, one had a sailor's hat, one had a deerstalker and one had a felt hat with a wide brim. Perhaps I had a different hat for different moods."

A primary school occupied Dutfield's Yard's remains. Children played where Elizabeth exited life's bloody stage.

"Whereas there was only nine days between Polly and Annie's murder, Liz died twenty-two days after Annie on the thirtieth of September. They say Annie's mutilation satisfied me more than Polly's death. But it didn't silence the urges for ever."

I stepped down from my ladder so they could see Elizabeth behind me. She smiled and raised her skirts. It wasn't her company I desired. With her hands occupied, I gripped her throat until she became limp. I placed her on the ground and slit her throat.

"Regrettably, I couldn't spend quality time with Liz. Had I not been disturbed, Catharine Eddowes may have lived a long, penniless life. Instead, she was the star of that night's bloody encore."

A horse and cart moved through the darkness, the hoof beats echoing as though Death had come to pay his respects. "Louis Diemschutz entered the yard at one a.m. with his pony and cart. The pony shied at something, but the night was blacker than my soul and blinded Diemschutz. He prodded the object with his whip, discovering Liz's body. She was still warm. His pony continued to be nervous so he believed I was lurking. Quick! We must flee before they catch us."

The group chased me to Mitre Square. Now part of a Memorial Garden for cremated remains, it was one of the few crime scenes to retain its name and cobbled street. Whitechapel had spent over a century trying to wash the bloodstains from its past. Every night, tour guides peeled back its modern skin, exposing its ancient wounds.

A woman waited beneath the trees behind a brick flower planter. She was five foot tall, her auburn hair hidden beneath her black straw bonnet.

"Catharine Eddowes wasn't known for being drunk or a prostitute. She was well educated with a long-term partner, John Kelly. However, on Sunday, September thirtieth, she was arrested for drunkenness and released at one a.m. At one thirty-five, she was seen talking to a man believed to be a sailor. He was about thirty years old and five foot seven." I gestured to myself. "The similarities are uncanny." My group laughed. "Catharine had her hand on his chest." I took her hand, placing it on my chest.

"Ten minutes later, PC Edward Watkins found her body."

I wrapped my hands around her throat. Her eyes widened as she faced the grim reality of her own mortality. When she'd surrendered consciousness, I lowered her then opened her carotid artery. I removed her right earlobe before starting my artistic work on her face, cutting through her left lower eyelid then her right one. I slashed through the bridge of her nose, down to her right jaw, almost splitting her face. Then I chopped the tip off her nose.

I pierced her upper lip, following it with a gash parallel to her lower lip before carving triangular flaps in her cheeks. Starting from her pubic area, I parted her abdomen up to her breastbone then across, leaving her navel intact. I stabbed her groin then slashed her thighs.

"It's like playing a gruesome version of Operation. But without the buzzer."

My knife slipped inside her, freeing her intestines. Placing them by her right shoulder, I cut two feet from her colon, putting it between her left arm and her body. I plunged my knife into her liver and pancreas before stealing her left kidney. Then I removed most of her womb.

"Dr Frederick Gordon Brown, the police surgeon, believed I had medical knowledge as I knew the kidney's location and how to remove it from the front, rather than the side, without damaging other organs. Catharine died instantly from her severed jugular, and the other wounds to her throat ensured there was no blood on her or me, despite the grisly mutilation. As skilled as I undoubtedly was, this would've taken longer than the ten minutes between the witness seeing Catharine, and Watkins finding her body."

My dwindling guests didn't seem to appreciate my recreation of her death. I'd promised them the real tour. People thought they craved reality, but they really wanted the romantic version.

"The true horror of my crimes isn't so fascinating after watching them for real, is it? Murder is more tantalising when it's not committed in front of you."

"I'll have nightmares," someone muttered. "If I sleep."

"You're safe." I smiled at him. "I only killed women. Equality wasn't popular then. Our next stop is Goulston Street, where the piece of bloodied apron was found with the famous graffiti 'the Juwes are the men that will not be blamed for nothing'."

I took them to the doors that were once the archway to Wentworth Model Dwellings. "The message was written on the black brick fascia edging of the open doorway which led to the basements of numbers 108 to 119. PC Alfred Long found the message and apron at 2.55 a.m."

"Did Jack write the message?" a woman asked.

"Perhaps. To divert the police's attention. But it would make more sense to write it by the victims." I beckoned. "Follow me to thirteen Miller's Court where we'll time travel to November the ninth, 1888 and meet beautiful Mary Jane Kelly, a twenty-five-year-old prostitute originally from Ireland. She moved to Wales as a child, later living and working as a prostitute in Cardiff. Eventually, Fate brought her here. To me." My smile twisted. "If you thought Catharine Eddowes' death was bad, I suggest you refrain from eating between now and our next destination. You are about to witness the horrifying brutality that earned me the name 'Jack the Ripper'."

"I can't watch this one," another man murmured to his friend. "This scene was a bloodbath."

People who abandoned a tour didn't get their money back. The website stated this was no ordinary tour. Real murders didn't come with refunds.

The group shadowed me to where the most famous victim had lived and died. Dorset Street was now a private alley running between a car park and warehouses, but where Mary died wasn't important. It was the how that people remembered.

"This warehouse stands on the spot where Miller's Court was." I unlocked the shutters and pushed them up. "So I bought it." Opening the door, I ushered everyone inside. Thirteen Miller's Court stood before us, exactly as it was in 1888.

Mary greeted me with a kiss, took my arm and led me into her home. I led her to her deathbed.

Mary undressed to her chemise, folded her clothes and placed them on a chair. Her boots sat in front of her fireplace. She lay on the bed, beckoning me.

"This was my vilest murder. Some people believe she was my true intended victim, hence the savagery, and there appeared to be no victims after her. But here, I could work undisturbed. There were no patrolling policemen or drunks to catch me. I could finally achieve my best work. Mary's room was locked when police arrived. They smashed the door open with an axe handle. What they found haunted them to their dying days."

I strangled Mary until the fight left her body then I severed her carotid artery. Blood gushed out in a crimson flood. As she lay dying, I created my masterpiece. I hacked off the tissue around her neck, exposing the bone and nicking two vertebrae. After carving jagged cuts into her arms, I partially removed her nose, cheeks, eyebrows and ears. Even her mother wouldn't recognise her. Maybe that's why her family never attended her funeral.

I flayed the skin off her abdomen. Sliding the blade under the skin of her left thigh, I peeled it to the knee. Turning my attentions to her right thigh, I revealed her bone. Running footsteps alerted me to fleeing guests. I hoped they visited my shopfront. I was proud of my Jack the Ripper gift shop. The long bladed letter openers were my particular favourite. The crime scene map tea towels always sold well and the squeaky toy kidney in a box addressed to George Lusk with the infamous "From Hell" letter was a popular stocking filler at Christmas. Murders were less grisly with merchandise.

I sliced off Mary's breasts, placing one under her head and the other by her right foot. One woman sat against a wall, her pale face betraying her revulsion. I opened Mary's stomach and removed her organs. I arranged the uterus and kidneys together then positioned her liver between her feet and her intestines by her right side. After placing her spleen by her left side, I rose, laying the skin from her thighs and stomach on a table.

I removed her heart. "I was never caught. Some people say I fled to America, others say Mary Kelly quenched my bloodlust and my need to kill. Maybe I was hanged for another crime, the hangman oblivious to the fiend on his gallows. Maybe I ended up in an asylum." I adopted a creepy voice. "Maybe I still stalk Whitechapel's streets, preying on those who step into my shadow. Serial killers *can't* stop. Not unless they're caught or die. Once they've unleashed the demon inside them, it can't be shackled back in its cage.

"Some believe the letters sent to the police and newspapers were hoaxes, others believe they were genuine. Was I a doctor? A butcher? A student wishing to practise the surgery I'd read about in textbooks? Some random madman who travelled the country slaughtering women and displaying their organs like a macabre art exhibition? Nobody will ever truly know the mystery behind the world's most famous serial killer. Even though the streets that bore my bloody shame no longer exist, my memory will live for ever."

I raised Mary Kelly's heart. Blood dribbled down my hand. "You've been a great audience. I hope you enjoyed my unique journey into Whitechapel's vicious past. Remember, the next time you hear footsteps behind you, it may be me. As long as my legend lives, I can never die."

I bowed. My group applauded as I showed them out then slipped into the shadows, leaving the present alone with the past.

Whitechapel today was unrecognisable from the Whitechapel of 1888. A date forever etched into people's minds. Few people achieved Jack the Ripper's fame. Modern celebrities only sustained it for a few decades. A name remembered through centuries was truly special.

I prowled my tour's route, revisiting the women's deathbeds. A man walked through Catharine Eddowes, who guarded her crime scene, awaiting her fatal destiny. History always repeated itself. Street names had changed, buildings had been torn down and replaced but the ground remembered its past as it drank the spilled blood of the slain.

My footsteps echoed through the darkened streets. Laughter escaped the shadows. A man scurried past and ducked into the Ten Bells. A woman stumbled towards me moments later, adjusting her short sequinned skirt.

"All right, darling? Looking for a good time?" She eyed me. "You're that Jack the Ripper impersonator. You gonna take me into the alley and do bad things to me?"

One thing that had changed was prostitutes' clothing. Jack from 1888 would never have encountered sequins and thongs. Taking her hand, I led her down the alley that was once Dorset Street, her stilettos threatening to pitch her into the gutter. We stopped outside my warehouse. Although it was tempting to re-enact my favourite murder inside, it would be foolish.

"What's your name?" she asked.

"People call me Jack."

Her eyes widened as my fingers slipped around her neck, choking her. I slashed her throat before she could scream. Blood streaked her skin, staining her parka's fake fur as I reawakened the nightmare that had plagued Whitechapel. I carved open her stomach, removing her organs and displaying them artistically around her cooling body. Reliving the murders with my victims' ghosts merely eased the yearning. Only fresh blood could cure it. I dipped my gloved finger into her blood and wrote on the dirty warehouse wall:

JACK IS THE MAN
WHO WILL NOT BE BLAMED FOR NOTHING

No life haunted her glazed eyes. Only my reflection.

The true face of Jack the Ripper.

Madame X
Nicky Peacock

The sound of slapping flesh drew his attention. Groaning and straining against the wall of the alley before him, was a man thrusting against a shadowed figure. The doctor stopped his quick strides, and stared for a moment. His plump black leather bag was damp and heavy in his hand, and the bitter London night air was betraying his fast, hard breaths. He felt his own groin stir at the sight, until the shadow's head lolled towards him into the dim light, and he found himself caught in her glazed dead-eyed stare.

He shivered then awkwardly pushed past the couple. A few paces on, he stopped and checked the address on a crumpled piece of paper, then looked up at the tall thin building looming before him. He wondered how the best bordello in London was to be found in the grimiest part of Whitchapel, although the term "best" was probably subjective, and certainly not referring to its décor.

He reached out, he pulled at the door's big brass knocker, its clang momentarily masking the rhythmic grunting still emanating from nearby the alley. He waited; the cold starting to settle into his still bones. Nothing happened. He scratched his forehead beneath his top hat and waited. He slammed the knocker again, this time with more vigour. Pulling out his pocket watch, he checked the time. He had slipped away early from his mortuary post – if another victim turned up within the hour, his early absence would be discovered. Maybe London's notorious serial killer would take the night off tonight, that is, if he was still sweetly sated from his previous red deeds.

With a theatrical creaking, the door gently swung open and he was greeted by a woman dressed in dated fineries. A spindly black cigarette clung to the cracks in her scarlet lipstick, like a sick spider trying to escape her mouth. She looked him up and down and half smiled. "Come in, my dear, it's a cold night tonight." She ushered him into the house, then peered out down towards the alley beyond.

"I told you," she shouted, "Molly, don't you go plying your rat-bitten trade round my establishment!"

"Ah, please, Ms Lilly." Molly edged herself out from the still pumping patron so she could make eye contact. "It's dangerous out here, Jack's still on the loose."

"Not my problem. Now move your fat arse, before I call the police on ya!" Scowling, she slammed the door then turned to the doctor. "Well, darling boy, tell me your deepest desires and let's start making 'em come to life."

"I don't normally come to places like this." He pulled his hat down a little further and refused to meet her roving eyes.

"Of course you don't, darling," she replied with a red-painted smile that invaded the natural line of her cadaverous lips.

"I came because I wanted to examine this . . . woman that you have."

"Oh, you mean Madame X? You want to examine Madame X."

He pulled up his doctor's bag for her to check. She gave it a cursory glance.

"You don't want to look inside? See what I'm carrying?"

"For any one of my other girls I would. Just the other day a client managed to slash open the forearm of his concubine and remove part of her bone – a souvenir he'd said."

"Did you call the police?"

"No. I just charged him extra. Turned out she didn't really need that bit of bone to work."

He looked away, but found it hard to rest his eyes on anything in the near darkness; he scanned the hallway for an oil lamp.

She raised an eyebrow at his disgust. "It's not like I invited in Jack the Ripper." She laughed then moved to turn up the oil lamp beside them. It spluttered back to life, seemingly to run more on willpower than oil.

"Come with me, Doctor. Madame X is in demand and you are already eating into your hour."

He followed the woman through the overtly elaborate house. Covered in faded red velvet and soiled brass. On the surface it looked expensive and decadent, it was only when you examined the furniture and wall hangings further that you discovered the artwork were all poor fakes, and there were tiny mice bites dotted through the dirty velvet.

"I've had princes here you know," she whispered, her thinning gloved hand trailing the gold-plated banister of the staircase.

He tried to ignore her as best he could. Examine the woman and get out, get back to his new wife, Nancy, that was his plan, although the sway of the owner's lacy bustle in front of him made his analytical mind start to deviate somewhat . . .

"They all look like you, when they first come in." She turned to him. "They're disgusted the first time."

"First and last time, Ms . . ."

"Just call me Lilith," she replied.

She led him further into the bowels of the house; each corridor giving off a ripe smell of decay and sex. Each architectural artery of the building seemed painted in a more vivid scarlet hue. Moans escaped through the cracks beneath the doors. Some were born of ecstasy, some pain; he didn't linger long enough to identify which was which.

"We cater for all types here," Lilith said through a grin. She then stopped and pointed towards another thin narrow staircase. "Madame X is up there. Here." She handed him a big brass key. "Lock up when you're finished." She held her now-empty hand open and he shoved a few coins into it. She weighed them in her palm, then turned and was gone, the black taffeta and lace of her gown melting into the darkness.

Each step towards the door seemed to take him forever to make. He breathed deeply and instantly regretted it, the sudden smell of rot rammed up into his nostrils.

The door was small and narrow, yet somehow still imposing. He put his ear to it. There was only silence beyond.

"I doubt you'll hear anything, she's a quiet one – till someone else is in the room with her."

He turned to see a young woman dressed in a tight corset and garters. She was only partially dressed, yet held herself like a petticoat-gilded princess.

"I love my wife," he muttered. He had meant to finish the sentence, yet the words stuck to his mouth like rotten chewing tobacco.

"My, my, if I had a shilling for every time a man told me that. Actually, come to think of it, I really do have a shilling for every time." She laughed and began to walk up the small steps, so she could face him. "Madame X is quite a ride, what makes me think you need some quick instruction? I'm Rosy, and I got some time to kill, if you need the extra pair of hands?"

"Apologies, miss, I'm only here to examine her. I'm a doctor."

"You're young for a doctor," she whispered, then lifted his left hand, "newlywed too?" She traced her index finger over the thin gold ring.

"Nancy will be expecting me soon. I must get on . . ." He turned and opened the door. He briefly took in the scene before him, then felt his eyes widen. His bag dropped from his grip to the floor.

Rosy pushed past him and picked up his bag, "Ain't she something?"

Madame X was not what he had expected; no more than twenty-five years old. She lay naked and tied spreadeagled on an awkwardly shaped four-poster bed. Her skin was shiny and white like a new-born pearl spat into existence by a pained oyster. Her long auburn hair was a flood of blood-red curls and slight pink freckles were dusted over her cheeks and breasts. Her eyes were pure white with no irises, and she had a small well-trimmed thatch of slick red curls between her legs.

"Why is she tied?" The doctor drew in a breath and slowly eased himself towards Madame X, like he was approaching a growling stray dog.

"She gets a little excitable."

As he moved closer to the bed, he noticed Madame X had no finger-nails and her lips drooped over pale red toothless gums.

"What of her teeth and fingernails? Did they fall out?" He fumbled in his pockets for his notebook and began to write down what he saw.

"Naw, we took them out. Like I said, she gets a bit excited."

The doctor narrowed his eyes. "Where did she come from? Did you know her before she got sick?"

Rosy sauntered to the side of the bed then snaked an arm under the doctor's coat. He shook her off and moved away. "I met her the night Lilith brought her home. There was a rumour that *she* was there."

"There?"

"When ol' Jack killed Mary Kelly. Carved her up like a side of Sunday beef, he did. Madame X was her roommate. She was hiding under the bed the whole time . . . Some say she didn't even have red hair before that day, dyed by all her friend's blood as it dripped off the bed."

"She was there? Then she is in shock, if she saw what happened. She could identify the killer." The doctor rushed to the bed and started to pull at Madame X's eyelids. She groaned at the touch and raised her hips.

"She wants you, doctor. It's the only thing that keeps her happy."

"Happy? Is that why she's tied up and unable to escape this den of depravity?"

Rosy slowly sat on the edge of the bed, her lace-covered buttocks spreading slightly as she arched her back "One man's depravity is another's saving grace."

"What's her real name?"

"I told you, I don't know her."

"Can you hear me, Madame?" The doctor gently moved Madame X's head from side to side. He then checked her pulse, but found none. "Pass me my bag, please."

Rosy bent and picked up his bag. "Looks like the one the papers say Jack carries," she whispered.

"Inside is a stethoscope, hand it to me, please."

Nimbly, she moved her fingers about in the bag then produced the right equipment. She handed it to the doctor who quickly put it to work.

No sound found his ears.

"She has no pulse." He moved back, Madame X's strange eyes vaguely following him.

"You've still got thirty minutes of your hour left, doctor. Maybe you should use that time more productively." Rosy edged towards him, her heavy breasts pushing rolls of tight flesh over her straining corset.

The doctor took the bag from her; he rifled in it and found a thermometer. He gently held Madame X's head up, and slipped it into her mouth. She spat it out.

"Think you need to try another hole, doctor." Rosy laughed.

He squeezed his eyes shut, opened them then rocked Madame X to her side, as far as her bounds would allow. He stared at her peach-shaped ass, and felt a familiar heat warming his thighs.

"Like what you see?" Rosy got up and wedged herself behind him. She snaked her hands around his waist and felt for his hard cock and heavy balls. "I think you do . . ."

"Please, stop it," he whispered.

"You could easily move my hand."

But he didn't move her hand; instead, he imagined her hand travelling further to grasp his tingling erection. A small groan escaped his lips.

She took her hand back and pushed him out of her way. Taking the thermometer, Rosy put it in her mouth and tenderly sucked it; she then spread Madame X's buttocks with one hand and, with slow, sensual precision, eased the saliva-slick thermometer into the dark cavity. Lazily, she began to pump it in and out.

Another moan escaped the doctor, but he hid it with a cough.

"You know," Rosy said, without turning her attention away from her work, "you're wound kind of tight for a newlywed."

The doctor turned and checked his pocket watch.

"You're not alone," Rosy said, still easing the thermometer in and out, "I see it all the time. A virgin marries the woman of his dreams, then when it comes to the dirty deed, he's scared of defiling his beautiful pedestal-dwelling goddess."

The doctor was thoughtful for a moment, then tore his eyes from the bed and delved into the depths of his leather bag. He pulled out an empty syringe.

He turned back to find Madame X gently rocking her body back and forth on the thermometer. "Hold her still."

Rosy stopped and pulled the instrument out. She put her arm over Madame X's shoulders and let the doctor take a blood sample.

"That's odd," he whispered, pulling out the syringe. "I have blood, but there was none seeping from the puncture wound."

"You know, Doc, I've got a cure for what ails you." Rosy took the syringe from him and placed it carefully in his bag. "Let's improve your bedside manner. Madame X here is just itching to get you inside." She pulled at the doctor's coat, then his shirt. She unbuttoned his trousers and pulled at his briefs. Before he could even protest, he was naked and his cock was rigid and glistening in the lamplight.

Rosy pulled Madame X onto her back; she groaned a little in protest and a strange string of vowels escaped her lips.

"Let me educate you. So you can please that new wife of yours." Rosy bent and pushed her own knickers down, she stepped out of them and pressed herself against him. "Don't worry, we'll only cover the basics, just to nudge you on your way."

She glided her body down his, their flesh becoming warm and tight together; the juxtaposition of the hard material of the corset and her soft skin making him harder. She knelt before him and, with a grin, bent her smile to his shaft. She licked it up and down, her hands behind her back, she explored his salty skin. She twirled her tongue over the smooth soft skin and suckled on the head. He yelped in surprise, but did not move away. Instead, his hands instinctively found the back of her head to urge her for more.

Rosy pursed her lips and softly blew on his cooling cock. She then nibbled the length of him, nipping at his shaft and following the line of its bulging blue vein. Sighing, she then tasted each of his sex-laden balls, sucking in each one.

Madame X moaned and Rosy stopped her exploration.

The doctor put his hand to his forehead and mopped his brow with his sweatier palm; he mumbled some sort of prayer then bent to lift his discarded clothes.

"Your time's not up yet." Rosy kicked the clothes out of his reach and took his hand. She led him to the bed. "Just lay on top of her, nature will sort out the rest."

He blinked then did what she said. He gently laid his weight down on Madame X, who pulled at her tethered hands and bucked her groin to his. His cock nestled itself between her soft wet folds and he pushed himself up.

"Close your eyes," Rosy climbed onto his back and put her hands over his eyes. "Imagine your beloved beneath you."

He thought of Nancy, her long flaxen hair and narrow hips. Her clear grey eyes that were clouded mirrors of her innocence. "No, I can't . . ."

Rosy pushed her groin down on his ass plunging him into Madame X's sticky pussy.

The doctor groaned and stayed still.

Tutting, Rosy turned around so she was straddling his shoulders and facing his ass, she then plunged her tongue into his anus. Instinctively, he lifted to her and slightly out of the slick red-curled pussy below. Rosy pushed him back down then plunged her tongue inside him again, spreading his ass cheeks so she could allow her tongue better access. Continuing this rhythm, his body began to take over and the thrusts became more frequent and much more urgent. Rosy straddled his back and rode his every lift, now keeping her tongue in his hole; she grabbed his hips and punctuated his every plunge by digging her nails deeper into his fleshy buttocks.

Madame X pushed her pussy up to meet his slick stiff cock. The doctor looked down at her white-eyed stare. She snapped her gummy lips up at him, and even though his sensibilities recoiled, his body made him rut faster and harder against her white waxy skin.

Rosy, now content the doctor was beyond stopping, removed her tongue and began to slide it up his spine.

"Oh, God!" he groaned.

"God doesn't hear you here, Doctor," Rosy whispered, her breathy words cooling her saliva on his skin. Finishing her trail at the nape of his neck, she moved over and off the doctor's body, her slippery pussy lingering in front of his now contorting face.

She grabbed his head, pulling his eyes to meet hers, and watched as he released himself, just as Madame X strained upward and gummed at Rosy's swollen, unused lips.

A sweet second of elation shuddered through the doctor's body, then he realized the horror of what had just happened.

"Get off me, whore!" He pushed Rosy off the bed and scrambled off Madame X, who moaned and pulled her body up to keep contact with his skin.

"You'll thank me later, Doctor, you and your pretty new wife." Rosy stood up and smoothed down her crumpled corset.

Shaking his head, he fumbled into his clothes, grabbed his bag then ran for the stairs. The rest of the bordello was a blur of stained red velvet and the echo of fervent cries as he bolted into the dirty fog-engulfed streets of London. Blindly still, he pushed himself back down the now vacant alley. He could barely fit the breadth of his shoulders between the dirty walls. He angled himself so he could maintain his urgency, parts of the dirty bricks crumbling against his force. Work would have to wait, the dead have no urgency; he had to get home, now.

Upon reaching his house he knocked and found himself suddenly staring at Nancy. Those grey eyes scanning his dishevelled appearance. A small candle held in her hands illuminating her curvy form beneath her frilly white night gown.

"What happened? You look like hell and smell like a lavatory."

He looked down at his half-buttoned shirt and the horse faeces coating his boots.

"I was . . ."

Nancy raised an eyebrow.

"I just . . . I had a bad night. Let me in?"

She rolled her eyes and stepped aside to allow him through the door. "Get off all your clothes and take a bath, before you come to bed."

He watched her work her way down the corridor, the light she carried growing dimmer the further she went.

Slowly, he undressed. He bathed in cold water, scrubbing at his whole body till his skin looked like month-old meat. When he closed his eyes, he saw the milky whites of Madame X as he invaded her cool slithery folds. How had it happened? He had fallen to temptation so quickly, even though his intentions had been pure, but it had felt so good. Never before had he imagined something missing in his life, until he'd felt his spent cock slide from Madame X's pussy. Sandwiched between two whores, he'd finally experienced a climax to his ever-building feelings for Nancy. Something he'd wanted to do with her. They had all moaned together; he so longed to hear Nancy let out a song of trembling vowels as he rutted into her warm, moist womanhood.

After pulling on his robe, he grabbed his bag and strode into her darkened bedroom. Nancy lay curled beneath the covers. He slid behind her, cupping her body with his.

"You smell better at least, go to sleep."

"Nancy, let's not wait any longer," he whispered, nibbling at her ear.

She breathed out a sigh and turned to him. "OK, I love you, darling."

His lips reached for hers and they kissed in a familiar hesitant, gentle way. His cock, still cold from the bath, twitched to life. His hand snaked between her thighs so he could feel that same wetness from earlier. But there was nothing and she recoiled from him.

"Don't do that, your hand is cold." She wriggled to create a gap between their bodies.

He moved closer. "Lie back, Nancy, put your arms and legs out like a jumping jack."

"What are you talking about?" She giggled a little and he noticed that in the semi-light of the bedroom, she looked just like an angel.

The doctor shuffled off the bed and, when he stood, he found his cock heavily falling forward.

"What's wrong?" she asked, concern filling her eyes.

He loved her, he'd always wanted her. But Nancy was so perfect, she wasn't a whore who should spread herself beneath him and allow him to desecrate her in such a carnal manner.

"Please talk to me, darling," Nancy pleaded, edging towards him off the bed. They stared at one another for a moment, then Nancy tugged up her nightdress and pulled it off over her head to sit naked before him. "It's OK, please come back to bed."

His normal rationality slowly began to sink into a sea of lubricated skin and sweet release. He remembered the feel of Rosy's mouth and Madame X's pussy. He wanted that feeling again; he wanted Nancy to feel it too.

"Close your eyes," he whispered.

She did what he asked.

He crept back across the room and gathered Nancy's naked body in his arms. He moved her to the middle of the bed. Carefully, he placed her arms and legs out wide, kissing each limb as he did. He laid himself on top of her to let nature take its course, and it did. His velvety member sought out Nancy's now-wet opening. He pushed slowly inside. It was tighter and warmer than Madame X's and the sensation alone made him believe that he had been right to wait until now. They both gasped together and Nancy angled her head to kiss him. A sweet rhythm began to swell between them. She pulled her legs up to grip his hips, allowing him deeper access. A beautiful calm fell over the doctor as he claimed his wife's virginity, a calm swiftly broken when searing pain spread across his bottom lip. He recoiled, pulling himself out of her. He put his hand to his lip and it came back bloody. "You bit me!"

Nancy giggled then started to holler manically. Holding her naked sides, she fell off the bed. In the dark it was hard to see, so he leaned across to the table lamp and teased it to life. It was dim but better. He pulled her back on to the bed.

"Nancy," he whispered, as he pushed her down onto the rumpled sheets. He looked into her grey eyes and she smiled; she was more playful than even the whores from Whitechapel.

Using his hips, he edged her legs apart again. He then plunged his cock into her. She groaned, louder than he knew she was capable of, so he thrust harder, his balls slapping against her groin. Her nails raked his back, drawing blood, but the pain merged with the pleasure and he bent to kiss her. Her teeth grazed his swollen lip again so he pulled back. Her eyes were paler than he remembered, but that thought was soon forgotten as she writhed beneath him, drawing his unyielding cock even deeper into her. Her head lolled a little and, when he tried to kiss her again, she snapped at him, her teeth clattering together. He lifted her right leg and withdrew completely, then swivelled her on to her stomach. Her ass was white and plump. He once again manoeuvred himself back into her warm, wet, fleshy sleeve. She leaned against him and he began a steady rhythm, almost mirroring the sound he'd heard in the alley earlier that night. Nancy moaned and writhed as he leaned forward and caught her breasts. He rolled each of her rigid nipples beneath his fingers. He then felt a blissful spasm ride his body as he pumped inside her, one last time.

He fell on top of her, pinning her down. She still moaned. He withdrew and rolled her over. "Nancy?" Her eyes were milky white and her peaches and cream complexion was now just creamy. She reached towards him and tried to grab him. He jumped off the bed. "Nancy!"

She jumped up to stand on the bed, her legs at awkward angles and her head cocked to one side. She leaped off the bed and on to him, her mouth trying to find purchase on his skin.

"What are you doing?" he yelled and rolled out from under her. He scrambled out of the bedroom and, still naked, down the stairs and towards the front door. Nancy screamed and ran after him, grunting and reaching out to pull at his flesh.

As he got to the door, it suddenly burst open and the doctor was face to face with a man in black velvet cape, top hat and a bag similar to his own.

"Stand aside!" boomed the man.

The doctor lost his footing and fell back on to the floor. Nancy flung herself on top of him. She was foaming at the mouth and chopping like a rabid dog.

The caped man yanked Nancy's hair, pulling her off the doctor. He then brought a scalpel from out of his pocket and slit her throat. She fell to the ground clutching at the wound.

"Nancy!" screamed the doctor.

"Don't be a fool, man. She was infected."

"What?"

The man held out his hand and the doctor took it. "The whores' disease turns them into undead beasts. Spreads like a mother, if you don't catch it quick. Now where did she catch it from? She doesn't look the type to frequent whores' alley?"

"I . . ."

"Yes? Oh, and Christ, man, put on some damn clothes." He threw his cape in a swirling fashion across the doctor's naked shoulders.

"We went to the bordello down the street in Whitechapel. They have a girl there, called Madame X."

"God damn it, must I slit every whore's throat in Whitechapel?"

"I can show you." The doctor pulled the cloak about him.

"Good show, we need to get to this Madame X fast, stop the infection before it starts. If we don't, London could be overrun with the undead in a matter of days."

Nancy's blood had now oozed its way across the floor and started to pool at the doctor's feet. Her body was still writhing and for the first time that night he clearly knew what he should do.

"There was another whore, Rosy. She needs to die too."

"Good, we need to kill all those infected," said the man as he wiped Nancy's blood off his gloved hand and onto a silk hanky.

"OK, we'll kill them all." The doctor narrowed his eyes. "What's your name?"

"They call me Jack. Now hop to it, man, there's work to be done."

The Ripper is You
Alvaro Zinos-Amaro

———

Murder the First. [*Superficial charm. Absence of delusions or nervousness. Lack of remorse or shame.*]

In the chilly dark, M spots her coming out of the Frying Pan public house, 207 Brick Lane, at 1.07 a.m., observes her from a cautious distance in her telltale "jolly" black bonnet as she traipses down to Wilmott's, 18 Thrawl Street, and M is sure she's the target.

The woman is not the only tipsy "unfortunate" looking to sell her services for three pence – the price of a tall glass of gin – on this cold night of 31 August 1888. She's not even the only one with a black bonnet. Other similarly dressed prostitutes frequent these streets. In fact, M herself is wearing a bonnet and playing the part of a "fallen woman." Twice she has been approached by ruddy-cheeked men, first perplexed then angered by her retreat, which a part of her regrets. (How would it have felt? M wonders. But then, what would her observers have made of such unprofessionalism?) Yet despite the clusters of inebriated women, M is convinced that the woman in her sights is Mary Ann Nichols – Polly – whom M has studied in great detail. Everything about her fits the profile.

Polly is five feet three inches tall, forty-two years old but younger looking, her dark complexion marred by a small forehead scar and cratered by saucy brown eyes. Her forehead is covered by unkempt, dark-brown hair going grey, and her teeth – those still in place – are discoloring. Polly is clad in two petticoats, a reddish-brown ulster with seven large brass buttons and a brown linsey frock and white chest flannel. And, of course, completing the outfit is the black straw bonnet trimmed in black velvet, the bonnet Polly believes will turn her fate around.

So well has M familiarized herself with Polly that her first glimpse of her feels like seeing a long-lost friend (the admittedly rare breed of acquaintance one will shortly stab to death). Recognition sparks giddiness in M, a sense of wild possibility. Polly has no idea who M is, of course, and doesn't look at her at all, but M doesn't take it personally. The relationship may be entirely one-sided right now, but during the next two hours Polly will get to know M in the most intimate terms possible.

M walks from Wilmott's to grime-coated Whitechapel High Street, and there she hovers near the corner of Osborn Street. Polly appears at 2.22 a.m., right on schedule, and clearly the worse for wear. She's alone. Very drunk. Her friend Ellen Holland materializes from a nearby street, as though out of thin air. M is close enough to overhear them, but not so close that they notice or care. Ellen is on her way home. Polly asks her what she's been doing, and Ellen, somewhat evasively, tells her she went to see the effect of the fire that broke out in the morning at Shadwell Dry Dock. Perhaps, M speculates, the destruction visible in the fire's wake speaks to Ellen as a metaphor for her own life. Polly and Ellen speak for eight minutes, during which time Polly sneezes once and Ellen, after deep coughing, spits onto the street twice. M remembers reading that bronchial disease is the main cause of death in Whitechapel at this time, and she can feel the smog's wispy fingers reaching into her chest. Total realism. She suppresses the urge to cough. The clock at St Mary's, across the road, strikes at 2.30 a.m. M shivers at its sound, intrinsically beautiful and solemn, in this instance an inimitable chime of imminent doom. Then Ellen is on her way, and Polly staggers down Whitechapel Road, M discreetly tailing her. After several unproductive encounters with men in which she hears Polly cackle and slobber, M sees that they have wended their way to Buck's Row, which for much of its cobbled length is narrow and gloomy. They are now a short distance from Bethnal Green.

It's 3.17 a.m.

That gives M about twenty minutes.

Perfect.

M doesn't believe she'll need more than sixteen, but it's best not to be overconfident.

M smiles and approaches Polly. She calls out to her, interrupting whatever drink-fueled dream Polly is entertaining as she leans against the side of a dosshouse, clumsily holding up her petticoats to reveal thighs as pale and gibbous as the moon.

"'Ow d'yer know me name?" Polly enquires, swinging towards M.

"A creature as pretty as you? It would be difficult to forget." M steps closer now, only a foot away.

Polly straightens and leans forward. "You sound funny, like a Yank. 'Ave we met?"

"Not directly."

"Then 'ow?"

"Your fame precedes you," M says, turning towards the building, drawing Polly in sideways.

"My fame?"

M nods.

Polly laughs. "My fame!" she repeats. "Or my name?" She laughs again, a bright warm laugh that sputters into a cough.

"I can help you achieve that fame," M says. "I can help you take your place in the history books. Give me your hand."

Polly steps back tentatively, but M proffers her hand, and on her fingertips is her secret weapon, sparkling nail polish with an intricate pattern of golden dots framing the side of each nail.

"So pretty," Polly whispers. " N'vr seen anythin' like 'em!"

Polly takes M's hand, and M feels a surge at the contact, that brush of skin on skin, each of them clammy, but for different reasons.

"And look at my other one," M says, pulling Polly into the looming shadows, and, as Polly cocks her head to study the fast-moving hand, she sees too late the flash of a long, narrow knife's blade.

M is quick, efficient, in this as in every other aspect of her life. She cuts Polly's throat and blood gushes out. Polly's legs twitch and M catches her, smoothly, gracefully, like both of them have rehearsed this, which in a twisted way is true. Then M carries Polly forward a few steps, until they are right across the entrance to a stable yard – Mr Brown's stables.

This is to be Polly's final resting place.

M sets her down with practiced ease, careful not to inadvertently create bruises where none should be. As blood continues to pour from Polly's throat, she believes she can make out Polly trying to say something, but the raspy sound dies amidst the gargles.

M pauses a moment and looks into Polly's eyes. They stare at her in piercing mute pain, asking the one unanswered – unanswerable – question. "You want to know why it had to be you, don't you?" M says, caressing Polly's hair as though it were a doll's. "That's a mystery we're bound to share. I don't know why any more than you do. But it happened before, and now it's happening again."

Polly's breathing is rapid and irregular. She tries to struggle up, but M easily holds her down. "We're almost done," she says encouragingly. "You're doing splendidly. I couldn't have asked for anything more."

The light from the street lamp on the opposite end of the street is poor. No one has walked by. M feels confident. Polly's wide eyes now stare up at someplace beyond M. She lapses into unconsciousness. M cuts her neck again, causing fresh blood to spurt forth, making it look like an attempted decapitation. Then she rolls up Polly's petticoats – one grey wool, the other flannel – up to her waist and stabs her twice, methodically, cleanly, in the vagina. Blood sluices down her legs, warm and slick, drenching Polly's black ribbed woolen stockings, dripping from her men's side spring boots, off their cut uppers and down their steel-tipped heels.

M then slashes Polly's abdomen with rapid, forceful swings of her sharp knife.

Crouching, she observes her handiwork.

A few minor touches remain.

She changes the angle of Polly's body on the footway, so that Polly now lies lengthways along it, then delicately tilts Polly's head towards the east and places her cooling left hand in contact with the gate. M opens both of Polly's clenched fists and extends her legs apart.

This is how Polly is to be found.

Yes. Very good.

M is satisfied with her performance.

The *Daily Star* will sensationalize M's act with a feature story titled, "A REVOLTING MURDER/ANOTHER WOMAN FOUND HORRIBLY MUTILATED IN WHITECHAPEL/GHASTLY CRIMES BY A MANIAC," a story containing a long paragraph about "The Ghastliness Of This Cut," claiming that two deep slashes in the abdomen could only be "The Deed Of A Maniac." It might have been true the first time, but it is nonsense now. M is no maniac, and though trembling from the physical effort and the intensity of her attention to detail, she feels strong. In control. She has given it her all. Let them evaluate all they want. She's sure that she will be chosen over her rivals, and she's ready to claim her reward.

M stands up, takes a final look, and walks away, heading in the opposite direction of the cart driver who is to find Polly – not quite dead, but beyond salvation – on the filthy cobblestones in precisely three minutes, her immobile body looking from a distance like nothing more than a tarpaulin.

Murder the Second. [*Antisocial behavior without apparent compunction. Unresponsiveness in general interpersonal relations.*]

Pasty skin, plump round cheeks.

Dour expression.

Sunken eyes.

Unsmiling now as in the picture from 1869, the year of Annie and John Chapman's wedding.

It takes J a few minutes to convince himself it's her. She's put on weight since the photograph, and she stoops. Her attire is correct: black figured jacket down to her knees, a brown bodice, a black skirt and a pair of lace boots.

Then J notices the bruise over her right temple and it seals the deal. It's her.

He knows that two more bruises, each thumb-sized – sustained during Annie's recent fight with her friend Eliza Cooper – darken the fore part of the top of her chest. J is sure they're there, though he can't see them yet.

He'll see them soon enough.

J glances around. Crossingham's, 35 Dorset Street. Four small floors for one hundred and fourteen occupants (J has barely studied for this, but he has a sharp memory for numbers). Dark Annie is sharing a pint of beer with William Stevens, a painter. J is busy being nobody about two feet behind them. He pretends to be distracted, but nothing is lost on him. He finds a lot about this place and time surprising. That's the result of a choice, of course, to not immerse himself in extensive prep. A calculated risk. J prefers to operate by instinct. Live in the moment, not according to some baroque script. He'll succeed by demonstrating his ability to improvise.

The furniture is uncomfortable, half-rotted wood. Everything decrepit. Smells repulsive. A stench wafts up from the cellar. J imagines a pit full of shit, the only sanitation this place can afford. Windows are broken, covered with old rags. For some time J fixes his gaze on a patch of wall from which hangs soiled paper, and he watches strings of vermin disappear behind it.

Nobody seems to mind the squalor, the stench, the bugs. It's warm here. Fire in the grate. There's company, or at least warm bodies. Drinks. Laughter, some.

And pills. Annie has a little box of them. She's placed them on the table, and William is looking at her with an expression of dumb concern, worried but not wanting responsibility. She must be sick, J figures. Lungs, probably. (Then he remembers: The membranes of Annie's brain are also diseased, but that will only be discovered later.) It's her illness, more than alcohol consumption, that explains her awful appearance, her bloatedness, wheezing. She and the painter talk.

Drink. Talk. He reaches for the pillbox, she pulls it back. The box breaks. She fetches a scrap of envelope from the kitchen floor to mend it or to transfer its contents – J is close enough to see the red splotch of a postmark on it. He checks the time. 12.31 a.m. About four and a half hours left.

J licks his lips.

Annie leaves.

J moves from one stool to another. Legs itch; probably lice from a mattress fragment opposite the stool.

Ten minutes pass.

Now the painter takes off.

Another ten.

Ten more.

Ten again.

Four minutes later, Annie returns.

She looks around, frowning.

Then she heads out again.

J downs the rest of his beer and follows her.

The night smog and smell of nearby urine are a welcome relief from the previous miasma.

Dark Annie enters Little Paternoster Row, and that's when J realizes she's being followed by someone besides him. J ducks into a side street and allows the pursuer to pass him.

John Evans, he somehow recalls. Funny that, another J. Night watchman. Sent after Annie by Crossingham's deputy, Timothy Donovan. J rolls the names off his tongue. They sound fictional, like liquor brands. He's impressed himself by remembering them.

Then J sees Annie turn towards Christ Church. John Evans is momentarily distracted by someone else he knows. By the time he resumes his trek Annie is gone, and he desists.

J passes him.

He makes a sharp left the first chance he has on Church Street and his legs eat up the two blocks to Hanbury Street with appetite. A fornicating couple on the corner opposite the Ten Bells public house pay no heed to the rapid clip of his boots. He returns the favor, fixing his eyes straight ahead.

And now here he is, at Hanbury Street, and there she is.

Dark Annie, about to become so much darker.

She seems to be in a kind of daze, confused. She seems to want to say something to a man coming out of number twenty-nine, but the man has a hard time understanding her slurred speech. J keeps his distance. Annie heads off toward the corner. Good time for J to study number twenty-nine's backyard. His playground-to-be.

The building, located on the north side of the street, is three floors. It was once used by weavers – J's brain keeps tossing up nuggets – but steam power did away with the hand loom and the building was converted into dwellings. Grot now. Like the neighbors. Yellow paint peeling, like a venereal disease on skin. "Mrs A. Richardson, packing case-maker" in cadaverous white letters above a single front door.

He steps through the door.

Hallway ahead. Staircase on the left, on the right a passage twenty-five feet long, one foot wide. In he goes. Leads to a rear door.

Bare floorboards. Creaky, but he redistributes his weight, pulls himself in. Vigilance. Stealth. Undetected he advances.

Rear door is unlocked. Swings open into a yard.

The yard.

Two steps down into it.

One, two. Buckle my shoe.

Yard is small, fourteen square feet maybe. Patches of bare earth and uneven stone paving. Close wooden palings, about five and a half feet high, fencing it off on both sides from the adjoining yards. He peeks over. Next door is number twenty-seven. No one around – yet. They'll get a good view later.

In the far left-hand corner, opposite the back door, a woodshed. Convenient. Won't go to waste.

On the right there's a lavatory. Privy, these people call it. It will see some real private things tonight, J thinks.

He turns around. Fence is rotting but will hold.

No exits.

J rehearses his actions, pushing against an imaginary Annie, anticipating the confrontation. Mentally, prepares himself to be scratched, maybe bitten. Knife is in his jacket pocket. He looks inside the shed, calculating. Good. Room enough.

Then he sits on the upper of the two steps and imagines himself dissolving into his surroundings. Very still, inconspicuous, black clothes against blackness of night. Calm. Centered in on something profound, immaterial, an unknowable *something* at the core of him.

Time passes, maybe minutes, maybe a couple of hours. He's not anxious.

She'll come.

Rêverie singing in his brain, future as melody. Bright, wealthy vision beckoning to him. Glowing sing-song of recognition. Of the power he deserves and will be awarded. Respect. Applause. Hearty congratulations. He will rise, alone. Jealous co-workers, and above all the rivals in this final trial, will acknowledge his superiority, concede defeat. More applause. And then another sound, less pleasant – *her* voice. Pricking J's fantasy. A moment of resentful dejection on J's part and then he tenses, feels himself become wired with anticipation.

Quick; retreats into the darkness of the hallway; presses himself flat against the wall; holds his breath, feels his ribcage lock down, tight against the skin of his chest.

Dark Annie approaching.

Closer, closer.

He can hear her breath now, ragged, besotted, sick.

Closer.

In she comes.

Five steps and he swoops down and envelops her, his strong hand clamped down on her mouth, other arm on her neck, shoving her body forward while he jolts back her head, into the yard they stumble.

The struggle is ferocious, as he expected, but he settles into it like a runner at the outset of a marathon. Detached, relentless. She claws at him, she gyrates with improbable torque, bends under him, gets out the word, "No," and, amused, he pushes her hard. She reels back, trips on those two steps, but he catches her, it would be no fun if she were to careen back and split her skull, then what would be left for him to do?

The rest of it – once he pulls out the knife as he shoves her upright, grabs her by the chin and cuts into her neck, unsparingly – goes by in a kind of white daze and it seems to go on very long and much to his surprise it never makes him sick or even gag and by the end of it she is a mangled bloody mess.

There are moments during the cutting that he wonders what his friends will say. With profound relief, he remembers he has none, only people who think of him as a friend but have no idea what he really thinks of them.

Blood is on the back wall of the house, smeared on the wooden palings, rapidly clotting. J rests Annie's left arm on her left breast, right arm lying down on her right side, her head towards the house, feet towards the woodshed, leaves her skirts raised. Part of her small intestines, which have slipped from J's hands several times after excising them from her – an incredibly annoying incident, this slipping, that provokes his peevishness – he drops down and piles them up by her right side, above her right shoulder, connected to the still internal remnants. There are three, maybe four scratches, below her lower jaw, on her left side, running in the direction opposite the incisions in her throat. And bruising. Plenty of bruising from their little dance.

But this is merely his visible handiwork, and quite incomplete, for J is taking some souvenirs with him, as per his instructions.

They weigh heavy in his black, blood-moistened bag.

The sun, up soon. By 6 a.m. Annie's mutilated corpse will be found. Time for a discreet exit.

Hoisting the bag that contains Annie's uterus, a section of her vagina and bladder, J marches nimbly out of the courtyard and back into Hanbury Street, all of which will soon fade around him, to be replaced by a much more welcoming though no less toxic reality.

He's ready for it.

Murders the Third and Fourth. [*A disregard for laws and social mores. A disregard for the rights of others. Private life impersonal, trivial, and poorly integrated. A tendency to display violent behavior.*]

The mantra plays inside K's head with numbing regularity:

The ripper is you.

But the hammer's head of these words clanging against K's consciousness is not the clean, ringing chord of a victory blow; more like the dissonant tone of a hollow strike. Maybe, K wonders, it's because the words themselves are hollow.

Perhaps not only the words.

Maybe she's hollow too.

Don't doubt yourself! That's part of the test.

A test that is no longer an abstraction, no longer a complex set of theoretical parameters and protocols to review in a Spartan, air-conditioned room with bright lights and recessed sensor panels. The test is very much a reality now, one that has swirled into existence all around K at the prodding of one of her supervisor's commands, mystifying her for the first few instants with its overwhelming sensory detail. *Your body is not really here*, K reminds herself. Useless. Her body is a slave to her brain, and her brain believes that it is *here*, in the dwindling hours of Sunday the twenty-ninth of September, 1888, in Whitechapel, London, and so for all intents and purposes she *is* here.

Outcast London.

Also referred to as The Abyss.

K walks down Berner Street, takes a look at Dutfield's Yard, shivers, keeps going. Her next stop is Mitre Square, Aldgate, in the City of

London. When she reaches this destination another tremor passes through her, this time more severe.

These are the two places where K is supposed to do her work: the slaughter of Elizabeth Stride – born in Sweden with the name of Elisabeth Gustafsdotter and nicknamed Long Liz, Annie Fitzgerald, Epileptic Annie, Hippy Lip Annie and Mother Gum – and Catherine Eddowes, alias Kate Kelly or Kate Conway.

The infamous *double event*.

Stride's body is to be discovered shortly after 1 a.m., in a courtyard off Berner Street, at the rear gate leading to the International Working Men's Club. Her throat will be slashed, but there will be no further mutilations, implying an interruption in the killer's work. *Sadismus interruptus*, K thinks.

Eddowes, in her black straw bonnet trimmed with green and black velvet, is to die less than an hour later, on her way from the Bishopsgate police station to her lodging house on Flower and Dean Street. Eddowes will suffer. Her throat will be cut all the way to the bone; her face will be slashed; as will her pelvic area and stomach be pierced and gutted, intestines yanked out and cast over her right shoulder and left arm, uterus and left kidney gluttonously removed.

What was going through the Ripper's mind on that night? K asks herself. It's a relevant question because *his* mindset should be hers. She should be recreating his matrix of thought within her own mind.

The ripper is you.

The words are weaker than before. Not so much a hammer now as pelting rain.

Unfocused, K lets her legs decide where she'll go next. A short time later, she's in an area south of Whitechapel High Street that some call "Little Odessa," dominated, they claim, by Jewish "greeners." Wentworth Street, Old Montague Street, other places in the environs form a Jewish ghetto. To K's untrained eye these streets look, save for the Jewish writing on some of the signs, much like the rest. Elizabeth Stride's lodging-house deputy, Elizabeth Tanner, will claim that Stride often performed cleaning work for the Jews; Michael Kidney, a waterside laborer whom Stride met and began living with in 1885, will state that she could speak Yiddish. Everything K sees begins to remind her of Stride or Eddowes in one way or another.

The effect deepens. The more K journeys in the night, the more the places around her become a web of associations, a topography of icons and imprints of what she knows has happened and will happen again, this time at K's own hands. She drags herself back to Berner Street, circles the neighborhood a few times, touring Fairclough Street, Sander Street, Batty Street, Christian Street, on and on. She stops at the places where Stride will be sighted by William Marshall, James Brown, Israel Schwartz, Matthew Packer. She visits the Beehive public house, seeking out some ineluctable quality in the air, some predestination of violence. She finds only people going about their somewhat drunken business.

The ripper is you.

Now the words feel small enough, light enough, to fight against. *What if* this *is what they're looking for after all?* Not blind obedience but *thoughtful dissent.* Independent thinking.

K has the power to change the story. Every national daily and weekly reported the Ripper's heinous deeds in excruciating detail. The decadence spread, fanning morbid interest wherever the news traveled, all the way across Europe. One graphic image showed the victims lying on their backs, divided by a torn paper edge that simulated the effect of a knife penetrating the human body. But K can choose to undo all this, at least in this world. Let them live. Let them shuffle through this recreation of their arduous, violent, disease-infested lives for as long as she's here.

K sits at the Nelson Beer House.

Is that Stride who just walked by?

Yes.

Very well.

K decides. She will do as she pleases.

And she pleases to do nothing.

Stride continues on her merry route.

Are approbatory notes hastily being made, K wonders a few moments later, *recommendations and decisions whispered in the observation center?* She is showing them that she is capable of going her own way, after all.

And that's why she believes they'll promote her and not one of her lame, sir-yes-sir rivals.

Murder the Fifth. [*Pathological egocentricity and inability to love. General poverty in major affective reactions.*]

A solitary gas lamp, mounted on the wall opposite Mary Jane Kelly's room, lights Miller's Court behind the house at twenty-six Dorset Street. C stands there under its dim glow catching her breath, visualizing herself doing what she needs to do in the next few minutes. Not easy. Nope. But then, nothing worth doing ever is.

On the way here, C has darted past two pubs on Dorset Street: on the Commercial Street end she's jogged past the Britannia, a beer house in which Annie Chapman, a victim assigned to one of M's rivals, was drinking on the night of her death, and in the middle of the street C has hurried by the ancient Blue Coat Boy. At the other end is the Horn of Plenty, which she would like to have visited, but no time. C has also passed Thomas Bowyer's home at number thirty-seven and John McCarthy's shop at number twenty-seven, places of interest to her but which again must remain unexplored. Her entry into this Whitechapel "rookerie" on 9 November 1888, has apparently been planned to measure her stress tolerance in a way she wasn't warned about. Twenty-four year-old Mary Jane Kelly dies inside her dingy bedroom at 3.42 a.m., and C found herself here at 3.32 a.m., barely giving her enough time to figure out her exact location and get to the appropriate place. *Breathe*, C tells herself. *In and out. You're here now. You're ready. In. Out.*

The whole situation is messed up, though, no matter how she looks at it. The plan called for her to be inside the lodging hours ago, to secure an invitation from Kelly into her room. Now C is going to have to force her way in. She sighs and pries the door to thirteen Miller's Court open with one of her pocket tools.

How can she be expected to conduct the symphony of bodily destruction her notes call for with what little time remains? C hovers outside Kelly's room, angry, frustrated. Her heart flutters in a weird arrhythmia. To remove Kelly's viscera and heart, to cut away the flesh from her thighs, to thoroughly flay her, attempt a decapitation, slice off both of her breasts, lop off her nose and arrange her abdominal organs on the bedside table, these aren't tasks C can rush! They require balance, planning, a fine attunement of inner and outer forces.

C feels light-headed.

You've prepared.

Get on with it.

Breathe.

In and out.

But she doesn't feel prepared.

She reaches out to touch the door handle, heart in overdrive—

And then everything goes black.

The chairman glances in quick succession at each of the four candidates sitting at the conference room table, ensuring he has their undivided attention. He needn't have bothered. An asteroid could be laying waste to the beautiful skyscrapers visible through the room's tinted window and none of the candidates would experience the slightest distraction.

The chairman, smiling with his gray eyes, his short gray hair perfectly parted to one side, is a study in manicured composure, practiced affability. His beige suit jacket is plain except for a single gold pin adorning the right lapel, a one-of-a-kind corporate emblem and memento of his years of tireless service.

"You have all done extraordinarily well," the chairman begins, and though the words may be rehearsed, he sounds genuinely thrilled when he speaks them. That same thrill passes through the candidates now, an invisible electric eel darting from person to person. "Only once before in my career – some fifty years ago now – have I seen this level of commitment and dedication from job applicants." He doesn't bother to describe the occasion he's alluding to, which some of the candidates automatically assume was the selection process that led to the chairman himself being hired into the company. "Only one of you is being selected for the role of Mergers and Acquisitions Executive Officer, but all of you have demonstrated remarkable tenacity, and those of you not chosen can still look forward to plenty of other exciting opportunities within our senior leadership team."

Now the chairman turns to his right and channels his full attention on Ciara. "You faced perhaps the most challenging version of the assessment, and you acquitted yourself impressively," the chairman says. Then he pauses, a cataclysmic interruption of reality for Ciara. "Unfortunately, you were competitively outperformed." The world has resumed but Ciara no longer feels like she's a part of it. "My lead interview specialists will walk you through the technical details of your stress test and your results. You should be proud. I look forward to our next interaction."

That's it. Ciara's dismissal. Two months of the most grueling, nerve-shattering interviewing she's ever experienced have come to a screeching halt with the curt nod of a slim man in his sixties, old enough to be her father, whose attention is already fixed on the next candidate.

"One question if I may," Ciara asks, rising, pale.

The chairman raises an eyebrow.

"My simulation ended before I had a chance to complete the mission," she says. "I was wondering—"

"We anticipated your system might react poorly to what was forthcoming."

"But . . . I wasn't given the chance to show that . . . I mean . . ." She stops herself, blushing.

"Thank you," the chairman says in a soft voice.

She turns around and leaves the conference room.

The chairman turns to his left. "Karam, your results indicate excellent originality of thought. However, my interview leads deemed that you strayed too far outside the required parameters. I'm sure we'll be running into each other again soon."

The chairman never *runs into* anyone, of course, save those whose paths he has carefully orchestrated to cross. "Thank you for the opportunity," Karam says, her voice steady. She bows once, rises, and leaves.

"That leaves only you two, Myriam and Jacob. You represent the cream of the crop. The absolute elite. I'm confident that either of you could fully handle the responsibilities of the imminent takeover of Visio Sigma, which will represent this company's largest acquisition yet."

Myriam nods, while Jacob is still. They both know the takeover will be a hostile one. Their selection process has been expertly designed to determine that they have the right skills for such a demanding – yet delicate – situation.

For a moment the chairman says nothing further, and the candidates begin to wonder if perhaps they are both, somehow, being chosen for the role.

But no. It is another little test.

Myriam has leaned forward several millimeters, unable to contain her curiosity. Jacob hasn't moved. The winner is implicit in these responses.

"Myriam," the chairman says, and her world unravels around her at the mention of the single, calmly spoken word, a word that should be familiar and evocative of *her* but instead sounds like three foreign syllables indecipherably strung together. The bloodrush in her ears is so intense during the next few seconds she can barely make out the chairman's words. "Your absence of delusions or nervousness during the test were unparalleled. Your lack of remorse or shame were equally outstanding. However, based on the level of your preparation before the evaluation, we were hoping you'd achieve even higher scores. My tech staff will walk you through the details. Thank you so much for your interest in this position, and I look forward to tracking your progress through our senior team."

Myriam stands up, face expressionless, and walks away.

"Jacob Tesija, congratulations. I hereby formally offer you the position of Mergers and Acquisitions Executive Officer."

The chairman stands and extends his hand. Jacob likewise stands and shakes it. "I accept," he says, as they both sit back down.

The chairman appears contemplative for an instant, then stares directly into Jacob's black eyes. "I realize this psychometric evaluation was extremely taxing, and is likely the most, ah, *unique* ocular-rift simulation you'll ever experience in a professional environment. But we needed to be sure that we had the right person for the job. Someone whose unwavering focus and ability to single-mindedly execute our vision was never in question. You possess every skill we've been looking for. I'm positive you'll manage this twenty-seven-billion-dollar takeover flawlessly. I'm not exaggerating when I say that we're lucky to have you."

Jacob allows himself a smile. Something he has been holding back comes to him then: the experience of cutting into Dark Annie's neck, and everything that followed that initial slice. In the test he passed through the carnage in a strange white daze, a denial, himself but not himself, observer and participant but neither. Now that changes. His actions buffet and penetrate him. Jacob relives every moment in graphic detail, and this time he is not disconnected, not depersonalized in the slightest. This is him, and this is what he's done. The sensations wash over his body like baptismal waters. He can hardly contain the ecstasy of what it signifies about his abilities, his potential.

Unchained – that's what he is.

Liberated.

Unlimited.

"I'm ready," Jacob says.

Trespass
Sally Spedding

Klodawa. Congress Poland. Saturday, 22 November 1879, 4 p.m.

Thirty-four-year-old Aniela Bielski trudged towards her lodgings in Dziadowice's Jewish quarter with not only the weight of her two full shopping baskets slowing her down, but also her thoughts. She'd just caught sight of two of her pupils from the Immanuel School dragging a scraggy-looking sheep and a sack of hay away from the early morning market. The last people she wanted to see after a week disrupted by bad weather and a dead starling – seemingly intact – left on her class register during yesterday morning's geography lesson.

For a moment, she was tempted to intervene. Persuade the boys to return the protesting creature to its seller, because, to her knowledge, neither had a garden or even a yard in which to keep it. However, instinct told her to walk on by, keeping her back to the pair. One endlessly chattering, the other as usual, silent.

Number three, Aleja Ogrod couldn't come soon enough, and, once she'd let herself in and climbed to the first floor where her bare front window overlooked the street, she was unnerved to see the two schoolboys standing outside, staring upwards. The poor sheep was still protesting. Its tongue hanging from its mouth while from the other end, dark green liquid dripped onto the trampled snow. Whether a ewe or a ram, she couldn't tell, what with that long tail and straggling fleece. Besides, not all rams had horns.

Aniela ducked sideways, leaving a noticeable patch of condensation on the glass, yet still able to see the silent one raise his hand and wave his white, tapering fingers in what a stranger might assume was a friendly gesture. But not her. She'd known both boys for two years, when she'd been an emergency replacement for an unwell Piotr Wolmark who'd never got better. His throat and lungs damaged by daily wear and tear on those youngsters stunted by their families' Hasidic faith, with few prospects of work in such a one-eyed town. Why, she lubricated her own throat every evening with several small glasses of Scheidam's Aromatic Shnapps. Also to keep the stinging cold at bay.

One day, she told herself while unloading her potatoes, cabbage and other items on to the kitchen table, she'd divorce Chaim Bielsky, become a Gentile and leave for Canada, where immigrants were in short supply. There, she'd pursue another career – this time in law – and become an advocate for orphaned children. At school, these were the boys she was most drawn towards to help and, every year, the local King David Charity would deliver their latest crop of twelve-year-olds, often with only the clothes they stood up in.

As she rinsed the potatoes in the chipped stone sink under a dribble of water from the single tap, she observed the progress of both four-teen-year-olds and their distressed sheep until they turned into the Ogrod Itshak Mayer – a park used by vagrants and drifters even in winter – and disappeared from view. She also noticed the sky turn yellow and, by the time her potatoes were dry, a fresh snowfall had begun.

Eight o'clock, and steam from the vegetable soup cooking on the small, iron stove did little to keep a luminous moon from filling her main living area, casting her few belongings in a queasy glow. She'd repeat-edly written to her landlord in Poznan for a nice thick curtain, but never received a reply. Only when the one chimney had become blocked, causing noxious fumes to fill the house, did he finally send someone round.

With her simple meal over, and her second glass of schnapps inside her, Aniela added a log to the stove, cleared the wooden table and fetched her hairbrush from what could hardly be called a bedroom. More a cupboard with space only for a narrow bed and a shelf above it for clothes and items she couldn't keep in the freezing shared lavatory and basin outside the back door.

The hairbrushing ritual was a necessary end to a gruelling week, as if each gentle tug of the bristles represented a problem expunged. Free of its tortoisehell combs, her thick, straight mane fell beyond her shoulders. Its unusual colour ranged from corn to barley depending upon the light. Her shield, untouched by any hairdresser, except on the eve of her wedding eight years ago, when her mother – now dead – had insisted on it.

Ouch.

The brush stalled behind her left ear where a snowball had landed during morning break. The silent perpetrator smiling apologies, waving those same tapering fingers as if she was his friend and he'd made a silly mistake. The bristles held fast until she twisted the brush this way and that to free them and their strange harvest. A densely tangled ball of hairs which, when placed on the table, seemed alive. To move of its own accord, unlike that wretched starling, with its scaly legs stuck up in the air. Its eyes squeezed shut.

Had the silent one been responsible? Or Hersz, his garrulous friend, who even though he'd been adopted last December, still wore dead men's shoes? Or any other of the pupils who passed through her classroom three times a week? While placing the knot of hair in her silver-plated Memory Box, she resolved to speak to Dr Korek, the head teacher, about the incident to ensure it wasn't repeated. As for the bird, she'd immediately carried it outside her schoolroom and buried it amongst summer's black, wilted remains.

With her brush clean and hair loosely piled on top of her head in readiness for bed, Aniela decided to spend the intervening minutes checking through copies of her current pupils' records inherited on 1 October 1877.

It wasn't fear of paperwork that had kept their leather folder with its gold star on the cover unopened. Rather, until Thursday afternoon, the need to disturb them hadn't yet arisen.

The leather was freckled by damp. Its clasps rusted where once they'd sparkled and, inside, the smell that escaped wasn't of paper and ink, but as if a grave had been disturbed.

Having regained her composure, Aniela extracted all the handwritten sheets and rearranged them in alphabetical order. Clearly her predecessor hadn't felt such things mattered, but orderliness and cleanliness had been instilled in her as being next to godliness. Her mother again, while supervising that taming of her only child's wild hair.

Soon, the two sheets she wanted lay in front of her.

HERSZ EILENBERG believed to be 12 years 5 months. No birth certificate. Origins unknown. King David Charity, Klodawa, from June 10th 1865–October 1st 1877. Circumcised July 1865. Adopted by Sarah and Benjamin Eilenberg on December 20th 1878. Address; 52, Aleja Benesh, Klodawa. Both weavers at the Kletzki factory. No other children. A talkative, friendly boy. Nature-lover, with an interest in chess and an innate ability in Mathematics. A tendency to be easily led has been noted. PW.

ARON MORDKE KOZMINSKI aged 12 years 2 months. Born Klodawa. Birth Certificate signed and dated September 11th 1865. Circumcised shortly after birth. Not entirely successfully. Father, Abraham, a tailor; mother, Golda, housewife. Address; 12, Droga Mojzesz Isserles, Klodawa. Five older siblings, one of whom, Iciek Szyme Kozminski studied here from October 1862–1867. Aron is a highly strung, inarticulate boy, yet on occasions displaying a certain covert rebelliousness which has been noted and will be acted upon if it breaches our Code of Conduct. However, he may yet surprise us all. PW.

How could she disagree with Piotr Wolmark's brief comments? She couldn't, and this gave her further reason to see Dr Korek when he was next available. She also wondered who'd paid for that sheep. It wasn't a lamb, after all, and if a ewe, could prove valuable to breed from. Neither boy came from well-to-do families, and she knew this query would continue to puzzle her until she found out.

The moon had gone, leaving an icy darkness, sucking the drab dwellings opposite into invisibility where not a single lamp glowed. Aniela shivered as she tidied away the files, leaving those particular two on top of the others. Once the clasps were clicked shut, she poured herself another drink and checked there was enough wood in the stove to last until morning. She also wondered where that sheep had ended up, and what the dispossessed were doing for warmth in that inhospitable park. How, compared to them, she was fortunate to have rooms, albeit sharing the house with two other single men. One a miner, the other a cook. Keeping themselves to themselves.

She rinsed out her glass and, for a few moments, warmed her nightdress by the stove's minimal heat, debating whether to visit the inconvenient lavatory or use her late father's chamber pot. An oriental affair harbouring ingrained stains and decorated with snarling dragons. The dragons won, because that earlier encounter with the schoolboys had unnerved her. And who was to say the one with those odd fingers wouldn't be hanging around, waiting for her? Throwing more snowballs. Smiling apologies as if they were friends?

No.

She used the chamber pot, rinsed it out and buttoned up her nightdress to her chin, aware that it needed a wash, but not when it would take a week to dry. She then pulled back the thick quilt on her bed and patted her piled-up hair to check it was secure. As she did so, she stopped without quite knowing why, until a tiny recollection eked into her tiredness, hovering like a persistent mote in the eye . . .

On Thursday afternoon, once her geography lesson had ended and her class departed, she'd suddenly sensed she wasn't alone. Yes, it was rumoured that the unquiet spirit of thirteen-year-old Henryk Bogen who'd hanged himself in that very room in June, still lingered, but she'd neither seen nor heard it. On the contrary, the four walls she'd covered with maps of faraway cities and landscapes made her classroom the least bleak of all.

Something or someone was touching her hair, which, for school, was always restrained in a neat French pleat. She'd spun round and, in that split second, had seen the dark space of her store cupboard behind her and a familiar hand swiftly withdrawn.

"Who's there?" she'd called out, but only the shuffle of feet and the closing of its opposite door replied.

Shabbat, 23 November, 10 a.m.

Aniela slept later than usual, after a night of turmoil in which lines of screaming chickens and sheep despatched by swift Shechita knives, left a widening lake of blood on what had resembled her main room's floor.

Not only that, but her nightdress had twisted round her body as if she'd been a mere spindle, while the warm quilt had long slid from sight. Not a good start to the day in which she'd planned a visit to the synagogue for its Minyan service followed by a train ride to Poznan to see her cousin with ideas for Hanukkah.

Instead, having again used the chamber pot then the sink for a wash, she dressed in her warmest clothes, including a hand-knitted hat that covered her ears, and thicker gloves than yesterday to protect her erratic circulation. In one coat pocket lay a small notebook and pencil. In the other, her purse. As she let herself out of number three and locked the door behind her, a hollow feeling suddenly took hold. After that hair-touching incident on Thursday afternoon, hadn't the key to her store cupboard's two doors been missing from the lock?

Another item for discussion with Dr Korek. A bachelor whose quarters above the Science department boasted the latest in modern comforts. Also, it was said, a fine collection of cigars.

*   *   *

A few kicks from her boot soon covered the sheep's dark green legacy with snow, and she began tracking the threesome's crisply defined prints. By the time she'd reached the park, however, these had become indistinct, mingling with others and, in places, appeared to have been deliberately erased.

Now what?

Her shadow preceded her as she made her way towards what was normally a small boating lake where several youngsters were attempting to cross its icy skin. Her question to the nearest child – a girl in a bright orange hat – brought a laugh of disbelief. This attracted another who joined in, before shouting, "Those boys must be mad! No one touches sheep from that market. They're unclean. Full of worms." She then imitated being sick.

Nevertheless, Aniela thanked them and moved away, studying the ground for even the smallest strand of hay and any further droppings. So preoccupied was she, that she failed to notice a tall, caped figure approaching from behind.

"Are you looking for something?" The accent too gutteral for a Russian. "Can I help?"

She looked up to see a clean-shaven man of around her age, with remarkably blue eyes. The smell of sweat and spirits obvious. A rough sleeper, she decided. But not from the area. Since her devoutly religious husband had abandoned her for a woman young enough to be his daughter, she'd become mistrustful of men. Particularly Orthodox believers with full beards and the long *peyot*. Most of the teaching staff, in fact. But this man was different. Interestingly so. "Maybe," she replied, before adding why she was there, careful not to give any names.

"I did notice something," he said finally, blowing on his bare hands. "But I was also trying to light a small fire, and had to watch the first flame carefully."

"Please," Aniela urged, feeling sorry for him, but needing to move things on. "Even the smallest detail might be useful."

"I think they went that way." He pointed at a plantation of bare sycamores. "Towards the river. The sheep was making a terrible din . . ."

Having thanked him, she pulled her purse from her pocket to give him the few *glotych* that were left. "You look frozen," she added. "I'm sorry I can't give any more."

With ice-cold fingers he scooped the coins from her open hand, and seemed about to cry. "You're an angel, do you know that?" And then, before she'd had time to deny it, or return the purse to her pocket, he'd set off with a rangy stride back towards Dziadowice. A German, of that she was suddenly sure.

Having missed her usual breakfast of bread and honey, Aniela's stomach grumbled loudly enough to be heard. Worse, as she forced herself through deeper snow towards those trees, her boots began to let in water. Her toes to solidify.

Soon, only the hint of two sets of tracks remained. One human, one definitely not. So, if that stranger *had* been right and seen two boys, where had the other one gone?

Despite her winter clothes, Aniela shivered again, seeing the half-frozen Rgilewka River barely distinguishable from its snowy banks. Here lay the half-buried remains of fishing trips and autumn picnics. A discarded scarf blown into the trees, and beyond, farmland of the lower plain dotted with black barns like tombstones.

Not a trace of anything useful to her search, save for a small, rust-coloured stain on the snow near her feet. Then another further on, and another until they became bigger, more intense and continous leading into a grove formed by a semicircle of those same trees. Their lower branches scraped the ground. Some freshly snapped as if they'd been obstacles to something dragged more deeply out of sight of the riverbank.

My God.

Aniela stared as if her latest dream had become horribly real. Stared and stared until last night's potato soup crept up her throat and into her mouth. She groaned, trembling as nature took its lurching course, then ran on numb legs back along the bank to the relative normality of the park.

Her pace was still unsteady on her frozen toes as she reached the front door of fifty-two, Aleja Benesh. A neat, narrow house at the end of a row behind the recently rebuilt synagogue. On one side it was joined to an identical property. On the other, a covered shack in a fenced-off area selling old sewing machines and the like. As she waited for someone to answer her impatient knock, the sun passed behind an iron-grey cloud, instantly adding to the chill.

"Come on. Come on," she muttered to herself, until at last hearing Hersz Eilenberg's distinctive voice.

"If it's Mama and Papa you want, they're at work," he called out.

"It's me, Pani Bielski." Her married surname still sounded wrong.

Silence.

Was he suddenly scared? And then she noticed the front room's curtains parting to reveal a fearful face before being snatched shut. Aniela thought that would be the end of it, but no. Seconds later and inch by inch, the door opened.

"Yes?" said the orphan, looking her up and down. A tremble to his lower lip.

"May I come in, just for a few moments?" The trace of sick was still on her breath and she swallowed twice. Meanwhile, panic had swept across Hersz's fleshed-out features. So different to those of his best friend.

"Er . . ." He glanced behind him as though he wasn't alone after all. "No, I've been told not to. Sorry. What's it about?"

Aniela let a young family pass by before beginning her account of finding the dismembered ewe, still tethered. How she'd recognised those thin legs, the thick, dirty fleece beneath what remained of its belly. How her throat had also been slit and several internal organs appeared missing. The sheer amount of blood. The pain in its dead eyes.

"Could it have been a fox?" He gasped. "Or a wolf?"

"I hardly think a wolf or other predator was responsible for those injuries." ⁻

The orphan had paled even more. A hand flew over his mouth and stayed there as she asked, "So was it you who took her from the park to the river?"

"No! Him, him," he burbled from behind his palm. "Said he knew somewhere nice for the time being. I agreed because I was already late home for synagogue. And, if I'm ever late, well, it's either the boot or the stick . . ."

"You know it's a sin to lie?" She'd met his adoptive parents. The kindest of people, with only his welfare at heart. "And I don't really want to involve Dr Korek at this stage. Or the police, do I?"

He removed his hand from his mouth and lowered his head. As far as she could tell, there wasn't the tiniest speck of blood on him anywhere. Even though his clothes were the same as yesterday's.

"My parents have never hit me. I shouldn't have said that."

Just then, an elderly neighbour appeared, wielding his broom, and began vigorously pushing snow in her direction. But she mustn't be distracted. "Hersz, listen to me," she whispered. "I saw you *both* with that sheep. And whoever sold her also knows. So, what's the rest of the story?"

"Near the end of the park, he told me to leave him and the sheep alone. Or else."

"Aron?"

Just to make sure.

"Yes."

"Or else what?"

"He didn't say." Hersz sniffed. "Didn't need to."

"And who'd paid for the poor creature?"

Another silence. Aniela waited, aware of her cold, wet feet. The neighbour finally went indoors.

"*I* did. Two roubles. I get money for clearing up round the weaving machines after school."

"I see."

He began to sob. Loudly, expressively. His shoulders heaving up and down. Aniela reached out and steadied the lad, promising not to breathe a word to anyone of her visit or about the sheep, but that if he was threatened again, she'd step in. That seemed to calm him, but then he unexpectedly shut the door, denying her the chance to also ask about the dead starling and her store cupboard's missing key.

Desperate for something with which to sweeten her mouth, she left number fifty-two and headed towards the westernmost end of the Jewish quarter, mentally preparing herself to face a tribe of Kozminskis whose mother in particular was known for plain speaking and lack of sentimentality. As Aniela approached the alleyway leading to a terrace of brick-built dwellings hosting enormous chimneys and small upper balconies, she couldn't ignore the Church of the Assumption of the Blessed Virgin Mary looming up beyond. Nevertheless, she also kept her eyes open for the slightest clue that the house she wanted might be occupied.

There was none. Even its front step had been swept clean of snow, and those footprints scattered nearby could have been anybody's. No smoke from the chimney either. No movement at all, just a silent stillness broken only by the odd passer-by and the church's sudden, bone-rattling peal of midday bells. Each reminding her how controlling most religions were, yet actually protecting no one. How she'd denounce it all once in Canada. For now, however, she must be seen to be a good Jew – although a frowned-upon separated one – and attend the afternoon's service at four o'clock incase Dr Korek's spies were out hunting.

ABRAM JOZEF KOZMINSKI TAILOR.
ALL SIZES. ALL OCCASIONS
PROMPT ATTENTION.

The notice, set in front of a black blind filling the front window, confirmed this to be the correct address. But what now? Should she use the shapely brass door knocker or wait around? And, with each empty second that passed, her resolve began to fade.

Just as she was about to abandon her mission, a solid tap connected with her shoulder, followed by the distinct smell of mint. She half turned to see Hersz Eilenberg's best friend, smartly dressed from top to toe with the obligatory *Kippot* perched on his crown of smooth, black hair. His high cheekbones glowed pink and a sly smile revealed a clear sweet caught between his lips.

"Pani Bielski, good morning." He ejected the sweet into his bare palm, then into his coat pocket. "I'd have carried your baskets yesterday morning if I could. I'm sorry."

"That's kind of you, Aron, but you and Hersz seemed to have your hands full."

An intense frown instantly aged him. "I thought that's why you were here. To complain."

This unfathomable boy who rarely spoke unless prompted, had derailed what she'd planned to say. Whether deliberately or not, was hard to tell.

"Why would I do that?"

He stared at her hair that had escaped her hat. "Because I don't think you like me."

She blinked. "Of course I do." Yet it sounded unconvincing.

Suddenly, he mimicked the sheep's loud baa, making her start.

"Was that good?" he asked.

"Excellent."

His smile hid his teeth. "I insisted to Hersz that you see her. I know you like animals."

"Did you also know she was a ewe?"

"Was?" He frowned again.

"Is."

"Of course. I chose her."

"Well, she seemed to have other ideas about leaving the market." Aniela kept her tone light. Her expression friendly. "I hope she's all right."

He glanced around as if expecting someone else to arrive, then said, "She is. But it was all Hersz's idea to buy her. He had the money, even to pay for a shed or some grazing. He thought she could mate with a ram, and then . . ."

"Lambs?"

He nodded. "An economic project, he said. Everyone eats lamb." His pointed tongue slid across his top lip.

"But *you* took her to the river?"

His thick, black eyebrows rose. "Did *he* say that?"

"I'm just guessing, because you seem quite involved with her. *Engaged* is the word . . ."

"Yes, I am," he said with pride. "And tomorrow after school, I'll find her somewhere permanent to live. She has enough hay to last today, because after dinner, I've to visit my aunt and uncle. "

"Good," said Aniela, finding it harder than ever to hide her terrible secret. "As long as she's looked after." Saying that made her feel sick all over again, and he surely must have recognised something different in her voice.

Just then, they were joined by a striking young woman with long, equally dark hair and the same, almost feline, features as he. Their spontaneously fierce embrace lasted long enough for Aniela to realise that whoever this person was, she was very welcome indeed.

"Matilda," he announced once they'd separated. "My next-to-youngest sister. And this," he added, pointing to Aniela, "is my geography teacher from school."

Nameless, she noticed, but nevertheless, she politely shook the newcomer's hand, then made her excuses to leave.

Having walked almost to the end of the alleyway, she turned to see his fingers lingering on that curly mass of hair tumbling from beneath his sister's stylish felt hat.

At the end of the synagogue service during which Aniela had dwelt more on the grisly scene at the riverbank than any holy words from the

Torah, she hastened towards the exit, keen to escape the stifling piety. On approaching the wide-open door, she noticed Dr Korek already outside. He was speaking to a stout, middle-aged couple whom she recognised from a parents' and guardians' gathering at the school on a sun-filled day in June. Then, that garden created in memory of Jews previously excluded from the town had been in full bloom. The talk full of hope for the school's future, and of local prosperity within Congress Poland. But few seemed to realise what dangerous clouds were gathering beyond its borders.

This time, it was with a growing sense of foreboding that Aniela obeyed her employer's signal to join them. Although the Kozminskis' waistlines had changed, their deep, brown eyes remained as sharp as before, and not a word was wasted during the introductions. Their faces bore the colour of mushrooms grown in darkness. Buried, more like, which in a sense was true. He in his workroom, she tending to a large family, even though three of their adult children had left home. Icieck to London seven years ago, so she'd heard.

"We're very pleased with Aron, aren't we?" said Dr Korek upon seeing Aniela. "He's coming along well, especially in Geography and Biology. Dissection seems to be his forte there, and only last week he gave an excellent demonstration on a dead toad."

"He keeps talking about it," said his mother, heavily corseted beneath her brown coat. "But we drew the line when he asked if Betsy's kitten might be next."

A brief silence followed, and large, soft snowflakes appeared from nowhere, settling on the four heads. Aniela shivered for too long.

"He also thinks healthy people should leave their bodies for medical advancement," added Dr Korek, stamping his well-shod feet on the unswept snow. He then addressed his member of staff. "Has Aron mentioned that to you?"

"Not yet," she said. "And, to be truthful, I find him something of an enigma."

"An *enigma*?" challenged the boy's father, pulling at his greying beard. "That's *quite* the wrong word to use. You must know his middle name's Mordke, meaning warrior. Someone who'll fight for our survival. Not be an enigma."

Dr Korek's steely eyes were on her. She was a butterfly on a pin, but not quite dead.

"Did you happen to notice any blood on his clothing yesterday?" she ventured, because that possibility and the boy's minty breath was all she could think of.

The couple coughed, clearly embarrassed by the question, and began to edge away. But Dr Korek gripped her arm while bidding them farewell then faced her. Anger quivering every open pore in his red cheeks. "What was the meaning of that, may I ask? And you'd better have a good answer. No, on second thoughts, see me tomorrow immediately after prayers. Urjasz Lozinski can stand in for you."

Aniela returned to her lodgings as darkness fell. Nothing was making sense, except for one slip of Golda Kozminski's tongue.

Kitten.

Having relit the stove, revived the circulation in her feet and gulped down two glasses of her aromatic saviour, she stood by her main room's window for a few minutes to reassure herself that no one was lurking outside. Least of all those two pupils.

The street had been muffled by further snow, and it was a lone pony and trap that made its way towards the town's centre, occasionally sliding from right to left, then righting itself. Aniela extracted her notebook and pencil from her coat pocket. The combination of the alcohol and warmth from the new log soon encouraged her to write down everything that had happened since Thursday afternoon. She made sure her handwriting stayed legible and to each occurrence was added the date and time. This activity seemed to restore some order and control to what was quickly becoming the opposite, and once she'd reexamined the two boys' files, added a few notes of her own.

Observations, not judgements. Why she was doing this, she wasn't quite sure. But she had no choice. Her conscience seemed to demand it.

Bang! Bang! Bang!

She shot up in her chair.

Who on earth was punishing the front door like that? She dropped her pencil and slipped on it as she ran to the window. When she finally reached it, kept her face to one side and forgot to breathe.

The not-so-silent boy.

Less smartly dressed than before. His upturned face even paler than those of his mother and father as he stood beneath the street lantern's mean glow. "At the synagogue today, why did you ask my parents if I'd blood on my clothes yesterday? Why?" His angry voice raised even more. "What's *wrong* with you?" He banged the door again, this time causing her ground-floor neighbour, built like a tank, to order him away, threatening the police.

The schoolboy sloped off, occasionally glancing back in her direction. A lanky figure diminishing with every stride, but not the effect he was having on her already troubled mind. Did he or didn't he know what had happened to the sheep? Hard to tell. Either way, she was convinced this violent, public outburst had been to warn her off.

Aniela ventured downstairs to thank the miner, whose face still bore smears of black dust. She explained that nuisance was one of her pupils at the Immanuel School, and how their misunderstanding would soon be cleared up.

"Better had," he muttered. "Because if he shows his face here again when I'm around, he'll regret it."

Monday, 24 November, 8 a.m.

Aniela arrived at the barely warm school deliberately early so that she could, after a restless, nervy night thinking of toads and kittens, prepare herself for her meeting with Dr Korek. He was sure to make it a one-sided affair, but she had nothing to lose, and, feeling dizzy and hungry, sat at her desk to re-examine the tailor's son's classwork in a different light. Last year it had featured a study of Africa. His written work was consistently neat and concise, with illustrations of spear-carriers and other hunters small, but vivid. Red his favourite colour, as were the hairstyles of various tribeswomen. So different in form and texture to most of northern Europe's inhabitants.

Then, on page eighteen, she suddenly paused. How could she have forgotten?

Her forefinger rested on a patch of black, crinkly fibres stuck with glue in the margin above a brief sentence in block capitals. ALL ARE APES.

Aniela found her magnifying glass and peered more closely, soon realising this particular sample hadn't come from any human head.

How strange.

She must have been in a hurry at the time. April always the busiest part of the year, with examinations and later, visits to place of interest. She would never have let this sample or the comment go unnoticed, and yet her *A* grade and *Well done!* was writ large.

"Pani Bielski?"

She jumped, slamming the pages shut as Urjasz Lozinski, dark as lignum, peered round her door, blowing on his hands. "Doctor Korek's mother's been taken ill in the night. It looks serious." He then glanced at the dully glowing stove in the corner. "You mustn't get cold. Shall I get someone to relight it?"

"No thank you. But there is something you could do, as the boy's in your class."

"Who?"

"Hersz Eilenberg. Can you ask him – in private, please – to see me here at eleven o'clock? On his own?"

The family man from Kola looked puzzled. "I'll try."

The long drawn-out siren for morning prayers made him draw back and disappear, but fired her determination to look further at 'The Warrior's' offerings.

*   *   *

For some reason, he wasn't in school, and her first two lessons passed off peaceably enough, with no one surmising where he might be. Then, at exactly eleven o'clock, the orphan appeared, finishing off a mouthful of something, and looking decidedly nervous. Aniela smiled to reassure him and indicated the wooden bench nearest her desk. "I appreciate your coming," she said, as he avoided her eyes. "And it won't take long, but I need a little more of your help. Very important help."

"No," he said. "I can't. I know what it's about, and . . ."

"And?"

He shifted on the bench, unsure where to place his hands. Seconds were ticking away on the clock over the stove.

"Aron touched my hair on Friday," she pre-empted him. "And then ran away. I also think he stole my storeroom key and left a dead bird on my register, the day before. How would *you* feel about that?"

"Hair?" He finally made eye contact, and she saw how, despite being fourteen, he was still young and vulnerable. How perhaps she shouldn't be doing this. But those mid-brown eyes had widened as if she'd struck a chord. "Didn't you know?"

"Know what?"

The coals in the stove also came to life, causing a flurry of sparks behind its bleary, glass doors.

"He sometimes cuts his sister's hair and keeps a bit of it on him always. *And* from down below. I've seen it."

"With scissors?"

"He used a knife once, but it wasn't as good."

"What kind of knife?"

He drew an imaginary S in the air.

Aniela deliberately remained expressionless, recalling the two siblings' fond encounter yesterday morning. Then page eighteen in that geography book. "You mean Matilda?"

Hersz nodded. "And he sleeps in the same bed as her. And . . . and . . ." A sudden blush covered his cheeks. He looked down at his hands.

"Please go on. I'm listening."

"Her blood. You know, what comes out every month. He likes the smell of it. He told me. And there's something else he does." The boy pointed between his legs, making jerking movements with an open fist. "Forgive me for showing you, Pani Bielski, but he can't leave it alone, even though he says it hurts."

Aniela shrunk inwardly at the grotesque images that had been conjured up, and almost missed a tall shadow lingering by the nearest window, before suddenly gliding away.

The orphan had seen it too, and sprung to his feet.

"That was *him*!" He fixed on her, more scared than ever. "Where can I hide? He'll realise why I'm here with you. Telling tales . . ."

She glanced behind her at the storeroom.

No key.

"Come with me," she hissed, feeling her limbs stiffen. The laundry room used for the school's few boarders led off the far corner of the classroom and into the dining area where there was always company.

Not today.

"I want my mama," murmured Hersz, whitening.

"Then hurry."

She accompanied him home to a grateful but anxious Sarah Eilenberg. Having warned her of the tailor's son and begged her to keep him safe, Aniela then negotiated the hardened snow through the deserted park, towards the Rgilewka River.

The disembowelled sheep had vanished, yet someone had frantically tried to cover all traces. But not quite. With trembling fingers, she retrieved a small, metal ring with the number twenty-two stamped into it. The seller's tag, perhaps? She could always check at next Saturday's market.

Aniela then moved nearer the water's edge where churned-up grass, hay and snow led to an area of broken ice continuing further along the river. Here, to her horror, a sheep's open muzzle protruded above its surface.

While her beating pulse seemed to slow her down, within minutes she was in her own street and recklessly sliding and skidding to reach her door as soon as possible.

Once unlocked, she pushed her way into the small hallway and was about to secure the door behind her, when the half-familiar smell of sweat, spirits and something sickly sweet, reached her nose.

"*Guten Tag, mein Engel . . .*"

The German.

Could he have seen her in her classroom? Followed her to Hersz's house?

Like yesterday, he'd appeared as if from nowhere; those same blue eyes shining with what seemed genuine pleasure. A wide smile showing perfect teeth. But something about his mouth made her shudder, for each corner revealed an unmistakable curl of dried blood. He also wore rough gloves streaked with dark red. The definite source of that smell . . .

Her question died in her throat.

"I had to eat," he explained with a shrug. "Anyone else in my position would have done the same. And did you notice the blue mark made by a ram on her rump? There was a lamb inside, almost ready to be born. It was delicious."

Before she could react to this casual confession, he'd kicked the front door shut behind him and pushed her hard against the stairs. With both his hands clamped around her throat, she spotted the squared-off end of a blood-smeared knife poking unseen from a pocket in his cape.

Shechita . . .

Too late to cry out or fight him off. Her spinning consciousness had become solid black.

"*Schmutzig Jude!*" He spat on her face. "Like all the rest of them. And this is just the start . . ."

Monday, 1 December 1879
ATTENTION!
Well-respected teacher murdered.

On the evening of Monday, 24 November, the badly mutilated body of Aniela Bielski was found by Leon Marczewski, a miner, also living at 3, Aleja Ogrod in Klodawa's Dziadowice quarter. Tributes have been paid by those who knew her, including Dr Jan Korek, Head Teacher of the Immanuel School where she had taught Geography for two years. Also, fourteen-year-old Aron Kozminski of 12, Droga Mojzez Isserles, whose school records and other material found at his teacher's address, led to lengthy police questioning in connection with this and a similar crime involving a sheep. Upon release, the distressed schoolboy admitted, "I will never, ever be able to forget the brutal loss of someone with such beautiful hair, or that gentle ewe and her innocent lamb who I helped save from slaughter."

While the search for the ruthless killer and the weapon continues, citizens are warned to remain vigilant and immediately report anything of interest to the police.

IMMANUEL SCHOOL, KLODAWA.
Wednesday, 17 December 1879.From the office of
Dr Jan Korek.

It is with regret that before this school
closes for Hanukkah, I have to inform all
staff that two of our most promising pupils
will not be returning to us next year. Hersz
Eilenberg and his adoptive parents will be
leaving for New York next week, while Aron

Kozminski plans to help in his father's tailoring business, while the family too, make plans for a more settled future.

Please also note that at her cousin's insistence, Aniela Bielski's mortal remains will be transferred to Poznan for re-internment on Saturday. The deceased's husband, Chaim Bielski, formerly resident near Warsaw, is believed to have recently left for France.

In the Wake of the Autumn Storm
Adrian Cole

Back then, in the late summer of 1970, I was twenty-four, not long out of university, and I had a new job in the heart of the City with, my peers assured me, very good prospects. I had landed a post on the highly successful monthly magazine, *The Informer*. Or rather, my father's contacts in the business world had got me the job. Everyone said it was a great time to sign up, given that the Tories had – surprisingly – dethroned the Labour Party to win the June election. Pay rises and prosperity, we'd all be rolling in filthy lucre.

My editor, Laurence Beaumont, who was not so many years older than me, was the son of a member of the House of Lords, himself a close friend of my father's. Laurence was extremely good at his job, a ruthless, tireless operator, who worked his team hard to winkle out the best of the gossip with which to regale an avid audience – *The Informer* had a circulation at that time of well into six figures, and no self-respecting household was without a subscription. Laurence, primed no doubt by his father, was keen for me to do well, but it was in his nature to test the mettle of his new recruits.

He called me into his office, poured me a coffee, lit us both a cigarette and studied me openly, as though he would quickly spot any weaknesses and lay them bare. His eyes were as sharp as a hawk's, his hunting instincts no less disarming. He told me he'd got hold of a possible story.

"May be nothing in it, old chap. These things sometimes fizzle out. Then again, they can turn out to be pure gold. Don't know about this one. You've got interesting connections. Ever heard of a Lady Constance Grandage? Country seat in Somerset. Super estate, by all accounts."

I admitted to a vague knowledge of the name. "I don't think she's been circulating in society circles for some time, if ever," I said. "Isn't she rather old?"

"Indeed. Ninety-five to be precise. My old man had a letter from her and she wants to write her memoirs, or at least part of them. A scandal that will rock the upper echelons of society, so she claims. Could be complete tosh, or it might allow us to blot a few escutcheons. Fancy a trip out there? Nice coup if it turns out to be a juicy one."

One didn't refuse Laurence and, although my initial enthusiasm was hardly bubbling over, I accepted the task and made my plans accordingly. Having established contact with Lady Grandage through the offices of the magazine, I duly received a formal invitation to visit her and so drove down to Somerset. The house was quite a pile, set within countless acres of rich, verdant countryside. It put me in mind of Longleat, although there were no intrusive tourists here.

I was to stay in a luxurious suite of rooms, for as many days as necessary, during which time I was free to roam the grounds, escorted or not, as I chose, at any time that Lady Grandage was indisposed. In the event, for a woman of advanced years, she proved remarkably enthused, and told me her story in long, precise details. We sat in one of the libraries, a huge, sumptuous room, filled with beautiful, doubtless priceless, books from Lord knew when, and whose walls also sported dramatic paintings, mostly battle scenes in which our ancestors were heroically sacrificing themselves against alien hordes.

In an atmosphere of Victorian pomp and circumstance, my nonagenarian host unveiled her story. I was allowed to take notes, and sat scribbling away as she talked, her voice strong and clear, her whole body, though small, charged with the energy of events and the excitement that went with it. For reasons that will become obvious, she told me she had changed the names of all those relevant to her story.

This is what she told me.

I may as well begin by revealing to you something that may shock you, although, as you are a youth of today, I suspect I'm being naïve to say so. My mother (let us call her Dolly) was a prostitute, and in Victorian England that had nothing of the glamour of the high society call girls I understand you may find in London now. Dolly and her close circle of friends all lived in a particularly insalubrious part of London, and without the income from their trade would have lived very brief lives. Most of them, Dolly included, had become prostitutes in their early teens, in some cases much younger.

Dolly was more fortunate than most, although given the life she led and the privations she was subjected to, that is probably an ironic comment. I say it because she began life as a very attractive girl. It made her popular with the clients, in particular one group of them. Men of substance, men of influence, men of position and power. Among them were members of the government, even some of the nobility, which will hardly surprise you. One of these, Lord Montague Bullstone, took a real shine to Dolly, so much so that he made arrangements for her to be kept apart from the others and used solely for his requirements. In return, Dolly had everything she wanted, that is, excluding her freedom.

She was able to dress well, keep herself clean, healthy and well fed. Indeed, she retained her looks and her figure, presided over by the watchful eyes of Lord Montague's retainers. On the infrequent occasions when she was permitted to leave the neat and tidy place of residence set up for her, she had to revert to clothing more in keeping with the drabs of the area. She led a double life, but at least she was able to communicate, to some extent, with her less fortunate friends. Her relationship with Lord Bullstone continued for a few years. He had a wife and family and a fine career, mixing as he did with the highest circles – indeed, he was a friend of the Royal Family. However, for all this, he was besotted with Dolly. Those of his friends who were party to his peccadillo, urged him to put her aside rather than risk a scandal should the matter become public. As you can imagine, a man in Lord Bullstone's position does have enemies.

He was adamant, however, and would not give up his love, no matter how compromising it could have become. Inevitably, Dolly, even though she had always been careful, fell pregnant. It would have been a simple matter for an abortion to have been arranged and indeed, the operation would have been performed by as professional and accomplished a surgeon as the times could provide. Lord Bullstone would have none of it. He was, perhaps laughably, perhaps commendably, to be a proud father. For all his sins and duplicity, he loved Dolly and any child she bore him would receive a similar quota of his devotion.

Unfortunately, affairs did not go well. Dolly was attended by the most competent people her lover could provide, but the birth was difficult, in fact, disastrous for Dolly. She presented Lord Bullstone with a daughter, but died in the bloody and protracted process. I am sure that there were those present who would have been quick to consign me – for it was me – to the river or some other immediate grave, but my father would have wrought dreadful reprisals on anyone responsible for such an act.

I was given to a surrogate mother, one of several kept women, and, as far as the world was concerned, I was just another child in the wretched scheme of things. I was, however, under the ever-watchful and protective eyes of my father's retainers. My new mother was poor, but received enough of a financial supplement to her daily work as a cleaner to keep her from the streets and selling her body. Even so, she was expected to give herself to the pleasure of my father's retainers at such times as it suited them to use her. I came to understand such things when I was very young, but in that place, it could hardly have been hidden from me and, worse, I assumed it to be a normal part of life.

I saw my father from time to time and he was always kind and caring, explaining that he had an important, secret position in society that would not allow him to exhibit me to the world. I understood only what I was told. I had no reason, then, to question him. He seemed altogether an awesome figure, worthy of respect, worship almost. My surrogate mother was careful never to speak out against him when he had left us.

It was not until I was thirteen – the age at which my father had first began his relationship with my mother – that his attitude towards me changed. I knew about sex – hadn't I witnessed it, clandestinely, many times when my father's men had used my surrogate mother, regardless of whether it gave her pleasure? I was uneasy about it, but I confess to having been intrigued. So that when my father began to express his love for me in newer, more physical terms, I was to some extent pliant. By the time he took full advantage of me, there was little I could do to resist. I was afraid, thinking that if I did not obey him, I would be rejected, probably cast out to live like the poorer women, where anyone would be able to use me. My father's attentions seemed a better option.

I became an obsession for him. I knew about his wife and family and he broke down and cried about how she did not love him, but preferred the company of other men, to his shame. I was little more than a child and I felt sorry for him, taken in as I was by the usual lover's protestations. Although our coition was a sin, he was never cruel or unkind. I was able to close myself off, shutting myself into an inner state of mind when he used me. I lived well, though more and more I was kept from the world I had known. Such friends as I had were no longer available to me. I was moved to a town house, under the care of a matronly woman, Mrs Bellairs. She knew most things, but said nothing.

Something dark and unpleasant had seeded itself in me, an unspoken reaction to my situation, but I held it in check and played my part as well as I was able. The house was luxurious by any standards and I now enjoyed a private education, which I exploited fully. I learned to speak in a new way and, well, if you are familiar with Shaw's *Pygmalion*, you'll understand me when I say I was not altogether unlike Miss Doolittle. My father created a new role for me, that of a relative's daughter, this fictitious relative and her husband having died in an unfortunate accident. Thus he had taken on the guise of being my guardian. His close friends knew the truth, of course, but this was not the place for it.

There were parties and gatherings, some related to Lord Bullstone's work and his meteoric career. I was not permitted to attend them, of course, but the nature of the house was such that it was never difficult for me to spy on some of what transpired. I was not interested in the various sexual liaisons, enacted in private rooms, but more in the gossip and news of the outside world. In particular, I wanted to find out about something that had become a deep shadow clouding the world of the city at that time.

It was 1888. There had been a number of terrible killings – atrociously bloody murders – in Whitechapel, an area that I knew well from my childhood. I knew, too, some of the women who walked its streets. Doubtless Dolly would have known them, too. But for the grace of God, any of them could have been the victims of this prowling horror. London was aghast, word of the murderer having spread like a virus throughout its higher and lower echelons. The police were baffled. The murderer mocked them. The world went in terror of this monster, this Jack the Ripper.

I gleaned all this from gossip at Lord Bullstone's parties as I made myself a shadow around the groups, the wives, the politicians, the society set. It excited them as much as it appalled them. They waited almost eagerly for news of the Ripper's next revolting act. One night, in the early hours of the morning to be precise, Lord Bullstone had a visitor, accompanied by three other men I had seen before and whom I knew to be from the higher levels of society, men of tremendous wealth and power.

I recall the date. It was November the ninth, a Friday. My father had taken me to his bed, his work for the week over, and he liked to enjoy sex with me before his other weekend amusements. We were both asleep at the time of the visit, which was at about 5 a.m. He was roused by his most discreet servants and quickly forgot about me in the excitement surrounding his visitors. Something about the affair piqued my curiosity and I dressed and slipped downstairs and secreted myself in an ante-room beyond the private drawing room in which he entertained his guests. I was able to stand behind the door and peer through its crack where it adjoined the jamb. I could hear their words very distinctly.

The principal visitor was a man I had seen on a few occasions, although briefly. He was Duke Julian Hammerford, a relation of certain members of the Royal Family. He was not tall, was some thirty-five years old and had a noticeably weak chin and piggish eyes, oddly close together. He wore very expensive clothes, visible clearly as he had tossed aside his coat, which one of the men with him was at great pains to fold up and remove in some haste. As I studied the figures beside the fire, which had been lit and now blazed brightly, I saw, with some surprise, the blood on the shirt of the Duke. A lot of blood. Indeed, my father had already sent for his most trusted servant to bring a change of clothes.

"What has happened?" said my father.

The duke seemed to be struggling for breath. "It came over me again. I tell you, Monty, you cannot imagine what it is like. It grips me in a vice of desire. I swear to you I was only seeking the usual carnal pleasures. So much is available in Whitechapel."

"You've killed again?" said my father, his voice like ice.

The other two men with him stared at the Duke, apparently unmoved, but when I saw their faces I could see they were deeply unsettled by what they already knew.

"Yes! I had the butcher's knife with me. I used it, again and again!" The man closed his eyes and shuddered and I realised with revulsion that he was reliving with *intense pleasure* the vileness of his act, which he described now. I shrank back. The man was a maniac, completely without morals or scruples. To have used his weapon so wildly and repeatedly marked him as a monster, a man who had crossed the bounds of humanity into some beastly, demonic realm. And yet my father and the other men listened to him and accepted what he said.

"Where?" said my father. "Where did this happen? What street?"

For a moment the duke looked bemused, licking his lips and wiping the runnels of perspiration from his brow. The excitement of reliving his ghastly exploits had got the better of him. "Uh, it was off Aldgate and Whitechapel Road. I think it was Commercial Street, or near it."

"Keep everyone well away from there," said my father. "Get the word out, Stanton. Warn anyone who might be in the area to get as far from that accursed area as they can. Who was with him?"

The third man nodded. "Not in the house. I was in the carriage, waiting. I didn't see—"

"You may thank God for that, sir," said my father. "No doubt we shall all hear more of this as the day wears on. Where is the knife?"

"Disposed of already," was the reply.

"Burn all the clothes. Everything. Get him back to one of his houses and prime everyone, as before. Julian, we cannot go on protecting you. This business has to stop, dammit. All these false trails we lay for you, the red herrings, the notes, sooner or later the police will catch on."

"I know, I know! It's so difficult." He started to cry and, to my amazement, my father put an arm around him, consoling him. This creature from Hell, who disembowelled and shredded the women of the streets, being pitied! I could bear it no longer and withdrew.

I was still awake, an hour later, when my father returned to my bed. He intended to feign sleep and leave me later, as though the events of the early morning had never occurred. He must have felt me shrinking back, the revulsion that coursed through me now at his nearness.

"Whatever is it?" he said. The embers of the fire were burning low in the grate. He went to them, took a spill and lit a candle, setting it on a table beside the bed. I could see his face, the lines of stress, as he hovered over me.

"How can you defend him?" I whispered.

It was as though I had applied a knife to him. His face had become a grim mask, fear and a deep unease limned by the garish light. "You . . . saw?"

I nodded.

"You must never speak of this."

"Answer me."

He sighed deeply. "No one must know. He is a member of the Royal Family. They know nothing of his illness. Those of us who do know are trying to save him from himself. If news of this reaches the press, the outside world, it will be catastrophic for the queen. We dare not let it become known. Do you understand that?"

"You cannot allow him such freedom."

"No, of course not. We will find a way of confining him. Tonight will be his last act. You must say nothing to anyone. We would all be ruined." He was dressing hurriedly now, the panic in his voice evident. "Also, if others became aware that you knew his identity, they would expect me to . . . deal with you."

"You mean kill me? Dispose of me? I would disappear and no one would be any the wiser, is that what you are saying?"

He threw himself on the bed beside me and gripped my hands. "No, no, never that! I would rather die than lose you, my darling! Don't say such things. Don't say anything. Leave this to me. Erase it all from your mind."

He left me, doubtless to attend to the aftermath of the duke's terrible acts. It gave me time to consider what I should do. My anger and my disgust at the night's revelations ignited a feverishness within me, a dark resolve. It was as though the events of the night had heated up my own buried frustrations, fuel to a sudden blaze of resentment.

By the time I rose and went about my day's activities, which on a Saturday consisted mainly of reading or painting, at which I had become passably proficient, my father had gone into the city. Word of the night's horrors had not formally reached the house, although I knew that it would not be long before they did. I nurtured a plan and, having refined its details in my mind, sought out Mrs Bellairs, the principal housekeeper.

She was a strict, austere woman, passably educated but from a working background and there was no doubt in my mind that she understood well enough the true relationship between me and the master of the house, although she would not have known he was my father. We spoke only as occasion demanded and she was a little wary of me. Resentful too, I am sure.

I found her in one of the smaller drawing rooms, attending to various daily chores. I closed the door behind me so that we were alone and unlikely to be disturbed.

"Mrs Bellairs," I said. "I need your help in certain matters."

She favoured me with her cold stare. "Of course, my lady, as you wish."

"I need to visit a certain part of the city and I need to do so clandestinely." She knew my circumstances, that I was not allowed anywhere except when escorted by the designated retainers of Lord Bullstone. To ask her aid in defiance of this would usually have met with immediate refusal. She said nothing, but her expression spoke for her. I was a precocious thirteen-year-old and I was asking the impossible.

"Before that," I went on, notwithstanding her iciness, "I require you to obtain certain information for me. About a close friend of Lord Bullstone. Duke Julian Hammerford. You know the man?"

"I don't know about that, my lady. I know of the duke, of course. But as for information about him, it would not be for me to betray any confidences."

"You are aware of certain incidents in the city, certain unpleasant murders?"

For a moment her glassy coolness melted and she shuddered. The very thought of the work of the Ripper cut most people to the quick. "I'm sure I'd rather not discuss such things, my lady. You should not distress yourself with—"

"What if I told you that I know his identity? What if I imparted it to you? And if I told you it is a secret so terrible that Lord Bullstone would want it guarded with his very life?"

"What are you saying, my lady!" She was appalled and made no attempt now to hide her shock.

"Under such circumstances, anyone who knew the identity of the monster at work in our city would themselves be in danger. Such a person would be a threat to Lord Bullstone. Not one he would tolerate."

"Why are you doing this?" she said, aghast.

"I mean you no harm, Mrs Bellairs. I want your help. Grant it me and I will ensure that Lord Bullstone is not made aware that you know the identity of the man known as Jack the Ripper."

"I have no idea who he is!"

"I have already told you."

She gasped, her hands clasped together in horror and made several attempts to speak, until at last she managed, "Tell me again what it is you want."

"Firstly you must find out as much as you can about Duke Julian Hammerford. In particular, I want his address, or if there are more than one in the city, all of them. I want to know about his regular movements. What clubs does he frequent, what theatres, if any? I want that information very soon."

She nodded slowly. I was certain she had her own contacts among the servants of other houses to enable her to glean the information for me.

"Once I have that, I wish to visit an area where I spent a lot of my youth, although I would scarcely consider myself an adult. You will arrange for me to slip away, deceive my guards, and spend some time away. Make some pretence that I am ill, confined to my room, seen only by you, anything you wish. Lord Bullstone will be away himself for at least a week. I will not be missed if you handle the matter discreetly. When I return, there will be no need to discuss the affair. You may then put it from your mind and go about your business."

"Where is it you wish to visit, my lady?"

"Whitechapel."

She blanched again. "Lord have mercy, but that's where—"

"It need not concern you. I have good friends there. I'll not be harmed. So, will you do these things?"

She had no choice, deeply disturbed though she was.

*   *   *

Whether Mrs Bellairs was prompted by sheer terror or by a lurid fascination for the gruesomeness of the reign of the man they called the Ripper, or both, she did as charged by me and within two days provided me with the information I wanted concerning Duke Hammerford. After that she arranged for me to visit Whitechapel. In the event, she proved singularly adept at deceiving Lord Bullstone's retainers as to my situation and they were not aware that I had been secretly able to slip my leash and leave the house for the best part of a day. I spent it with the unfortunates of that bleak district, some of whom I knew, but who hardly remembered me.

The information I imparted to them was enough to win their approval and confidence. I may have been little more than a child in most people's eyes, but the nature of my life and the cold circumstances surrounding me had sharpened my senses and hardened me into a darker spirit. My resolve was fixed, my heart devoid of warmth.

Two days after my return to Lord Bullstone's house, where I settled back into the routine set out for me, there was a message, brought to me by a nervous Mrs Bellairs. I had shared none of my endeavours with her, merely used her as an aide to my movements.

"I am to tell you," she said, "that a certain person is being held in Whitechapel, as you instructed."

"Then I must go there. It will be the last time, Mrs Bellairs. Afterwards, your role in these matters will be at an end."

She was clearly relieved and carried out the last of her instructions without fuss. She was afraid of me, and although I bore her no malice, it was necessary to make use of her fear. So I visited Whitechapel once more and left Mrs Bellairs in the safe hands of some friends, where she was obliged to await my return.

My contacts, two young women who were already losing that youth, given the grim nature of their daily work, met me. They were scarcely able to contain their excitement, eager to see this business through. I am certain that half the populace of London would have stood beside us had they known what we intended. It was a suitably foggy night, the air reeking with it, the night wrapping us in its folds, clammy and acrid, a perfect occasion for a meeting with a monster.

The house we went to looked derelict, its windows boarded up, its roof sagging. We passed down an alley beside it that stank of rubbish and urine. We negotiated a sagging gate and went into a narrow yard, where two other women were waiting for us, as ragged and filthy as those who had brought me. They both favoured me with gap-toothed grins, but I remained to all intents and purposes cold and emotionless. Part of me was detached from this, standing back and observing, a stiffening of resolve.

Inside the back room, a bare, foul-smelling place with soot-blackened walls, a few candles cast a wavering glow over the small group of people who were gathered, not unlike a coven of witches. There was only one man here, and he was tied to a bed, his arms and legs outstretched in a vague cruciform. They had gagged him and I looked down into those eyes, those piggish, close-set eyes, as they widened in horror. His body was shaking, his face dripping with perspiration.

"I know who you are," I told him. "I know you by another name than Duke Julian Hammerford. I knew you would come again to Whitechapel. It was not difficult to prepare a reception this time."

The gag made it impossible for him to scream, but nevertheless he attempted to do it and bite through the gag in the process.

I turned to the gathered women. I could see that they had brought the things I had asked for. Each of them held the butchering knives.

"Strip him," I told them and waited while his shoes and every last shred of clothing were ripped from the outspread duke. His fat, oily body gleamed in the candle glow, shaking uncontrollably. He had lost control of his bladder, soaking the dirty mattress on which he was spreadeagled, the stench of the urine only adding to the eagerness of the women to begin.

I had read of the Ripper's bloody handiwork in newspapers at Lord Bullstone's that I was not supposed to have seen. The women here all knew the grisly and disgusting nature of that work – the disembowelling, the carving up of the bodies, the removal of organs. It was not difficult to duplicate the work. If any of the women who undertook it now were revolted by it, or felt the remotest spark of compassion, they hid it well, drowning it in the lake of blood that flowed from their victim. I would have joined them, but they were content to let me stand aside and watch.

And watch I did. I will not pretend that it was anything but utterly vile. The man was cut open, ripped apart, his eyes almost leaping from their sockets in terror and agony, until their light dimmed in death. When it was over, the charnel house scene duplicated the ghastly scenes that he had presented to the world when he had set upon his own victims. An eye for an eye, a tooth for a tooth and, in this case, an organ for an organ.

The bonds that had bound him were removed, as was the gag. Quickly the women dispersed, myself with them. The fog had closed in and few people dared to venture out. It was unlikely that the slaughtered man would be discovered by accident this night. I knew that he would have been brought to Whitechapel in a private carriage, as many of his breeding were, but his servants would have a long vigil.

I had known that the duke's retainers, waiting with his carriage, would spare no efforts to find their master. The very last thing they would have wanted was for him to have been found by others, especially if he had been in a compromising position. They were permitted to scour Whitechapel frantically for the remains of the night, until, an hour after dawn, one of our company tipped them off that there was a body in a certain deserted house. We had made sure that when the Duke's retainers found him there would be no mistaking him. His head had not been mutilated or marked.

I had also known that the duke's retainers would do everything in their power to divert the attention of the police away from his death. If such a ghastly scenario as they had discovered were to get into the press, or be made known to his family and son, especially his royal connections, it would be disastrously embarrassing. They sent, as I knew they would, for my father. He, of course, used all the power at his disposal to throw a blanket over the whole affair. The corpse, in all its scattered horror, was removed from that place, which was duly scrubbed. Indeed, the house was pulled down, the scene of the crime buried. The police knew nothing of the death and the sudden disappearance of Duke Julian Hammerford became an altogether different mystery. The press speculated, as they will, and heroic efforts were made to find the missing duke. His retainers were silent and swore that they had not been called upon to transport him anywhere prior to his disappearance.

The whole affair slowly died down.

My father, who had been extremely agitated, gradually regained his self-control. His own private investigations into what had really occurred had come to nothing. In spite of my reassurances to Mrs Bellairs that no more would be said about the matter – she knew about the "disappearance", of course, although she was insensible to its detail – she resigned her post and found another placement, some distance from us in the city.

One evening, I found my father in his study, reading through some papers. It was not a room that I usually visited, but for once I had a specific purpose. I had with me a small casket, a rather beautiful object, wrought in pure silver. It had been purloined especially for me, one of a number of items stolen from the household of a member of the gentry, and not one that was likely to be greatly missed by its opulent owner.

"My dear, I did ask you not to disturb me when I'm working in here," said my father, with an admonishing, though not severe glance.

"I know," I said, holding out the little casket. "But I wanted to give you this little gift."

Any disapproval he felt at my presence dissipated as he stood up and took the gift. "That's very kind of you. Wherever did you obtain such a thing?"

I smiled. "Surely a woman is allowed some secrets."

He made no attempt to remind me that I was child. Perhaps he never thought of me that way. He opened the casket and unwrapped the content. I watched his face turn to chalk as he realized what it was.

"What in God's name—?" he blurted, almost dropping the casket. He held it away from him, repulsed.

I knew what it was, of course, having put it there, but I played my part, screwing up my face. "I have lately been having lessons in biology from my tutor," I said, quite casually.

He looked at me, totally bemused.

"Unless I am mistaken, sir, that is a liver. A human liver."

My father withdrew from his affairs for several days after that and hardly anyone saw him, certainly not I. He may have unravelled the mystery, and even my part in it, but he chose not to see me. Of course, he would have understood all too well that the grisly organ that I had presented to him was that of his former colleague. I expected to be summoned in due course, and either interrogated brutally, even killed. I would have accepted such a thing, given that I had been party to ridding the world of that vilest of creatures, the Duke of Hammerford.

However, my father's obsession with me had not dimmed. He could not bring himself to dispense with me. It may even have been that in some perverted way my crime provided a certain piquancy to our relationship. Nothing about him and his depravity, or that of any of his distinguished colleagues, would have surprised me. As it was, he decided to close the matter of the Duke's death.

"I am concerned for you," my father told me, some months later. "As long as you live here in the city, you are in danger. You know the identity of – well, let us not dwell on it, but you understand me. If it were ever to be found out that you held such a secret, you would be under threat from obvious parties. Not from me, never that."

I nodded, letting him speak.

"For this reason, I have decided to move you. I shall set you up in one of my country estates. I have done very well in political circles, as you know. The Marquis of Salisbury himself has praised me and I think it will not be too long before I am promoted to even higher status. I will send you to Somerset. You will be confined there, but I promise you, my dear, you will enjoy life even more than you do here. You will lack for nothing."

Except my freedom, as always, I thought.

And so it has been. I have lived here for all these years and, indeed, I have outlived him and all his illustrious fellows. The line of Lord Bullstone died out some years ago. I have said nothing of those events of 1888 in Whitechapel until now. It is a secret that has never been revealed to a soul, and I suspect that until I shared it with you, I have been the sole possessor of its knowledge. I have not long to live and, while I am alive, I shall deny everything. After I am gone, well, you may make of it what you will. By all means tell the world.

That's how Lady Grandage left it. My time with her was ended. Like one of her retainers, I was dismissed.

I didn't have the easiest of nights, my brain swirling with numerous images from the extraordinary tale I'd been told. It was all perfectly plausible, of course, but my immediate problem would be establishing its veracity. It was certainly a suitably lurid tale for *The Informer*, but unless I was careful it would sound like another "improbable fiction".

I sat alone in the ridiculously oversized breakfast room of the country house, pondering my next move over several cups of rich coffee. While I was sitting there, my main guide, a fellow by the name of Alan Foster, approached and coughed as though uneasy about disturbing me. It reminded me of the isolated and almost redundant way of life that people like Lady Grandage had enjoyed.

"I really am very sorry about this, sir, but I'm afraid there is some rather unfortunate news this morning."

Ironically, I had a feeling I knew what he was going to say.

"It's Lady Grandage, sir. I'm afraid she passed away in the night."

"I'm sorry to hear that. She was quite a character."

"She had made good preparations, sir, so matters will be put in hand at once. Please do not feel the need to leave until you are quite ready."

"That's fine. As a matter of fact, we'd concluded our interview. My business here is done."

Foster slipped a long white envelope from his breast pocket. "Not quite, sir." He smiled and proffered the letter. "Lady Grandage specifically asked me to give you this when you left. Would you like any more coffee?"

"No, that's fine."

He left me and I slit the letter open. It was from Lady Grandage and contained a last addendum to her story and I scanned her beautiful script.

None of my revelations will account for anything, it said, *without some kind of proof. I told you I had used different names in my story. So here is the real name of the man they called Jack the Ripper.*

I stared at the name, my flesh going very cold. Lady Grandage had saved the last, brutal, cut until last. It was the name of my great-great-grandfather.